Ø - 1/21 - 4/23

THE BEST OF
JULES de GRANDIN

20 CLASSIC OCCULT DETECTIVE STORIES

SEABURY QUINN

Night Shade Books
New York

Night Shade books may be purchased in bulk at special discounts for sales promotion, corporate gifts, fund-raising, or educational purposes. Special editions can also be created to specifications. For details, contact the Special Sales Department, Night Shade Books, 307 West 36th Street, 11th Floor, New York, NY 10018 or info@skyhorsepublishing.com.

Night Shade Books® is a registered trademark of Skyhorse Publishing, Inc.®, a Delaware corporation.

Visit our website at www.nightshadebooks.com.

10 9 8 7 6 5 4 3 2 1

Library of Congress Cataloging-in-Publication Data is available on file.

Print ISBN: 978-1-949102-26-0
Ebook ISBN: 978-1-949102-42-0

Cover illustration by Donato Giancola
Cover design by Claudia Noble

Printed in the United States of America

TABLE OF CONTENTS

Introduction by George A. Vanderburgh and Robert E. Weinberg ix

The Isle of Missing Ships (*Weird Tales*, February 1926) 1
The House of Horror (*Weird Tales*, July 1926) 33
The Great God Pan (*Weird Tales*, October 1926) 51
Restless Souls (*Weird Tales*, October 1928) 63
The Black Master (*Weird Tales*, January 1929*) 89
The Devil's Rosary (*Weird Tales*, April 1929†) 115
The House without a Mirror (*Weird Tales*, November 1929) 143
Stealthy Death (*Weird Tales*, November 1930) 169
Satan's Stepson (*Weird Tales*, September 1931) 199
The Bleeding Mummy (*Weird Tales*, November 1932) 249
The Thing in the Fog (*Weird Tales*, March 1933‡) 273
The Hand of Glory (*Weird Tales*, July 1933‡) 311
The Mansion of Unholy Magic (*Weird Tales*, October 1933) 339
Red Gauntlets of Czerni (*Weird Tales*, December 1933‡) 367
The Jest of Warburg Tantavul (*Weird Tales*, September 1934) 393
Hands of the Dead (*Weird Tales*, January 1935) 415
Witch-House (*Weird Tales*, November 1936‡) 441
Suicide Chapel (*Weird Tales*, June 1938‡) 469
The House Where Time Stood Still (*Weird Tales*, March 1939) 495
The Green God's Ring (*Weird Tales*, January 1945) 525

*Cover by Curtis C. Senf
†Cover by Hugh Rankin
‡Cover by Margaret Brundage

To
PETER RUBER
with fond memories of our good times and travels

To
AUGUST W. DERLETH
with admiration of his multifaceted writing talent

To
CHARLES EMERSON (Vincent) STARRETT
The Last Bookman, born in Toronto, lived in Chicago,
and a founding member of The Baker Street Irregulars

Introducing the Sherlock Holmes and Hercule Poirot of Supernatural, Speculative Fantasy & Macabre Fiction

by George A. Vanderburgh and Robert E. Weinberg

Weird Tales, the self-described "Unique Magazine," and one of the most influential Golden Age pulp magazines in the first half of the twentieth century, was home to a number of now-well-recognized names, including Robert Bloch, August Derleth, Robert E. Howard, H. P. Lovecraft, Clark Ashton Smith, and Manly Wade Wellman.

But among such stiff competition was another writer, more popular at the time than all of the aforementioned authors, and paid at a higher rate because of it. Over the course of ninety-two stories and a serialized novel, his most endearing character captivated pulp magazine readers for nearly three decades, during which time he received more front cover illustrations accompanying his stories than any of his fellow contributors.

The writer's name was Seabury Quinn, and his character was the French occult detective Jules de Grandin.

Perhaps you've never heard of de Grandin, his indefatigable assistant Dr. Trowbridge, or the fictional town of Harrisonville, New Jersey. Perhaps you've never even heard of Seabury Quinn (or maybe only in passing, as a historical footnote in one of the many essays and reprinted collections of Quinn's now-more-revered contemporaries). Certainly, de Grandin was not the first occult detective—Algernon Blackwood's John Silence, Hodgson's Thomas Carnacki, and Sax Rohmer's Moris Klaw preceded him—nor was he the last, as Wellman's John Thunstone, Margery Lawrence's Miles Pennoyer, and Joseph Payne Brennan's Lucius Leffing all either overlapped with the end of de Grandin's run or followed him. And without doubt de Grandin shares more than a passing resemblance to both Sir Arthur Conan Doyle's Sherlock Holmes (especially with his Dr. Watson-like sidekick) and Agatha Christie's Hercule Poirot.

Indeed, even if you were to seek out a de Grandin story, your options over the years would have been limited. Unlike Lovecraft, Smith, Wellman, Bloch, and other *Weird Tales* contributors, the publication history of the Jules de Grandin tales is spotty at best. In 1966, Arkham House printed roughly 2,000 copies of *The Phantom-Fighter*, a selection of ten early works. In the late 1970s, Popular Library published six paperback volumes of approximately thirty-five assorted tales, but they are now long out of print. In 2001, the specialty press The Battered Silicon Dispatch Box released an oversized, three-volume hardcover set of every de Grandin story (the first time all the stories had been collected), and, while still in production, the set is unavailable to the general trade.

So, given how obscure Quinn and his character might seem today, it's justifiably hard to understand how popular these stories originally were, or how frequently new ones were written. But let the numbers tell the tale: from October 1925 (when the very first de Grandin story was released) to December 1933, a roughly eight-year span, de Grandin stories appeared in an incredible sixty-two of the ninety-six issues that *Weird Tales* published, totaling well-over three-quarters of a million words. Letter after letter to the magazine's editor demanded further adventures from the supernatural detective.

If Quinn loomed large in the mind of pulp readers during the magazine's heyday, then why has his name fallen on deaf ears since? Aside from the relative unavailability of his work, the truth is that Quinn has been successfully marginalized over the years by many critics, who have often dismissed him as simply a hack writer. The de Grandin stories are routinely criticized as being of little worth, and dismissed as unimportant to the development of weird fiction. A common argument, propped up by suspiciously circular reasoning, concludes that Quinn was not the most popular writer for *Weird Tales*, just the most prolific.

These critics seem troubled that the same audience who read and appreciated the work of Lovecraft, Smith, and Howard could also enjoy the exploits of the French ghostbuster. And while it would be far from the truth to suggest that the literary merits of the de Grandin stories exceed those of some of his contemporaries' tales, Quinn was a much more skillful writer, and the adventures of his occult detective more enjoyable to read, than most critics are willing to acknowledge. In the second half of the twentieth century, as the literary value of some pulp-fiction writers began to be reconsidered, Quinn proved to be the perfect whipping boy for early advocates attempting to destigmatize weird fiction: He was the hack author who churned out formulaic prose for a quick paycheck. Anticipating charges that a literary reassessment of Lovecraft would require reevaluating the entire genre along with him, an arbitrary line was quickly drawn in the sand, and as the standard-bearer of pulp fiction's popularity, the creator of Jules de Grandin found himself on the wrong side of that line.

First and foremost, it must be understood that Quinn wrote to make money, and he was far from the archetypal "starving artist." At the same time that his Jules de Grandin stories were running in *Weird Tales*, he had a similar series of detective stories publishing in *Real Detective Tales*. Quinn was writing two continuing series at once throughout the 1920s, composing approximately twenty-five thousand words a month on a manual typewriter. Maintaining originality under such a grueling schedule would be difficult for any author, and even though the de Grandin stories follow a recognizable formula, Quinn still managed to produce one striking story after another. It should also be noted that the tendency to recycle plots and ideas for different markets was very similar to the writing practices of *Weird Tales*'s other prolific and popular writer, Robert E. Howard, who is often excused for these habits, rather than criticized for them.

Throughout his many adventures, the distinctive French detective changed little. His penchant for amusingly French exclamations was a constant through all ninety-three works, as was his taste for cigars and brandy after (and sometimes before) a hard day's work, and his crime-solving styles and methods remained remarkably consistent. From time to time, some new skill or bit of knowledge was revealed to the reader, but in most other respects the Jules de Grandin of "The Horror on the Links" was the same as the hero of the last story in the series, published twenty-five years later.

> He was a perfect example of the rare French blond type, rather under medium height, but with a military erectness of carriage that made him look several inches taller than he really was. His light-blue eyes were small and exceedingly deep-set, and would have been humorous had it not been for the curiously cold directness of their gaze. With his wide mouth, light mustache waxed at the ends in two perfectly horizontal points, and those twinkling, stock-taking eyes, he reminded me of an alert tomcat.

Thus is de Grandin described by Dr. Trowbridge in the duo's first meeting in 1925. His personal history is dribbled throughout the stories: de Grandin was born and raised in France, attended medical school, became a prominent surgeon, and in the Great War served first as a medical officer, then as a member of the intelligence service. After the war, he traveled the world in the service of French Intelligence. His age is never given, but it's generally assumed that the occult detective is in his early forties.

Samuel Trowbridge, on the other hand, is a typical conservative small-town doctor of the first half of the twentieth century (as described by Quinn, he is a cross between an honest brother of George Bernard Shaw and former Chief Justice of the United States Charles Evans Hughes). Bald and bewhiskered, most— if not all—of his life was spent in the same town. Trowbridge is old-fashioned and somewhat conservative, a member of the Knights Templar, a vestryman in the Episcopal Church, and a staunch Republican.

While the two men are dissimilar in many ways, they are also very much alike. Both are fine doctors and surgeons. Trowbridge might complain from time to time about de Grandin's wild adventures, but he always goes along with them; there is no thought, ever, of leaving de Grandin to fight his battles alone. More than any other trait, though, they are two men with one mission, and perhaps for that reason they remained friends for all of their ninety-three adventures and countless trials.

The majority of Quinn's de Grandin stories take place in or near Harrisonville, New Jersey, a fictional community that rivals (with its fiends, hauntings, ghouls, werewolves, vampires, voodoo, witchcraft, and zombies) Lovecraft's own Arkham, Massachusetts. For more recent examples of a supernatural-infested community, one need look no further than the modern version of pulp-fiction narratives . . . television. *Buffy the Vampire Slayer*'s Sunnydale, California, and *The Night Strangler*'s Seattle both reflect the structural needs of this type of supernatural narrative.

Early in the series, de Grandin is presented as Trowbridge's temporary house guest, having travelled to the United States to study both medicine and modern police techniques, but Quinn quickly realized that the series was due for a long run and recognized that too much globe-trotting would make the stories unwieldy. A familiar setting would be needed to keep the main focus of each tale on the events themselves. Harrisonville, a medium-sized town outside New York City, was completely imaginary, but served that purpose.

Most of the de Grandin stories feature beautiful girls in peril. Quinn discovered early on that Farnsworth Wright, *Weird Tales*'s editor from 1924 to 1940, believed nude women on the cover sold more copies, so when writing he was careful to always feature a scene that could translate to appropriately salacious artwork. Quinn also realized that his readers wanted adventures with love and romance as central themes, so even his most frightening tales were given happy endings (. . . of a sort).

And yet the de Grandin adventures are set apart from the stories they were published alongside by their often explicit and bloody content. Quinn predated the work of Clive Barker and the splatterpunk writers by approximately fifty years, but, using his medical background, he wrote some truly terrifying horror stories; tales like "The House of Horror" and "The House Where Time Stood Still" feature some of the most hideous descriptions of mutilated humans ever set down on paper. The victims of the mad doctor in "The House of Horror" in particular must rank near the top of the list of medical monstrosities in fiction.

Another element that set Quinn's occult detective apart from others was his pioneering use of modern science in the fight against ancient superstitions. De Grandin fought vampires, werewolves, and even mummies in his many adventures, but oftentimes relied on the latest technology to save the day. The Frenchman put it best in a conversation with Dr. Trowbridge at the end of "The Blood-Flower":

"And wasn't there some old legend to the effect that a werewolf could only be killed with a silver bullet?"

"Ah, bah," he replied with a laugh. "What did those old legend-mongers know of the power of modern firearms? . . . When I did shoot that wolfman, my friend, I had something more powerful than superstition in my hand. *Morbleu*, but I did shoot a hole in him large enough for him to have walked through."

Quinn didn't completely abandon the use of holy water, ancient relics, and magical charms to defeat supernatural entities, but he made it clear that de Grandin understood that there was a place for modern technology as well as old folklore when it came to fighting monsters. Nor was de Grandin himself above using violence to fight his enemies. Oftentimes, the French occult investigator served as judge, jury and executioner when dealing with madmen, deranged doctors, and evil masterminds. There was little mercy in his stories for those who used dark forces.

While sex was heavily insinuated but rarely covered explicitly in the pulps, except in the most general of terms, Quinn again was willing to go where few other writers would dare. Sexual slavery, lesbianism, and even incest played roles in his writing over the years, challenging the moral values of the day.

In the end, there's no denying that the de Grandin stories are pulp fiction. Many characters are little more than assorted clichés bundled together. De Grandin is a model hero, a French expert on the occult, and never at a loss when battling the most evil of monsters. Dr. Trowbridge remains the steadfast companion, much in the Dr. Watson tradition, always doubting but inevitably following his friend's advice. Quinn wrote for the masses, and he didn't spend pages describing landscapes when there was always more action unfolding.

The Jules de Grandin stories were written as serial entertainment, with the legitimate expectation that they would not be read back to back. While all of the adventures are good fun, the best way to properly enjoy them is over an extended period of time. Plowing through one story after another will lessen their impact, and greatly cut down on the excitement and fun of reading them. One story a week, which would stretch out this entire five-volume series over two years, might be the perfect amount of time needed to fully enjoy these tales of the occult and the macabre. They might not be great literature, but they don't pretend to be. They're pulp adventures, and even after seventy-five years, the stories read well.

Additionally, though the specific aesthetic values of *Weird Tales* readers were vastly different than those of today's readers, one can see clearly see the continuing allure of these types of supernatural adventures, and the long shadow that they cast over twentieth and early twenty-first century popular culture. Sure, these stories are formulaic, but it is a recipe that continues to be popular to this day. The formula of the occult detective, the protector who stands between us and the monsters of the night, can be seen time and time again in the urban fantasy and paranormal romance categories of commercial fiction, and is prevalent in today's television and movies. Given the ubiquity and contemporary popularity of this type of narrative, it's actually not at all surprising that Seabury Quinn was the most popular contributor to *Weird Tales*.

We are proud to present this volume collecting the best Jules de Grandin stories written by Seabury Quinn, organized chronologically, as they originally appeared in *Weird Tales* magazine.

This volume has been graced by tremendous artwork from renowned artist Donato Giancola, who has given Quinn's legendary character an irresistible combination of grace, cunning and timelessness. We couldn't have asked for a better way to introduce "the occult Hercule Poirot" to a new generation of readers.

Finally, if Seabury Quinn is watching from above, and closely scrutinizing the shelves of bookstores, he would undoubtedly be pleased as punch, and proud as all get-out, to find his creation, Dr. Jules de Grandin, rising once again in the minds of readers around the world, battling the forces of darkness . . . wherever, whoever, or whatever the nature of their evil might be.

When the Jaws of Darkness Open,
Only Jules de Grandin Stands in Satan's Way!

Robert E. Weinberg
Chicago, Illinois, USA

and

George A. Vanderburgh
Lake Eugenia, Ontario, Canada

23 September 2016

THE BEST OF
JULES DE GRANDIN

20 CLASSIC OCCULT DETECTIVE STORIES

The Isle of Missing Ships

I

THE *Mevrouw*, SUMATRA-BOUND OUT of Amsterdam, had dropped the low Holland coast an hour behind that day in 1925, when I recognized a familiar figure among the miscellany of Dutch colonials. The little man with the erect, military carriage, trimly waxed mustache and direct, challenging blue eyes was as conspicuous amid the throng of over-fleshed planters, traders and petty administrators as a *fleur-de-lis* growing in the midst of a cabbage patch.

"For the Lord's sake, de Grandin! What are you doing here?" I demanded, seizing him by the hand. "I thought you'd gone back to your microscopes and test tubes when you cleared up the Broussac mystery."

He grinned at me like a blond brother of Mephistopheles as he linked his arm in mine and caught step with me. "*Eh bien*," he agreed with a nod, "so did I; but those inconsiderate Messieurs Lloyd would not have it so. They must needs send me an urgent message to investigate a suspicion they have at the other end of the earth.

"I did not desire to go. The summer is come and the blackbirds are singing in the trees at St. Cloud. Also, I have much work to do; but they tell me: 'You shall name your own price and no questions shall be asked,' and, *hélas*, the franc is very low on the exchange these days.

"I tell them, 'Ten pounds sterling for each day of my travels and all expenses.' They agree. *Voilà*. I am here."

I looked at him in amazement. "Lloyds? Ten pounds sterling a day?" I echoed. "What in the world—?"

"*La, la!*" he exclaimed. "It is a long story, Friend Trowbridge, and most like a foolish one in the bargain, but, at any rate, the English money is sound. Listen"—he sank his voice to a confidential whisper—"you know those Messieurs Lloyd, *hein?* They will insure against anything from the result of one of your

American political elections to the loss of a ship in the sea. That last business of theirs is also my business, for the time.

"Of late the English insurers have had many claims to pay—claims on ships which should have been good risks. There was the Dutch Indiaman *Van Damm*, a sound little iron ship of twelve thousand tons displacement. She sail out of Rotterdam for Sumatra, and start home heavy-laden with spices and silks, also with a king's ransom in pearls safely locked in her strong box. Where is she now?" He spread his hands and shrugged expressively. "No one knows. She was never heard of more, and the Lloyds had to make good her value to her owners.

"There was the French steamer *l'Orient*, also dissolved into air, and the British merchantman *Nightingale*, and six other sound ships gone—all gone, with none to say whither, and the estimable Messieurs Lloyd to pay insurance. All within one single year. *Parbleu*, it is too much! The English company pays its losses like a true sportsman, but it also begins to sniff the aroma of the dead fish. They would have me, Jules de Grandin, investigate this business of the monkey and tell them where the missing ships are gone.

"It may be for a year that I search; it may be for only a month, or, perhaps, I spend the time till my hair is as bald as yours, Friend Trowbridge, before I can report. No matter; I receive my ten pounds each day and all incidental expenses. Say now, are not those Messieurs Lloyd gambling more recklessly this time than ever before in their long career?"

"I think they are," I agreed.

"But," he replied with one of his elfish grins, "remember, Trowbridge, my friend, those Messieurs Lloyd were never known to lose money permanently on any transaction. *Morbleu!* Jules de Grandin, as the Americans say, you entertain the hatred for yourself!"

The *Mevrouw* churned and wallowed her broad-beamed way through the cool European ocean, into the summer seas, finally out upon the tropical waters of Polynesia. For five nights the smalt-blue heavens were ablaze with stars; on the sixth evening the air thickened at sunset. By ten o'clock the ship might have been draped in a pall of black velvet as a teapot is swathed in a cozy, so impenetrable was the darkness. Objects a dozen feet from the porthole lights were all but indistinguishable, at twenty feet they were invisible, and, save for the occasional phosphorescent glow of some tumbling sea denizen, the ocean itself was only an undefined part of the surrounding blackness.

"Eh, but I do not like this," de Grandin muttered as he lighted a rank Sumatra cigar from the ship steward's store and puffed vigorously to set the fire going: "this darkness, it is a time for evil doings, Friend Trowbridge."

He turned to a ship's officer who strode past us toward the bridge. "Is it that we shall have a storm, Monsieur?" he asked. "Does the darkness portend a typhoon?"

"No," returned the Dutchman. "Id iss folcanic dust. Some of dose folcano mountains are in eruption again and scatter steam and ash over a hundred miles. Tomorrow, perhaps, or de nex' day, ve are out of id an' into de zunzhine again."

"Ah," de Grandin bowed acknowledgment of the information, "and does this volcanic darkness frequently come at this latitude and longitude, Monsieur?"

"Ja," the other answered, "dese vaters are almost alvays cofered; de chimneys of hell poke up through de ocean hereabouts, *Mijnheer.*"

"*Cordieu!*" de Grandin swore softly to himself. "I think he has spoken truth, Friend Trowbridge. Now if—*Grand Dieu*, see! What is that?"

Some distance off our port bow a brand of yellow fire burned a parabola against the black sky, burst into a shower of sparks high above the horizon and flung a constellation of colored fireballs into the air. A second flame followed the first, and a third winged upward in the wake of the second. "Rockets," de Grandin announced. "A ship is in distress over there, it would seem."

Bells clanged and jangled as the engine room telegraph sent orders from the bridge; there was a clanking of machinery as the screws churned in opposite directions and the steering mechanism brought the ship's head about toward the distress signals.

"I think we had best be prepared, my friend," de Grandin whispered as he reached upward to the rack above us and detached two kapok swimming jackets from their straps. "Come, slip this over your shoulders, and if you have anything in your cabin you would care to save, get it at once," he advised.

"You're crazy, man," I protested, pushing the life preserver away. "We aren't in any danger. Those lights were at least five miles away, and even if that other ship is fast on a reef our skipper would hear the breakers long before we were near enough to run aground."

"*Nom d'un nom!*" the little Frenchman swore in vexation. "Friend Trowbridge, you are one great zany. Have you no eyes in that so empty head of yours? Did you not observe how those rockets went up?"

"How they went up?" I repeated. "Of course I did; they were fired from the deck—perhaps the bridge—of some ship about five miles away."

"So?" he replied in a sarcastic whisper. "Five miles, you say? And you, a physician, do not know that the human eye sees only about five miles over a plane surface? How, then, if the distressed ship is five miles distant, could those flares have appeared to rise from *a greater height than our own deck?* Had they really a masthead, at that distance—they should have appeared to rise across the horizon. As it was, they first became visible at a considerable height."

"Nonsense," I rejoined; "whoever would be setting off rockets in midair in this part of the world?"

"Who, indeed?" he answered, gently forcing the swimming coat on me. "That question, *mon ami*, is precisely what those Messieurs Lloyd are paying me ten pounds a day to answer. Hark!"

Distinctly, directly in our path, sounded the muttering roar of waves breaking against rocks.

Clang! The ship's telegraph shrieked the order to reverse, to put about, to the engine room from the bridge.

Wheels and chains rattled, voices shouted hoarse orders through the dark, and the ship shivered from stem to stern as the engine struggled hysterically to break our course toward destruction.

Too late! Like a toy boat caught in a sudden wind squall, we lunged forward, gathering speed with each foot we traveled. There was a rending crash like all the crockery in the world being smashed at once, de Grandin and I fell headlong to the deck and shot along the smooth boards like a couple of ball players sliding for second base, and the stout little *Mevrouw* listed suddenly to port, sending us banging against the deck rail.

"Quick, quick, my friend!" de Grandin shouted. "Over the side and swim for it. I may be wrong, *prie-Dieu* I am, but I fear there will be devil's work here anon. Come!" He lifted himself to his feet, balanced on the rail a moment, then slipped into the purple water that swirled past the doomed ship's side a scant seven feet below us.

I followed, striking out easily toward the quiet water ahead, the kapok jacket keeping me afloat and the rushing water carrying me forward rapidly.

"By George, old fellow, you've been right this far," I congratulated my companion, but he shut me off with a sharp hiss.

"Still, you fool," he admonished savagely. "Keep your silly tongue quiet and kick with your feet. Kick, kick, I tell you! Make as great commotion in the water as possible—*nom de Dieu!* We are lost!"

Faintly luminous with the phosphorescence of tropical sea water, something seeming as large as a submarine boat shot upward from the depths below, headed as straight for my flailing legs as a sharpshooter's bullet for its target.

De Grandin grasped my shoulder and heaved me over in a clumsy back somersault, and at the same time thrust himself as deeply into the water as his swimming coat would permit. For a moment his fiery silhouette mingled with that of the great fish and he seemed striving to embrace the monster, then the larger form sank slowly away, while the little Frenchman rose puffing to the surface.

"*Mordieu!*" he commented, blowing the water from his mouth, "that was a near escape, my friend. One little second more and he would have had your leg in his belly. Lucky for us, I knew the pearl divers' trick of slittin' those fellows' gills with a knife, and luckier still I thought to bring along a knife to slit him with."

"What was it?" I asked, still bewildered by the performance I had just witnessed. "It looked big enough to be a whale."

He shook his head to clear the water from his eyes as he replied. "It was our friend, *Monsieur le Requin*—the shark. He is always hungry, that one, and such morsels as you would be a choice titbit for his table, my friend."

"A shark!" I answered incredulously. "But it couldn't have been a shark, de Grandin, they have to turn on their backs to bite, and that thing came straight at me."

"Ah, *bah!*" he shot back disgustedly. "What old wives' tale is that you quote? *Le requin* is no more compelled to take his food upside down than you are. I tell you, he would have swallowed your leg up to the elbow if I had not cut his sinful gizzard in two!"

"Good Lord!" I began splashing furiously. "Then we're apt to be devoured any moment!"

"Possibly," he returned calmly, "but not probably. If land is not too far away that fellow's brethren will be too busy eating him to pay attention to such small fry as us. *Grace à Dieu*, I think I feel the good land beneath our feet even now."

It was true. We were standing armpit-deep on a sloping, sandy beach with the long, gentle swell of the ocean kindly pushing us toward the shore. A dozen steps and we were safely beyond the tide-line, lying face down upon the warm sands and gulping down great mouthfuls of the heavy, sea-scented air. What de Grandin did there in the dark I do not know, but for my part I offered up such unspoken prayers of devout thanksgiving as I had never breathed before.

My devotions were cut short by a sputtering mixture of French profanity.

"What's up?" I demanded, then fell silent as de Grandin's hand closed on my wrist like a tightened tourniquet.

"Hark, my friend," he commanded. "Look across the water to the ship we left and say whether or no I was wise when I brought us away."

Out across the quiet lagoon inside the reef the form of the stranded *Mevrouw* loomed a half shade darker than the night, her lights, still burning, casting a fitful glow upon the crashing water at the reef and the quiet water beyond. Two, three, four, half a dozen shades gathered alongside her; dark figures, like ants swarming over the carcass of a dead rat, appeared against her lights a moment, and the stabbing flame of a pistol was followed a moment later by the reports of the shots wafted to us across the lagoon. Shouts, cries of terror, screams of women in abject fright followed one another in quick succession for a time, then silence, more ominous than any noise, settled over the water.

Half an hour, perhaps, de Grandin and I stood tense-muscled on the beach, staring toward the ship, waiting expectantly for some sign of renewed life. One by one her porthole lights blinked out; at last she lay in utter darkness.

"It is best we seek shelter in the bush, my friend," de Grandin announced matter-of-factly. "The farther out of sight we get the better will be our health."

"What in heaven's name does it all mean?" I demanded as I turned to follow him.

"Mean?" he echoed impatiently. "It means we have stumbled on as fine a nest of pirates as ever cheated the yardarm. When we reached this island, Friend Trowbridge, I fear we did but step from the soup kettle into the flame. *Mille tonneres*, what a fool you are, Jules de Grandin! You should have demanded fifty pounds sterling a day from those Messieurs Lloyd! Come, Friend Trowbridge, let us seek shelter. Right away, at once, immediately."

2

THE SLOPING BEACH GAVE way to a line of boulders a hundred yards inland, and these in turn marked the beginning of a steady rise in the land, its lower portion overgrown with bushes, loftier growth supplanting the underbrush as we stumbled upward over the rocks.

When we had traversed several hundred rods and knocked nearly all the skin from our legs against unexpectedly projecting stones, de Grandin called a halt in the midst of a copse of wide-leafed trees. "We may as well rest here as elsewhere," he suggested philosophically. "The pack will scarcely hunt again tonight."

I was too sleepy and exhausted to ask what he meant. The last hour's events had been as full of surprises to me as a traveling carnival is for a farmhand.

It might have been half an hour later, or only five minutes, judging by my feelings, that I was roused by the roar of a muffled explosion, followed at short intervals by two more detonations. "*Mordieu!*" I heard de Grandin exclaim. "Up, Friend Trowbridge. Rise and see!" He shook me roughly by the shoulder, and half dragged me to an opening in the trees. Out across the lagoon I saw the hulk of the *Mevrouw* falling apart and sliding into the water like a mud bank attacked by a summer flood, and round her the green waters boiled and seethed as though the entire reef had suddenly gone white hot. Across the lagoon, wave after swelling wave raced and tumbled, beating on the glittering sands of the beach in a furious surf.

"Why—" I began, but he answered my question before I could form it.

"Dynamite!" he exclaimed. "Last night, or early this morning, they looted her, now they dismantle the remains with high explosives; it would not do to let her stand there as a sign-post of warning for other craft. *Pardieu!* They have system, these ones. Captain Kidd and Blackbeard, they were but freshmen in crime's college, Friend Trowbridge. We deal with postgraduates here. Ah"—his small, womanishly slender hand caught me by the arm—"observe, if you please; what is that on the sands below?"

Following his pointing finger with my eyes, I made out, beyond a jutting ledge of rocks, the rising spiral of a column of wood smoke. "Why," I exclaimed delightedly "some of the people from the ship escaped, after all! They got to shore and built a fire. Come on, let's join them. Hello, down here; hello, hello! You . . ."

"Fool!" he cried in a suppressed shout, clapping his hand over my mouth. "Would you ruin us altogether, completely, entirely? *Le bon Dieu* grant your ass's bray was not heard, or, if heard, was disregarded!"

"But," I protested, "those people probably have food, de Grandin, and we haven't a single thing to eat. We ought to join them and plan our escape."

He looked at me as a school teacher might regard an unusually backward pupil. "They have food, no doubt," he admitted, "but what sort of food, can you answer me that? Suppose—*nom d'un moinçau, regardez-vous!*"

AS IF IN ANSWER to my hail, a pair of the most villainous-looking Papuans I had ever beheld came walking around the rocky screen beyond which the smoke rose, looked undecidedly toward the heights where we hid, then turned back whence they had come. A moment later they reappeared, each carrying a broad-bladed spear, and began climbing over the rocks in our direction.

"Shall we go to meet them?" I asked dubiously. Those spears looked none too reassuring to me.

"*Mais non!*" de Grandin answered decidedly. "They may be friendly; but I distrust everything on this accurst island. We would better seek shelter and observe."

"But they might give us something to eat," I urged. "The whole world is pretty well civilized now, it isn't as if we were back in Captain Cook's day."

"Nevertheless," he returned as he wriggled under a clump of bushes, "we shall watch first and ask questions later."

I crawled beside him and squatted, awaiting the savages' approach.

But I had forgotten that men who live in primitive surroundings have talents unknown to their civilized brethren. While they were still far enough away to make it impossible for us to hear the words they exchanged as they walked, the two Papuans halted, looked speculatively at the copse where we hid, and raised their spears menacingly.

"*Ciel!*" de Grandin muttered. "We are discovered." He seized the stalk of one of the sheltering plants and shook it gently.

The response was instant. A spear whizzed past my ear, missing my head by an uncomfortably small fraction of an inch, and the savages began clambering rapidly toward us, one with his spear poised for a throw, the other drawing a murderous knife from the girdle which constituted his sole article of clothing.

"*Parbleu!*" de Grandin whispered fiercely. "Play dead, my friend. Fall out from the bush and lie as though his spear had killed you." He gave me a sudden push which sent me reeling into the open.

I fell flat to the ground, acting the part of a dead man as realistically as possible and hoping desperately that the savages would not decide to throw a second spear to make sure of their kill.

Though my eyes were closed, I could feel them standing over me, and a queer, cold feeling tingled between my shoulder blades, where I momentarily expected a knife thrust.

Half opening one eye, I saw the brown, naked shins of one of the Papuans beside my head, and was wondering whether I could seize him by the ankles and drag him down before he could stab me, when the legs beside my face suddenly swayed drunkenly, like tree trunks in a storm, and a heavy weight fell crashing on my back.

STARTLED OUT OF MY sham death by the blow, I raised myself in time to see de Grandin in a death grapple with one of the savages. The other one lay across me, the spear he had flung at us a few minutes before protruding from his back directly beneath his left shoulder blade.

"A *moi*, Friend Trowbridge!" the little Frenchmen called. "Quick, or we are lost."

I tumbled the dead Papuan unceremoniously to the ground and grappled with de Grandin's antagonist just as he was about to strike his dirk into my companion's side.

"*Bien, très bien!*" the Frenchman panted as he thrust his knife forward, sinking the blade hilt-deep into the savage's left armpit. "Very good, indeed, Friend Trowbridge. I have not hurled the javelin since I was a boy at school, and I strongly misdoubted my ability to kill the one with a single throw from my ambush, but, happily, my hand has not lost its cunning. *Voilà*, we have a perfect score to our credit! Come, let us bury them."

"But was it necessary to kill the poor fellows?" I asked as I helped him scrape a grave with one of his victim's knives. "Mightn't we have made them understand we meant them no harm?"

"Friend Trowbridge," he answered between puffs of exertion as he dragged one of the naked bodies into the shallow trench we had dug, "never, I fear me, will you learn the sense of the goose. With fellows such as these, even as with the shark last night, we take necessary steps for our own protection first.

"This interment which we make now, think you it is for tenderness of these *canaille*? Ah, *non*. We bury them that their friends find them not if they come searching, and that the buzzards come not flapping this way to warn the others of what we have done. Good, they are buried. Take up that one's spear and come with me. I would investigate that fire which they have made."

We approached the heights overlooking the fire cautiously, taking care to remain unseen by any possible scout sent out by the main party of natives. It was more than an hour before we maneuvered to a safe observation post. As we crawled over the last ridge of rock obstructing our view I went deathly sick at my stomach and would have fallen down the steep hill, had not de Grandin thrown his arm about me.

Squatting around a blazing bonfire in a circle, like wolves about the stag they have run to earth, were perhaps two dozen naked savages, and, bound upright to a stake fixed in the sand, was a white man, lolling forward against the restraining cords with a horrible limpness. Before him stood two burly Papuans, the war clubs in their hands, red as blood at the tips, telling the devil's work they had just completed. It was blood on the clubs. The brown fiends had beaten their helpless captive's head in, and even now one of them was cutting the cords that held his body to the stake.

But beyond the dead man was a second stake, and, as I looked at this, every drop of blood in my body seemed turned to liquid fire, for, lashed to it, mercifully unconscious, but still alive, was a white woman whom I recognized as the wife of a Dutch planter going out from Holland to join her husband in Sumatra.

"Good God, man!" I cried. "That's a woman; a white woman. We can't let those devils kill *her!*"

"Softly, my friend," de Grandin cautioned, pressing me back, for I would have risen and charged pell-mell down the hill. "We are two, they are more than a score; what would it avail us, or that poor woman, were we to rush down and be killed?"

I TURNED ON HIM IN amazed fury. "You call yourself a Frenchman," I taunted, "yet you haven't chivalry enough to attempt a rescue? A fine Frenchman you are!"

"Chivalry is well—in its place," he admitted, "but no Frenchman is so foolish as to spend his life where there is nothing to be bought with it. Would it help her if we, too, were destroyed, or, which is worse, captured and eaten also? Do we, as physicians, seek to throw away our lives when we find a patient hopelessly sick with phthisis? But no, we live that we may fight the disease in others—that we may destroy the germs of the malady. So let it be in this case. Save that poor one we can not; but take vengeance on her slayers we can and will. I, Jules de Grandin, swear it. Ha, she has it!"

Even as he spoke one of the cannibal butchers struck the unconscious woman over the head with his club. A stain of red appeared against the pale yellow of her hair, and the poor creature shuddered convulsively, then hung passive and flaccid against her bonds once more.

"Par le sang du diable," de Grandin gritted between his teeth, "if it so be that the good God lets me live, I swear to make those *sales bouchers* die one hundred deaths apiece for every hair in that so pitiful woman's head!"

He turned away from the horrid sight below us and began to ascend the hill. "Come away, Friend Trowbridge," he urged. "It is not good that we should look upon a woman's body served as meat. *Pardieu*, almost I wish I had followed your so crazy advice and attempted a rescue; we should have killed some of them so! No matter, as it is, we shall kill all of them, or may those Messieurs Lloyd pay me not one penny."

3

FEELING SECURE AGAINST DISCOVERY by the savages, as they were too engrossed in their orgy to look for other victims, we made our way to the peak which towered like a truncated cone at the center of the island.

From our station at the summit we could see the ocean in all directions and get an accurate idea of our surroundings. Apparently, the islet was the merest point of land on the face of the sea—probably only the apex of a submarine volcano. It was roughly oval in shape, extending for a possible five miles in length by two-and-a-quarter miles at its greatest width, and rising out of the ocean with a mountainous steepness, the widest part of the beach at the water-line being not more than three or four hundred feet. On every side, and often in series of three or four, extended reefs and points of rock (no doubt the lesser peaks of the mountain whose un-submerged top constituted the island) so that no craft larger than a whaleboat could hope to come within half a mile of the land without having its bottom torn out by the hidden semi-submerged crags.

"*Nom d'un petit bonhomme!*" de Grandin commented. "This is an ideal place for its purpose, *c'est certain*. Ah, see!"—he drew me to a ridge of rock which ran like a rampart across the well-defined path by which we had ascended. Fastened to the stone by bolts were three sheet-iron troughs, each pointing skyward at an angle of some fifty degrees, and each much blackened by smoke stains. "Do you see?" he asked. "These are for firing rockets—observe the powder burns on them. And here"—his voice rose to an excited pitch and he fairly danced in eagerness—"see what is before us!"

UP THE PATH, ALMOST at the summit of the peak, and about twenty-five feet apart, stood two poles, each some twelve feet in height and fitted with a pulley and lanyard. As we neared them we saw that a lantern with a green globe rested at the base of the right-hand stake, while a red-globed lamp was secured to the rope of the left post "Ah, clever, clever," de Grandin muttered, staring from one pole to the other. "Observe, my friend. At night the lamps can be lit and hoisted to the tops of these masts then gently raised and lowered. Viewed at a distance against the black background of this mountain they will simulate a ship's lights to the life. The unfortunate mariner making for them will find his ship fast on these rocks while the lights are still a mile or more away, and—too well we know what happens then. Let us see what more there is, eh?"

Rounding the peak we found ourselves looking down upon the thatched beehive-roofs of a native village, before which a dozen long Papuan canoes were beached on the narrow strip of sand. "Ah," de Grandin inspected the cluster of huts, "it is there the butchers dwell, eh? That will be a good spot for us to avoid, my friend. Now to find the residence of what you Americans call the master mind. Do you see aught resembling a European dwelling, Friend Trowbridge?"

I searched the greenery below us, but nowhere could I descry a roof. "No," I answered after a second inspection, "there's nothing like a white man's house down there; but how do you know there's a white man here, anyway?"

"Ho, ho," he laughed, "how does the rat know the house contains a cat when he hears it mew? Think you those *sacré* eaters of men would know enough to set up such devil's machinery as this, or that they would take care to dynamite the wreck of a ship after looting it? No, no, my friend, this is white man's work, and very bad work it is, too. Let us explore."

Treading warily, we descended the smooth path leading to the rocket-troughs, looking sharply from left to right in search of anything resembling a white man's house. Several hundred feet down the mountain the path forked abruptly, one branch leading toward the Papuan village, the other running to a narrow strip of beach bordering an inlet between two precipitous rock walls. I stared and stared again, hardly able to believe my eyes, for, drawn up on the sand and made fast by a rope to a ringbolt in the rock was a trim little motor-boat, flat-bottomed for navigating the rock-strewn waters in safety, broad-beamed for mastering the heavy ocean swells, and fitted with a comfortable, roofed-over cabin. Forward, on the little deck above her sharp clipper bow, was an efficient looking Lewis gun mounted on a swivel, and a similar piece of ordnance poked its aggressive nose out of the engine cockpit at the stern.

"*Par la barbe d'un bouc vert*," de Grandin swore delightedly, "but this is marvelous, this is magnificent, this is superb! Come, Friend Trowbridge, let us take advantage of this miracle; let us leave this hell-hole of an island right away, immediately, at once. *Par—*" The exclamation died, half uttered, and he stared past me with the expression of a superstitious man suddenly face-to-face with a sheeted specter.

4

"SURELY, GENTLEMEN," said a suave voice behind me, "you are not going to leave without permitting me to offer you some slight hospitality? That would be ungenerous."

I turned as though stung by a wasp and looked into the smiling eyes of a dark-skinned young man, perhaps thirty years of age. From the top of his spotless *topi* to the tips of his highly polished tan riding boots he was a perfect model of the well-dressed European in the tropics. Not a stain of dust or travel showed on his spruce white drill jacket or modishly cut riding breeches, and as he waved his silver-mounted riding crop in greeting, I saw his slender hands were carefully manicured, the nails cut rather long and stained a vivid pink before being polished to the brightness of mother-of-pearl.

De Grandin laid his hand upon the knife at his belt, before he could draw it, a couple of beetle-browed Malays in khaki jackets and *sarongs* stepped from the bushes bordering the path and leveled a pair of business-like Mauser rifles at us. "I wouldn't," the young man warned in a blasé drawl, "I really wouldn't, if I were you. These fellows are both dead shots and could put enough lead in you to sink you forty fathoms down before you could get the knife out of its sheath, much less into me. Do you mind, really?" He held out his hand for the weapon. "Thank you, that is much better"—he tossed the blade into the water of the inlet with a careless gesture—"really, you know, the most frightfully messy accidents are apt to happen with those things."

De Grandin and I eyed him in speechless amazement, but he continued as though our meeting were the most conventional thing imaginable.

"Mr. Trowbridge—pardon my assumption, but I heard your name called a moment ago—will you be good enough to favor me with an introduction to your friend?"

"I am Dr. Samuel Trowbridge, of Harrisonville, New Jersey," I replied, wondering, meanwhile, if I were in the midst of some crazy dream, "and this is Dr. Jules de Grandin, of Paris."

"So good of you," the other acknowledged with a smile. "I fear I must be less frank than you for the nonce and remain veiled in anonymity. However, one really must have some sort of designation, mustn't one? So suppose you know me for the present as Goonong Besar. Savage, unchristian-sounding sort of name, I'll admit, but more convenient than calling, 'hey, you!' or simply whistling when you wish to attract my attention. Eh, what? And now"—he made a slight bow—"if you will be so kind as to step into my humble burrow in the earth . . . Yes, that is it, the doorway right before you."

Still under the menacing aim of the Malays' rifles, de Grandin and I walked through the cleft in the rock, traversed a low, narrow passage, darker than a windowless cellar, made a sharp turn to the left, and halted abruptly, blinking our eyes in astonishment.

Before us, seeming to run into infinity, was a wide, long apartment paved with alternate squares of black and white marble, colonnaded down each side with double rows of white-marble pillars and topped with a vaulted ceiling of burnished copper plates. Down the center of the corridor, at intervals of about twenty feet, five silver oil lamps with globes of finely cut crystal hung from the polished ceiling, making the entire room almost as bright as equatorial noon.

"Not half bad, eh?" our host remarked as he viewed our astonishment with amusement. "This is only the vestibule, gentlemen; you really have no idea of the wonders of this house under the water. For instance, would either of you care to retrace your steps? See if you can find the door you came in."

We swung about, like soldiers at the command of execution, staring straight at the point where the entranceway should have been. A slab of marble, firm and solid as any composing the walls of the room, to all appearances, met our gaze; there was neither sign nor remote evidence of any door or doorway before us.

Goonong Besar chuckled delightedly and gave an order to one of his attendants in the harsh, guttural language of Malaya. "If you will look behind you, gentlemen," he resumed, again addressing us, "you will find another surprise."

We wheeled about and almost bumped into a pair of grinning Malay lads who stood at our elbows.

"These boys will show you to your rooms." Goonong Besar announced. "Kindly follow them. It will be useless to attempt conversation, for they understand no language but their native speech, and as for replying, unfortunately, they lack the benefits of a liberal education and can not write, while . . ." he shot a quick order to the youths, who immediately opened their mouths as though yawning. Both de Grandin and I gave vent to exclamations of horror. The boys mouths gaped emptily. Both had had their tongues cut off at the roots.

"You see," Goonong went on in the same musical, slightly bored voice, "these chaps can't be a bit of use to you as gossips, they really can't.

"I think I can furnish you with dinner clothes, Dr. de Grandin, but"—he smiled apologetically—"I'm afraid you, Dr. Trowbridge, are a little too—er—corpulent to be able to wear any garments made for me. So sorry! However, no doubt we can trick you out in a suit of whites Captain Van Thun—er, that is, I'm sure you can be accommodated from our stores. Yes.

"Now, if you will follow the guides, please"—he broke off on a slightly interrogative note and bowed with gentle courtesy toward each of us in turn—"you will excuse me for a short time, I'm sure."

Before we could answer, he signaled his two attendants, and the three of them stepped behind one of the marble columns. We heard a subdued click, as of two pieces of stone coming lightly together.

"But, Monsieur, this is incredible, this is monstrous!" de Grandin began, striding forward. "You shall explain, I demand—*Cordieu*, he is gone!"

He was. As though the wall had faded before his approach, or his own body had dissolved into ether, Goonong Besar had vanished. We were alone in the brilliantly lighted corridor with our tongueless attendants.

Nodding and grinning, the lads signaled us to follow them down the room. One of them ran a few paces ahead and parted a pair of silken curtains, disclosing a narrow doorway through which only one could go at a time. Obeying the lad's gestures, I stepped through the opening, followed by de Grandin and our dumb guides.

The lad who had held aside the curtains for us ran ahead a few paces and gave a strange, eerie cry. We looked sharply at him, wondering what the utterance portended, and from behind us sounded the thud of stone on stone. Turning, we saw the second Malay grinning broadly at us from the place where the doorway had been. I say "had been" advisedly, for, where the narrow arched door had pierced the thick wall a moment before, was now a solid row of upright marble slabs, no joint or crack showing which portion of the wall was solid stone and which cunningly disguised door.

"*Sang du diable!*" de Grandin muttered. "But I do not like this place. It reminds me of that grim fortress of the Inquisition at Toledo where the good fathers, dressed as demons, could appear and disappear at will through seeming solid walls and frighten the wits out of and the true faith into superstitious heretics."

I suppressed a shudder with difficulty. This underground house of secret doors was too reminiscent of other practises of the Spanish Inquisition besides the harmless mummery of the monks for my peace of mind.

"*Eh bien*," de Grandin shrugged, "now we are here we may as well make the best of it. Lead on, *Diablotins*"—he turned to our dark-skinned guides—"we follow."

We were standing in a long, straight passage, smoothwalled with panels of polished marble, and, like the larger apartment, tiled with alternate squares of black and white. No doorways led off the aisle, but other corridors crossed it at right angles at intervals of thirty to thirty-five feet. Like the larger room, the passage was lighted by oil lamps swung from the ceiling.

Following our guides, we turned to the right down a passageway the exact duplicate of the first, entered a third corridor, and, after walking a considerable distance, made another turn and stopped before a narrow curtained archway. Through this we entered a large square room, windowless, but well lighted by lamps and furnished with two bedsteads of bamboo having strong China matting on them in lieu of springs or mattress. A low bamboo dressing table, fitted with a mirror of polished metal, and several reed chairs constituted the residue of the furniture.

One of the boys signed to us to remove our clothes, while the other ran out, returning almost immediately dragging two sheet-iron bath tubs after him. Placing these in the center of the room he left us again, and reappeared in a few minutes with a wheeled contrivance something like a child's express wagon in which stood six large earthen jars, four containing warm water, the other two cold.

We stepped into the tubs and the lads proceeded to rub us down with an oily liquid, strongly perfumed with sandalwood and very soothing to feel. When this had been well worked into our skins the lads poured the contents of the warm-water jars over us, splashing us thoroughly from hair to feet, then sluiced us off with a five-gallon douche of almost ice-cold water. Towels of coarse native linen were unfolded, and in less than five minutes we were as thoroughly cleansed, dried and invigorated as any patron of a Turkish bath at home.

I felt rather dubious when my personal attendant produced a clumsy native razor and motioned me to be seated in one of the cane chairs, but the lad proved a skillful barber, light and deft of touch and absolutely speechless—a great improvement upon the loquacious American tonsorialist, I thought.

Dinner clothes and a suit of carefully laundered white drill, all scented with the pungent, pleasing odor of clove husks, were brought in on wicker trays, and as we put the finishing touches on our toilet one of the lads produced a small casket of polished cedar in which reposed a layer of long, black cigars, the sort which retail for a dollar apiece in Havana.

"*Nom d'un petit bonhomme!*" de Grandin exploded as he exhaled a lungful of the fragrant smoke; "this is marvelous; it is magnificent; it is superb—but I like it not, Friend Trowbridge."

"Bosh," I responded, puffing in placid content, "you're afraid of your shadow, de Grandin! Why, man, this is wonderful—think where we were this morning, shipwrecked, pursued by man-eaters, with starvation as the least of our perils, and look at us now, both dressed in clean clothes, with every attention and convenience we could have at home, and safe, man, safe."

"Safe?" he answered dubiously. "'Safe,' do you say? Did you apprehend, my friend, how our host, that so mysterious Monsieur Goonong, almost spoke of Captain Van Thun when the question of clothing you came up?"

"Why, now you speak of it, I do remember how he seemed about to say something about Captain Something-or-Other, and apparently thought better of it," I agreed. "But what's that to do with us?"

The little Frenchman came close to me and sank his voice to a scarcely audible whisper: "Captain Franz Van Thun," he breathed, "was master of the Dutch Indiaman *Van Damm*, which sailed from Rotterdam to Sumatra, and was lost, as far as known, *with all on board*, on her homeward voyage."

"But—" I protest.

"*She-s-sh!*" he cut me off. "Those servant boys are beckoning: come, we are wanted elsewhere."

I looked up at the two mutes, and shuddered at sight of the leering grins on their faces.

5

THE LADS LED US through another bewildering series of corridors till our sense of location was completely obfuscated, finally paused, one on each side of an archway, and, bowing deeply, signaled us to enter.

We strode into a long, marble-tiled room which, unlike every other apartment in the queer house, was not brilliantly lighted. The room's sole illumination was furnished by the glow of fourteen wax candles set in two seven-branched silver candelabra which stood at opposite ends of a polished mahogany table of purest Sheraton design, its waxed surface giving back reflections of crystal, and silver dinner service fit for the table of a king.

"Ah, gentlemen," Goonong Besar, arrayed in immaculate evening clothes, greeted us from the farther end of the room. "I hope you have brought good appetites with you. I'm fairly ravenous, for my part. Will you join me?"

The same Malay servitors who had accompanied him at our meeting stood behind him now, their semi-military khaki jackets and sarongs exchanged for costumes of freshly ironed white linen and their rifles replaced by a pair of large-caliber Luger pistols which each wore conspicuously tucked in his scarlet silk cummerbund.

"Sorry I can't offer you a cocktail," our host apologized as we seated ourselves, "but ice is not among the improvements available in my modest little menage, unfortunately. However, we find the sea caves do quite well as refrigerators and I think you'll find this chilled wine really acceptable as a substitute. Ah"—he looked diffidently from one of us to the other, finally fixing his gaze on me—"will you be good enough to ask the blessing, Dr. Trowbridge? You look as if you might be experienced in that line."

Startled, but greatly reassured by the request, I bowed my head and repeated the customary formula, almost springing from my chair with amazement as I opened my eyes at the prayer's end. While de Grandin and I had bent above the table during grace, the servants had pulled back the rich *batik* with which the wall facing us was draped, revealing a series of heavy plate glass panels against which the ocean's green waters pressed. We are looking directly on to the sea bottom.

"Jolly clever idea, what?" Goonong Besar inquired smiling at our surprised faces. "Thought it all up myself; like to see the little finny fellows swim past, you know. Had a beastly hard time getting workmen to do the job for me, too; but all sorts of unbelievable persons trickle into these islands from time to time—architects gone *ga-ga* with drink, skilled artisans in all the trades and what-not—I finally managed to collect the men I wanted."

"But, Monsieur, the expense," de Grandin protested with typical Gallic logic, "it must have been prodigious!"

"Oh, no," the young man answered negligently. "I had to feed the beggars, of course, but most of 'em were habituated to native food, and that's not very expensive."

"But their salaries," de Grandin persisted; "why Monsieur, this house is a work of genius, a marvel of engineering; even drink-ruined architects and engineers capable of producing such a place as this would demand fabulous fees for their services—and the laborers, the men who cut and polished the marble here, they must have been numerous as an army; their wages would be ruinous."

"Most of the marble was salvaged from deserted Dutch colonial palaces," Goonong Besar replied. "You know, Holland built a mighty empire in these islands a century or so ago, and her planters lived in palaces fit for kings. When the empire crumbled the planters left, and he who cared to might help himself to their houses, wholly or in part. As for wages"—he waved a jeweled hand carelessly—"I am rich, but the wages made no great inroads on my fortune. Do you remember your medieval history, Dr. de Grandin?"

"Eh? But certainly," the Frenchman responded, "but . . ."

"Don't you recall, then, the precaution the nobles, ecclesiastical as well as temporal, took to insure the secrecy of their castle or cathedral plans?" He paused, smiling quizzically at de Grandin.

"*Parbleu!* But you would not; you could not, you would not dare!" the Frenchman almost shouted, half rising from his chair and staring at our host as though a mad dog sat in his place.

"Nonsense, of course I would—and did," the other replied good-humoredly. "Why not? The men were bits of human flotsam, not worth salvaging. And who was to know? Dead men are notoriously uncommunicative, you know. Proverbially so, in fact."

"But, you tell this to me?" de Grandin looked at him incredulously.

Our host's face went perfectly expressionless as he stared directly at de Grandin for a period while one might count five slowly, then his dark, rather sullen face lighted with a smile. "May I offer you some more wine, my dear doctor?" he asked.

I LOOKED ALTERNATELY AT MY companions in wonderment. Goonong Besar had made some sinister implication which de Grandin had been quick to comprehend, I knew, and their subsequent conversation concerning dead men telling no tales contained a thinly veiled threat; but try as I would I could not find the key to their enigmatic talk. "Medieval castles and cathedrals? Dead men tell no tales?" I repeated to myself. What did it all mean?

Goonong Besar broke in on my thought: "May I offer you a bit more of this white meat, Dr. Trowbridge?" he asked courteously. "Really, we find this white meat" (the words were ever, so slightly emphasized) "most delicious. So tender and well flavored, you know. Do you like it?"

"Very much, thank you," I replied. "It's quite different from anything I've ever tasted. In a way it reminds me of delicate young pork, yet it's different, too. Is it peculiar to the islands, Mr. Goonong?"

"Well—er"—he smiled slightly as he cut a thin slice of the delicious roast and placed it on my plate—"I wouldn't say it is peculiar to our islands, though we have an unusual way of preparing it in this house. The natives hereabouts refer to the animal from which it comes as 'long pig'—really a disgusting sort of beast while living; but quite satisfactory when killed and properly cooked. May I serve you again, Dr. de Grandin?" He turned toward the Frenchman with a smile.

I sat suddenly upright in utter, dumfounded amazement as I beheld Grandin's face. He was leaning forward in his chair, his fierce little blue eyes very round and almost protruding from his head, his weather-tanned cheeks gone the color of putty as he stared at our host like a subject regarding a professional hypnotist. "*Dieu, grand Dieu!*" he ejaculated in a choking whisper. "'Long pig,' did you say? *Sang de St. Denis!* And I have eaten it!"

"My dear chap, are you ill?" I cried, leaping from my chair and hastening to his side. "Has your dinner disagreed with you?"

"*Non, non!*" he waved me away, still speaking that choking whisper. "Sit down, Friend Trowbridge, sit down; but *par l'amour de Dieu*, I beseech you, eat no more of that accurst meat, at least not tonight."

"Oh, my dear sir!" Goonong Besar protested mildly. "You have spoiled Dr. Trowbridge's appetite, and he was enjoying this delicious white meat so much, too. This is really too bad, you know. Really, it is!"

He frowned at the silver meat platter before him a moment, then signaled one of his attendants to take it away, adding a quick command in Malayan as he did so.

"Perhaps a little entertainment will help us forget this unfortunate *contretemps*," he suggested. "I have sent for Miriam. You will like her, I fancy. I have great hopes for her; she has the makings of a really accomplished *artiste*, I think."

The servant who had taken away the meat returned and whispered something in our host's ear. As he listened, Goonong Besar's thin, well-bred face took on such an expression of fury as I had never before seen displayed by a human being. "What?" he shouted, forgetting, apparently, that the Malay did not understand English. "I'll see about this—we'll soon see who says 'must' and 'shall' in this house."

He turned to us with a perfunctory bow as he rose. "Excuse me, please," he begged. "A slight misunderstanding has arisen, and I must straighten it out. I shan't keep you waiting long, I hope; but if you wish anything while I am gone, Hussein"—he indicated the Malay who stood statue-still behind his chair—"will attend your wants. He speaks no English, but you can make him understand by signs, I think."

"Quick, de Grandin, tell me before he comes back," I besought as Goonong, accompanied by one of the Malays, left the room.

"Eh?" replied the Frenchman, looking up from an absorbed contemplation of the tableware before him. "What is it you would know, my friend?"

"What was all that word-juggling about medieval builders and dead men telling no tales?" I demanded.

"Oh, that?" he answered with a look of relief. "Why, do you not know that when a great lord of the Middle Ages commissioned an architect to build a castle for him it was almost tantamount to a death sentence? The architect, the master builders, even the principal workmen, were usually done to death when the building was finished in order that they might not divulge its secret passages and hidden defenses to an enemy, or duplicate the design for some rival noble."

"Why—why, then, Goonong Besar meant he killed the men who built this submarine house for him!" I ejaculated, horror-stricken.

"Precisely," de Grandin answered, "but, bad as that may be, we have a more personal interest in the matter. Did you notice him when I showed surprise he should confess his guilt to us?"

"Good heavens, yes!" I answered. "He meant—"

"That, though still breathing, we are, to all intents dead men," de Grandin supplied.

"And that talk of 'white meat,' and 'long pig'?" I asked.

He drew a shuddering breath, as though the marble-lined cavern had suddenly gone icy-cold. "Trowbridge my friend," he answered in a low, earnest whisper, "you must know this thing; but you must control yourself, too. Not by word or sign must you betray your knowledge. Throughout these devil-ridden islands, wherever the brown fiends who are their natives eat men, they refer to the cannibal feast as a meal of long pig. That so unfortunate man we saw dead at the stake this morning, and that pitiful Dutch woman we saw clubbed to death— they, my friend, were 'long pigs.' That was the *white meat* this devil out of lowest hell set before us this night. That is the food we have eaten at this accurst table!"

"My God!" I half rose from my chair, then sank back, overcome with nausea. "Did we—do you suppose—was it *her* flesh—?"

"S-s-sh!" he warned sharply. "Silence, my friend; control yourself. Do not let him see you know. He is coming!"

As though de Grandin's words had been a theatrical cue for his entrance, Goonong Besar stepped through the silken portieres at the doorway beyond the table, a pleased smile on his swarthy face. "So sorry to keep you waiting," he apologized. "The trouble is all adjusted now, and we can proceed with our entertainment. Miriam is a little diffident before strangers, but I—er—persuaded her to oblige us." He turned toward the door through which he had entered and waved his hand to someone behind the curtains.

Three Malays, one a woman bent with age and hideously wrinkled, the other two vacant-faced youths, came through the doorway at his gesture. The woman, bearing a section of bamboo fitted with drumheads of rawhide at each end, led the way, the first boy rested his hand on her shoulder, and the second lad, in turn, held tightly to his companion's jacket. A second glance told us the reason for this procedure. The woman, though aged almost to the point of paralysis, possessed a single malignant, blood-shot eye; both boys were sightless, their scarred and sunken eyelids telling mutely of eyeballs gouged from their faces by unskilled hands which had torn the surrounding tissues as they ripped the optics from the quivering flesh.

"Ha-room; ha-room!" cried the old crone in a cracked treble, and the two blind boys seated themselves cross-legged on the marble floor. One of them raised a reed pipe to his lips, the other rested a sort of zither upon his knees, and each began trying his instrument tentatively, producing a sound approximating the complaints of a tomcat suffering with cholera morbus.

"Ha-room; ha-room!" the hag cried again, and commenced beating a quick rhythm on her drum, using her fingertips and the heels of her hands alternately for drumsticks. "Tauk-auk-a—tauk-auk-a—tauk-auk-a!" the drum-beats boomed hollowly, the first stroke heavily accented, the second and third following in such quick succession that they seemed almost indivisible parts of one continuous thrumming.

Now the pipe and zither took up the tribal tune, and a surge of fantastic music swirled and eddied through the marble-walled apartment. It was unlike anything I had ever heard, a repetitious, insistent, whining of tortured instruments, an air that pleaded with the hearers' evil nature to overthrow restraint and give the beast within him freedom, a harmony that drugged the senses like opium or the extract of the cola-nut. The music raced and soared, faster, shriller and higher, the painted-silk curtains swung apart and a girl glided out upon the tessellated pavement.

SHE WAS YOUNG—SIXTEEN, OR seventeen at the most—and the sinuous, lithe grace of her movements was as much due to healthy and perfectly co-ordinated muscles as to training. The customary sarong of the islands encased her nether limbs, but, instead of the native woman's jacket, her sarong was carried up beyond the gold six-inch wide belt about her waist and tightly wrapped about her bosom so that it formed a single comprehensive garment covering her from armpits to ankles. Save for a chaplet of blazing cabochon rubies about her slender throat, her neck and shoulders were bare, but ornaments in the form of flexible golden snakes with emerald eyes twined up each arm from elbow to shoulder, and bangles of pure, soft gold, hung with triple rows of tiny hawk-bells, circled her wrists. Other bangles, products of the finest goldsmiths of India, jangled about her white ankles above the pearl-encrusted slippers of amethyst velvet, while the diamond aigrette fastened comb-fashion in her sleekly parted black hair was worth a king's ransom. Fit to ransom a monarch, too, was the superb blue-white diamond of her nose-stud, fixed in her left nostril, and the rope of pearls which circled her waist and hung swaying to the very hem of her sarong of Philippine pineapple gauze was fit to buy the Peacock Throne of the Grand Mogul himself.

Despite the lavishly applied cosmetics, the antimony which darkened her eyelids to the color of purple grape skins, the cochineal which dyed her lips and cheeks a brilliant scarlet and the powdered charcoal which traced her eyebrows in continuous, fluted line across her forehead, she was beautiful with the rich, ripe beauty of the women who inspired Solomon of old to indite his *Song of Songs*. None but the Jewish race, or perhaps the Arabian, could have produced a woman with the passionate, alluring beauty of Miriam, the dancer in the house beneath the sea.

Back and forth across the checkered floor the girl wove her dance, tracing patterns intricate as lace from Canary or the looms of spiders over the marble with the soft soles of her velvet slippers, the chiming bells at her wrists and ankles keeping time to the calling, luring tune of the old hag and her blind musicians with the consummate art of a Spanish castanet dancer following the music with her hand cymbals.

At last the dance was done.

Shaking like a leaf with the intoxication of her own rhythmic movements, Miriam flung herself full length face downward, before Goonong Besar, and lay upon the marble floor in utter, abject self-abasement.

What he said to her we did not understand, for the words were in harsh Malayan, but he must have given her permission to go, for she rose from her prostration like a dog expecting punishment when its master relents, and ran from the room, bracelets and anklets ringing time to her panic flight, pearls clicking together as they swayed with the motion of her *sarong*.

The old crone rose, too, and led her blind companions from the room, and we three sat staring at each other under the winking candles' light with the two impassive Malay guards standing motionless behind their master's chair.

"Do you think she is beautiful?" Goonong Besar asked as he lighted a cigarette and blew a cloud of smoke toward the copper ceiling.

"Beautiful?" de Grandin gasped, "*Mon Dieu*, Monsieur, she is wonderful, she is magnificent, she is superb. Death of my life, but she is divine! Never have I seen such a dancer; never such, such—*nom de Dieu*, I am speechless as the fish! In all the languages I know there are no words to describe her!"

"And you, Dr. Trowbridge, what do you think of my little Miriam?" Goonong addressed me.

"She is very lovely," I acknowledged, feeling the words foolishly inadequate.

"Ha, ha," he laughed good-naturedly. "Spoken with true Yankee conservatism, by Jove.

"And that, gentlemen," he continued, "leads us to an interesting little proposition I have to make you. But first you will smoke? You'll find these cigars really good. I import them from Havana." He passed the polished cedar humidor across the table and held a match for us to light our selections of the expensive tobacco.

"Now, then," he commenced, inhaling a deep lungful of smoke, "first a little family history, then my business proposition. Are you ready, gentlemen?"

De Grandin and I nodded, wondering mutely what the next chapter in this novel of incredible surprises would be.

6

"WHEN WE MET so auspiciously this afternoon," our host began in his pleasant voice, "I requested that you call me Goonong Besar. That, however, is what we might call, for want of a better term, merely my *nom de l'ile*. Actually gentlemen, I am the Almost Honorable James Abingdon Richardson."

"*Parbleu*, Monsieur," de Grandin demanded, "how is it you mean that, 'the Almost Honorable'?"

The young man blew a cloud of fragrant smoke toward the room's copper ceiling and watched it float upward a moment before he replied: "My father was an English missionary, my mother a native princess. She was not of the Malay blood, but of the dominant Arab strain, and was known as Laila, Pearl of the Islands.

"My father had alienated himself from his family when he and an elder sister deserted the Church of England and, embracing a dissenting creed, came to Malay to spread the gospel of repentance or damnation among the heathen in their blindness."

He drew thoughtfully at his cigar and smiled rather bitterly as he resumed: "He was a fine figure of a man, that father of mine, six feet tall, blue-eyed and curly-haired, with a deep, compelling voice and the fire of fanaticism burning in his heart. The natives, Arab and Malay alike, took to his fiery gospel as the desert dwellers of Arabia once listened to the preaching of Mohammed, the camel driver. My grandfather, a pirate prince with a marble palace and a thousand slaves of his own, was one of the converts, and came to the mission bringing his ten-year-old daughter, Laila, with him. He left her at the mission school to learn the gentle teachings of the Prophet of Nazareth. She stayed there four years."

Again our host paused, puffing silently at his cigar, seemingly attempting to marshal his thoughts. "I believe I said my father was a dissenting clergyman? Yes, so I did, to be sure. Had he been a member of the established church things might have been different. The established English clergy are bad enough, with their fox hunting and general worldliness, but they're usually sportsmen. When she was a scant fifteen years old—women of the East mature more rapidly than your Western women, you know—Laila, the Pearl of the Islands, came back to her father's palace of marble and cedar, bearing a little boy baby in her arms. The charitable Christian sister of the missionary had driven her out of the mission settlement when she learned that she (the sister) was about to have a little nephew whose birth was not pre-sanctified by a wedding ring.

"The old pirate prince was furious. He would have put his daughter and her half-caste child to death and swooped down on the mission with fire and dagger, but my mother had learned much of Christian charity during her stay at the school. She was sure, if she went to my father with as many pearls as her hands could hold, and with a dowry of rubies strung round her neck, he would receive her as his wife—er—make an honest woman of her, as the saying goes.

"However, one thing and another prevented her return to the mission for three years, and when we finally got there we found my reverend sire had taken an English lady to wife.

"Oh, he took the jewels my mother brought—no fear of his refusing—and in return for them he permitted us to live in the settlement as native hangers-on. She, a princess, and the daughter of generations of princesses, scrubbed floors and baked bread in the house presided over by my father's wife and I, my father's first-born son, duly christened with his name, fetched and carried for my father's younger sons.

"They were hard, those days at the mission school. The white boys who were my half-brothers overlooked no chance to remind me of mother's shame and my own disgrace. Humility and patience under affliction were the lessons my mother and I had ground into us day by day while we remained there.

"Then, when I was a lad of ten years or so, my father's cousin, Viscount Abingdon, broke his neck at a fox hunt, and, as he died without issue, my father became a member of England's landed gentry, and went back home to take over the title and the entails. He borrowed on his expectancy before he left and offered my mother money to have me educated as a clerk in some trader's store, but my mother, for all her years of servitude, was still a princess of royal blood. Also she remembered enough Scripture to quote, 'Thy money perish with thee.' So she spat in his face and went back to the palace of her father, telling him that her husband was dead.

"I was sent to school in England—oh, yes, I'm a public school man, Winchester, you know—and I was down from my first term at Cambridge when the war broke out in 1914.

"Why should I have fought for England? What had England or the English ever done for me? It was the call of the blood—the English blood—perhaps. At any rate I joined up and was gazetted to a London regiment. Everything was death or glory those days, you know. 'For King and Country,' and all that sort of tosh. Racial lines were wiped out, and every man, whatever his color or creed, was for the common cause. Rot!

"I came into the officers' mess one night after a hard day's drill, and was presented to a young man from one of the guards regiments. 'Lieutenant Richardson,' my captain said, 'this is Lieutenant Richardson. Queer coincidence, you chaps are both James Abingdon Richardson. Ought to be great pals on that account, what?'

"The other Lieutenant Richardson looked me over from head to foot, then repeated distinctly, so everyone in the room could hear and understand. 'James, my boots need polishing. Attend to it.' It was the same order he had given me at the mission school a hundred times when we were lads together. He was Lieutenant the Honorable James Abingdon Richardson, *legitimate* eldest son of Viscount Abingdon. I was . . ."

He broke off, staring straight before him a moment, then: "There was a devil of a row. Officers weren't supposed to beat other officers into insensibility in company mess, you know. I was dismissed from the service, and came back to the islands.

"My grandfather was dead; so was my mother. I was monarch of all I surveyed—if I was willing not to look too far—and since my return I have consecrated my life to repaying my debt to my father on such of his race as crossed my path.

"The hunting has been fairly good, too. White men are such fools! Ship after ship has run aground on the rocks here, sometimes in answer to my signal rockets, sometimes mistaking the red and green lamps on the hill up yonder for ships' lights.

"It's been profitable. Nearly every ship so far has contained enough loot to make the game distinctly worth the trouble. I must admit your ship was somewhat of a disappointment in respect of monetary returns, but then I have had the pleasure of your company; that's something.

"I keep a crew of Papuans around to do the dirty work, and let 'em eat a few prisoners now and then by way of reward—don't mind an occasional helping of 'long pig' myself, as a matter of fact, provided it's a white one.

"But"—he smiled unpleasantly—"conditions aren't ideal, yet. I still have to install electricity in the house and rig up a wireless apparatus—I could catch more game that way—and then there's the question of women. Remember how Holy Writ says, 'It is not good for man to dwell alone'? I've found it out, already.

"Old Umera, the woman who played the drum tonight, and the slave girl, Miriam, are the only women in the establishment, thus far, but I intend to remedy that soon. I shall send to one of the larger islands and buy several of the most beautiful maidens available within the next few months, and live as befits a prince—a pirate prince, even as my grandfather was.

"Now, white men"—his suave manner dropped from him like a mask let down, and implacable hatred glared from his dark eyes—"this is my proposition to you. Before I establish my seraglio it is necessary that I possess suitable furniture. I can not spare any of my faithful retainers for the purpose of attending my women, but you two come into my hands providentially. Both of you are surgeons—you shall perform the necessary operations on each other. It is a matter of indifference to me which of you operates first—you may draw straws for the privilege if you wish—but it is my will that you do this thing, and my will is law on this island."

Both de Grandin and I looked at him in speechless horror, but he took no notice of amazement. "You may think you will refuse," he told us, "but you will not. Captain Van Thun, of the Dutch steamer *Van Damm*, and his first mate were offered the same chance and refused it. They chose to interview a little pet I keep about the premises as an alternative: But when the time for the interview came both would gladly have reconsidered their decision. This house is the one place in the world where a white man must keep his word, willy-nilly. Both of them were obliged to carry out their bargain to the letter—and I can not say the prestige of the pure Caucasian breed was strengthened by the way they did it.

"Now, I will give you gentlemen a greater opportunity for deliberation than I gave the Dutchmen. You shall first be allowed to see my pet, then decide whether you will accept my offer or not. But I warn you beforehand, whatever decision you make must be adhered to.

"Come." He turned to the two armed Malays who stood behind his chair and barked an order. Instantly de Grandin and I were covered by their pistols, and the scowling faces behind the firearms' sights told us we might expect no quarter if the order to fire were given.

"Come," Goonong Besar—or Richardson—repeated imperiously, "walk ahead, you two, and remember, the first attempt either of you makes to escape will mean a bullet through his brain."

WE MARCHED DOWN A series of identical corridors as bewildering as the labyrinth of Crete, mysterious stone doors thudding shut behind us from time to time, other doors swinging open in the solid walls as our guards pressed cunningly concealed springs in the walls or floor. Finally we brought up on a sort of colonnaded porch, a tiled footpath bordered with a low stone parapet from which a row of carved stone columns rose to a concave ceiling of natural stone. Below the balcony's balustrade stretched a long, narrow pool of dead-motionless water between abrupt vertical walls of rock, and, some two hundred feet away, through the arch of a natural cave, the starlit tropical sky showed like a little patch of freedom before our straining eyes. The haze which had thickened the air the previous night must have cleared away, for rays of the bright, full moon painted a "path to Spain" over the waters at the cavern's mouth, and sent sufficient light as far back as our balcony to enable us to distinguish an occasional tiny ripple on the glassy surface below us.

"Here, pretty, pretty!" our captor called, leaning forward between two columns. "Come up and see the brave white men who may come to play with you. Here, pretty pet; come up, come up!"

We stared into the purple waters like lost souls gazing on the hell prepared for them, but no motion agitated the depths.

"Sulky brute!" the half-caste exclaimed, and snatched a pistol from the girdle of one of his attendants. "Come up," he repeated harshly. "Damn you, come when I call!" He tossed the weapon into the pool below.

De Grandin and I uttered a gasp of horror in unison, and I felt his nails bite into my arm as his strong slender fingers gripped me convulsively.

A S THOUGH THE PISTOL had been superheated and capable of setting the water in the cave boiling by its touch, the deep, blue-black pool beneath us suddenly woke to life. Ripples—living, groping ripples—appeared on the pool's smooth face and long, twisting arms, sinuous as snakes, thick as fire-hose, seemed waving just under the surface, flicking into the air now and again and displaying tentacles roughened with great, wart-like protuberances. Something like a monster bubble, transparent-gray like a jelly-fish, yet, oddly, spotted like an unclean reptile, almost as big around as the umbrellas used by teamsters on their wagons in summer-time, and, like an umbrella, ribbed at regular intervals, rose from the darker water, and a pair of monstrous, hideous white eyes, large as dinner plates, with black pupils large as saucers, stared greedily, unwinkingly, at us.

"*Nom de Dieu de nom de Dieu!*" de Grandin breathed. "The sea-devil; the giant octopus!"

"Quite so," Goonong Besar agreed affably, "the giant octopus. What he grasps he holds forever, and he grasps all he can reach. A full-grown elephant thrown into that water would have no more chance of escape than a minnow—or, for unpleasant example, than you gentlemen would. Now, perhaps you realize why Captain Van Thun and his first officer wished they had chosen to enter my—er—employ, albeit in a somewhat extraordinary capacity. I did not afford them a chance of viewing the alternative beforehand, as I have you, however. Now that you have had your chance, I am sure you will take the matter under serious advisement before you refuse.

"There is no hurry; you will be given all tonight and tomorrow to arrive at a decision. I shall expect your answer, at dinner tomorrow. Good gentlemen, my boys will show you to your room. Good night, and—er—may I wish you pleasant dreams?"

With a mocking laugh he stepped quickly back into the shadows, we heard the sound we had come to recognize as the closing of one of the hidden stone doors, and found ourselves alone upon the balcony over-looking the den of the giant octopus.

"*Bon Dieu!*" de Grandin cried despairingly, "Trowbridge, my friend, they make a mistake, those people who insist the devil dwells in hell. *Parbleu!* What is that?"

The noise which startled him was the shuffling of bare brown feet. The tongueless youths who acted as our *valets de chambre* were coming reluctantly toward us down the passageway, their eyes rolling in fearful glances toward the balustrade beyond which the devil of the sea lurked in his watery lair.

"*En bien,*" the Frenchman shrugged, "it is the two devilkins again. Lead on, *mes enfants*; any place is better than this threshold of hell."

7

"AND NOW," HE ANNOUNCED as he dropped into one of the bedroom's wicker chairs and lighted a cigarette, "we are in what you Americans would call a tight fix, Friend Trowbridge. To accede to that half-caste hellion's proposition would be to dishonor ourselves forever—that is unthinkable. But to be eaten up by that so infernal octopus, that, too, is unthinkable. *Morbleu*, had I known then what I know now I should have demanded one thousand pounds a day from those Messieurs Lloyd and then refused their offer. As your so splendid soldiers were wont to say during the war, we are, of a surety, S.O.L., my friend."

Beneath the bamboo bedstead across the room a slight rustling sounded. I looked apathetically toward the bed, indifferent to any fresh horror which might appear; but, wretched as I was, I was not prepared for the apparition which emerged.

Stripped of her gorgeous raiment of pineapple gauze, a *sarong* and jacket of the cheapest native cotton inadequately covering her glorious body, an ivory-wood button replacing her diamond nose-stud, her feet bare and no article of jewelry adorning her, Miriam, the dancer, crept forth and flung herself to her knees before de Grandin.

"Oh, Monsieur," she begged in a voice choked with tears, "have pity on me, I implore you. Be merciful to me, as you would have another in your place be pitiful to your sister, were she in mine."

"*Morbleu*, child, is it of me you ask pity?" de Grandin demanded. "How can I, who can not even choose my own death, show compassion to you?"

"Kill me," she answered fiercely. "Kill me now, while yet there is time. See, I have brought you this"—from the folds of her scanty sarong she drew a native kris, a wavy-bladed short sword with a razor edge and needle point.

"Stab me with it," she besought, "then, if you wish, use it on your friend and yourself; there is no other hope. Look about you, do not you see there is no way of dying in this prison room? Once on a time the mirror was of glass, but a captive white man broke it and almost succeeded in cutting his wrists with the pieces until he died. Since then Goonong Besar has had a metal mirror in this room."

"*Pardieu*, you are right, child!" de Grandin agreed as he glanced at the dressing table over which the metal mirror hung. "But why do you seek death? Are you, too, destined for the octopus?"

She shuddered. "Some day, perhaps, but while I retain my beauty there is small fear of that. Every day old Umera, the one-eyed she-devil, teaches me to dance, and when I do not please her (and she is very hard to please) she beats me with bamboo rods on the soles of my feet till I can scarcely bear to walk. And Goonong Besar makes me dance for him every night till I am ready to drop, and if I do not smile upon him as I dance, or if I grow weary too soon, so that my feet lag before he gives me permission to stop, he beats me.

"Every time a ship is caught in his trap he saves some of the officers and makes me dance before them, and I know they are to be fed to the fish-devil, yet I must smile upon them, or he will beat me till my feet bleed, and the old woman will beat me when he is weary of it.

"My father was French, Monsieur, though I, myself, was born in England of a Spanish mother. We lost all our money in the war, for my father kept a goldsmith's shop in Rheims, and the *sale boche* stole everything he had. We came to the islands after the war, and my father made money as a trader. We were returning home on the Dutch ship *Van Damm* when Goonong Besar caught her in his trap.

"Me he kept to be taught to dance the dances of the islands and to be tortured—see, he has put a ring in my nose, like a native woman's." She lifted a trembling hand to the wooden peg which kept the hole pierced in her nose from growing together when she was not wearing her jeweled stud. "My father—oh, God of Israel!—he fed to the devil-fish before my eyes and told me he would serve me the same way if I proved not submissive to his will in all things.

"And so, Monsieur," she ended simply, "I would that you cause me to die and be out of my unhappiness."

As the girl talked, de Grandin's face registered every emotion from amazement to horror and compassion. As she completed her narrative he looked thoughtful. "Wait, wait, my pretty one," he besought, as she would have forced the *kris* into his hand. "I must think. *Pardieu!* Jules de Grandin, you silly fool, you must think now as never before." He sank his face in his hands and bowed his chin nearly to his knees.

"Tell me, my little cabbage," he demanded suddenly, "do they let you out of this accurst house by daylight, *hein?*"

"Oh, yes," she responded. "I may go or come as I will when I am not practicing my dances or being beaten. I may go anywhere on the island I wish, for no one, not even the cannibals who live on the shore, would dare lay his little finger on me for fear of the master. I belong to Goonong Besar, and he would feed anyone who touched his property to the great fish-devil."

"And why have you never sought to die by your own hand?" de Grandin asked suspiciously.

"Jews do not commit suicide," she answered proudly. "To die by another's hand is not forbidden—Jephthah's daughter so died—but to go from life with your hands reddened with your own blood is against the law of my fathers."

"Ah, yes, I understand," he agreed with a short nod. "You children of Jacob shame us so-called Christians in the way you keep your precepts, child. *Eh bien,* 'tis fortunate for all us you have a strong conscience, my beautiful.

"Attend me: In your walks about this never-enough-to-be-execrated island have you observed, near the spot where the masts which carry the false ship's lights stand, certain plants growing, plants with shining leaves and a fruit like the unripe apple which grows in France—a low bush with fruit of pale green?"

The girl wrinkled her white forehead thoughtfully, then nodded twice. "Yes," she replied, "I have seen such a plant."

"*Très bien,*" he nodded approvingly, "the way from this evil place seems to open before us, *mes amis.* At least, we have the sporting chance. Now listen, and listen well, my little half-orange, for upon your obedience rests our chance of freedom.

"Tomorrow, when you have a chance to leave this vestibule of hell, go you to the place where those fruits like apples grow and gather as many of them as you can carry in your *sarong.* Bring these fruits of the *Cocculus indicus* to the house and mash them to a pulp in some jar which you must procure. At the dinner hour, pour the contents of that jar into the water where dwells the devil-fish. Do not fail us, my little pigeon, for upon your faithful performance of your trust our lives, and yours, depend, *pardieu!* If you do but carry out your orders we shall feed that Monsieur Octopus such a meal as he will have small belly for, *parbleu!*

"When you have poured all the crushed fruit into the water, secret yourself in the shadows near by and wait till we come. You can swim? Good. When we do leap into the water, do you leap also, and altogether we shall swim to that boat I was about to borrow when we met this so excellent Monsieur Goonong-Besar-James-Abingdon-Richardson-Devil. *Cordieu,* I think that Jules de Grandin is not such a fool as I thought he was!

"Good night, fairest one, and may the God of your people, and the gentle Mary, too, guard you this night, and all the nights of your life."

8

"GOOD EVENING, GENTLEMEN," GOONONG Besar greeted as we entered the dining room next evening; "have you decided upon our little proposition?"

"But certainly," de Grandin assured him. "If we must choose between a few minutes' conversation with the octopus and a lifetime, or even half an hour's sight of your neither-black-nor-white face, we cast our vote for the fish. He, at least, does what he does from nature; he is no vile parody of his kind. Let us go to the fish-house *tout vite, Monsieur*. The sooner we get this business completed, the sooner we shall be rid of you!"

Goonong Besar's pale countenance went absolutely livid with fury. "You insignificant little fool," he cried, "I'll teach you to insult me! *Ha-room!*" he sent the call echoing through the marble-lined cave. "You'll not be so brave when you feel those tentacles strangling the life out of your puny body and that beak tearing your flesh off your bones before the water has a chance to drown you."

He poured a string of burning orders at his two guards, who seized their rifles and thrust them at us. "Off, off to the grotto!" he shrieked, beside himself with rage. "Don't think you can escape the devil-fish by resisting my men. They won't shoot to kill; they'll only cripple you and drag you to the pool. Will you walk, or shall we shoot you first and pull you there?"

"Monsieur," de Grandin drew himself proudly erect, "a gentleman of France fears no death a Malay *batard* can offer. Lead on!"

Biting his pale lips till the blood ran to keep from screaming with fury, Goonong Besar signaled his guards, and we took up our way toward the sea monster's lair.

"*La bon Dieu* grant *la belle juive* has done her work thoroughly," de Grandin whispered as we came out upon the balcony. "I like not this part of our little playlet, my friend. Should our plan have failed, *adieu*." He gave my hand a hasty pressure.

"Who goes first?" Goonong Besar asked as we halted by the balustrade.

"*Pardieu*, you do!" de Grandin shouted, and before anyone was aware of his intention he dashed one of his small hard fists squarely into the astonished half-caste's face, seized him about the waist and flung him bodily into the black, menacing water below.

"In, Friend Trowbridge!" he called, leaping upon the parapet. "Dive and swim—it is our only chance!"

I waited no second bidding, but jumped as far outward as possible, striking out vigorously toward the far end of the cave, striving to keep my head as near water level as possible, yet draw an occasional breath.

Horror swam beside me. Each stroke I took I expected one of the monster's slimy tentacles to seize me and drag me under; but no great, gray bubble rose from the black depths, no questing arms reached toward me. For all we could observe to the contrary, the pool was as harmless as any of the thousands of rocky caves which dot the volcanic coast of Malaya.

Bullets whipped and tore the water around us, striking rocky walls and singing off in vicious ricochets; but the light was poor, and the Malay marksmen emptied their pieces with no effect.

"*Triomphe!*" de Grandin announced, blowing the water from his mouth in a great, gusty sigh of relief as we gained the shingle outside the cave. "Miriam, my beautiful one, are you with us?"

"Yes," responded a voice from the darkness. "I did as you bade me, Monsieur, and the great fish-devil sank almost as soon as he thrust his snake-arms into the fruit as it floated on the water. But when I saw he was dead I did not dare wait; but swam out here to abide your coming."

"It is good," de Grandin commended. "One of those bullets might easily have hit you. They are execrable marksmen, those Malays, but accidents do occur.

"Now, Monsieur," he addressed the limp bundle he towed behind him in the water, "I have a little business proposition to make to *you*. Will you accompany us, and be delivered to the Dutch or British to be hanged for the damned pirate you are, or will you fight me for your so miserable life here and now?"

"I cannot fight you now," Goonong Besar answered, "you broke my arm with your cowardly jiu jitsu when you took advantage of me and attacked me without warning."

"Ah, so?" de Grandin replied, helping his captive to the beach. "That is unfortunate, for—*Mordieu*, scoundrel, would you do so!"

The Eurasian had suddenly drawn a dagger from his coat and lunged viciously at de Grandin's breast.

With the agility of a cat the Frenchman evaded the thrust, seized his antagonist's wrist, and twisted the knife from his grasp. His foot shot out, he drove his fist savagely into Goonong's throat, and the half-caste sprawled helplessly on the sand.

"Attend Mademoiselle!" de Grandin called to me. "It is not well for her to see what I must do here."

There was the sound of a scuffle, then a horrible gargling noise, and the beating of hands and feet upon the sands.

"*Fini!*" de Grandin remarked nonchalantly, dipping his hands in the water and cleansing them of some dark stains.

"You . . . ?" I began.

"*Mais certainement*," he replied matter-of-factly. "I slit his throat. What would you have? He was a mad dog; why should he continue to live?"

Walking hurriedly along the beach, we came to the little power-boat moored in the inlet and set her going.

"Where to?" I asked as de Grandin swung the trim little craft around a rocky promontory.

"Do you forget, *cher* Trowbridge, that we have a score to settle with those cannibals?" he asked.

We settled it. Running the launch close inshore, de Grandin shouted defiance to the Papuans till they came tumbling out of their cone-shaped huts like angry bees from their hives.

"*Sa ha, messieurs*," de Grandin called, "we give you food of another sort this night. Eat it, *sacré canaille*; eat it!" The Lewis machine-gun barked and sputtered, and a chorus of cries and groans rose from the beach.

"IT IS WELL," HE announced as he resumed the wheel. "They eat no more white women, those ones. Indeed, did I still believe the teachings of my youth, I should say they were even now partaking of the devil's hospitality with their late master."

"But see here," I demanded as we chugged our way toward the open water, "what was it you told Miriam to put in the water where the octopus was, de Grandin?"

He chuckled. "Had you studied as much biology as I, Friend Trowbridge, you would recognize that glorious plant, the *Cocculus indicus*, when you saw it. All over the Polynesian islands the lazy natives, who desire to obtain food with the minimum of labor, mash up the berry of that plant and spread it in the water where the fish swim. A little of it will render the fish insensible, a little more will kill him as dead as the late lamented Goonong Besar. I noticed that plant growing on the island, and when our lovely Jewess told me she could go and come at will I said to me, 'By the George, why not have her poison that great devil-fish and swim to freedom?' *Voilà tout!*"

A PASSING DUTCH STEAMER PICKED us up two days later. The passengers and crew gaped widely at Miriam's imperial beauty, and wider still at de Grandin's account of our exploits. "*Pardieu!*" he confided to me one night as we walked the deck, "I fear those Dutchmen misbelieve me, Friend Trowbridge. Perhaps I shall have to slit their ears to teach them to respect the word of a Frenchman."

IT WAS SIX MONTHS later that a Western Union messenger entered my consulting room at Harrisonville and handed me a blue-and-white envelope. "Sign here," he ordered.

I tore the envelope open, and this is what I read:

Miriam made big sensation in Folies Bérgères tonight. Felicitations.— de Grandin

The House of Horror

"**M**orbleu, Friend Trowbridge, have a care," Jules de Grandin warned as my lurching motor car almost ran into the brimming ditch beside the rain-soaked road.

I wrenched the steering wheel viciously and swore softly under my breath as I leaned forward, striving vainly to pierce the curtains of rain which shut us in.

"No use, old fellow," I confessed, turning to my companion, "We're lost; that's all there is to it."

"Ha," he laughed shortly, "do you just begin to discover that fact, my friend? *Parbleu*, I have known it this last half-hour."

Throttling my engine down, I crept along the concrete roadway, peering through my streaming windshield and storm curtains for some familiar landmark, but nothing but blackness, wet and impenetrable, met my eyes.

Two hours before, that stormy evening in 192–, answering an insistent 'phone call, de Grandin and I had left the security of my warm office to administer a dose of toxin anti-toxin to an Italian laborer's child who lay, choking with diphtheria, in a hut at the workmen's settlement where the new branch of the railroad was being put through. The cold, driving rain and the Stygian darkness of the night had misled me when I made the detour around the railway cut, and for the past hour and a half I had been feeling my way over unfamiliar roads as futilely as a lost child wandering in the woods.

"*Grace à Dieu*," de Grandin exclaimed, seizing my arm with both his small, strong hands, "a light! See, there it shines in the night. Come, let us go to it. Even the meanest hovel is preferable to this so villainous rain."

I peeped through a joint in the curtains and saw a faint, intermittent light flickering through the driving rain some two hundred yards away.

"All right," I acquiesced, climbing from the car, "we've lost so much time already we probably couldn't do anything for the Vivianti child, and maybe these people can put us on the right road, anyway."

Plunging through puddles like miniature lakes, soaked by the wind-driven rain, barking our shins again and again on invisible obstacles, we made for the light, finally drawing up to a large, square house of red brick fronted by an imposing white-pillared porch. Light streamed out through the fanlight over the white door and from the two tall windows flanking the portal.

"*Parbleu*, a house of circumstance, this," de Grandin commented, mounting the porch and banging lustily at the polished brass knocker.

I wrinkled my forehead in thought while he rattled the knocker a second time. "Strange, I can't remember this place," I muttered. "I thought I knew every building within thirty miles, but this is a new one . . ."

"Ah bah!" de Grandin interrupted. "Always you must be casting a wet blanket on the parade, Friend Trowbridge. First you insist on losing us in the midst of a *sacré* rainstorm, then when I, Jules de Grandin, find us a shelter from the weather, you must needs waste time in wondering why it is you know not the place. *Morbleu*, you will refuse shelter because you have never been presented to the master of the house, if I do not watch you, I fear."

"But I ought to know the place, de Grandin," I protested. "It's certainly imposing enough to . . ."

My defense was cut short by the sharp click of a lock, and the wide, white door swung inward before us.

We strode over the threshold, removing our dripping hats as we did so, and turned to address the person who opened the door.

"Why . . ." I began, and stared about me in open-mouthed surprise.

"Name of a little blue man!" said Jules de Grandin, and added his incredulous stare to mine.

As FAR AS WE could see, we were alone in the mansion's imposing hall. Straight before us, perhaps for forty feet, ran a corridor of parquetry flooring, covered here and there by rich-hued Oriental rugs. White-paneled walls, adorned with oil paintings of imposing-looking individuals, rose for eighteen feet or so to a beautifully frescoed ceiling, and a graceful curving staircase swept upward from the farther end of the room. Candles in cut glass sconces lighted the high-ceilinged apartment, the hospitable glow from a log fire burning under the high white marble mantel lent an air of homely coziness to the place, but of anything living, human or animal, there was no faintest trace or sign.

Click! Behind us, the heavy outer door swung to silently on well-oiled hinges and the automatic lock latched firmly.

"Death of my life!" de Grandin murmured, reaching for the door's silver-plated knob and giving it a vigorous twist. "*Par la moustache du diable*, Friend Trowbridge, it is locked! Truly, perhaps it had been better if we had remained outside in the rain!"

"Not at all, I assure you, my dear sir," a rich mellow voice answered him from the curve of the stairs. "Your arrival was nothing less than providential, gentlemen."

Coming toward us, walking heavily with the aid of a stout cane, was an unusually handsome man attired in pajamas and dressing gown, a sort of nightcap of flowered silk on his white head, slippers of softest morocco on his feet.

"You are a physician, sir?" he asked, glancing inquiringly at the medicine case in my hand.

"Yes," I answered. "I am Dr. Samuel Trowbridge, from Harrisonville, and this is Dr. Jules de Grandin, of Paris, who is my guest."

"Ah," replied our host, "I am very, very glad to welcome you to Marston Hall, gentlemen. It so happens that one—er—my daughter, is quite ill, and I have been unable to obtain medical aid for her on account of my infirmities and the lack of a telephone. If I may trespass on your charity to attend my poor child, I shall be delighted to have you as my guests for the night. If you will lay aside your coats"—he paused expectantly. "Ah, thank you"—as we hung our dripping garments over a chair—"you will come this way, please?"

We followed him up the broad stairs and down an upper corridor to a tastefully furnished chamber where a young girl—fifteen years of age, perhaps—lay propped up with a pile of diminutive pillows.

"Anabel, Anabel, my love, here are two doctors to see you," the old gentleman called softly.

The girl moved her fair head with a weary, peevish motion and whimpered softly in her sleep, but gave no further recognition of our presence.

"And what have been her symptoms, if you please, *Monsieur?*" de Grandin asked as he rolled back the cuffs of his jacket and prepared to make an examination.

"Sleep," replied our host, "just sleep. Some time ago she suffered from influenza; lately she has been given to fits of protracted slumber from which I can not waken her. I fear she may have contracted sleeping sickness, sir. I am told it sometimes follows influenza."

"H'm." De Grandin passed his small, pliable hands rapidly over the girl's cheeks in the region of the ears, felt rapidly along her neck over the jugular vein, then raised a puzzled glance to me. "Have you some laudanum and aconite in your bag, Friend Trowbridge?" he asked.

"There's some morphine," I answered, "and aconite; but no laudanum."

"No matter," he waved his hand impatiently, bustling over to the medicine case and extracting two small phials from it. "No matter, this will do as well. Some water, if you please, *Monsieur,*" he turned to the father, a medicine bottle in each hand.

"But, de Grandin"—I began, when a sudden kick from one of his slender, heavily-shod feet nearly broke my shin—"de Grandin, do you think that's the proper medication?" I finished lamely.

"Oh, *mais oui*, undoubtedly," he replied. "Nothing else would do in this case. Water, if you please, *Monsieur*," he repeated, again addressing the father.

I STARED AT HIM IN ill-disguised amazement as he extracted a pellet from each of the bottles and quickly ground them to powder while the old gentleman filled a tumbler with water from the porcelain pitcher which stood on the chintz-draped wash-stand in the corner of the chamber. He was as familiar with the arrangement of my medicine case as I was, I knew, and knew that my phials were arranged by numbers instead of being labeled. Deliberately, I saw, he had passed over the morphine and aconite, and had chosen two bottles of plain, unmedicated sugar of milk pills. What his object was I had no idea, but I watched him measure out four teaspoonfuls of water, dissolve the powder in it, and pour the sham medication down the unconscious girl's throat.

"Good," he proclaimed as he washed the glass with meticulous care. "She will rest easily until the morning, *Monsieur*. When daylight comes we shall decide on further treatment. Will you now permit that we retire?" He bowed politely to the master of the house, who returned his courtesy and led us to a comfortably furnished room farther down the corridor.

"SEE HERE, DE GRANDIN," I demanded when our host had wished us a pleasant good-night and closed the door upon us, "what was your idea in giving that child an impotent dose like that . . . ?"

"S-s-sh!" he cut me short with a fierce whisper. "That young girl, *mon ami*, is no more suffering from encephalitis than you or I. There is no characteristic swelling of the face or neck, no diagnostic hardening of the jugular vein. Her temperature was a bit subnormal, it is true—but upon her breath I detected the odor of chloral hydrate. For some reason, good I hope, but bad I fear, she is drugged, and I thought it best to play the fool and pretend I believed the man's statements. *Pardieu*, the fool who knows himself no fool has an immense advantage over the fool who believes him one, my friend."

"But . . ."

"But me no buts, Friend Trowbridge; remember how the door of this house opened with none to touch it, recall how it closed behind us in the same way, and observe this, if you will." Stepping softly, he crossed the room, pulled aside the chintz curtains at the window and tapped lightly on the frame which held the thick plate glass panes. "*Regardez vous*," he ordered, tapping the frame a second time.

Like every other window I had seen in the house, this one was of the casement type, small panes of heavy glass being sunk into latticelike frames. Under de Grandin's directions I tapped the latter, and found them not painted wood, as I had supposed, but stoutly welded and bolted metal. Also, to my surprise, I found the turnbuckles for opening the casement were only dummies, the metal frames being actually securely bolted to the stone sills. To all intents, we were as firmly incarcerated as though serving a sentence in the state penitentiary.

"The door . . ." I began, but he shook his head.

Obeying his gesture, I crossed the room and turned the handle lightly. It twisted under the pressure of my fingers, but, though we had heard no warning click of lock or bolt, the door itself was as firmly fastened as though nailed shut.

"Wh—why," I asked stupidly, "what's it all mean, de Grandin?"

"*Je ne sais quoi*," he answered with a shrug, "but one thing I know: I like not this house, Friend Trowbridge. I . . ."

Above the hissing of the rain against the windows and the howl of the sea-wind about the gables, there suddenly rose a scream, wire-edged with inarticulate terror, freighted with utter, transcendental anguish of body and soul.

"*Cordieu!*" He threw up his head like a hound hearing the call of the pack from far away. "Did you hear it, too, Friend Trowbridge?"

"Of course," I answered, every nerve in my body trembling in horripilation with the echo of the hopeless wail.

"Pardieu," he repeated, "I like this house less than ever, now! Come, let us move this dresser before our door. It is safer that we sleep behind barricades this night, I think."

We blocked the door, and I was soon sound asleep.

"Trowbridge, Trowbridge, my friend"—de Grandin drove a sharp elbow into my ribs—"wake up, I beseech you. Name of a green goat, you lie like one dead, save for your so abominable snoring!"

"Eh?" I answered sleepily, thrusting myself deeper beneath the voluminous bedclothes. Despite the unusual occurrences of the night I was tired to the point of exhaustion, and fairly drunk with sleep.

"Up; arise, my friend," he ordered, shaking me excitedly. "The coast is clear, I think, and it is high time we did some exploring."

"Rats!" I scoffed, disinclined to leave my comfortable couch. "What's the use of wandering about a strange house to gratify a few unfounded suspicions? The girl might have been given a dose of chloral hydrate, but the chances are her father thought he was helping her when he gave it. As for these trick devices for opening and locking doors, the old man apparently lives here alone and has installed these mechanical aids to lessen his work. He has to hobble around with a cane, you know."

"Ah!" my companion assented sarcastically. "And that scream we heard, did he install that as an aid to his infirmities, also?"

"Perhaps the girl woke up with a nightmare," I hazarded, but he made an impatient gesture.

"Perhaps the moon is composed of green cheese, also," he replied. "Up, up and dress; my friend. This house should be investigated while yet there is time. Attend me: But five minutes ago, through this very window, I did observe *Monsieur* our host, attired in a raincoat, depart from his own front door, and without his cane. *Parbleu*, he did skip, as agilely as any boy, I assure you. Even now he is almost at the spot where we abandoned your automobile. What he intends doing there I know not. What I intend doing I know full well. Do you accompany me or not?"

"Oh, I suppose so," I agreed, crawling from the bed and slipping into my clothes. "How are you going to get past that locked door?"

He flashed me one of his sudden smiles, shooting the points of his little blond mustache upward like the horns of an inverted crescent. "Observe," he ordered, displaying a short length of thin wire. "In the days when a woman's hair was still her crowning glory, what mighty deeds a lady could encompass with a hairpin! *Pardieu*, there was one little *grisette* in Paris who showed me some tricks in the days before the war! Regard me, if you please."

Deftly he thrust the pliable loop of wire into the key's hole, twisting it tentatively back and forth, at length pulling it out and regarding it carefully. "*Très bien*," he muttered as he reached into an inside pocket, bringing out a heavier bit of wire.

"See," he displayed the finer wire, "with this I take an impression of that lock's tumblers, now"—quickly he bent the heavier wire to conform to the waved outline of the lighter loop—"*voilà*, I have a key!"

And he had. The lock gave readily to the pressure of his improvised key, and we stood in the long, dark hall, staring about us half curiously, half fearfully.

"This way, if you please," de Grandin ordered; "first we will look in upon *la jeunesse*, to see how it goes with her."

We walked on tiptoe down the corridor, entered the chamber where the girl lay, and approached the bed.

SHE WAS LYING WITH her hands folded upon her breast in the manner of those composed for their final rest, her wide, periwinkle-blue eyes staring sightlessly before her, the short, tightly curled ringlets of her blonde, bobbed hair surrounding her drawn, pallid face like a golden nimbus encircling the ivory features of a saint in some carved ikon.

My companion approached the bed softly, placing one hand on the girl's wrist with professional precision. "Temperature low, pulse weak," he murmured, checking off her symptoms. "Complexion pale to the point of lividity—ha, now for the eyes; sleeping, her pupils should have been contracted, while they should now be dilate—*Dieu de Dieu!* Trowbridge, my friend, come here.

"Look," he commanded, pointing to the apathetic girl's face. "Those eyes—*grand Dieu*, those eyes! It is sacrilege, nothing less."

I looked into the girl's face, then started back with a half-suppressed cry of horror. Asleep, as she had been when we first saw her, the child had been pretty to the point of loveliness. Her features were small and regular, clean-cut as those of a face in a cameo, the tendrils of her light-yellow hair had lent her a dainty, ethereal charm comparable to that of a Dresden china shepherd-ess. It had needed but the raising of her delicate, long-lashed eyelids to give her face the animation of some laughing sprite playing truant from fairyland.

Her lids were raised now, but the eyes they unveiled were no clear, joyous windows of a tranquil soul. Rather, they were the peepholes of a spirit in tor-ment. The irises were a lovely shade of blue, it is true, but the optics themselves were things of horror. Rolling grotesquely to right and left, they peered futilely in opposite directions, lending to her sweet, pale face the half-ludicrous, wholly hideous expression of a bloating frog.

"Good heavens!" I exclaimed, turning from the deformed girl with a feeling of disgust akin to nausea; "What a terrible affliction!"

De Grandin made no reply, but bent over the girl's still form, gazing intently at her malformed eyes. "It is not natural," he announced. "The muscles have been tampered with, and tampered with by someone who is a master hand at surgery. Will you get me your syringe and some strychnine, Friend Trowbridge? This poor one is still unconscious."

I HASTENED TO OUR BEDROOM and returned with the hypodermic and stim-ulant, then stood beside him, watching eagerly, as he administered a strong injection.

The girl's narrow chest fluttered as the powerful drug took effect, and the pale lids dropped for a second over her repulsive eyes. Then, with a sob which was half moan, she attempted to raise herself on her elbow, fell back again, and, with apparent effort, gasped, "The mirror, let me have the mirror! Oh, tell me it isn't true; tell me it was a trick of some sort. Oh, the horrible thing I saw in the glass couldn't have been I. Was it?"

"*Tiens, ma petite*," de Grandin replied, "but you speak in riddles. What is it you would know?"

"He—he"—the girl faltered weakly, forcing her trembling lips to frame the words—"that horrible old man showed me a mirror a little while ago and said the face in it was mine. Oh, it was horrible, horrible!"

"Eh? What is this?" de Grandin demanded on a rising note. "'He'? 'Horrible old man'? Are you not his daughter? Is he not your father?"

"No," the girl gasped, so low her denial was scarcely audible. "I was driving home from Mackettsdale last—oh, I forget when it was, but it was at night—and my tires punctured. I—I think there must have been glass on the road, for the shoes were cut to ribbons. I saw the light in this house and came to ask for help. An old man—oh, I thought he was so nice and kind!—let me in and said he was all alone here and about to eat dinner, and asked me to join him. I ate some—some—oh, I don't remember what it was—and the next thing I knew he was standing by my bed, holding a mirror up to me and telling me it was my face I saw in the glass. Oh, please, *please*, tell me it was some terrible trick he played on me. I'm not truly hideous, am I?"

"*Morbleu!*" de Grandin muttered softly, tugging at the ends of his mustache. "What is all this?"

To the girl he said: "But of course not. You are like a flower, *Mademoiselle*. A little flower that dances in the wind. You . . ."

"And my eyes, they aren't—they aren't"—she interrupted with piteous eagerness—"please tell me they aren't . . ."

"*Mais non, ma chère*," he assured her. "Your eyes are like the *pervenche* that mirrors the sky in springtime. They are . . ."

"Let—let me see the mirror, please," she interrupted in an anxious whisper. "I'd like to see for myself, if you—oh, I feel all weak inside . . ." She lapsed back against the pillow, her lids mercifully veiling the hideously distorted eyes and restoring her face to tranquil beauty.

"*Cordieu!*" de Grandin breathed. "The chloral re-asserted itself none too soon for Jules de Grandin's comfort, Friend Trowbridge. Sooner would I have gone to the rack than have shown that pitiful child her face in a mirror."

"But what's it all mean?" I asked. "She says she came here, and . . ."

"And the rest remains for us to find out, I think," he replied evenly. "Come, we lose time, and to lose time is to be caught, my friend."

DE GRANDIN LED THE way down the hall, peering eagerly into each door we passed in search of the owner's chamber, but before his quest was satisfied he stopped abruptly at the head of the stairs. "Observe, Friend Trowbridge," he ordered, pointing a carefully manicured forefinger to a pair of buttons, one white, one black, set in the wall. "Unless I am more mistaken than I think I am, we have here the key to the situation—or at least to the front door."

He pushed vigorously at the white button, then ran to the curve of the stairs to note the result.

Sure enough, the heavy door swung open on its hinges of cast bronze, letting gusts of rain drive into the lower hall.

"*Pardieu*," he ejaculated, "we have here the open sesame; let us see if we possess the closing secret as well! Press the black button, Trowbridge, my friend, while I watch."

I did his bidding, and a delighted exclamation told me the door had closed.

"Now what?" I asked, joining him on the stairway.

"U'm," he pulled first one, then the other end of his diminutive mustache meditatively; "the house possesses its attractions, Friend Trowbridge, but I believe it would be well if we went out to observe what our friend, *le vieillard horrible*, does. I like not to have one who shows young girls their disfigured faces in mirrors near our conveyance."

Slipping into our raincoats we opened the door, taking care to place a wad of paper on the sill to prevent its closing tightly enough to latch, and scurried out into the storm.

As we left the shelter of the porch a shaft of indistinct light shone through the rain, as my car was swung from the highway and headed toward a depression to the left of the house.

"*Parbleu*, he is a thief, this one!" de Grandin exclaimed excitedly. "*Holà, Monsieur!*" He ran forward, swinging his arms like a pair of semaphores. "What sort of business is it you make with our *moteur?*"

The wailing of the storm tore the words from his lips and hurled them away, but the little Frenchman was not to be thwarted. "*Pardieu*," he gasped, bending his head against the wind-driven rain, "I will stop the scoundrel if—*nom d'un coq*, he has done it!"

Even as he spoke the old man flung open the car's forward door and leaped, allowing the machine to go crashing down a low, steep embankment into a lake of slimy swamp-mud.

For a moment the vandal stood contemplating his work, then burst into a peal of wild laughter more malignant than any profanity.

"*Parbleu*, robber, Apache! You shall laugh from the other side of your mouth!" de Grandin promised, as he made for the old man.

But the other seemed oblivious of our presence. Still chuckling at his work, he turned toward the house, stopped short as a sudden heavy gust of wind shook the trees along the roadway, then started forward with a yell of terror as a great branch, torn bodily from a towering oak tree came crashing toward the earth.

He might as well have attempted to dodge a meteorite. Like an arrow from the bow of divine justice, the great timber hurtled down, pinning his frail body to the ground like a worm beneath a laborer's brogan.

"Trowbridge, my friend," de Grandin announced matter-of-factly, "observe the evil effects of stealing motor cars."

WE LIFTED THE HEAVY bough from the prostrate man and turned him over on his back. De Grandin on one side, I on the other, we made a hasty examination, arriving at the same finding simultaneously. His spinal column was snapped like a pipestem.

"You have some last statement to make, *Monsieur?*" de Grandin asked curtly. "If so, you had best be about it, your time is short."

"Y—yes," the stricken man replied weakly. "I—I meant to kill you, for you might have hit upon my secret. As it is, you may publish it to the world, that all may know what it meant to offend a Marston. In my room you will find the documents. My—my pets—are—in—the—cellar. She—was—to—have—been—one—of—them."

The pauses between his words became longer and longer, his voice grew weaker with each labored syllable. As he whispered the last sentence painfully there was a gurgling sound, and a tiny stream of blood welled up at the corner of his mouth. His narrow chest rose and fell once with a convulsive movement, then his jaw dropped limply. He was dead.

"Oh ho," de Grandin remarked, "it is a hemorrhage which finished him. A broken rib piercing his lung. U'm? I should have guessed it. Come, my friend, let us carry him to the house, then see what it was he meant by that talk of documents and pets. A pest upon the fellow for dying with his riddle half explained! Did he not know that Jules de Grandin can not resist the challenge of a riddle? *Parbleu*, we will solve this mystery, *Monsieur le Mort*, if we have to hold an autopsy to do so!"

"Oh, for heaven's sake, hush, de Grandin," I besought, shocked at his heartlessness. "The man is dead."

"Ah bah!" he returned scornfully. "Dead or not, did he not steal your motor car?"

WE LAID OUR GRUESOME burden on the hall couch and mounted the stairs to the second floor. With de Grandin in the lead we found the dead man's room and began a systematic search for the papers he had mentioned, almost with his last breath. After some time my companion unearthed a thick, leather-bound portfolio from the lower drawer of a beautiful old mahogany highboy, and spread its wide leaves open on the white-counterpaned bed.

"Ah," he drew forth several papers and held them to the light, "we begin to make the progress, Friend Trowbridge. What is this?"

He held out a newspaper clipping cracked from long folding and yellowed with age. It read:

ACTRESS JILTS SURGEON'S CRIPPLED
SON ON EVE OF WEDDING

Declaring she could not stand the sight of his deformity, and that she had engaged herself to him only in a moment of thoughtless pity, Dora Lee, well-known variety actress, last night repudiated her promise to marry John Biersfield Marston, Jr., hopelessly crippled son of Dr. John Biersfield Marston, the well-known surgeon and expert osteologist. Neither the abandoned bridegroom nor his father could be seen by reporters from the *Planet* last night.

"Very good," de Grandin nodded, "we need go no farther with that account. A young woman, it would seem, once broke her promise to marry a cripple, and, judging from this paper's date, that was in 1896. Here is another, what do you make of it?"

The clipping he handed me read as follows:

SURGEON'S SON A SUICIDE

Still sitting in the wheel-chair from which he has not moved during his waking hours since he was hopelessly crippled while playing polo in England ten years ago, John Biersfield Marston, son of the famous surgeon of the same name, was found in his bedroom this morning by his valet. A rubber hose was connected with a gas jet, the other end being held in the young man's mouth.

Young Marston was jilted by Dora Lee, well-known vaudeville actress, on the day before the date set for their wedding, one month ago. He is reported to have been extremely low-spirited since his desertion by his fiancée.

Dr. Marston, the bereaved father, when seen by reporters from the *Planet* this morning, declared the actress was responsible for his son's death and announced his intention of holding her accountable. When asked if legal proceedings were contemplated, he declined further information.

"So?" de Grandin nodded shortly. "Now this one, if you please." The third clipping was brief to the point of curtness:

WELL-KNOWN SURGEON RETIRES

Dr. John Biersfield Marston, widely known throughout this section of the country as an expert in operations concerning the bones, has announced his intention of retiring from practice. His house has been sold, and he will move from the city.

"The record is clear so far," de Grandin asserted, studying the first clipping with raised eyebrows, "but—*morbleu*, my friend, look, look at this picture. This Dora Lee, of whom does she remind you? Eh?"

I took the clipping again and looked intently at the illustration of the article announcing young Marston's broken engagement. The woman in the picture was young and inclined to be overdressed in the voluminous, fluffy mode of the days before the Spanish-American War.

"U'm, no one whom I know . . ." I began, but halted abruptly as a sudden likeness struck me. Despite the towering pompadour arrangement of her blonde hair and the unbecoming straw sailor hat above the coiffure, the woman in the picture bore a certain resemblance to the disfigured girl we had seen a half-hour before.

The Frenchman saw recognition dawn in my face, and nodded agreement. "But of course," he said. "Now, the question is, is this young girl whose eyes are so out of alignment a relative of this Dora Lee, or is the resemblance a coincidence, and if so, what lies behind it? *Hein?*"

"I don't know," I admitted, "but there must be some connection . . ."

"Connection? Of course there is a connection," de Grandin affirmed, rummaging deeper in the portfolio. "A-a-ah! What is this? *Nom d'un nom*, Friend Trowbridge, I think I smell the daylight! Look!"

He held a full page story from one of the sensational New York dailies before him, his eyes glued to the flowing type and crude, coarse-screened half-tones of half a dozen young women which composed the article.

"WHAT HAS BECOME OF THE MISSING GIRLS?" I read in boldfaced type across the top of the page.

"*Are sinister, unseen hands reaching out from the darkness to seize our girls from palace and hovel, shop, stage and office?*" the article asked rhetorically. "*Where are Ellen Munro and Dorothy Sawyer and Phyllis Bouchet and three other lovely, light-haired girls who have walked into oblivion during the past year?*"

I read to the end the sensational account of the girls' disappearances. The cases seemed fairly similar; each of the vanished young women had failed to return to her home and had never been accounted for in any manner, and in no instance, according to the newspaper, had there been any assignable reason for voluntary departure.

"*Parbleu*, but he was stupid, even for a journalist!" de Grandin asserted as I completed my inspection of the story. "Why, I wager even my good Friend Trowbridge has already noticed one important fact which this writer has treated as though it were as commonplace as the nose on his face."

"Sorry to disappoint you, old chap," I answered, "but looks to me as though the reporter had covered the case from every possible angle."

"Ah? So?" he replied sarcastically. "*Morbleu*, we shall have to consult the oculist in your behalf when we return home, my friend. Look, look I beseech you, upon the pictures of these so totally absent and unaccounted for young women, *cher ami*, and tell me if you do not observe a certain likeness among them, not only a resemblance to each other, but to that Mademoiselle Lee who jilted the son of Dr. Marston? Can you see it, now I have pointed it out?"

"No—wh—why, yes—yes, of course!" I responded, running my eye over the pictures accompanying the story. "By the Lord Harry, de Grandin, you're right;

you might almost say there is a family resemblance between these girls! You've put your fingers on it, I do believe."

"*Hélas*, no!" he answered with a shrug. "I have put my finger on nothing as yet, my friend. I reach, I grope, I feel about me like a blind man tormented by a crowd of naughty little boys, but nothing do the poor fingers of my mind encounter. *Pah!* Jules de Grandin, you are one great fool! Think, think, stupid one!"

He seated himself on the edge of the bed, cupping his face in his hands and leaning forward till his elbows rested on his knees.

Suddenly he sprang erect, one of his elfish smiles passing across his small, regular features. "*Nom d'un chatrouge*, my friend, I have it—I have it!" he announced. "The pets—the pets that old stealer of motor cars spoke of! They are in the basement! *Pardieu*, we will see those pets, *cher* Trowbridge; with our four collective eyes we will see them. Did not that so execrable stealer declare she was to have been one of them? Now, in the name of Satan and brimstone, whom could he have meant by 'she' if not that unfortunate child with eyes like *la grenouille?* Eh?"

"Why . . ." I began, but he waved me forward.

"Come, come; let us go," he urged. "I am impatient, I am restless, I am not to be restrained. We shall investigate and see for ourselves what sort of pets are kept by one who shows young girls their deformed faces in mirrors and—*Parbleu!*—steals motor cars from my friends."

Hurrying down the main stairway, we hunted about for the cellar entrance, finally located the door and, holding above our heads a pair of candles from the hall, began descending a flight of rickety steps into a pitch-black basement, rock-walled and, judging by its damp, moldy odor, unfloored save by the bare, moist earth beneath the house.

"*Parbleu*, the dungeons of the château at Carcassonne are more cheerful than this," de Grandin commented as he paused at the stairs' foot, holding his candle aloft to, make a better inspection of the dismal place.

I suppressed a shudder of mingled chill and apprehension as I stared at the blank stone walls, unpierced by windows or other openings of any sort, and made ready to retrace my steps. "Nothing here," I announced. "You can see that with half an eye. The place is as empty as . . ."

"Perhaps, Friend Trowbridge," he agreed, "but Jules de Grandin does not look with half an eye. He uses both eyes, and uses them more than once if his first glance does not prove sufficient. Behold that bit of wood on the earth yonder. What do you make of it?"

"U'm—a piece of flooring, maybe," I hazarded.

"Maybe yes, maybe no," he answered. "Let us see."

Crossing the cellar, he bent above the planks, then turned to me with a satisfied smile. "Flooring does not ordinarily have ringbolts in it, my friend," he remarked bending to seize the iron ring which was made fast to the boards by a stout staple.

"Ha!" As he heaved upward the planks came away from the black earth, disclosing a board-lined well about three feet square and of uncertain depth. An almost vertical ladder of two-by-four timbers led downward from the trap-door to the well's impenetrable blackness.

"*Allons*, we descend," he commented, turning about and setting his foot on the topmost rung of the ladder.

"Don't be a fool," I advised. "You don't know what's down there."

"True"—his head was level with the floor as he answered—"but I shall know, with luck, in a few moments. Do you come?"

I sighed with vexation as I prepared to follow him.

A T THE LADDER'S FOOT he paused, raising his candle and looking about inquiringly. Directly before us was a passageway through the earth, ceiled with heavy planks and shored up with timbers like the lateral workings of a primitive mine.

"Ah, the plot shows complications," he murmured, stepping briskly into the dark tunnel. "Do you come, Friend Trowbridge?"

I followed, wondering what manner of thing might be at the end of the black, musty passage, but nothing but fungus-grown timbers and walls of moist, black earth met my questing gaze.

De Grandin preceded me by some paces, and, I suppose, we had gone fifteen feet through the passage when a gasp of mingled surprise and horror from my companion brought me beside him in two long strides. Fastened with nails to the timbers at each side of the tunnel were a number of white, glistening objects, objects which, because of their very familiarity, denied their identity to my wondering eyes. There was no mistaking the things; even a layman could not have failed to recognize them for what they were. I, as a physician, knew them even better. To the right of the passage hung fourteen perfectly articulated skeletons of human legs, complete from foot to ilium, gleaming white and ghostly in the flickering light of the candles.

"Good heavens!" I exclaimed.

"*Sang du diable!*" Jules de Grandin commented. "Behold what is there, my friend," he pointed to the opposite wall. Fourteen bony arms, complete from hand to shoulder-joint, hung pendulously from the tunnel's upright timbers.

"*Pardieu,*" de Grandin muttered, "I have known men who collected stuffed birds and dried insects; I have known those who stored away Egyptian mummies—even the skulls of men long dead—but never before have I seen a collection of arms and legs! *Parbleu*, he was *caduc*—mad as a hatter, this one, or I am much mistaken."

"So these were his pets?" I answered. "Yes, the man was undoubtedly mad to keep such a collection, and in a place like this. Poor fellow . . ."

"*Nom d'un canon!*" de Grandin broke in; "what was that?"

From the darkness before us there came a queer, inarticulate sound, such as a man might make attempting to speak with a mouth half-filled with food, and, as though the noise had wakened an echo slumbering in the cavern, the sound was repeated, multiplied again and again till it resembled the babbling of half a dozen overgrown infants—or an equal number of full grown imbeciles.

"Onward!" Responding to the challenge of the unknown like a warrior obeying the trumpet's call to charge, de Grandin dashed toward the strange noise, swung about, flashing his candle this side and that, then:

"*Nom de Dieu de nom de Dieu!*" he almost shrieked. "Look, Friend Trowbridge, look and say that you see what I see, or have I, too, gone mad?"

Lined up against the wall was a series of seven small wooden boxes, each with a door composed of upright slats before it, similar in construction to the coops in which country folk pen brooding hens—and no larger. In each of the hutches huddled an object, the like of which I had never before seen, even in the terrors of nightmare.

The things had the torsos of human beings, though hideously shrunken from starvation and encrusted with scales of filth, but there all resemblances to mankind ceased. From shoulders and waist there twisted flaccid tentacles of unsupported flesh, the upper ones terminating in flat, paddle-like flippers which had some remote resemblance to hands, the lower ones ending in almost shapeless stubs which resembled feet, only in that each had a fringe of five shriveled, unsupported protuberances of withered flesh.

On scrawny necks were balanced caricatures of faces, flat, noseless chinless countenances with horrible crossed or divergent eyes, mouths widened almost beyond resemblance to buccal orifices and—horror of horrors!—elongated, split tongues protruding several inches from the lips and wagging impotently in vain efforts to form words.

"Satan, thou art outdone!" de Grandin cried as he held his candle before a scrap of paper decorating one of the cages after the manner of a sign before an animal's den at the zoo. "Observe!" he ordered, pointing a shaking finger at the notice.

I looked, then recoiled, sick with horror. The paper bore the picture and name of Ellen Munro, one of the girls mentioned as missing in the newspaper article we had found in the dead man's bedroom.

Beneath the photograph was scribbled in an irregular hand: "*Paid 1-25-97.*"

Sick at heart we walked down the line of pens. Each was labeled with the picture of a young and pretty girl with the notation, "*Paid*," followed by a date. Every girl named as missing in the newspaper was represented in the cages.

Last of all, in a coop somewhat smaller than the rest, we found a body more terribly mutilated than any. This was marked with the photograph and name of Dora Lee. Beneath her name was the date of her "payment," written in bold red figures.

"*Parbleu*, what are we to do, my friend?" de Grandin asked in an hysterical whisper. "We can not return these poor ones to the world, that would be the worst form of cruelty; yet—yet I shrink from the act of mercy I know they would ask me to perform if they could speak."

"Let's go up," I begged. "We must think this thing over, de Grandin, and if I stay here any longer I shall faint."

"*Bien*," be agreed, and turned to follow me from the cavern of horrors.

"It is to consider," he began as we reached the upper hall once more. "If we give those so pitiful ones the stroke of mercy we are murderers before the law, yet what service could we render them by bringing them once more into the world? Our choice is a hard one, my friend."

I nodded.

"*Morbleu*, but he was clever, that one," the Frenchman continued, half to me, half to himself. "What a surgeon! Fourteen instances of Wyeth's amputation of the hip and as many more of the shoulder—and every patient lived, lived to suffer the tortures of that hell-hole down there! But it is marvelous! None but a madman could have done it.

"Bethink you, Friend Trowbridge. Think how the mighty man of medicine brooded over the suicide of his crippled son, meditating hatred and vengeance for the heartless woman who had jilted him. Then—snap! went his great mentality, and from hating one woman he fell to hating all, to plot vengeance against the many for the sin of the one. And, *cordieu*, what a vengeance! How he must have laid plans to secure his victims; how he must have worked to prepare that hell-under-the-earth to house those poor, broken bodies which were his handiwork, and how he must have drawn upon the great surgical skill which was his, even in his madness, to transform those once lovely ones into the visions of horror we have just beheld! Horror of horrors! To remove the bones and let the girls still live!"

He rose, pacing impatiently across the hall. "What to do? What to do?" he demanded, striking his open hands against his forehead.

I followed his nervous steps with my eyes, but my brain was too numbed by the hideous things I had just seen to be able to respond to his question.

I looked hopelessly past him at the angle of the wall by the great fireplace, rubbed my eyes and looked again. Slowly, but surely, the wall was declining from the perpendicular.

"De Grandin," I shouted, glad of some new phenomenon to command my thoughts, "the wall—the wall's leaning!"

"Eh, the wall?" be queried. "*Pardieu*, yes! It is the rain; the foundations are undermined. Quick, quick, my friend! To the cellars, or those unfortunate ones are undone!"

We scrambled down the stairs leading to the basement, but already the earth floor was sopping with water. The well leading to the madman's sub-cellar was more than half full of bubbling, earthy ooze.

"Mary, have pity!" de Grandin exclaimed. "Like rats in a trap, they did die. God rest their tired souls"—he shrugged his shoulders as he turned to retrace his steps—"it is better so. Now, Friend Trowbridge, do you hasten aloft and bring down that young girl from the room above. We must run for it if we do not wish to be crushed under the falling timbers of this house of abominations!"

THE STORM HAD SPENT itself and a red, springtime sun was peeping over the horizon as de Grandin and I trudged up my front steps with the mutilated girl stumbling wearily between us. We had managed to flag a car when we got out.

"Put her to bed, my excellent one," de Grandin ordered Nora, my house-keeper, who came to meet us enveloped in righteous indignation and an outing flannel nightgown. "*Parbleu*, she has had many troubles!"

In the study, a glass of steaming whisky and hot water in one hand, a vile-smelling French cigarette in the other, he faced me across the desk. "How was it you knew not that house, my friend?" he demanded.

I grinned sheepishly. "I took the wrong turning at the detour," I explained, "and got on the Yerbyville Road. It's just recently been hard-surfaced, and I haven't used it for years because it was always impassable. Thinking we were on the Andover Pike all the while, I never connected the place with the old Olmsted Mansion I'd seen hundreds of times from the road."

"Ah, yes," he agreed, nodding thoughtfully, "a little turn from the right way, and—*pouf!*—what a distance we have to retrace."

"Now, about the girl upstairs," I began, but he waved the question aside.

"The mad one had but begun his devil's work on her," he replied. "I, Jules de Grandin, will operate on her eyes and make them as straight as before, nor will I accept one penny for my work. Meantime, we must find her kindred and notify them she is safe and in good hands.

"And now"—he handed me his empty tumbler—"a little more whisky, if you please, Friend Trowbridge."

The Great God Pan

"**B**UT OF COURSE, MY friend," Jules de Grandin conceded as he hitched his pack higher on his shoulders and leaned forward against the grade of the wooded hill, "I grant you American roads are better than those of France; but look to what inconvenience these same good roads put us. Everything in America is arranged for the convenience of the motorist—the man who covers great distances swiftly. Your roads are the direct result of motorized transportation for the millions, and, consequently, you and I must tramp half the night and very likely sleep under the stars, because there is no inn to offer shelter.

"Now in France, where roads were laid out for stage-coaches hundreds of years before your Monsieur Ford was dreamed of, there is an abundance of resting places for the pedestrian. Here—" He spread his hands in an eloquent gesture of deprecation.

"Oh, well," I comforted, "we started out on a hiking trip, you know, and we've had mighty fine weather so far. A night in the open won't do us any harm. That cleared place at the top of the hill looks like a good spot to make camp."

"Eh, yes, I suppose so," he acquiesced as he breasted the crown of the hill and paused for breath. "*Parbleu*," he gazed about him, "I fear we trespass, Friend Trowbridge! This is no natural glade, it has been cleared for human habitation. Behold!" He waved his arm in a commanding gesture.

"By George, you're right!" I agreed in disappointment as I surveyed the clearing.

"The trees—beech, birch and poplar—had been cut away for the space of an acre or more, and the stumps removed, the cleared land afterward being sown with grass as smooth and well cared for as a private estate's lawn. Twenty yards ahead a path of flat, smooth stones was laid in the sod, running from a dense thicket of dwarf pine and rhododendron across the sward to a clump of tall, symmetrical cedars standing almost in the center of the clearing. Through the dark, bearded boughs of the evergreens we caught the fitful gleam of lights as the soft summer-evening breeze swayed the branches."

"Too bad," I murmured; "guess we'll have to push on a little farther for our bivouac."

"*Mille cochons, non!*" de Grandin denied. "Not I. *Parbleu*, but my feet faint from exhaustion, and my knees cry out for the caress of Mother Earth with a piety they have not known these many years! Come, let us go to the proprietor of that mansion and say, '*Monsieur*, here are two worthy gentleman tramps who crave the boon of a night's lodging and a meal, also a bath and a cup of wine, if that so entirely detestable Monsieur Volstead has allowed you to retain any.' He will not refuse us, my friend. *Morbleu*, a man with the charity of a Senegalese idol would not turn us away in the circumstances! I shall ask him with tears in my voice—*pardieu*, I shall weep like a lady in the cinema; I shall wring my hands and entreat him! Never fear, my friend, we shall lodge in yonder house this night, or Jules de Grandin goes supperless to a bed of pine-needles."

"Humph, I hope your optimism is justified," I grunted as I followed him across the close-cropped lawn to the stone path and marched toward the lights in the cedars.

We had progressed a hundred feet or so along the path when a sudden squealing cry, followed by a crashing in the thicket at the clearing edge, stopped us in our tracks. Something fluttering and white, gleaming like a ghost in the faint starlight, broke through the bushes, and a soft slapping noise, as though someone were beating his hands lightly and quickly together, sounded as the figure approached us.

"Oh, sirs, run, run for your lives, it—it's *Pan!*" the girl called in a frightened voice as she came abreast of us. "Run, run, if you want to live; *he's* there, I tell you! I saw his face among the leaves!"

One of de Grandin's small, slender hands rose with an involuntary gesture to stroke his little blond mustache as he surveyed our admonisher. She was tall and built with a stately, statuesque beauty which was doubly enhanced by the simple white linen garment which fell in straight lines from her lovely bare shoulders to her round, bare ankles. The robe was bound about the waist with a corded girdle which crossed above her breast, and was entirely sleeveless, though cut rather high at the neck, exposing only a few inches of white throat. Her feet, narrow and high-arched, and almost as white as the linen of her robe, were innocent of any covering, and I realized that the slapping sound I had heard was the impact of her bare soles on the stones of the path as she ran.

"*Tiens, Mademoiselle*," de Grandin declared with a bow, "you are as lovely as Pallas Athene herself. Who is it has dared frighten you? *Cordieu*, I shall do myself the honor of twisting his unmannerly nose!"

"No, no!" the girl besought in a trembling voice. "Do not go back, sir, *please!* I tell you Pan—the Great God Pan, Himself—is in those bushes. I went to bathe in the fountain a few minutes ago, and as I came from the water I—I saw his face grinning at me between the rhododendron bushes! It was only for a second, and I was so frightened I did not look again, but—oh, let us go to the house! Hurry, hurry, or we may see him in good earnest, and—" She broke off with a shudder and turned from us, walking hurriedly, but with consummate grace, toward the knot of cedars before us.

"*Sacré nom!*" de Grandin murmured as he fell in behind her. "Is it that we have arrived at a home for the feeble-minded, Friend Trowbridge, or is this beautiful one a goddess from the days of old? *Nom d'un coq*, she speaks the English like an American, but her costume, her so divine beauty, they are things of the days when Pygmalion hewed living flesh from out the lifeless marble!"

T HE MURMUR OF FEMININE voices, singing softly in unison, came to us as we made our way through the row of cedar trees and approached the house. The building was almost square, as well as we could determine in the uncertain light, constructed of some sort of white or light-colored stone, and fronted by a wide portico with tall pillars topped with Doric capitals. The girl ran lightly up the three wide steps leading to the porch, her bare feet making no sound on the stone treads, and we followed her, wondering what sort of folk dwelt in this bit of classic Greece seemingly dropped from some other star in the midst of the New Jersey woods.

"*Morbleu!*" de Grandin exclaimed softly in wonderment as we paused at the wide, doorless entrance. Inside the house, or temple, was a large apartment, almost fifty feet square, paved with alternate slabs of white and grey-green stone. In the center stood a square column of black stone, some three feet in height, topped by an urn of some semi-transparent substance in which a light glowed dimly. The place was illuminated by a series of flaring torches hung in rings let into the walls, their uncertain, flickering light showing us a circle of ten young women, dressed in the same simple classic costume as that worn by the girl we had met outside, kneeling about the central urn, their faces bowed modestly toward the floor, white arms raised above their heads, hands bent inward toward the center of the room. As we stood at gaze the girl who had preceded us hurried soundlessly across the checkered pavement and sank to her knees, inclining her shapely head and raising her arms in the same position of mute adoration assumed by the others.

"Name of a sacred pig!" de Grandin whispered. "We have here the votaries, but the hierophant, where is he?"

"There, I think," I answered, nodding toward the lighted urn in the pavement's center.

"*Parbleu*, yes," my companion assented, "and a worthy one for such a class, *n'est-ce-pas?*"

Standing beside the central altar, if such it could be called, was a short, pudgy little man, clothed in a short *chiton* of purple cloth bordered about neck, sleeves and bottom with a zig-zag design of gold braid. His bald head, gleaming in the torchlight, was crowned with a wreath of wild laurel, and a garland of roses hung about his fat, creased neck like an overgrown Hawaiian *lei*. Clasped in the crook of his left elbow was a zither, or some similar musical instrument, while a little stick, ending in a series of curved teeth, something like the fingers of a Japanese back-scratcher, was clasped in his dimpled right hand.

"Come, my children," the comic little man exclaimed in a soft, unctuous voice, "let us to our evening worship. Beauty is love, love beauty; that is all ye know and all ye need to know. Come, Chloë, Thisbe, Daphne, Clytie, let us see how well you know the devotion of beauty!"

He waved his stick like a monarch gesturing with his scepter, and drew its claw-tipped end across the strings of his zither, striking a chord, whereat the kneeling girls began singing, or, rather, humming, a lilting, swinging tune vaguely reminiscent of Mendelssohn's *Spring Song,* and four of their number leaped nimbly to their feet, ran lightly to the center of the room, joined hands in a circle and began a dance of light, lithe grace.

Faster and faster their white feet whirled in the convolutions of the dance, their graceful arms weaving patterns of living beauty as they swung in time to the measures of the song. They formed momentary tableaux of sculptural loveliness, only to break apart instantly into quadruple examples of individual posturing such as would have set an artist mad with delight.

The music ceased on a long-drawn, quavering note, the four dancers ran quickly back to their positions in the circle, and dropped again to their knees, extending their arms above their heads and bending their supple hands inward.

"It is well," the fat little man pronounced oracularly. "The day is done; let us to our rest."

The girls rose with a subdued rustling of white garments and separated into whispering, laughing groups, while the little man posed more pompously than ever beside the lighted urn.

"*Tiens*, Friend Trowbridge," de Grandin whispered with a chuckle, "do you behold how this bantam would make a peacock of himself? He is vain, this one. Surely, we shall spend the night here!

"*Monsieur*," he emerged from the shadow of the doorway and advanced toward the absurd figure posturing beside the urn, "we are two weary travelers, lost in the midst of these woods, without the faintest notion of the direction of the nearest inn. Will you not, of your so splendid generosity, permit that we spend the night beneath your roof?"

"Eh, what's that?" the other exclaimed with a start as he beheld the little Frenchman for the first time. "What d'ye want? Spend the night here? No, no; I can't have that. Get my school talked about. Couldn't possibly have it. Never have any men in this place."

"Ah, but *Monsieur*," de Grandin replied smoothly, "you do forget that you are already here. If it were but a question of having male guests at this so wonderful school of the arts, is not the reputation of the establishment already ruined? Surely a gentleman with so much of the appeal to beauty as *Monsieur* unquestionably possesses would cause much gossip if he were not so well known for his discretion. And, *Monsieur's* discretion being already so firmly established, who would dare accuse him of anything save great-heartedness if he did permit two wanderers—and medical men in the bargain—to remain overnight in his house? Permit me, *Monsieur*; I am Dr. Jules de Grandin, of the Sorbonne, and this is Dr. Samuel Trowbridge, of Harrisonburg, New Jersey, both entirely at your good service, *Monsieur*."

The little fellow's fat face creased in a network of wrinkles as he regarded de Grandin with a self-satisfied smirk. "Ah, you appreciate the pure beauty of our school?" he remarked with almost pathetic eagerness. "I am Professor Judson—Professor Herman Judson, sir—of the School of the Worship of Beauty. These—ah—young ladies whom you have seen here tonight are a few of my pupils. We believe that the old ideals—the old thought—of ancient Greece is a living, motivating thing today, just as it was in centuries gone by. We assert sir, that the religion of beauty which actuated the Greeks is still a living, vital thing. We believe that the old gods are not dead; but come to those who woo them with the ancient rite of song and the dance. In fine, sir, we are pagans—apostles of the religion of neo-paganism!"

He drew himself up to his full height, which could not have exceeded five feet six inches, and glared defiantly at de Grandin, as though expecting a shocked protest at his announcement.

The Frenchman's smile became wider and blander than ever. "Capital, *Monsieur*," he congratulated. "Anyone with the eye of a blind man could see that you are the very personality to head such an incontestably sensible school of thought. The expertness with which your pupils perform their dances shows that they have a teacher worthy of all your claims. We do felicitate you most heartily, *Monsieur*. Meantime"—he slipped the pack from his shoulders and lowered it to the pavement—"you will undoubtlessly permit that we shall pass the night here? No?"

"We-ell," the professor's doubt gave way slowly, "you seem to be more appreciative than the average modern barbarian. Yes, you may remain here overnight; but you must be off in the morning—early in the morning, mind you. Never do to have the neighbors seeing strange men coming from this place. Understand?"

"Perfectly, *Monsieur*," de Grandin answered with a bow. "And, if we might make so bold, may we trespass on your hospitality for a bite—the merest morsel of food?"

"U'm, pay for it?" the other demanded dubiously.

"But assuredly," de Grandin replied, producing a roll of bills. "It would cause us the greatest anguish, I do assure you, if it were ever said that we accepted the hospitality of the great Professor 'Erman Judson without making adequate return."

"Very well," the professor assented, and hurried through a door at the farther end of the apartment, returning in a few minutes with a tray of cold roast veal, warm, ripe apples, a loaf of white bread and a jug of more than legally strong, sour wine.

"Ah," de Grandin boasted as he washed down a sandwich with a draft of the acid liquor, "did I not tell you we should spend the night here, Friend Trowbridge?"

"You certainly made good your promise," I agreed as I shoved the remains of my meal from me, undid my pack and prepared to pillow my head on my rolled-up jacket. "See you in the morning, old fellow."

"Very good," he agreed. "Meantime, I go out of doors to smoke a last cigarette before I join you in sleep."

I MIGHT HAVE SLEPT AN hour, perhaps a little more, when a sharp, insistent poke in my ribs woke me sufficiently to understand the words whispered fiercely in my ear. "Trowbridge, Trowbridge, my friend," Jules de Grandin breathed so low I could scarcely make out the syllables. "This house, it is not all as it should be, I fear me."

"Eh, what's that?" I demanded sleepily, sitting up and blinking half comprehendingly at his dim outline in the semidarkness of the big room.

"S-s-sh, not so loud," he cautioned, then leaned nearer, speaking rapidly: "Do you know from whence your English word 'panic' comes, my friend?"

"What?" I demanded in disgust. "Did you wake me up to discuss etymology—after a day's hiking? Good Lord, man—"

"Be still!" he ordered sharply; then, inconsistently, "Answer me, if you please; whence comes that word?"

"Hanged if I know," I replied, "and I'm hanged if I care a whoop, either. It can come from the Cannibal Islands, for all I—"

"Quiet!" he commanded, then hurried on: "In the old days when such things were, my friend, Pan, the god of Nature, was very real to the people. They believed, firmly, that whoso saw Pan after nightfall, that one died instantly. Therefore, when a person is seized with a blind, unreasoning fear; even to this day, we say he has a panic. Of what consequence is this?

Remember, my friend, the young lady whom we did meet as we approached this house told us she had seen Pan's face grinning at her from out the bushes as she bathed. Is it not so?"

"I guess so," I answered, putting my head back on my improvised pillow and preparing to sleep while he talked.

But he shook my shoulder with a sharp, imperative gesture. "Listen, my friend," he besought, "when I did go out of doors to smoke my cigarette, I met one of those beautiful young women who frequent this temple of the new heathenism, and engaged her in conversation. From her I learned much, and some of it sounds not good to my ears. For instance, I learn that this Professor Herman Judson is a much misunderstood man. Oh, but yes. The lawyers, they have misunderstood him many times. Once they misunderstood him so that he was placed in the state's prison for deceiving gullible women with fortune-telling tricks. Again he was misunderstood so that he went to the Bastille for attempting to secure some money which a certain deceased lady's heirs believed should have gone to them—which *did* go to them eventually."

"Well, what of it?" I growled. "That's no affair of ours. We're not a committee on the morals of dancing masters, are we?"

"Eh, are we not so?" he replied. "I am not entirely sure of that, my friend. I fear we, too, are about to misunderstand this Professor Judson. Some other things I find out from that young lady with the Irish nose and the Greek costume. This professor he has founded this school of dancing and paganism, taking for his pupils only young women who have no parents or other near relations, but much money. He is not minded to be misunderstood by heirs-at-law. What think you of that, *hein?*"

"I think he's got more sense than we gave him credit for," I replied.

"Undoubtlessly," he agreed, "very much more; for also I discovered that *Monsieur le Professeur* has had his school regularly incorporated, and has secured from each of his pupils a last will and testament in which she does leave the bulk of her estate to the corporation."

"Well," I challenged, giving up hope of getting my sleep till he had talked himself out, "what of it? The man may be sincere in his attempt to found some sort of aesthete cult, and he'll need money, for the project."

"True, quite true," he conceded, nodding his head like a China mandarin, "but attend me, Friend Trowbridge; while we walked beneath the stars I did make an occasion to take that young lady's hand in mine, and—"

"You old rake!" I cut in, grinning, but he shut me off with a snort of impatience.

"— and that was but a ruse to feel her pulse," he continued. "*Parbleu*, my friend, her heart did race like the engine of a *moteur!* Not with emotion for me—never think it, for I did talk to her like a father or uncle, well, perhaps more like a cousin—but because it is of an abnormal quickness. Had I a stethoscope with me I could have told more, but as it is I would wager a hundred dollars that she suffers a chronic myocarditis, and the prognosis of that ailment is always grave, my friend. Think you a moment—what would happen if that young girl with a defective heart should see what she took to be the face of the great god Pan peering at her from the leaves, as the lady we first saw declared she did? Remember, these children believe in the deities of old, my friend."

"By George!" I sat bolt upright. "Do you mean—you don't mean that—"

"No, my friend, as yet I mean nothing," he replied evenly, "but it would be well if we emulated the cat, and slept with one eye and both ears open this night. Perhaps"—he shrugged his shoulders impatiently—"who knows what we may see in this house where the dead gods are worshiped with song and the dance?"

A MARBLE PAVEMENT IS A poor substitute for a bed, even when the sleeper is thoroughly fatigued from a long day's tramp, and I slept fitfully, troubled by all manner of unpleasant dreams. The forms of lithe, classically draped young girls dancing about a fire-filled urn alternated with visions of goat-legged, grinning satyrs in my sleep as I rolled from side to side on my hard bed; but the sudden peal of devilish laughter, quavering sardonically, almost like the bleating of a goat, was the figment of no dream. I sat suddenly up, wide-awake, as a feminine scream, keen-edged with the terror of death, rent the tomblike stillness of the early morning, and ten white-draped forms came rushing in the disorder of abject fright into the room about us.

Torches were being lighted, one from another, and we beheld the girls, their tresses unloosed from the classic fillets which customarily bound them, their robes hastily adjusted, huddled fearfully in a circle about the glowing urn, while outside, in the moonless night, the echo of that fearful scream seemed wandering blindly among the evergreens.

"Professor, Professor!" one of the girls cried, wringing her hands in an agony of apprehension. "Professor, where are you? Chloë's missing, Professor!"

"Eh, what is it that you say?" de Grandin demanded, springing up and gazing questioningly about him. "What is this? One of your number missing! And the professor, too? *Parbleu*; me, I shall investigate this! Do you attend the young ladies, Friend Trowbridge. I, Jules de Grandin, shall try conclusions with whatever god or devil accosts the missing one!"

"Wait a minute," I cautioned. "The professor will be here in a moment. You can't go out there now; you haven't any gun."

"Ha, have I not?" he replied sarcastically, drawing the heavy, blue-steel pistol from his jacket pocket. "Friend Trowbridge, there are entirely too many people of ill repute who desire nothing more than the death of Jules de Grandin to make it safe for me to be without a weapon at any time. Me, I go to investigate."

"Never mind, sir," the smooth, oily voice of Professor Judson sounded from the door at the rear of the room as he marched with short-legged dignity toward the altar. "Everything is all right, I assure you.

"My children," he turned to the frightened girls, "Chloë has been frightened at the thought of Pan's presence. It is true that the great god of all Nature hovers ever near his worshipers, especially at the dark of the moon, but there is nothing to fear.

"Chloë will soon be all right. Meantime, let us propitiate Pan by prayer and sacrifice. Thetis, bring hither a goat!" He turned his small, deep-set eyes on the young girl we had met as we entered the grounds, and waved a pudgy hand commandingly.

The girl went white to the lips, but with a submissive bow she hurried from the room, returning in a moment leading a half-grown black goat by a string, a long, sharp butcher-knife and a wide, shallow dish under her free arm.

She led the animal to the altar where the professor stood, gave the leading string into his hand and presented the sacrificial knife, then knelt before him, holding the dish beneath the terrified goat's head, ready to catch the blood when the professor should have cut the creature's throat.

It was as if some beady, madness-compelling fume had suddenly wafted into the room. For a single breathless moment the other girls looked at their preceptor and his kneeling acolyte with a gaze of fear and disgust, their tender feminine instincts rebelling at the thought of the warm blood soon to flow, then, as a progressive, contagious shudder seemed to run through them, one after another, they leaped wildly upward with frantic, frenzied bounds as though the stones beneath their naked feet were suddenly turned white-hot, beating their hands together, waving their arms convulsively above their heads, bending forward till their long, unbound hair cascaded before their faces and swept the floor at their feet, then leaping upward again with rolling, staring eyes and wantonly waving arms. With a maniac shriek one of them seized the bodice of her robe and rent it asunder, exposing her breasts, another tore her gown from hem to hips in half a dozen places, so that streamers of tattered linen draped like ribbons about her rounded limbs as she sprang and crouched and sprang again in the abandon of her voluptuous dance.

And all the while, as madness seemed to feed on madness, growing wilder and more depraved each instant, they chanted in a shrill, hysterical chorus:

Upon thy worshipers now gaze,
    Pan, Pan, Io Pan,
To thee be sacrifice and praise,
    Pan, Pan, to Pan.
Give us the boon of the seeing eye,
That we may behold ere yet we die
The ecstasies of thy mystery,
    Pan, Pan, *Pan!*

Repeated insistently, with maniacal fervor, the name "Pan" beat against the air like the rhythm of a tom-tom. Its shouted repetition seemed to catch the tempo of my heart-beats; despite myself I felt an urging, strong as an addict's craving for his drug, to join in the lunatic dance, to leap and shout and tear the encumbering clothing from my body as I did so.

The professor changed his grip from the goat's tether to its hind legs. He swung the bleating animal shoulder-high, so that as it held its head back its throat curved above the dish held by the girl, who twitched her shoulders and swayed her body jerkily in time to the pagan hymn as she knelt at his feet.

"Oh, Pan, great goat-god, personification of all Nature's forces, immortal symbol of the ecstasy of passion, to Thee we make the sacrifice; to Thee we spill the blood of this victim," the professor cried, his eyes gleaming brilliantly in the reflection of the torches and the altar fire. "Behold, goat of thy worshiper's flock, we—"

"*Zut!* Enough of this; *cordieu*, too much!" de Grandin's furious voice cut through the clamor as a fire-bell stills the noise of street traffic. "Hold your hand, accursed of heaven, or by the head of St. Denis, I scatter your brains in yonder dish!" His heavy pistol pointed unwaveringly at the professor's bald head till the terrified man unloosed his hold upon the squirming goat.

"To your rooms, my little ones," de Grandin commanded, his round, blazing eyes traveling from one trembling girl to another. "Be not deceived, God is not mocked. Evil communications corrupt good manners—*parbleu, Monsieur*, I do refer to you and no one else—" he glowered at the professor. "And you, Mademoiselle," he called to the kneeling girl, "do you put down that dish and have nothing to do with this sacrifice of blood. Do as I say. I, Jules de Grandin, command it!

"Now, *Monsieur le Professeur*," he waved his pistol to enforce his order, "do you come with me and explore these grounds. If we find your great god Pan I shall shoot his evil eyes from out his so hideous head. If we do not find him, *morbleu*, it were better for you that we find him, I damn think!"

"Get outa my house!" Professor Judson's mantle of culture ripped away, revealing the coarse fibre beneath it; "I'll not have any dam' Frenchman comin' around here an'—"

"Softly, *Monsieur*, softly; you will please remember there are ladies present," de Grandin admonished, motioning toward the door with his pistol. "Will you come with me, or must I so dispose of you that you can not ran away until I return? I could most easily shoot through one of your fat legs."

Professor Judson left the altar of Pan and accompanied de Grandin into the night. I do not know what took place out under the stars, but when the Frenchman returned some ten minutes later, he carried the inert form of the eleventh young woman in his arms, and the professor was not with him.

"Quickly, Friend Trowbridge," he commanded as he laid the girl on the pavement, "give me some of the wine left from our supper. It will help this poor one, I think. Meantime"—he swung his fierce, unwinking gaze about the clustering circle of girls—"do you young ladies assume garments more fitted for this day and age, and prepare to evacuate this house of hell in the morning. Dr. Trowbridge and I shall remain here until the day, and tomorrow we notify the police that this place is permanently closed forever."

IT WAS A GRIM, hard task we had bringing the unconscious girl out of her swoon, but patience and the indomitable determination of Jules de Grandin finally induced a return of consciousness.

"Oh, oh, I saw Pan—Pan looked at me from the leaves!" the poor child sobbed hysterically as she opened her eyes.

"*Non, non, ma chère*," de Grandin assured her. "'Twas but a papier-mâché mask which the so odious one placed in the branches of the bush to terrify you. Behold, I will bring it to you that you may touch it, and know it for the harmless thing it is!"

He darted to the doorway of the temple, returning instantly with the hideous mask of a long, leering face, grinning mouth stretched from pointed ear to pointed ear, short horns rising from the temples and upward-slanting eyes glaring in fiendish malignancy. "It is ugly, I grant you," he admitted, flinging the thing upon the pavement and grinding it beneath his heavily booted heel, "but see, the foot of one who fears them not is mightier than all the gods of heathendom. Is it not so?"

The girl smiled faintly and nodded.

DE GRANDIN WAS OUT of the house at sunup, and returned before nine o'clock with a fleet of motor cars hastily commandeered from a roadhouse garage which he discovered a couple of miles down the road. "Remember, *Mesdemoiselles*," he admonished as the cars swung away from the portico of the temple with the erstwhile pupils of the School of Neopaganism, "those wills and testaments, they must be revoked forthwith. The detestable one, he has the present copies, but any will which you wish to make will revoke those he holds. Leave your money to found a vocal school for Thomas cats, or for a gymnasium for teaching young frogs to leap, but bequeath it to some other cause than this temple of false gods, I do implore you."

"Ready, sport?" the driver of the car reserved for us demanded, lighting a cigarette and flipping the match toward the temple steps with a disdainful gesture.

"In one moment, my excellent one," de Grandin answered as he turned from me and hurried into the house. "Await me, Friend Trowbridge," he called over his shoulder; "I have an important mission to perform."

"WHAT THE DICKENS DID you run back into that place for when the chauffeur was all ready to drive us away?" I demanded as we bowled over the smooth road toward the railway station.

He turned his unwinking cat's stare on me a moment, then his little blue eyes sparkled with a gleam of elfin laughter. "*Pardieu*, my friend," he chuckled, "that Professor Judson, I found a trunkful of his clothes in the room he occupied, and paused to burn them all. Death of my life, I did rout him from the premises in that Greek costume he wore last night, and when he returns he will find naught but glowing embers of his modern garments! What a figure he will cut, walking into a haberdasher's clothed like Monsieur Nero, and asking for a suit of clothes. *La, la*, could we but take a motion picture of him, our eternal fortunes would be made!"

Restless Souls

"TEN THOUSAND SMALL GREEN devils! What a night; what an odious night!" Jules de Grandin paused beneath the theater's porte-cochère and scowled ferociously at the pelting rain.

"Well, summer's dead and winter hasn't quite come," I reminded soothingly. "We're bound to have a certain amount of rain in October. The autumnal equinox—"

"May Satan's choicest imps fly off with the autumnal equinox!" the little Frenchman interrupted. "*Morbleu*, it is that I have seen no sun since God alone knows when; besides that, I am most abominably hungry!"

"That condition, at least, we can remedy," I promised, nudging him from the awning's shelter toward my parked car. "Suppose we stop at the Café Bacchanale? They usually have something good to eat."

"Excellent, capital," he agreed enthusiastically, skipping nimbly into the car and rearranging the upturned collar of his raincoat. "You are a true philosopher, *mon vieux*. Always you tell me that which I most wish to hear."

They were having an hilarious time at the cabaret, for it was the evening of October 31, and the management had put on a special Halloween celebration. As we passed the velvet rope that looped across the entrance to the dining room a burst of Phrygian music greeted us, and a dozen agile young women in abbreviated attire were performing intricate gyrations under the leadership of an apparently boneless damsel whose costume was principally composed of strands of jangling hawk-bells threaded round her neck and wrists and ankles.

"Welsh rabbit?" I suggested. "They make a rather tasty one here." He nodded almost absent-mindedly as he surveyed a couple eating at a nearby table.

At last, just as the waiter brought our bubbling-hot refreshment: "Regard them, if you will, Friend Trowbridge," he whispered. "Tell me what, if anything, you make of them."

The girl was, as the saying goes, "a knockout." Tall, lissome, lovely to regard, she wore a dinner dress of simple black without a single hint of ornament except a single strand of small matched pearls about her slim and rather long throat. Her hair was bright chestnut, almost copper-colored, and braided round her small head in a Grecian coronal, and in its ruddy frame her face was like some strange flower on a tall stalk. Her darkened lids and carmined mouth and pale cheeks made an interesting combination.

As I stole a second glance at her it seemed to me she had a vague yet unmistakable expression of invalidism. Nothing definite, merely the combination of certain factors which pierced the shell of my purely masculine admiration and stock response from my years of experience as a medical practitioner—a certain blueness of complexion which meant "interesting pallor" to the layman but spelled imperfectly oxidized blood to the physician; a slight tightening of the muscles about the mouth which gave her lovely pouting lips a pathetic droop; and a scarcely perceptible retraction at the junction of cheek and nose which meant fatigue of nerves or muscles, possibly both.

Idly mingling admiration and diagnosis, I turned my glance upon her escort, and my lips tightened slightly as I made a mental note: "Gold digger!" The man was big-boned and coarse-featured, bullet-headed and thick-necked, and had the pasty, toad-belly complexion of one who drinks too much and sleeps and exercises far too little. He hardly changed expression as the girl talked eagerly in a hushed whisper. His whole attitude was one of proprietorship, as if she were his thing and chattel, bought and paid for, and constantly his fishy eyes roved round the room and rested covetously on attractive women supping at the other tables.

"I do not like it, me," de Grandin's comment brought my wandering attention back. "It is both strange and queer; it is not right."

"Eh?" I returned. "Quite so; I agree with you. It's shameful for a girl like that to sell—or maybe only rent—herself to such a creature—"

"*Non, non*," he interrupted testily. "I have no thought of censoring their morals, such are their own affair. It is their treatment of the food that intrigues me."

"Food?" I echoed.

"*Oui-da*, food. On three distinct occasions they have ordered refreshment, yet each time they allowed it to grow cold; let it remain untouched until the *garçon* carried it away. I ask you, is that right?"

"Why—er—" I temporized, but he hurried on.

"Once as I watched I saw the woman make as though to lift a goblet to her lips, but the gesture of her escort halted her; she set the beverage down untasted. What sort of people ignore wine—the living soul of the grape?"

"Well, are you going to investigate?" I asked, grinning. I knew his curiosity was well-nigh as boundless as his self-esteem, and should not have been too greatly surprised if he had marched to the strange couple's table and demanded an explanation.

"Investigate?" he echoed thoughtfully. "Um. Perhaps I shall."

He snapped the pewter lid of his beer-mug back, took a long, pensive draught, then leant forward, small round eyes unwinkingly on mine. "You know what night this is?" he demanded.

"Of course, it's Halloween. All the little devils will be out stealing garden gates and knocking at front doors—"

"Perhaps the larger devils will be abroad, too."

"Oh, come, now," I protested, "you're surely not serious—"

"By blue, I am," he affirmed solemnly. "*Regardez, s'il vous plaît.*" He nodded toward the pair at the adjoining table.

Seated directly opposite the strange couple was a young man occupying a table by himself. He was a good-looking, sleek-haired youngster of the sort to be found by scores on any college campus. Had de Grandin brought the same charge of food wastage against him that he had leveled at the other two he would have been equally justified, for the boy left an elaborate order practically untasted while his infatuated eyes devoured every line of the girl at the next table.

As I turned to look at him I noted from the corner of my eye that the girl's escort nodded once in the same direction, then rose and left the table abruptly. I noticed as he walked toward the door that his walk was more like the rapid amble of an animal than the step of a man.

The girl half turned as she was left alone and under lowered lashes looked at the young man so indifferently that there was no mistaking her intent.

De Grandin watched with what seemed bleak disinterest as the young man rose to join her, and, save for an occasional covert glance, paid no attention as they exchanged the inane amenities customary in such cases, but when they rose to leave a few minutes later he motioned me to do likewise. "It is of importance that we see which way they go," he told me earnestly.

"Oh, for goodness' sake, be sensible!" I chided. "Let them flirt if they want to. I'll warrant she's in better company now than she came in with—"

"*Précisément,* exactly, quite so!" he agreed. "It is of that 'better company' I think when I have the anxiety."

"H'm, that *was* a tough-looking customer she was with," I conceded. "And for all her innocent-looking prettiness she might be the bait in a badger-game—"

"A badger-game? *Mais oui,* my friend. A game-of-the-badger in which the stakes are infinitely high!" Of the ornate doorman he demanded, "That couple, that young man and woman—they did go what way, *Monsieur le Concierge?*"

"Huh?"

"The young man and young woman—you saw them depart? We would know their direction—" a crumpled dollar bill changed hands, and the doorman's memory revived miraculously.

"Oh, them. Yeah, I seen 'em. They went down th' street that-away in a big black taxi. Little English feller drivin' 'em. Looked like th' feller's made a mash. He'll *get* mashed, too, if th' tough bimbo 'at brought th' broad in ketches 'im messin' round with her. That gink's one awful mean-lookin' bozo, an'—"

"Assuredly," de Grandin agreed. "And this *Monsieur le Gink* of whom you speak, he went which way, if you please?"

"He come outer here like a bat outer hell 'bout ten minutes ago. Funny thing 'bout him, too. He was walkin' down th' street, an' I was watchin' him, not special, but just lookin' at him, an' I looked away for just a minute, an' when I looked back he was gone. He wasn't more'n half way down th' block when I last seen him, but when I looked again he wasn't there. Dam' if I see how he managed to get round th' comer in that time."

"I think that your perplexity is justified," de Grandin answered as I brought the car to a stop at the curb, then, to me: "Hasten, Friend Trowbridge. I would that we get them in sight before they are lost in the storm."

IT WAS A MATTER of only a few minutes to pick up the tail light of the big car in which the truants sped toward the outskirts of town. Occasionally we lost them, only to catch them again almost immediately, for their route led straight out Orient Boulevard toward the Old Turnpike. "This is the craziest thing we've ever done," I grumbled. "There isn't any more chance that we'll catch them than—great Scott, they've stopped!"

Improbably, the big car had drawn up at the imposing Canterbury Gate of Shadow Lawn Cemetery.

De Grandin leant forward in his seat like a jockey in the saddle. "Quick, hurry, make all speed, my friend!" he besought. "We must catch them before they alight!"

Try as I would my efforts were futile. Only an empty limousine and a profanely bewildered chauffeur awaited us when we drew up at the burying ground, our engine puffing like a winded horse.

"Which way, my friend—where did they go?" de Grandin vaulted from the car before we had come to a full stop.

"Inside th' graveyard!" answered the driver. "What th' hell d'ye know about that? Bringin' me way out here where th' devil says 'Good Night!' an' leavin' me as flat as a dam' pancake." His voice took on a shrill falsetto in imitation of a woman's. "'You needn't wait for us, driver, we'll not be com' back,' she says. Good God A' mighty, who th' hell but dead corpses goes into th' cemet'ry an' don't come back?"

"Who, indeed?" the Frenchman echoed, then, to me: "Come, Friend Trow-bridge, we must hasten, we must find them all soon, or it is too late!"

SOLEMN AS THE PURPOSE to which it was dedicated, the burial park stretched dark and forbidding about us as we stepped through the grille in the imposing stone gateway. The curving ravelled avenues, bordered with double rows of hem-locks, stretched away like labyrinthine mazes, and the black turf with its occa-sional corrugations of mounded graves or decorations of pallid marble, sloped upward from us, seemingly to infinity.

Like a terrier on the scent de Grandin hurried forward, bending now and then to pass beneath the downward-swaying bough of some rain-laden ever-green, then hurrying still faster.

"You know this place, Friend Trowbridge?" he demanded during one of his brief halts.

"Better than I want to," I admitted. "I've been here to several funerals."

"Good!" he returned. "You can tell me then where is the—how do you call him?—the receiving vault?"

"Over there, almost in the center of the park," I answered, and he nodded understandingly, then took up his course, almost at a run.

Finally we reached the squat grey-stone receiving mausoleum, and he tried one of the heavy doors after another. "A loss!" he announced disappointedly as each of the tomb's great metal doors defied his efforts. "It seems we must search elsewhere."

He trotted to the open space reserved for parking funeral vehicles and cast a quick appraising look about, arrived at a decision and started like a cross-country runner down the winding road that led to a long row of family mausoleums. At each he stopped, trying the strong metal gratings at its entrance, peering into its gloomy interior with the aid of his pocket flashlight.

Tomb after tomb we visited, till both my breath and patience were exhausted. "What's all this nonsense?" I demanded. "What're you looking for—"

"That which I fear to find," he panted, casting the beam of his light about. "If we are balked—ah? Look, my friend, look and tell me what it is you see."

In the narrow cone of light cast by his small electric torch I descried a dark form draped across the steps of a mausoleum. "Wh-why, it's a man!" I exclaimed.

"I hope so," he replied. "It may be we shall find the mere relic of one, but—ah? So. He is still breathing."

Taking the flashlight from him I played its ray on the still form stretched upon the tomb steps. It was the young man we had seen leave the café with the strange woman. On his forehead was a nasty cut, as though from some blunt instrument swung with terrific force—a blackjack, for instance.

Quickly, skillfully, de Grandin ran his supple, practised hands over the youngster's body, pressed his fingers to his pulse, bent to listen at his chest. "He lives," he announced at the end of his inspection, "but his heart, I do not like it. Come; let us take him hence, my friend."

"AND NOW, *mon brave*," he demanded half an hour later when we had revived the unconscious man with smelling salts and cold applications, "perhaps you will be good enough to tell us why you left the haunts of the living to foregather with the dead?"

The patient made a feeble effort to rise from the examination table, gave it up as too difficult and sank back. "I thought I was dead," he confessed.

"U'm?" the Frenchman regarded him narrowly. "You have not yet answered our question, young Monsieur."

The boy made a second attempt to rise, and an agonized expression spread over his face, his hand shot up to his left breast, and he fell back, half lolling, half writhing on the table.

"Quick, Friend Trowbridge, the amyl nitrite, where is it?" de Grandin asked.

"Over there," I waved my hand toward the medicine cabinet. "You'll find some three-minim capsules in the third bottle."

In a moment he secured the pearly little pellets, crushed one in his handkerchief and applied it to the fainting boy's nostrils. "Ah, that is better, *n'est-ce-pas*, my poor one?" he asked.

"Yes, thanks," the other replied, taking another deep inhalation of the powerful restorative, "much better." Then, "How'd you know what to give me? I didn't think—"

"My friend," the Frenchman interrupted with a smile, "I was practising the treatment of angina pectoris when you were still unthought of. Now, if you are sufficiently restored, you will please tell us why you left the Café Bacchanale, and what occurred thereafter. We wait."

Slowly, assisted by de Grandin on one side and me on the other, the young man descended from the table and seated himself in an easy chair. "I'm Donald Rochester," he introduced himself, "and this was to have been my last night on earth."

"Ah?" Jules de Grandin murmured.

"Six months ago." the young man continued, "Dr. Simmons told me I had angina pectoris. My case was pretty far advanced when he made his diagnosis, and he gave me only a little while to live. Two weeks ago he told me I'd be lucky to see the month out, and the pain was getting more severe and the attacks more frequent; so today I decided to give myself one last party, then go home and make a quick, clean job of it."

"Damn!" I muttered. I knew Simmons, a pompous old ass, but a first-rate diagnostician and a good heart man, though absolutely brutal with his patients.

"I ordered the sort of meal they haven't allowed me in the last half year," Rochester went on, "and was just about to start enjoying it when—when I saw her come in. Did"—he turned from de Grandin to me as if expecting greater understanding from a fellow countryman—"did you see her, too?" An expression of almost religious rapture overspread his face.

"Perfectly, *mon vieux*," de Grandin returned. "We all saw her. Tell us more."

"I always thought this talk of love at first sight was a lot of tripe, but I'm cured now. I even forgot my farewell meal, couldn't see or think of anything but her. If I'd had even two more years to live, I thought, nothing could have kept me from hunting her out and asking her to marry—"

"*Précisément*, assuredly, quite so," the Frenchman interrupted testily. "We do concede that you were fascinated, Monsieur; but, for the love of twenty thousand pale blue monkeys, I entreat you tell us what you did, not what you thought."

"I just sat and goggled at her sir. Couldn't do anything else. When that big brute she was with got up and left and she smiled at me, this poor old heart of mine almost blinked out, I tell you. When she smiled a second time there wasn't enough chain in the country to keep me from her.

"You'd have thought she'd known me all her life, the way she fell in step when we went out of the café. She had a big black car waiting outside and I climbed right in with her. Before I knew it, I was telling her who I was, how long I had to live, and how my only regret was losing her, just when I'd found her. I—"

"*Parbleu*, you told her that?"

"I surely did, and a lot more—blurted out that I loved her before I knew what I was about."

"And she—"

"Gentlemen, I'm not sure whether I ought to have delirium or not with this disease, but I'm pretty sure I've had a touch of something. Now, I want you to know I'm not crazy before I tell you the rest; but I might have had a heart attack or something, then fallen asleep and dreamed it."

"Say on, Monsieur," de Grandin ordered rather grimly. "We listen."

"Very well. When I said I loved her that girl just put her hands up to her eyes—like this—as if to wipe away some unshed tears. I half expected she'd be angry, or maybe giggle, but she didn't. All she said was, 'Too late—oh, too late!'

"'I know it is,' I answered. 'I've already told you I'm as good as dead, but I can't go west without telling you how I feel.'

"Then she said, 'Oh, no, it's not that, my dear. That's not at all what I meant. For I love you, too, though I've no right to say so—I've no right to love anyone—it's too late for me, too.'

"After that I just took her in my arms and held her tight, and she sobbed as if her heart would break. Finally I asked her to make me a promise. 'I'll rest better in my grave if I know you'll never go out with that ugly brute I saw you with tonight,' I told her, and she let out a little scream and cried harder than ever.

"Then I had the awful thought that maybe she was married to him, and that was what she meant when she said it was too late. So I asked her point blank.

"She said something devilish queer then. She told me, 'I must go to him whenever he wants me. Though I hate him as you can never understand; when he calls I have to go. This is the first time I've ever gone with him, but I must go again, and again, and again! She kept screaming the word till I stopped her mouth with kisses.

"Presently the car stopped and we got out. We were at some sort of park, I think, but I was so engrossed in helping her compose herself I didn't notice much of anything.

"She led me through a big gate and down a winding road. At last we stopped before some sort of lodge-house, and I took her in my arms for one last kiss.

"I don't know whether the rest of it really happened or whether I passed out and dreamed it. What I thought happened was this: Instead of putting her lips against mine, she put them around them and seemed to draw the very breath out of my lungs. I could feel myself go faint, like a swimmer caught in the surf and mauled and pounded till the breath's knocked out of him, and my eyes seemed blinded with a sort of mist; then everything went sort o' dark green round me, and I began sagging at the knees. I could still feel her arms round me, and remember being surprised at her strength, but it seemed as if she'd transferred her lips to my throat. I kept getting weaker and weaker with a sort of languorous ecstasy, if that means anything to you. Rather like sinking to sleep in a soft dry bed with a big drink of brandy tucked under your belt after you're dog-tired with cold and exposure. Next thing I knew I'd toppled over and fallen down the steps with no more strength in my knees than a rag doll has. I must have got an awful crack on the head when I went down, for I passed out completely, and the next thing I remember was waking to find you gentlemen working over me. Tell me, did I dream it all? I'm—just—about—played—out."

The sentence trailed off slowly, as if he were falling to sleep, and his head dropped forward while his hands slipped nervelessly from his lap, trailing flaccidly to the floor.

"Has he gone?" I whispered as de Grandin sprang across the room and ripped his collar open.

"Not quite," he answered. "More amyl nitrite, if you please; he will revive in a moment, but go home he shall not unless he promises not to destroy himself. *Mon Dieu*, destroyed he would be, body and soul, were he to put a bullet through his brain before—ah-*ha*? Behold, Friend Trowbridge, it is even as I feared!"

Against the young man's throat there showed two tiny perforated wounds, as though a fine needle had been thrust through a fold of skin.

"H'm," I commented. "If there were four of them I'd say a snake had bitten him."

"She has! Name of a little blue man, she has!" he retorted. "A serpent more virulent and subtle than any which goes on its belly has sunk her fangs in him; he is envenomed surely as if he had been a victim of a cobra's bite; but by the wings of Jacob's Angel we shall thwart her, my friend. We shall show her Jules de Grandin must be reckoned with—her, and that fish-eyed paramour of hers as well, or may I eat stewed turnips for my Christmas dinner and wash them down with ditch-water!"

It was a serious face he showed at breakfast the next day. "You have perhaps a half hour's liberty this morning?" he asked as he drained his fourth cup of coffee.

"H'm, I suppose so. Anything special you'd like to do?"

"There is, indeed. I should like to go again to Shadow Lawn Cemetery. I would examine it by daylight, if you please."

"Shadow Lawn?" I echoed in amazement. "What in this world—"

"Only partially," he interrupted. "Unless I am much more mistaken than I think our business has as much to do with the next world as this. Come; you have your patients to attend, I have my duties to perform. Let us go."

The rain had vanished with the night and a bright November sun was shining when we reached the graveyard. Making straight for the tomb where we had found young Rochester the night before, de Grandin halted and inspected it carefully. On the lintel of the massive doorway he invited my attention to the single incised word:

HEATHERTON

"U'm?" he nursed his narrow pointed chin between a thoughtful thumb and forefinger. "That name I must remember, Friend Trowbridge."

Inside the tomb, arranged in two superimposed rows, were the crypts containing the remains of deceased Heathertons, each sealed by a white marble slab set with cement in a bronze frame, a two-lined legend telling the name and vital data of the occupant. The withering remains of a wreath clung by a knot of ribbon to the bronze ring-bolt ornamenting the marble panel of the farthest crypt, and behind the desiccating circle of roses and ruscus leaves I made out:

ALICE HEATHERTON
Sept. 28, 1926—Oct. 2, 1948

"You see?" he asked.

"I see a girl named Alice Heatherton died a month ago at the age of twenty-two," I admitted, "but what that has to do with last night is more than I can—"

"Of course," he broke in with a chuckle somehow lacking merriment. "But certainly. There are many things you do not see, my old one, and there are many more at which you blink your eyes, like a child passing over the unpleasant pages of a picture book. Now, if you will be so kind as to leave me, I shall interview *Monsieur l'Intendant* of this so lovely park, and several other people as well. If possible I shall return in time for dinner, but"—he raised his shoulders in a fatalistic shrug—"at times we must forego a meal in deference to duty. Yes, it is unfortunately so."

THE CONSOMMÉ HAD GROWN cold and the roast lamb kiln-dried in the oven when the stutter of my study telephone called me. "Trowbridge, my friend," de Grandin's voice, shrill with excitement, came across the wire, "meet me at Adelphi Mansions quickly as you can. I would have you for witness!"

"Witness?" I echoed. "What—" A sharp click notified me he had hung up and I was left bewildered at the unresponsive instrument.

He was waiting for me at the entrance of the fashionable apartment house when I arrived, and refused to answer my impatient questions as he dragged me through the ornate entrance and down the rug-strewn foyer to the elevators. As the car shot upward he reached in his pocket and produced a shiny thumb-smudged photograph. "This I begged from *Le Journal,*" he explained. "They had no further use for it."

"Good heavens!" I exclaimed as I looked at the picture. "Wh—why, it's—"

"Assuredly it is," he answered in a level tone. "It is the girl we saw last night beyond a doubt; the girl whose tomb we visited this morning; the girl who gave the kiss of death to the young Rochester."

"But that's impossible! She—"

His short laugh interrupted. "I was convinced you would say just that, Friend Trowbridge. Come, let us hear what Madame Heatherton can tell us."

A trim Negro maid in black-and-white uniform answered our summons and took our cards to her mistress. As she left the rather sumptuous reception room I glanced covertly about, noting rugs from China and the Near East, early American mahogany and an elaborately wrought medieval tapestry depicting a scene from the *Nibelungenlied* with its legend in formal Gothic text: "*Hic Siegfriedum Aureum Occidunt*—Here They Slay Siegfried the Golden."

"Dr. Trowbridge? Dr. de Grandin?" the soft, cultured voice recalled me from my study of the fabric as an imposing white-haired lady entered.

"Madame, a thousand pardons for this intrusion!" de Grandin clicked his heels together and bowed stiffly from the hips. "Believe me, we have no desire to trespass on your privacy, but a matter of the utmost importance brings us. You will forgive me if I inquire of the circumstances of your daughter's death, for I am of the *Sûreté* of Paris, and make investigation as a scientific research."

Mrs. Heatherton was, to use an overworked expression, a "perfect lady." Nine women out of ten would have frozen at de Grandin's announcement, but she was the tenth. The direct glance the little Frenchman gave her and his evident sincerity, combined with perfect manners and immaculate dress, carried conviction. "Please be seated, gentlemen," she invited. "I cannot see where my poor child's tragedy can interest an officer of the Paris secret police, but I've no objection to telling all I can; you could get a garbled version from the newspapers anyway.

"Alice was my youngest child. She and my son Ralph were two years apart, almost to the day. Ralph graduated from Cornell year before last, majoring in civil engineering, and went to Florida to take charge of some construction work. Alice died while visiting him."

"But—forgive my seeming rudeness, Madame—your son, is not he also deceased?"

"Yes," our hostess assented. "He is dead, also. They died almost together. There was a man down there, a fellow townsman of ours, Joachim Palenzeke— not the sort of person one knows, but Ralph's superior in the work. He had something to do with promoting the land development, I believe. When Alice went to visit Ralph this person presumed on his position and the fact that we were all from Harrisonville, and attempted to force his attentions on her."

"One sees. And then?" de Grandin prompted softly.

"Ralph resented his overtures. Palenzeke made some insulting remarks— some scurrilous allusions to Alice and me, I've been told, and they fought. Ralph was a small man, but a thoroughbred. Palenzeke was almost a giant, but a thoroughgoing coward. When Ralph began to get the better of him he drew a pistol and fired five shots into my poor son's body. Ralph died the next day after hours of terrible suffering.

"His murderer fled to the swamps where it would be difficult to track him with hounds, and according to some Negro squatters he committed suicide, but there must have been some mistake, for—" she broke off, pressing her crumpled handkerchief to her mouth, as if to force back the sobs.

De Grandin reached from his chair and patted her hand gently, as if consoling a child. "Dear lady," he murmured, "I am distressed, believe me, but also please believe me when I say I do not ask these so heart-breaking questions idly. Tell me, if you will, why you believe the story of this vile miscreant's suicide an error."

"Because—because he was seen again! He killed Alice!"

"*Nom d'un nom!* Do you say so?" His comment was a suppressed shout. "Tell me, tell me, Madame, how came this vileness about? This is of the great importance; this explains much which was inexplicable. Say on, *chère Madame*, I implore you!"

"Alice was prostrated at the tragedy of Ralph's murder—somehow, she seemed to think she was responsible for it—but in a few days she recovered enough to make preparations to return home with his body.

"There was no railway nearer than fifteen miles, and she wanted to catch an early train, so she set out by motor the night before her train was due. As she drove through a length of lonely, unlighted road between two stretches of undrained swampland someone emerged from the tall reeds—we have the chauffeur's statement for this—and leaped upon the running-board. He struck the driver senseless with a single blow, but not before he had been recognized. It was Joachim Palenzeke. The car ran into the swamp when the driver lost consciousness, but fortunately for him the mud was deep enough to stall the machine, though not deep enough to engulf it. He recovered in a short time and raised the alarm.

"A sheriff's posse found them both next morning. Palenzeke had apparently slipped in the bog while trying to escape and been drowned. Alice was dead—from shock, the doctors said. Her lips were terribly bruised, and there was a wound on her throat, though not serious enough to have caused death; and she had been—"

"Enough! No more, Madame, I entreat you! *Sang de Saint Denis*, is Jules de Grandin a monster that he should roll a stone upon a mother's breaking heart? *Dieu de Dieu, non!* But tell me, if you can, and then I shall ask you no more—what became of this ten-thousand-times-damned—your pardon, Madame!—this so execrable *cochon* of a Palenzeke?"

"They brought him home for burial," Mrs. Heatherton replied softly. "His family is very wealthy. Some of them were bootleggers during prohibition, some are real estate speculators, some are politicians. He had the most elaborate funeral ever seen in the local Greek Orthodox Church—they say the flowers alone cost more than five thousand dollars—but Father Apostolakos refused to say Mass over him, merely recited a short prayer, and denied him burial in the consecrated part of the church cemetery."

"Ah!" de Grandin looked meaningfully at me, as if to say, "I told you as much!"

"This may interest you, too, though I don't know," Mrs. Heatherton added: "A friend of mine who knows a reporter on the *Journal*—newspapermen know everything," she added with simple naïveté, "told me that the coward really must have tried suicide and failed, for there was a bullet-mark on his temple, though of course it couldn't have been fatal, since they found him drowned in the swamp. Do you suppose he could have wounded himself purposely where those Negro swamp-dwellers could see, so that the story of his suicide would get about and the officers stop looking for him?"

"Quite possibly," de Grandin agreed as he rose. "Madame, we are your debtors more than you suspect, and though you cannot know it, we have saved you at least one pang this night. *Adieu, chère Madame*, and may the good God watch over you—and yours." He laid his lips to her fingers and bowed himself from the room.

As we passed through the outer door we caught the echo of a sob and Mrs. Heatherton's despairing cry: "Me and mine—there are no 'mine.' All, all are gone!"

"*La Pauvre!*" de Grandin murmured as he closed the door softly. "All the more reason for *le bon Dieu's* watchfulness, though she knows it not!"

"Now what?" I demanded, dabbing furtively at my eyes with my handkerchief.

The Frenchman made no effort to conceal his tears. They trickled down his face as if he had been a half-grown schoolboy. "Go home, my friend," he ordered. "Me, I shall consult the priest of that Greek Church. From what I hear of him he must be a capital fellow. I think he will give credence to my story. If not, *parbleu*, we must take matters into our own hands. Meantime, crave humble pardon from the excellent Nora for having neglected her dinner and ask that she prepare some slight refreshment, then be ready to accompany me again when we shall have regaled ourselves. *Nom d'un canard vert*, we have a busy night before us, my old and rare!"

IT WAS NEARLY MIDNIGHT when he returned, but from the sparkle in his eyes I knew he had successfully attended to some of his "offices."

"*Barbe d'une chèvre*," he exclaimed as he disposed of his sixth cold lamb sandwich and emptied his eighth glass of Ponte Canet, "that Father Apostolakos is no man's fool, my friend. He is no empty-headed modern who knows so much that he knows nothing; a man versed in the occult may talk freely with him and be understood. Yes. He will help us."

"U'm?" I commented noncommittally, my mouth half-filled with lamb sandwich.

"Precisely," he agreed, refilling his glass and lifting another sandwich from the tray. "Exactly, my friend. The good *papa* is supreme in matters ecclesiastical, and tomorrow he will give the necessary orders without so much as 'by your leave' from the estimable ex-bootleggers, real estate dealers and politicians who compose the illustrious Palenzeke clan. The sandwiches are all gone, and the bottle empty? Good, then let us be upon our way."

"Where?" I demanded.

"To the young Monsieur Rochester's. Me, I would have further talk with that one."

As we left the house I saw him transfer a small oblong packet from his jacket to his overcoat. "What's that?" I asked.

"A thing the good father lent me. I hope we shall have no occasion to use it, but it will prove convenient if we do."

A LIGHT MIST, DAPPLED HERE and there with chilling rain, was settling in the streets as we set off for Rochester's. Half an hour's cautious driving brought us to the place, and as we drew up at the curb the Frenchman pointed to a lighted window on the seventh floor. "That burns in his suite," he informed me. "Can it be he entertains at this hour?"

The night elevator operator snored in a chair in the lobby, and, guided by de Grandin's cautious gesture, I followed his lead up the stairs. "We need not announce our coming," he whispered as we rounded the landing of the sixth floor. "It is better that we come as a surprise, I think."

Another flight we climbed silently, and paused before the door of Rochester's apartment. De Grandin rapped once softly, repeated the summons more authoritatively, and was about to try the knob when we heard footsteps beyond the panels.

Young Rochester wore a silk robe over his pyjamas, his hair was somewhat disarranged, but he looked neither sleepy nor particularly pleased to see us.

"We are unexpected, it seems," de Grandin announced, "but we are here, nevertheless, Be kind enough to stand aside and let us enter, if you please."

"Not now," the young man refused. "I can't see you now. If you'll come back tomorrow morning—"

"This is tomorrow morning, *mon vieux*," the little Frenchman interrupted. "Midnight struck an hour ago." He brushed past our reluctant host and hurried down the long hall to the living room.

The room was tastefully furnished in typically masculine style, heavy chairs of hickory and maple, Turkish carpets, a table with a shaded lamp, a long couch piled with pillows before the fireplace in which a bed of cannel coal glowed in a brass grate. An after-tang of cigarette smoke hung in the air, but mingled with it was the faint, provocative scent of heliotrope.

De Grandin paused upon the threshold, threw his head back and sniffed like a hound at fault. Directly opposite the entrance was a wide arch closed by two Paisley shawls hung lambrequinwise from a brass rod, and toward this he marched, his right hand in his topcoat pocket, the ebony cane which I knew concealed a sword blade held lightly in his left.

"De Grandin!" I cried in shocked protest, aghast at his air of proprietorship.

"Don't!" Rochester called warningly. "You mustn't—"

The hangings at the archway parted and a girl stepped from between them. The long, close-clinging gown of purple tissue she wore was almost as diaphanous as smoke, and through it we could see the white outlines of her body. Her copper-colored hair flowed in a cloven tide about her face and over smooth bare shoulders. Halted in the act of stepping, one small bare foot showed its blue-veined whiteness in sharp silhouette against the rust-red of the Borkhara rug.

As her eyes met de Grandin she paused with a sibilant intake of breath, and her eyes widened with a look of fright. It was no shamefaced glance she gave him; no expression of confusion at detected guilt or brazen attempt at facing out a hopelessly embarrassing situation. Rather, it was the look of one in dire peril, such a look as she might have given a rattlesnake writhing toward her.

"So!" she breathed, and I could see the thin stuff of her gown grow tight across her breasts. "So you know! I was afraid you would, but—" She broke off as he took another step toward her and swerved until his right-hand coat pocket was within arm's length of her.

"Mais oui, mais oui, Mademoiselle la Morte," he returned, bowing ceremoniously, but not removing his hand from his pocket. "I know, as you say. The question now arises, 'What shall we do about it?'"

"See here," Rochester flung himself between them, "what's the meaning of this unpardonable intrusion—"

The little Frenchman turned to him, a look of mild inquiry on his face. "You demand an explanation? If explanations are in order—"

"See here, damn you, I'm my own man, and not accountable to anyone. Alice and I love each other. She came to me tonight of her own free will—"

"En vérité?" the Frenchman interrupted. "How did she come, Monsieur?"

The young man seemed to catch his breath like a runner struggling to regain his wind at the end of a hard course. "I—I went out for a little while," he faltered, "and when I came back—"

"My poor one!" de Grandin broke in sympathetically. "You do lie like a gentleman, but also you lie very poorly. You are in need of practice. Attend me, I will tell you how she came: This night, I do not know exactly when, but well after sundown, you heard a knock-rap at your window or door, and when you looked out, voilà, there was the so lovely demoiselle. You thought you dreamed, but once again the pretty fingers tap-tapped at the windowpane, and the soft, lovely eyes looked love at you, and you opened your door or window and bade her enter, content to entertain the dream of her, since there was no chance of her coming in the flesh. Tell me, young Monsieur, and you, too, lovely Mademoiselle, do I not recite the facts?"

Rochester and the girl stared at him in amazement. Only the quivering of the young man's eyelids and the trembling of the girl's sensitive lips gave testimony he had spoken accurately.

For a moment there was a tense, vibrant silence; then with a little gasping cry the girl lurched forward on soft, soundless feet and dropped to her knees before de Grandin. "Have pity—be merciful!" she begged. "Be merciful to me as you may one day hope for mercy. It's such a little thing I ask. You know what I am; do you also know who I am, and why I am now—now the accursed thing you see?" She buried her face in her hands. "Oh, it's cruel—too cruel!" she sobbed. "I was so young; my whole life lay before me. I'd never known real love until it was too late. You can't be so unkind as to drive me back now; you *can't!*"

"*Ma pauvre!*" de Grandin laid his hand upon the girl's bowed, shining head. "My innocent, poor lamb who met the butcher ere you had the lambkin's right to play! I know all there is to know of you. Your sainted mother told me far more than she dreamed this evening. I am not cruel, my little lovely one; I am all sympathy and sorrow, but life is cruel and death is even crueller. Also, you know what the inevitable end must be if I forebear to do my duty. If I could work a miracle I would roll back the gates of dead, and bid you live and love until your natural time had come to die, but—"

"I don't care what the end must be!" the girl blazed, sinking back until she sat upon the upturned soles of her bare feet. "I only know that I've been cheated out of every woman's birthright. I've found love now, and I want it; I want it! He's mine, I tell you, mine—" She cowered, groveling before him—"Think what a little thing I'm asking!" Inching forward on her knees she took his hand in both of hers and fondled it against her cheek. "I'm asking just a little drop of blood now and then; just a little, tiny drop to keep my body whole and beautiful. If I were like other women and Donald were my lover he'd be glad to give me a transfusion—to give me a whole pint or quart of his blood any time I needed it. Is it so much, then, when I ask only an occasional drop? Just a drop now and then, and once in a while a draft of living breath from his lungs to—"

"To slay his poor sick body, then destroy his young, clean soul!" the Frenchman interrupted softly. "It is not of the living that I think so much, but of the dead. Would you deny him quiet rest in his grave when he shall have lost his life because of you? Would you refuse him peaceful sleep until the dawn of God's Great Tomorrow?"

"O-o-oh!" the cry wrung from her writhing lips was like the wail of a lost spirit. "You're right—it is his soul we must protect. I'd kill that, too, as mine was killed that night in the swamps. Oh, pity, pity me, dear Lord! Thou who didst heal the lepers and despised not the Magdalen, have pity on me, the soiled, the unclean!"

Scalding tears of agony fell between the fingers of her long, almost transparent hands as she held them before her eyes. Then: "I am ready," she announced, seeming to find courage for complete renunciation. "Do what you must to me. If it must be the knife and stake, strike quickly. I shall not scream or cry, if I can help it."

For a long moment he looked in her face as he might have looked in the casket of a dear friend. "*Ma pauvre,*" he murmured compassionately. "My poor, brave, lovely one!"

Abruptly he turned to Rochester. "Monsieur," he announced sharply, "I would examine you. I would determine the state of your health."

We stared at him astounded as he proceeded to strip back the—young man's pyjamas jacket and listen carefully at his chest, testing by percussion, counting the pulse action, then feeling slowly up and down the arm. "U'm" he remarked judicially at the end of the examination, "you are in bad condition, my friend. With medicines, careful nursing, and more luck than the physician generally has, we might keep you alive another month. Again, you might drop over any moment. But in all my life I have never given a patient his death warrant with more happiness."

Two of us looked at him in mute wonder; it was the girl who understood. "You mean," she trilled, laughter and a light the like of which there never was on land or sea breaking in her eyes, "you mean that I can have him till—"

He grinned at her delightedly. There was a positively gleeful chuckle in his voice as he replied: "Precisely, exactly, quite so, Mademoiselle." Turning from her he addressed Rochester.

"You and Mademoiselle Alice are to love each other as much as you please while life holds out. And afterwards"—he stretched his hand out to grasp the girl's fingers—"afterwards I shall do the needful for you both. Ha, *Monsieur Diable*, I have tricked you nicely; Jules de Grandin had made one great fool of hell!" He threw his head back and assumed an attitude of defiance, eyes flashing, lips twitching with excitement and elation.

The girl bent forward, took his hand and covered it with kisses. "Oh, you're kind—kind!" she sobbed brokenly. "No other man in all the world, knowing what you know, would have done what you have done!"

"*Mais non, mais certainement non, Mademoiselle*," he agreed imperturbably. "You do forget that I am Jules de Grandin."

"Come, Trowbridge, my friend," he admonished, "we obtrude here most unwarrantably. What have we, who drained the purple wine of youth long years ago, to do with those who laugh and love the night away? Let us go."

Hand in hand, the lovers followed us to the hall, but as we paused upon the threshold—

Rat-tat-tat! something struck the fog-glazed window, and as I wheeled in my tracks I felt the breath go hot in my throat. Beyond the window, seemingly adrift in the fog, there was a human form. A second glance told me it was the brutal-faced man we had seen at the café the previous night. But now his ugly, evil face was like the devil's, not merely a wicked man's.

"*Eh bien*, Monsieur, is it you, indeed?" de Grandin asked nonchalantly. "I thought you might appear, so I am ready for you.

"Do not invite him in," he called the sharp command to Rochester. "He cannot come in unbidden. Hold your beloved, place your hand or lips against her mouth, lest she who is his thing and chattel, however unwillingly, give him permission to enter. Remember, he cannot cross the sill without the invitation of someone in this room!"

Flinging up the sash he regarded the apparition sardonically. "What have you to say, *Monsieur le Vampire*, before I send you hence?" he asked.

The thing outside mouthed at us, very fury robbing it of words. At last: "She's mine!" it shrieked. "I made her what she is, and she belongs to me. I'll have her, and that dough-faced, dying thing she holds in her arms, too. All, all of you are mine! I shall be king, I shall be emperor of the dead! Not you nor any mortal can stop me. I am all-powerful, supreme, I am—"

"You are the greatest liar outside burning hell," de Grandin cut in icily. "As for your power and your claims, Monsieur Monkey-Face, tomorrow you shall have nothing, not even so much as a little plot of earth to call a grave. Meanwhile, behold this, devil's spawn; behold and be afraid!"

Whipping his hand from his topcoat pocket he produced a small flat case like the leather containers sometimes used for holding photographs, pressed a concealed spring and snapped back its top. For a moment the thing in the night gazed at the object with stupefied, unbelieving horror; then with a wild cry fell backward, its uncouth motion somehow reminding me of a hooked bass.

"You do not like it, I see," the Frenchman mocked. "*Parbleu*, you stinking truant from the charnel-house, let us see what nearer contact will effect!" He stretched his hand out till the leather-cased object almost touched the phantom face outside the window.

A wild, inhuman screech echoed, and as the demon face retreated we saw a weal of red across its forehead, as if the Frenchman had scored it with a hot iron.

"Close the windows, *mes amis*," he ordered casually as though nothing hideous hovered outside. "Shut them tight and hold each other close until the morning comes and shadows flee away. *Bonne nuit!*"

"For heaven's sake," I besought as we began our homeward drive, "what's it all mean? You and Rochester called that girl Alice, and she's the speaking image of the girl we saw in the café last night. But Alice Heatherton is dead. Her mother told us how she died this evening; we saw her tomb this morning. Are there two Alice Heathertons, or is this girl her double—"

"In a way," he answered. "It was Alice Heatherton we saw back there, my friend, yet not the Alice Heatherton of whom her mother spoke this evening, nor yet the one whose tomb we saw this morning—"

"For God's sake," I burst out, "stop this damned double-talk! Was or was it not Alice Heatherton—"

"Be patient, my old one," he counseled. "At present I can not tell you, but later I will have a complete explanation—I hope."

Daylight was just breaking when his pounding on my bedroom door roused me from coma-like sleep. "Up, Friend Trowbridge!" he shouted, punctuating his summons with another knock. "Up and dress as quickly as may be. We must be off at once. Tragedy has overtaken them!"

Scarcely knowing what I did I stumbled from the bed, felt my way into my clothes and, sleep still filming my eyes, descended to the lower hall where he waited in a perfect frenzy of excitement.

"What's happened?" I asked as we started for Rochester's.

"The worst," he answered. "Ten minutes ago I was awakened by the telephone. 'It is for Friend Trowbridge,' I told me. 'Some patient with the *mal de l'estamac* desires a little paregoric and much sympathy. I shall not waken him, for he is all tired with the night's exertions.' But still the bell kept ringing, and so I answered it. My friend, it was Alice. *Hélas*, as strong as her love was, her bondage was still stronger. But when the harm was done she had the courage to call us. Remember that when you come to judge her."

I would have paused for explanation, but he waved me on impatiently. "Make haste; oh, hurry, hurry!" he urged. "We must go to him at once. Perhaps it is even now too late."

There was no traffic in the streets, and we made the run to Rochester's apartment in record time. Almost before we realized it we were at his door once more, and this time de Grandin stood upon no ceremony. Flinging the door open he raced down the hall and into the living room, pausing at the threshold with a sharp indrawn breath. "So!" he breathed. "He was most thorough, that one."

The place was a shambles. Chairs were overturned, pictures hung awry, bits of broken bric-à-brac were strewn about, the long throw-cover of the center table had been jerked off, overturning the lamp and scattering ashtrays and cigarette boxes indiscriminately.

Donald Rochester lay on the rug before the dead fire, one leg bent queerly under him, his right arm stretched out flaccidly along the floor and bent at a sharp right angle at the wrist.

The Frenchman crossed the room at a run, unclasping the lock of his kit as he leaped. Dropping to his knees he listened intently at the young man's chest a moment, then stripped back his sleeve, swabbed his arm with alcohol and thrust the needle of his hypodermic through a fold of skin. "It is a desperate chance I take," he muttered as he drove the plunger home, "but the case is urgent; *le bon Dieu* knows how urgent."

Rochester's eyelids fluttered as the powerful stimulant took effect. He moaned and turned his head with great effort, but made no move to rise. As I knelt beside de Grandin and helped him raise the injured man I understood the cause of his lethargy. His spine had been fractured at the fourth dorsal veterbra, paralysis resulting.

"Monsieur," the little Frenchman whispered softly, "you are going fast. Your minutes are now more than numbered on the circle of the watch-face. Tell us, tell us quickly, what occurred." Once more he injected stimulant into Rochester's arm.

The young man wet his blued lips with the tip of his tongue, attempted a deep breath, but found the effort too great. "It was he—the fellow you scared off last night," he whispered hoarsely.

"After you'd gone Alice and I lay on the hearth rug, counting our minutes together as a miser counts his gold. I heaped coals on the fire, for she was chilled, but it didn't seem to do any good. Finally she began to pant and choke, and I let her draw breath from me. That revived her a little, and when she'd sucked some blood from my throat she seemed almost herself again, though I could feel no movement of her heart as she lay against me.

"It must have been just before daybreak—I don't know just when, for I'd fallen asleep in her arms—when I heard a clattering at the window, and some-one calling to be let in. I remembered your warning, and tried to hold Alice, but she fought me off. She ran to the window and flung it up as she called, 'Enter, master; there is none to stop you now.'

"He made straight for me, and when she realized what he was about she tried to stop him, but he flung her aside as if she were a rag doll—took her by the hair and dashed her against the wall. I heard her bones crack as she struck it.

"I grappled with him, but I was no more his match than a three-year-old child was mine. He threw me down and broke my arms and legs with his feet. The pain was terrible. Then he grabbed me up and hurled me to the floor again, and after that I felt no pain, except this dreadful headache. I couldn't move, but I was conscious, and the last thing I remember was seeing Alice stepping out the window with him, hand in hand. She didn't even look back."

He paused a moment, fighting desperately for breath, then, still lower, "Oh, Alice—how could you? And I loved you so!"

"Peace, my poor one," bade de Grandin. "She did not do it of her own accord. That fiend holds her in bondage she cannot resist. She is his thing and chattel more completely than ever black slave belonged to his master. Hear me; go with this thought uppermost in your mind: She loved you, she loves you. It is because she called us we are here now, and her last word was one of love for you. Do you hear me? Do you understand? 'Tis sad to die, *mon pauvre*, but surely it is some-thing to die loving and beloved. Many a man lives out his whole life without as much, and many there are who would trade a whole span of four score gladly for five little minutes of the ecstasy that was yours last night.

"Monsieur Rochester—do you hear me?" he spoke sharply, for the young man's face was taking on the greyness of impending death.

"Ye-es. She loves me—she loves me. Alice!" With the name sighing on his lips his facial muscles loosened and his eyes took on the glazed, unwinking stare of eyes that see no more.

De Grandin gently drew the lids across the sightless eyes and raised the fallen jaw, then set about straightening the room with methodical haste. "As a licensed practitioner you will sign the death certificate," he announced matter-of-factly. "Our young friend suffered from angina pectoris. This morning he had an attack, and after calling us fell from the chair on which he stood to reach his medicine, thereby fracturing several bones. He told us this when we arrived to find him dying. You understand?"

"I'm hanged if I do," I denied. "You know as well as I—"

"That the police would have awkward questions to address to us," he reminded me. "We were the last ones to see him alive. Do you conceive that they would credit what we said if we told them the truth?"

Much as I disliked it, I followed his orders to the letter and the poor boy's body was turned over to the ministrations of Mortician Martin within an hour.

As Rochester had been an orphan without known family de Grandin assumed the role of next friend, made all arrangements for the funeral, and gave orders that the remains be cremated without delay, the ashes to be turned over to him for final disposition.

Most of the day was taken up in making these arrangements and in my round of professional calls. I was thoroughly exhausted by four o'clock in the afternoon, but de Grandin, hustling, indefatigable, seemed fresh as he had been at daybreak.

"Not yet, my friend," he denied as I would have sunk into the embrace of an easy chair, "there is yet something to be done. Did not you hear my promise to the never-quite-to-be-sufficiently-anathematized Palenzeke last night?"

"Eh, your promise?"

"*Précisément.* We have one great surprise in store for that one."

Grumbling, but with curiosity that overrode my fatigue, I drove him to the little Greek Orthodox parsonage. Parked at the door was the severely plain black service wagon of a funeral director, its chauffeur yawning audibly at the delay in getting through his errand.

De Grandin ran lightly up the steps, gained admission and returned in a few minutes with the venerable priest arrayed in full canonicals. "*Allons mon enfant,*" he told the chauffeur, "be on your way; we follow."

Even when the imposing granite walls of the North Hudson Crematory loomed before us I failed to understand his hardly suppressed glee.

All arrangements had apparently been made. In the little chapel over the retort Father Apostolakos recited the orthodox burial office, and the casket sank slowly from view on the concealed elevator provided for conveying it to the incineration chamber below.

The aged priest bowed courteously to us and left the building, seating himself in my car, and I was about to follow when de Grandin motioned to me imperatively. "Not yet, Friend Trowbridge," he told me. "Come below and I will show you something."

We made our way to the subterranean chamber where incineration took place. The casket rested on a low wheeled track before the yawning cavern of the retort, but de Grandin stopped the attendants as they were about to roll it into place. Tiptoeing across the tiled floor he bent above the casket, motioning me to join him.

As I paused beside him I recognized the heavy, evil features of the man we had first seen with Alice, the same bestial, furious face which had mouthed curses at us from outside Rochester's window the night before. I would have drawn back, but the Frenchman clutched me firmly by the elbow, drawing me still nearer the body.

"*Tiens, Monsieur le Cadavre*," he whispered as he bent above the dead thing, "what think you of this, *hein?* You who would be king and emperor of the dead, you who boasted that no power on earth could balk you—did not Jules de Grandin promise you that you should have nothing, not even one poor plot of earth to call a grave? Pah, murderer and ravisher of women, man-killer, where is now your power? Go—go through the furnace fire to hell-fire, and take this with you!" He pursed his lips and spat full in the cold upturned visage of the corpse.

It might have been a trick of overwrought nerves or an optical illusion produced by the electric lights, but I still believe I saw the dead, long-buried body writhe in its casket and a look of terrible, unutterable hate disfigure the waxen features.

He stepped back, nodding to the attendants, and the casket slid noiselessly into the retort. A whirring sounded as the pressure pump was started, and in a moment came the subdued roar of oil-flames shooting from the burners.

He raised his narrow shoulders in a shrug. "*C'est une affaire finie.*"

It was somewhat after midnight when we made our way once more to Shadow Lawn Cemetery. Unerringly as though going to an appointment, de Grandin led the way to the Heatherton family mausoleum, let himself through the massive bronze gates with a key he had procured somewhere, and ordered me to stand guard outside.

Lighted by the flash of his electric torch he entered the tomb, a long cloth-covered parcel clasped under his arm. A moment later I heard the clink of metal on metal the sound of some heavy object being drawn across the floor; then, as I grew half hysterical at the long continued silence, there came the short, half-stifled sound of a gasping cry, the sort of cry a patient in the dental chair gives when a tooth is extracted without anaesthetic.

Another period of silence, broken by the rasp of heavy objects being moved, and the Frenchman emerged from the tomb, tears streaming down his face. "Peace," he announced chokingly. "I brought her peace, Friend Trowbridge, but oh! how pitiful it was to hear her moan, and still more pitiful to see the lovely, live-seeming body shudder in the embrace of relentless death. It is not hard to see the living die, my old one, but the dead! *Mordieu*, my soul will be in torment every time I think of what I had to do tonight for mercy's sake!"

JULES DE GRANDIN CHOSE a cigar from the humidor and set it glowing with the precision that distinguished his every movement. "I grant you the events of the last three days have been decidedly queer," he agreed as he sent a cloud of fragrant smoke ceilingward. "But what would you? All that lies outside our everyday experience is queer. To one who has not studied biology the sight of an amoeba beneath the microscope is queer; the Eskimos undoubtlessly thought Monsieur Byrd's airplane queer; we think the sights which we have seen these nights queer. It is our luck—and all mankind's—that they are.

"To begin: Just as there exist today certain protozoa which are probably identical with the earliest forms of life on earth, so there are still, though constantly diminishing in numbers, certain holdovers of ancient evil. Time was when earth swarmed with them—devils and devilkins, imps, satyrs and demons, elementals, werewolves and vampires. All once were numerous; all, perhaps, exist in considerable numbers to this day, though we know them not, and most of us never so much as hear of them. It is with the vampire that we had to deal this time. You know him, no?

"Strictly, he is an earthbound soul, a spirit which because of manifold sins and wickedness is bound to the world wherein it once worked evil and cannot take itself to its proper place. He is in India in considerable numbers, also in Russia, Hungary, Romania and throughout the Balkans—wherever civilization is very old and decadent, there he seems to find a favorable soil. Sometimes he steals the body of one already dead; sometimes he remains in the body which he had in life, and then he is most terrible of all, for he needs nourishment for that body, but not such nourishment as you or I take. No, he subsists on the life force of the living, imbibed through their blood, for the blood is the life. He must suck the breath from those who live, or he cannot breathe; he must drink their blood, or he dies of starvation. And here is where the danger rises: a suicide, one who dies under a curse, *or one who has been inoculated with the vampire virus* by having his blood sucked by a vampire, becomes a vampire after death. Innocent of all wrong he may be, often is, yet he is doomed to tread the earth by night, preying ceaselessly upon the living, ever recruiting the grisly ranks of his tribe. You apprehend?

"Consider this case: This *sacré* Palenzeke, because of his murder and suicide, perhaps partly because of his Slavic ancestry, maybe also because of his many other sins, became a vampire when he killed himself to death. Madame Heatherton's informant was correct, he had destroyed himself; but his evil body and more evil soul remained in partnership, ten thousand times a greater menace to mankind than when they had been partners in their natural life.

"Enjoying the supernatural power of his life-in-death, he rose from the swamplands, waylaid Mademoiselle Alice, assaulted her chauffeur, then dragged her off into the bog to work his evil will on her, gratifying at once his bestial lust, his vampire's thirst for blood and his revenge for her rejection of his wooing. When he had killed her, he had made her such a thing as he was. More, he had gained dominion over her. She was his toy, his plaything, his automaton, without will or volition of her own. What he commanded she must do, however much she hated doing it. You will recall, perhaps, how she told the young Rochester that she must go out with the villain, although she hated him? Also, how she bade him enter the apartment where she and her beloved lay in love's embrace, although his entrance meant her lover's undoing?

"Now, if the vampire added all the powers of living men to his dead powers we should have no defense, but fortunately he is subject to unbreakable laws. He can not independently cross the thread of a running stream, he must be carried; he can not enter any house or dwelling until invited by someone therein; he can fly through the air, enter at keyholes and window-chinks, or through the crack of the door, but he can move about only at night—between sunset and cock-crow. From sunrise to dark he is only a corpse, helpless as any other, and must lie corpse-dead in his tomb. At such times he can easily be slain, but only in certain ways. First, if his heart be pierced by a stake of ash and—his head severed from his body, he is dead in good earnest, and can no more rise to plague us. Second, if he can be completely burned to ashes he is no more, for fire cleanses all things.

"Now, with this information, fit together the puzzle that so mystifies you: the other night at the Café Bacchanale I liked the looks of that one not at all. He had the face of a dead man and the look of a born villain, as well as the eye of a fish. Of his companion I thoroughly approved, though she, too, had an other-worldly look. Wondering about them, I watched them from my eye's tail, and when I observed that they ate nothing I thought it not only strange, but menacing. Normal people do not do such things; abnormal people usually are dangerous.

"When Palenzeke left the young woman, after indicating she might flirt with the young Rochester, I liked the look of things a little less. My first thought was that it might be a game of decoy and robbery—how do you call him?—the game of the badger? Accordingly, I thought it best to follow them to see what we should see. *Eh bien*, my friend, we saw a plenty, *n'est-ce-pas?*

"You will recall young Rochester's experience in the cemetery. As he related it to us I saw at once what manner of foeman we must grapple with, though at that time I did not know how innocent Mademoiselle Alice was. Our information from Madame Heatherton confirmed my worst fears. What we beheld at Rochester's apartment that night proved all I had imagined, and more.

"But me, I had not been idle meantime. Oh, no. I had seen the good Father Apostolakos and told him what I had learned. He understood at once, and made immediate arrangements to have Palenzeke's foul body exhumed and taken to the crematory for incineration. He also lent me a sacred *ikon*, the blessèd image of a saint whose potency to repel demons had more than once been proved. Perhaps you noticed how Mademoiselle Alice shrank from me when I approached her with the relic in my pocket? And how the restless soul of Palenzeke flinched from it as flesh recoils from white-hot iron?

"Very well. Rochester loved this woman already dead. He himself was moribund. Why not let him taste of love with the shade of the woman who returned his passion for the few days he had yet to live? When he died, as die he must, I was prepared to treat his poor clay so that, though he were already half a vampire from the vampire's kisses on his throat, he could yet do no harm. You know I have done so. The cleansing fire has rendered Palenzeke impotent. Also, I had pledged myself to do as much for the poor, lovely, sinned-against Alice when her brief aftermath of earthly happiness should have expired. You heard me promise her, and I have kept my word.

"I could not bear to hurt her needlessly, so when I went to her with stake and knife tonight I took also a syringe loaded with five grains of morphine and gave her an injection before I began my work. I do not think she suffered greatly. Her moan of dissolution and the portion of her poor body as the stake pierced through her heart, they were but reflex acts, not signs of conscious misery."

"But look here," I objected, "if Alice were a vampire, as you say, and able to float about after dark, how comes it that she lay in her casket when you went there tonight?"

"Oh, my friend," tears welled up in his eyes, "she waited for me.

"We had a definite engagement; the poor one lay in her casket, awaiting the knife and stake which should set her free from bondage. She—she smiled at me and pressed my hand when I had dragged her from the tomb!"

He wiped his eyes and poured an ounce or so of cognac into a bud-shaped inhaler. "To you, young Rochester, and to your lovely lady," he said as he raised the glass in salute. "Though there be neither marrying nor giving in marriage where you are, may your restless souls find peace and rest eternally—together."

The fragile goblet shattered as he tossed it, emptied, into the fireplace.

The Black Master

1

J ULES DE GRANDIN POURED a thimbleful of Boulogne cognac into a wide-mouthed glass and passed the goblet back and forth beneath his nose with a waving motion, inhaling the rich, fruity fumes from the amber fluid. "*Eh bien*, young *Monsieur*," he informed our visitor as he drained the liqueur with a slow, appreciative swallow and set the empty glass on the tabouret with a scarcely suppressed smack of his lips, "this is of interest. Pirate treasure, you do say? *Parbleu—c'est presque irresistible*. Tell us more, if you please."

Eric Balderson looked from the little Frenchman to me with a half-diffident, deprecating smile. "There really isn't much to tell," he confessed, "and I'm not at all sure I'm not the victim of a pipe-dream, after all. You knew Father pretty well, didn't you, Dr. Trowbridge?" he turned appealingly to me.

"Yes," I answered, "he and I were at Amherst together. He was an extremely levelheaded sort of chap, too, not at all given to daydreaming, and—"

"That's what I'm pinning my faith on," Eric broke in. "Coming from anyone but Dad the story would be too utterly fantastic to—"

"*Mordieu*, yes, *Monsieur*," de Grandin interrupted testily, "we do concede your so excellent *père* was the ultimate word in discretion and sound judgment, but will you, for the love of kindly heaven, have the goodness to tell us all and let us judge for ourselves the value of the communication of which you speak?"

Eric regarded him with the slow grin he inherited from his father, then continued, quite unruffled, "Dad wasn't exactly what you'd call credulous, but he seemed to put considerable stock in the story, judging from his diary. Here it is." From the inside pocket of his dinner-coat he produced a small book bound in red leather and handed it to me. "Read the passages I've marked, will you please, Doctor," he asked. "I'm afraid I'd fill up if I tried to read Dad's writing aloud. He—he hasn't been gone very long, you know."

Adjusting my pince-nez, I hitched a bit nearer the library lamp and looked over the age-yellowed sheets covered with the fine, angular script of my old classmate:

8 Nov. 1898—Old Robinson is going fast. When I called to see him at the Seaman's Snug Harbor this morning I found him considerably weaker than he had been yesterday, though still in full possession of his faculties. There's nothing specifically wrong with the old fellow, save as any worn-out bit of machinery in time gets ready for the scrap-heap. He will probably go out sometime during the night, quite likely in his sleep, a victim of having lived too long.

"Doctor," he said to me when I went into his room this morning, "ye've been mighty good to me, a poor, worn-out old hulk with never a cent to repay all yer kindness; but I've that here which will make yer everlastin' fortune, providin' ye're brave enough to tackle it."

"That's very kind of you, John," I answered, but the old fellow was deadly serious.

"'Tis no laughin' matter, Doctor," he returned as he saw me smile. "'Tis th' truth an' nothin' else I'm tellin' ye—I'd 'a' had a go at it meself if it warn't that seafarin' men don't hold with disturbin' th' bones o' th' dead. But you, bein' a landsman, an' a doctor to boot, would most likely succeed where others have failed. I had it from my gran'ther, sir, an' he was an old man an' I but a lad when he gave it me, so ye can see 'tis no new thing I'm passin' on. Where he got it I don't know, but he guarded it like his eyes an' would never talk about it, not even to me after he'd give it to me."

With that he asked me to go to his ditty-box and take out a packet done up in oiled silk, which he insisted I take as partial compensation for all I'd done for him.

I tried to tell him the home paid my fee regularly, and that he was beholden to me for nothing, but he would not have it; so, to quiet the old man, I took the plan for my "everlastin' fortune" before I left.

9 Nov. 1898—Old John died last night, as I'd predicted, and probably went with the satisfied feeling that he had made a potential millionaire of the struggling country practitioner who tended him in his last illness. I must look into the mysterious packet by which he set such store. Probably it's a chart for locating some long-sunk pirate ship or unburying the loot of Captain Kidd, Blackbeard, or some other old sea-robber. Sailormen a generation ago were full of such yarns, and recounted them so often they actually came to believe them.

10 Nov. '98—I was right in my surmise concerning old John's legacy, though it's rather different from the usual run of buried-treasure maps.

Some day, when I've nothing else to do, I may go down to the old church in Harrisonville and actually have a try at the thing. It would be odd if poor Eric Balderson, struggling country practitioner, became a wealthy man overnight. What would I do first? Would a sealskin dolman for Astrid or a new side-bar buggy for me be the first purchase I'd make? I wonder.

"H'm," I remarked as I put down the book. "And this old seaman's legacy, as your father called it—"

"Is here," Eric interrupted, handing me a square of ancient, crackling vellum on which a message of some kind had been laboriously scratched. The edges of the parchment were badly frayed, as though with much handling, though the indentures might have been the result of hasty tearing in the olden days. At any rate, it was a tattered and thoroughly decrepit sheet from which I read:

in yᵉ name of yᵉ most Holie Trinitie

    I, Richard Thompson, being a right synfull manne and near unto mine ende do give greeting and warning to whoso shall rede herefrom. Ye booty which my master whose name no manne did rightly know, but who was surnamed by some ye Black Master and by somme Blackface ye Merciless, lyes hydden in divers places, but ye creame thereof is laid away in ye churchyard of St. Davides hard by Harrisons village. There, by daye and by nite do ye dedde stand guard over it for ye Master sealed its hydinge place both with cement and with a curse which he fondlie sware should be on them & on their children who violated ye sepulchre without his sanction. Yet if any there be who dare defye ye curse (as I should not) of hym who had neither pitie ne mercie ne lovingkindness at all, let hm go unto ye burrieing ground at dedde of nite at ye season of dies natalis invicti & obey ye direction. Further hint I dast not gyvve, for fear of him who lurks beyant ye portales of lyffe to hold to account such of hys servants as preceded him not in dethe. And of your charity, ye who rede this, I do charge and conjure ye that ye make goode and pieous use of ye Master hys treasure and that ye expend such part of ye same as may be fyttinge for masses for ye good estate of Richard Thompson, a synnfull man dieing in terror of his many iniquities & of ye tongueless one who waites himme across ye borderline

    When ye star shines from ye tree
    Be it as a sign to ye.
    Draw ye fourteen cubit line
    To ye entrance unto lyfe
    Whence across ye graveyard sod
    See spotte cursed by man & God.

"It looks like a lot of childish nonsense to me," I remarked with an impatient shrug as I tossed the parchment to de Grandin. "Those old fellows who had keys to buried treasure were everlastingly taking such care to obscure their meaning in a lot of senseless balderdash that no one can tell when they're serious and when they're perpetrating a hoax. If—"

"*Cordieu*," the little Frenchman whispered softly, examining the sheet of frayed vellum with wide eyes, holding it up to the lamplight, then crackling it softly between his fingers. "Is it possible? But yes, it must be—Jules de Grandin could not be mistaken."

"Whatever are you maundering about?" I interrupted impatiently. "The way you're looking at that parchment anyone would think—"

"Whatever anyone would think, he would be far from the truth," de Grandin cut in, regarding us with the fixed, unwinking stare which meant deadly seriousness. "If this plat be a *mauvaise plaisanterie*—how do you call it? the practical joke?—it is a very grim one indeed, for the parchment on which it is engraved is human skin."

"What?" cried Eric and I in chorus.

"Nothing less," de Grandin responded. "Me, I have seen such parchments in the Paris *musée*; I have handled them, I have touched them. I could not be mistaken. Such things were done in the olden days, my friends. I think, perhaps, we should do well to investigate this business. Men do not set down confessions of a sinful life and implore the possible finders of treasure to buy masses for their souls on human hide when they would indulge in pleasantries. No, it is not so."

"But—" I began, when he shut me off with a quick gesture.

"In the churchyard of Saint David's this repentant Monsieur Richard Thompson did say. May I inquire, Friend Trowbridge, if there be such a church in the neighborhood? Assuredly there was once, for does he not say, 'hard by Harrison's village,' and might that not have been the early designation of your present city of Harrisonville?"

"U'm—why, yes, by George!" I exclaimed. "You're right, de Grandin. There *is* a Saint David's church down in the old East End—a Colonial parish, too; one of the first English churches built after the British took Jersey over from the Dutch. Harrisonville was something of a seaport in those days, and there was a bad reef a few miles offshore. I've been told the church was built and endowed with the funds derived from salvaging cargo from ships stranded on the reef. The parish dates back to 1670 or '71, I believe."

"H'm-m." De Grandin extracted a vile-smelling French cigarette from his black-leather case, applied a match to it and puffed furiously a moment, then slowly expelled a twin column of smoke from his nostrils. "And '*dies natalis invicti*' our so scholarly Monsieur Richard wrote as the time for visiting this churchyard. What can that be but the time of Bonhomme Noël—the Christmas season?

Parbleu, my friends, I think, perhaps, we shall go to that churchyard and acquire a most excellent Christmas gift for ourselves. Tonight is December 22, tomorrow should he near enough for us to begin our quest. We meet here tomorrow night to try our fortune, *n'est-ce-pas?*"

Crazy and harebrained as the scheme sounded, both Eric and I were carried away by the little Frenchman's enthusiasm, and nodded vigorous agreement.

"*Bon*," he cried, "*très bon!* One more drink, my friends, then let us go dream of the golden wheat awaiting our harvesting."

"But see here, Dr. de Grandin," Eric Balderson remarked, "since you've told us what this message is written on this business looks more serious to me. Suppose there's really something in this curse old Thompson speaks of? We won't be doing ourselves much service by ignoring it, will we?"

"Ah bah," returned the little Frenchman above the rim of his half-drained glass. "A curse, you do say. Young *Monsieur*, I can plainly perceive you do not know Jules de Grandin, A worm-eaten fig for the curse! Me, I can curse as hard and as violently as any villainous old sea-robber who ever sank a ship or slit a throat!"

2

THE BLEAK DECEMBER WIND which had been moaning like a disconsolate banshee all afternoon had brought its threatened freight of snow about nine o'clock and the factory- and warehouse-lined thoroughfares of the unfashionable part of town where old Saint David's church stood were noiseless and white as ghost-streets in a dead city when de Grandin, Eric Balderson and I approached the churchyard pentice shortly before twelve the following night. The hurrying flakes had stopped before we left the house, however, and through the wind-driven pluvial clouds the chalk-white winter moon and a few stars shone frostily.

"*Cordieu*, I might have guessed as much!" de Grandin exclaimed in exasperation as he tried the iron grille stopping the entrance to the church's little close and turned away disgustedly. "Locked—locked fast as the gates of hell against escaping sinners, my friends," he announced. "It would seem we must swarm over the walls, and—"

"And get a charge of buckshot in us when the caretaker sees us," Eric interrupted gloomily.

"No fear, *mon vieux*," de Grandin returned with a quick grin. "Me, I have not been idle this day. I did come here to reconnoiter during the afternoon—*morbleu*, but I did affect the devotion at evensong before I stepped outside to survey the terrain!—and many things I discovered. First, this church stands like a lonely outpost in a land whence the expeditionary force has been withdrawn. Around here are not half a dozen families enrolled on the parish register. Were it not for churchly pride and the fact that heavy endowments of the past make it possible to support this chapel as a mission, it would have been closed long ago. There is no resident sexton, no *curé* in residence here. Both functionaries dwell some little distance away. As for the *cimetière*, no interments have been permitted here for close on fifty years. The danger of grave-robbers is *nil*, so also is the danger of our finding a night watchman. Come, let us mount the wall."

It was no difficult feat scaling the six-foot stone barricade surrounding Saint David's little God's Acre, and we were standing ankle-deep in fresh snow within five minutes, bending our heads against the howling midwinter blast and casting about for some starting-point in our search.

Sinking to his knees in the lee of an ancient holly tree, de Grandin drew out his pocket electric torch and scanned the copy of Richard Thompson's cryptic directions. "H'm," he murmured as he flattened the paper against the bare ground beneath the tree's outspread, spiked branches, "what is it the estimable Monsieur Thompson says in his so execrable poetry? 'When the star shines from the tree.' Name of three hundred demented green monkeys, when *does* a star shine from a tree, Friend Trowbridge?"

"Maybe he meant a Christmas tree," I responded with a weak attempt at flippancy, but the little Frenchman was quick to adopt the suggestion.

"*Morbleu*, I think you have right, good friend," he agreed with a nod. "And what tree is more in the spirit of Noël than the holly? Come, let us take inventory."

Slowly, bending his head against the wind, yet thrusting it upward from the fur collar of his greatcoat like a turtle emerging from its shell every few seconds, he proceeded to circle every holly and yew tree in the grounds, observing them first from one angle, then another, going so near that he stood within their shadows, then retreating till he could observe them without withdrawing his chin from his collar. At last:

"*Nom d'un singe vert*, but I think I have it!" he ejaculated. "Come and see."

Joining him, we gazed upward along the line indicated by his pointing finger. There, like a glass ornament attached to the tip of a Yuletide tree, shone and winked a big, bright star—the planet Saturn.

"So far, thus good," he murmured, again consulting the cryptogram. "'Be it as a sign to ye,' says our good Friend Thompson. *Très bien, Monsieur*, we have heeded the sign—now for the summons.

"'Draw ye fourteen cubit line'—about two hundred and fifty-two of your English inches, or, let us say, twenty-one feet," he muttered. "Twenty-one feet, yes; but which way? 'To the entrance unto life.' U'm, what *is* the entrance to life in a burying-ground, *par le mort d'un chat noir*? A-a-ah? Perhaps yes; why not?"

As he glanced quickly this way and that, his eyes had come to rest on a slender stone column, perhaps three feet high, topped by a wide, bowl-like capital. Running through the snow to the monument, de Grandin brushed the clinging flakes from the bowl's lip and played the beam of his flashlight on it. "You see?" he asked with a delighted laugh.

Running in a circle about the weathered stone was the inscription:

SANCTVS, SANCTVS, SANCTVS
Vnleff a man be borne again of VVater &
Ye Holy Spirit he fhall in nowife . . .

The rest of the lettering had withered away with the alternate frosts and thaws of more than two hundred winters.

"Why, of course!" I exclaimed with a nod of understanding. "A baptismal font—'the entrance unto life,' as old Thompson called it."

"My friend," de Grandin assured me solemnly, "there are times when I do not entirely despair of your intellect, but where shall we find that much-cursed spot of which *Monsieur*—"

"Look, look, for God's sake!" croaked Eric Balderson, grasping my arm in his powerful hand till I winced under the pressure. "Look there, Dr. Trowbridge—*it's opening!*"

The moon, momentarily released from a fetter of drifting clouds, shot her silver shafts down to the clutter of century-old monuments in the churchyard, and, twenty feet or so from us, stood one of the old-fashioned boxlike grave-markers of Colonial times. As we looked at it in compliance with Eric's panic-stricken announcement, I saw the stone panel nearest us slowly slide back like a shutter withdrawn by an invisible hand.

"Sa-ha, it lies this way, then?" de Grandin whispered fiercely, his small, white teeth fairly chattering with eagerness. "Let us go, my friends; let us investigate. Name of a cockroach, but this is the *bonne aventure!*

"No, my friend," he pushed me gently back as I started toward the tomb, "Jules de Grandin goes first."

It was not without a shudder of repulsion that I followed my little friend through the narrow opening in the tomb, for the air inside the little enclosure was black and terrible, and solid-looking as if formed of ebony. But there was no chance to draw back, for close behind me, almost as excited as the Frenchman, pressed Eric Balderson.

The boxlike tomb was but the bulkhead above a narrow flight of stone stairs, steep-pitched as a ship's accommodation ladder, I discovered almost as soon as I had crawled inside, and with some maneuvering I managed to turn about in the narrow space and back down the steps.

Twenty steps, each about eight inches high, I counted as I descended to find myself in a narrow, stone-lined passageway which afforded barely room for us to walk in single file.

Marching ahead as imperturbably as though strolling down one of his native boulevards, de Grandin led the way, flashing the ray from his lantern along the smoothly paved passage. At length:

"We are arrived, I think," he announced. "And, unless I am mistaken, as I hope I am, we are in a *cul-de-sac*, as well."

The passage had terminated abruptly in a blank wall, and there was nothing for us to do, apparently, but edge around and retrace our steps. I was about to suggest this when a joyous exclamation from de Grandin halted me.

Feeling along the sandstone barrier, he had sunk to his knees, prodded the stone tentatively in several places, finally come upon a slight indentation, grooved as though to furnish hand-hold.

"Do you hold the light, Friend Trowbridge," he directed as he thrust the ferrule of his ebony cane into the depression and gave a mighty tug. "Ah, *parbleu*, it comes; it comes—we are not yet at the end of our tape!"

Resisting only a moment, the apparently solid block of stone had slipped back almost as easily as a well-oiled trap-door, disclosing an opening some three and a half feet high by twenty inches wide.

"The light, my friend—shine the light past me while I investigate," de Grandin breathed, stooping almost double to pass through the low doorway.

I bent as far forward as I could and shot the beam of light over his head, and lucky for him it was I did so, for even as his head disappeared through the cleft he jerked back with an exclamation of dismay. "Ha, villain, would you so?" he rasped, snatching the keen blade from his sword cane and thrusting it through the aperture with quick, venomous stabs.

At length, having satisfied himself that no further resistance offered beyond the wall, he sank once more to his bended knees and slipped through the hole. A moment later I heard him calling cheerfully, and, stooping quickly, I followed him, with Eric Balderson, making heavy work at jamming his great bulk through the narrow opening, bringing up the rear. De Grandin pointed dramatically at the wall we had just penetrated.

"*Morbleu*, he was thorough, that one," he remarked, inviting our attention to an odd-looking contrivance decorating the stones.

It was a heavy ship's boom, some six feet long, pivoted just above its center to the wall so that it swung back and forth like a gigantic pendulum. Its upper end was secured to a strand of heavily tarred cable, and fitted with a deep notch, while to its lower extremity was securely bolted what appeared to be the fluke from an old-fashioned ship's anchor, weighing at least three stone and filed and ground to an axlike edge. An instant's inspection of the apparatus showed us its simplicity and diabolical ingenuity. It was secured by a brace of wooden triggers in a horizontal position above the little doorway through which we had entered, and the raising of the stone-panel acted to withdraw the keepers till only a fraction of their tips supported the boom.

Pressure on the sill of the doorway completed the operation, and sprung the triggers entirely back, permitting the timber with its sharpened iron tip to swing downward across the opening like a gigantic headsman's ax, its knife-sharp blade sweeping an arc across the doorway's top where the head of anyone entering was bound to be. But for the warning furnished by the beam of light preceding him, and the slowness of the machine's operation after a century or more of inactivity, de Grandin would have been as cleanly decapitated by the descending blade as a convict lashed to the cradle of a guillotine.

"But what makes the thing work?" I asked curiously. "I should think that whoever set it in place would have been obliged to spring it when he made his exit. I can't see—"

"S-sst!" the Frenchman cut me off sharply, pointing to the deadly engine.

Distinctly, as we listened, came the sound of tarred hawsers straining over pulley-wheels, and the iron-shod beam began to rise slowly, once more assuming a horizontal position.

I could feel the short hairs at the back of my neck rising in company with the boom as I watched the infernal spectacle, but de Grandin, ever fearless, always curious, wasted no time in speculation. Advancing to the wall, he laid his hand upon the cable, tugging with might and main, but without visible effect on the gradually rising spar. Giving over his effort, he laid his ear to the stones, listened intently a moment, then turned to us with one of his quick, elfish smiles. "He was clever, as well as wicked, the old villain who invented this," he informed us. "Behold, beyond this wall is some sort of a mechanism worked by running water, my friends. When the trigger retaining this death-dealer is released, water is also undoubtlessly permitted to run from a cask or tank attached to the other end of this rope. When the knife-ax has descended and made the unwelcome visitor shorter by a head, the flowing water once more fills the tank, hoists the ax again to its original position, and *pouf!* he are ready to behead the next unin-vited guest who arrives. It are clever, yes. I much regret that we have not the time to investigate the mechanism, for I am convinced something similar opens the door through which we entered—perhaps once each year at the season of the ancient Saturnalia—but we did come here to investigate something entirely quite different, eh, Friend Balderson?"

Recalled to our original purpose, we looked about the chamber. It was almost cubical in shape, perhaps sixteen feet long by as many wide, and slightly less in height. Save the devilish engine of destruction at the entrance, the only other fixture was a low coffin-like block of stone against the farther wall.

Examining this, we found it fitted with hand-grips at the sides, and two or three tugs at these heaved the monolith up on end, disclosing a breast-high, narrow doorway into a second chamber, somewhat smaller than the first, and reached by a flight of some five or six stone steps.

Quickly descending these, we found ourselves staring at a long stone sarcophagus, bare of all inscription and ornament, save the grisly emblem of the "Jolly Roger," or piratical skull and thigh-bones, graven on the lid where ordinarily the name-plate would have rested, and a stick of dry, double-forked wood, something like a capital X in shape, which lay transversely across the pirate emblem.

"Ah, what have we here?" inquired de Grandin coolly, approaching the coffin and prying at its lid with his cane-sword.

To my surprise, the top came away with little or no effort on our part, and we stared in fascination at the unfleshed skeleton of a short, thick-set man with enormously long arms and remarkably short, bandy legs.

"Queer," I muttered, gazing at the relic of mortality. "You'd have thought anyone who went to such trouble about his tomb and its safeguards would have been buried in almost regal raiment, yet this fellow seems to have been laid away naked as the day he was born. This coffin has been almost airtight for goodness knows how many years, and there ought to be some evidence of cerements left, even if the flesh has moldered away."

De Grandin's little blue eyes were shining with a sardonic light and his small, even teeth were bared beneath the line of his miniature golden mustache as he regarded me. "Naked, unclothed, without fitting cerements, do you say, Friend Trowbridge?" he asked. Prodding with his sword blade between the skeleton's ribs a moment, he thrust the flashlight into my grip with an impatient gesture and put both hands elbow-deep into the charnel box, rummaging and stirring about in the mass of nondescript material on which the skeleton was couched. "What say you to this, and these—and these?" he demanded.

My eyes fairly started from my face as the electric torch ray fell on the things which rippled and flashed and sparkled between the little Frenchman's white fingers. There were chains of gold encrusted with rubies and diamonds and greenly glowing emeralds; there were crosses set with amethyst and garnet which any mitered prince of the church might have been proud to wear; there were ear- and finger-rings with brilliant settings in such profusion that I could not count them, while about the sides of the coffin were piled great stacks of broad gold pieces minted with the effigy of his most Catholic Majesty of Spain, and little hillocks of unset gems which sparkled and scintillated dazzlingly.

"Regal raiment did you say, Friend Trowbridge?" de Grandin cried, his breath coming fast as he viewed the jewels with ecstasy. "*Cordieu*, where in all the world is there a monarch who takes his last repose on such a royal bed as this?"

"It—it's real!" Balderson breathed unbelievingly. "It wasn't a pipe-dream, after all, then. We're rich, men—*rich!* Oh, Marian, if it only weren't too late!"

De Grandin matter-of-factly scooped up a double handful of unset gems and deposited them in his overcoat pocket. "What use has this old *drôle* for all this wealth?" he demanded. "*Mordieu*, we shall find better use for it than bolstering up dead men's bones! Come, my friends, bear a hand with the treasure; it is high time we were leaving this—Trowbridge, my friend, watch the light!"

Even as he spoke I felt the flashlight slipping from my fingers, for something invisible had struck me a numbing blow across the knuckles. The little lantern fell with a faint musical tinkle into the stone coffin beside the grinning skull and we heard the soft plop as its airless bulb exploded at contact with some article of antique jewelry.

"Matches—strike a light, someone, *pour l'amour de Dieu!*" de Grandin almost shrieked. "It is *nécessaire* that we have light to escape from this so abominable place without having our heads decapitated!"

I felt for my own flashlight, but even as I did so there was a faint hissing sound, the sputter of a safety match against its box, and—the breath of a glowing furnace seemed suddenly to sweep the room as the heavy, oppressive air was filled with dancing sheets of many-colored flames and a furious detonation shook the place. As though seized in some giant fist, I felt myself lifted bodily from the floor and hurled with devastating force against the wall, from which I rebounded and fell forward senseless on the stone-paved floor.

"TROWBRIDGE—TROWBRIDGE, GOOD, KIND FRIEND, tell us that you survive!" I heard de Grandin's tremulous voice calling from what seemed a mile or more away as I felt the fiery trickle of brandy between my teeth.

"Eh? Oh, I'm all right—I guess," I replied as I sat up and forced the little Frenchman's hip-flask from my lips. "What in the world happened? Was it—"

"*Morbleu*," laughed my friend, his spirits already recovered, "I thought old Bare-bones in the coffin yonder had returned from hell and brought his everlasting fires with him. We, my friends, are three great fools, but Jules de Grandin is the greatest. When first I entered this altogether detestable tomb, I thought I smelled the faint odor of escaping illuminating-gas, but so great was my curiosity before we forced the coffin, and so monstrous my cupidity afterward, that I dismissed the matter from my mind. Assuredly there passes close by here some main of the city's gas pipes, and there is a so small leak in one of them. The vapor has penetrated the graveyard earth in small quantities and come into this underground chamber. Not strong enough to overpower us, it was none the less in sufficient concentration to explode with one great *boom* when Friend Balderson struck his match. Fortunately for us, the doors behind are open, thus providing expansion chambers for the exploding gas. Otherwise we should have been annihilated altogether entirely.

"Come, the gas has blown away with its own force and we have found Friend Trowbridge's flashlight. *Mordieu*, my ten fingers do itch most infernally to be at the pleasant task of counting this ill-gotten wealth!"

CRAMBLING OVER THE CEMETERY wall was no light task, since each of us had filled his pockets with Spanish gold and jewels until he scaled almost twice his former weight, and it was necessary for Balderson and de Grandin to boost me to the wall crest, then for de Grandin to push from below while I lent a hand from above to help Balderson up, and finally for the pair of us to drag the little Frenchman up after us.

"Lucky for us the wind has risen and the snow recommenced," de Grandin congratulated as we made our way down the deserted street, walking with a rolling gait, like heavy-laden ships in a high sea; "within an hour the snow inside the cemetery will be so drifted that none will know we visited there tonight. Let us hail a taxi, *mes amis*; I grow weary bearing this great weight of wealth about."

3

"NAME OF A SMALL green rooster," Jules de Grandin exclaimed delightedly, his little blue eyes shining with elation in the light of the library lamp, "we are rich, my friends, rich beyond the wildest dreams of Monte Cristo! Me, I shall have a Parisian *appartement* which shall be the never-ending wonder of all beholders; a villa on the Riviera; a ducal palace in Venice—no less!—and—*grand Dieu*, what is that?"

Above the wailing of the storm-wind, half obliterated by the keening blasts, there came to us from the street outside the scream of a woman in mortal terror: "Help—help—ah, help!" the last desperate appeal so thin and high with panic and horror that we could scarce distinguish it from the skirling of the gale.

"Hold fast—courage—we come! we come!" de Grandin shouted, as he burst through the front door, cleared the snow-swept porch with a single bound and raced hatless into the white-swathed street. "Where are you Madame?" he cried, pausing at the curb and looking expectantly up and down the deserted highway. "Call out, we are here!" For another moment he searched the desolate street with his gaze; then, "Courage!" he cried, vaulting a knee-high drift and rushing toward a dark, huddled object lying in the shifting snow a hundred feet or so away.

Balderson and I hurried after him but he had already raised the woman's lolling head in the crook of his elbow and was preparing to administer stimulant from his ever-ready flask when we arrived.

She was a young girl, somewhere between seventeen and twenty to judge by her face, neither pretty nor ill-favored, but with the clean, clear complexion of a well-brought-up daughter of lower middle-class people. About her flimsy party dress was draped a cloth coat, wholly inadequate to the chill of the night, trimmed with a collar of nondescript fur, and the hat which was pushed back from her blond bobbed hair was the sort to be bought for a few dollars at any department store.

De Grandin bent above her with all the deference he would have shown a duchess in distress. "What was it, *Mademoiselle?*" he asked solicitously. "You did call for assistance—did you fall in the snow? Yes?"

The girl looked at him from big, terrified eyes, swallowed once convulsively, then murmured in a low, hoarse whisper: "His eyes! Those terrible eyes—they—ah, Jesus! Mercy!" In the midst of a pitiful attempt to sign herself with the cross, her body stiffened suddenly, then went limp in the Frenchman's arms; her slender bosom fluttered once, twice, then flattened, and her lower jaw fell slowly downward, as if in a half-stifled yawn. Balderson, layman that he was, mistook her senseless, imbecile expression for a bit of ill-timed horseplay and gave a half-amused titter. De Grandin and I, inured to vigils beside the moribund, recognized the trade mark stamped in those glazed, expressionless eyes and that drooping chin.

"*Ad te, Domine*—" the Frenchman bent his blond head as he muttered the prayer. Then: "Come, my friends, help me take her up. We must bear her in from the storm, then notify the police. Ha, something foul has been abroad this night; it were better for him if he runs not crosswise of the path of Jules de Grandin, *pardieu!*"

Breakfast was a belated meal next morning, for it was well after three o'clock before the coroner's men and police officers had finished their interrogations and taken the poor, maimed clay that once was gay little Kathleen Burke to the morgue for official investigation. The shadow of the tragedy sat with us at table, and none cared to discuss future joyous plans for squandering the pirate treasure. It was de Grandin who waked us from our gloomy reveries with a half-shouted exclamation.

"*Nom d'un nom*—another!" he cried. "Trowbridge, Balderson, my friends, give attention! Hear, this item from *le journal*, if you please:

Two Girls Victims of Fiend

Early this morning the police were informed of two inexplicable murders in the streets of Harrisonville. Kathleen Burke, 19, of 17 Bonham Place, was returning from a party at a friend's house when Drs. Trowbridge and de Grandin, of 993 Susquehanna Avenue, heard her screaming for help and rushed out to offer assistance, accompanied by Eric Balderson, their house guest. They found the girl in a dying condition, unable to give any account of her assailant further than to mumble something concerning his eyes. The body was taken to the city morgue for an inquest which will be held today.

Rachel Müller, 26, of 445 Essex Avenue, a nurse in the operating-room at Mercy Hospital, was returning to her home after a term of special night duty a few minutes before 3 A.M. when she was set upon from behind by a masked man wearing a fantastic costume which she described to the police as consisting of a tight-fitting coat, loose, baggy pantaloons and high boots, turned down at the top, and a stocking-cap on his head. He seized her by the throat, and she managed to fight free, whereupon he attacked her with a dirk-knife, inflicting several wounds of a serious nature. Officer Timothy Dugan heard the woman's outcries and hurried to her rescue, finding her bleeding profusely and in a serious condition. He administered first aid and rang for an ambulance in which she was removed to Casualty Hospital, where she was unable to give a more detailed description of her attacker. She died at 4:18 this morning. Her assailant escaped. The police, however, claim to be in possession of several reliable clues and an arrest is promised in the near future.

"What say you to that, my friends?" the Frenchman demanded. "Me, I should say we would better consult—"

"Sergeant Costello, sor," Nora McGinnis, my household factotum, announced from the breakfast room door as she stood aside to permit the burly, red-haired Irishman to enter.

"Ah, bonjour, Sergent," de Grandin greeted with a quick smile. "Is it that you come to lay the clues to the assassin of those two unfortunate young women before us?"

Detective Sergeant Jeremiah Costello's broad, red face went a shade more rubescent as he regarded the diminutive Frenchman with an affectionate grin. "Sure, Dr. de Grandin, sor, 'tis yerself as knows when we're handin' out th' straight goods an' when we're peddlin' th' bull," he retorted. "Ain't it th' same wid th' johnny darmes in Paree? Sure, it is. Be gorry, if we had so much as one little clue, rayliable or not, we'd be huggin' an' kissin' ourselves all over th' place, so we would. 'Tis fer that very reason, an' no other, I'm after troublin' ye at yer breakfast this marnin'. Wud ye be willin' to listen to th' case, as far as we know it, I dunno?"

"Say on, mon vieux," de Grandin returned, his eyes shining and sparkling with the joy of the born manhunter in the chase. "Tell us all that is in your mind, and we may together arrive at some solution. Meantime, may I not make free of Dr. Trowbridge's hospitality to the extent of offering you a cup of coffee?"

"Thanks, sor, don't mind if I do," the detective accepted, "it's mortal cold outside today."

"Now to begin wid, we don't know no more about who committed these here murthers, or, why he done it, than a hog knows about a holiday, an' that's a fact. They tell me at headquarters that th' little Burke gur-rl (God rest her soul!) said something about th' felly's eyes to you before she died, an' Nurse Müller raved about th' same thing, though she was able to give some little bit of dayscription of him, as well. But who th' divil would be goin' around th' streets o' nights murtherin' pore, definseless young women—it's cases like this as makes policemen into nervous wrecks, Dr. de Grandin, sor. Crimes o' passion an' crimes committed fer gain, they're meat an' drink to me, sor—I can understand 'em—but it's th' divil's own job runnin' down a johnny who goes about committin' murthers like this. Sure, 'tis almost always th' sign of a loose screw in his steerin' gear, sor, an' who knows where to look fer 'im? He might be some tough mug, but 'tisn't likely. More apt to be some soft-handed gentleman livin' in a fine neighborhood an' minglin' wid th' best society. There's some queer, goin's on among th' swells, sor, an' that's gospel; but we can't go up to every bur-rd that acts funny at times an' say, 'Come wid me, young felly me lad; it's wanted fer th' murther o' Kathleen Burke an' Rachel Müller ye are,' now can we?"

"Hélas, non," the Frenchman agreed sympathetically. "But have you no clue of any sort to the identity of this foul miscreant?"

"Well, sor, since ye mention it, we have one little thing," the sergeant replied, delving into his inside pocket and bringing forth a folded bit of paper from which he extracted a shred of twisted yarn. "Would this be manin' annything to ye?" he asked as he handed it to de Grandin.

"U'm," the little Frenchman murmured thoughtfully as he examined the object carefully. "Perhaps, I can not say at once. Where did you come by this?"

"'Twas clutched in Nurse Müller's hand as tight as be-damned when they brought her to th' hospital, sor," the detective replied. "We're not sure 'twas from th' murtherer's fancy-dress costume, o' course, but it's better'n nothin' to go on."

"But yes—most certainly," de Grandin agreed as he rose and took the find to the surgery.

For a few minutes he was busily engaged with jeweler's loop and microscope; finally he returned with the shred of yarn partly unraveled at one end. "It would seem," he declared as he returned the evidence to Costello, "that this is of Turkish manufacture, though not recent. It is a high grade of angora wool; the outer scales have smooth edges, which signifies the quality of the fleece. Also, interwoven with the thread is a fine golden wire. I have seen such yarn, the wool cunningly intermixed with golden threads, used for tarboosh tassels of wealthy Moslems. But the style has not prevailed for a hundred years and more. This is either a very old bit of wool, or a cunning simulation of the olden style—I am inclined to think the former. After all, though, this thread tells little more than that the slayer perhaps wore the headgear of a Mohammedan. The nurse described him as wearing a stocking-cap or toboggan, I believe. In her excitement and in the uncertain light of early morning a fez might easily be mistaken for such a piece of headgear."

"Then we're no better off than we were at first?" the Irishman asked disappointedly.

"A little," de Grandin encouraged. "Your search has narrowed somewhat, for you need only include among your suspects those possessing genuine Turkish fezzes a hundred years or more old."

"Yeah," commented Costello gloomily. "An' after we've run all them down, all we haf ter do is go down ter th' seashore an' start countin' th' grains o' sand."

"*Tiens*, my friend, be not so downcast," de Grandin bade. "Like your so magnificent John Paul Jones, we have not yet commenced to fight. Come, *Sergent*, Trowbridge, let us to the morgue. Perhaps we shall discover something there, if the pig-clumsy physicians have not already spoiled matters with their autopsy knives.

"Balderson, *mon brave*, do you remain to guard that which requires watching. You have small stomach for the things Friend Trowbridge and I shall shortly look upon."

SIDE BY SIDE IN the zinc-lined drawers of the city morgue's refrigerator lay the bodies of Kathleen Burke and Rachel Müller. De Grandin bent above the bodies, studying the discolorations on their throats in thoughtful silence. "U'm," he commented, as he turned to me with a quizzical expression, "is there not something these contusions have in common, Friend Trowbridge?"

Leaning forward, I examined the dark, purplish ridges banding both girls' throats. About the thickness of a lead-pencil, they ran about the delicate white skins, four on the left side, one on the right, with a small circular patch of discoloration in the region of the larynx, showing where the strangler had rested the heel of his hand as a fulcrum for his grip. "Why," I began, studying the marks carefully, "er, I can't say that I notice—by George, yes! The center finger of the throttler's hand was amputated at the second joint!"

"*Précisément*," the Frenchman agreed. "And which hand is it, if you please?"

"The right, of course; see how his thumb pressed on the right side of his victim's throats."

"*Exactement*, and—"

"And that narrows Costello's search still more," I interrupted eagerly. "All he has to do now is search for someone with half the second finger of his right hand missing, and—"

"And you do annoy me excessively," de Grandin cut in frigidly. "Your interruptions, they vex, they harass me. If I do not mistake rightly, we have already found him of the missing finger; at least, we have seen him."

I looked at him in open-mouthed amazement. Men afflicted with mysterious sadistic impulses, I knew, might move in normal society for years without being subject to suspicion, but I could recall no one of our acquaintance who possessed the maimed hand which was the killer's trade mark. "You mean—?" I asked blankly.

"Last night, or early this morning, *mon vieux*," he returned. "You, perhaps, were too immediately concerned with dodging exploding gases to take careful note of all we saw in the charnel chamber beneath the ground, but me, I see everything. *The right middle finger of the skeleton we found in the coffin with the treasure was missing at the second joint.*"

"You're joking!" I shot back incredulously.

For answer he pointed silently to the still, dead forms before us. "Are *these* a joke, my friend?" he demanded. "*Cordieu*, if such they be, they are an exceedingly grim jest."

"But for heaven's sake," I demanded, "how could that skeleton leave its tomb and wander about the streets? Anyhow, Nurse Müller declared it was a man who attacked her, not a skeleton. And skeletons haven't eyes, yet poor little Kathleen spoke of her assailant's eyes the first thing when we found her."

He turned his back on my expostulations with a slight shrug and addressed himself to the morgue master. "Have they arrived at the precise causes of death, *Monsieur?*" he asked.

"Yes, sir," the official replied. "The little Burke girl died o' heart failure consequent upon shock. Miss Müller died from loss o' blood an'—"

"Never mind, my friend, it is enough," de Grandin interrupted. "Strangulation was present in both cases, but apparently was not the primary cause of either death. That was all I desired to learn."

"Trowbridge, my friend," he assured me as we parted at the mortuary door, "he practises."

"Practises—who?" I demanded. But de Grandin was already out of earshot, walking down the street at a pace which would have qualified him for entry in a professional pedestrians' race.

4

THE CONSOMMÉ WAS GROWING cold in the tureen, Balderson and I were becoming increasingly aware of our appetites, and Nora McGinnis was on the verge of nervous prostration as visions of her elaborate dinner spoiling on the stove danced before her mind's eye when Jules de Grandin burst through the front door, a film of snowflakes from the raging storm outside decorating his shoulders like the ermine on a judge's gown. "Quick, Friend Trowbridge," he ordered as he drew up his chair to the table, "fill my plate to overflowing. I hunger, I starve, I famish. Not so much as one little crumb of luncheon has passed my lips this day."

"Find out anything?" I asked as I ladled out a liberal portion of smoking chicken broth.

"*Cordieu*, I shall say so, and he who denies it is a most foul liar!" he returned with a grin. "Observe this, if you please."

From his pocket he produced an odd-looking object, something like a fork of dried weed or a root of desiccated ginger, handing it first to me, then to Eric Balderson for inspection.

"All right, I'll bite—what is it?" Eric admitted as the little Frenchman eyed us in turn expectantly.

"*Mandragora officinalis*—mandrake," he replied with another of his quick smiles. "Have you not seen it before?—"

"U'm"—I searched the pockets of my memory a moment—"isn't this the thing we found on the old pirate's coffin last night?"

"Exactly, precisely, quite so!" he replied delightedly, patting his hands together softly as though applauding at a play. "You have it right, good friend; but last night we were too much concerned with saving our silly heads from the swinging ax, with finding gold and gems, and similar useless things to give attention to matters of real importance. Behold, my friends, with this bit of weed-root and these, I shall make one *sacré singe*—a monkey, no less—of that so vile murderer who terrorizes the city and slays inoffensive young women in the right. Certainly." As he finished speaking, he thrust his hand into another pocket and brought forth a dozen small conical objects which he pitched onto the table-cloth with a dramatic gesture.

"Bullets!" Balderson remarked wonderingly. "What—"

"Bullets, no less," de Grandin agreed, taking a pair of the little missiles into his hand and joggling them up and down playfully. "But not such bullets as you or Friend Trowbridge have seen before, I bet me your life. Attend me: These are silver, solid silver, without a trace of alloy. *Eh bien*, but I did have the fiend's own time finding a jeweler who would undertake to duplicate the bullets of my pistol in solid silver on such short notice. But at last, *grâce à Dieu*, I found him, and he fashioned these so pretty things to my order and fitted them into the shells in place of the nickel-plated projectiles. For good measure I ordered him to engrave each one with a cross at its tip, and then, on my way home, I did stop at the church of Saint Bernard and dip them each and every one into the font of *eau bénite*. Now, I damn think, we shall see what we shall see this night."

"What in the world—" I began, but he shut me off with upraised hand.

"The roast, Friend Trowbridge," he implored, "for dear friendship's sake, carve me a liberal portion of the roast and garnish it well with potatoes. Do but permit that I eat my fill, and, when the time arrives, I shall show you such things as to make you call yourself one colossal liar when you recall them to memory!"

Sergeant Costello, thoroughly disgruntled at hours of vigil in the snowy night and completely mystified, was waiting for us beside the entrance to Saint David's churchyard. "Sure, Dr. de Grandin, sor," he announced as he stepped from the shelter of the pentice, blowing on his numbed fingers, "'tis th' divil's own job ye gave me tonight. Me eyes have been skinned like a pair o' onions all th' night long, but niver a bit o' annyone comin' in or out o' th' grave-yard have I seen."

"Very good, my friend," de Grandin commented. "You have done most well, but I fear me one will attempt to pass you, and by the inward route, before many minutes have gone. You will kindly await our outcoming, if you please, and we shall be no longer than necessary, I assure you."

Forcing the sliding door of the tombstone, we hastened down the stairway to the burial chamber in de Grandin's wake, sprung the guarding ax at the entrance of the first room and crept into the inner cavern. One glance was sufficient to confirm our suspicions. The stone coffin was empty.

"Was—was it like this when you were here today?" I faltered.

"No," de Grandin answered, "he lay in his bed as calmly as a babe in its cradle, my friend, *but he lay on his side.*"

"On his side? Why, that is impossible! The skeleton was on its back when we came here last night and we didn't move it. How came the change of posture?"

"*Tiens*, who can say?" he replied. "Perhaps he rests better that way. Of a certainty, he had lain long enough on his posterior to have become tired of it. It may be—*sssh!* Lights out. To your quarters!"

Balderson and I rushed to opposite corners of the room, as de Grandin had previously directed, our powerful electric bull's-eye lanterns shut off, but ready to flood the place with light at a second's notice. De Grandin stationed himself squarely in line with the door, his head thrust forward, his knees slightly bent, his entire attitude one of pleased anticipation.

What sixth sense had warned him of approaching danger I know not, for in the absolute quiet of the pitch dark chamber I could hear no sound save the low, short breaths of my two companions and the faint trickle-trickle of water into the tank of the beheading machine which guarded the entrance of the farther room. I was about to speak, when:

Bang! The muffled detonation of a shot fired somewhere above ground sounded startlingly, followed by another and still another; then the rasping, high-pitched cackle of a maniacal laugh, a scraping, shuffling step on the nar-row stone stairs, and:

"Lights, *pour l'amour de Dieu*, lights!" de Grandin shrieked as something—some malign, invisible, unutterably wicked *presence* seemed suddenly to fill the chamber, staining the inky darkness still more black with its foul effluvium.

As one man Balderson and I snapped up the shutters of our lanterns, and the converging beams displayed a frightful tableau.

Crouched at the low entrance of the cavern, like a predatory beast with its prey, was a fantastic figure, a broad, squat—almost humpbacked—man arrayed in leathern jerkin, Turkish fez and loose, baggy pantaloons tucked into hip-boots of soft Spanish leather. About his face, mask-like, was bound a black-silk kerchief with two slits for eyes, and through the openings there glowed and glittered a pair of baleful orbs, green-glossed and vitreous, like those of a cat, but fiercer and more implacable than the eyes of any feline.

Over one malformed shoulder, as a miller might carry a sack of meal, the creature bore the body of a girl, a slight, frail slip of femininity with ivory face and curling hair of deepest black, her thin, frilly party dress ripped to tatters, one silver slipper fallen from her silk-sheathed foot, the silver-tissue bandeau which bound her hair dislodged so that it lay half across her face like the bandage over the eyes of a condemned felon.

"*Monsieur le Pirate*," de Grandin greeted in a low, even voice, "you do roam afield late, it seems. We have waited overlong for you."

The mask above the visitant's face fluttered outward with the pressure of breath behind it, and we could trace the movement of jaws beneath the silk, but no word of answer came to the Frenchman's challenge.

"Ah—so? You choose not to talk?" de Grandin queried sarcastically. "Is it perhaps that you prefer deeds to words? *C'est bien!*" With a quick, skipping step he advanced several paces toward the creature, raising his pistol as he moved.

A peal of sardonic, tittering laughter issued from beneath the mask. Callous as a devil, the masked thing dropped the girl's lovely body to the stone floor, snatched at the heavy hanger in his belt and leaped straight for de Grandin's throat.

The Frenchman fired even as his antagonist charged, and the effect of his shot was instantaneous. As though he had run against a barrier of iron, the masked pirate stopped in mid-stride and staggered back an uncertain step, but de Grandin pressed his advantage. "Ha, you did not expect this, *hein?*" he demanded with a smile which was more like a snarl. "You who defy the bullets of policemen and make mock of all human resistance thought you would add one more victim to your list, *n'est-ce-pas, Monsieur?* Perhaps, *Monsieur, le Mort-félon*, you had not thought of Jules de Grandin?"

As he spoke he fired another shot into the cowering wretch, another, and still another until eight silver balls had pierced the cringing thing's breast.

As the final shot went home the fantastical, terrible shape began to change before our eyes. Like the cover of a punctured football the gaudy, archaic costume began to wrinkle and wilt, the golden-tasseled fez toppled forward above the masked face and the black-silk handkerchief itself dropped downward, revealing the unfleshed countenance of a grinning skull.

"Up with him, my friends," de Grandin shouted. "Pitch him into his coffin, clamp down the lid—here, lay the root of mandrake upon it! So! He is in again, and for all time.

"Now, one of you, take up poor *Mademoiselle* and pass her through the door to me.

"Very well, *Sergent*, we come and bring the young lady with us!" he cried as Costello's heavy boots sounded raspingly on the stone steps outside. "Do not attempt to enter—it is death to put your head through the opening!"

A moment later, with the girl's body wrapped in the laprobe, we were driving toward my house, ignoring every speed regulation in the city ordinances.

5

SERGEANT COSTELLO LOOKED ASKANCE at the rug-wrapped form occupying the rear seat of my car. "Say, Dr. de Grandin, sor," he ventured with another sidewise glance at the lovely body, "hadn't we best be notifyin' th' coroner, an'"— he gulped over the word—"an' gittin' a undertaker fer this here pore young lady?"

"Coroner—undertaker? À bas les croque-morts! Your wits are entirely absent harvesting the wool of sheep, *cher sergent*. The only undertaker of which she stands in need is the excellent Nora McGinnis, who shall give her a warm bath to overcome her chill after Friend Trowbridge and I have administered stimulants. Then, unless I mistake much, we shall listen to a most remarkable tale of adventure before we restore her to the arms of her family."

HALF AN HOUR LATER our fair prize, revived by liberal doses of aromatic ammonia and brandy, thoroughly warmed by a hot sponge and alcohol rub administered by the competent Nora, and with one of de Grandin's vivid flowered-silk dressing-gowns slipped over the sorry remnants of her tattered party costume, sat demurely before our library fire. As she entered the room, Eric Balderson, who had not seen her face before, because of the bandeau which obscured it in the cave, gave a noticeable start, then seemed to shrink back in his corner of the ingle-nook.

Not so Jules de Grandin. Swinging one well-tailored leg across the corner of the library table, he regarded the young lady with a level, unwinking stare till the sustained scrutiny became embarrassing. Finally:

"*Mademoiselle*, you will have the kindness to tell us exactly what has happened to you this night, so far as you can remember," he ordered.

The girl eyed him with a tremulous smile a moment; then, taking a deep breath, launched on her recital like a child speaking a piece in school.

"I'm Marian Warner," she told us. "We live in Tunlaw Street—I think Dr. Trowbridge knows my father, Fabian Warner."

I nodded agreement, and she continued.

"Tonight I went to a Christmas Eve party at Mr. and Mrs. Partridge's. It was a masquerade affair, but I just wore a domino over my evening dress, since we were to unmask at midnight, anyway, and I thought I'd feel more comfortable in 'citizen's clothes' than I would dancing in some sort of elaborate costume.

"There wasn't anything unusual about the party, or about the first part of the evening, that I remember, except, of course, everyone was talking about the mysterious murder of those two poor women.

"They danced a German just before midnight, and I was pretty hot from the running around, so I stepped into the conservatory to slip out of my domino a moment and cool off.

"I'd just taken the gown off when I felt a touch on my arm, and turning round found a man staring into my face. I thought he must be one of the guests, of course, though I couldn't remember having seen him. He wore a jerkin of bright red leather with a wide black belt about his waist, a red fez with gold-and-black tassel, and loose trousers tucked into tall boots. His face was concealed with a black-silk handkerchief instead of a regular mask, and, somehow, there was something menacing and terrifying about him. I think it must have been his eyes, which glittered in the light like those of an animal at night.

"I started back from him, but he edged after me, extending his hand to stroke my arm, and almost fawning on me. He made queer, inarticulate sounds in his throat, too.

"'Go away,' I told him. 'I don't know you and I don't want to. Please leave me alone.' By that time he'd managed to crowd me into a corner, so that my retreat into the house was cut off, and I was getting really frightened.

"'If you don't let me go, I'll scream,' I threatened, and then, before I had a chance to say another word, out shot one of his hands—ugh, they were big and thin and long, like a gorilla's!—and grasped me by the throat.

"I tried to fight him off, and even as I did so there flashed through my mind the description Miss Müller gave of her murderer. Then I knew. I was helpless in the grasp of the killer! That's all I remember till I regained consciousness with Dr. Trowbridge's housekeeper drying me after my bath and you gentlemen standing outside the door, ready to help me downstairs.

"Did they catch him—the murderer?" she added with true feminine curiosity.

"But of course, *Mademoiselle*," de Grandin assured her gravely. "I was on his trail. It was impossible he should escape.

"Attend me, my friends," he ordered, slipping from his seat on the table and striding to the center of the room like a lecturer about to begin his discourse. "Last night, when we entered that accursed tomb, I had too many thoughts within my so small brain to give full attention to any one of them. In my hurry

I did overlook many important matters. That root of mandrake, by example, I should have suspected its significance, but I did not. Instead, I tossed it away as an unconsidered trifle.

"Mandrake, or mandragora, my friends, was one of the most potent charm-drugs in the ancient pharmacopoeia. With it the barren might be rendered fecund; love forgotten might be reawakened; deep and lasting coma might be induced by it. Does not that Monsieur Shakespeare make Cleopatra say:

'Give me to drink of mandragora,
That I might sleep out this great gap of time
My Antony is away'?

"Most certainly. Moreover, it had another, and less frequent use. Placed upon the grave of one guilty of manifold sins, *it would serve to keep his earthbound spirit from walking.* You perceive the connection.

"When we cast aside that root of mandragora, we did unseal a tomb which was much better left unopened, and did release upon the world a spirit capable of working monstrous evil. Yes. This 'Black Master,' I do know him, Friend Trowbridge.

"When we looked upon the poor relics of those slain women, I noticed at once the peculiarity of the bruises on their throats. '*Parbleu,*' I say to me, 'the skeleton which we saw last night, he had a hand so maimed as to leave a mark like this. Jules de Grandin, we must investigate.'

"'Make it so,' I reply to me in that mental conversation, and so, Friend Trowbridge, when I left you I did repair instantly to that cursed tomb and look about. There, in his coffin of stone, lay the skeleton of the 'Black Master,' but, as I have already been at pains to tell you, on his side, not as we left him lying the night before. '*Mordieu,* this are not good, this are most badly strange,' I inform me. Then I look about and discover the bit of mandrake root, all shriveled and dried, and carelessly tossed to one side where we left it when Friend Trowbridge let fall his light. I—"

"By the way, de Grandin," I put in. "Something hit me a paralyzing blow on the knuckles before I let my flashlight fall; have you any idea what it was?"

He favored me with a momentary frown, then: "But certainly," he responded. "It were a bit of stone from the ceiling. I saw it detach itself and cried a warning to you, even as it fell, but the loss of our light was of such importance that I talked no more about your injury. Now to resume:

"'Can we not now seal him in the tomb with the mandrake once more?' I ask me as I stand beside that coffin today, but better judgment tells me not to attempt it. This old-time sea-devil, he have been able to clothe his bony frame with seeming habiliments of the flesh. He are, to all intents and purposes, once more alive, and twice as wicked as before on account of his long sleep. I shall kill his fantasmal body for good and all before I lock him once and forever in the tomb again.

"'But how shall we slay him so that he be really-truly dead?' I ask me.

"Then, standing beside the coffin of that old, wicked pirate, I think and think deeply. 'How were the were-wolves and witches, the wizards and the war-locks, the bugbears and goblins of ancient times slain in the olden days?' I ask, and the answer comes back, 'With bullets of silver.' Attend me, my friends."

Snatching a red leather volume from the near-by shelf he thumbed quickly through its pages. "Hear what your Monsieur Whittier say in one of his so lovely poems. In the olden times, the garrison of a New England fort was beset by

> . . . a spectral host, defying stroke of
> steel and aim of gun;
> Never yet was ball to slay them in the
> mold of mortals run!
> Midnight came; from out the forest moved
> a dusky mass that soon
> Grew to warriors, plumed and painted,
> grimly marching in the moon.
> "Ghosts or witches," said the captain, "thus
> I foil the Evil One!"
> And *he rammed a silver button from his*
> *doublet down his gun.*

"Very good. I, too, will thus foil the Evil One and his servant who once more walks the earth. I have told you how I had the bullets made to my order this day. I have recounted how I baptized them for the work they were to do this night. Yourselves saw how the counter-charm worked against that servitor of Satan, how it surprised him when it pierced his phantom breast, how it made of him a true corpse, and how the seeming-flesh he had assumed to clothe his bare bones while he worked his evil was made to melt away before the bullets of Jules de Grandin. Now, doubly dead, he lies sealed by the mandrake root within his tomb for evermore.

"Friend Balderson, you have been most courteously quiet this long time. Is there no question you would care to ask?"

"You told Dr. Trowbridge you knew the 'Black Master,'" Eric replied. "Can you tell us something about him—"

"Ah, *parbleu*, but I can!" de Grandin interrupted. "This afternoon, while the excellent jeweler was turning out my bullets, I repaired to the public library and discovered much of that old villain's life and deeds. Who he was nobody seems to know. As to what he was, there is much fairly accurate conjecture.

"A Turk he was by birth, it is generally believed, and a most unsavory follower of the false Prophet. Even in sinful Stamboul his sins were so great that he was deprived of his tongue by way of punishment. Also, he was subjected to another operation not wholly unknown in Eastern countries. This latter, instead of rendering him docile, seemed to make a veritable demon of him. Never would he permit his crews to take prisoners, even for ransom. Sexless himself, he forbade the presence of women—even drabs from Maracaibo and Panama—aboard his ships, save for one purpose. That was torture. Whenever a ship was captured, he fetched the female prisoners aboard, and after compelling them to witness the slaughter of their men folk, with his own hands he put them to death, often crushing life from their throats with his maimed right hand. Does not his history fit squarely with the things we have observed these last two nights? The accounts declare, 'The time and place of his death are uncertain, but it is thought he died somewhere near the present city of Newark and was buried somewhere in Jersey. A vast treasure disappeared with him, and speculation concerning its hiding-place rivals that of the famous buried hoard of Captain Kidd.'

"Now, it is entirely probable that we might add something of great interest to that chronicle, but I do not think we shall, for—"

Absorbed in the Frenchman's animated narrative, Eric Balderson had moved from his shadowed corner into the zone of light cast by the reading-lamp, and as de Grandin was about to finish, Marian Warner interrupted him with a little cry of incredulous delight. "Eric," she called. "Eric Balderson! Oh, my dear, I've wondered and worried so much about you!"

A moment later she had flown across the room, shedding de Grandin's purple lizard-skin slippers as she ran, put both hands on the young man's shoulders, and demanded, "Why did you go away, dear; didn't you kno—"

"Marian!" Eric interrupted hoarsely. "I didn't dare ask your father. I was so wretchedly poor, and there seemed no prospect of my ever getting anywhere—you'd been used to everything, and I thought it would be better for us both if I just faded out of the picture. But"—he laughed boyishly—"I'm rich, now, dear—one of the richest men in the country, and—"

"Rich or poor, Eric dear, I love you," the girl interrupted as she slipped both arms about his neck and kissed him on the lips.

Jules de Grandin's arms shot out like the blades of a pair of opening shears. With one hand he grasped Sergeant Costello's arm; the other snatched me by the elbow. "Come away, foolish ones," he hissed. "What have we, who left our loves in Avalon long years ago, to do with such as they? *Pardieu*, to them we are a curse, a pest, an abomination; we do incumber the earth!

"Await me here," he ordered as we concluded our march to the consulting-room. "I go, but I return immediately."

In a moment he came tripping down the stairs, a magnificent glowing ruby, nearly as large as a robin's egg, held daintily between his thumb and forefinger. "For their betrothal ring," he announced proudly. "See, it is the finest in my collection."

"Howly Mither, Dr. de Grandin, sor, are ye, a jinny from th' *Arabeen Nights*, to be passin' out jools like that whenever a pair o' young folks gits engaged?" demanded Sergeant Costello, his big blue eyes almost popping from his head in amazement.

"Ah, *mon sergent*," the little Frenchman turned one of his quick, elfish smiles on the big Irishman, "you have as yet seen nothing. Before you leave this house tonight Friend Trowbridge and I shall fill every pocket of your clothes to overflowing with golden coin from old Spain; but e'er we do so, let us remember it is Christmas."

With the certainty of one following a well-worn path, he marched to the medicine closet, extracted a bottle of peach brandy and three glasses, and filled them to the brim.

"To your very good and long-lasting health, my friend," he pledged, raising his glass aloft. "*Joyeux Noël!*"

The Devil's Rosary

M Y FRIEND JULES DE Grandin was in a seasonably sentimental mood. "It is the springtime, Friend Trowbridge," he reminded as we walked down Tonawanda Avenue. "The horse-chestnuts are in bloom and the blackbirds whistle among the branches at St. Cloud; the tables are once more set before the cafés, and—*grand Dieu, la belle creature!*" He cut short his remarks to stare in undisguised admiration at a girl about to enter an old-fashioned horse-drawn victoria at the curb.

Embarrassed, I plucked him by the elbow, intent on drawing him onward, but he snatched his arm away and bounded forward with a cry, even as my fingers touched his sleeve. "Attend her, my friend," he called; "she faints!"

As she seated herself on the taupe cushions of her carriage, the girl reached inside her silver mesh bag, evidently in search of a handkerchief, fumbled a moment among the miscellany of feminine fripperies inside the reticule, then wilted forward as though bludgeoned.

"*Mademoiselle*, you are ill, you are in trouble, you must let us help you!" de Grandin exclaimed as he mounted the vehicle's step. "We are physicians," he added in belated explanation as the elderly coachman turned and favored us with a hostile stare.

The girl was plainly fighting hard for consciousness. Her face had gone death-gray beneath its film of delicate make-up, and her lips trembled and quavered like those of a child about to weep, but she made a brave effort at composure. "I—I'm—all—right—thank—you," she murmured disjointedly. "It's—just—the—heat—" Her protest died half uttered and her eyelids fluttered down as her head fell forward on de Grandin's ready shoulder.

"*Morbleu*, she has swooned!" the little Frenchman whispered. "To Dr. Trowbridge's house—993 Susquehanna Avenue!" he called authoritatively to the coachman. "*Mademoiselle* is indisposed." Turning to the girl he busied himself making her as comfortable as possible as the rubber-tired vehicle rolled smoothly over the asphalt roadway.

She was, as de Grandin had said, a "belle créature." From the top of her velour hat to the pointed tips of her suede pumps she was all in gray, a platinum fox scarf complementing the soft, clinging stuff of her costume, a tiny bouquet of early-spring violets lending the sole touch of color to her ensemble. A single tendril of daffodil-yellow hair escaped from beneath the margin of her close-fitting hat lay across a cheek as creamy-smooth and delicate as a babe's.

"Gently, my friend," de Grandin bade as the carriage stopped before my door. "Take her arm—so. Now, we shall soon have her recovered."

In the surgery he assisted the girl to a chair and mixed a strong dose of aromatic ammonia, then held it to the patient's blanched lips.

"Ah—so, she revives," he commented in a satisfied voice as the delicate, violet-veined lids fluttered uncertainly a moment, then rose slowly, unveiling a pair of wide, frightened purple eyes.

"Oh—" the girl began in a sort of choked whisper, half rising from her seat, but de Grandin put a hand gently on her shoulder and forced her back.

"Make haste slowly, *ma belle petite*," he counseled. "You are still weak from shock and it is not well to tax your strength. If you will be so good as to drink this—" He extended the glass of ammonia toward her with a bow, but she seemed not to see it. Instead, she stared about the room with a dazed, panic-stricken look, her lips trembling, her whole body quaking in a perfect ague of unreasoning terror. Somehow, as I watched, I was reminded of a spectacle I had once witnessed at the zoo when Rajah, a thirty-foot Indian python, had refused food, and the curators, rather than lose a valuable reptile by starvation, overrode their compunctions, and thrust a poor, helpless white rabbit into the monster's glass-walled den.

"I've seen it; I've seen it; *I've seen it!*" She chanted the litany of terror, each repetition higher, more intense, nearer the boundary of hysteria than the one before.

"*Mademoiselle!*" de Grandin's peremptory tone cut her terrified iteration short. "You will please not repeat meaningless nothings to yourself while we stand here like a pair of stone monkeys. What is it you have seen, if you please?"

The unemotional, icy monotone in which he spoke brought the girl from her near-hysteria as a sudden dash of cold water in the face might have done. "This!" she cried in a sort of frenzied desperation as she thrust her hand into the mesh bag pendent from her wrist. For a moment she ransacked its interior with groping fingers; then, gingerly, as though she held something live and venomous, brought forth a tiny object and extended it to him.

"U'm?" he murmured non-committally, taking the thing from her and holding it up to the light as though it were an oddity of nature.

It was somewhat smaller than a hazel-nut, smooth as ivory, and stained a brilliant red. Through its axis was bored a hole, evidently for the purpose of accommodating a cord. Obviously, it was one of a strand of inexpensive beads, though I was at a loss to say of what material it was made. In any event, I could see nothing about the commonplace little trinket to warrant such evident terror as our patient displayed.

Jules de Grandin was apparently struck by the incongruity of cause and effect, too, for he glanced from the little red globule to the girl, then back again, and his narrow, dark eyebrows raised interrogatively. At length: "I do not think I apprehend the connection," he confessed. "This"—he tapped the tiny ball with a well manicured forefinger—"may have deep significance to you, *Mademoiselle*, but to me it appears—"

"Significance?" the girl echoed. "It has! When my mother was drowned in Paris, a ball like this was found clutched in her hand. When my brother died in London, we found one on the counterpane of his bed. Last summer my sister was drowned while swimming at Atlantic Highlands. When they recovered her body, they found one of these terrible beads hidden in her bathing-cap!" She broke off with a retching sob and rested her arm on the surgery table, pillowing her face on it and surrendering herself to a paroxysm of weeping.

"Oh, I'm doomed," she wailed between blanching lips. "There's no help for me, and—I'm too young; I don't want to die!"

"Few people do, *Mademoiselle*," de Grandin remarked dryly. "However, I see no cause of immediate despair. Over an hour has passed since you discovered this evil talisman, and you still live. So much for the past. For the future you may trust in the mercy of heaven and the cleverness of Jules de Grandin. Meantime, if you are sufficiently recovered, we shall do ourselves the honor of escorting you home."

UNDER DE GRANDIN'S ADROIT questioning we learned much of the girl's story during our homeward drive. She was Haroldine Arkright, daughter of James Arkright, a wealthy widower who had lately moved to Harrisonville and leased the Broussard mansion in the fashionable west end. Though only nineteen years old, she had spent so much time abroad that America was more foreign to her than France, Spain or England.

Born in Waterbury, Connecticut, she had lived there during her first twelve years, and her family had been somewhat less than moderately well-to-do. Her father was an engineer, and spent much time abroad. Occasionally, when his remittances were delayed, the family felt the pinch of undisguised poverty. One day her father returned home unexpectedly, apparently in a state of great agitation. There had been mysterious whisperings, much furtive going and coming; then the family entrained for Boston, going immediately to the Hoosac Tunnel Docks and taking ship for Europe.

She and her sister were put to school in a convent at Rheims, and though they had frequent and affectionate letters from their parents, the communications came from different places each time; so she had the impression her elders led a Bedouin existence.

At the outbreak of the war the girls were taken to a Spanish seminary, where they remained until two years before, when they joined their parents in Paris.

"We'd lived there only a little while," she continued, "when two gendarmes came to our apartment one afternoon and asked for Daddy. One of them whispered something to him and he turned white as a sheet; then, when the other took something from his pocket and showed it, Daddy fell over in a dead faint. It wasn't till several hours later that we children were told. Mother's body had been found floating in the Seine, and one of those horrible little red balls was in her hand. That was the first we ever heard of them.

"Though Daddy was terribly affected by the tragedy, there was something we couldn't understand about his actions. As soon as the *Pompes Funèbres* (the municipal undertakers) had conducted the services, he made arrangements with a solicitor to sell all our furniture, and we moved to London without stopping to pack anything but a few clothes and toilet articles.

"In London we took a little cottage out by Garden City, and we lived—it seemed to me—almost in hiding; but before we'd lived there a year my brother Philip died, and—they found the second of these red beads lying on the cover of his bed.

"Father seemed almost beside himself when Phil died. We left—fled would be a better word—just as we had gone from Paris, without stopping to pack a thing but our clothes. When we arrived in America we lived in a little hotel in downtown New York for a while, then moved to Harrisonville and rented this house furnished.

"Last summer Charlotte went down to the Highlands with a party of friends, and—" she paused again, and de Grandin nodded understandingly.

"Has *Monsieur* your father ever taken you into his confidence?" he asked at length. "Has he, by any chance, told you the origin of these so mysterious little red pellets and—"

"Not till Charlotte drowned," she cut in. "After that he told me that if I ever saw such a ball anywhere—whether worn as an ornament by some person, or among my things, or even lying in the street—I was to come to him at once."

"U'm?" he nodded gravely. "And have you, perhaps, some idea how this might have come into your purse?"

"No. I'm sure it wasn't there when I left home this morning, and it wasn't there when I opened my bag to put my change in after making my purchases at Braunstein's, either. The first I saw of it was when I felt for a handkerchief after getting into the carriage, and—oh, I'm terribly afraid, Dr. de Grandin. I'm too young to die! It's not fair; I'm only nineteen, and I was to have been married this June and—"

"Softly, *ma chère*," he soothed. "Do not distress yourself unnecessarily. Remember, I am with you."

"But what can you do?" she demanded. "I tell you, when one of these beads appears anywhere about a member of our family, it's too late for—"

"*Mademoiselle*," he interrupted, "it is never too late for Jules de Grandin—if he be called in time. In your case we have—" His words were drowned by a sudden angry roar as a sheet of vivid lightning tore across the sky, followed by the bellow of a deafening crash of thunder.

"*Parbleu*, we shall be drenched!" de Grandin cried, eyeing the cloud-hung heavens apprehensively. "Quick, Trowbridge, *mon vieux*, assist Mademoiselle Haroldine to alight. I think we would better hail a taxi and permit the coachman to return alone with the carriage.

"One moment, if you please, *Mademoiselle*," he ordered as the girl took my outstretched hand; "that little red ball which you did so unaccountably find in your purse, you will let me have it—a little wetting will make it none the less interesting to your father." Without so much as a word of apology, he opened the girl's bag, extracted the sinister red globule and deposited it between the cushions of the carriage seat, then, with the coachman's aid, proceeded to raise the vehicle's collache top.

As the covered carriage rolled rapidly away, he raised his hand, halting a taxicab, and calling sharply to the chauffeur: "Make haste, my friend. Should you arrive at our destination before the storm breaks, there is in my pocket an extra dollar for you."

The driver earned his fee with compound interest, for it seemed to me we transgressed every traffic ordinance on the books in the course of our ride, cutting corners on two wheels, racing madly in the wrong direction through one-way streets, taking more than one chance of fatal collision with passing vehicles.

The floodgates of the clouds were just opening, and great torrents of water were cataracting down when we drew up beneath the Arkright porte-cochère, and de Grandin handed Haroldine from the cab with a ceremonious bow, then turned to pay the taxi-man his well-earned bonus.

"*Mordieu*, our luck holds excellently well—" he began as we turned toward the door, but a blaze of lightning more savage than any we had seen thus far and the roaring detonation of a thunderclap which seemed fairly to split the heavens blotted out the remainder of his sentence.

The girl shrank against me with a frightened little cry as the lightning seared our eyes, and I sympathized with her terror, for it seemed to me the flash must have struck almost at our feet, so nearly simultaneous were fire and thunder, but a wild, half-hysterical laugh from de Grandin brought me round with an astonished exclamation.

The little Frenchman had rushed from the shelter of the mansion's porch and pointed dramatically toward the big stone pillars flanking the entrance to the grounds. There, toppled on its side as though struck fairly by a high-explosive shell, lay the victoria we had ordered to follow us, the horses kicking wildly at their shattered harness, the coachman thrown a clear dozen feet from his vehicle, and the carriage itself reduced to splinters scarcely larger than match-staves.

Heedless of the drenching rain, we raced across the lawn and halted by the prostrate postilion. Miraculously, the man was not only living, but regaining consciousness as we reached him. "Glory be to God!" he exclaimed piously as we helped him to his feet. "'Tis only by th' mercy o' heaven I'm still a livin' man!"

"*Eh bien*, my friend"—de Grandin gave his little blond mustache a sharp twist as he surveyed the ruined carriage—"perhaps the stupidity of hell may have something to do with it. Look to your horses; they seem scarcely worse off than yourself, but they may be up to mischief if they remain unchaperoned."

Once more beneath the shelter of the porte-cochère, as calmly as though discussing the probability of the storm's abatement, he proposed: "Let us go in, my friends. The horses and coachman will soon be all right. As for the carriage"—he raised his narrow shoulders in a fatalistic shrug—"*Mademoiselle*, I hope *Monsieur* your father carried adequate insurance on it."

2

THE LITTLE FRENCHMAN LAID his hand on the polished brass handle of the big oak door, but the portal held its place unyieldingly, and it was not till the girl had pressed the bell button several times that a butler who looked as if his early training had been acquired while serving as guard in a penitentiary appeared and paid us the compliment of a searching inspection before standing aside to admit us.

"Your father's in the living-room, Miss Haroldine," he answered the girl's quick question, then followed us half-way down the hall, as though reluctant to let us out of sight.

Heavy draperies of mulberry and gold brocade were drawn across the living-room windows, shutting out the lightning flashes and muffling the rumble of the thunder. A fire of resined logs burned cheerfully in the marble-arched fireplace, taking the edge from the early-spring chill; electric lamps under painted shades spilled pools of light on Turkey carpets, mahogany shelves loaded with ranks of morocco-bound volumes and the blurred blues, reds and purples of Oriental porcelains. On the walls the dwarfed perfection of several beautifully executed miniatures showed, and in the far corner of the apartment loomed the magnificence of a massive grand piano.

James Arkright leaped from the overstuffed armchair in which he had been lounging before the fire and whirled to face us as we entered the room, almost, it seemed to me, as though he were expecting an attack. He was a middle-aged man, slender almost to the point of emaciation, with an oddly parchmentlike skin and a long, gaunt face rendered longer by the iron-gray imperial pendant from his chin. His nose was thin and high-bridged, like the beak of a predatory bird, and his ears queer, Panesque appendages, giving his face an odd, impish look. But it was his eyes which riveted our attention most of all. They were of an indeterminate color, neither gray nor hazel, but somewhere between, and darted continually here and there, keeping us constantly in view, yet seeming to watch every corner of the room at the same time. For a moment, as we trooped into the room, he surveyed us in turn with that strange, roving glance, a light of inquiring uncertainty in his eyes fading to a temporary relief as his daughter presented us.

As he resumed his seat before the fire the skirt of his jacket flicked back and I caught a fleeting glimpse of the corrugated stock of a heavy revolver holstered to his belt.

The customary courtesies having been exchanged we lapsed into a silence which stretched and lengthened until I began to feel like a bashful lad seeking an excuse for bidding his sweetheart adieu. I cleared my throat, preparatory to making some inane remark concerning the sudden storm, but de Grandin forestalled me.

"*Monsieur*," he asked as his direct, unwinking stare bored straight into Arkright's oddly watchful eyes, "when was it you were in Tibet, if you please?"

The effect was electric. Our host bounded from his chair as though propelled by an uncoiled spring, and for once his eyes ceased to rove as he regarded the little Frenchman with a gaze of mixed incredulity and horror. His hand slipped beneath his jacket to the butt of the concealed weapon, but:

"Violence is unnecessary, my friend," de Grandin assured him coolly. "We are come to help you, if possible, and besides, I have you covered"—he glanced momentarily at the bulge in his jacket pocket where the muzzle of his tiny Ortgies automatic pressed against the cloth—"and it would be but an instant's work to kill you several times before you could reach your pistol. Very good"—he gave one of his quick, elfish smiles as the other subsided into his chair—"we do make progress.

"You wonder, perhapsly, how comes it I ask that question? Very well. A half-hour or so ago, when *Mademoiselle* your lovely daughter was recovered from her fainting-spell in Dr. Trowbridge's office, she tells us of the sinister red bead she has found in her purse, and of the evil fortune such little balls have been connected with in the past.

"I, *Monsieur*, have traveled a very great much. In darkest Africa, in inner-most Asia, where few white men have gone and lived to boast of it, I have been there. Among the head-hunters of Papua, beside the upper, banks of the Ama-zon, Jules de Grandin has been. *Alors*, is it so strange that I recognize this so mysterious ball for what it is? *Parbleu*, in disguise I have fingered many such in the lamaseries of Tibet!

"*Mademoiselle's* story, it tells me much; but there is much more I would learn from you if I am to be of service. You were once poor. That is no disgrace. You suddenly became rich; that also is no disgrace, nor is the fact that you traveled up and down the world almost constantly after the acquisition of your fortune necessarily confession of wrongdoing. But"—he fixed his eyes challengingly on our host—"but what of the other occurrences? How comes it that *Madame* your wife (God rest her spirit!) was found floating in the Seine with such a red ball clutched in her poor, dead hand?

"Me, I have recognized this ball. It is a bead from the rosary of a Buddhist lama of that devil-ridden gable of the world we call Tibet. How came *Madame* to be grasping it? Who knows?

"When next we see one of these red beads, it is on the occasion of the sud-den sad death of the young *Monsieur*, your son.

"Later, when you have fled like one pursued to America and settled in this small city which nestles in the shadow of the great New York, comes the death of your daughter, Mademoiselle Charlotte—and once more the red ball appears.

"This afternoon Mademoiselle Haroldine finds the talisman of impending doom in her purse and forthwith swoons in terror. Dr. Trowbridge and I succor her and are conveying her to you when a storm arises out of a clear sky. We change vehicles and I leave the red bead behind. All goes well until—*pouf!*—a bolt of lightning strikes the carriage in which the holder of this devil's rosary seems to ride, and demolishes it. But horses and coachman are spared. *Cordieu*, it is more than merely strange; it is surprising, it is amazing, it is astonishing! One who does not know what Jules de Grandin knows would think it incom-prehensible.

"It is not so. I know what I have seen. In Tibet I have seen those masked devil-dancers cause the rain to fall and the winds to blow and the lightning bolts to strike where they willed. They are worshipers of the demons of the air, my friends, and it was not for nothing the wise old Hebrews named Satan, the rejected of God, the Prince of the Powers of the Air. No.

"Very well. We have here so many elements that we need scarcely guess to know what the answer is. *Monsieur* Arkright, as the roast follows the fish and coffee and cognac follow both, it follows that you once wrested from the lamas of Tibet some secret they wished kept; that by that secret you did obtain much wealth; and that in revenge those old heathen monks of the mountains follow you and yours with implacable hatred. Each time they strike, it would appear, they leave one of these beads from the red rosary of vengeance as sign and seal of their accomplished purpose. Am I not right?" He looked expectantly at our host a moment; then, with a gestured application for permission from Haroldine, produced a French cigarette, set it alight and inhaled its acrid, ill-flavored smoke with gusto.

JAMES ARKRIGHT REGARDED THE little Frenchman as a respectable matron might look at the blackmailer threatening to disclose an indiscretion of her youth. With a deep, shuddering sigh he slumped forward in his chair like a man from whom all the resistance has been squeezed with a single titanic pressure. "You're right, Dr. de Grandin," he admitted in a toneless voice, and his eyes no longer seemed to take inventory of everything about him. "I *was* in Tibet; it was there I stole the *Pi Yü* Stone—would God I'd never seen the damned thing!"

"Ah?" murmured de Grandin, emitting a twin column of mordant smoke from his narrow nostrils. "We make progress. Say on, *Monsieur*; I listen with ears like the rabbit's. This *Pi Yü* Stone, it is what?"

Something like diffidence showed in Arkright's face as he replied, "You won't believe me, when I've told you."

De Grandin emitted a final puff of smoke and ground the fire from his cigarette against the bottom of a cloisonné bowl. "*Eh bien, Monsieur*," he answered with an impatient shrug, "it is not the wondrous things men refuse to credit. Tell the ordinary citizen that Mars is sixty million miles from the earth, and he believes you without question. Hang up a sign informing him that a fence is newly painted, and he must needs smear his finger to prove your veracity. Proceed, if you please."

"I was born in Waterbury," Arkright began in a sort of half-fearful, half-stubborn monotone, "and educated as an engineer. My father was a Congregational clergyman, and money was none too plentiful with us; so, when I completed my course at Sheff, I took the first job that offered. They don't pay any too princely salaries to cubs just out of school, you know, and the very necessity of my finding employment right away kept me from making a decent bargain for myself.

"For ten years I sweated for the N.Y., N.H.&H., watching most of my classmates pass me by as though I stood stone-still. Finally I was fed up. I had a wife and three children, and hardly enough money to feed them, let alone give them the things my classmates' families had. So, when I got an offer from a British house to do some work in the Himalayas it looked about as gorgeous to me as the fairy godmother's gifts did to Cinderella. It would get me away from America and the constant reminders of my failure, at any rate.

"The job took me into upper Nepal and I worked at it for close to three years, earning the customary vacation at last. Instead of going down into India, as most of the men did, I pushed up into Tibet with another chap who was keen on research, and a party of six Bhotia bearers. We had no particular goal in mind, but we'd been so fed up on stories of the weird happenings in those mountain lamaseries, we thought we'd go up and have a look—see on our own.

"There was some good shooting on the way, and what few natives we ran into were harmless enough if you kept 'em far enough away to prevent their cooties from climbing aboard you; so we really didn't get much excitement out of the trip, and had about decided it was a bust when we came on a little lamasery perched like an eagle's nest on the edge of an enormous cliff.

"We managed to scramble up the zigzag path to the place, and had some difficulty getting in, but at last the ta-lama agreed we might spend the night there.

"They didn't seem to take any particular notice of us after we'd unslung our packs in the courtyard, and we had the run of the place pretty much to ourselves. Clendenning, my English companion, had knocked about Central Asia for upward of twenty years, and spoke several Chinese dialects as well as Tibetan, but for some reason he'd played dumb when we knocked at the gates and let our head man interpret for us.

"About four o'clock in the afternoon he came to me in a perfect fever of excitement. 'Arkright, old boy,' he whispered, 'this blighted place is simply filthy with gold—raw, virgin gold!'

"'You're spoofing,' I told him; 'these poor old duffers are so God-awful poor they'd crawl a mile on their bare knees and elbows for a handful of copper cash.'

"'*Cash* my hat!' he returned. 'I tell you, they've got great heaps and stacks of gold here; gold enough to make our perishing fortunes ten times over if we could shift to get the blighted stuff away. Come along, I'll show you.'

"He fairly dragged me across the courtyard where our duffle was stored, through a low doorway, and down a passage cut in the solid rock. There wasn't a lama or servant in sight as we made our way through one tunnel after another; I suppose they were so sure we couldn't understand their lingo that they thought it a waste of time to watch us. At any rate, no one offered us any interruption while we clambered down three or four flights of stairs to a sort of cavern which had been artificially enlarged to make a big, vaulted cellar.

"Gentlemen"—Arkright looked from de Grandin to me and back again— "I don't know what it is, but something seems to get into a white man's blood when he goes to the far corners of the world. Men who wouldn't think of stealing a canceled postage stamp at home will loot a Chinese or Indian treasure house clean and never stop to give the moral aspects of their actions a second thought. That's the way it was with Clendenning and me. When we saw those stacks of golden ingots piled up in that cave like firewood around the sides of a New England woodshed, we just went off our heads. Nothing but the fact that the two of us couldn't so much as lift, much less carry, a single one of the bars kept us from making off with the treasure that minute.

"When we saw we couldn't carry any of it off we were almost wild. Scheme after scheme for getting away with the stuff was broached, only to be discarded. Stealth was no go, for we'd be sure to be seen if we tried to lead our bearers down the tunnels; force was out of the question, for the lamas outnumbered us ten to one, and the ugly-looking knives they wore were sufficient warning to us not to get them roused.

"Finally, when we were almost insane with futile planning, Clendenning suggested, 'Come on, let's get out of this cursed place. If we look around a little we may find a cache of jewels—we wouldn't need a derrick to carry off a couple of Imperial quarts of them, at any rate.'

"The underground passages were like a Cretan labyrinth, and we lost our way more than once while we stumbled around with no light but the flicker of Clendenning's electric torch, but after an hour or more of floundering over the damp, slippery stones of the tunnels, we came to a door stopped with a curtain of yak's hide. A fat, shaven-headed lama was sitting beside it, but he was sound asleep and we didn't trouble to waken him.

"Inside was a fair-sized room, partly hollowed out of the living rock, partly natural grotto. Multicolored flags draped from the low ceiling, each emblazoned with prayers or mottoes in Chinese ideographs or painted with effigies of holy saints or gods and goddesses. Big bands of silk cloth festooned down the walls. On each side of the doorway were prayer wheels ready to be spun, and a plate of beaten gold with the signs of the Chinese zodiac was above the lintel. On both sides of the approach to the altar were low, red-lacquered benches for the lamas and the choir. Small lamps with tiny, flickering flames threw their rays on the gold and silver vessels and candlesticks. At the extreme end of the room, veiling the sanctuary, hung a heavy curtain of yellow silk painted with Tibetan inscriptions.

"While we were standing there, wondering what our next move would be, the shuffle of feet and the faint tinkle of bells came to us. 'Quick,' Clendenning ordered, 'we mustn't be caught here!' He ran to the door, but it was too late, for the monk on guard was already awake, and we could see the faint gleam of light from candles borne in procession at the farther end of the corridor.

"What happened next was the turning-point in our lives, gentlemen. Without stopping to think, apparently, Clendenning acted. Snatching the heavy Browning from his belt he hit the guardian monk a terrific blow over the head, dragged him through the doorway and ripped off his robe. 'Here, Arkright, put this on!' he commanded as he lugged the unconscious man's body into a dark corner of the room and concealed himself behind one of the wall draperies.

"I slipped the yellow gown over my clothes and squatted in front of the nearest prayer wheel, spinning the thing like mad.

"I suppose you've already noticed I've a rather Mongolian cast of features?" he asked with a bleak smile.

"*Nom d'un fusil, Monsieur,* let us not discuss personal pulchritude or its lack, if you please!" de Grandin exclaimed testily. "Be so good as to advance with your narrative!"

"It wasn't vanity which prompted the question," Arkright replied. "Even with my beard, I'm sometimes taken for a Chinaman or a half-caste. In those days I was clean-shaven, and both Clendenning and I had had our heads shaved for sanitary reasons before setting out on our trip; so, with the lama's robe pulled up about my neck, in the dim light of the sanctuary I passed very well for one of the brotherhood, and not one of the monks in the procession gave me so much as a second glance.

"The ta-lama—I suppose you'd call him the abbot of the community—led the procession into the temple and halted before the sanctuary curtain. Two subordinate lamas pulled the veil aside, and out of the dim light from the flickering lamps there gradually appeared the great golden statue of Buddha seated in the Golden Lotus. The face of the image was indifferent and calm with only the softest gleam of light animating it, yet despite the repose of the bloated features it seemed to me there was something malignant about the countenance.

"Glancing up under my brows as I turned the prayer wheel, I could see the main idol was flanked on each side by dozens of smaller statues, each, apparently, of solid gold.

The ta-lama struck a great bronze gong with a padded drumstick to attract the Buddha's attention to his prayer; then closed his eyes, placed his hands together before his face and prayed. As his sleeve fell away, I noticed a rosary of red beads, like those I was later to know with such horror, looped about his left wrist.

"The subordinate lamas all bent their foreheads to the floor while their master prayed standing before the face of Buddha. Finally, the abbot lowered his hands, and his followers rose and gathered at the foot of the altar. He opened a small, ovenlike receptacle beneath the calyx of the Golden Lotus and took from it a little golden image which one of his subordinates placed among the ranks of subsidiary Buddhas to the right of the great idol. Then he replaced the golden statuette with another exactly like it, except fashioned of lead, closed the sliding door to the little cavity and turned from the altar. Then, followed by his company, he marched from the chapel, leaving Clendenning and me in possession.

"It didn't take us more than a minute to rush up those altar steps, swing back the curtain and open the door under the Golden Lotus, you may be sure.

"Inside the door was a compartment about the size of a moderately large gas stove's oven, and in it were the little image we had seen the ta-lama put in and half a dozen bars of lead, iron and copper, each the exact dimensions of the golden ingots we'd seen in the treasure chamber.

"I said the bars were lead, copper and iron, but that's a misstatement. All of them *had* been composed of those metals, *but every one was from a quarter to three-fourths solid gold.* Slowly, as a loaf of bread browns by degrees in a bake-oven, these bars of base metal were being transmuted into solid, virgin gold.

"Clendenning and I looked at each other in dumfounded amazement. We knew it couldn't be possible, yet there it was, before our eyes.

"For a moment Clendenning peered into the alchemist's cabinet, then suddenly gave a low whistle. At the extreme back of the 'oven' was a piece of odd-looking substance about the size of a child's fist; something like jade, something like amber, yet differing subtly from each. As Clendenning reached his hand into the compartment to indicate it with his finger the diamond setting of a ring he wore suddenly glowed and sparkled as though lit from within by living fire.

"'For Gawd's sake!' he exclaimed. 'D'ye see what it is, Arkright? It's the Philosopher's Stone, or I'm a Dutchman!'"

"The Philosopher's Stone?" I queried puzzled.

De Grandin made a gesture of impatience, but Arkright's queer, haunted eyes were on me, and he failed to notice the Frenchman's annoyance.

"Yes, Dr. Trowbridge," he replied. "The ancient alchemists thought there was a substance which would convert all base metals into gold by the power of its magical emanations, you know. Nearly all noted magi believed in it, and most of them attempted to make it synthetically. Many of the things we use in everyday life were discovered as by-products while the ancient were seeking to perfect the magic formula. Bötticher stumbled on the method of making Dresden porcelain while searching for the treasure; Roger Bacon evolved the composition of gunpowder in the same way; Gerber discovered the properties of acids, Van Helmont secured the first accurate data on the nature of gases and the famous Dr. Glauber discovered the medicinal salts which bear his name in the course of experiments in search of the Stone.

"Oddly enough, the ancients were on the right track all the while, though, of course, they could not know it; for they were wont to refer to the Stone as a sub-stratum—from the Latin *sub* and *stratus*, of course, signifying something spread under—and hundreds of years later scientists actually discovered the uranium oxide we know as pitchblende, the chief source of radium.

"Clendenning must have realized the queer substance in the altar was possessed of remarkable radioactive properties, for instead of attempting to grasp it in his fingers, as I should have done, he seized two of the altar candlesticks, and holding them like a pair of pincers, lifted the thing bodily from its setting; then, taking great care not to touch it, wrapped and rewrapped it in thin sheets of gold stripped from the altar ornaments. His data were incomplete, of course, but his reasoning, or perhaps his scientifically trained instinct, was accurate. You see, he inferred that since the 'stone' had the property of transmuting base metals with which it came in near contact into gold, gold would in all probability be the one element impervious to its radioactive rays, and consequently the only effective form of insulation. We had seen the ta-lama and his assistants grasp the little image of Buddha so recently transformed from lead to gold with their bare hands, so felt reasonably sure there would be no danger of radium burns from gold recently in contact with the substance, while there might be grave danger if we used anything but gold as wrappings for it.

"Clendenning was for strangling the lama we had stunned when we saw the procession headed toward the chapel, but I persuaded him to tie and gag the fellow and leave him hidden in the shrine; so when we had finished this we crept through the underground passages to the courtyard where our Bhotias were squatting beside the luggage and ordered them to break camp at once.

"The old ta-lama came to bid us a courteous good-bye and refused our offered payment for our entertainment, and we set off on the trail toward Nepal as if the devil were on our heels. He was, though we didn't know it then.

"Our way was mostly downhill, and everything seemed in our favor. We pushed on long after the sun had set, and by ten o'clock were well past the third *tach-davan*, or pass, from the lamasery. When we finally made camp Clendenning could hardly wait for our tent to be pitched before experimenting with our loot.

"Unwrapping the strange substance, we noticed that it glowed in the half-light of the tent with a sort of greenish phosphorescence, which made Clendenning christen it *Pi Yü*, which is Chinese for jade, and by that name we knew it thereafter. We put a pair of pistol bullets inside the wrappings, and lay down for a few hours' sleep with the *Pi Yü* between us. At five the next morning when we routed out the bearers and prepared to get under way, the entire leaden portions of the cartridges had been transmuted to gold and the copper powder-jackets were beginning to take on a decided golden glint. Forcing the shells off, we found the powder with which the cartridges were charged had become pure gold dust. This afforded us some valuable data. Lead was transmuted more quickly than copper, and semi-metallic substances like gunpowder were apparently even more susceptible than pure metals, though the powder's granular form might have sped its transmutation.

"We drove the bearers like slave-masters that day, and they were on the point of open mutiny when evening came. Poor devils, if they'd known what lay behind there'd have been little enough need to urge them on.

"Camp had been made and we had all settled down to a sleep of utter exhaustion when I first heard it. Very faint and far away it was, so faint as to be scarcely recognizable, but growing louder each second—the rumbling whistle of a wind of hurricane velocity shrieking and tearing down the passes.

"I kicked Clendenning awake, and together we made for a cleft in the rocks, yelling to our Bhotias to take cover at the same time. The poor devils were too waterlogged with sleep to realize what we shouted, and before we could give a second warning the thing was among them. Demonical blasts of wind so fierce we could almost see them shrieked and screamed and howled through the camp, each gust seeming to be aimed with dreadful accuracy. They whirled and twisted and tore about, scattering blazing logs like sparks from bursting firecrackers, literally tearing our tents into scraps no larger than a man's hand, picking up beasts and men bodily and hurling them against the cliff-walls till they were battered out of all semblance of their original form. Within five minutes our camp was reduced to such hopeless wreckage as may be seen only in the wake of a tornado, and Clendenning and I were the only living things within a radius of five miles.

"We were about to crawl from our hiding-place when something warned me the danger was not yet past and I grabbed at Clendenning's arm. He pulled away, but left the musette bag in which the *Pi Yü* was packed in my hand. Next moment he walked to the center of the shambles which had been our camp and began looking around in a dazed sort of way. Almost as he came to a halt, a terrific roar sounded and the entire air seemed to burn with the fury of a bursting lightning-bolt. Clendenning was wiped out as though he had never been—torn literally to dust by the unspeakable force of the lightning, and even the rock where he had stood was scarred and blackened as though water-blasted. But the terrible performance didn't stop there. Bolt after bolt of frightful lightning was hurled down like an accurately aimed barrage till every shred of our men, our yaks, our tents and our camp paraphernalia had not only been milled to dust, but completely obliterated.

"How long the artillery-fire from the sky lasted I do not know. To me, as I crouched in the little cave between the rocks, it seemed hours, years, centuries. Actually, I suppose, it kept up for something like five minutes. I think I must have fainted with the horror of it at the last, for the next thing I knew the sun was shining and the air was clear and icy-cold. No one passing could have told from the keenest observation that anything living had occupied our campsite in years. There was no sign or trace—absolutely none—of human or animal occupancy to be found. Only the cracked and lightning-blackened rocks bore witness to the terrible bombardment which had been laid down.

"I wasted precious hours in searching, but not a shred of cloth or flesh, not a lock of hair or a congealed drop of blood remained of my companions.

"The following days were like a nightmare—one of those awful dreams in which the sleeper is forever fleeing and forever pursued by something unnamably horrible. A dozen times a day I'd hear the skirling tempests rushing down the passes behind and scuttle to the nearest hole in the rocks like a panic-stricken rabbit when the falcon's shadow suddenly appears across its path. Sometimes I'd be storm-bound for hours while the wind howled like a troop of demons outside my retreat and the lightning-strokes rattled almost like hailstones on the rubble outside. Sometimes the vengeful tempest would last only a few minutes and I'd be released to fly like a mouse seeking sanctuary from the cat for a few miles before I was driven to cover once more.

"There were several packs of emergency rations in the musette bag, and I made out for drink by chipping off bits of ice from the frozen mountain springs and melting them in my tin cup, but I was a mere rack of bones and tattered hide encased in still more tattered clothes when I finally staggered into an outpost settlement in Nepal and fell babbling like an imbecile into the arms of a *sowar* sentry.

"The lamas' vengeance seemed confined to the territorial limits of Tibet, for I was unmolested during the entire period of my illness and convalescence in the Nepalese village.

"When I was strong enough to travel I was passed down country to my outfit, but I was still so ill and nervous that the company doctor gave me a certificate of physical disability and I was furnished with transportation home.

"I'd procured some scrap metal before embarking on the P. and O. boat, and in the privacy of my cabin I amused myself by testing the powers of the *Pi Yü*. Travel had not altered them, and in three days I had about ten pounds of gold where I'd had half that weight of iron.

"I was bursting with the wonderful news when I reached Waterbury, and could scarcely wait to tell my wife, but as I walked up the street toward my house an ugly, Mongolian-faced man suddenly stepped out from behind a roadside tree and barred my way. He did not utter a syllable but stood immovable in the path before me, regarding me with such a look of concentrated malice and hatred that my breath caught fast in my throat. For perhaps half a minute he glared at me, then raised his left hand and pointed directly at my face. As his sleeve fell back, I caught the gleam of a string of small, red beads looped round his wrist. Next instant he turned away and seemed to walk through an invisible door in the air—one moment I saw him, the next he had disappeared. As I stood staring stupidly at the spot where he had vanished, I felt a terrific blast of ice-cold wind blowing about me, tearing off my hat and sending me staggering against the nearest front-yard fence.

"The wind subsided in a moment, but it had blown away my peace of mind forever. From that instant I knew myself to be a marked man, a man whose only safety lay in flight and concealment.

"My daughter has told you the remainder of the story, how my wife was first to go, and how they found that accursed red bead which is the trade mark of the lamas' blood-vengeance clasped in her hand; how my son was the next victim of those Tibetan devils' revenge, then my daughter Charlotte; now she, too, is marked for destruction. Oh, gentlemen"—his eyes once more roved restlessly about—"if you only knew the inferno of terror and uncertainty I've been through during these terrible years, you'd realize I've paid my debt to those mountain fiends ten times over with compound interest compounded tenfold!'"

Our host ended his narrative almost in a shriek, then settled forward in his chair, chin sunk on breast, hands lying flaccidly in his lap, almost as if the death of which he lived in dread had overtaken him at last.

In the silence of the dimly lit drawing-room the logs burned with a softly hissing crackle; the little ormolu clock on the marble mantel beat off the seconds with hushed, hurrying strokes as though it held its breath and went on tiptoe in fear of something lurking in the shadows. Outside the curtained windows the subsiding storm moaned dismally, like an animal in pain.

Jules de Grandin darted his quick, birdlike glance from the dejected Arkright to his white-lipped daughter, then at me, then back again at Arkright. "*Tiens, Monsieur,*" he remarked, "it would appear you find yourself in what the Americans call one damn-bad fix. *Sacré bleu,* those ape-faced men of the mountains know how to hate well, and they have the powers of the tempest at their command, while you have nothing but Jules de Grandin.

"No matter; it is enough. I do not think you will be attacked again today. Make yourselves as happy as may be, keep careful watch for more of those damnation red beads, and notify me immediately one of them reappears. Meantime I go to dinner and to consult a friend whose counsel will assuredly show us a way out of our troubles. *Mademoiselle, Monsieur,* I wish you a very good evening." Bending formally from the hips, he turned on his heel and strode from the drawing-room.

"Do you think there was anything in that cock-and-bull story of Arkright's?" I asked as we walked home through the clear, rain-washed April evening.

"Assuredly," he responded with a nod. "It has altogether the ring of truth, my friend. From what he tells us, the *Pi Yü* Stone which he and his friend stole from the men of the mountain is merely some little-known form of radium, and what do we know of radium, when all is said and done? *Barbe d'un pou,* nothing or less!

"True, we know the terrific and incessant discharge of etheric waves consequent on the disintegration of the radium atoms is so powerful that even such known and powerful forces as electrical energy are completely destroyed by it. In the presence of radium, we know, non-conductors of electricity become conductors, differences of potential cease to exist and electroscopes and Leyden jars fail to retain their charges. But all this is but the barest fraction of the possibilities.

"Consider: Not long ago we believed the atom to be the ultimate particle of matter, and thought all atoms had individuality. An atom of iron, for instance, was to us the smallest particle of iron possible, and differed distinctly from an atom of hydrogen. But with even such little knowledge as we already have of radioactive substances we have learned that all matter is composed of varying charges of electricity. The atom, we now believe, consists of a proton composed of a charge of positive electricity surrounded by a number of electrons, or negative charges, and the number of these electrons determines the nature of the atom. Radium itself, if left to itself, disintegrated into helium, finally into lead. Suppose, however, the process be reversed. Suppose the radioactive emanations of this *Pi Yü* which Monsieur Arkright thieved away from the lamas, so affect the balance of protons and electrons of metals brought close to it as to change their atoms from atoms of zinc, lead or iron to atoms of pure gold. All that would be needed to do it would be a rearrangement of protons and electrons. The hypothesis is simple and believable, though not to be easily explained. You see?"

"No, I don't," I confessed, "but I'm willing to take your word for it. Meantime—"

"Meantime we have the important matter of dinner to consider," he interrupted with a smile as we turned into my front yard. "*Pipe d'un chameau*, I am hungry like a family of famished wolves with all this talk."

3

"TROWBRIDGE, *mon vieux*, THEY are at their devil's work again—have you seen the evening papers?" de Grandin exclaimed as he burst into the office several days later.

"Eh—what?" I demanded, putting aside the copy of Corwin's monograph on Multiple Neuritis and staring at him. "Who are 'they,' and what have 'they' been up to?"

"Who? Name of a little green man, those devils of the mountains, those Tibetan priests, those servants of the *Pi Yü* Stone!" he responded. "Peruse *le journal*, if you please." He thrust a copy of the afternoon paper into my hand, seated himself on the corner of the desk and regarded his brightly polished nails with an air of deep solicitude. I read:

GANGLAND SUSPECTED IN BEAUTY'S DEATH
Police believe it was to put the seal of eternal silence on her rouged lips that pretty Lillian Conover was "taken for a ride" late last night or early this morning. The young woman's body, terribly beaten and almost denuded of clothing, was found lying in one of the bunkers of the Sedgemoor Country Club's golf course near the Albemarle Pike shortly after six o'clock this morning by an employee of the club. From the fact that no blood was found near the body, despite the terrible mauling it had received, police believe the young woman had been "put on the spot" somewhere else, then brought to the deserted links and left there by the slayers or their accomplices.

The Conover girl was known to have been intimate with a number of questionable characters, and had been arrested several times for shoplifting and petty thefts. It is thought she might have learned something of the secrets of a gang of bootleggers or hijackers and threatened to betray them to rival gangsters, necessitating her silencing by the approved methods of gangland.

The body, when found, was clothed in the remnants of a gray ensemble with a gray fox neck-piece and a silver mesh bag was still looped about one of her wrists. In the purse were four ten-dollar bills and some silver, showing conclusively that robbery was not the motive for the crime.

The authorities are checking up the girl's movements on the day before her death, and an arrest is promised within twenty-four hours.

"U'm?" I remarked, laying down the paper.

"U'm?" he mocked. "May the devil's choicest imps fly away with your 'u'ms,' Friend Trowbridge. Come, get the car; we must be off."

"Off where?"

"Beard of a small blue pig, where, indeed, but to the spot where this so unfortunate girl's dead corpse was discovered?" Delay not, we must utilize what little light remains!"

The bunker where poor Lillian Conover's broken body had been found was a banked sand-trap in the golf course about twenty-five yards from the highway. Throngs of morbidly curious sightseers had trampled the smoothly kept fairways all day, brazenly defying the "PRIVATE PROPERTY—NO TRESPASSING" signs with which the links were posted.

To my surprise, de Grandin showed little annoyance at the multitude of footprints about, but turned at once to the business of surveying the terrain. After half an hour's crawling back and forth across the turf, he rose and dusted his trouser knees with a satisfied sigh.

"*Succès!*" he exclaimed, raising his hand, thumb and forefinger clasped together on something which reflected the last rays of the sinking sun with an ominous red glow. "Behold, *mon ami*, I have found it; it is even as I suspected."

Looking closely, I saw he held a red bead, about the size of a small hazelnut, the exact duplicate of the little globule Haroldine Arkright had discovered in her reticule.

"Well?" I asked.

"*Barbe d'un lièvre*, yes; it is very well, indeed," he assented with a vigorous nod. "I was certain I should find it here, but had I not, I should have been greatly worried. Let us return, good friend; our quest is done."

I knew better than to question him as we drove slowly home; but my ears were open wide for any chance remark he might drop. However, he vouchsafed no comment till we reached home; then he hurried to the study and put an urgent call through to the Arkright mansion. Five minutes later he joined me in the library, a smile of satisfaction on his lips. "It is as I thought," he announced. "Mademoiselle Haroldine went shopping yesterday afternoon and the unfortunate Conover girl picked her pocket in the store. Forty dollars was stolen—forty dollars *and a red bead!*"

"She told you this?" I asked. "Why—"

"*Non, non,*" he shook his head. "She did tell me of the forty dollars, yes; the red bead's loss I already knew. Recall, my friend, how was it the poor dead one was dressed, according to the paper?"

"Er—"

"*Précisément.* Her costume was a cheap copy, a caricature, if you please, of the smart ensemble affected by Mademoiselle Haroldine. Poor creature, she plied her pitiful trade of pocket-picking once too often, removed the contents of Haroldine's purse, including the sign of vengeance which had been put there, *le bon Dieu* knows how, and walked forth to her doom. Those who watched for a gray-clad woman with the fatal red ball seized upon her and called down their winds of destruction, even as they did upon the camp of Monsieur Arkright in the mountains of Tibet long years ago. Yes, it is undoubtlessly so."

"Do you think they'll try again?" I asked. "They've already muffed things twice, and—"

"And, as your proverb has it, the third time is the charm," he cut in. "Yes, my friend, they will doubtlessly try again, and again, until they have worked their will, or been diverted. We must bend our energies toward the latter consummation."

"But that's impossible!" I returned. "If those lamas are powerful enough to seek their victims out in France, England and this country and kill them, there's not much chance for the Arkrights in flight, and it's hardly likely we'll be able to argue them out of their determination to exact payment for the theft of their—"

"*Zut!*" he interrupted with a smile. "You do talk much but say little, Friend Trowbridge. Me, I think it highly probable we shall convince the fish-faced gentlemen from Tibet they have more to gain by foregoing their vengeance than by collecting their debt."

4

HARRISONVILLE'S NEWEST CITIZEN HAD delayed her debut with truly feminine capriciousness, and my vigil at City Hospital had been long and nerve-racking. Half an hour before I had resorted to the Weigand-Martin method of ending the performance, and, shaking with nervous reaction, took the red, wrinkled and astonishingly vocal morsel of humanity from the nurse's hands and laid it in its mother's arms; then, nearer exhaustion than I cared to admit, set out for home and bed.

A rivulet of light trickled under the study door and the murmur of voices mingled with the acrid aroma of de Grandin's cigarette came to me as I let myself in the front door. "*Eh bien*, my friend," the little Frenchman was asserting, "I damn realize that he who sups with the devil must have a long spoon; therefore I have requested your so invaluable advice.

"Trowbridge, *mon vieux*," his uncannily sharp ears recognized my tread as I stepped softly into the hall, "may we trespass on your time a moment? It is of interest."

With a sigh of regret for my lost sleep I put my obstetrical kit on a chair and pushed open the study door.

Opposite de Grandin was seated a figure which might have been the original of the queer little manikins with which Chinese ivory-carvers love to ornament their work. Hardly more than five feet tall, his girth was so great that he seemed to overflow the confines of the armchair in which he lounged. His head, almost totally void of hair, was nearly globular in shape, and the smooth, hairless skin seemed stretched drum-tight over the fat with which his skull was generously upholstered. Cheeks plump to the point of puffiness almost forced his oblique eyes shut; yet, though his eyes could scarcely be seen, it required no deep intuition to know that they always saw. Between his broad, flat nose and a succession of chins was set, incongruously a small, sensitive mouth, full-lipped but mobile, and drooping at the corners in a sort of perpetual sad smile.

"Dr. Feng," de Grandin introduced, "this is my very good friend, Dr. Trowbridge. Trowbridge, my friend, this is Dr. Feng Yuin-han, whose wisdom is about to enable us to foil the machinations of those wicked ones who threaten Mademoiselle Haroldine. Proceed, if you please, *cher ami*," he motioned the fat little Chinaman to continue the remark he had cut short to acknowledge the introduction.

"It is rather difficult to explain," the visitor returned in a soft, unaccented voice, "but if we stop to remember that the bird stands midway between the reptile and the mammal we may perhaps understand why it is that the cock's blood is most acceptable to those elemental forces which my unfortunate superstitious countrymen seek to propitiate in their temples. These malignant influences were undoubtedly potent in the days we refer to as the age of reptiles, and it may be the cock's lineal descent from the pterodactyl gives his blood the quality of possessing certain emanations soothing to the tempest spirits. In any event, I think you would be well advised to employ such blood in your protective experiments."

"And the ashes?" de Grandin put in eagerly.

"Those I can procure for you by noon tomorrow. Camphor wood is something of a rarity here, but I can obtain enough for your purpose, I am sure."

"*Bon, très bon!*" the Frenchman exclaimed delightedly. "If those camel-faces will but have the consideration to wait our preparations, I damn think we shall tender them the party of surprise. Yes. *Parbleu*, we shall astonish them!"

Shortly after noon the following day an asthmatic Ford delivery wagon bearing the picture of a crowing cockerel and the legend

P. GRASSO

Vendita di Pollame Vivi

on its weatherworn leatherette sides drew up before the house, and an Italian youth in badly soiled corduroys and with a permanent expression indicative of some secret sorrow climbed lugubriously from the driver's seat, took a covered two-gallon can, obviously originally intended as a container for Quick's Grade A Lard, from the interior of the vehicle and advanced toward the front porch.

"Docta de Grandin 'ere?" he demanded as Nora McGinnis, my household factotum, answered his ring.

"No, he ain't," the indignant Nora informed him, "an' if he wuz, 'tis at th' back door th' likes o' you should be inquirin' fer 'im!"

The descendant of the Cæsars was in no mood for argument. "You taka dissa bucket an' tella heem I breeg it—Pete Grasso," he returned, thrusting the lard tin into the scandalized housekeeper's hands. "You tella heem I sella da han, I sella da roosta, too, an' I keela heem w'an my customers ask for it; but I no lika for sella da blood. No, *santissimo Dio*, not me! *Perchè il sangue è la vita*—how you say? Da blood, he are da life; I not lika for carry heem aroun'."

"Howly Mither, is it blood ye're afther givin' me ter hold onto?" exclaimed Nora in rising horror. "Ye murtherin' dago, come back 'ere an' take yer divilish—"

But P. Grasso, dealer in live poultry, had cranked his decrepit flivver into a state of agitated life and set off down the street, oblivious of the choice insults which Mrs. McGinnis sent in pursuit of him.

"Sure, Dr. Trowbridge, sor," she confided as she entered the consulting-room, the lard tin held at arm's length, "'tis th' fine gintleman Dr. de Grandin is entirely; but he do be afther doin' some crazy things at times. Wud ye be afther takin' charge o' this mess o' blood fer him? 'Tis meself as wouldn't touch it wid a fifthy-foot pole, so I wouldn't, once I've got it out o' me hands!"

"Well," I laughed as I espied a trim little figure turning into my front yard, "here he comes now. You can tell him your opinion of his practises if you want."

"Ah, Docthor, darlin', ye know I'd niver have th' heart to scold 'im," she confessed with a shamefaced grin. "Sure, he's th'—"

The sudden hysterical cachinnation of the office telephone bell cut through her words, and I turned to the shrilling instrument.

For a moment there was no response to my rather impatient "Hello?"; then dimly, as one entering a darkened room slowly begins to descry objects about him, I made out the hoarse, rale-like rasp of deep-drawn, irregular breathing.

"Hello?" I repeated, more sharply.

"Dr. Trowbridge," a low, almost breathless feminine voice whispered over the wire, "this is Haroldine Arkright. Can you come right over with Dr. de Grandin? Right away? Please. It—it's *here!*"

"Right away!" I called back, and wheeled about, almost colliding with the little Frenchman, who had been listening over my shoulder.

"Quick, speed, haste!" he cried, as I related her message. "We must rush, we must hurry, we must fly, my friend! There is not a second to lose!"

As I charged down the hall and across the porch to my waiting car he stopped long enough to seize the lard tin from beside my desk and two bulky paper parcels from a hall chair, then almost trod on my heels, in his haste to enter the motor.

5

"Not here, *Monsieur*, if you please," de Grandin ordered as he surveyed the living-room where Arkright and his daughter awaited us. "Is there no room without furniture, where we can meet the foeman face to face? I would fight over a flat terrain, if possible."

"There's a vacant bedroom on the next floor," Arkright replied, "but—"

"No buts, if you please; let us ascend at once, immediately, right away!" the Frenchman interrupted. "Oh, make haste, my friends! Your lives depend upon it, I do assure you!"

About the floor of the empty room de Grandin traced a circle of chicken's blood, painting a two-inch-wide ruddy border on the bare boards, and inside the outer circle he drew another, forcing Haroldine and her father within it. Then, with a bit of rag, he wiped a break in the outside line, and opening one of his paper parcels proceeded to scatter a thin layer of soft, white wood-ashes over the boards between the two circles.

"Now, *mon vieux*, if you will assist," he turned to me, ripping open the second package and bringing to light a tin squirt-gun of the sort used to spray insecticide about a room infested with mosquitoes.

Dipping the nozzle of the syringe into the blood-filled lard tin, he worked the plunger back and forth a moment, then handed the contrivance to me. "Do you stand at my left," he commanded, "and should you see footprints in the ashes, spray the fowl's blood through the air above them. Remember, my friend, it is most important that you act with speed."

"Footprints in the ashes—" I began incredulously, wondering if he had lost his senses, but a sudden current of glacial air sweeping through the room chilled me into silence.

"Ah! of the beautiful form is *Mademoiselle*, and who was I to know that cold wind of Tibetan devils would display it even more than this exquisite *robe d'Orient?*" said de Grandin.

Clad in a wondrous something, she explained fright had so numbed her that dressing had been impossible.

"When did you first know they were here?" de Grandin whispered, turning his head momentarily toward the trembling couple inside the inner circle, then darting a watchful glance about the room as though he looked for an invisible enemy to materialize from the air.

"I found the horrible red ball in my bath," Haroldine replied in a low, trembling whisper. "I screamed when I saw it, and Daddy got up to come to me, and there was one of them under his ash-tray; so I telephoned your house right away, and—"

"*S-s-st!*" the Frenchman's sibilant warning cut her short. "*Garde à vous*, Friend Trowbridge! *Fixe!*" As though drawing a saber from its scabbard he whipped the keen steel sword blade from his walking-stick and swished it whiplike through the air. "The cry is still '*On ne passe pas!*' my friends!"

There was the fluttering of the tiny breeze along the bedroom floor, not like a breeze from outside, but an eery, tentative sort of wind, a wind which trickled lightly over the doorsill, rose to a blast, paused a moment in reconnaissance, then crept forward experimentally, as though testing the strength of our defenses.

A light, pit-pattering noise, as though an invisible mouse were circling the room, sounded from the shadows; then, to my horrified amazement, there appeared the print of a broad, naked foot in the film of ashes de Grandin had spread upon the floor!

Wave on wave of goose-flesh rose on my arms and along my neck as I watched the first print followed by a second, for there was no body above them, no sign nor trace of any alien presence in the place; only, as the keys of a mechanical piano are depressed as the strings respond to the notes of the reeling record, the smooth coating of ashes gave token of the onward march of some invisible thing.

"Quick, my friend, shoot where you see the prints!" de Grandin cried in a shrill, excited voice, and I thrust the plunger of my pump home, sending out a shower of ruddy spray.

As invisible ink takes form when the paper is held before a flame, there was suddenly outlined in the empty air before us the visage of—

"*Sapristi!* 'Tis Yama himself, King of Hell! God of Death! *Holà, mon brave*," de Grandin called almost jocularly as the vision took form wherever the rain of fowl's blood struck, "it seems we meet face to face, though you expected it not. *Nom d'un porc*, is this the courtesy of your country? You seem not overjoyed to meet me.

"Lower, Friend Trowbridge," he called from the corner of his mouth, keeping wary eyes fixed upon the visitant, "aim for his legs; there is a trick I wish to show him."

Obediently, I aimed the syringe at the footless footprints in the ashes, and a pair of broad, naked feet sprang suddenly into view.

"*Bien*," the Frenchman commended, then with a sudden forward thrust of his foot engaged the masked Mongolian's ankle in a grapevine twist and sent the fellow sprawling to the floor. The blue and gold horror that was the face of Yama came off, disclosing a leering, slant-eyed lama.

"Now, *Monsieur*," de Grandin remarked, placing his sword-point against the other's throat directly above the palpitating jugular vein, "I damn think perhaps you will listen to reason, *hein?*"

The felled man gazed malignantly into his conqueror's face, but neither terror nor surrender showed in his sullen eyes.

"*Morbleu*, he is a brave savage, this one," de Grandin muttered, then lapsed into a wailing, singsong speech the like of which I had never heard.

A look of incredulous disbelief, then of interest, finally of amazed delight, spread over the copper-colored features of the fallen man as the little Frenchman progressed. Finally he answered with one or two coughing ejaculations, and at a sign from de Grandin rose to his feet and stood with his hands lifted above his head.

"Monsieur Arkright," the Frenchman called without taking his eyes from his captive, "have the goodness to fetch the *Pi Yü* Stone without delay. I have made a treaty with this emissary of the lamas. If you return his treasure to him at once he will repair forthwith to his lamasery and trouble you and yours no more."

"But what about my wife, and my children these fiends killed?" Arkright expostulated. "Are they to go scot-free? How do I know they'll keep their word? I'm damned if I'll return the *Pi Yü!*"

"You will most certainly be killed if you do not," de Grandin returned coolly. "As to your damnation, I am a sinful man, and do not presume to pronounce judgment on you, though I fear the worst unless you mend your morals. Come, will you return this man his property, or do I release him and bid him do his worst?"

Muttering imprecations, Arkright stepped across the barrier of blood, left the room and returned in a few minutes with a small parcel wrapped in what appeared to be thin plates of gold.

De Grandin took it from his hand and presented it to the Tibetan with a ceremonious bow.

"*Ki lao yeh hsieh ti to lo*," the yellow man pressed his clasped hands to his breast and bowed nearly double to the Frenchman.

"*Parbleu*, yes, and Dr. Trowbridge, too," my little friend returned, indicating me with a wave of his hand.

The Tibetan bent ceremoniously toward me as de Grandin added, "*Ch'i kan.*"

"What did he say?" I demanded, returning the Asiatic's salute.

"He says, 'The honorable, illustrious sir has my heartfelt thanks,' or words to that effect, and I insist that he say the same of you, my friend," de Grandin returned. "Name of a small green pig, I do desire that he understand there are two honorable men in the room besides himself.

"*En avant, mon brave,*" he motioned the Tibetan toward the door with his sword, then lowered his point with a flourish, saluting the Arkrights with military punctilio.

"Mademoiselle Haroldine," he said, "it is a great pleasure to have served you. May your approaching marriage be a most happy one.

"Monsieur Arkright, I have saved your life, and, though against your will, restored your honor. It is true you have lost your gold, but self-respect is a more precious thing. Next time you desire to steal, permit that I suggest you select a less vengeful victim than a Tibetan brotherhood. *Parbleu*, those savages they have no sense of humor at all! When a man robs them, they take it with the worst possible grace."

"**P**ipe d'un chameau"—Jules de Grandin brushed an imaginary fleck of dust from the sleeve of his dinner jacket and refilled his liqueur glass—"it has been a most satisfactory day, Friend Trowbridge. Our experiment was one grand, unqualified success; we have restored stolen property to its rightful owners, and I have told that Monsieur Arkright what I think of him."

"U'm," I murmured. "I suppose it's all perfectly clear to you, but I'm still in the dark about it all."

"Perfectly," he agreed with one of his quick, elfin smiles. "Howeverly, that can be remedied. Attend me, if you please:

"When first we interviewed Mademoiselle Haroldine and her father, I smelt the odor of Tibet in this so strange business. Those red beads, they could have come from but one bit of jewelry, and that was the rosary of a Buddhist monk of Tibet. Yes. Now, in the course of my travels in that devil-infested land, I had seen those old lamas do their devil-dances and command the elements to obey their summons and wreak vengeance on their enemies. 'Very well,' I tell me, 'if this be a case of lamas' magic, we must devise magic which will counteract it.'

"'Of course,' I agree with me. 'For every ill there is a remedy. Men living in the lowlands know cures for malaria; those who inhabit the peaks know the cure for mountain fever. They must do so, or they die. Very well, is it not highly probable that the Mongolian people have their own safeguards against these mountain devils? If it were not so, would not Tibet completely dominate all China?'

"'You have right,' I compliment me, 'but whom shall we call on for aid?'

"Thereupon I remember that my old friend, Dr. Feng Yuin-han, whom I have known at the Sorbonne, is at present residing in New York, and it is to him I send my message for assistance. *Parbleu*, when he comes he is as full of wisdom as a college professor attempts to appear! He tells me much in our nighttime interview before you arrive from your work of increasing the population. I learn from him, for instance, that when these old magicians of the mountains practise their devil's art, they automatically limit their powers. Invisible they may become, yes; but while invisible, they may not overstep a pool, puddle or drop of chicken blood. For some strange reason, such blood makes a barrier which they can not pass and across which they can not hurl a missile nor send their destroying winds or devastating lightning-flashes. Further, if chicken blood be cast upon them their invisibility at once melts away, and while they are in the process of becoming visible in such circumstances their physical strength is greatly reduced. One man of normal lustiness would be a match for fifty of them half visible, half unseen because of fresh fowl's blood splashed on them.

"*Voilà* I have my grand strategy of defense already mapped out for me. From the excellent Pierre Grasso I buy much fresh chicken blood, and from Dr. Feng I obtain the ashes of the mystic camphor tree. The blood I spread around in an almost-circle, that our enemy may attack us from one side only, and inside the outer stockade of gore I scatter camphor wood ashes that his footprints may become visible and betray his position to us. Then, inside our outer ramparts, I draw a second complete circle of blood which the enemy can not penetrate at all, so that Monsieur Arkright, but most of all his so charming daughter, may be safe. Then I wait.

"Presently comes the foe. He circles our first line of defense, finds the break I have purposely left, and walks into our trap. In the camphor wood ashes his all-invisible feet leave visible footprints to warn of his approach.

"With your aid, then, I do spray him with the blood as soon as his footprints betray him, and make him visible so that I may slay him at my good convenience. But he are no match for me. *Non*, Jules de Grandin would not call it the sport to kill such as he; it would not be fair. Besides, is there not much to be said on his side? I think so.

"It was the cupidity of Monsieur Arkright and no other thing which brought death upon his wife and children. We have no way of telling that the identical man whom I have overthrown murdered those unfortunate ones, and it is not just to take his life for his fellows' crimes. As for legal justice, what court would listen believingly to our story? *Cordieu*, to relate what we have seen these last few days to the ordinary lawyer would be little better than confessing ourselves mad or infatuated with too much of the so execrable liquor which your prosperous bootleggers supply. Me, I have no wish to be thought a fool.

"Therefore, I say to me, 'It is best that we call this battle a draw. Let us give back to the men of the mountains that which is theirs and take their promise that they will no longer pursue Monsieur Arkright and Mademoiselle Haroldine. Let there be no more beads from the Devil's rosary scattered across their path.'

"Very good. I make the equal bargain with the Tibetan; his property is returned to him and—

"My friend, I suffer!"

"Eh?" I exclaimed, shocked at the tragic face he turned to me.

"*Nom d'un canon*, yes; my glass is empty again!"

The House without a Mirror

MY FRIEND JULES DE Grandin was in one of his gayest moods. Reclining against the plank seat of the john-boat he gazed with twinkling, bright blue eyes at the cloudless Carolina sky, tweaked the tips of his diminutive blond mustache till the waxed hairs thrust out to right and left of his small, thin-lipped mouth as sharply as a pair of twin fish-hooks, and gave vent to his own private translation of a currently popular song:

"Oui, nous n'avons plus de bananes;
Nous n'avons plus de bananes aujourd'hui!"

he caroled merrily.

"Say, looka yere, boss," protested our colored factotum from the boat's stern, "does yo' all want ter shoot enny o' dem birds, youh's best be cuttin' out dat music. Dese yere reed-birds is pow'ful skittish, wid so many no'then gemmen comin' dhown yere an' bangin' away all ober de place wid deir pump-guns, an—"

"*Là, là, mon brave,*" the little Frenchman interrupted, "of what importance is it whether we kill ten dozen or none at all of the small ones? Me, I had as soon return to Monsieur Gregory's lodge with empty bag as stagger homeward with a load of little feathered corpses. Have not these, God's little ones, a good right to live? Why should we slay them when our bellies are well filled with other things?"

The Negro boy regarded him in hang-jawed amazement. That anyone, especially a "gemman" from the fabulous "no'th," should feel compunction at slaughtering the reed-birds swarming among the wild rice was something beyond his comprehension. With an inarticulate grunt he thrust his ten-foot pole into the black mud bottom of the swamp canal and drove the punt toward a low-lying island at the farther end of the lagoon-like opening in the waterway. "Does yo' all crave ter eat now?" he asked. "Ef yuh does, dis yere lan' is as dry as enny 'round yere, an—"

"But of course," de Grandin assented, reaching for the well-filled luncheon hamper our host had provided. "I am well-nigh perished with hunger, and if Monsieur Gregory has furnished brandy as well as food—*Mordieu*, may the hairs of his head each become a waxen taper to light his way to glory when he dies!"

The hamper was quickly unpacked and we sat cross-legged on a slight eminence to discuss assorted sandwiches, steaming coffee from vacuum bottles and some fine old cognac from a generously proportioned flask.

A faint rustling in the short grass at de Grandin's elbow drew my attention momentarily from my half-eaten sandwich. "Look out!" I cried sharply.

"Lawd Gawd, boss, don' move!" the colored boy added in a horrified tone.

Creeping unnoticed through the short, sun-dried vegetation with which the island was covered, a huge brown moccasin had approached within a foot of the little Frenchman and paused, head uplifted, yellow, forked tongue flickering lambently from venom-filled mouth.

We sat in frozen stillness. A move from the Negro or me might easily have irritated the reptile into striking blindly; the slightest stirring by de Grandin would certainly have invited immediate disaster. I could hear the colored guide's breath rasping fearfully through his flaring nostrils; the pounding of my own heart sounded in my ears. I ran my tongue lightly over suddenly parched lips, noting, with that strange ability for minute inventory we develop at such times, that the membrane seemed rough as sandpaper.

Actually, I suppose, we held our statue-still pose less than a minute. To me it seemed a century. I felt the pupils of my eyes narrowing and ceasing to function as if I had just emerged from a darkened room into brilliant sunlight, and the hand which half raised the sandwich to my lips was growing heavy as a leaden fist when sudden diversion came.

Like a beam of light shot through a moonless night something whizzed through the still afternoon air from a thicket of scrub trees some thirty feet behind us; there was a sharp, clipping sound, almost like a pair of scissors snipping shut, and the deadly reptile's head struck the ground with a smacking impact. Next instant the foul creature's blotched body writhed upward, coiling and wriggling about a three-foot shaft of slender, flexible wood like the serpent round Mercury's caduceus. A feather-tipped arrow had cleft the snake through the neck an inch or less behind its ugly, wedged-shaped head, and pinned it to the earth.

"Thank you, friend," de Grandin cried, turning toward the direction from which the rescuing shaft had sped. "I know not who you are, but I am most greatly in your debt, for—"

He broke off, his lips refusing to frame another word, his small, round eyes staring unbelievingly at the visage which peered at us between the leaves.

The Negro boy followed the Frenchman's glance, emitted a single shrill, terrified yell, turned a half somersault backward, regaining his feet with the agility of a cat and scurrying down the mud-flat where our boat lay beached. "Lawdy Gawdy," he moaned, "hit's de *ha'nt*; hit's de swamp ha'nt, sho's yuh bo'n! Lawd Gawd, lemme git erway fr'm heah! Please, suh, Gawd, sabe me, sabe dis pore nigger fr'm de ha'nt!"

He reached our punt, clambered aboard and shoved off, thrusting his pole against the lagoon bottom and driving the light craft across the water with a speed like that of a racing motorboat. Ere de Grandin or I could more than frame a furious shout he rounded the curve of a dense growth of wild rice and disappeared as completely as though dissolved into the atmosphere.

The Frenchman turned to me with a grimace. "*Cordieu*," he remarked, "we would seem to be between the devil and the sea, Friend Trowbridge. Did you, by any chance, see what I saw a moment hence?"

"Ye-es; I think so," I assented. "If you saw something so dreadful no nightmare ever equaled it—"

"*Zut!*" he laughed. "Let us not be ungrateful. Ugly the face is, I concede; but its owner did us at least one good turn." He pointed to the still-writhing snake, pinned fast to the earth by the sharp-tipped arrow. "Come, let us seek the ugly one. Though he be the devil's own twin for ugliness, he is no less deserving of our thanks. Perhaps he will show further amiability and point out an exit from this doubly damned morass of mud and serpents."

Treading cautiously, lest we step upon another snake, we advanced to the clump of scrub trees whence the repulsive face had peered. Several times de Grandin hailed the unseen monster whose arrow had saved his life, but no answer came from the softly rustling bushes. At length we pushed our way among the shrubs, and reached the covert where our unknown friend had been concealed. Nothing rewarded our search, though we passed entirely through the coppice several times.

I was about ready to drop upon the nearest rotting log for a moment's rest when de Grandin's shrill cry hailed me. "*Regardez-vous*," he commanded, pointing to the black, greasy mud which sloped into the stagnant water.

Clearly outlined in the mire as though engraved with a sculptor's tool was the imprint of a tiny, mocassined foot, so small it could have been made only by a child or a daintily formed woman.

"Well—" I began, then paused for lack of further comment.

"Well, indeed, good friend," de Grandin assented with a vigorous nod. "Do not you understand its significance?"

"U'm—can't say I do," I confessed.

"Ah bah, you are stupid!" he shot back. "Consider: There is no sign of a boat having been beached here; there is nothing to which a boat could have been tied within ten feet of the water's edge. We have searched the island, we know we are alone here. What then? How came the possessor of this so lovely foot here, and *how did she leave?*"

"Hanged if I know," I returned.

"Agreed," he acquiesced, "but is it not fair to assume that she waded through yonder water to that strip of land? I think so. Let us test it."

We stepped into the foul marsh-water, felt the mud sucking at our boots, then realized that the bottom was firm enough to hold us. Tentatively, step by cautious step, we forded the forty-foot channel, finding it nowhere more than waist-deep, and, bedraggled, mud-caked and thoroughly uncomfortable, finally clambered up the loamy bank of the low peninsula which jutted into the marsh-lake opposite the island of our adventure.

"*Tiens*, it seems I was right, as usual, Friend Trowbridge," the Frenchman announced as we floundered up the bank to solid ground. Again, limned in the soft, moist earth, was a tiny, slender footprint, followed by others leading toward the rank-growing woods.

"I may be wrong," he admitted, surveying the trail, "but unless I am more mistaken than I think, we have but to follow our noses and these shapely tracks to extricate ourselves. Come; *allez vous en!*"

Simple as the program sounded, it was difficult of accomplishment. The guiding footprints trailed off and lost themselves among the dead, crackling leaves with which the wood was paved, and the thick-set trees and thicker under-growth disclosed nothing like a path. Beating the hampering bushes aside with our guns, staggering and crashing through thorny thickets by main strength and direct assault, we forced our way, turning aside from time to time as the land became spongy with seeping bogwater or an arm of the green, stagnant swamp barred our advance. We progressed slowly, striving to attain open country before darkness overtook us, but before we realized it twilight fell and we were obliged to admit ourselves hopelessly lost.

"No use, old chap," I advised. "The more we struggle, the deeper in we get; with night coming on our chances of being mired in the swamp are a hundred to one. Best make camp and wait for daylight. We can build a fire and—"

"May Satan bake me in his oven if we do!" de Grandin interrupted. "Are we the Babes in the Woods that we should lie down here and wait for death and the kindly ministrations of the robin-redbreasts! Come away, my friend; we shall assuredly win through!"

He returned to the assault with redoubled vigor, beat his way some twenty yards farther through the underbrush, then gave a loud, joyous hail.

"See what is arrived, Friend Trowbridge!" he called. "*Cordieu*, did I not promise we should find it?"

Heavy-footed, staggering with fatigue, I dragged myself to where he stood, and stared in amazement at the barrier barring our path.

Ten feet away stood an ancient wall, gray with weather and lichen-spotted with age. Here and there patches of the stucco with which it had originally been dressed had peeled away, exposing the core of antique firebrick.

"Right or left?" de Grandin asked, drawing a coin from his pocket. "Heads we proceed right; tails, left." He spun the silver disk in the air and caught it between his palms. "*Bon*, we go right," he announced, shouldering his gun and turning on his heel to follow the wall.

A few minutes' walk brought us to a break in the barrier where four massive posts of roughly dressed stone stood sentry. There should have been gates between them, but only ancient hand-wrought hinges, almost eaten away with rust, remained. Graven in the nearest pillar was an escutcheon on which had been carved some sort of armorial device, but the moss of many decades had smothered the crest so that its form was indistinguishable.

Beyond the yawning gateway stood a tiny, box-like gatekeeper's lodge, like the wall, constructed of brick faced with stucco. Tiles had scuffed from its antiquated roof, the panes of old, green bottle-glass were smashed from its leaded casements; the massive door of age-discolored oak leaned outward drunkenly, its sole support, a single lower hinge with joints long since solidified with rust.

Before us stretched the avenue, a mere unkept, overgrown trail straggling between two rows of honey locusts. Alternating shafts of moonlight and shadow barred its course like stripes upon a convict's clothes. Nothing moved among the trees, not even a moth or a bird belated in its homeward flight. Despite myself, I shivered as I gazed on the desolation of this place of bygone splendor. It was as if the ghosts of ten generations of long-dead gentlefolk rose up and bade us stay our trespassing steps.

"*Eh bien*, it is not cheerful," de Grandin admitted with a somewhat rueful grin, "but there is the promise of four walls and at least the remnant of a roof beyond. Let us see what we shall see, Friend Trowbridge."

We passed between the empty gate-pillars and strode up the driveway, traversing perhaps a hundred yards before we saw the house—a low, age-ravaged building of rough gray stone set in the midst of a level, untended grass plot and circled by a fourteen-foot moat filled with green, stagnant water in which floated a few despondent-looking lily pads. The avenue continued to a crumbling causeway, broke abruptly at the moat's lip, then took up its course to the grilled entrance of the house. Two tumbledown pillars reared astride the driveway at the farther side of the break, and swung between them, amazingly, was a mediæval drawbridge of stout oaken planks held up by strands of strong, almost new Manila hawser.

"*Grand diable*," the Frenchman murmured wonderingly, "a *château fort*—here! How comes it?"

"I don't know," I responded, "but here it is, and it's in tolerable repair—what's more, someone lives in it. See, there's a light behind that window."

He looked, then nodded briefly. "My friend," he assured me, "I damnation think we shall eat and sleep within walls tonight.

"*Allo*," he shouted through cupped hands, "*holà, là-haut*; we hunger, we thirst, we are lost; we are miserable!"

Twice more he hailed the silent house before lights stirred behind the narrow windows piercing its walls. Finally the iron grille guarding the door swung slowly outward and an elderly, stoop-shouldered man shuffled out, an old-fashioned bull's-eye lantern dangling in his left hand, a modern and efficient-looking repeating rifle cradled in the crook of his right elbow.

"Who calls?" he asked, peering through the darkness and pausing to flash his smoky lantern in our direction. "Who is it?"

"*Mordieu*, two weary, wayworn travelers, no more," de Grandin answered. "All afternoon we have battled with this *sacré* woodland, and lost ourselves most thoroughly. We are tired, *Monsieur*, we are enervated, and the magnitude of our hunger is matched only by that of our thirst."

"Where are you from?" the other challenged, placing his lamp on the ground and surveying us suspiciously.

"From the hunting-lodge of Monsieur Wardman Gregory. In a fortuneless moment we accepted his invitation to come South and hunt the detestable little birds which frequent these morasses. This afternoon our seventy-times-damned traitor of a guide fled from us, leaving us to perish in a wilderness infested by snakes and devil-faced monsters of the woods. Surely, you will not deny us shelter?"

"If you're Gregory's guests it's all right," the other returned, "but if you come from *him*—you needn't look for mercy if I find it out."

"*Monsieur*," de Grandin assured him, "half of what you say is intelligible, the other half is meaningless. The 'him' of whom you speak is a total stranger to us; but our hunger and fatigue is a real and present thing. Permit that we enter, if you please."

The master of the house eyed us suspiciously a second time; then he turned from his inspection and drew back the ratchet which held the hawser-drum. Creakingly, the drawbridge descended and bumped into place against its stone sill. "Come over," the old man called, taking up his gun and holding it in readiness, "but remember, the first false move you make means a bullet."

"*Parbleu*, he is churlish, this one," de Grandin whispered as we strode across the echoing planks.

Arrived beyond the moat, we assisted our unwilling host to rewind the ropes operating the bridge, and in compliance with a gesture containing more of suspicion than courtesy preceded him to the house.

THE BUILDING'S GRAY, BARE rooms were in keeping with its gray, dilapidated exterior; age and lack of care had more than softened the antique furnishings, it had reduced them to a dead level of tonelessness, without accent, making the big, stone-paved hall in which they stood seem empty and monotonous.

Our host put down his lantern and gun, then called abruptly: "Minerva—Poseidon—we have guests, prepare some food, make haste!"

Through a swinging door connecting with a rear apartment an ancient, wrinkled little yellow woman sidled, paused at the threshold and looked about her uncertainly. "Did yuh say we all has *guests*, Marse Jawge?" she asked incredulously.

"Yes," replied her master, "they've been traveling all day, too. Shake up something to eat, quickly."

"Yas, suh," she returned and scuttled back to her kitchen like a frightened rabbit scurrying into its burrow.

She reappeared in a few minutes, followed by an aged and intensely black little man, each of them bearing a tray on which were slices of cold roast fowl, fresh white bread, preserved fruits, coffee and decanters of red, home-made wine. These they set on the massive table occupying the center of the room, and spread fresh napkins of coarse but carefully bleached linen, then stood waiting attentively.

A certain fumbling ineptness in their movements made me glance sharply at them a second time. Realization was slow in coming, but when it burst upon me I could hardly repress an exclamation. Both the aged servants were stone-blind; only the familiarity of long association enabled them to move about the room with the freedom of those possessing vision. I glanced hastily at de Grandin, and noted that his narrow, expressive face was alight with curiosity as he beheld the expressionless, sightless eyes of the servants.

Our host accompanied us to table and poured a cup of coffee and a glass of wine for himself as soon as we began our attack on the more substantial portions of the menu. He was a man well advanced in years, thin-faced, lean and sun-burned almost to the point of desiccation. Time had not dealt gently with him; his long, high-cheeked face, rendered longer by the drooping gray mustache and imperial he affected, seemed to have been beaten into angularity by merciless hammer-blows of unkind fortune. His lips were thin, almost colorless and exceedingly bitter in expression; his deep-set, dark eyes glowed and smoldered with a light of perpetual anger mingled with habitual distrust. He wore a suit of coarse linen crash, poorly tailored but spotlessly clean; his white-cotton shirt had seen better days, though not recently, for its wristbands were frayed and tattered: at the edges, though it, too, was immaculate as though fresh from the laundress's hands.

Ravenous from his fast and the exhausting exercise of the afternoon de Grandin did voracious justice to the meal, but though his mouth was too full for articulate speech, his little, round blue eyes looked eloquent curiosity as they roved round the big, stone-floored hall, rested on the ancient, moldering tapestries and the dull Flemish oak furniture, and finally took minute inventory of our host.

The other noted the little Frenchman's wondering eyes and smiled with a sort of mournful pride. "The house dates from Jean Ribault's unfortunate attempt to colonize the coast," he informed us. "Georges Ducharme, an ancestor of mine, accompanied one of the unsuccessful expeditions to the New World, and when the colonists rose against their leaders at Port Royal, he and a few companions beat a path through the wilderness and finally settled here. This place was old when the foundations of Jamestown were laid. For almost four hundred years the Ducharmes have lived here, serving neither French king nor English, Federal Government nor Confederate States—they are and have always been a law unto themselves, accountable to none but their own consciences and God, sirs."

"U'm?" de Grandin cleared his mouth of roast pheasant and bread with a prodigious swallow, then helped himself to a generous stoup of home-made wine. "And you are the last of the Ducharmes, *Monsieur?*"

Quick suspicion was reborn in the other's dark, deep-set eyes as he regarded the Frenchman. For a moment he paused as a man may pause for breath before diving into a chilling stream; then, "Yes," he answered shortly. "I am the last of an ancient line. With me the house of Ducharme ceases to exist."

De Grandin tweaked the waxed ends of his tiny blond mustache after the manner of a well-fed tom-cat combing his whiskers. "Tell me, Monsieur Ducharme," he demanded as he chose a cigarette from his case with deliberate care and set it alight in the flame of one of the tall candles flickering on the table, "you have, presumably, passed the better part of your life here; of a certainty you are familiar with the neighborhood and its traditions. Have you, by any fortunate chance, heard of a certain monstrosity, a thing of infinite hideousness of appearance, which traverses the trackless wastes of these swamps? Today at noon I was all but exterminated by a venomous serpent, but a timely arrow—*an arrow*, mind you—shot from a near-by thicket, saved my life. Immediately I would have given thanks to the unknown archer who delivered me from the reptile, but when I turned to make acknowledgment, I beheld a face so vilely ugly, so exceedingly hideous, that it startled me to silence. *Eh bien*, it did more than that to our superstitious Negro guide. He shrieked something about a specter which haunts the swampland and fled incontinently, leaving us to face the wilderness alone—may seven foul fiends torment his spirit unceasingly in the world to come!

"Thereafter we did search for some trace of the ill-favored one, but nothing could we find save only a few footprints—*parbleu*, such footprints as a princess might have boasted to possess!" He bunched his slender fingers at his lips and wafted an ecstatic kiss toward the vaulted stone ceiling.

Ducharme made a queer, choking noise in his throat. "You—you found foot-prints! You—traced—them—here?" he asked in an odd, dry voice, rising and gripping his chair till the tendons showed in lines of high, white relief against the backs of his straining hands.

"By no means," de Grandin answered. "Though we did struggle like flies upon the *papier des mouches* to extricate ourselves from this detestable morass, we found neither sign nor trace of human thing until we were stopped by the wall which girdles your estate, for which last the good God be devoutly thanked!"

Ducharme bent a long, questioning look on the little Frenchman, then shrugged his shoulders. "No matter," he murmured as though speaking to him-self; "if you're *his* messengers I'll know it soon enough, and I'll know how to deal with you."

Aloud he announced: "You are probably tired after the day's exertions. If you've quite finished your repast, we may as well retire—we sleep early at Ducha-rme Hall."

Beside the newel-post of the wide, broad-stepped staircase curving upward from the hall stood a small oaken table bearing several home-dipped candles in standards of antique silver. Taking one of these, our host lit it from the can-delabrum on the dining-table, handed it to me, then repeated the process and supplied de Grandin with a taper. "I'll show you to your room," he offered with a courteous bow.

We trooped up the stairs, turned down a narrow, stone-paved corridor and, at Ducharme's invitation, entered a high-celled, stone-floored chamber lighted by a single narrow window with leaded panes of ancient greenish glass and fur-nished with a four-post canopied bed, a massive chest of deep-carven oak and two straight-backed cathedral chairs which would have brought their weight in gold at a Madison Avenue antique dealer's.

"I'll have Poseidon wait on you in the morning," our host promised. "In spite of his natural handicaps he makes an excellent valet." What seemed to me a cruel smile flickered across the thin, pale lips beneath his drooping mustache as he concluded the announcement, bowed politely and backed from the room, drawing the door soundlessly shut behind him.

For a moment I stood in the center of the little, narrow room, striving to make a survey of our surroundings by the light of our tallow dips; then, moved by a sudden impulse, I ran on tiptoe to the door, seized its ancient, hand-wrought handle and pulled with all my might. Firm as though nailed to its easing, it resisted my strongest effort. As I gave over the attempt to force the panels open and turned in panic to de Grandin I thought I heard the muted echo of a low, malicious chuckle in the darkened corridor outside.

"I say, de Grandin," I whispered, "do you realize we're caught here like flies in a spider-web?"

"Very probably," he replied, smothering a yawn. "What of it? If they slit our throats while we sleep we shall at least have the advantage of a few minutes' repose before bidding Saint Peter *bonjour.* Come, let us sleep."

But despite his assumed indifference I noticed that he placed one of the great carved chairs before the door in such manner that anyone entering the apartment would do so at imminent peril of barked shins, perhaps of a broken leg, and that he removed only his boots and jacket and lay down with his vicious little automatic pistol ready to his hand.

"TROWBRIDGE, *mon vieux*, AWAKE, arise and behold!" de Grandin's sharp whisper cut through my morning sleep. The early October day was well advanced, for a patch of warm golden sunlight lay in a prism-mottled field on the stone pavement of the room, little half-moons of opalescent coloring marking the curved lenses of the green bottle-glass of the casement through which the beams came. Gazing with fixed intensity at some object below, the little Frenchman stood at the half-opened window and motioned me to join him."

As I stepped across the chilled paving-blocks of the bedroom floor the high sweet notes of the polonaise from *Mignon* floated up to us, the singer taking the quadruple trills with the easy grace of a swallow skimming over sunlit water, never faltering in the vocal calisthenics which give pause to many a professional musician. "Wha—who—" I stammered wonderingly as I reached his side. "I thought Ducharme said—"

"*S-s-st!*" He cut me off. "Remark her; *c'est belle, n'est-ce-pas?*"

Just beyond the drawbridge, full in the rich flood of early-morning sunlight stood a girl, slim, straight and virginal as a hazel wand, her head thrown back, a perfect torrent of clear, wine-rich soprano melody issuing from her throat. Only the rippling cascade of her abundant, wavy auburn hair told her sex, for from feet to throat she was arrayed like a boy—small, sturdy woodsman's moccasins laced calf-high about her straight, slender legs, riding-breeches of brown corduroy belted about her slight waist by a wide girdle of soft brown leather, an olive-drab flannel shirt of military pattern, rolled elbow-high at the sleeves and open at the collar encasing her spare torso. Her back was to us as she trilled her joyous aubade to the rising sun, and I noticed that a leather baldric was swung across her left shoulder, a quiver of arrows with unstrung bow thrust among them laced to the wide suede strap.

Hands as white and delicately formed as any I had ever seen fluttered graciously in rhythm to the music as she poured her very heart out in song; as she ended on a high, true note, she wove her fingers together in a very ecstasy of self-engendered emotion, stood in lovely tableau a moment, then set off toward the forest with a swinging, graceful stride which told of long days spent in walking beneath the open sky with limbs unhampered by traveling-skirts and feet unfettered by modish shoes.

"De Grandin," I exclaimed, "can it be—is it possible—those little, mocass-ined feet, those arrows—can *she* be the archer who killed the snake yester—"

"You do forget the face we saw," he interrupted in a bleak, monotonous voice.

"But couldn't she—isn't it possible she wore a dreadful mask for some rea-son—"

"One wonders," he returned before I could complete my argument. "One also wonders who she is and what she does here."

"Yes, Ducharme distinctly told us he was the only one—"

"*Ah bah*," he cut in. "That Monsieur Ducharme, I think he flatters himself he fools us, Friend Trowbridge. Meanwhile—*allo?* Who calls?"

A soft, timid knock sounded on our door, followed by a second rap, then, after a discreet interval, a third.

"Hit's Poseidon, suh," the old Negro's voice answered quaveringly. "Marse Jawge, he done tol' me ter come up yere an' valet y'all dis mo'nin'. Is yuh ready fo' yo' baffs an' shaves, suhs? Ah done got de watah yere fo' yuh."

"By all means, enter, my excellent one," de Grandin replied, crossing to the door and flinging it back. With a start I noticed that it swung inward without resistance.

The old blind servant shuffled into the room, a towel and two old-fashioned razors in one hand, a porcelain basin clutched beneath his elbow and a pewter pitcher of steaming water in the other hand. "Ah'll shave yuh first, den drag in de baff, if yuh please, suh," he announced, turning his sightless eyes toward the corridor where a long, tin bathtub rested in readiness.

"*Bien non, mon brave*," de Grandin denied, "I shall shave myself, as I have done each day since my sixteenth year. Bring me the mirror, if you please."

"Mirruh, suh?" the servant queried. "Dey ain't no sech thing in de house, suh. Minervy an' me, we don' need nuffin like hit, an' Marse Jawge, he manage ter git erlong wid me ter shave him. Mis' Clarimonde, she ain't nebber seen 'er—oh, Lawdy, suh, please, *please*, suh, don' nebber tell Marse Jawge Ah said nuffin erbout—"

"*Tiens*, my friend," the Frenchman reassured, "fear nothing. The best of us sometimes make slips of the tongue. Your lapse from duty shall be safe in my keeping. Meanwhile, however excellently you may barber your master, I fear I must dispense with your services. Trowbridge, my friend, lend me your glasses, if you please."

"My glasses?" I repeated, in surprise. "What—"

"But certainly. Must one draw diagrams before you understand? Is Jules de Grandin a fool, or has he sense? Observe." Taking my spectacles from the carved chest, he fixed them to the back of one of the tall chairs, draping his jacket behind the lenses to make a dark background. Thus equipped he proceeded to regard his image in the primitive mirror while he spread the lather thickly over cheeks and chin, then scraped it off with the exquisitely sharp blade of the perfectly balanced English razor the blind servant handed him.

"*Très bon*," he announced with a satisfied smile. "Behold, I am my own valet this morning, nor has my complexion suffered so much as one little scratch. This old one here, he seems too innocent to practise any wrong on us, but—he who goes to dinner with the devil should take with him a long spoon. Me, I do not care to take unnecessary chances."

Following de Grandin's example, I shaved myself with the aid of my glasses-mirror, and one after the other we laved ourselves in the tubs of luke-warm water the ancient servitor dragged in from the hall.

"If y'all is ready, suhs," the Negro announced as we completed our toilets, "Ah'll 'scort yuh to de dinin'-room. Marse Jawge is waitin' yo' pleasure below."

"Ah, good morning, gentlemen," Ducharme greeted as we joined him in the main hall. I trust you enjoyed a good night's rest?"

The Frenchman eyed him critically. "I have had worse," he replied. "However, the sense of security obtained by well-bolted doors is not greatly heightened by knowledge that the locks operate from the further side, *Monsieur*."

A faint flush mounted our host's thin cheeks at de Grandin's thrust, but he chose to ignore it. "Minerva!" he cried sharply, turning toward the kitchen. "The gentlemen are down; bring in some breakfast."

The old, blind Negress emerged from her quarters with the promptness of a cuckoo coming from its cell as the clock strikes the hour, and placed great bowls of steaming cornmeal mush before us. Idly, I noticed that the pitcher for the milk accompanying the mush was of unglazed pottery and the pot in which the steaming coffee was served was of tarnished, dull-finished silver.

With a rather impatient gesture, Ducharme motioned us to eat and excused himself from joining us by saying he had breakfasted an hour or so before.

De Grandin's little eyes scarcely left our host's face as he ate ravenously, but though he seemed on the point of putting some question point-blank more than once, he evidently thought better of it, and held his peace.

"It's impossible for me to get a guide for you this morning, gentlemen," Ducharme apologized as we finished breakfast, "and it's hardly practicable for me to accompany you myself. However, if you'll be good enough to remain another day, I think—perhaps—I may be able to find someone to take you back to Gregory's. Provided, of course, you really wish to go there." Something like a sneer crossed his lips as he concluded, and de Grandin was on his feet instantly, his small face livid with rage.

"*Monsieur*," he protested, his little eyes snapping ominously, "on more than one occasion you have been good enough to intimate we are impostors. I have heard much of your vaunted Southern hospitality in the past, but the sample you display leaves much to be desired. If you will be so good as to stand aside we shall give ourselves the pleasure of shaking your dust from our feet forthwith. Meantime, since you have small liking for the post of social host, permit that we compensate you for our entertainment." His face still white with fury, he thrust his hand into his pocket, withdrew a roll of bills and tossed several on the table. "I trust that is sufficient," he added cuttingly. "Count it; if you desire more, more shall be forthcoming."

Ducharme had risen with de Grandin. As the Frenchman finished his tirade, he stepped quickly to the corner and snatched up his rifle. "If either of you attempts to leave this house before I give permission," he announced in a low, menacing voice, "so help me God, I'll blow his head off!" With a quick backward step he reached the door, slipped through it and banged it shut behind him.

"Are you going to stand this?" I demanded angrily, turning to de Grandin. "The man's mad—mad as a hatter. We'll be murdered before sunset if we don't get away!"

"I think not so," he returned, resuming his seat and lighting a cigarette. "As for killing us, he will need more speed than he showed just now. I had him covered from my pocket before he took up his gun, and could have stopped his words with a bullet any time I was so minded, but—I did not care to. There are things which interest me about this place, Friend Trowbridge, and I desire to remain until my curiosity is satisfied."

"But his insinuations—his insulting doubt—" I began.

"*Tiens*, it *was* well done was it not?" he interrupted with a self-satisfied smile. "*Barbe d'un chameau*, I play-acted so well I did almost deceive myself!"

"Then you weren't really angry—"

"Jules de Grandin is quick to anger, my friend, if the provocation be sufficient, but never has he bitten off his nose through desire to revenge himself upon his face. No. Another time I might have resented his boorishness. This morning I desire to remain more greatly than I wish to leave; but should I disclose my real desires he would undoubtlessly insist upon our going. *Alors*, I make the monkey business. To make our welcome doubly sure I deceive Monsieur Ducharme to think that leaving is our primary desire. *C'est très simple, n'est-ce-pas?*"

"I suppose so," I admitted, "but what earthly reason have you for wanting to stay in this confounded place?"

"One wonders," he returned enigmatically, blowing a twin cloud of smoke from his nostrils.

"One certainly does," I agreed angrily. "I, for one—"

He tossed his cigarette into his porringer and rose abruptly. "Is it of significance to you, my friend, that this *sacré* house contains not only not a single mirror, but not so much as one polished surface in which one may by any chance behold himself with the exception of the spectacles which adorn your kindly nose this minute? Or that the servants here are blind?" he added as I shook my head doubtfully. "Or that Monsieur Ducharme has deliberately attempted to mislead us into thinking that he, we and the two blind ones are the only tenants of the place?"

"It is mystifying," I agreed, "but I can't seem to fit the facts into any kind of pattern. Probably they're just coincidences, and—"

"Coincidence is the name we give to that we can not otherwise explain," he interrupted. "Me, I have arrived already at a theory, though much still remains obscure. At dinner tonight I shall let fly a random shot; who knows what it may bring down?"

DUCHARME KEPT OUT OF sight the remainder of the day, and it was not till well after dark we saw him again. We were just concluding our evening meal when he let himself in, a more amiable expression on his sour face than I had seen before.

"Dr. de Grandin, Dr. Trowbridge," he greeted as he placed his rifle in an angle of the wall and drew a chair up to the table, "I have to tender you my humblest apologies. My life has been a bitter one, gentlemen; and I live in daily dread of something I can not explain. However, if I tell you it is sufficient to make me suspicious of every stranger who comes near the house, you may understand something of the lack of courtesy I have shown you. I did doubt your word, sirs, and I renew my apologies for doing so. This morning, after warning you to stay indoors, I went to Gregory's—it's less than a three hours' trip, if you know the way—and made certain of your identity. Tomorrow, if you wish, I shall be happy to guide you to your friends."

The Frenchman bent along, speculative stare upon our host. At length: "You are satisfied from Monsieur Gregory's report that we are indeed physicians?" he asked.

"Of course—"

"Suppose I add further information. Would it interest you to know that I hold degrees from Vienna and the Sorbonne, that I have done much surgical work for the University of Paris, and that in the days after the Armistice I was among those who helped restore to pre-war appearance the faces of those noble heroes whose features had been burned away by Hunnish *flammenwerfer?*" He pronounced the last words with slow, impressive deliberation, his level, unwinking gaze fixed firmly on the dark, sullen eyes of our host.

Quick, incredulous fury flamed in the other's face. "You spying scoundrel— you damned sneak!" he cried, leaping from his chair and making for his rifle.

"Slowly!" De Grandin, too, was on his feet, his small, round eyes blazing with implacable purpose, his little, deadly pistol aimed unwaveringly at Ducharme's breast. "Greatly as I should regret it," he warned, "I shall kill you if you make one further move, *Monsieur*."

The other wavered, for there was no doubting de Grandin's sincerity.

"Ah, that is better," he remarked as Ducharme halted, then returned slowly to his seat. "Now we shall talk sense.

"A moment since, *Monsieur*," he continued as Ducharme dropped heavily into his chair and sank his face in his hands, "I did avail myself of what the Americans call the bluff. Consider, I am clever; the wool can not successfully be drawn across my eyes, and so I suspected what I now know for the truth. Yesterday an arrow saved my life; anon we found small footprints in the mud; last night when we arrived here we met with scant welcome from you, and inside the house we found you waited on by blinded servants. This morning, when I ask for a mirror that I may shave myself, your servant tells there is not one in all the house, and on sober thought I recall that I have seen no single polished surface wherein a man may behold his own image. Why is it? If strangers are unwelcome, if there be no mirrors here, if the servants be blind—is there not something hideous within these walls, something of which you know, but which you desire to be kept most secret? Again, you are not beautiful, but you would not necessarily be averse to regarding your reflection in a mirror. What then? Is it not, perhaps, I think, that you greatly desire that the ugly one—whoever it be—not only not be seen, but shall not see itself? It are highly probable.

"This morning I have seen a so lovely young girl attired for *le footing*, who sings divinely in the early sunlight. But I have not seen her face. No. However, she wears upon her back a bow and quiverful of arrows—and an arrow such as those saved me from the serpent yesterday, one little moment before we beheld the face of awful ugliness.

"Two and two invariably make four, *Monsieur*. You have said there is no other person but yourself and your servants in the house; but even as you doubted me, so I have doubted you. Indeed, from what I have seen, I know you have been untruthful; but I think you are so because of some great reason. And so I tell you of my work in restoring the wrecked faces of the soldiers of France.

"But I am no idle boaster. No. What I say is true. Call in the unfortunate young lady; I shall examine her minutely, and if it are humanly possible I shall remold her features to comeliness. If you do not consent you are a heartless, inhuman monster. Besides," he added matter-of-factly, "if you refuse I shall kill you and perform the operation anyway."

Ducharme gazed unbelievingly at him. "You really think you can do it?" he demanded.

"Have I not said it?"

"But, if you fail—"

"Jules de Grandin does not fail, *Monsieur*."

"Minerva!" Ducharme called. "Ask Miss Clarimonde to come here at once, please."

The old blind woman's slipshod footsteps sounded along the tiled floor of a back passage for a moment, then faded away as she slowly climbed a hidden flight of stairs.

For something like five minutes we sat silently. Once or twice Ducharme swallowed nervously, de Grandin's slim, white fingers drummed a noiseless, devil's tattoo on the table, I fidgeted nervously in my chair, removed my glasses and polished them, returned them to my nose, then snatched them off and fell to wiping them again. At length the light tap-tap of slippered feet sounded on the stairs and we rose together as a tall, graceful figure emerged from the stairway shadow into the aura of light thrown out by the candles.

"My daughter, gentlemen—Clarimonde, Dr. de Grandin; Dr. Trowbridge," Mr. Ducharme introduced in a voice gone thin and treble with nervousness. From the corner of my eye I could see him watching us in a sort of agony, awaiting the horror we were bound to show as the girl's face became visible.

I saw de Grandin's narrow, pointed chin jut forward as he set his jaw against the shock of the hideous countenance, then watched the indomitable will within him force his face into the semblance of an urbane smile as he stepped forward gallantly and raised the girl's slim, white hand to his lips.

The figure which stepped slowly, reluctantly, into the dull luminance of the candles was the oddest patch-work of grotesquerie I had ever seen. From feet to throat she was perfectly made as a sculptured Hebe, slim, straight, supple with the pliancy of youth and abundant health. Shoes of white satin and stockings of sheerest white silk complemented a straight, plain frock of oyster-white which assuredly had come from nowhere but Vienna or the Rue de la Paix; a Manila shawl, yellowed with years and heavily fringed, lay scarfwise over her ivory shoulders and arms; about her throat was clasped a single tight-fitting strand of large, lustrous pearls.

The sea-gems were the line of demarcation. It was as if by some sorcery of obscene surgery the lovely girl's head had been sheared off by a guillotine three inches above the clavicle and replaced by the foulest specimen from the stored-up monstrosities of a medical museum. The skin about the throat was craped and wrinkled like a toad's, and of the color of a tan boot on which black dressing has inadvertently been rubbed, then ineffectually removed. Above, the chin was firm and pointed, tapering downward from the ears in good lines, but the mouth extended a full five inches across the face, sweeping in a curving diagonal from left to right like a musical turn mark, one corner lifted in a perpetual travesty of a grin, the other sagging in a constant snarl. Between the spaces where the brows should have been the glabella was so enlarged that a protuberance almost like a horn stood out from the forehead, while the eyes, fine hazel, flecked with brown, were horrifically cocked at divergent angles so that it was impossible for her to gaze at an object directly before her without turning her head slightly to the side. The nose was long and curved, exaggeratedly high-bridged and slit down the outer side of each flaring nostril as the mouth of a hairlipped person is cleft. Like the throat, the entire face was integumented in coarse, loosely wrinkled skin of soiled brown, and, to make the contrast more shockingly incongruous, a mass of gleaming auburn hair, fine and scintillant as spun rose-gold, lay loosely coiled in a Grecian coronal above the repulsive countenance.

Had the loathsomeness been unrelieved by contrasting comeliness, the effect would have been less shocking; as it was, the hideous face inlaid between the perfect body and glowing, ruddy-diadem of hair was like the sacrilegious mutilation of a sacred picture—as though the oval of the Sistine Virgin's face were cut from the canvas and the sardonic, grinning features of a Punchinello thrust through the aperture.

To his everlasting credit, de Grandin did not flinch. Debonair as though at any social gathering, he bowed the monstrous creature to a chair and launched a continuous flow of conversation. All the while I could see his eyes returning again and again to the hideous countenance across the table, his keen surgeon's mind surveying the grotesque features and weighing his chances of success against the almost foregone certainty of failure.

THE ORDEAL LASTED SOMETHING like half an hour, and my nerves had stretched to the snapping point when sudden diversion came.

With a wild, frantic movement the girl leaped up, oversetting her chair, and faced us, her misdirected eyes rolling with a horrible ludicrousness in their sockets, tears of shame and self-pity welling from them and coursing down the sides of her grotesque face. Her wide, cavernous mouth opened obliquely and she gave scream after scream of shrill, tortured anguish. "I know; I know!" she cried frenziedly. "Don't think you've fooled me by taking all the mirrors from the house, Father! Remember, I go about the woods at will, and *there are pools of quiet water in the woods!* I know I'm hideous; I know I'm so repulsive that even the servants who wait on us must be blind! I've seen my face reflected in the moat and the swamp; I saw the horror in your eyes when you first looked at me, Dr. de Grandin; I noticed how Dr. Trowbridge couldn't bear even to glance at me just now without a shudder! Oh, God of mercy, why haven't I had courage to kill myself before?—Why did I live till I met strangers and saw them turn from me with loathing? Why—"

"*Mademoiselle*, be still!" de Grandin's sharp, incisive command cut through her hysterical words and stung her to silence. "You lament unnecessarily," he continued as she turned her goggling toad-eyes toward him. "*Monsieur*, your father, bids you come to us for a specific purpose; namely, that I inspect your countenance and give him my opinion as a surgeon concerning the possibility of cure. Attend me: I tell you I can so reshape your features that you shall be completely beautiful; you shall grace the salons of Washington, of New York, of Paris, and you shall have young men to do you honor and lay their kisses thick upon your hands and lips, and breathe their tales of love into your ears; you—"

A shriek of wild, incredulous laughter silenced him. "I? I have admirers— lovers? Dear God—the bitterness of the mockery! I am doomed to spend my life among the snakes and toads, the bats and salamanders of the swamps, a thing as hideous as the ugliest of them, cut off from all my kind, and—"

"Your fate may be a worse one, unless I can prevent it," Ducharme broke in with an odd, dry croaking voice.

We turned on him by common consent as he rasped his direful prophecy. His long, goat-like face was working spasmodically; I could see the tendons of his thin neck contracting as he swallowed nervously, and the sad, bitter lips beneath the drooping gray mustache twisted into a smile that was more than half a snarl as he gazed at de Grandin and his daughter in turn.

"You wondered why I greeted you with suspicion when you came asking food and shelter last night, gentlemen?" he asserted rather than asked, looking from the Frenchman to me. "This is why:

"As I told you last night, the Ducharmes have lived here since long before the first English colony was planted in Virginia. Although our plantation has been all but eaten up by the swamps, the family wealth holds out, and I am what is counted a rich man, even in these days of swollen fortunes. It was the custom of our family for generations to send their women to a convent at Rheims for education; the young men were sent to Oxford or Cambridge, Paris or Vienna, occasionally to Louvain or Heidelberg, and their training was completed by the grand tour.

"I followed the family tradition and studied at the Sorbonne when my under-graduate work at Oxford was completed. It was while I lived in Paris I met Ino-cencia. She was an *Argentina*—a native of the Argentine, a dancer in a cabaret, and as lovely a creature as ever set a man's blood afire. All the students were mad about her, but Ruiz, a fellow-countryman of hers, and I were the most favored of her coterie of suitors.

"Leandro Ruiz was a medical student, the son of an enormously wealthy cattleman, who took to surgery from an innate love of blood and suffering rather than from any wish to serve humanity or earn a livelihood, for he already had more money than he could ever spend, and as for humanitarianism, the devil himself had more of it.

"One night as I sat studying, there came a terrified rapping at my door, and Inocencia fell, rather than ran, into my rooms. She had struggled through the raging sleet-storm from Montmartre, and Ruiz was hot behind her. He had accosted her as she left the café, and demanded that she come forthwith and consort with him—there never was an honorable thought in the scoundrel's mind, and what he could not buy he was accustomed to take by force.

"I had barely time to lock and bar the door when Ruiz and three hired bullies came clamoring up the stairs and battered on the panels like werewolves shut out from their prey. Ha, I left my mark on him that night! As he stooped down to bawl obscenities through the keyhole I thrust, a sword-cane through the lock and blinded him in one eye. Despite his wound he hung around the door nearly all night, and it was not till two gendarmes threatened him and his companions with arrest for public disturbance that they slunk away.

"Next morning Inocencia and I arranged to be married, and as soon as the formalities of French-law could be complied with, we were wed and made a tour of Europe for our honeymoon. When we returned to Paris we heard Ruiz had contracted pneumonia the night he raged outside my quarters in the sleet, and had died and been buried in St. Sulpice. Ha, you may be sure we shed no tears at the news!

"I was nearly thirty, Inocencia barely twenty, when we married. It was not till ten years later that Clarimonde was born, and when at last we had a child to crown our union we thought our cup of joy was surely overflowing. God!" He paused, poured himself a goblet of wine and drained it to the bottom before continuing:

"No hired *bonne* was good enough to take our darling out; Inocencia herself accompanied her on every outing and filled the afternoons with recitals of the thousand cunning things our baby did and said while toddling in the park.

"One day they did not return. I was frantic and set the entire gendarmerie by the ears to search for them. Nowhere could we find a trace till finally my wife's dead body, partly decomposed, but still identifiable, was rescued from the Seine. Police investigation disclosed she had been murdered—her throat severed and her heart cut out, but not before a hundred and more disfiguring wounds had been inflicted with a knife.

"My baby's fate was still unknown, and I lived for weeks and months in a frenzy of mingled despair and hope till—" Again he paused; once more he filled and drained a wine-glass. Then: "At last my fears were set at rest. At daylight one morning the thin, pitiful wailing of a little frightened child sounded at my door, and when the *concierge* went to investigate she found Clarimonde lying there in a basket. Clarimonde, my Clarimonde, her mother's sole remaining souvenir, dressed in the baby garments she had worn the day she vanished, positively identified by the little, heart-shaped birthmark on the under side of her left arm, but, my God, how altered! Her face, gentlemen, was as you see it now, a dreadful, disfigured, mutilated mask of horror, warped and carved and twisted almost out of human semblance, save as the most grotesque caricature resembles the thing it parodies. And with her was a letter, a letter from Leandro Ruiz. The fiend had caused the report of his death to be given us, and bided his time through all the years, always studying and experimenting in plastic surgery that he might one day carry out his terrible revenge, watching Inocencia and Clarimonde when they least suspected it, familiarizing himself with their habits and ways so that he might best set his *apaches* on them and kidnap them when the time was ripe for his devil's vengeance. After dishonoring and torturing Inocencia, he killed her slowly—cut her heart from her living breast before he slashed her throat. The next three months he spent carefully disfiguring the features of our baby, adding horror on horror to the poor, helpless face as though he were a sculptor working out the details of a statue with slow, painstaking care. At last, when even he could think of nothing more to add to the devastation he had made, he laid the poor, mutilated mite on my doorstep with a note describing his acts, and containing the promise that all his life and all his boundless wealth would be devoted to making his revenge complete.

"You wonder how he could do more? Gentlemen, you can not think how vile humanity can be until you've known Leandro Ruiz. Listen: When Clarimonde reaches her twenty-first year, he said he would come for her. If death had taken him meanwhile, he would leave a sum of money to pay those who carried out his will. He, or his hirelings, would come for her, and though she hid behind locked doors and armed men, they would ravish her away, cut out her tongue to render her incapable of speech, *then exhibit her for hire in a freak show*—make my poor, disfigured baby girl the object of yokels' gawking curiosity throughout the towns and provinces of Europe and South America!

"I fled from Paris as Lot fled from Sodom, and brought my poor, maimed child to Ducharme Hall. Here I secured Minerva and Poseidon for servants, because both were blind and could not let fall any remarks which would make Clarimonde realize her deformity. I secured blind teachers and tutors; she is as well educated as any seminary graduate; every luxury that money could buy has been given her, but never has there been a mirror in Ducharme Hall, or anything which could serve as a mirror, since we came here from Paris.

"Now, gentlemen, perhaps you understand the grounds for my suspicions? Clarimonde was twenty-one this month."

Jules de Grandin twisted the fine, blond hairs of his diminutive mustache until they stood out in twin needle-points each side of his mouth, and fixed a level, unwinking stare upon our host. "*Monsieur,*" he said, "a moment hence I was all for going to the North; I would have argued to the death against a moment's delay which kept me from performing the necessary work to restore Mademoiselle Clarimonde's features to their pristine loveliness. Now, *parbleu*, five men and ten little boys could not drag me from this spot. We shall wait here, *Monsieur,* we shall stay here, rooted as firmly as the tallest oak in yonder forest, until this Monsieur Ruiz and his corps of assassins appear. Then"—he twisted the ends of his mustache still more fiercely, and the lightning-flashes in his little, round eyes were cold as arctic ice and hot as volcanic fire—"then, by damn, I think those seventy-six-thousand-times accursed miscreants shall find that he who would step into the hornet's nest would be advised to wear heavy boots. Yes; I have said it."

From that night Ducharme Hall was more like a castle under siege than ever. In terror of abduction Clarimonde no longer roamed the woods, and Mr. Ducharme, de Grandin or I was always on lookout for any strangers who might appear inside the walled park. A week, ten days passed quietly, and we resumed our plans for returning North, where the deformed girl's face could receive expert surgical treatment.

"I shall give Mademoiselle Clarimonde my undivided attention until all is accomplished," de Grandin told me as we lay in bed one evening while the October wind soughed and moaned through the locust-trees bordering the avenue and a pack of tempest-driven storm clouds harried the moon like hounds pursuing a fleeing doe. "With your permission I shall leave your house and take up residence in the hospital, Friend Trowbridge, and neither day nor night shall I be beyond call of the patient. I shall—

"*Attendez, voilà les assassins!*" Faintly as the scuffing of a dried twig against the house, there came the gentle sound of something scratching against the rubble-stone of the wall.

For a moment the Frenchman lay rigid; then with bewildering quickness he leaped from the bed, bundled the sheets and pillows together in simulation of a person covered with bedclothes, and snatched down one of the heavy silken cords binding back the draperies which hung in mildewed festoons, between the mahogany posts. "Silence!" he cautioned, tiptoeing across the chamber and taking his station beside the open casement. "No noise, my friend, but if it is possible, do you creep forward and peer out, then tell me what it is you see."

Cautiously, I followed his instructions, rested my chin upon the wide stone window-sill and cast a hurried glance down the wall.

Agilely as a cat, a man encased in close-fitting black jersey and tights was scaling the side of the house by aid of a hooked ladder similar to those firemen use. Behind him came a companion, similarly costumed and equipped, and even as I watched them I could not but marvel at the almost total silence in which they swarmed up the rough stones.

I whispered my discovery to de Grandin, and saw him nod once understandingly. "*Voleurs de nuit*—professional burglars," he pronounced. "He chose expert helpers, this one. Let us await them."

A moment later there was a soft, rubbing sound as a long steel hook, well wrapped in tire-tape, crept like a living thing across the window-sill, and was followed in a moment by a slender and none too clean set of fingers which reached exploringly through the casement.

In another instant a head covered by a tight-fitting black jersey cowl loomed over the sill, the masked eyes peered searchingly about the candlelit room; then, apparently satisfied that someone occupied the bed and slept soundly, the intruder crept agilely across the sill, landed on the stone floor with a soft thud and cleared the space between bed and window in a single feline leap.

There was the glint of candlelight on sharpened steel and a fiendish-looking stiletto flashed downward in a murderous arc and buried itself to the hilt in the pillow which lay muffled in the blankets where I had lain two minutes before.

Like a terrier pouncing on a rat de Grandin leaped on the assassin's shoulders. While awaiting the intruder's advent he had looped the strong curtain cord into a running noose, and as he landed on the other's back, driving his face down among the bedding and effectively smothering outcry, he slipped the strangling string about the burglar's throat, drew it tight with a single dexterous jerk, then crossed its ends and pulled them as one might pull the draw-string of a sack. "Ha, good *Monsieur le Meurtrier*," he whispered exultantly, "I serve you a dish for which you have small belly, *n'est-ce-pas?* Eat your fill, my friend, do not stint yourself, Jules de Grandin has plentiful supply of such food for you!

"So!" He straightened quickly and whipped the cord from his captive's throat. "I damnation think you will give us small trouble for some time, my friend. Attention, Friend Trowbridge, the other comes!"

Once more he took his place beside the window, once more he cast his strangling cord as a masked head protruded into the room. In a moment two black-clad, unconscious forms lay side by side upon the bed.

"Haste, my friend, *dépêchez vous*," he ordered, beginning to disrobe our prisoners as he spoke. "I do dislike to ruin Monsieur Ducharme's bedding, but we must work with what we have. Tear strips from the sheets and bind these unregenerate sons of pigs fast. There is no time to lose; a moment hence and we must don their disguises and perform that which they set out to do."

We worked feverishly, tying the two desperadoes in strip after strip of linen ripped from the sheets, gagging them, blindfolding them; finally, as an added precaution, lashing their hands and feet to the head—and footposts of the bed. Then, shedding our pajamas, we struggled into the tightfitting jerseys the prisoners had worn. The stocking-like garments were clammily wet and chilled me to the marrow as I drew them on, but the Frenchman gave me no time for complaint. "*Allons, en route*, make haste!" he ordered.

Leaving the unconscious thugs to such meditations as they might have upon regaining consciousness, we hastened to Ducharme's chamber.

"Fear not, it is I," de Grandin called as he beat imperatively on our host's door. "In our chamber repose two villains who gained entrance by means of scaling ladders—from the feel of their clothes, which we now wear, I should say they swam your moat. We go now to lower the drawbridge and let the master villain in. Do you be ready to receive him!"

"Holà!" he called a moment later as we let ourselves out the front door and lowered the drawbridge. "Come forth, all is prepared!"

Two men emerged from the darkness beyond the moat in answer to his hail, one a tall, stoop-shouldered fellow arrayed in ill-fitting and obviously new clothes, the other small, frail-looking, and enveloped from neck to high-heeled boots in a dark mackintosh or raincoat of some sort which hung about his spare figure like the cloak of a conspirator in a melodramatic opera. There was something infinitely wicked in the slouching truculent swagger of the big, stoop-shouldered bully, something which suggested brute strength, brute courage and brute ferocity; but there was something infinitely more sinister in the mincing, precise walk of his smaller companion, who advanced with an odd sort of gait, placing one foot precisely before the other like a tango dancer performing to the rhythm of inaudible music.

"Judas Iscariot and Company," de Grandin whispered to me as the queerly assorted couple set foot on the drawbridge; then with an imperative wave of his hand he beckoned them toward the house and set off up the driveway at a rapid walk. "We must not let them get close enough to suspect," he whispered, quickening his pace. "All cats are gray in the dark, and we much resemble their friends at a distance, but it is better that we take no chances."

Once or twice the other two called to us, demanding to know if we had encountered resistance, but de Grandin's only answer was another gesture, urging them to haste, and we were still some ten feet in the lead when we reached the door, swung it open and slipped into the house, awaiting the others' advent.

The candles burned with a flickering, uncertain light, scarcely more than staining the darkness flooding the big stone hall as the two men trailed us through the door. By the table, the candlelight falling full upon her mutilated face, stood Clarimonde Ducharme, her hideously distorted eyes rolling pathetically in their elongated sockets as she turned her head from side to side in an effort to get a better view of the intruders.

A shrill, cackling laugh burst from the smaller man. "Look at that; Henri," he bade, catching his breath with an odd, sucking sound. "Look at that. That's my work; isn't it a masterpiece?"

Mockingly, he snatched the wide-brimmed soft black-felt hat from his head, laid it over his heart, then swept it to the floor as he bowed profoundly to the girl. "Señorita hermosa, yo beso sus manos!" he declared, then burst into another cackle of cachinnating laughter. As he removed his headgear I observed he was bald as an egg, thickly wrinkled, and wore a monocle of dark glass in his right eye.

His companion growled an inarticulate comment, then turned toward us with an expectant look. "Now?" he asked. "Shall I do it now and get it over?"

"*Si, como no?*—certainly, why not?" the smaller man lisped. "They've served their purpose, have they not?"

"Right," the big man returned. "They did the job, and dead men tell no tales—"

There was murderous menace in every movement of his big body as he swaggered toward de Grandin. "Come, little duckie," he bade mockingly in *gamin* French, "come and be killed. We can't have you running loose and babbling tales of what you've seen tonight the first time you get your hide full of *vin ordinaire*. Say your prayers, if you know any; you've precious little time to do it. Come, duckie—" As he advanced he thrust his hand beneath his ill-fitting jacket and drew a knife of fearsome proportions, whetting it softly against the heel of his hand, smiling to himself as though anticipating a rare bit of sport.

De Grandin gave ground before the other's onslaught. Two or three backward running steps he took, increasing the distance between them, then paused.

With a flick of his left hand he swept the disguising hood from his features and smiled almost tenderly at the astonished bully. "*Monsieur,*" he announced softly, "it sometimes happens that the weasel discovers the duck he hunts to be an eagle in disguise. So it would seem tonight. You have three seconds to live; make the most of them. *Un—deux—trois!*" The spiteful, whip-like report of pistol sounded sharp punctuation to his third count, and the bravo stumbled back a step, an expression of amazement on his coarse face, a tiny bruised-looking circle almost precisely bisecting the line of heavy, black brows which met above his nose.

"Wha—what?" the smaller villain began in a strangled, frightened scream, wheeling on de Grandin and snatching at a weapon beneath his cloak.

But George Ducharme leaped out of the darkness like a lion avenging the slaughter of its mate and bore him, screaming madly, to the floor. "At last, Leandro Ruiz—at last!" he shouted exultantly, fastening his fingers on the other's thin, corded neck and pressing his thumb into the sallow, flaccid flesh. "At last I've got you! You killed my wife, you deformed my baby, you've made me live in a hell of fear for eighteen years; but now I've got you—*I've got you!*"

"*Eh bien,* have a care, *Monsieur,* you are unduly rough!" de Grandin protested, tapping Ducharme's shoulder gently, "Be careful I implore you!"

"What?" George Ducharme cried angrily, looking up at the diminutive Frenchman, but retaining his strangling hold on his foeman's throat. "D'ye mean I'm not to treat this dog as he deserves?"

The other's narrow shoulders rose nearly level with his ears in an eloquent shrug. "I did but caution you, my friend," he answered mildly. "When one is very angry one easily forgets one's strength. Be careful, or you kill him too swiftly.

"Come, Friend Trowbridge, the night is fine outside. Let us admire the view."

The prisoners in the bedroom were only too glad to take their departure without stopping to inquire concerning their late employer. From remarks they dropped while we hunted clothing to replace the conspicuous black tights of which we had relieved them, I gathered they had distrusted Ruiz's good faith, and insisted on payment in advance. That Monsieur Ruiz had left, leaving no address, and consequently would not be in position to extort return of his fee with the aid of the gigantic Henri was the best possible news we could have given them, and they took speedy farewell of us.

T HE FOLLOWING DAY DE Grandin and I set out for the North, accompanied by the Ducharmes. Clarimonde traveled closely veiled, and we occupied a drawing-room suite on the B. & O. fast train which bore us from Washington to Harrisonville. The first night in New Jersey was spent at my house, Clarimonde keeping closely to her room, lest Nora McGinnis, my faithful but garrulous Irish household factotum, behold her mutilated features and spread news of them along the kitchen-door telegraph line.

A suite of rooms at Mercy Hospital was engaged the following day, and true to his promise, de Grandin took up residence in the institution, eating sleeping and passing his entire time within half a minute's walk of his patient.

What passed in the private operating-room Ducharme's money made possible for his daughter's case I did not know, for the press of my own neglected practise kept me busy through most of the daylight hours, and de Grandin performed his work unassisted except by three special nurses who, like him, spent their entire time on duty in the special suite secured for Clarimonde.

Nearly three months passed before my office telephone shrilled one bright Sunday morning and de Grandin's excited voice informed me he was about to remove the bandages from his charge. Ten minutes later, out of breath, with haste, I stood in the comfortably furnished sitting-room of Clarimonde's suite, and stared fascinated at the little Frenchman who posed and postured beside his patient like a lecturer about to begin his discourse.

"My friends," he announced, sweeping the circle composed of Ducharme, the nurses and me with twinkling eyes, "this is one of the supreme moments of my life. Should my workmanship be successful, I shall proceed forthwith to get most vilely, piggishly intoxicated. If I have failed"—he paused dramatically, then drew a small, silver-mounted automatic pistol from his pocket and laid it on the table beside him—"if I have failed, Friend Trowbridge, I beseech you, write in the death certificate that, my suicide was induced by a broken heart. *Allons*."

With a pair of surgical scissors he slit the outermost layer of bandages about the girl's face and began unwinding the white gauze with slow, deliberate movements.

"*A-a-ah!*" The long-drawn exclamation came unbidden from all of us in chorus.

The wrinkled, blotched, leather-like skin which had covered the girl's face had, by some alchemy employed by de Grandin, been bleached to an incredibly beautiful shade of light, suntanned *écru*, smooth as country cream and iridescent as an alloy of gold and platinum. Above a high, straight brow of creamy whiteness her soft auburn hair was loosely dressed in a gleaming diadem of sun-stained metallic luster. But it was the strange, exotic molding of her features which brought our hearts into our eyes as we looked. Her high, straight forehead continued down into her perfectly formed nose without the slightest indication of a curve—like the cameo-fine formation of the most beautiful faces found on recovered artistic treasures of ancient Greece. With consummate skill the Frenchman had made the enlargement of her eyes an ally in his work, for while he had somewhat decreased the length of the cuts with which Ruiz had mutilated the girl's eyes, he had left the openings larger than normal and raised them slightly at the outer corners, imparting to the face which would have otherwise been somewhat too severe in its utter classicism a charming hint of Oriental piquancy. The mouth was still somewhat large, but perfect in its outline, and the lips were thin, beautifully molded lines of more than usual redness, in repose presenting an expression of singular sweetness, retracting only slightly when she smiled, giving her face an expression of languid, faint amusement which was as provocative in its appeal as the far-famed smile of Mona Lisa.

"My God—Clarimonde, you're *beautiful!*" Ducharme cried brokenly, and stumbled across the floor to drop kneeling before his daughter, burying his face in her lap and sobbing hysterically.

"*Pipe d'une souris!*" de Grandin pocketed his pistol and bent above his patient. "Jules de Grandin and none other shall have the first kiss from these so beautiful lips!" He placed a resounding salute upon the girl's scarlet mouth, then turned toward the adjoining room.

"Behind that door," he announced, "I have secreted several pints of the hospital's finest medicinal brandy, Friend Trowbridge. See to it, if you please, that I am not disturbed until I say otherwise. For the next four and twenty hours Jules de Grandin shall be delightfully engaged in acquiring the noblest case of delirium tremens the institution's staff has ever treated!"

Stealthy Death

1. The Second Murder

"PARADE—REST! SOUND OFF!" PLAYING in quick time, the academy band marched the field, executed a perfect countermarch and returned to its post at the right of the ordered ranks of cadets. As the bandsmen came to a halt the trumpets of the drum corps, gay with fringed tabards, belled forth the slow, appealing notes of retreat, and: "Battalion—'tention! Present—arms!" came the adjutant's command as "The Star-Spangled Banner" sounded and the national color floated slowly from its masthead.

Jules de Grandin's white-chamois gloved right hand cupped itself before his right ear in a French army salute, his narrow, womanish shoulders squared back and his little, pointed chin thrust up and forward as the evening sun picked half a thousand answering beams from the burnished bayonets on the presented rifles. "Parfait, exquis; magnifique!" he applauded. "C'est très beau, that, my friend. You have here a fine aggregation of young men. Certainly."

I nodded absently. My thoughts were not on the stirring spectacle of the parade, nor upon the excellence of Westover Military Academy's student body. I was dreading the ordeal which lay before me when, the parade dismissed, I must tell Harold Pancoast of his father's awful death. "He'll take it better than you, Doctor Trowbridge!" the widow had whispered between tremulous lips, and:

"Poor boy, this is tragic!" the headmaster had told me deprecatingly. "Won't you wait till after parade, Doctor? Pancoast is Battalion Adjutant, and I think it would be kinder to let him complete his duties at parade before we break the news."

"Confound it!" I complained bitterly more than once; "why did they have to give me this job? The family lawyer, or—"

"Mais non, my friend," de Grandin comforted. "It is the way of life. We are born in others' pain; we perish in our own, and between beginning and end stands the physician. We help them into the world, we watch beside their sick-beds, we make their exits into immortality as painless as possible—at the last we stay to comfort those who remain. These are the obligations of our trade." He sighed. "It is, *hélas*, too true. Had kindly heaven given me a son I should have sternly forbid him to study medicine—and I should most assuredly have cracked his neck had he done otherwise!"

The last gold rays of the dying October sun were slanting through the red and russet leaves of the tree-lined avenue leading to the administration building as we waited in the headmaster's office for young Pancoast. At last he came, sauntering easily along the red-brick walk, plainly in no haste to answer the official summons, laughing as only carefree youth can laugh, and looking with more than friendly regard into the face of his companion. Indeed, she was a sight to brighten any eye. A wistful, seeking look was on her features, her fine dark hair lay round her delicate, pale face like a somber nimbus, and the Chinese coat of quilted black satin she wore against the light evening chill was lined and collared with soft orange-pink which set off her brunette pallor to perfection. "*Parbleu*, he chooses nicely, that one," de Grandin approved as the lad bade his companion adieu with a smart military salute and turned to mount the steps to the headmaster's sanctum.

I drew a deep breath and braced myself, but I might have known the boy would take the blow like the gentleman he was. "Dead—*my* Dad?" he murmured slowly, unbelievingly as I concluded my evil tidings. "How? When?"

"Last night, *mon pauvre*," de Grandin took the conversation from me. "Just when, we do not know, but that he met his death by foul play there is no room for doubting. The steel of the assassin struck him from behind—a sneaking, cowardly blow, but a mighty one, *mon brave*—so that he died instantly, with-out pain or struggle. It is for us—you and us—to find the one responsible and give him up to justice. Yes. Certainly. You accept the challenge? Good! Bravely spoken, like the soldier and the gentleman you are; I do salute you—" He drew himself to rigid attention, raising his hand with precise military courtesy.

Admiringly, I saw the Gallic subtlety with which he had addressed the lad. Had I been telling him, I should have minimized the tragic aspects of his father's death as much as possible. The Frenchman, on the contrary, had thrown them brutally before the boy, and then, with sure psychology, diverted thoughts of grief and horror by holding out the lure of vengeance.

"You're right!" the youngster answered, his chin thrust forth belligerently. "I don't know who'd want to harm my Dad—he never hurt a fly that didn't bite him first—but when we find the one who did it, we—by God, sir, we'll hang him high as Haman!"

Arrangements were quickly made. Indefinite leave was granted Harold, and I parked my car before his dormitory while he completed hurried packing for the journey to his desolated home.

"Strikes me he's taking an unconscionable time to stuff his bags," I grumbled when we had waited upward of an hour. "Perhaps he's broken down, de Grandin—I've seen sturdier lads than he collapse like deflated balloons in similar circumstances—will you excuse me while I run in and see if he's all right?"

The little Frenchman nodded and I hastened to the upper-story room young Pancoast shared with a classmate.

"Pancoast? No, sir," his roommate replied to my hurried inquiry. "He came in about an hour ago and told me his trouble, then stuffed his gear into his kit bag there"—he indicated the great pigskin valise resting in a corner of the room—"and said he had to see some one before he left for home. I thought perhaps he'd decided to go on without his grip and would send for it later. Terrible thing, his father's death, wasn't it, sir?"

"Quite," I answered. "You've no idea where he went, or why, I suppose?"

The lad colored slightly. "I—" he began, then stopped, embarrassed.

"Out with it!" I ordered curtly. "His mother's on the verge of collapse at home, and he's needed there. It's the better part of three hours' steady drive, too."

"I'm not sure, sir," the cadet answered, evidently of divided mind whether to hold fast the confidence imposed in him or break the school's unwritten law in deference to the emergency. "I'm not *certain* where he went, but—well, he's been pretty spoony on a *femme* ever since the semester started, and—maybe—he ran over to say good-bye. But it shouldn't take him this long, and—"

"All right," I broke in brusquely, "never mind the details. Where's this young woman likely to be found? We're in a hurry, son." I bent and seized the waiting kit-bag as I spoke, then paused significantly at the door.

"I haven't her address, sir," the lad replied, "Panny never mentioned it to me, but you'll be likely to find him down in Rogation Walk—that's the little lane south of the campus by the old Military Road, you know—they usually meet there between retreat and tattoo."

"Very well, I'll hunt him there," I answered. "Thanks for the information. Good-night."

HAROLD PANCOAST LAY AS he had fallen, his uniform cap, top down, on the bricks of the shaded walk, the black-braided collar and gray shoulders of his blouse stained rusty red. Transversely across the back of his head, where hair-line joined the neck, gaped a long incised wound from which blood, already beginning to congeal, was welling freely, and in which there showed a trace of the grayish-white of cerebro-spinal fluid. His hands were stretched above him and clenched convulsively. The blow which struck him down must have been a brutally powerful one, delivered with some sharp, heavy instrument and wielded with monstrous force, for it had hacked its way half through the atlas of his spine and, glacing upward, cut deeply in the lower occiput. No need to ask if he were dead; the guillotine could scarcely have worked with more efficiency upon the poor lad's neck.

As I gazed at him in horror another horror crept over me. Though I had not inspected his father's injuries, Parnell, the coroner's physician, had described them with the ghoulish gusto of his trade, and there before me on the son there lay the very reproduction of the wound which cost the father's life not twenty hours earlier!

"Good heavens!" I gasped, and my pounding heart-beats almost stopped my breath. "This is devilish!"

I turned and raced along the quiet, tree-rimmed walk in search of Jules de Grandin.

2. The Third Murder

"SURE, DOCTOR DE GRANDIN, sor, 'tis, th' divil's own puzzle we've got here, an' no mistake," confided Detective Sergeant Jeremiah Costello as he knocked an inch of ash from his cigar and turned worried blue eyes on the diminutive Frenchman. "First off, we've got th' murther o' this here now Misther Pancoast— an' th' divil's own murther it were, too, sor—an' now we've got th' case of his kid to consider; though, th' blessèd saints be praised, *that* case is what ye might call academic, since it happened outside me jurisdiction entirely, an' catchin' o' th' scoundrel as done it is none o' me official business, unless, belike—"

Jules de Grandin nodded shortly. "It is very exceedingly belike, indeed, my friend," he interrupted. "Consider, if you please. What are the facts?" He raised his small left hand and spread the fingers fanwise, then counted on them in succession. "First we have this Monsieur Pancoast the elder, a fine and honest gentleman, if all reports be true. Very good. Night before last he leaves the dinner table for a meeting of his lodge, and drives off in his motor car. He shows no sign of worriment at the meeting; he is his usual smiling self. Very well. Precisely at eleven o'clock he leaves, for they have worked the third degree, and food is being served, but he is on a diet and can not stay to eat. That is too bad. Two fellow members see him enter his sedan and drive away toward home. What happens afterward we do not surely know; but in the morning he is found beside the door of his garage, face downward on the ground, and weltering in blood. His neck is chopped across the back, his spine is all but severed and the instrument of death has cloven through his skull and struck the *corpus dentatum* of his brain."

He nodded solemnly. "'Why has this thing been done?' I ask. To find the criminal in this case means we must find the motive, but where can it be found?

We can not say. This Monsieur Pancoast is a most estimable citizen, a member of the church and of the Rotary Club, a bank director, a one-time city councilman. Yet he is dead—murdered. The case is veiled in mystery.

"*Eh bien*, if the father's case is obscure, what shall we think of the son's? A fine young man, who had harmed no one, and whom no one could reasonably wish to harm. Yet he, too, is dead—murdered—and murdered with the same strange technique as that which killed his father.

"Attend me: You, *Sergent*, have seen much killing, both in war and peace; Trowbridge, my friend, you are a surgeon and anatomist; can either of you match the wounds which slew these poor ones in all of your experience?"

I shook my head. "Not I," I answered. "I can understand how a blow might be delivered in such a way as to cut the tip of the spine, or how the base of the skull could be cut through, but these wounds are beyond me. Parnell described Pancoast's injuries to me, and it seems they were identical with Harold's. His opinion was that no such upward-slanting blow could have been struck unless the victim lay prone, and even then the weapon used would have to be curved, like a carpenter's adz, for instance, to permit the course these incisions followed."

"*Ah bah*, Parnell, he is an old woman in trousers!" de Grandin shot back. "Better would he exercise such talents as he has in a butcher shop, I think. Consider him: He says the victim must be prone. *Grand dieu des cochons!* Did we not examine the poor *petit Monsieur*? But certainly. And did we not find him stretched face downward on the earth? Yes, again. But with his tight-clenched hands above his head, as though he clutched at nothing while he fell? Of course. His attitude was one of having fallen, and he who lies upon the earth must find it impossible to fall. *Voilà*, he was killed standing; for had he lain flat upon the ground when he was struck, he must inevitably have writhed in reflex death-agony when that blow shore through his spine and skull; but standing he would have made a single wild clutch for support, then stiffened as he fell upon his face. His nerves and muscles were disposed to hold him upright, and when death comes from sudden wounding of the brain, reaction of rigidity is almost instant. You have seen it, *Sergent*; so have I. A soldier in the charge, by example, is drilled through the head by a rifle ball. He staggers on a step or two, perhaps, and then he falls, or it is better to say he topples forward, stiff and straight as though at attention, and hours afterward his poor, dead hands still grasp his musket tightly. But if that same man lies on the earth when he meets death that way, the chances are nine hundred in a thousand that he will twist and writhe, at least in one final spasm, before he stiffens. But certainly. It is for that reason that the condemned one is strapped tight to the cradle of the guillotine. If he were not, the reflex nervous action consequent upon decapitation—which is no more than a sudden injury to the spine, my friends— would surely cause him to roll sidewise on the scaffold floor, and that would rob the execution of its dignity. Yes, it is undoubtlessly so."

"Well, be gob, sor, ye're makin' th' dose harder to take than ever," Costello muttered. "First ye tell us that th' same felly kilt th' both o' them; then ye demonstrate beyant th' shadder o' a doubt that no one livin' could 'a' struck th' blows as kilt 'em. What's th' answer, if anny?"

"*Hélas*, as yet there is none," de Grandin returned. "Tomorrow, when the funeral has been held, I shall investigate, and probably I shall be wiser when I finish. Until that time we only know that some one for some motive as yet unguessed has done away with son and father, and from the difficult technique of both the murders, I am most confident is was the same assassin who perpetrated them. As for the motive—"

"That's just it, sor," Costello interrupted. "There ain't none."

"*Précisément, mon vieux*, as I was saying, this seeming absence of motive may prove most helpful to us in our researches. It is better to be lost in the midst of impenetrable night than to be witch-led by will-o'-the-wisps. So in this case. With no false leads, we commence from the beginning—start from scratch, as your athletes say. Yes, it is better so."

"Ye—ye mean to say because there's nayther hide nor hair o' motive, nor rime nor reason to these here killin's, th' case is easier?" Costello demanded.

"You have removed the words from my lips, *mon brave*."

"Glory be to God—'tisn't Jerry Costello who'd like to see what ye'd be afther callin' a har-rd case, then!" the Irishman exclaimed.

The little Frenchman grinned delightedly. "Forgive me if I seem to jerk your leg, my old one," he apologized. "Let us gather here tomorrow at this time, and we shall talk more straightly to the point, for we shall then know what we know not now."

"Be gob, 'tis meself that's hopin' so," Costello responded with none too much optimism in his tone.

A MOTORCADE OF BLACK AND shining limousines was ranked beneath the Lombardy poplars which stood before the Pancoast house. Frock-coated gentlemen and ladies in subdued attire ascended the front steps, late floral deliveries were unostentatiously shunted to the kitchen door and signed for by a black-coated, gray-gloved gentleman. The air in the big drawing-room was heavy with the scent of carnations and tuberoses.

"Good afternoon, Doctor Trowbridge; how are you, Doctor de Grandin?" Coroner Martin, officiating in his private capacity of funeral director, met us in the hall. "There are two seats over by that window," he added in an undertone. "Take my advice and get them while you can, the air in here is thick enough to choke you."

"*Bien merci*," de Grandin murmured, treading an assortment of outstretched feet as he wove his way between the rows of folding chairs to the vacant seats beside the window. Arrived, he perched on the extreme forward rim of the chair, his silk hat held tenderly with both hands on his knees, his little, round blue eyes fixed unwinkingly upon the twin caskets of polished mahogany, as though he would drag their secrets from them by very force of will.

The funeral rites began. The clergyman, a man in early middle life who liked to think that Beecher's mantle had fallen on him, was more than generous with his words. Unrelated and entirely inapposite excerpts from Scripture were sandwiched between readings from the poets, his voice broke and quavered artistically as he spoke feelingly of "these our dear departed brethren;" when the time came for final prayer I was on the verge of sleep.

"*Capote d'une anguille,*" de Grandin murmured angrily, "does he take the good God for a fool? Must he be telling him these poor ones met their deaths by murder? Does *le bon Dieu* not yet know what everyone in Harrisonville already knows by heart? Bid him say 'Amen' and cease, Friend Trowbridge; my neck is breaking; I can no longer bow my head!"

"S-s-s-sh!" I ordered in a venomous whisper, reinforcing my order with a sharp dig of my elbow in his ribs. "Be quiet; you're irreverent!"

"*Mordieu,* I am worse; I am impatient," he breathed in my ear, and raised his head to cast a look of far from friendly import on the praying divine.

"Ah?" I heard him breathe between his teeth. "*A-a-ah?*" Abruptly he bowed his head again, but I could see his sidelong glance was fixed on some one seated by the farther window.

When the interminable service was at length concluded and the guests had filed out, de Grandin made excuse to stay. The motor cars had left, and only one or two assistants of the mortician remained to set the funeral room in order, but still he lingered in the hall. "This cabinet, my friend," he drew me toward an elaborate piece of furniture finished in vermilion lacquer and gold-leaf, "is it not a thing of beauty? And this"—he pointed to another piece of richly inlaid brass and tortoise-shell—"surely this is a work of art."

I shrugged impatiently. "Do you think it good taste to take inventory of the furniture at such a time?" I asked acidly.

"One wonders how they came here, and when," he answered, ignoring my remark; then, as a servant hurried by with brush and dustpan, "Can you tell me whence these came?" he asked.

The maid, a woman well past middle life, gave him a look which would have withered anyone but Jules de Grandin, but he met her frown with a smile of such frank artlessness that she relented despite herself.

"Yes, sir," she returned. "Mr. Carlin—Mr. Pancoast, sir—God rest him!—brought them home with him when he returned from India. We used to have a ruck of such-like things, but he sold 'most all of 'em; these two are all that's left."

"Indeed, then Monsieur Pancoast was once a traveler?"

"Well, I don't rightly know about that, sir. I only know the talk around the house; you see, I've only been here twenty years, and he came back long before that. It's only what Mrs. Hussy—she used to cook here, and had worked for the family long before I came—it's only what she told me that I know for certain, sir, and even that's just hearsay."

"*Bien*, quite so, *exactement*," he answered thoughtfully and slipped a folded bill into her hand. "And can you by some happy chance tell one where he may find this queen among cooks, this peerless Madame Hussé?"

"Yes, sir, that I can; she's living at the Bellefield Home. She bought an an-uty and—"

"A which?" de Grandin asked.

"An an-uty—a steady income, sir. She bought it when she left service and went to live at the home. She's past eighty years old, and—"

"*Parbleu*, then we must hurry if we wish to speak with her!" de Grandin interrupted with a bow. "I thank you for the information.

"Expect me when I return, my friend," he told me as we reached the street. "I may be early or I may be late; that depends entirely upon this Madame Hussé's powers as a conversationist. At any rate, it would be wiser if you did not wait for me at dinner."

IT WAS FORTUNATE WE did not wait on him, for nine o'clock had struck and dinner was long over when he came bursting in the door, his little round blue eyes alight with excitement, a smile of satisfaction on his lips. "Has the good Costello yet arrived?" he asked as he looked hastily around the study as though he half suspected the great Irishman might be hidden beneath the couch or desk.

"Not yet," I answered, "but—" The ringing of the doorbell cut me short, and the big detective entered. A parenthesis of worry-wrinkles lay between his brows, and the look he gave de Grandin was almost one of appeal.

"Well, Doctor de Grandin, sor," he remarked, brightening as he noted the little Frenchman's expression, "what's in th' news-bag? There's sumpin' up yer sleeve beside yer elbow, I can see it be th' look o' ye."

"You have right, my friend," de Grandin answered. "Did not I tell you that the absence of a motive was a cheerful sign for us? But yes. Attend me!

"At Monsieur Pancoast's late abode this afternoon I chanced to spy two objects of *vertu* the like of which we do not ordinarily find outside of museums. Jules de Grandin, he has traveled much, and what he knows he knows. The importation of such things is rare, for they are worth their weight in gold and—a thousand pardons if I give offense—Americans as a class are not yet educated to their beauty. Only those who have lived long in the East appreciate them, and few have brought them home. Therefore I asked a most excellently garrulous maidservant who was passing if she could tell me whence they came, and though she knew but little she gave to me the clue for which I searched, for she said first that Monsieur Pancoast brought them from India—which was not so—and that she had heard as much from a former cook, which was indubitably true.

"*Alors*, to Bellefield I did go to interview this Madame Hussé who had once been cook for Monsieur Pancoast, and she did tell me much. *Mais oui*, she told me a very great deal, indeed.

"She told me, by example, that he had studied for the ministry as a young man, and had gone to preach the Gospel in Burma. She had known him from a lad, and much surprised she was when he decided on the missioner's vocation, for he had been a—how do you say? a gay dog?—among the ladies, and such behavior as his and the minister's black coat did not seem to her in harmony.

"*Eh bien*, there is no sinner so benighted he can not see the light if he will but look toward it, and so it was with this one. Young Pancoast assumed the ministry and off he went to battle with the Evil One and teach the heathen to wear clothes.

"Now what transpired in the East she does not know; but that he returned home again and not with empty pockets, she knows full well, for great was the surprise of everyone when the erstwhile poor clergyman returned and set himself up in business. And he did prosper mightily. *Tiens*, it was the wonder of the city how everything he touched seemed transmuted into gold. Yes. And then, though well along in years for marrying, he wedded Mademoiselle Griggsby, whose father was most wealthy and whose social standing was above reproach. By her he had one son, whose name was Harold. Does not an explanation, or at least a theory, jump to your eye?"

"Because he married Griggsby's daughter an' had a son named Harold?" Costello asked with heavy sarcasm. "Well, no sor; I can't say as how me eye is troubled with any explanation jumpin' in it yet awhile."

"*Zut*, it is permissible to be stupid, but you abuse the privilege!" the little Frenchman snapped. "You know something of the East, I take it? Monsieur Kipling has nearly phrased it:

. . . somewheres East of Suez,
Where the best is like the worst,
And there ain't no Ten Commandments—

"Ah? You begin to perceive? In that sun-flogged land of Burma the best *is* like the worst, or becomes so shortly after arrival. The white man's morale—and morals—break down, the saint becomes a sinner overnight. The native men are worse than despicable, the native women—*eh bien*, who suffers hunger in an orchard or dies of thirst amid running brooks, my friends? Yes, strange things happen in the East. The laws of man may be enforced, but those of God are flouted. The man who is respectable at home has no shame in betraying any woman whose skin bears the sun's kiss marks or at turning any shabby deal which lines his purse with gold and takes him home again in affluence. No. *And Pancoast quit the ministry in Burma.* A Latin or a Greek or Anglican priest may not quit his holy orders unless he is ecclesiastically unfrocked, but clergymen of the Protestant sects may lay their office down as lightly as a businessman resigning his position. Pancoast did. He said as much to Madame Hussé when once he had a bursting-out of confidence. Remember, she had known him from a little lad.

"Now, what have you to say?"

"Well, sor," Costello answered slowly, "I know ye're speakin' truth about th' East. I served me time in th' Philippines, an' seen many a man go soft in morals underneath that sun, which ain't so different from th' sun in Burma. I'm afther thinkin', but—"

"There is a friend of Monsieur Pancoast, a boyhood chum, who went in business with him after his return," de Grandin broke in. "By good chance it may be that you know him; his name is Dalky, and he was associated with Pancoast until some ten years since, when they had a quarrel and dissolved their partnership. This Monsieur Dalky, perhaps, can be of ser—"

The strident ringing of the telephone cut through his narrative.

"It's you they want" I told Costello, handing him the instrument.

"Hullo? Sure—been here fer—Howly Mither, is it so? I'll be right over!"

He clashed the monophone into its hooks and turned on us with blazing eyes.

"Gentlemen," he announced, "here's wor-rk fer us, an' no time to delay. Whilst we've been settin' here like three dam' fools, talkin' o' this an' that, there's murther bein' done. 'Tis Missis Pancoast. They got her. Th' Lord help us—they've wiped out the whole family, sors, right beneath our very noses!"

3. The Message on the Card

THE SERVANT WE HAD talked with after the funeral met us in the hall when we reached the Pancoast home. "No, sir," she answered Costello's inquiries, "I can't tell you much about it. Mrs. Pancoast came back from the cemet'ry in a terrible state—not crying nor taking on, but sort o' all frozen up inside, you know. I didn't hear her speak a word, except once. She'd gone into her bow-duer upstairs and laid down on the couch, and along about four o'clock I thought maybe a cup o' tea might help her some, so I went up with it. She'd got up, and was standing looking at a picture o' Mr. Harold in his uniform that hung on the wall—an almost life-sized portrait it is. Just as I come into the room—I didn't knock, for I didn't want to disturb her if she was sleeping—she said, 'O, my baby; my belovèd baby boy!' Just that and nothing else, sir. No crying or anything, you understand. Then she turned and seen me standing there with the tea, and said,

'Thank you, Jane, put it on the table, please,' and went back and lay down on the couch. She was calm and collected as she always was, but I could see the heart of her was breaking inside her breast, all the same.

"She didn't come down to supper, of course, so I took some toast and eggs up to her. The tea I'd brought earlier was standing stone-cold on the table, sir; she hadn't poured a drop of it. When I went in she thanked me for the supper and had me set it on the table, and I left.

"It was something after nine o'clock, maybe, when the young woman called."

"Eh? A young woman? Do you tell me? This is of interest. Describe her, if you please," de Grandin ordered.

"I can't say as I can, sir," the woman answered. "She wasn't very tall, and she wasn't exactly what you'd call short, either. She was just medium, not tall nor short, thin nor fat. Her hair, as far as I could see, was dark, and her face was rather pale. I guess you'd call her pretty, though there was a sort o' queer, goggle-eyed expression to her that made me think—well, sir, you know how young folks are these days, what with Prohibition and cocktail parties and all—if I'd smelled anything, I'd have said she'd been drinking too much, but there wasn't any odor of alcohol about her, though she did have some kind o' strong, sweet perfume. She asked to see Mrs. Pancoast, and when I said I didn't think she could be seen, she said it was most urgent; that Mrs. Pancoast would surely see her if I'd take her card up. So she handed me a little note in an envelope—not just a visiting-card, sir—and I took it up, though I didn't feel right about doing it.

"Mrs. Pancoast didn't want to be bothered at first; told me to send the young lady away, but when she read what was written on the card her whole manner changed. She seemed all nervous and excited-like, right away, and told me to show the visitor right up.

"They stayed there talking about fifteen minutes, I should judge; then the two of 'em came down, the young lady still blear-eyed and sort o' dazed-looking and Mrs. Pancoast in an awful hurry. She was more excited than I'd ever seen her in all the twenty years I've worked here. It seemed to me like she was all trembly and twitching-like, sir. They got into the taxi, and—"

"Oh ho, there wuz a taxi, wuz there?" Costello interrupted.

"Why, yes, sir; didn't I say the young lady came in a taxi?"

"Ye did not; an' ye're neglecting to tell whether 'twas th' same one she came in that took them off, but—'

"Yes, sir, it was. She kept it waiting, sir."

"Oh, did she, now? I don't suppose ye noted its number?"

"No, sir, I didn't; but—"

"Or what kind it wuz—yellow, blue or—"

"I'm not exactly certain it *was* a taxi, sir, now I come to think of it. It was sort o' dark-colored, and—"

"An' had four wheels wid rubber tires on each o' em, I suppose? Ye're bein' mighty helpful to us, so ye are, I must say. Now git on wid it. What happened next?"

"Nothing happened, sir. They drove off and I went on about my work. First I tidied up the bow-duer and took away the supper tray—Mrs. Pancoast hadn't touched a bite—then I came downstairs and—"

"Howly St. Bridget! *Will* ye be gittin' on wid it?" Costello almost roared. "We'll admit fer th' sake o' argyment that ye done yer duties and done 'em noble, but what we're afther tryin' to find out, if ye'd please be so kind as to tell us, is when ye first found out Mrs. Pancoast had been kilt, and how ye found it out."

The woman's eyes snapped angrily. "I was coming to that," she answered tartly. "I'd come down to the basement to wash the supper things from Mrs. Pancoast's tray, when I heard a ringing at the lower front door—the tradesmen's door, you know. I went to answer it, for Cook had gone, and—oh, Mary, Mother! It was terrible!

"She lay there, gentlemen, head-foremost down the three steps that leads to the gate under the porch stairs, and blood was running all over the steps. I almost fainted, but luckily I remembered to call the coroner to come and take it—her, I mean—away. Oh, I'll never, never be able to go up those service steps again!"

"Ten thousand small and annoying active little blue devils!" de Grandin swore. "Do you tell me they took her away—removed the body before we had a chance to view it?"

"Yes, sir; of course. I knew the proper thing to do was not to touch it—her, I mean—until the coroner had come, so I 'phoned him right away and—"

"Oh, ye did, did ye?" Costello broke in. "I don't suppose ye ever heard that th' city pays policemen to catch those that commits murther? Ye called th' coroner and had him spoil what little clues we might o' found, an'—"

The goaded woman turned on him in fury. "The city may pay police to catch murderers," she blazed, "but if it does it's wasting its money on the likes o' you! Do you know who killed Mr. Carlin? No! Do you know who killed Mr. Harold? No! Will you find out who murdered poor, innocent Mrs. Pancoast? Don't make me laugh! You couldn't catch cold on a rainy day, let alone catch a sneaking murderer like the one which did these killings! You and your talk o' spoiled clues!" She tossed her head disdainfully. "Was I to leave the poor lady's remains laying by her own front door while you looked round for fingerprints and the like o' that? Not for all the police in Harrisonville would I—"

"*Tiens*, my friends, this is interesting, but not instructive. There is little to be gained from calling hard names, and time presses. Had you first notified the police, *Mademoiselle*, you would have rendered apprehension of the miscreants more certain, but as it is we must make the best of what we have to work with. No amount of weeping will restore spilled milk."

To Costello he added: "Let us inspect Madame Pancoast's boudoir. Perhaps we shall find something."

A BRIGHT FIRE BURNED BEHIND the brass fender in the cheerful apartment Maria Pancoast had quit to go to her death an hour earlier; pictures, mostly family portraits, adorned the walls, the windows were gay with bright-figured chintz. A glance at the mahogany table revealed nothing. The gayly painted wastebasket contained only a few stray wisps of crumpled notepaper; the Colonial escritoire which stood between the windows was kept with spinsterish neatness; nothing like a hastily opened note or visiting-card showed on its fresh green blotter.

"*Voilà*, my friends, I think I have it!" de Grandin cried, peering into the bed of glowing coke as he crouched on hands and knees before the fireplace. "It is burned, but—careful, very careful, my friend, a strong breath may destroy it!" He motioned Costello back, took up the brazen fire-tongs and, gently as a chemist might handle an explosive mixture, lifted a tiny curl of crackling gray-black ash from the blue flames. "*Prie Dieu* she wrote in ink!" he muttered as he bore his find to the table and laid it tenderly upon the sheet of clean white paper Costello spread before him.

The parchment shades were stripped from the lamps and at Costello's order Jane, the maid, ran to the dining-room to fetch stronger electric bulbs. Meanwhile de Grandin reached into his waistcoat pocket and took out a pair of delicate steel tweezers and a collapsible-framed jeweler's loop which he inserted in his right eye.

Carefully, almost without breathing, lest the gentle current of air from lips or nostrils destroy the carbonized cardboard, he turned the blackened relic underneath the lens of his glass.

"M—i—s—s— A—l—l," he spelled out slowly, then fell to studying the cone of blackened paper intently again. "No use, my friends, the printing is effaced by the fire beyond that part," he told us. "Now for the message on the card. If she used ink all is well, for the metallic pigment in it will have withstood the heat. If she wrote in pencil—we are luckless, I fear. Let us see."

For several minutes he turned the little cone of ash beneath the lights, then with a shrug of impatience laid it on the paper, and holding one end in a gentle, steady grip with the tweezers, dipped his fingers in a tumbler and let fall a drop of water on the charred pasteboard. The burned paper trembled like a living thing in torture as the liquid touched it, and a tiny crackling rose from it. But after a moment the moisture seemed to spread through the burned fiber, rendering it less brittle. Twice more he repeated the experiment, each time increasing the pressure of his tweezers. At length he succeeded in prying the cone of heat-contorted paper partly open.

"*Ah?*" he exclaimed exultantly. "It was prepared beforehand. See, she did use ink—thanks be to God!"

Again be studied the charred pasteboard and spelled out slowly: "lp—ho—ban—so—"

"Name of a name; it is plain as any flagpole!" he cried. "In vain is the evidence of crime burned, my friends. We have them, we know the bait by which they lured poor Madame Pancoast to her death! You see?" He turned bright eyes on Costello and me in turn.

"Not I," I answered.

"Nor I," the Irishman confessed.

"*Mordieu*, must I then teach school to you great stupid-heads?" he asked. "Consider:

"A young woman comes to see poor Madame Pancoast, scarcely four hours after she has laid away all that remained to her of son and husband. Would *Madame* be likely to see a stranger in such circumstances? Mademoiselle Jane, the maid, thought not, and she was undoubtlessly right. But Madame Pancoast saw this visitor. For why? Because of something written on a card. Now, what could move a woman with a shattered heart to see an unknown visitor—more, to go away with her, seemingly in a fever of impatience? The answer leaps to the eye. Certainly. It is this: Fill in the missing letters of these words, and though they make but fragments of a sentence, they speak to us in trumpet-tones. Four parts of words we have, the first of which is '*lp*.' Add two letters to it, and we have '*help*.' *N'est-ce-pas*? But certainly. Perform the same office for the other three and we have this portion of the message: '*help—who—husband—son.*' What more is needed? Tonight came one who promised—in writing, *grâce à Dieu*—to help the stricken wife and mother bring to justice the slayer of her husband and her son! Is it to be wondered that she went with her? *Pardieu*, though she had known for certainty that the path led to the death she met tonight, she would have gone. Yes.

"Madame Pancoast"—he wheeled and faced a portrait of the murdered woman which hung upon the wall and brought his hand up in salute—"your sacrifice shall not be in vain. Although they know it not, these vile miscreants who lured you to your death have paved the way for Jules de Grandin to seek them out. I swear it!"

To us he ordered peremptorily: "Come, let us go!"

"Where?" Costello and I demanded in chorus.

"To Monsieur Dalky's, of course. I think that he can do us a favor. I know we can do him one, if it be not already too late. *Allez-vous-en!*"

4. The Warning

"NO SIR, MR. DALKY's not in," the butler answered de Grandin's impatient inquiry. "He went out about fifteen or twenty minutes ago, and—

"Really, I couldn't say, sir," the man's manner was eloquent of outraged dignity as de Grandin demanded his employer's destination. "Mr. Dalky was not accustomed to tell me where he intended—"

"*Dix mille mousquites*, what do we care of his customs?" the Frenchman cut in. "This is of importance. We must know whither he went at once, right away—"

"I really couldn't say, sir," the butler returned imperturbably, and swung the door to.

"Listen here, young felly," Costello inserted the broad toe of his boot in the rapidly diminishing space between door and jamb and brought his broad shoulder against the panels, "d'ye see this?" He turned back the lapel of his jacket, displaying his badge. "Ye'll tell us where Dalky went, an' tell it quick, or else—"

Statement of the alternative was unnecessary. "I'll ask Mrs. Dalky, sir," the man began, but:

"Ye'll not," Costello denied. "Ye'll take us to her, an' we'll do our own askin', savvy?" The butler led us to the room where Mrs. Dalky sat beneath a reading-lamp conning the current issue of *The New Yorker*.

"A thousand pardons, *Madame*," de Grandin apologized, "but we come in greatest haste to consult Monsieur your husband. It is in relation to the so strange deaths of Monsieur Pancoast and—"

"Mr. Pancoast!" Mrs. Dalky dropped her magazine and her air of slight hauteur at once. "Why, that's what Herbert went to see about."

"Ten thousand crazy monkeys!" de Grandin swore beneath his breath, then, aloud: "When? Where, if you please? It is important!"

"We were sitting here reading," the lady replied, "when the telephone rang. Some one wanted to speak with Mr. Dalky privately, concerning the murder of Mr. Pancoast and his son. It seemed, from what I overheard, that this person had stumbled on the information accidentally and wanted to consult my husband about one or two phases of the case before they went to the police. Mr. Dalky wanted him to come here, but he said they must act at once if they were to catch the murderers, so he would meet my husband at Tunlaw and Emerson Streets in twenty minutes, then they could go directly to police headquarters, and—"

"Your pardon, *Madame*, we must go!" de Grandin almost shouted, and seizing Costello with one hand and me with the other, he fairly dragged us from the room.

"Rush, hasten, fly, my friend!" he bade me. "We have perhaps five little minutes of grace. Let us make the most of it. To those Tunlaw and Emerson Streets, with all celerity, if you please!"

The gleaming, baleful eyes of a city ambulance's red-lensed headlights bore down upon us from the opposite direction as we raced to the designated corner, and the *r-r-r-rang!* of its gong warned traffic from the road. A crowd had already begun to congregate at the curb, staring with hang-jawed wonder at something on the sidewalk.

"Jeez, Sergeant," exclaimed the patrolman who stood guard above the still figure lying on the concrete, "I never seen nothing like it. Talk about puttin' 'em on th' spot! Lookit this!" He put back the improvised shroud covering Dalky's features, and I went sick at the sight. The left side of the man's head, from brow to hair-line, was scooped away, like an apple bitten into, and from the awful, gaping wound flowed mingled blood and brain. "No need for you here, Doc," the officer added to the ambulance surgeon as the vehicle clanged to a halt and the white-jacketed intern elbowed his way through the crowd. "What this pore sucker needs is th' morgue wagon."

"How'd it happen?" Costello asked.

"Well, sir, it was all so sudden I can't rightly tell you," the patrolman answered. "I seen this here bird standin' on th' corner, kind o' lookin' round an' pullin' out his watch every once in a while, like he had a heavy date with some one, when all of a sudden a car comes rushin' round th' corner, goin' like th' hammers o' hell, an' before I knew it, it's swung up that way through Emerson Street, and this pore feller's layin' on th' sidewalk with half his face missin'." He passed a hand meditatively across his hard-shaven chin. "It musta been th' car hit 'im," he added, "though I can't see how it could 'a' cut him up that way, but I'd 'a' swore I seen sumpin sort o' jump out o' th' winder at him as th' automobile dashed past, just th' same. I suppose I'm all wet, but—"

"By no means, *mon vieux*," de Grandin interrupted. "What was it you saw flash from the passing car, if you please?"

"That's hard to say, sir," the officer responded. "I can say what it *looked* like, though."

"*Très bien*. Say on; we are all attention."

"Well, sit, don't think I'm a nut; but it *looked* like a sad-iron hitched onto a length o' clothesline. I'd 'a' swore some one inside th' car flung th' iron out th' winder, mashed th' pore chap in th' face with it, an' yanked it back—all in one motion, like. Course, it couldn't 'a' been, but—"

"What kind o' car wuz it?" demanded Costello.

"Looked like a taxi, sir. One o' them new, shiny black ones with a band o' red an' gold checkers runnin' round the tonneau, you know. It had more speed than any taxi I ever saw, an' it got clear away before I got a good look at it, for I was all taken up with this pore man, but—"

"All right, turn in your report when th' coroner's car comes for him," Costello ordered. "Annything y'ed like to ask, Doctor de Grandin?"

"I think not," the Frenchman answered. "But, if you please, I should like to have you put a guard in Mrs. Dalky's house. In no circumstances is anyone not known to the servants to be allowed to see her, and no telephone calls whatever are to be put through to her. You will do this?"

"H'm, I'll try, sor. If th' lady objects, o' course, there's nothin' we can do, for she's not accused o' crime, an' we can't isolate her that way agin her will; but I'll see what we can do.

"This burns me up," he added dismally. "Here this felly, whoever he is, goes an' pulls another murther off, right while we're lookin' at 'im, ye might say. It's monkeys he's makin' out o' us, nothin' less!"

"By no means," de Grandin denied. "True, he has accomplished his will, but for the purpose of his final apprehension, it is best that he seems to have the game entirely his own way. Our seeming inability to cope with him will make him bold, and boldness is akin to foolishness in a criminal. Consider: We were at fault concerning Monsieur Pancoast's murder; the murder of his son likewise gave us naught to go upon; almost while we watched he lured poor Madame Pancoast from her house and slew her, and as far as he can know, we know no more about the bait he used in her case than we knew of the other killings. Now comes Monsieur Dalky. The game seems all too easy; he thinks that he can kill at will and pass among us unsuspected and unmolested. Assuredly he will try the trick again, and when he does,—*parbleu*, the strongest pitcher comes to grief if it be taken to the well too often! Yes."

"What made ye think that Dalky'd be th' next to go?" Costello asked as we drove slowly through the quiet street to notify the widow.

"A little by-play which I chanced to notice at the funeral this afternoon," de Grandin answered. "It happened that I raised my head while the good clergyman was broadcasting endlessly, and as I did so I perceived a hand reach through the open window and drop a wad of paper at Monsieur Dalky's feet. He did not seem to notice it at first, and when he did he thrust it unread into his waistcoat pocket.

"There I was negligent, I grant you. I should have followed him and asked to see the contents of the note—for a note of some kind it was undoubtlessly. Why else should it have been dropped before him while he was at the funeral of his one-time partner? But I did not follow my intention. Although the incident intrigued me, I had more pressing business to attend to in searching out Monsieur Pancoast's antecedents that we might find some motive for his murder. It was not till I had interviewed Madame Hussé at the Bellefield Home that I learned of the former partnership between Pancoast and Dalky, and even then I did not greatly apprehend the danger to the latter; for though he was associated with the murdered man, he, at least, had never traveled to the East. But when the vengeful one slew Madame Pancoast, who was most surely innocent of any wrong, my fears for Monsieur Dalky were roused, and so we hastened to his house—too late, *hélas*."

We drove in silence a few moments, then: "What we have seen tonight confirms my suspicions almost certainly," he stated.

"Umph!" grunted Costello.

"Precisely, exactly, quite so. The chenay throwing-knife, do you know him?"

"Can't say I do."

"Very good. I do. On more than one occasion I had dodged him, and he requires artful dodging, I assure you. Yes. *Couteau de table du diable*—the devil's table knife—he has been called, and rightly so. Something like the bolo of your Filipinos it is, but with a curved blade, a blade not curved like a saber, but bent lengthwise, the point toward the hilt, so that the steel describes an arc. Sharpened on both edges like a razor—five inches across its widest part, weighted at the handle, it is the weapon of the devil—or of *Dakaits*, who are the foul fiend's half-brothers. They fling it with lightning speed and such force that it will sheer through iron—or one's skull. Then with a thin, tough cord of gut they pull it back again. Yes, it is true. Very well. Such a blade, Friend Trowbridge, hurled at a man's back would cut his spine and also cleave his lower skull. You apprehend me?"

"You mean it was a knife like that—"

"*Précisément.* No less. I did not at first identify it by the wound it made on the poor Pancoasts, but when I saw the so unfortunate Monsieur Dalky's cloven face, my memory bridged the gulf of years and bore me back to Burma—and the throwing-knives. With Pancoast's history in our minds, with these knife wounds to bear it out, the conclusion is obvious. The Oriental mind is flexible, but it is also conservative. Having started on a course of action, it will carry it through without the slightest deviation. I think we shall soon lay this miscreant by the heels, my friends."

"How?" Costello asked.

"Attend me carefully, and you shall see. Jules de Grandin has sworn an oath to poor, dead Madame Pancoast, and Jules de Grandin is no oath-breaker. By no means. No."

THE SHOCK WAS ALMOST more than Mrs. Dalky could bear. Both de Grandin and I were busy for upward of an hour with sedatives and soothing words. Meanwhile her condition simplified the Frenchman's program, for a police-woman who also held a nurse's license was installed beside her bed with orders to turn away all callers, and a plainclothes man was posted in the hall.

"And now, *mon vieux*," de Grandin told the butler, "you will please get me at once the formal coat and waistcoat Monsieur Dalky wore to the Pancoast funeral this afternoon. Hasten; my time is short and my temper shorter!"

Feverishly he turned the dead man's pockets out. In the lower left waistcoat was a tiny wad of crumpled rice-paper, the kind of thin, gray-white stuff which Eastern merchandise is wrapped in. Across it, roughly scrawled in red was the grotesque figure of a pointing man, a queer-looking figure in tight trousers and a conical cap, pointing with clenched fists at a row of smaller figurines. Obviously three of the smaller characters were men, their bifurcated garments proclaimed as much. Two more, judging by the crudely pictured skirts, were women. Two of the male figures had toppled over, the third and the two women stood erect.

"*Ha*, the implication here is plain. You see it?" de Grandin asked excitedly. "It was a warning, though the poor Dalky knew it not, apparently. Observe"—he tapped the two prone figures with his finger tip—"here lie the Pancoasts, *père et fils*. There, ready for the sacrifice is Madame Pancoast, and here is Monsieur Dalky, the sole remaining man. The last one in the group, the final woman, is who? Who but Madame Dalky, my friends? All, all are designed to die, and two are already dead, according to this drawing. Yes." He glared across the room as though in challenge to an invisible personage. "*Ha*, Monsieur Murderer, you may propose, but Jules de Grandin will dispose of this case and of you. I damn think I shall take you in your own trap and call your vengeance down on your own head. May Satan serve me stewed with parsley if I do not so!"

5. Allura

"SURE, IT WAS AN elegant job Coroner Martin did on Misther Dalky," Sergeant Costello commented as he stretched his feet to the fire of birch logs crackling on my study hearth and drew appreciatively at the cigar de Grandin gave him. "Were ye mindin' th' way he'd patched th' pore gentleman's face up so y'ed never notice how th' haythen murtherer done 'im in, Doctor Trowbridge, sor?"

I nodded. "Martin's a clever man at demi-surgery," I answered. "one of the best I've ever seen, and—"

"Excuse me, sor." Nora McGinnis, who is nominally my cook and household factotum, but who actually rules both my house and me with a hand of iron, appeared in the study doorway, "there's a lady in th' consultin'-room askin' to see Doctor de Grandin."

"Me?" the Frenchman asked. "You are sure? I do not practise medicine here; it must be Doctor Trowbridge whom she—"

"Th' divil a bit," Nora contradicted. "Sure, she's askin' fer th' little gentleman wid light hair an' a waxed mustache, an' Doctor Trowbridge has nayther light nor anny kind o' hair, nor does he wax his mustache."

"You win, *ma belle*, certainly it is I," de Grandin answered with a laugh and rose to follow her.

A moment later he rejoined us, walking softly as a cat, his little round blue eyes alight with excitement. "Trowbridge, Costello, my friends," he whispered almost soundlessly, "come quietly, *comme une souris*, and see who is within. Adhere your ears to the keyhole, my friends, and likewise your eyes; I would that you should hear, as well as see!" He turned and left us and, as quietly as we could, we followed through the passage.

The writing-lamp burned on my office desk, its emerald shade picking out a spot of glowing green in the shadows of the room, and de Grandin moved it deftly so that its light fell full upon the visitor, yet left his face in dusk. At the door between the surgery and consulting-room we paused and watched the tables. Despite myself I started as my eyes rested on the face turned toward the Frenchman.

Devoid of rouge or natural coloring, save for the glowing carmine of the painted lips, the face was pale as death's own self and the texture of the fine white skin seemed more that of a Dresden blond than a brunette, although the hair beneath the modishly small hat was almost basalt-black. The nose was delicate, with slender nostrils that seemed to palpitate above the crimson lips. The face possessed a strange, compelling charm, its ivory pallor enhanced by the shadow of the long, silken lashes that lay against the cheeks, half veiling, half revealing purple eyes which slanted downward at the outer corners, giving the countenance a quaint, pathetic look. "It's she!" I murmured, forgetting that Costello could not understand, since he had never looked on her before. But I recognized her instantly. When first I saw her, she had walked with Harold Pancoast, an hour or less before he met his tragic death.

"It is my uncle, sir," she told de Grandin as we halted at the door. "He suffers from an obscure disease he contracted in the Orient years ago. The attacks are more violent at changes of the season—spring and autumn always affect him— and at present he's suffering acutely. We've had several doctors already, but none of them seems to understand the case. Then we heard of you." She folded her slender pale hands in her lap and looked placidly at him, and it seemed to me there was an odd expression in her gaze, like that of a person just aroused and still heavy with sleep, or one suffering from a dose of some narcotic drug.

The little Frenchman twisted the waxed tips of his diminutive blond mustache, obviously much pleased. "How was it they bade you come to me, *Mademoiselle?*" he asked.

"We heard—my uncle heard, that is—that you were a great traveler and had studied in the clinics of the East. He thought if anyone could give him relief it would be you." There was a queer, indefinable quality to her speech, her words were short, close-clipped, and seemed to stand out individually, as though each were the expression of a separate thought, and her semivowels and aspirates seemed insufficiently stressed.

For a long moment de Grandin studied her, and I thought I saw a look of wondering speculation in his face as he gazed directly into her luminous dark-blue eyes. Then: "Very well, *Mademoiselle*, I will come," he assented. "Do but wait a moment while I write out this prescription—" he took a pad of notepaper from the corner of the blotter and drew it towards him.

Crash! The atmosphere seemed shattered by the detonation and the room was plunged in sudden darkness.

I leaped forward, but a sharp, warning hiss from de Grandin stopped me in my tracks, and next instant I felt his little hand against my shoulder, pushing me insistently back to my hiding-place. Hardly had I regained the shelter of the door when the lights in the ceiling chandelier snapped on, flooding the room with brightness. Amazement almost froze me as I looked.

Calm and unmoved as a graven image the girl sat in her chair, her mild, impersonal gaze still fixed on Jules de Grandin. No charge in expression or attitude had taken place, though the desk lamp lay shattered on the floor, its shade and bulbs smashed into a thousand fragments.

"Right away, Mademoiselle," de Grandin remarked, as though he also were unaware of any untoward happening. "Come, let us go."

A long, black taxicab, its tonneau banded with squares of alternate gold and red, stood waiting at the curb before my door. The engine must have been running all the while, for de Grandin and the girl had hardly entered before it was away, traveling at a furious pace.

"Howly Moses, Trowbridge, sor, can't ye tell me what it's all about?" Costello asked as we re-entered the consulting-room and gazed upon the havoc.

"I'm afraid not," I returned, "but it looks as though a twenty-dollar lamp has been ruined, and—" I stopped, gazing at the two white spots upon my green desk-blotter. One was a woman's visiting card, engraved in neat block letters:

MISS ALLURA BATA

The other was a scribbled note from Jules de Grandin:

Friend Trowbridge:

In vain is the net spread in the sight of any bird, and I am not caught napping by their ruse. I think the murderer suspects I am too hot upon his trail, and has decided to dispose of me; but his chances of success are small. Await me. I shall return.

J. DE G.

"Lord knows I hope his confidence is justified," I exclaimed fervently. The thought of my little friend entering the lair of the pitiless killer appalled me.

"Wurra, if I'd 'a' known it he'd never gone off wid her unless I went along," Costello added. "He's a good little divil, Doctor Trowbridge, sor, an' if they do 'im injury, I'll—"

"Merci, my friend, you are most complimentary," de Grandin's laughing voice came from the doorway. "You did think I had the chance of the sparrow in the cat's mouth, hein? Eh bien, I fear this sparrow proved a highly indigestible morsel, in that event. Yes.

"If by any chance you should go to a corner, not so far away, my friend, you will find there a taxicab in a most deplorable state of disrepair. It is not healthy for the chauffeur to try conclusions with a tree, however powerful his motor may be. As for that one—" he paused, and there was something more of grimness than merriment in his smile.

"Where is he?" Costello asked. "If he tried any monkey-business—"

"*Tiens*, he surely did," de Grandin interrupted, "but with less success than a monkey would have had, I think. As for his present whereabouts"—he raised his narrow shoulders in an expressive shrug—"let us be charitable and say he is in heaven, although I fear that would be too optimistic. Perhaps I should have waited, but I had but little time to exercise my judgment, and so I acted quickly. I did not like the way he put speed to his motor the moment we had entered it, and as he was increasing the distance between you and me with each turn of his wheels, I acted on an impulse and struck him on the head. I struck him very hard, I fear, and struck him with a blackjack. It seemed to bother him considerably, for he lost control of his wheel immediately and ran into a tree. The vehicle stopped suddenly, but he continued on. The windshield intervened, but he continued on his way. Yes. He was a most unpleasant sight when last I looked at him.

"It took but half my eye," he continued, "to tell me the fellow was a foreigner, an Indian or Burmese. The trap was evidently well oiled, but so was I. *Alors*, I did escape.

"*Eh bien*, they are clever, those ones. It was a taxicab I entered, a new and pretty taxicab with lines of red and gold squares round its tonneau. The wrecked car from which I crawled a few minutes later had no such marks. No. By a device easily controlled from the driver's cab a shutter, varnished black to match the body of the car, could be instantly raised over the red and golden checkers, thus transforming what was patently a taxicab into a sumptuous private limousine. Had I not come back, you might have searched long for the taxi I was last seen in, but your search would have been in vain. It was a taxi, so the maid thought, which bore poor Madame Pancoast to her death, and it was a taxi, according to the officer, from which the death-knife was hurled at Monsieur Dalky, but neither of them could identify it accurately, and if instant chase had been given in either instance, the vehicle could have changed its identity almost while the pursuers watched, and gotten clean away. A clever scheme, *n'est-ce-pas?*"

"Well, sor, I'll be—" began Costello.

"Where's the girl?" I interrupted.

He looked at us with something like wonder in his eyes. "Do you recall how she sat stone-still, and seemed to notice not at all when I hurled your desk-lamp to the floor, and plunged the room in darkness?" he asked irrelevantly. "You saw that, for all she seemed to notice, nothing had happened, and that she took up the conversation where we left off when I turned on the lights again?"

"Yes, but where *is*—"

"*Parbleu*, you have as yet seen nothing, or at the most, but very little," he returned. "Come."

The girl sat calmly on the sofa in the study, her lovely, violet eyes staring with bovine placidity into the fire.

The little Frenchman tiptoed in and took up his position before her. "*Mademoiselle?*" he murmured questioningly.

"Doctor de Grandin?" she asked, turning her odd, almost sightless gaze on him.

"Yes, *Mademoiselle*."

"I've come to see you about my uncle. He suffers from an obscure disease he contracted in the Orient years ago. The attacks are most violent at changes of the season—spring and autumn always affect him—and at present he is suffering acutely. We've had several doctors already, but none of them seems to understand the case. Then we heard of you."

Sergeant Costello and I looked at her, then at each other in mute astonishment. Obviously unaware that she had seen him before, the girl had stated her errand in the precise words employed in the consulting-room not half an hour earlier.

The Frenchman looked at me above her head and his lips formed a single soundless word: "Morphine."

I regarded him questioningly a moment, and he repeated the silent disyllable, holding his hand beside his leg and going through the motion of making an injection at the same time, then glancing significantly at the girl.

I nodded understandingly at last and went to fetch the drug. She seemed not to be aware of what transpired as I took a fold of skin between my thumb and finger, pinched it lightly, and thrust the needle in.

"We heard—my uncle heard, that is—that you were a great traveler and had studied in the clinics of the East," she was telling de Grandin as I shot the plunger home, and still repeating her message parrotwise, word for word as she had delivered it before, she fell asleep beneath the power of three-quarters of a grain of alkaloid of *somniferum*.

6. The Death-Dealer

"AND NOW, MY EXCELLENT one," de Grandin told Costello as he and I returned from putting the unconscious girl to bed, "I would that you telephone headquarters and have them send us two good men and a *chien de police* without delay. We shall need them, I damn think, and that without much waiting, for the spider will be restless when the fly comes not, and will undoubtlessly be seeking explanations here."

"Be dad, sor, if he comes here lookin' for flies he'll find a flock o' horseflies, an' th' kind that can't be fooled, at that!" Costello answered with a grin as he picked up the 'phone.

"Now, *mes amis*, YOU can not be too careful," de Grandin warned the two patrolmen who answered Costello's summons. "This is a vicious one we deal with, and a clever one, as well. He thinks no more of murder than you or I consider the extermination of a bothersome gnat, and he is also quick and subtle. Yes. It is late for anyone to call. Should a visitor mount the steps, one of you inquire his business, but let the other keep well hidden and have his pistol ready. At the first hostile move you shoot, and shoot to hit. Remember, he has already killed three men and a defenseless woman. No mercy is deserved by such as he."

The officers nodded understandingly, and we disposed our forces for defense. Costello, de Grandin and I were to join the policemen alternately on the outside watch, relieving each other every hour. The two remaining in the house were to stay in the room where the girl Allura lay in drugged sleep, for the Frenchman had a theory the killer would attempt to find her if he managed to elude the guard outside. "She who was bait for us will now be bait for him," he stated as he concluded arrangements. "Let us proceed, my friends, and remember what I said, let no false notions of the preciousness of life delay your hands—*he* is troubled with no such scruples, I assure you."

Midnight passed and one o'clock arrived, still no indications of the visitant's approach. Costello had gone to join the outside guard, I lounged and yawned in the armchair by the bed where Allura lay, de Grandin lighted cigarette from cigarette, beat a devil's tattoo on his chair-arm and gazed impatiently at his watch from time to time.

"I'm afraid it's no use, old chap," I told him. "This fellow probably took fright when his messenger and chauffeur failed to return—he's very likely putting as much distance between himself and us as possible this very minute. If—"

Bang! the thunderous detonation drowned my voice as an explosion, almost under our window, shook the air. I leaped to my feet with a cry, but:

"Not the window, my friend—keep away, it is death!" de Grandin warned, seizing me by the arm and dragging me back. "This way—it is safest!"

As we raced downstairs the sharp, staccato discharge of a revolver sounded, followed by a mocking laugh. The Frenchman opened the front door, and dropping to his hands and knees glanced out into the night. Another pistol shot, followed by a cry of pain, sounded from the farther end of the yard; then the deep, ferocious baying of the police dog and a crashing in the rhododendron bushes told us contact of some sort had been made with the enemy.

"D'je get hit, Clancy?" called one of the policemen, charging across the lawn.

"Never mind me, git *him!*" the other cried, and his mate rushed toward the thicket where the savage dog was worrying something. A nightstick flashed twice in the rays of a street lamp, and two dull, heavy thuds told us the locust club struck flesh both times.

"Here he is, Sergeant!" the patrolman called. "Shall I bring 'im in?"

"Sure, let's have a look at him," Costello answered. "Are ye hurt bad, Clancy?"

"Not much, sir," the other answered. "He flang a knife or sumpin at me, but Ludendorff jumped 'im so quick it spoilt his aim. I could do with a bit o' bandage, though."

While Costello and the uninjured policeman dragged the infuriated dog from the unconscious man and prepared to bring him into the house, de Grandin and I assisted Clancy to the surgery. He was bleeding profusely from a long crescent-shaped incised wound in the right shoulder, but the injury was superficial, and a first-aid pack of boric and salicylic acid held in place by a figure-eight bandage quickly reduced the hemorrhage.

"I'll say he's cute, sir," Clancy commented as de Grandin deftly pinned the muslin bandage into place. "We none o' us suspected he was anywheres around—he must 'a' walked on his hands, for he surely didn't make no footsteps we could hear—when all of a sudden we heard sumpin go *bang!* alongside th' house, an' a flare o' fire like a Fourth o' July rocket went up. I yanks out me gun an' fires, like you told us, an' then some one laughs at me, right behind me back, an' sumpin comes whizzin' through th' air like a little airplane an' I feels me shoulder getting numb an' blood a-runnin' down me arm.

"Lucky thing for me old Ludendorff was with me. The son-of-a-gun could make a monkey out o' me, flingin' his contact bomb past me an' drawin' me out in th' open with me back turned to 'im, so's he could fling his knife into me, but he couldn't fool th' dawg. No, sir! He smelt th' feller forty feet away an' made a bee-line for him, draggin' 'im down before you could say Jack Robinson."

The Frenchman nodded. "You were indeed most fortunate," he agreed. "In a few minutes the ambulance will come, and you may go. Meantime—you will?"

"I'm tellin' th' cock-eyed world I will!" Officer Clancy responded as de Grandin moved the brandy bottle and a glass toward him. "Say, Doc, they can cut me up every night o' th' week, if I git this kind o' medicine afterward!"

"*Mon vieux*, your comrade waits in the next room," de Grandin told the other officer. "He is wounded but happy, and I suspect you would like to join him—" he glanced invitingly through the opened door, and as the officer beheld the treatment Clancy was taking for his hurt, he nearly overset the furniture in hasty exit.

"Now, my friends—to business," the Frenchman cried as he closed the surgery door on the policemen and turned to eye our prisoner.

I held a bottle of sal volatile under the man's nose, and in a moment a twitching of the nostrils and fluttering of lids told us he was coming round. He clutched both chair-arms and half heaved himself upright, but:

"Slowly my friend; when your time comes to depart, you will not go alone," de Grandin ordered, digging the muzzle of his pistol into the captive's ribs. "Be seated, rest yourself, and give us information which we much desire, if you please."

"Yes, an' remember annything ye say may be used agin ye at yer trial," Costello added officially.

"Pains of a dyspeptic Billy-goat! Must you always spoil things?" de Grandin snapped, but:

"It's quite all right sir, the game seems played, and I appear to have lost," the prisoner interrupted. "What is it you would like to know?"

He was a queer figure, one of the queerest I had ever seen. A greatcoat of plum-colored cloth, collared and cuffed with kolinsky, covered him from throat to knees, and beneath the garment his massive legs, arrayed in light gray trousers, stuck forward woodenly, as though his joints were stiff. He was big, huge; wide of shoulder, deep of chest and almost obscenely gross of abdomen. His head was oversized, even for his great body, and nearly round, with out-jutting, sail-like ears. Somehow, his face reminded me of one of those old Japanese terror-masks, mahogany-colored, mustached with badger hair, and snarling malignantly. A stubble of short, gray hair covered his scalp, the fierce gray mustache above his month was stiff as bristles from a scrubbing-brush, and the smile he turned on Jules de Grandin was frozen cruelty warmed by no slightest touch of human pity, while terrible, malignant keenness lurked in his narrow, onyx-black eyes. A single glance at him convinced me that the ruthless murderer of four innocent people was before us, and that his trail of murder would be ended only with his further inability to kill. He waved a hand, loosely, wagging it from the wrist as though it were attached to his forearm by a well-oiled hinge, and I caught the gleam of a magnificent octagonal emerald—a gem worth an emperor's ransom—on his right forefinger. "What was it you wished to know?" he repeated. Then: "May I smoke?"

The Frenchman nodded assent, but kept the prisoner covered with his weapon until sure he meant to draw nothing more deadly than a silver cigarette case from his pocket.

"Begin at the beginning, if you please, Monsieur," he bade. "We know how you did slay Monsieur Pancoast and his poor son, and how you murdered his defenseless widow, also the poor Monsieur Dalky, but why, we ask to know. For why should four people you had never seen be victims of your lust for killing? Speak quickly; we have not long to wait."

The prisoner smiled, and once again I felt the chills run down my back at sight of the grimace.

"East is East and West is West,
And never the twain shall meet."

he quoted ironically. "I suppose it's no use attempting to make you share my point of view?"

"That depends on what your viewpoint is," de Grandin answered. "You killed them—why?"

"Because they deserved it richly," the other returned calmly. "Listen to this charming little story, if you can spare the time:

"I was born in Mangadone. My father was a *chetty*—they call them *bania* in India. A money-lender—usurer—in fine. You know the breed; unsavory lot they are, extracting thirty and forty per cent on loans and keeping whole generations in their debt. Yes, my father was one of them.

"He was Indian by birth, but took up trade in Burma, and flourished at it like the proverbial green bay tree. His ideas for me, though, were different from the usual Indian's. He wanted me to be a *burra sahib*—a 'somebody,' as you say. So when the time came he packed me off to England and college to study Shakespeare and the musical classes, but particularly law and finance. I came back a licensed barrister and with a master's degree in economics.

"But"—again his evil smile moved across his features—"I came back to a desolated home, as well. My father had a daughter by a second wife, a lovely little thing called Mumtaj, meaning moonflower. He cherished her, was rather more fond of her than the average benighted Indian is of his girl-children; and because of the wealth he had amassed, looked forward to a brilliant match for her.

"'Man proposes but God disposes,' it has been said, you know. In this case it was the White Man's God, through one of his accredited ministers, who disposed. In the local American mission was an earnest young *sahib* known as the Reverend Carlin Pancoast, a personable young man who wrestled mightily with Satan, and made astonishing progress at it. My father was liberal-minded; he saw much good in the ways of the *sahiblog*, believing that our ancient customs were outmoded; so it was not difficult to induce him to send my little sister Moonflower to the mission school.

"But though he was progressive, my father still adhered to some of the old ways. For instance, he kept the bulk of his wealth in precious metals and jewels, and much of it in gold and silver currency—this last was necessary in order to have ready cash for borrowers, you see. So it was not very difficult for Pancoast *Thakin* and my sister to lay hands on gold and jewels amounting to three lakhs of rupees—about a hundred thousand dollars—quite a respectable little sum, and virtually every farthing my father had.

"They fled to China, 'cross the bay,' where no one was too inquisitive and British extradition would not reach, except in the larger cities. Then they went inland and to the sea by boat. At Shanghai they parted. It was impossible for a *sahib*, especially an American preacher-*sahib*, to take a black girl home with him as wife. But it was not at all embarrassing for him to take home her father's money, which she had stolen for him, plus my sister's *purchase price*.

"What? Oh, dear me, yes. He sold her. She was 'damaged goods,' of course, but proprietors of the floating brothels that ply the China coasts and rivers aren't over-particular concerning the kind of woman-flesh they buy, provided the price is low enough. So the Reverend Pancoast *Sahib* was rid of an embarrassing incumbrance, and in a little cash to boot by the deal. Shrewd businessmen, these Yankees.

"My father was all for prosecuting in the *sahibs'* way, but I had other plans. A few odd bits of precious metals were dug up here and there—literally dug up, gentlemen, for Mother Earth is Mother India's most common safe deposit vault—and with these we began our business life all over again. I profited by what I'd learned in England, and we prospered from the start. In fifteen years we were far wealthier than when the Reverend Carlin Pancoast eloped with my father's daughter and fortune.

"But as the Chinese say, 'we had lost face'—the memory of the insult put on us by the missionary still rankled, and I began to train myself to wipe it out. From fakirs I learned the arts of hypnotism and jugglery, and from *Dakaits* whom I hired at fabulous prices I acquired perfect skill at handling the throwing-knife. Indeed, there was hardly a *budmash* in all lower Burma more expert in the murderer's trade than I when I had completed my training.

"Then I came here. Before the bloody altar of Durga—you know her as Kali, goddess of the *thags*—I took an oath that Pancoast and all his tribe should perish at my hands, and that everyone who had profited by what he stole from my father should also die.

"And—I can't expect you to appreciate this subtlety—I brought along a very useful tool in addition to my knives. I called her Allura. Not bad, eh? She certainly possesses allure, if nothing else.

"I found her in a London slum, a miserable, undernourished brat without known father and with a gin-soaked female swine for mother. I bought her for thirty shillings, and could have had her for half that, except it pleased me to make sure her dam would drink herself to death, and so I gave her more cash than she had ever seen at one time for the child.

"I almost repented of my bargain at first, for the child, though beautiful according to Western standards, was very meagerly endowed with brains, almost a half-wit, in fact. But afterward I thanked whatever gods may be that it was so.

"Her simplicity adapted her ideally to my plan, and I began to practise systematically to kill what little mind she had, substituting my own will for it. The scheme worked perfectly. Before she had reached her twelfth year she was nothing but a living robot—a mechanism with no mind at all, but perfectly responsive to my lightest wish. With only animal instinct to guide her to the simplest vital acts, she would perform any task I set her to, provided I explained in detail just what she was to do. I've sent her on a five-hundred-mile journey, had her buy a particular article in a particular shop, and return with it, as if she were an intelligent being; then, when the task was done, she lapsed once more into idiocy, for she has become a mere idiot whenever the support of my will is withdrawn.

"It was rare sport to send her to be made love to by Pancoast's cub. The silly moon-calf fell heels over head in love with her at sight, and every day I made her rehearse everything he said—she did it with the fidelity of a gramophone—and told her what to say and do at their next meeting. When I had disposed of his father I had Allura bring the son to a secluded part of the campus and—how is it you say in French, Doctor de Grandin? Ah, yes, there I administered the *coup de grâce*. It was really droll. She didn't even notice when I cut him down, just stood there, looking at the spot where he had stood, and saying, 'Poor Harold; dear Harold; I'm so sorry, dear!'

"She was useful in getting Pancoast's widow out of the house and into my reach, too.

"Dalky I handled on my own, using the telephone in approved American fashion to 'put him on the spot,' as your gangsters so quaintly phrase it.

"Your activities were becoming annoying, though, Doctor de Grandin, so I reluctantly decided to eliminate you. Tell me, how did you suspect my trap? Did Allura fail? She never did before."

"I fear you underestimated my ability to grasp the Oriental viewpoint, my friend." de Grandin answered dryly. "Besides, although it had been burned, I rescued Mademoiselle Allura's card from Madame Pancoast's fire, and read the message on it. That, and the warning we found in Monsieur Dalky's waistcoat pocket—I saw it thrown through the window to him at the Pancoast funeral— these gave me the necessary clues. Now, if you have no more to say, let us be going. The Harrisonville *gendamerie* will be delighted to provide you entertainment, I assure you."

"A final cigarette?" the prisoner asked, selecting one of the long, ivory-tipped paper tubes from his case with nice precision.

"*Mais oui*, of course," de Grandin agreed, and held his flaming lighter forward.

"I fear you *do* underestimate the Oriental mind, after all, de Grandin," the prisoner laughed, and thrust half the cigarette into his mouth, then bit it viciously.

"*Mille diables*, he has tricked us!" the Frenchman cried as a strong odor of peach kernels flooded the atmosphere and the captive lurched forward spasmodically, then fell back in his chair with gaping month and staring, death-glazed eyes. "He was clever, that one. All camouflaged within his cigarette he had a sac of hydrocyanic acid. Less than one grain produces almost instant death; he had a least ten times that amount ready for emergency.

"*Eh bien*, my friend," he turned to Costello with a philosophical shrug, "it will save the state the expense of a trial and of electric current to put him to death. Perhaps it is better so. Who knows?"

"What about the girl, Allura?" I asked.

He pondered a moment, then: "I hope he was mistaken," he returned. "If she could be made intelligent by hypnotism, as he said, there is a chance her seeming idiocy may be entirely cured by psychotherapy. It is worth the trial, at all events. Tomorrow we shall begin experiments.

"Meantime, I go."

"Where?" Costello and I asked together.

"Where?" he echoed, as though surprised at our stupidity. "Where but to see if those so thirsty gentlemen of the police have left one drink of brandy in the bottle for Jules de Grandin, *pardieu!*"

Satan's Stepson

1. The Living Dead

"Horns of a little blue devil!" Jules de Grandin bent his head against the sleet-laden February wind and clutched madly at my elbow as his feet all but slipped from under him. "'We are three fools, my friends. We should be home beside our cheerful fire instead of risking our necks going to this *sacré* dinner on such a night."

"*Comment ça va, mon Jules,*" demanded Inspector Renouard, "where is your patriotism? Tonight's dinner is in honor of the great General Washington, whose birthday it is. Did not our own so illustrious Marquis de Lafayette—"

"*Monsieur le Marquis* is dead, and we are like to be the same before we find our way home again," de Grandin cut in irritably. "As for the great Washington, I think no more of him for choosing this so villainous month in which to be born. Now me, I selected May for my *début*; had he but used a like discretion—"

"*Misère de Dieu*, see him come! He is a crazy fool, that one!" Renouard broke in, pointing to a motor car racing toward us down the avenue.

We watched the vehicle in open-mouthed astonishment. To drive at all on such a night was risking life and limb, yet this man drove as though contending for a record on the racing track. Almost abreast of us, he applied his brakes and swerved sharply to the left, seeking to enter the cross street. The inevitable happened. With a rending of wood and metal the car skidded end for end and brought up against the curb, its right rear wheel completely dished, its motor racing wildly as the rimless spokes spun round and round.

"*Mordieu*, you are suicidal, my friend!" de Grandin cried, making his way toward the disabled vehicle with difficulty. "Can I assist you? I am a physician, and—"

A woman's hysterical scream cut through his offer. "Help—save me— they're—" Her cry died suddenly as a hand was clapped over her mouth, and a hulking brute of a man in chauffeur's leather coat and vizored cap scrambled from the driver's cab and faced the Frenchman truculently. "*Yékhat!* Be off!" he ordered shortly. "We need no help, and—"

"Don't parley with him, Dimitri!" a heavy voice inside the tonneau commanded. "Break his damned neck and—"

"'*Cré nom!* With whose assistance will you break my neck, *cochon?*" de Grandin asked sharply. "Name of a gun, make but one step toward me, and—"

The giant chauffeur needed no further invitation. As de Grandin spoke he hurled himself forward, his big hands outstretched to grasp the little Frenchman's throat. Like a bouncing ball de Grandin rose from the ground, intent on meeting the bully's rush with a kick to the pit of the stomach, for he was an expert at the French art of foot-boxing, but the slippery pavement betrayed him. Both feet flew upward and he sprawled upon his back, helpless before the larger man's attack.

"À *moi, mon Georges!*" he called Renouard. "*Je suis perdu!*"

Practical policeman that he was, Renouard lost no time in answering de Grandin's cry. Reversing the heavy walking-stick which swung from his arm he brought its lead-loaded crook down upon the chauffeur's head with sickening force, then bent to extricate his friend from the other's crushing bulk.

"The car, into the *moteur*, my friend!" de Grandin cried. "A woman is in there; injured, perhaps; perhaps—"

Together they dived through the open door of the limousine's tonneau, and a moment later there came the sound of scuffling and mingled grunts and curses as they fought desperately with some invisible antagonist.

I rushed to help them, slipped upon the sleet-glazed sidewalk, and sprawled full length as a dark body hurtled from the car, cannoned into me and paused a moment to hurl a missile, then sped away into the shadows with a mocking laugh.

"Quick, Friend Trowbridge, assist me; Renouard is hit!" de Grandin emerged from the wrecked car supporting the Inspector on his arm.

"*Zut!* It is nothing—a scratch!" Renouard returned. "Do you attend to her, my friend. Me, I can walk with ease. Observe—" he took a step and collapsed limply in my arms, blood streaming from a deeply incised wound in his left shoulder.

Together de Grandin and I staunched the hemorrhage as best we could, then rummaged in the ruined car for the woman whose screams we had heard when the accident occurred.

"She is unconscious but otherwise unhurt, I think," de Grandin told me. "Do you see to Georges; I will carry her—*prie-Dieu* I do not slip and kill us both!"

"But what about this fellow?" I asked, motioning toward the unconscious chauffeur. "We oughtn't leave him here. He may freeze or contract pneumonia—"

"*Eh bien*, one can but hope," de Grandin interrupted. "Let him lie, my friend. The sleet may cool his ardor—he who was so intent on breaking Jules de Grandin's neck. Come, it is but a short distance to the house. Let us be upon our way; *allez-vous-en!*"

A RUGGED CONSTITUTION AND THE almost infinite capacity for bearing injury which he had developed during years of service with the *gendarmerie* stood Inspector Renouard in good stead. Before we had reached the house he was able to walk with my assistance; by the time he had had a proper pack and bandage applied to his wound and absorbed the better part of a pint of brandy he was almost his usual debonair self.

Not so our other patient. Despite our treatment with cold compresses, sal volatilis and aromatic ammonia it was nearly half an hour before we could break the profound swoon in which she lay, and even then she was so weak and shaken we forbore to question her.

At length, when a slight tinge of color began to show in her pale cheeks de Grandin took his station before her and bowed as formally as though upon a ballroom floor. "*Mademoiselle*," he began, "some half an hour since we had the happy privilege of assisting you from a motor wreck. This is Doctor Samuel Trowbridge, in whose office you are; I am Doctor Jules de Grandin, and this is our very good friend, Inspector Georges Jean Jacques Joseph-Marie Renouard, of the *Sûreté Générale*, all of us entirely at your service. If *Mademoiselle* will be so kind as to tell us how we may communicate with her friends or family we shall esteem it an honor—"

"Donald!" the young woman interrupted breathlessly. "Call Donald and tell him I'm all right!"

"*Avec plaisir*," he agreed with another bow. "And this Monsieur Donald, he is who, if you please?"

"My husband."

"Perfectly, *Madame*. But his name?"

"Donald Tanis. Call him at the Hotel Avalon and tell him that I—that Sonia is all right, and where I am, please. Oh, he'll be terribly worried!"

"But certainly, *Madame*, I fully understand," he assured her. Then:

"You have been through a most unpleasant experience. Perhaps you will be kind enough to permit that we offer you refreshment—some sherry and biscuit— while *Monsieur* your husband comes to fetch you? He is even now upon his way."

"Thank you so much," she nodded with a wan little smile, and I hastened to the pantry in search of wine and biscuit.

Seated in an easy-chair before the study fire, the girl sipped a glass of Duff Gordon and munched a pilot biscuit while de Grandin, Renouard and I studied her covertly. She was quite young—not more than thirty, I judged—and lithe and slender in stature, though by no means thin, and her hands were the whitest I had ever seen. Ash-blond her complexion was, her skin extremely fair and her hair that peculiar shade of lightness which, without being gray, is nearer silver than gold. Her eyes were bluish gray, sad, knowing and weary, as though they had seen the sorrow and futility of life from the moment of their first opening.

"You will smoke, perhaps?" de Grandin asked as she finished her biscuit. As he extended his silver pocket lighter to her cigarette the bell shrilled imperatively and I hastened to the front door to admit a tall, dark young man whose agitated manner labeled him our patient's husband even before he introduced himself.

"My dear!" he cried, rushing across the study and taking the girl's hand in his, then raising it to his lips while de Grandin and Renouard beamed approvingly.

"Where—how—" he faltered in his question, but his worshipful glance was eloquent.

"Donald," the girl broke in, and though the study was almost uncomfortably warm she shuddered with a sudden chill, "*it was Konstantin!*"

"Wha—*what?*" he stammered in incredulous, horrified amazement. "My dear, you surely can't be serious. Why, he's *dead!*"

"No, dear," she answered wearily, "I'm not jesting. It was Konstantin. There's no mistaking it. He tried to kidnap me.

"Just as I entered the hotel dining-room a waiter told me that a gentleman wanted to see me in the lobby; so, as I knew you had to finish dressing, I went out to him. A big, bearded man in a chauffeur's leather uniform was waiting by the door. He told me he was from the Cadillac agency; said you had ordered a new car as a surprise for my birthday, but that you wanted me to approve it before they made delivery. It was waiting outside, he said, and he would be glad if I'd just step out and look at it.

"His accent should have warned me, for I recognized him as a Russian, but there are so many different sorts of people in this country, and I was so surprised and delighted with the gift that I never thought of being suspicious. So I went out with him to a gorgeous new limousine parked about fifty feet from the porte-cochère. The engine was running, but I didn't notice that till later.

"I walked round the car, admiring it from the outside; then he asked if I'd care to inspect the inside of the tonneau. There seemed to be some trouble with the dome light when he opened the door for me, and I was half-way in before I realized some one was inside. Then it was too late. The chauffeur shoved me in and slammed the door, then jumped into the cab and set the machine going in high gear. I never had a chance to call for help.

"It wasn't till we'd gone some distance that my companion spoke, and when he did I almost died of fright. There was no light, and he was so muffled in furs that I could not have recognized his face anyway, but his voice—and those corpse-hands of his—I knew them! It was Konstantin.

"'*Jawohl, meine liebe Frau,*' he said—he always loved to speak German to torment me—'it seems we meet again, *nicht wahr?*'

"I tried to answer him, to say something—anything—but my lips and tongue seemed absolutely paralyzed with terror. Even though I could not see, I could feel him chuckling in that awful, silent way of his.

"Just then the driver tried to take a curve at high speed and we skidded into the curb. These gentlemen were passing and I screamed to them for help. Konstantin put his hand over my mouth, and at the touch of his cold flesh against my lips I fainted. The next I knew I was here and Doctor de Grandin was offering to call you, so—" She paused and drew her husband's hand down against her cheek. "I'm frightened, Donald—terribly frightened," she whimpered. "Konstantin—"

Jules de Grandin could stand the strain no longer. During Mrs. Tanis' recital I could fairly see his ungovernable curiosity bubbling up within him; now he was at the end of his endurance.

"*Pardonnez-moi, Madame*," he broke in, "but may one inquire who this so offensive Konstantin is?"

The girl shuddered again, and her pale cheeks went a thought paler.

"He—he is my husband," she whispered between blenched lips.

"But, *Madame*, how can it be?" Renouard broke in. "Monsieur Tanis, he is your husband, he admits it, so do you; yet this Konstantin, he is also your husband. *Non*, my comprehension is unequal to it."

"But Konstantin is *dead*, I tell you," her husband insisted. "I saw him die—I saw him in his coffin—"

"Oh, my darling," she sobbed, her lips blue with unholy terror, "you saw *me* dead—coffined and buried, too—but I'm living. Somehow, in some way we don't understand—"

"*Comment?*" Inspector Renouard took his temples in his hands as though suffering a violent headache. "Jules, my friend, tell me I can not understand the English," he implored. "You are a physician; examine me and tell me my faculties are failing, my ears betraying me! I hear them say, I think, that Madame Tanis has died and been buried in a grave and coffin; yet there she sits and—"

"Silence, *mon singe*, your jabbering annoys one!" de Grandin cut him short. To Tanis he continued:

"We should be grateful for an explanation, if you care to offer one, for *Madame's* so strange statement has greatly puzzled us. It is perhaps she makes the pleasantry at our expense, or—"

"It's no jest, I assure you, sir," the girl broke in. "I *was* dead. My death and burial are recorded in the official archives of the city of Paris, and a headboard, marks my grave in Saint Sébastien, but Donald came for me and married—"

"*Eh bien, Madame*, either my hearing falters or my intellect is dull," de Grandin exclaimed. "Will you repeat your statement once again, slowly and distinctly, if you please? Perhaps I did not fully apprehend you."

2. Inferno

Despite herself the girl smiled. "What I said is literally true," she assured him. A pause, then: "We hate to talk of it, for the memory horrifies us both, but you gentlemen have been so kind I think we owe you an explanation.

"My name was Sonia Malakoff. I was born in Petrograd, and my father was a colonel of infantry in the Imperial Army, but some difficulty with a superior officer over the discipline of the men led to his retirement. I never understood exactly what the trouble was, but it must have been serious, for he averted court-martial and disgrace only by resigning his commission and promising to leave Russia forever.

"We went to England, for Father had friends there. We had sufficient property to keep us comfortable, and I was brought up as an English girl of the better class.

"When the War broke out Father offered his sword to Russia, but his services were peremptorily refused, and though he was bitterly hurt by the rebuff, he determined to do something for the Allied cause, and so we moved to France and he secured a noncombatant commission in the French Army. I went out as a V.A.D. with the British.

"One night in '16 as our convoy was going back from the advanced area an air attack came and several of our ambulances were blown off the road. I detoured into a field and put on all the speed I could. As I went bumping over the rough ground I heard some one groaning in the darkness. I stopped and got down to investigate and found a group of Canadians who had been laid out by a bomb. All but two were dead and one of the survivors had a leg blown nearly off, but I managed to get them into my van with my other *blessés* and crowded on all the gas I could for the dressing-station.

"Next day they told me one of the men—the poor chap with the mangled leg—had died, but the other, though badly shell-shocked, had a good chance of recovery. They were very nice about it all, gave me a mention for bringing them in, and all that sort of thing. Captain Donald Tanis, the shell-shocked man, was an American serving with the Canadians. I went to see him, and he thanked me for giving him the lift. Afterward they sent him to a recuperation station on the Riviera, and we corresponded regularly, or as regularly as people can in such circumstances, until—" she paused a moment, and a slight flush tinged her pallid face.

"*Bien oui,*" de Grandin agreed with a delighted grin. "It was love by correspondence, *n'est-ce-pas, Madame?* And so you were married? Yes?"

"Not then," she answered. "Donald's letters became less frequent, and—and of course I did what any girl would have done in the circumstances, made mine shorter, cooler and farther apart. Finally our correspondence dwindled away entirely.

"The second revolution had taken place in Russia and her new masters had betrayed the Allies at Brest-Litovsk. But America had come into the war and things began to look bright for us, despite the Bolsheviks' perfidy. Father should have been delighted at the turn events were taking, but apparently he was disappointed. When the Allies made their July drive in '18 and the Germans began retreating he seemed terribly disturbed about something, became irritable or moody and distrait, often going days without speaking a word that wasn't absolutely necessary.

"We'd picked up quite a few friends among the émigrés in Paris, and Father's most intimate companion was Alexis Konstantin, who soon became a regular visitor at our house. I always hated him. There was something dreadfully repulsive about his appearance and manner—his dead-white face, his flabby, fish-cold hands, the very way he dressed in black and walked about so silently—he was like a living dead man. I had a feeling of almost physical nausea whenever he came near me, and once when he laid his hand upon my arm I started and screamed as though a reptile had been put against my flesh.

"When Donald's letters finally ceased altogether, though I wouldn't admit it, even to myself, my heart was breaking. I loved him, you see," she added simply.

"Then one day Father came home from the War Department in a perfect fever of nervousness. 'Sonia,' he told me, 'I have just been examined by the military doctors. They tell me the end may come at any time, like a thief in the night. I want you to be provided for in case it comes soon, my dear. I want you to be married.'

"'But Father, I don't want to marry,' I replied. 'The war's not over yet, though we are winning, and I've still my work to do with the ambulance section. Besides, we're well enough off to live; there's no question of my having to marry for a home; so—'

"'But that's just it,' he answered. 'There is. That is exactly the question, my child. I—I've speculated; speculated and lost. Every kopeck we had has gone. I've nothing but my military pay, and when that stops, as it must stop directly the war is won, we're paupers.'

"I was surprised, but far from terrified. 'All right,' I told him, 'I'm strong and healthy and well educated, I can earn a living for us both.'

"'At what?' he asked sarcastically. 'Typing at seventy shillings a week? As nursery governess at five pounds per month with food and lodging? No, my dear, there's nothing for it but a rich marriage, or at least a marriage with a man able to support us both while I'm alive and keep you comfortably after that.'

"I thought I saw a ray of hope. 'We don't know any such man,' I objected. 'No Frenchman with sufficient fortune to do what you wish will marry a dowerless girl, and our Russian friends are all as poor as we, so—'

"'Ah, but there is such a man,' he smiled. 'I have just the man, and he is willing—no, anxious—to make you his wife.'

"My blood seemed to go cold in my arteries as he spoke, for something inside me whispered the name of this benefactor even before Father pronounced it: Gaspardin Alexis Konstantin!

"I wouldn't hear of it at first; I'd sooner wear my fingers out as seamstress, scrub tiles upon my knees or walk the pavements as a *fille de joie* than marry Konstantin, I told him. But though I was English bred I was Russian born, and Russian women are born to be subservient to men. Though I rebelled against it with every atom of my being, I finally agreed, and so it was arranged that we should marry.

"Father hurried me desperately. At the time I thought it was because he didn't want me to have time to change my mind, but—

"It was a queer wedding day; not at all the kind I'd dreamed of. Konstantin was wealthy, Father said, but there was no evidence of wealth at the wedding. We drove to and from the church in an ancient horse-drawn taximeter cab and my father was my only attendant. An aged *papa* with one very dirty little boy as acolyte performed the ceremony. We had only the cheap silver-gilt crowns owned by the church—none of our own—and not so much as a single spray of flowers for my bridal bouquet."

"The three of us came home together and Konstantin sent the *concierge* out for liquor. Our wedding breakfast consisted of brandy, raw fish and tea! Both Father and my husband drank more than they ate. I did neither. The very sight of Konstantin was enough to drive all desire of food away, even though the table had been spread with the choicest dainties to be had from a fashionable caterer.

"Before long, both men were more than half tipsy and began talking together in low, drunken mutterings, ignoring me completely. At last my husband bade me leave the room, ordering me out without so much as looking in my direction.

"I sat in my bedroom in a sort of chilled apathy. I imagine a condemned prisoner who knows all hope of reprieve is passed waits for the coming of the hangman as I waited there.

"My half-consciousness was suddenly broken by Father's voice. 'Sonia, Sonia!' he called, and from his tone I knew he was beside himself with some emotion.

"When I went into the dining-room my father was trembling and wringing his hands in a perfect agony of terror, and tears were streaming down his cheeks as he looked imploringly at Konstantin. 'Sonia, my daughter,' he whispered, 'plead with him. Go on your knees to him, my child, and beg him—pray him as you would pray God, to—'

"'Shut up, you old fool,' my husband interrupted. 'Shut up and get out—leave me alone with my bride.' He leered drunkenly at me.

"Trembling as though with palsy, my father rose humbly to obey the insolent command, but Konstantin called after him as he went out: 'Best take your *pistolet, mon vieux*. You'll probably prefer it to *le peloton d'exécution*.'

"I heard Father rummaging through his chest in the bedroom and turned on Konstantin. 'What does this mean?' I asked. 'Why did you say he might prefer his own pistol to the firing-party?'

"'Ask him,' he answered with a laugh, but when I attempted to join my father he thrust me into a chair and held me there. 'Stay where you are,' he ordered. 'I am your master, now.'

"Then my British upbringing asserted itself. 'You're not my master; no one is!' I answered hotly. 'I'm a free woman, not a chattel, and—'

"I never finished. Before I could complete my declaration he'd struck me with his fist and knocked me to the floor, and when I tried to rise he knocked me down again. He even kicked me as I lay there.

"I tried to fight him off, but though he was so slightly built he proved strong as a prize-fighter, and my efforts at defense were futile. They seemed only to arouse him to further fury, and he struck and kicked me again and again. I screamed to my father for help, but if he heard me he made no answer, and so my punishment went on till I lost consciousness.

"My bridal night was an inferno. Sottish with vodka and drunk with passion, Konstantin was a sadistic beast. He tore—actually ripped—my clothing off; covered me with slobbering, drunken caresses from lips to feet, alternating maudlin, obscene compliments with scurrilous insults and abuse, embracing and beating me by turns. Twice I sickened under the ordeal and both times he sat calmly by, drinking raw vodka from the bottle and waiting till my nausea passed, then resumed my torment with all the joy a mediæval Dominican might have found in torturing a helpless heretic.

"It was nearly noon next day when I woke from what was more a stupor of horror and exhaustion than sleep. Konstantin was nowhere to be seen, for which I thanked God as I staggered from the bed and sought a nightrobe to cover the shameless nudity he had imposed on me.

"'I'll not stand it,' I told myself as, my self-respect somewhat restored by the garment I'd slipped on, I prepared a bath to wash the wounds and bruises I'd sustained during the night.

"Then all my new-found courage evaporated as I heard my husband's step outside, and I cringed like any odalisk before her master as he entered—groveled on the floor like a dog which fears the whip.

"He laughed and tossed me a copy of the Paris edition of *The Daily Mail*. 'You may be interested in that obituary,' he told me, 'the last paragraph in the fourth column.'

"I read it, and all but fainted as I read, for it told how my father had been found that morning in an obscure street on the left bank. A bullet wound in the head pointed to suicide, but no trace of the weapon had been found, for thieves had taken everything of value and stripped the body almost naked before the gendarmes found it.

"They gave him a military funeral and buried him in a soldier's grave. His service saved him from the Potter's Field, but the army escort and I were his only mourners. Konstantin refused to attend the services and forbade my going till I had abased myself and knelt before him, humbly begging for permission to attend my father's funeral and promising by everything I held sacred that I would be subservient to him in every act and word and thought forever afterward if only he would grant that one poor favor.

"That evening he was drunk again, and most ill-natured. He beat me several times, but offered no endearments, and I was glad of it, for his blows, painful as they were, were far more welcome than his kisses.

"Next morning he abruptly ordered me to rejoin my unit and write him every day, making careful note of the regiments and arms of service to which the wounded men I handled belonged, and reporting to him in detail.

"I served two weeks with my unit, then the Commandant sent for me and told me they were reducing the personnel, and as I was a married woman they deemed it best that I resign at once. 'And by the bye, Konstantin,' she added as I saluted and turned to go, 'you might like to take these with you—as a little souvenir, you know.' She drew a packet from her drawer and handed it to me. It was a sheaf of fourteen letters, every one I'd written to my husband. When I opened them outside I saw that every item of intelligence they contained had been carefully blocked out with censor's ink.

"Konstantin was furious. He thrashed me till I thought I'd not have a whole bone left.

"I took it as long as I could; then, bleeding from nose and lips, I tried to crawl from the room.

"The sight of my helplessness and utter defeat seemed to infuriate him still further. With an animal-snarl he fairly leaped on me and bore me down beneath a storm of blows and kicks.

"I felt the first few blows terribly; then they seemed to soften, as if his hands and feet were encased in thick, soft boxing-gloves. Then I sank face-downward on the floor and seemed to go to sleep.

"When I awoke—if you can call it that—I was lying on the bed, and everything seemed quiet as the grave and calm as Paradise. There was no sensation of pain or any feeling of discomfort, and it seemed to me as if my body had grown curiously lighter. The room was in semi-darkness, and I noticed with an odd feeling of detachment that I could see out of only one eye, my left. 'He must have closed the right one with a blow,' I told myself, but, queerly, I didn't feel resentful. Indeed, I scarcely felt at all. I was in a sort of semi-stupor, indifferent to myself and everything else.

"A scuffle of heavily booted feet sounded outside; then the door was pushed open and a beam of light came into the room, but did not reach to me. I could tell several men had entered, and from their heavy breathing and the scraping sounds I heard, I knew they were lugging some piece of heavy furniture.

"'Has the doctor been here yet?' one of them asked.

"'No,' some one replied, and I recognized the voice of Madame Lespard, an aged widow who occupied the flat above. 'You must wait, gentlemen, the law—'

"'À bas the law!' the man replied. 'Me, I have worked since five this morning, and I wish to go to bed.'

"'But gentlemen, for the love of heaven, restrain yourselves!' Madame Lespard pleaded. 'La pauvre belle créature may not be—'

"'No fear,' the fellow interrupted. 'I can recognize them at a mile. Look here.' From somewhere he procured a lamp and brought it to the bed on which I lay. 'Observe the pupils of the eyes,' he ordered, 'see how they are fixed and motionless, even when I hold the light to them.' He brought the lamp within six inches of my face, flashing its rays directly into my eye; yet, though I felt its luminance, there was no sensation of being dazzled.

"Then suddenly the light went out. At first I thought he had extinguished the lamp, but in a moment I realized what had actually happened was that my eyelid had been lowered. Though I had not felt his finger on the lid, he had drawn it down across my eye as one might draw a curtain!

"'And now observe again,' I heard him say, and the scratch of a match against a boot-sole was followed by the faint, unpleasant smell of searing flesh.

"'Forbear, Monsieur!' old Madame Lespard cried in horror. 'Oh, you are callous—inhuman—you gentlemen of the pompes funèbres!'

"Then horrifying realization came to me. A vague, fantasmal thought which had been wafting in my brain, like an unremembered echo of a long-forgotten verse, suddenly crystallized in my mind. These men were from the pompes funèbres—the municipal undertakers of Paris—the heavy object they had lugged in was a coffin—my coffin! They thought me dead!

"I tried to rise, to tell them that I lived, to scream and beg them not to put me in that dreadful box. In vain. Although I struggled till it seemed my lungs and veins must burst with effort, I could not make a sound, could not stir a hand or finger, could not so much as raise the eyelid the undertaker's man had lowered!

"'Ah, bon soir, Monsieur le Médicin!' I heard the leader of the crew exclaim. 'We feared you might not come tonight, and the poor lady would have to lie un-coffined till tomorrow.'

"The fussy little municipal doctor bustled up to the bed on which I lay, flashed a lamp into my face and mumbled something about being overworked with la grippe killing so many people every day. Then he turned away and I heard the rustle of papers as he filled in the blanks of my certificate of death. If I could have controlled any member of my body I would have wept. As it was, I merely lay there, unable to shed a single tear for the poor unfortunate who was being hustled, living, to the grave.

"Konstantin's voice mingled with the others'. I heard him tell the doctor how I had fallen head-first down the stairs, how he had rushed wildly after me and borne me up to bed, only to find my neck was broken. The lying wretch actually sobbed as he told his perjured story, and the little doctor made perfunctory, clucking sounds of sympathy as he listened in attentively and wrote the death certificate—the warrant which condemned me to awful death by suffocation in the grave!

"I felt myself lifted from the bed and placed in the pine coffin, heard them lay the lid above me and felt the jar as they drove home nail after nail. At last the task was finished, the *entrepreneurs* accepted a drink of brandy and went away, leaving me alone with my murderer.

"I heard him take a turn across the room, heard the almost noiseless chuckle which he gave whenever he was greatly pleased, heard him scratch a match to light a cigarette; then, of a sudden, he checked his restless walk and turned toward the door with a short exclamation.

"'Who comes?' he called as a measured tramping sounded in the passageway outside.

"'The military police!' his hail was answered. 'Alexis Konstantin, we make you arrested for espionage. Come!'

"He snarled like a trapped beast. There was the *click* of a pistol-hammer, but the gendarmes were too quick for him. Like hounds upon the boar they leaped on him, and though he fought with savage fury—I had good cause to know how strong he was!—they overwhelmed him, beat him into submission with fists and saber-hilts and snapped steel bracelets on his wrists.

"All fight gone from him, cursing, whining, begging for mercy—to be allowed to spend the last night beside the body of his poor, dead wife!—they dragged him from the room and down the stairs. I never saw him again—until tonight!"

The girl smiled sadly, a trace of bitterness on her lips. "Have you ever lain awake at night in a perfectly dark room and tried to keep count of time?" she asked. "If you have, you know how long a minute can seem. Imagine how many centuries I lived through while I lay inside that coffin, sightless, motionless, soundless, but with my sense of hearing abnormally sharpened. For longer years than the vilest sinner must spend in purgatory I lay there thinking—thinking. The rattle of carts in the streets and a slight increase in temperature told me day had come, but the morning brought no hope to me. It meant only that I was that much nearer the Golgotha of my Via Dolorosa.

"At last they came. 'Where to?' a workman asked as rough hands took up my coffin and bore me down the stairs.

"'Saint Sébastien,' the *premier ouvrier* returned, 'her husband made arrangements yesterday. They say he was rich. *Eh bien*; it is likely so; only the wealthy and the poor dare have funerals of the third class.'

"Over the cobbles of the streets the little, one-horse hearse jolted to the church, and at every revolution of the wheels my panic grew. 'Surely, *surely* I shall gain my self-control again,' I told myself. 'It can't be that I'll lie like this until—' I dared not finish out the sentence, even in my thoughts.

"The night before, the waiting had seemed endless. Now it seemed the shambling, half-starved nag which drew the hearse was winged like Pegasus and made the journey to the cemetery more swiftly than the fastest airplane.

"At last we halted, and they dragged me to the ground, rushed me at break-neck speed across the cemetery and put me down a moment while they did something to the coffin. What was it? Were they making ready to remove the lid? Had the municipal doctor remembered tardily how perfunctory his examination had been, and conscience-smitten, rushed to the cemetery to snatch me from the very jaws of the grave?

"'We therefore commit her body to the earth—earth to earth, ashes to ashes, dust to dust—' the priest's low sing-song came to me, muffled by the coffin-walls. Too late I realized the sound I heard had been only the knotted end of the lowering-rope falling on the coffin top as the workmen drew a loop about the case.

"The priest's chant became fainter and fainter. I felt myself sinking as though upon a slowly descending lift, while the ropes sawed and rasped against the square edges of the coffin, making noises like the bellow of a cracked bass viol, and the coffin teetered crazily from side to side and scraped against the raw edges of the grave. At last I came to rest. A jolt, a little thud, a final scraping noise, and the lowering-ropes were jerked free and drawn underneath the coffin and out of the grave. The end had come, there was no more—

"A terrible report, louder than the bursting of a shell, exploded just above my chest, and the close, confined air inside the coffin shook and trembled like the air in a dugout when hostile flyers lay down an air-barrage. A second shock burst above my face—its impact was so great I knew the coffin lid must surely crack beneath it—then a perfect drum-fire of explosions as clod on roaring clod struck down upon the thin pine which coffined me. My ears were paralyzed with the continuous detonations, I could feel the constantly increasing weight of earth pressing on my chest, my mouth, my nostrils. I made one final effort to rouse myself and scream for help; then a great flare, like the bursting of a star-shell, enveloped me and the last shred of sensation went amid a blaze of flame and roar of thunder.

"Slowly I fought back to consciousness. I shuddered as the memory of my awful dream came back to me. I'd dreamed that I was dead—or, rather, in a trance—that men from the *pompes funèbres* came and thrust me into a coffin and buried me in Saint Sébastien, and I had heard the clods fall on the coffin lid above me while I lay powerless to raise a hand.

"How good it was to lie there in my bed and realize that it had only been a dream! There, with the soft, warm mattress under me, I could lie comfortably and rest till time had somewhat softened the terror of that nightmare; then I would rise and make a cup of tea to soothe my frightened nerves; then go again to bed and peaceful sleep.

"But how dark it was! Never, even in those days of air-raids, when all lights were forbidden, had I seen a darkness so absolute, so unrelieved by any faintest ray of light. I moved my arms restlessly. To right and left were hard, rough wooden walls that pressed my sides and interfered with movement. I tried to rise, but fell back with a cry of pain, for I had struck my brow a violent blow. The air about me was very close and damp; heavy, as though confined under pressure.

"Suddenly I knew. Horror made my scalp sting and prickle and the awful truth ran through me like an icy wave. It was no dream, but dreadful fact. I had emerged from the coma which held me while preparations for my funeral were made; at last I was awake, mistress of my body, conscious and able to move and scream aloud for help—but none would ever hear me. I was coffined, shut up beneath a mound of earth in Saint Sébastien Cemetery—buried alive!

"I called aloud in agony of soul and body. The dreadful reverberation of my voice in that sealed coffin rang back against my ears like thunder-claps tossed back by mountain peaks.

"Then I went mad. Shrieking, cursing the day I was born and the God Who let this awful fate befall me, I writhed and twisted, kicked and struggled in the coffin. The sides pressed in so closely that I could not raise my hands to my head, else I had torn my hair out by the roots and scratched my face to the bone, but I dug my nails into my thighs through the flimsy drapery of my shroud and bit my lips and tongue until my mouth was choked with blood and my raving cries were muted like the gurglings of a drowning man. Again and yet again I struck my brow against the thin pine wood, getting a fierce joy from the pain. I drew up my knees as far as they could go and arched my body in a bow, determined to burst the sepulcher which held me or spend my faint remaining spark of life in one last effort at escape. My forehead crashed against the coffin lid, a wave of nausea swept over me and, faint and sick, I fell back to a merciful unconsciousness.

"The soft, warm sunlight of September streamed through an open window and lay upon the bed on which I lay, and from the table at my side a bowl of yellow roses sent forth a cloud of perfume. 'I'm surely dead,' I told myself. 'I'm released from the grave at last. I've died and gone—where? Where was I? If this were heaven or paradise, or even purgatory, it looked suspiciously like earth; yet how could I be living, and if I were truly dead, what business had I still on earth?

"Listlessly I turned my head. There, in American uniform, a captain's bars gleaming on his shoulders, stood Donald, my Donald, whom I'd thought lost to me forever. 'My dear,' I whispered, but got no farther, for in a moment his arms were round me and his lips were pressed to mine."

Sonia paused a moment, a smile of tenderest memory on her lips, the light that never was on sea or land within her eyes. "I didn't understand at all," she told us, "and even now I only know it second-hand. Perhaps Donald will tell you his part of the story. He knows the details better than I."

3. La Morte Amoureuse

The leaping flames behind the andirons cast pretty highlights of red and orange on Donald Tanis and his wife as they sat hand in hand in the love seat beside the hearth rug. "I suppose you gentlemen think I was pretty precipitous in love-making, judging from the record Sonia's given," the young husband began with a boyish grin, "but you hadn't watched beside her bed while she hovered between sanity and madness as I had, and hadn't heard her call on me and say she loved me. Besides, when she looked at me that afternoon and said, 'My dear!' I knew she loved me just as well as though she'd taken all day long to tell me."

De Grandin and Renouard nodded joint and most emphatic approval. "And so you were married?" de Grandin asked.

"You bet we were," Donald answered. "There'd have been all sorts of red tape to cut if we'd been married as civilians, but I was in the army and Sonia wasn't a French citizeness; so we went to a friend of mine who was a padre in one of our outfits and had him tie the knot. But I'm telling this like a newspaper story, giving the ending first. To begin at the start:

"The sawbones in the hospital told me I was a medical freak, for the effect of the bursting 'coalbox' on me was more like the bends, or caisson disease, than the usual case of shell-shock. I didn't go dotty, nor get the horrors; I wasn't even deafened to any extent, but I did have the most God-awful neuralgic pains with a feeling of almost overwhelming giddiness whenever I tried to stand. I seemed as tall as the Woolworth tower the minute I got on my feet, and seven times out of ten I'd go sprawling on my face two seconds after I got out of bed. They packed me off to a convalescent home at Biarritz and told me to forget I'd ever been mixed up in any such thing as a war.

"I did my best to follow orders, but one phase of the war just wouldn't be forgotten. That was the plucky girl who'd dragged me in that night the Fritzies tried to blow me into Kingdom Come. She'd been to see me in hospital before they sent me south, and I'd learned her name and unit, so as soon as I was up to it I wrote her. Lord, how happy I was when she answered!

"You know how those things are. Bit by bit stray phrases of intimacy crept into our notes, and we each got so that the other's letters were the most important things in life. Then Sonia's notes became less frequent and more formal; finally they hinted that she thought I was not interested any more. I did my best to disabuse her mind of *that* thought, but the letters came farther and farther apart. At last I decided I'd better tell her the whole truth, so I proposed by mail. I didn't like the idea, but there I was, way down in the Pyrénées, unable to get about, except in a wheel-chair, and there she was somewhere on the west front. I couldn't very well get to her to tell her of my love, and she couldn't come to me—and I was dreadfully afraid I'd lose her.

"Then the bottom dropped out of everything. I never got an answer to that letter. I didn't care a hang what happened to me then; just sat around and moped till the doctors began to think my brain must be affected, after all.

"I guess about the only thing that snapped me out of it was America's coming in. With my own country sending troops across, I had a definite object in life once more; to get into American uniform and have a last go at the Jerries. So I concentrated on getting well.

"It wasn't till the latter part of July, though, that they let me go, and then they wouldn't certify me for duty at the front. 'One more concussion and you'll go blotto altogether, lad,' the commandant told me before I left the nursing-home, and he must have put a flea in G.H.Q.'s. ear, too, for they turned me down cold as caviar when I asked for combatant service.

"I'd made a fair record with the Canadians, and had a couple of good friends in the War Department, so I drew a consolation prize in the form of a captaincy of infantry with assignment to liaison duty with the *Censure Militaire*.

"The French officers in the bureau were first-rate scouts and we got along famously. One day one of 'em told me of a queer case they'd had passed along by the British M.I. It seemed there was a queer sort of bird, a Russian by the name of Konstantin, who'd been making whoopee for some time, but covering up his tracks so skillfully they'd never been able to put salt on his tail. He'd been posing as an *émigré* and living in the Russian colony in Paris, always with plenty of money, but no visible employment. After the way the Bolshies had let the Allies down everything Russian was regarded with suspicion, and this bird had been a source of several sleepless nights for the French Intelligence. Finally, it seemed, they'd got deadwood on him.

"An elderly Russian who'd been billeted in the censor's bureau and always been above suspicion had been found dead in the streets one morning, a suicide, and the police had hardly got his body to the morgue when a letter from him came to the chief. In it he confessed that he'd been systematically stealing information from censored documents and turning it over to Konstantin, who was really an agent for the Soviets working with the Heinies. Incidentally, the old fellow named several other Russians who'd been corrupted by Konstantin. It seemed his game was to lend them money when they were hard up, which they generally were, then get them to do a little innocuous spying for him in return for the loan. After that it was easy. He had only to threaten to denounce them in order to keep them in his power and make them go on gathering information for him, and of course the poor fish were more and more firmly entangled in the net with each job they did for him.

"Just why old Captain Malakoff chose to kill himself and denounce Konstantin wasn't clear, but the Frenchman figured that his conscience had been troubling him for some time and he'd finally gotten to the point where he couldn't live with it any longer.

"I'd been sitting back, not paying much attention to Lieutenant Fouchet's story, but when he mentioned the suicide's name my interest was roused. Of course, Malakoff isn't an unusual Russian name, but this man had been an officer in the Imperial army in his younger days, and had been taken in the French service practically as an act of charity. The details seemed to fit my case. 'I used to know a girl named Malakoff,' I said. 'Her father was in the censorship, too, I believe.'

"Fouchet smiled in that queer way he had, showing all his teeth at once beneath his little black mustache. I always suspected he was proud of the bridge work an American dentist had put in for him. 'Was the young lady's name Sonia, by any chance?' he asked.

"That brought me up standing. 'Yes,' I answered.

"'Ah? It is doubtless the daughter of our estimable suicide, in that case,' he replied. 'Attend me: Two weeks ago she married with this Konstantin while she was on furlough from her unit at the front. Almost immediately after her marriage she rejoined her unit, and each day she has written her husband a letter detailing minutely the regiments and arms of service to which the wounded men she carried have belonged. These letters have, of course, been held for us by the British, and *voilà*, our case is complete. We are prepared to spring our trap. Captain Malakoff we buried with full military honors; no one suspects he has confessed. Tonight or tomorrow we all arrest this Konstantin and his accomplices.' He paused and smiled unpleasantly; then: 'It is dull work for the troops stationed here in Paris,' he added. 'They will appreciate a little target practice.'

"'But—but what of Sonia—Madame Konstantin?' I asked.

"'I think that we can let the lady go,' he said. 'Doubtless she was but a tool in her husband's hands; the same influence which drove her father from his loyalty may have been exerted on her; he is a very devil with the women, this Konstantin. Besides, several of his aides have confessed, so we have ample evidence on which to send him to the firing-party without the so pitiful little spy-letters his wife wrote to him. She must be dismissed from the service, of course, and never may she serve in any capacity, either with the civil or military governments, but at least she will be spared a court-martial and public disgrace. Am I not kind, my friend?'

"A few days later he came to me with a serious face. 'The man Konstantin has been arrested,' he said, 'but his wife, *hélas*, she is no more. The night before last she died in their apartment—fell down the stairs and broke her lovely neck, I'm told—and yesterday they buried her in Saint Sébastien. Courage, my friend!' he added as he saw my face. 'These incidents are most regrettable, but—there is much sorrow in the world today—*c'est la guerre*.'

"He looked at me a moment; then: 'You loved her?' he asked softly.

"'Better than my life,' I answered. 'It was only the thought of her that brought me through—she dragged me in and saved my life one night out by Lens when the Jerries knocked me over with an air-bomb.'

"'*Mon pauvre garçon!*' he sympathized. Then: 'Consider me, my friend, there is a rumor—oh, a very unsubstantiated rumor, but still a rumor, that poor Madame Konstantin did not die an entirely natural death. An aged widow-neighbor of hers has related stories of a woman's cries for mercy, as though she were most brutally beaten, coming from the Konstantin apartment. One does not know this is a fact. The old talk much, and frequently without good reason, but—'

"'The dog!' I interrupted. 'The cowardly dog, if he hit Sonia I'll—'

"Fouchet broke in. 'I shall attend the execution tomorrow,' he informed me. 'Would not you like to do the same?'

"Why I said yes I've no idea, but something, some force outside me, seemed to urge me to accept the invitation, and so it was arranged that I should go.

"A few hooded street lamps were battling ineffectually with the foggy darkness when we arrived at the Santé Prison a little after three next morning. Several motor cars were parked in the quadrangle and a sergeant assigned us seats in one of them. After what seemed an interminable wait, we saw a little knot of people come from one of the narrow doors leading into the courtyard—several officers in blue and black uniforms, a civilian handcuffed to two gendarmes, and a priest—and enter a car toward the head of the procession. In a moment we were under way, and I caught myself comparing our motorcade to a funeral procession on its way to the cemetery.

"A pale streak of dawn was showing in the east, bringing the gabled roofs and towers out in faint silhouette as we swung into the Place de la Nation. The military chauffeurs put on speed and we were soon in the Cours de Vincennes, the historic old fortification looming gloomy and forbidding against the sky as we dashed noiselessly on to the *champ d'execution*, where two companies of infantry in horizon blue were drawn up facing each other, leaving a narrow lane between. At the farther end of this aisle a stake of two-by-four had been driven into the turf, and behind and a little to the left stood a two-horse black-curtained van, from the rear of which could be seen protruding the butt of a deal coffin, rough and unfinished as a hardware merchant's packing-case. A trio of unshaven workmen in black smocks lounged beside the wagon, a fourth stood at the horses' heads.

"As our party alighted a double squad of musicians stationed at the lower end of the files of troops tossed their trumpets upward with a triple flourish and began sounding a salute and the soldiers came to present arms. I could see the tiny drops of misty rain shining like gouts of sweat on the steel helmets and bayonet blades as we advanced between the rows of infantry. A chill of dread ran up my spine as I glanced at the soldiers facing us on each side. Their faces were grave and stern, their eyes harder than the bayonets on their rifles. Cold, implacable hatred, pitiless as death's own self, was in every countenance. This was a spy, a secret enemy of France, who marched to his death between their perfectly aligned ranks. The wet and chilly morning air seemed surcharged with an emanation of concentrated hate and ruthlessness.

"When the prisoner was almost at the stake he suddenly drew back against the handcuffs binding him to his guard and said something over his shoulder to the colonel marching directly behind him. The officer first shook his head, then consulted with a major walking at his left, finally nodded shortly. 'Monsieur le Capitaine,' a dapper little sub-lieutenant saluted me, 'the prisoner asks to speak with you. It is irregular, but the colonel has granted permission. However, you may talk with him only in the presence of a French officer'—he looked coldly at me, as though suspecting I were in some way implicated in the spy's plots—'you understand that, of course?'

"'I have no wish to talk with him—' I began, but Fouchet interrupted.

"'Do so, my friend,' he urged. 'Who knows, he may have news of Madame Sonia, your morte amoureuse. Come.

"'I will act as witness to the conversation and stand surety for Captain Tanis,' he added to the subaltern with frigid courtesy.

"They exchanged polite salutes and decidedly impolite glares, and Fouchet and I advanced to where the prisoner and the priest stood between the guarding gendarmes.

"Even if I had known nothing of him—if I'd merely passed him casually on the boulevard—Konstantin would have repelled me. He was taller than the average and thin with a thinness that was something more than the sign of malnutrition; this skeletal gauntness seemed to have a distinct implication of evil. His hat had been removed, but from neck to feet he was arrayed in unrelieved black, a black shirt bound round the collar with a black cravat, a black serge suit of good cut and material, shoes of dull-black leather, even gloves of black kid on his long, thin hands. He had a sardonic face, long, smooth-shaven, its complexion an unhealthy yellowish olive. His eyes were black as carbon, and as lacking in luster, overhung by arched brows of intense, dead black, like his hair, which was parted in the middle and brushed sharply back from the temples, leaving a point at the center of the forehead. This inverted triangle led down to a long, hooked nose, and that to a long, sharp chin. Between the two there ran a wide mouth with thin, cruel lips of unnatural, brilliant red, looking, against the sallow face, as though they had been freshly rouged. An evil face it was, evil with a fathomless understanding of sin and passion, and pitiless as the visage of a predatory beast.

"He smiled briefly, almost imperceptibly, as I approached. 'Captain Donald Tanis, is it not?' he asked in a low, mocking voice.

"I bowed without replying.

"'*Monsieur le Capitaine*,' he proceeded, 'I have sent for you because I, of all the people in the world, can give you a word of comfort—and my time for disinterested philanthropy grows short. A little while ago I had the honor to take to wife a young lady in whom you had been deeply interested. Indeed I think we might make bold to say you were in love with her, *nicht wahr?*'

"As I still returned no answer he opened that cavernous, red-lipped mouth of his and gave a low, almost soundless chuckle, repulsive as the grinning of a skull.

"'*Jawohl*,' he continued, 'let us waive the tender confession. Whatever your sentiments were toward her, there was no doubt of hers toward you. She married me, but it was you she loved. The marriage was her father's doing. He was in my debt, and I pressed him for my pound of flesh, only in this instance it was a hundred pounds or so of flesh—his daughter's. He'd acted as an agent of mine at the *Censure Militaire* until he'd worn out his usefulness, so I threatened to denounce him unless he would arrange a marriage for me with the charming Sonia. Having gotten what I wanted, I had no further use for him. The sad-eyed old fool would have been a wet blanket on the ardor of my honeymoon. I told him to get out—gave him his choice between disposing of himself or facing a French firing-squad.

"'It seems now that he chose to be revenged on me at the same time he gave himself the happy dispatch. Dear, dear, who would have thought the sniveling old dotard would have had the spirit?

"'But we digress and the gentlemen grow impatient,' he nodded toward the file of troops. 'We Russians have a saying that the husband who fails to beat his wife is lacking in outward manifestation of affection.' He chuckled soundlessly again. 'I do not think my bride had cause for such complaint.

"'What would you have given,' he asked in a low, mocking whisper, 'to have stood in my place that night three weeks ago? To have torn the clothing off her shuddering body, to have cooled her fevered blushes with your kisses, then melted her maidenly coolness with burning lips—to have strained her trembling form within your arms, then, in the moment of surrender, to have thrust her from you, beaten her down, hurled her to the floor and ground her underfoot till she crept suppliant to you on bare and bleeding knees, holding up her bruised and bleeding face to your blows or your caresses, as you chose to give them—utterly submissive, wholly, unconditionally yours, to do with as you wished?'

"He paused again and I could see little runnels of sweat trickling down his high, narrow brow as he shook with passion at the picture his words had evoked.

"'*Nu*,' he laughed shortly. 'I fear my love became too violent at last. The fish in the pan has no fear of strangling in the air. I can tell you this without fear of increasing my penalty. Sonia's death certificate declares she died of a broken neck resulting from a fall downstairs. Bah! She died because I beat her! I beat her to death, do you hear, my fish-blooded American, my chaste, chivalrous worshiper of women, and as she died beneath my blows, she called on you to come and save her!

"'You thought she stopped her letters because she had grown tired? Bah, again. She did it out of pride, because she thought that you no longer cared. At my command her father intercepted the letters you sent to her Paris home—I read them all, even your halting, trembling proposal, which she never saw or even suspected. It was amusing, I assure you.

"'You've come to see me die, *hein*? Then have your fill of seeing it. *I* saw Sonia die; heard her call for help to the lover who never came, saw her lower her pride to call out to the man she thought had jilted her as I rained blow on blow upon her!'

"Abruptly his manner changed, he was the suave and smooth-spoken gentleman once more. '*Auf Wiedersehen, Herr Hauptmann!*' he bid me with a mocking bow.

"'I await your pleasure, *Messieurs*,' he announced, turning to the gendarmes.

"A detail of twelve soldiers under the command of a lieutenant with a drawn sword detached itself from the nearer company of infantry, executed a left wheel and came to halt about five meters away, their rifles at the order, the bayonets removed. The colonel stepped forward and read a summary of the death sentence, and as we drew back the gendarmes unlatched their handcuffs and bound the prisoner with his back against the post with a length of new, white rope. A handkerchief was bound about his eyes and the gendarmes stepped back quickly.

"'*Garde à vous!*' the firing-party commander's voice rang out.

"'*Adieu pour ce monde, mon Lieutenant*, do not forget the *coup de grâce!*' Konstantin called airily.

"The lieutenant raised his sword and swung it downward quickly; a volley rang out from the platoon of riflemen.

"The transformation in the prisoner was instant and horrible. He collapsed, his body sagging weakly at the knees, as a filled sack collapses when its contents are let out through a cut, then sprawled full length face-downward on the ground, for the bullets had cut the rope restraining him. But on the turf the body writhed and contorted like a snake seared with fire, and from the widely opened mouth there came a spate of blood and gurgling, strangling cries mingled with half-articulate curses.

"A corporal stepped forward from the firing-party, his heavy automatic in his hand. He halted momentarily before the widening pool of blood about the writhing body, then bent over, thrust the muzzle of his weapon into the long black hair which, disordered by his death agonies, was falling about Konstantin's ears, and pulled the trigger. A dull report, like the popping of a champagne cork, sounded, and the twisting thing upon the ground gave one convulsive shudder, then lay still.

"'This is the body of Alexis Konstantin, a spy, duly executed in pursuance of the sentence of death pronounced by the military court. Does anyone lay claim to it?' announced the commandant in a steady voice. No answer came, though we waited what seemed like an hour to me.

"'À vos rangs!' Marching in quick time, the execution party filed past the prostrate body on the blood-stained turf and rejoined its company, and at a second command the two units of infantry formed columns of fours and marched from the field, the trumpet sounding at their head.

"The black-smocked men dragged the coffin from the black-curtained van, dumped the mangled body unceremoniously into it, and the driver whipped his horses into a trot toward the cemetery of Vincennes where executed spies and traitors were interred in unmarked graves.

"'A queer one, that,' an officer of the party which had accompanied the prisoner to execution told us as we walked toward our waiting cars. 'When we left the Santé he was almost numb with fright, but when I told him that the *coup de grâce*—the mercy shot—was always given on occasions of this kind, he seemed to forget his fears and laughed and joked with us and with his warders till the very minute when we reached the field. *Tiens*, he seemed to have a premonition that the volley would not at once prove fatal and that he must suffer till the mercy shot was given. Do you recall how he reminded the platoon commander to remember the shot before the order to fire was given? Poor devil!'"

"Ah?" said Jules de Grandin. "A-ah? Do you report that conversation accurately, my friend?"

"Of course I do," young Tanis answered. "It's stamped as firmly on my mind as if it happened yesterday. One doesn't forget such things, sir."

"*Précisément, Monsieur*," de Grandin agreed with a thoughtful nod. "I did but ask for verification. This may have some bearing on that which may develop later, though I hope not. What next, if you please?"

Young Tanis shook his head as though to clear an unhappy memory from his mind. "Just one thought kept dinning in my brain," he continued. "'Sonia is dead—Sonia is dead!' a jeering voice seemed repeating endlessly in my ear.

'She called on you for help and you failed her!' By the time we arrived at the censor's bureau I was half mad; by luncheon I had formed a resolve. I would visit Saint Sébastien that night and take farewell of my dead sweetheart—she whom Fouchet had called my *morte amoureuse*.

"The light mist of the morning had ripened into a steady, streaming downpour by dark; by half-past eleven, when my fiacre let me down at Saint Sébastien, the wind was blowing half a gale and the rain drops stung like whip-lashes as they beat into my face beneath the brim of my field hat. I turned my raincoat collar up as far as it would go and splashed and waded through the puddles to the pentice of the tiny chapel beside the cemetery entrance. A light burned feebly in the intendant's cabin, and as the old fellow came shuffling to open the door in answer to my furious knocks, a cloud of super-heated, almost fetid air burst into my face. There must have been a one per cent concentration of carbon monoxide in the room, for every opening was tightly plugged and a charcoal brazier was going full blast.

"He blinked stupidly at me a moment; then: 'M'sieur l'Americain?' he asked doubtfully, looking at my soaking hat and slicker for confirmation of his guess. 'M'sieur has no doubt lost his way, n'est-ce-pas? This is the cemetery of Saint Sébastien—'

"'Monsieur l'Americain has not lost his way, and he is perfectly aware this is the cemetery of Saint Sébastien,' I assured him. Without waiting for the invitation I knew he would not give, I pushed by him into the stuffy little cabin and kicked the door shut. 'Would the estimable *fossoyeur* care to earn a considerable sum of money—five hundred—a thousand francs—perhaps?' I asked.

"'*Sacré Dieu*, he is crazy, this one,' the old man muttered. 'Mad he is, like all the Yankees, and drunk in the bargain. Help me, blessed Mother!'

"I took him by the elbow, for he was edging slowly toward the door, and shook a bundle of hundred-franc notes before his staring eyes. 'Five of these now, five more when you have fulfilled your mission, and not a word to anyone!' I promised.

"His little shoe-button eyes shone with speculative avarice. 'M'sieur desires that I help him kill some one?' he ventured. 'Is it perhaps that M'sieur has outside the body of one whom he would have secretly interred?'

"'Nothing as bad as that,' I answered, laughing in spite of myself, then stated my desires baldly. 'Will you do it, at once?' I finished.

"'For fifteen hundred francs, perhaps—' he began, but I shut him off.

"'A thousand or nothing,' I told him.

"'*Mille tonnerres*, M'sieur, you have no heart,' he assured me. 'A poor man can scarcely live these days, and the risk I run is great. However,' he added hastily as I folded the bills and prepared to thrust them back into my pocket, 'however, one consents. There is nothing else to do.' He slouched off to a corner of the hut and picked up a rusty spade and mattock. 'Come, let us go,' he growled, dropping a folded burlap sack across his shoulders.

"The rain, wind-driven between the leafless branches of the poplar trees, beat dismally down upon the age-stained marble tombs and the rough, unsodded mounds of the ten-year concessions. Huddled by the farther wall of the cemetery, beneath their rows of ghastly white wooden signboards, the five- and three-year concessions seemed to cower from the storm. These were the graves of the poorer dead, one step above the tenants of the Potter's Field. The rich, who owned their tombs or graves in perpetuity, slept their last long sleep undisturbed; next came the rows of ten-year concessionaires, whose relatives had bought them the right to lie in moderately deep graves for a decade, after which their bones would be exhumed and deposited in a common charnel-house, all trace of their identity lost. The five-year concessionnaires' graves were scarcely deeper than the height of the coffins they enclosed, and their repose was limited to half a decade, while the three-year concessions, placed nearest the cemetery wall, were little more than mounds of sodden earth heaped over coffins sunk scarce a foot underground, destined to be broken down and emptied in thirty-six months. The sexton led the way to one of these and began shoveling off the earth with his spade.

"His tool struck an obstruction with a thud and in a moment he was wrenching at the coffin top with the flat end of his mattock.

"I took the candle-lantern he had brought and flashed its feeble light into the coffin. Sonia lay before me, rigid as though petrified, her hands tight-clenched, the nails digging into the soft flesh of her palms, little streams of dried blood running from each self-inflicted wound. Her eyes were closed—thank heaven!— her mouth a little open, and on her lips there lay a double line of bloody froth.

"'Grand Dieu!' the sexton cried as he looked past me into the violated coffin. 'Come away, quickly, M'sieur; it is a vampire that we see! Behold the life-like countenance, the opened mouth all bloody from the devil's breakfast, the hands all wet with human blood! Come, I will strike it to the heart with my pickax and sever its unhallowed head with my spade, then we shall fill the grave again and go away all quickly. O, Sainte Vierge, have pity on us! See, M'sieur, I do begin!' He laid the spur-end of his mattock against Sonia's left breast, and I could see the flimsy crêpe night robe she wore by way of shroud and the soft flesh beneath dimple under the iron's weight.

"'Stop it, you fool!' I bellowed, snatching his pickax and bending forward. 'You shan't—' Some impulse prompted me to rearrange the shroud where the muddy mattock had soiled it, and as my hand came into contact with the beloved body I started. *The flesh was warm.*

"I thrust the doddering old sexton back with a tremendous shove and he landed sitting in a pool of mud and water and squatted there, mouthing bleating admonitions to me to come away.

"Sinking to my knees beside the grave I put my hand against her breast, then laid a finger on her throat beneath the angle of the jaw, as they'd taught us in first-aid class. There was no doubt of it. Faint as the fluttering of a fledgling thrust prematurely from its nest and almost perished with exposure, but still perceptible, a feeble pulse was beating in her breast and throat.

"A moment later I had snatched my raincoat off, wrapped it about her, and, flinging a handful of banknotes at the screaming sexton, I clasped her flaccid body in my arms, sloshed through the mud to the cemetery wall and vaulted over it.

"I found myself in a sort of alley flanked on both sides by stables, a pale light burning at its farther end. Toward this I made, bending almost double against the driving rain in order to shield my precious burden from the storm and to present the poorest target possible if the sexton should procure a gun and take a pot-shot at me.

"It seemed as though I waded through the rain for hours, though actually I don't suppose I walked for more than twenty minutes before a prowling taxi hailed me. I jumped into the vehicle and told the man to drive to my quarters as fast as his old rattletrap would go, and while we skidded through the sodden streets I propped Sonia up against the cushions and wrapped my blouse about her feet while I held her hands in mine, chafing them and breathing on them.

"Once in my room I put her into bed, piled all the covers I could about her, heated water and soaked some flannel cloths in it and put the hot rolls to her feet, then mixed some cognac and water and forced several spoonfuls of it down her throat.

"I must have worked an hour, but finally my clumsy treatment began to show results. The faintest flush appeared in her cheeks, and a tinge of color came to the pale, wounded lips which I'd wiped clean of blood and bathed in water and cologne when I first put her into bed.

"As soon as I dared leave her for a moment I hustled out and roused the *concierge* and sent her scrambling for a doctor. It seemed a week before he came, and when he did he merely wrote me a prescription, looked importantly through his *pince-nez* and suggested that I have him call next morning.

"I pleaded illness at the bureau and went home from the surgeon's office with advice to stay indoors as much as possible for the next week. I was a sort of privileged character, you see, and got away with shameless malingering which would have gotten any other fellow a good, sound roasting from the sawbones. Every moment after that which I could steal from my light duties at the bureau I spent with Sonia. Old Madame Couchin, the *concierge*, I drafted into service as a nurse, and she accepted the situation with the typical Frenchwoman's aplomb.

"It was September before Sonia finally came back to full consciousness, and then she was so weak that the month was nearly gone before she could totter out with me to get a little sunshine and fresh air in the *bois*. We had a wonderful time shopping at the Galleries Lafayette, replacing the horrifying garments

Madame Couchin had bought for us with a suitable wardrobe. Sonia took rooms at a little *pension*, and in October we were—

"*Ha, parbleu*, married at last!" Jules de Grandin exclaimed with a delighted chuckle. "*Mille crapauds*, my friend, I thought we never should have got you to the parson's door!"

"Yes, and so we were married," Tanis agreed with a smile.

The girl lifted her husband's hand and cuddled it against her cheek. "Please, Donald dear," she pleaded, "please don't let Konstantin take me from you again."

"But, darling," the young man protested, "I tell you, you must be mistaken.

"Mustn't she, Doctor de Grandin?" he appealed. "If I saw Konstantin fall before a firing-party and saw the corporal blow his brains out, and saw them nail him in his coffin, he *must* be dead, mustn't he? Tell her she can't be right, sir!"

"But, Donald, you saw *me* in *my* coffin, too—" the girl began.

"My friends," de Grandin interrupted gravely, "it may be that you both are right, though the good God forbid that it is so."

4. Menace Out of Bedlam

Donald and Sonia Tanis regarded him with open-mouthed astonishment. "You mean it's possible Konstantin might have escaped in some mysterious way, and actually come here?" the young man asked at last.

The little Frenchman made no answer, but the grave regard he bent on them seemed more ominous than any vocally expressed opinion.

"But I say," Tanis burst out, as though stung to words by de Grandin's silence, "he can't take her from me. I can't say I know much about such things, but surely the law won't let—"

"*Ah bah!*" Inspector Renouard's sardonic laugh cut him short. "The law," he gibed, "what is it? *Parfum d'un chameau.* I think in this country it is a code devised to give the criminal license to make the long nose at honest men. Yes.

"A month and more ago I came to this so splendid country in search of one who has most richly deserved the kiss of Madame Guillotine, and here I catch him red-handed in most flagrant crime. 'You are arrest,' I tell him. 'For wilful murder, for sedition and subornation of sedition and for stirring up rebellion against the Republic of France I make you arrested.' *Voilà.*

"I take him to the Ministry of Justice. '*Messieurs*,' I say, 'I have here a very noted criminal whom I desire to return to French jurisdiction that he may suffer according to his misdoings.' Certainly.

"*Alors*, what happens? The gentlemen at the *Palais de Justice* tell me: 'It shall be even as you say.'

"Do they assist me? *Hélas*, entirely otherwise. In furtherance of his diabolical designs this one has here abducted a young American lady and on her has committed the most abominable assault. For this, say the American authorities, he must suffer.

"'How much?' I ask. 'Will his punishment be death?'

"'Oh, no,' they answer me. 'We shall incarcerate him in the *bastille* for ten years; perhaps fifteen.'

"'*Bien alors*,' I tell them, 'let us compose our differences amicably. Me, I have traced this despicable one clear across the world, I have made him arrested for his crimes; I am prepared to take him where a most efficient executioner will decapitate his head with all celerity. *Voilà tout*; a man dies but once, let this one die for the crime which is a capital offense by the laws of France, and which is not, but should be capital by American law. That way we shall both be vindicated.' Is not my logic absolute? Would not a three-year-old child of most deficient intellect be convinced by it? Of course; but these ones? *Non*.

"'We sympathize with you,' they tell me, 'but *tout la même* he stays with us to expiate his crime in prison.' Then they begin his prosecution.

"*Grand Dieu*, the farce that trial is! First come the lawyers with their endless tongues and heavy words to make fools of the jury. Next comes a corps of doctors who will testify to anything, so long as they are paid. 'Not guilty by reason of insanity,' the verdict is, and so they take him to a madhouse.

"Not only that," he added, his grievance suddenly becoming vocal again, "they tell me that should this despicable one recover from his madness, he will be discharged from custody and may successfully resist extradition by the Government of France. Renouard is made the fool of! If he could but once get his hands on this criminal, Sun Ah Poy, or if that half-brother of Satan would but manage to escape from the madhouse that I might find him unprotected by the attendants—"

Crash! I ducked my head involuntarily as a missile whistled through the sleet-drenched night, struck the study window a shattering blow and hurtled across the room, smashing against the farther wall with a resounding crack.

Renouard, the Tanises and I leaped to our feet as the egg-like object burst and a sickly-sweet smell permeated the atmosphere, but Jules de Grandin seemed suddenly to go wild. As though propelled by a powerful spring he bounded from the couch, cleared the six feet or so separating him from Sonia in a single flying leap and snatched at the trailing drapery of her dinner frock, ripping a length of silk off with a furious tug and flinging it veilwise about her head. "Out—for your lives, go out!" he cried, covering his mouth and nose with a wadded handkerchief and pushing the girl before him toward the door.

We obeyed instinctively, and though a scant ten seconds intervened between the entry of the missile and our exit, I was already feeling a stinging sensation in my eyes and a constriction in my throat as though a ligature had been drawn around it. Tears were streaming from Renouard's and Tanis' eyes, too, as we rushed pell-mell into the hall and de Grandin slammed the door behind us. "What—" I began, but he waved me back.

"Papers—newspapers—all you have!" he ordered hysterically, snatching a rug from the hall floor and stuffing it against the crack between the door and sill.

I took a copy of the *Evening News* from the hall table and handed it to him, and he fell to tearing it in strips and stuffing the cracks about the door with fierce energy. "To the rear door," he ordered. "Open it and breath as deeply as you may. I do not think we were exposed enough to do us permanent injury, but fresh air will help, in any event.

"I humbly beg your pardon, Madame Tanis," he added as he joined us in the kitchen a moment later. "It was most unconventional to set on you and tear your gown to shreds the way I did, but"—he turned to Tanis with a questioning smile—"perhaps *Monsieur* your husband can tell you what it was we smelled in the study a moment hence."

"I'll tell the world I can," young Donald answered. "I smelt that stuff at Mons, and it darn near put me in my grave. You saved us; no doubt about it, Doctor de Grandin. It's tricky, that stuff."

"*What* is?" I asked. This understanding talk of theirs got on my nerves.

"Name of a thousand pestiferous mosquitoes, yes, what was it?" Renouard put in.

"Phosgene gas—COCl2" de Grandin answered. "It was among the earliest of gases used in the late war, and therefore not so deadly as the others; but it is not a healthy thing to be inhaled, my friend. However, I think that in a little while the study will be safe, for that broken window makes a most efficient ventilator, and the phosgene is quickly dissipated in the air. Had he used mustard gas—*tiens*, one does not like to speculate on such unpleasant things. No."

"He?" I echoed. "Who the dickens are you talking—"

There was something grim in the smile which hovered beneath the upturned ends of his tightly waxed wheat-blond mustache. "I damn think Friend Renouard has his wish," he answered, and a light which heralded the joy of combat shone in his small blue eyes. "If Sun Ah Poy has not burst from his madhouse and come to tell us that the game of hide-and-go-seek is on once more I am much more mistaken than I think. Yes. Certainly."

The whining, warning *whe-e-eng!* of a police car's siren sounded in the street outside and heavy feet tramped my front veranda while heavy fists beat furiously on the door.

"Ouch, God be praised, ye're all right, Doctor de Grandin, sor!" Detective Sergeant Jeremiah Costello burst into the house, his greatcoat collar turned up round his ears, a shining film of sleet encasing the black derby hat he wore habitually. "We came here hell-bent for election to warn ye, sor," he added breathlessly. "We just heard it ourselves, an'—"

"*Tiens*, so did we!" de Grandin interrupted with a chuckle.

"Huh? What're ye talkin' of, sor? I've come to warn ye—"

"That the efficiently resourceful Doctor Sun Ah Poy, of Cambodia and elsewhere, has burst the bonds of bedlam and taken to the warpath, *n'est-ce-pas?*" de Grandin laughed outright at the Irishman's amazed expression.

"Come, my friend," he added, "there is no magic here. I did not gaze into a crystal and go into a trance, then say, 'I see it all—Sun Ah Poy has escaped from the asylum for the criminal insane and comes to this place to work his mischief.' Indeed no. Entirely otherwise. Some fifteen minutes gone the good Renouard expressed a wish that Doctor Sun might manage his escape so that the two might come to grips once more, and hardly had the words flown from his lips when a phosgene bomb was merrily tossed through the window, and it was only by a hasty exit we escaped the inconvenience of asphyxiation. I am not popular with many people, and there are those who would shed few tears at my funeral, but I do not know of one who would take pleasure in throwing a stink-bomb through the window to stifle me. No, such clever tricks as that belong to Doctor Sun, who loves me not at all, but who dislikes my friend Renouard even more cordially. *Alors*, I deduce that Sun Ah Poy is out again and we shall have amusement for some time to come. Am I correct?"

"Check an' double check, as th' felly says," Costello nodded. "'Twas just past dark this evenin' whilst th' warders wuz goin' through th' State Asylum, seein' everything wuz shipshape for th' night, sor, that Doctor Sun did his disappearin' act. He'd been meek as anny lamb ever since they took him to th' bughouse, an' th' orderlies down there had decided he warn't such a bad actor, afther all. Well, sor, th' turnkey passed his door, an' this Doctor Sun invites him in to see a drawin' he's made. He's a clever felly wid his hands, for all his bein' crippled, an' th' boys at th' asylum is always glad to see what he's been up to makin'.

"Th' pore chap didn't have no more chance than a sparry in th' cat's mouth, sor. Somewhere th' Chinese divil had got hold of a table-knife an' ground it to a razor edge. One swipe o' that across th' turnkey's throat an' he's floppin' round th' floor like a chicken wid its head cut off, not able to make no outcry for th' blood that's stranglin' him. A pore nut 'cross th' corridor lets out a squawk, an' Doctor Sun ups an' cuts *his* throat as cool as ye'd pare a apple for yer luncheon, sor. They finds this out from another inmate that's seen it all but had sense enough in his pore crazy head to keep his mouth shut till afther it's all over.

"Ye know th' cell doors ain't locked, but th' different wards is barred off from each other wid corridors between. This Doctor Sun takes th' warder's uniform cap as calm as ye please and claps it on his ugly head, then walks to th' ward door an' unlocks it wid th' keys he's taken from th' turnkey. Th' guard on duty in th' corridor don't notice nothin' till Sun's clear through th' door;

then it's too late, for Sun stabs 'im to th' heart before he can so much as raise his club, an' beats it down th' corridor. There's a fire escape at th' other end o' th' passage—one o' them spiral things that works like a slide inside a sheet-iron cylinder, ye know. It's locked, but Sun has th' key, an' in a moment he's slipped inside, locked th' door behind him an' slid down faster than a snake on roller skates. He's into th' grounds an' over th' wall before they even know he's loose, an' he must o' had confederates waitin' for him outside, for they heard th' roar of the car runnin' like th' hammers o' hell whilst they're still soundin' th' alarm.

"O' course th' State Troopers an' th' local police wuz notified, but he seems to 'a' got clean away, except—"

"Yes, except?" de Grandin prompted breathlessly, his little, round blue eyes sparkling with excitement.

"Well, sor, we don't rightly *know* it wuz him, but we're suspectin' it. They found a trooper run down an' kilt on th' highway over by Morristown, wid his motorcycle bent up like a pretzel an' not a whole bone left in his body. Looks like Sun's worrk, don't it, sor?"

"Assuredly," the Frenchman nodded. "Is there more to tell?"

"Nothin' except he's gone, evaporated, vanished into thin air, as th' sayin' is, sor; but we figured he's still nursin' a grudge agin Inspector Renouard an' you, an' maybe come to settle it, so we come fast as we could to warn ye."

"Your figuring is accurate, my friend," de Grandin answered with another smile. "May we trespass on your good nature to ask that you escort Monsieur and Madame Tanis home? I should not like them to encounter Doctor Sun Ah Poy, for he plays roughly. As for us—Renouard, Friend Trowbridge and me—we shall do very well unguarded for tonight. Good Doctor Sun has shot his bolt; he will not he up to other tricks for a little time, I think, for he undoubtlessly has a hideaway prepared, and to it he has gone. He would not linger here, knowing the entire *gendarmerie* is on his heels. No. To hit and run, and run as quickly as he hits, will be his policy, for a time, at least."

5. Desecration

"Doctor de Grandin—gentlemen!" Donald Tanis burst into the breakfast room as de Grandin, Renouard and I were completing our morning meal next day. "Sonia—my wife—she's gone!"

"Eh? What is it you tell me?" de Grandin asked. "Gone?"

"Yes, sir. She rides every morning, you see, and today she left for a canter in the park at six o'clock, as usual. I didn't feel up to going out this morning, and lay abed rather late. I was just going down to breakfast when they told me her horse had come back to the stable—alone."

"Oh, perhaps she had a tumble in the park," I suggested soothingly. "Have you looked—"

"I've looked everywhere," he broke in. "Soldiers' Park's not very large, and if she'd been in it I'd have found her long ago. After what happened last night, I'm afraid—"

"*Morbleu, mon pauvre*, you fear with reason," de Grandin cut him short. "Come, let us go. We must seek her—we must find her, right away, at once; without delay, for—"

"If ye plaze, sor, Sergeant Costello's askin' for Doctor de Grandin," announced Nora McGinnis, appearing at the breakfast room door. "He's got a furrin gentleman wid him," she amplified as de Grandin gave an exclamation of impatience at the interruption, "an' says as how he's most partic'lar to talk wid ye a minit."

Father Pophosepholos, shepherd of the little flock of Greeks, Lithuanians and Russians composing the congregation of St. Basil's Church, paused at the doorway beside the big Irish policeman with uplifted hand as he invoked divine blessing on the inmates of the room, then advanced with smiling countenance to take the slim white fingers de Grandin extended. The aged *papa* and the little Frenchman were firmest friends, though one lived in a thought-world of the Middle-Ages, while the other's thoughts were modern as the latest model airplane.

"My son," the old man greeted, "the powers of evil were abroad last night. The greatest treasure in the world was ravished from my keeping, and I come to you for help."

"A treasure, *mon père?*" de Grandin asked.

Father Pophosepholos rose from his chair, and we forgot the cheap, worn stuff of his purple cassock, his broken shoes, even the pinchbeck gold and imitation amethyst of his pectoral cross as he stood in patriarchal majesty with upraised hands and back-thrown head. "The most precious body and blood of our blessed Lord," he answered sonorously. "Last night, between the sunset and the dawn, they broke into the church and bore away the holy Eucharist." For a moment he paused, then in all reverence echoed the Magdalen's despairing cry: "They have taken away my Lord, and I know not where they have laid Him!"

"*Ha*, do you say it?" The momentary annoyance de Grandin had evinced at the old priest's intrusion vanished as he gazed at the cleric with a level stare of fierce intensity. "Tell me of the sacrilege. All—tell me all. Right away; at once, immediately. I am all attention!"

Father Pophosepholos resumed his seat and the sudden fire which animated him died down. Once more he was a tired old man, the threadbare shepherd of a half-starved flock. "I saw you smile when I mentioned a treasure being stolen from *me*," he told de Grandin gently. "You were justified, my son, for St. Basil's is a poor church, and I am poorer still. Only the faith which is in me sustains me through the struggle. We ask no help from the public, and receive none; the rich

Latins look on us with pity, the Anglicans sometimes give us slight assistance; the Protestant heretics scarcely know that we exist. We are a joke to them, and, because we're poor, they sometimes play mischievous pranks on us—their boys stone our windows, and once or twice when parties of their young people have come slumming they have disturbed our services with their thoughtless laughter or ill-bred talking during service. Our liturgy is only meaningless mummery to them, you see.

"But this was no childish mischief, not even the vandalism of irreverent young hoodlums!" his face flushed above its frame of gray beard. "This was deliberately planned and maliciously executed blasphemy and sacrilege!

"Our rubric makes no provision for low mass, like the Latins'," he explained, "and daily celebration of the Eucharist is not enjoined; so, since our ceremony of consecration is a lengthy one, we customarily celebrate only once or twice a week, and the pre-sanctified elements are reserved in a tabernacle on the altar.

"This morning as I entered the sanctuary I found everything in disorder. The veils had been torn from the table, thrown upon the floor and fouled with filth, the ikon of the Virgin had been ripped from the reredos and the tabernacle violated. They had carried off the elements together with the chalice and paten, and in their place had thrust into the tabernacle the putrefying carcass of a cat!" Tears welled in the old man's eyes as he told of the sacrilege.

Costello's face went brick-red with an angry flush, for the insult put upon the consecrated elements stung every fiber of his nature. "Bad cess to 'em!" he muttered. "May they have th' curse o' Cromwell!"

"They took my chasuble and cope, my alb, my miter and my stole," the priest continued, "and from the sacristy they took the deacon's vestments—"

"*Grand Dieu*, I damn perceive their game!" the little Frenchman almost shouted. "At first I thought this might be but an act of wantonness performed by wicked boys. I have seen such things. Also, the chalice and the paten might have some little value to a thief; but this is no mere case of thievery mixed with sacrilege. *Non*. The stealing of the vestments is conclusive proof.

"Tell me, *mon père*," he interrupted himself with seeming irrelevance, "it is true, is it not, that only the celebrant and the deacon are necessary for the office of consecration? No subdeacon is required?"

The old priest nodded wonderingly.

"And these elements were already consecrated?"

"They were already consecrated," the clergyman returned. "Presanctified, we call it when they are reserved for future services."

"Thank God, no little one then stands in peril," de Grandin answered.

"*Mon père*, it gives me greatest joy to say I'll aid in tracking down these miscreants. Monsieur Tanis, unless I am more greatly mistaken than I think, there is direct connection between your lady's disappearance and this act of sacrilege. Yes, I am sure of it!" He nodded several times with increasing vigor.

"But, my dear fellow," I expostulated, "what possible connection can there be between—"

"*Chut!*" he cut me short. "This is the doing of that villain Konstantin! Assuredly. The wife he has again abducted, though he has not attempted to go near the husband. For why? *Pardieu*, because by leaving Monsieur Donald free he still permits the wife one little, tiny, ray of hope. With vilest subtlety he holds her back from the black brink of despair and suicide that he may force her to compliance to his will by threats against the man she loves. *Sacré nom d'un artichaut*, I shall say yes! Certainly; of course."

"You—you mean he'll make Sonia go with him—leave me—by threats against my life?" young Tanis faltered.

"*Précisément.* That and more, I fear, Monsieur," de Grandin answered somberly.

"But what worse can he do than that? You—you don't think he'll kill her, do you?" the husband cried.

The little Frenchman rose and paced the study a moment in thoughtful silence. At last: "Courage, *mon brave*," he bade, putting a kindly hand on Tanis' shoulder. "You and Madame Sonia have faced perils—even the perils of the grave—before. Take heart! I shall not hide from you that your present case is as desperate as any you have faced before; but if my guess is right, as heaven knows I hope it is not, your lady stands in no immediate bodily peril. If that were all we had to fear we might afford to rest more easily; as it is—"

"As it is," Renouard cut in, "let us go with all celerity to St. Basil's church and look to see what we can find. The trail grows cold, *mon* Jules, but—"

"But we shall find and follow it," de Grandin interrupted. "*Parbleu*, we'll follow it though it may lead to the fire-doors of hell's own furnaces, and then—"

The sharp, insistent ringing of the telephone broke through his fervid prophecy.

"This is Miss Wilkinson, supervisor at Casualty Hospital, Doctor Trowbridge," a professionally precise feminine voice informed me. "If Detective Sergeant Costello is at your office, we've a message for him. Officer Hornsby is here, about to go on the table, and insists we put a message through to Sergeant Costello at once. We've already called him at headquarters, and they told us—"

"Just a minute," I bade. "It's for you, Sergeant," I told Costello, handing him the instrument.

"Yes," Costello called into the mouthpiece. "Yes; uh-huh. *What?* Glory be to God!"

He swung on us with flushing face and blazing eyes. "'Twas Hornsby," he announced. "He wuz doin' relief traffic duty out at Auburndale an' Gloucester Streets, an' a car run 'im down half an hour ago. There wuz no witnesses to th' accident, an' Hornsby couldn't git th' license number, but just before they struck 'im he seen a felly ridin' in th' car.

"You'll be rememberin' Hornsby wuz in th' raidin' party that captured this here Doctor Sun?" he asked de Grandin.

The Frenchman nodded.

"Well, sor, Hornsby's got th' camera eye. He don't forget a face once he's seen it, even for a second, an' he tells me Doctor Sun wuz ridin' in th' car that bowled 'im over. They run 'im down deliberate, sor, an' Sun Ah Poy was ridin' wid a long, tall, black-faced felly wid slantin' eyebrows an' a pan like th' pictures ye see o' Satan in th' chur-rches, sor!"

"And what was this one doing with his pan?" Renouard demanded. "Is it that—"

"Pan," Costello shouted, raising his voice as many people do when seeking to make clear their meaning to a foreigner, "'twas his pan I'm speaking of. Not *a* pan; *his* pan—his mush—his map—his puss, ye know.

"*Pas possible!* The miscreant held a pan of mush for his cat to eat, and a map, also, while his motor car ran down the gendarme?"

"Oh, go sit in a tree—*no!*" Costello roared. "It's his face I'm afther tellin' ye of. Hornsby said he had a face—a face, git me; a face is a pan an' a pan's a face— like th' divil's, an' he wuz ridin' in th' same car wid this here now Doctor Sun Ah Poy that's made his getaway from th' asylum! Savvy?"

"Oh, *mais oui,*" the Frenchman grinned. "I apprehend. It is another of the so droll American idioms which you employ. *Oui-da*; I perceive him."

"'Tis plain as anny pikestaff they meant to do 'im in deliberately," Costello went on, "an' they like to made good, too. Th' pore felly's collarbone is broke, an' so is several ribs; but glory be to heaven, they wuz goin' so fast they bumped 'im clean out o' th' road an' onto th' sidewalk, an' they kep' on goin' like th' hammers o' hell widout waitin' to see how much they'd hurt 'im."

"You hear, my friends?" de Grandin cried, leaping to his feet, eyes flashing, diminutive, wheat-blond mustache twitching with excitement like the whiskers of an angry tomcat. "You heard the message of this gloriously devoted officer of the law who sends intelligence to Costello even as he waits to go upon the oper-ating-table? What does it mean? I ask. No, I demand what does it mean?

"Sun Ah Poy rides in a car which maims and injures the police, and with him rides another with a face like Satan's. *Mordieu, mes amis,* we shall have hunting worthy of our utmost skill, I think.

"*Sun Ah Poy and Konstantin have met and combined against us!* Come, my friends, let us take their challenge.

"Come, Renouard, my old one, this is more than mere police work. The enemy laughs at our face, he makes the thumb-nose at us and at all for which we stand. Forward to the battle, *brave comrade. Pour la France!*"

6. Allies Unawares

Four of us—de Grandin, Renouard, Donald Tanis and I—sat before my study fire and stared gloomily into the flames. All day the other three, accompanied by Costello, had combed the city and environs, but neither sign nor clue, trail nor trace of the missing woman could they find.

"By heaven," Tanis cried, striking his forehead with his hand in impotent fury, "it looks as if the fellow were the devil himself!"

"Not so bad a guess, *mon brave*," de Grandin nodded gloomily. "Certain it is he is on friendly terms with the dark powers, and, as usual, Satan is most kindly to his own."

"*Ah bah, mon Jules*," Renouard rejoined, "you do but make a bad matter so much worse with your mumblings of Satan and his cohorts. Is it not sufficient that two poor ladies of this town are placed in deadly peril without your prating of diabolical opponents and—"

"*Two* ladies?" Tanis interrupted wonderingly. "Why, has he abducted some one else—"

"*Bien non*," Renouard's quick explanation came. "It is of another that I speak, *Monsieur*. This Konstantin, who has in some way met with Sun Ah Poy and made a treaty of alliance with him, has taken your poor lady for revenge, even as he sought to do when first we met him, but Sun Ah Poy has also reasons to desire similar vengeance of his own, and all too well we know how far his insane jealousy and lust will lead him. Regard me, if you please: As I have previously told you, I came across the world in search of Sun Ah Poy, and took him bloody-handed in commission of a crime of violence. Clear from Cambodia I trailed him, for there he met, and having met, desired a white girl-dancer in the mighty temple shrine at Angkor. Just who she was we do not know for certain, but strongly circumstantial evidence would indicate she was the daughter of a missionary gentleman named Crownshield, an American, who had been murdered by the natives at the instigation of the heathen priests and whose widowed mother had been spirited away and lodged within the temple until she knew the time of woman and her child was born. Then, we suppose, the mother, too, was done to death, and the little white girl reared as a *bayadère*, or temple-dancer.

"The years went on, and to Cambodia came a young countryman of yours, a citizen of Harrisonville, who met and loved this nameless mystery of a temple *coryphée*, known only as Thi-bah, the dancing-woman of the temple, and she returned his passion, for in Cambodia as elsewhere, like cries aloud to like, and this milk-skinned, violet-eyed inmate of a heathen shrine knew herself not akin to her brown-faced fellow members of the temple's *corps du ballet*.

"*Enfin*, they did elope and hasten to the young man's home in this city, and on their trail, blood-lustful as a tiger in the hunt, there followed Sun Ah Poy, determined to retake the girl whom he had purchased from the priests; if possi-ble to slay the man on whom her favor rested, also. *Parbleu*, and as the shadow follows the body when the sun is low, Renouard did dog the footsteps of this Sun Ah Poy. Yes.

"*Tiens*, almost the wicked one succeeded in his plans for vengeance, but with the aid of Jules de Grandin, who is a clever fellow, for all his stupid looks and silly ways, I captured him and saved the little lady, now a happy wife and an American citizeness by marriage and adoption.

"How I then fared, how this miscreant of a Sun Ah Poy made apes and monkeys of the law and lodged himself all safely in a madhouse, I have already related. How he escaped and all but gave me my quietus you know from personal, first-hand experience. Certainly.

"Now, consider: Somewhere in the vicinage there lurk these two near-mad men with twin maggots of jealousy and vengeance gnawing at their brains. Your so unfortunate lady is already in their power—Konstantin has scored a point in his game of passion and revenge. But I know Sun Ah Poy. A merchant prince he was in former days, the son of generations of merchant princes, and Chinese merchant princes in the bargain.

"Such being so, I know all well that Sun Ah Poy has not united forces with this Konstantin unless he is assured of compensation. My death? *Pouf*, a baga-telle! Me he can kill—at least, he can attempt my life—whenever he desires, and do it all unaided. Last night we saw how great his resource is and how casually he tossed a stink-bomb through the window by way of telling me he was at liberty once more. No, no, my friend; he has not joined with Konstantin merely to he assured that Renouard goes home in one of those elaborate containers for the dead your undertakers sell. On the contrary. He seeks to regain the custody of her who flouted his advances and ran off with another man. Thus far his pur-pose coincides with Konstantin's. They both desire women whom other men have won. One has succeeded in his quest, at least for the time being; the other still must make his purpose good. Already they have run down a *gendarme* who stood in their way—thus far they work in concert. Beyond a doubt they will continue to be allies till their plans are consummated. Yes."

The clatter of the front-door knocker silenced him, and I rose to answer the alarm, knowing Nora McGinnis had long since gone to bed.

"Is there a feller named Renyard here?" demanded a hoarse voice as I swung back the door and beheld a most untidy taximan in the act of assaulting the knocker again.

"There's a gentleman named Renouard stopping here," I answered coldly. "What—"

"A'right, tell 'im to come out an' git his friend, then. He's out in me cab, drunk as a hard-boiled owl, an' won't stir a foot till this here Renyard feller comes fer 'im. Tell 'im to make it snappy, will yuh, buddy. This here Chinaman's so potted I'm scared he's goin' to—"

"A Chinaman?" I cut in sharply. "What sort of Chinaman?"

"A dam' skinny one, an' a mean one, too. Orderin' me about like I wuz a servant or sumpin', an'—"

"Renouard—de Grandin!" I called over my shoulder. "Come here, quickly, please! There's a Chinaman out there in that cab—'a skinny Chinaman,' the driver calls him—and he wants Renouard to come out to him. D'ye suppose—"

"*Sacré nom d'un porc*, I damn do!" de Grandin answered. To the taximan he ordered:

"Bring in your passenger at once, my friend. We can not come out to him; but—"

"Say, feller, I ain't takin' no more orders from a Frog than I am from a Chink, git me?" the cabman interposed truculently. "You'll come out an' git this here drunk, an' like it, or else—"

"*Précisément*; or else?" de Grandin shot back sharply, and the porchlight's rays gleamed on the wicked-looking barrel of his small but deadly automatic pistol. "Will you obey me, or must I shoot?"

The taximan obeyed, though slowly, with many a backward, fearful glance, as though he did not know what instant the Frenchman's pistol might spit death. From the cab he helped a delicate, bent form muffled to the ears in a dark over-coat, and assisted it slowly up the steps. "Here he is," he muttered angrily, as he transferred his tottering charge to Renouard's waiting hands.

The shrouded form reeled weakly at each step as de Grandin and Renouard assisted it down the hall and guided it to an armchair by the fire. For a moment silence reigned within the study, the visitant crouching motionless in his seat and wheezing asthmatically at intervals. At length de Grandin crossed the room, took the wide brim of the black-felt hat which obscured the man's face in both his hands and wrenched the headgear off.

"Ah?" he ejaculated as the light struck upon the caller's face. "A-a-ah? I thought as much!"

Renouard breathed quickly, almost with a snort, as he beheld the livid coun-tenance turned toward him. "Sun Ah Poy, thou species of a stinking camel, what filthy joke is this you play?" he asked suspiciously.

The Chinaman smiled with a sort of ghastly parody of mirth. His face seemed composed entirely of parchment-like skin stretched drum-tight above the bony processes; his little, deep-set eyes were terrible to look at as empty sockets in a skull; his lips, paper-thin and bloodless, were retracted from a set of broken and discolored teeth. The countenance was as lifeless and revolting as the mummy of Rameses in the British Museum, and differed from the dead man's principally in that it was instinct with conscious evil and lacked the majesty and repose of death.

"Does this look like a jest?" he asked in a low, faltering voice, and with a twisted, claw-like hand laid back a fold of his fur overcoat. The silken Chinese blouse within was stained with fresh, warm blood, and the gory spot grew larger with each pulsation of his heart.

"*Morbleu*, it seems you have collided with just retribution!" de Grandin commented dryly. "Is it that you are come to us for treatment, by any happy chance?"

"Partly," the other answered as another horrifying counterfeit of mirth writhed across his livid mouth. "Doctor Jules de Grandin is a surgeon and a man of honor; the oath of Aesculapius and the obligation of his craft will not allow him to refuse aid to a wounded man who comes to him for succor, whoever that man may be."

"*Eh bien*, you have me there," de Grandin countered, "but I am under no compulsion to keep your presence here a secret. While I am working on your wound the police will be coming with all haste to take you back in custody. You realize that, of course?"

We cut away his shirt and singlet, for undressing him would have been too hazardous. To the left, between the fifth and sixth ribs, a little in front of the mid-axillary line, there gaped a long incised wound, obviously the result of a knife-thrust. Extensive hemorrhage had already taken place, and the patient was weakening quickly from loss of blood. "A gauze pack and styptic collodion," de Grandin whispered softly, "and then perhaps ten minims of adrenalin; it's all that we can do I fear. The state will save electric current by this evening's work, my friend; he'll never live to occupy the chair of execution."

The treatment finished, we propped the patient up with pillows. "Doctor Sun," de Grandin announced professionally, "it is my duty to inform you that death is very near. I greatly doubt that you will live till morning."

"I realize that," the other answered weakly, "nor am I sorry it is so. This wound has brought me back my sanity, and I am once again the man I was before I suffered madness. All I have done while I was mentally deranged comes back to me like memories of a disagreeable dream, and when I think of what I was, and what I have become, I am content that Sun Ah Poy should die.

"But before I go I must discharge my debt—pay you my fee," he added with another smile, and this time, I thought, there was more of gentleness than irony in the grimace. "My time is short and I must leave some details out, but such facts as you desire shall be yours," he added.

"This morning I met Konstantin the Russian as I fled the police, and we agreed to join forces to combat you. He seemed to be a man beset, like me, by the police, and gladly did I welcome him as ally." He paused a moment, and a quick spasm of pain flickered in his face, but he fought it down. "In the East we learn early of some things the Western world will never learn," he gasped. "The lore of China is filled with stories of some beings whose existence you deride.

Yet they are real, though happily they become more rare each day. Konstantin is one of them; not wholly man, nor yet entirely demon, but a dreadful hybrid of the two. Not till he'd taken me to his lair did I discover this—he is a servant of the Evil One.

"It cost my life to come and tell you, but *he must be exterminated*. My life for his; the bargain is a trade by which the world will profit. What matters Sun Ah Poy beside the safety of humanity? Konstantin is virtually immortal, but he *can* be killed. Unless you hunt him out and slay him—"

"We know all this," de Grandin interrupted; "at least, I have suspected it. Tell us while you have time where we may find him, and I assure you we shall do to him according to his sins—"

"Old Shepherd's Inn, near Chestertown—the old, deserted place padlocked three years ago for violation of the Prohibition law," the Chinaman broke in. "You'll find him there at night, and with him—go there before the moon has set; by day he is abroad, and with him goes his captive, held fast in bonds of fear, but when the moon has climbed the heavens—" He broke off with a sigh of pain, and little beads of perspiration shone upon his brow. The man was going fast; the pauses between his words were longer, and his voice was scarcely louder than a whisper.

"Renouard"—he rolled his head toward the Inspector—"in the old days you called me friend. Can you forget the things I did in madness and say good-bye to the man you used to know—will you take my hand, Renouard? I can not hold it out to you—I am too weak, but—"

"Assuredly, I shall do more, *mon vieux*," Renouard broke in. "*Je vous salue!*" He drew himself erect and raised his right hand in stiff and formal military greeting. Jules de Grandin followed suit.

Then, in turn, they took the dying man's hand in theirs and shook it solemnly.

"Shades—of—honorable—ancestors, comes—now—Sun—Ah—Poy to be among—you!" the Oriental gasped, and as he finished speaking a rattle sounded in his throat and from the corners of his mouth there trickled thin twin streams of blood. His jaw relaxed, his eyes were set and glazed, his breast fluttered once or twice, then all was done.

"Quicker than I thought," de Grandin commented as he lifted the spare, twisted body from the chair and laid it on the couch, then draped a rug over it. "The moment I perceived his wound I knew the pleural wall was punctured, and it was but a matter of moments before internal hemorrhage set in and killed him, but my calculations erred. I would have said half an hour; he has taken only eighteen minutes to die. We must notify the coroner," he added practically. "This news will bring great happiness to the police, and rejoice the newspapers most exceedingly, as well."

"I wonder how he got that wound?" I asked.

"You wonder?" he gave me an astonished glance. "Last night we saw how Konstantin can throw a knife—Renouard's shoulder is still sore in testimony of his skill. The wonder is he got away at all. I wish he had not died so soon; I should have liked to ask him how he did it."

7. Though This Be Damnation

Shepherd's Inn was limned against the back-drop of wind-driven snow like the gigantic carcass of a stranded leviathan. Remote from human habitation or activity, it stood in the midst of its overgrown grounds, skeletal remains of small summer-houses where in other days Bacchus had dallied drunkenly with Aphrodite stood starkly here and there among the rank-grown evergreens and frost-blasted weeds; flanking the building on the left was a row of frontless wooden sheds where young bloods of the nineties had stabled horse and buggy while reveling in the bar or numerous private dining-rooms upstairs; a row of hitching-posts for tethering the teams of more transient guests stood ranked before the porch. The lower windows were heavily barred by rusted iron rods without and stopped by stout wooden shutters within. Even creepers seemed to have felt the blight which rested on the place, for there was no patch of ivy green upon the brickwork which extended upward to the limit of the lower story.

Beneath a wide-boughed pine we paused for council. "Sergeant," de Grandin ordered, "you and Friend Trowbridge will enter at the rear—I have here the key which fits the door. Keep watchful eyes as you advance, and have your guns held ready, for you may meet with desperate resistance. I would advise that one of you precede the other, and that the first man hold the flashlight, and hold it well out from his body. Thus, if you're seen by Konstantin and he fires or flings a knife at the light, you will suffer injury only to your hand or arm. Meanwhile, the one behind will keep sharp watch and fire at any sound or movement in the dark—a shotgun is most pleasantly effective at any range which can be had within a house.

"Should you come on him unawares, shoot first and parley afterward. This is a foul thing we face tonight, my friends—one does not parley with a rattlesnake, neither does one waste time with a viper such as this. Non, by no means. And as you hope for pardon of your sins, shoot him but once; no matter what transpires, you are not to fire a second shot. Remember.

"Renouard and I shall enter from the front and work our way toward you. You shall know when we are come by the fact that our flashlight will be blue— the light in that I give you will be red, so you may shoot at any but a blue light, and we shall blaze away whenever anything but red is shown. You understand?"

"Perfectly, sor," the Irishman returned.

We stumbled through the snow until we reached the rear door and Costello knelt to fit the key into the lock while I stood guard above him with my gun.

"You or me, sor?" he inquired as the lock unlatched, and even in the excitement of the moment I noted that its mechanism worked without a squeak.

"Eh?" I answered.

"Which of us carries th' light?"

"Oh. Perhaps I'd better. You're probably a better shot than I."

"O.K. Lead th' way, sor, an' watch your shtep. I'll be right behint ye."

Cautiously we crept through the service hall, darting the red rays of our flash to left and right, through the long-vacant dining-room, finally into the lobby at the front. As yet we saw no sign of Konstantin nor did we hear a sound betokening the presence of de Grandin or Renouard.

The foyer was paved with flagstones set in cement sills, and every now and then these turned beneath our feet, all but precipitating us upon our faces. The air was heavy and dank with that queer, unwholesome smell of earth one associates with graves and tombs; the painted woodwork was dust-grimed and dirty and here and there wallpaper had peeled off in leprous strips, exposing patches of the corpse-gray plaster underneath. From the center of the hall, slightly to the rear, there rose a wide grand staircase of wood. A sweep of my flashlight toward this brought an exclamation of surprise from both of us.

The central flight of stairs which led to the landing whence the side-flights branched to left and right, was composed of three steps and terminated in a platform some six feet wide by four feet deep. On this had been placed some sort of packing-case or table—it was impossible to determine which at the quick glance we gave it, and over this was draped a cover of some dark material which hung down nearly to the floor. Upon this darker covering there lay a strip of linen cloth and upright at the center of the case was fixed some sort of picture or framed object, while at either end there stood what I first took to be candelabra, each with three tall black candles set into its sockets. "Why," I began in a whisper, it looks like an—"

"Whist, Doctor Trowbridge, sor, there's some one comin'!" Costello breathed in my ear. "Shall I let 'em have it?" I heard the sharp click of his gunlock in the dark.

"There's a door behind us," I whispered back. "Suppose we take cover behind it and watch to see what happens? If it's our man and he comes in here, he'll have to pass us, and we can jump out and nab him; if it's de Grandin and Renouard, we'll hail them and let them know there's no one in the rear of the house. What d'ye say?"

"A'right," he acquiesced. "Let's go."

We stepped back carefully, and I heard Costello fumbling with the door. "O.K., sor, it's open," he whispered. "Watch your shtep goin' over th' sill; it's a bit high."

I followed him slowly, feeling my way with cautious feet, felt his big bulk brush past me as he moved to close the door; then:

"Howly Moses!" he muttered. "It's a trap we're in, sor! It were a snap-lock on th' door. Who th' devil'd 'a' thought o' *that?*"

He was right. As the door swung to there came a faint, sharp click of a spring lock, and though we strained and wrenched at the handle, the strong oak panels refused to budge.

The room in which we were imprisoned was little larger than a closet, windowless and walled with tongue-and-groove planks in which a line of coat hooks had been screwed. Obviously at one time it had functioned as a sort of cloak room. For some reason the management had fancied decorations in the door, and some five feet from the floor twin designs of interlacing hearts had been bored through the panels with an auger. I blessed the unknown artist who had made the perforations, for they not only supplied our dungeon generously with air but made it possible for us to see all quarters of the lobby without betraying our proximity.

"Don't be talkin', sor," Costello warned. "There's some one comin'!"

The door across the lobby opened slowly, and through it, bearing a sacristan's taper, came a cowled and surpliced figure, an ecclesiastical-looking figure which stepped with solemn pace to the foot of the staircase, sank low in genuflection, then mounted to the landing and lit the candles on the right, retreated, genuflected again, then lit companion candles at the left.

As the wicks took fire and spread a little patch of flickering luminance amid the dark, my first impression was confirmed. The box-like object on the stairs was an altar, clothed and vested in accordance, with the rubric of the Orthodox Greek Church; at each end burned a trinity of sable candles which gave off an unpleasant smell, and in the center stood a gilt-framed ikon.

Now the light fell full upon the sacristan's face and with a start I recognized Dimitri, the burly Russian Renouard had felled the night we first met Konstantin and Sonia.

The leering altar-wait retired, backed reverently from the parodied sanctuary, returned to the room whence he had entered, and in a moment we heard the sound of chanting mingled with the sharp, metallic clicking of a censer's chains.

Again Dimitri entered, this time swinging a smoking incense-pot, and close behind him, vested as a Russian priest, walked a tall, impressive figure. Above his sacerdotal garb his face stood out sharply in the candles' lambent light, smooth-shaven, long-jawed, swarthy of complexion. His coal-black eyes were deep-set under curiously arched brows; his lusterless black hair was parted in the middle and brushed abruptly backward, leaving a down-pointing triangle in the center of his high and narrow forehead which indicated the commencement of a line which was continued in the prominent bowed nose and sharp, out-jutting chin. It was a striking face, a proud face, a face of great distinction, but a face so cruel and evil it reminded me at once of every pictured image of the devil which I had ever seen. Held high between his upraised hands the evil-looking man bore carefully a large chalice of silver-gilt with a paten fitted over it for cover.

The floating cloud of incense stung my nostrils. I sniffed and fought away a strong impulse to sneeze. And all the while my memory sought to classify that strong and pungent odor. Suddenly I knew. On a vacation trip to Egypt I had spent an evening at an Arab camp out in the desert and watched them build their fires of camel-dung. That was it, the strong smell of ammonia, the faintly sickening odor of the carbonizing fumet!

Chanting slowly in a deep, melodious voice, his attendant chiming in with the responses, the mock-priest marched to the altar and placed the sacred vessels on the fair cloth where the candle-rays struck answering gleams from their cheap gilding. Then with a deep obeisance he retreated, turned, and strode toward the doorway whence he came.

Three paces from the portal he came to pause and struck his hands together in resounding claps, once, twice, three times; and though I had no intimation what I was about to see, I felt my heart beat faster and a curious weakness spread through all my limbs as I waited breathlessly.

Into the faint light of the lobby, vague and nebulous as a phantom-form half seen, half apprehended, stepped Sonia. Slowly, with an almost regal dignity she moved. She was enfolded from white throat to insteps in a long and cling-ing cloak of heavily embroidered linen which one beautiful, slim hand clutched tight round her at the breast. Something familiar yet queerly strange about the garment struck me as she paused. I'd seen its like somewhere, but never on a woman—the candlelight struck full upon it, and I knew. It was a Greek priest's white-linen over-vestment, an alb, for worked upon it in threads of gold and threads of silver and threads of iridescent color were double-barred Lorraine crosses and three mystic Grecian letters.

"Are you prepared?" the pseudo-priest demanded as he bent his lusterless black eyes upon the girl's pale face.

"I am prepared," she answered slowly. "Though this be damnation to my soul and everlasting corruption to my body, I am prepared, if only you will promise me that he shall go unharmed!"

"Think well," the man admonished, "this rite may be performed only with the aid of a woman pure in heart—a woman in whom there can be found no taint or stain of sin—who gives herself willingly and without reserve, to act the part I call on you to play. Are *you* such an one?"

"I am such an one," she answered steadily, though a ripple of heart-breaking horror ran across her blenching lips, even as they formed the words.

"And you make the offer willingly, without reserve?" he taunted. "You know what it requires? What the consequences to your flesh and soul must be?" With a quick motion he fixed his fingers in her short, blond hair and bent her head back till he gazed directly down into her upturned eyes. "*Willingly?*" he grated. "Without reserve?"

"Willingly," she answered with a choking sob. "Yes, willingly, ten thousand times ten thousand times I offer up my soul and body without a single reservation, if you will promise—"

"Then let us be about it!" he broke in with a low, almost soundless laugh.

Dimitri, who had crouched before the altar, descended with his censer and bowed before the girl till his forehead touched the floor. Then he arose and wrapped the loose ends of his stole about him and passed the censer to the other man, while from a fold of his vestments he drew a strange metal plate shaped like an angel with five-fold outspread wings, and this he waved above her head while she moved slowly toward the altar and the other man walked backward, facing her and censing her with reeking fumes at every step.

A gleam of golden slippers shone beneath her cloak as she approached the lowest of the altar steps, but as she halted for a moment she kicked them quickly off and mounted barefoot to the sanctuary, where she paused a breathless second and blessed herself, but in reverse, commencing at a point below her breast and making the sign of the cross upside-down.

Then on her knees she fell, placing both hands upon the altar-edge and dropping her head between them, and groveled there in utter self-abasement while in a low but steady voice she repeated words which sent the chills of horror through me.

I had not looked inside a Greek book for more than thirty years, but enough of early learning still remained for me to translate what she sang so softly in a firm, sweet voice:

My soul doth magnify the Lord,
And my spirit hath rejoiced
In God my Savior,
For He hath regarded the lowliness
Of His handmaiden . . .

The canticle was finished. She rose and dropped the linen cloak behind her and stretched her naked body on the altar, where she lay beneath the candles' softly glowing light like some exquisite piece of carven Carrara marble, still, lifeless, cold.

Chalice and paten were raised and placed upon the living altar-cloth, their hard, metallic weight denting the soft breasts and exquisite torso, their silver-gilt reflecting little halos of brightness on the milk-white skin. The vested man's voice rose and fell in what seemed to me an endless chant, his kneeling deacon's heavy guttural intoning the response. On, endlessly on, went the deep chant of celebration, pausing a breathless moment now and then as the order of the service directed that the celebrant should kiss the consecrated place of sacrifice, then hot and avid lips pressed shrinking, wincing flesh.

Now the rite was ended. The priest raised high the chalice with its hallowed contents and turned his back upon the living altar with a scream of cachinnating laughter. "Lucifer, Lord of the World and Prince Supreme of all the Powers of the Air, I hold thy adversary in my hands!" he cried. "To Thee the Victory, Mighty Master, Puissant God of Hell—behold I sacrifice to Thee the Nazarene! His blood be on our heads and on our children's—"

"*Eh bien, Monsieur*, I know not of your offspring, but blood assuredly shall be on your head, and that right quickly!" said Jules de Grandin, appearing suddenly in the darkness at the altar-side. A stab of lurid flame, a sharp report, and Konstantin fell forward on his face, a growing smear of blood-stain on his forehead.

A second shot roared answer to the first, and the crouching man in deacon's robes threw up both hands wildly, as though to hold himself by empty air, then leaned slowly to the left, slid down the altar steps and lay upon the floor, a blotch of moveless shadow in the candlelight.

Inspector Renouard appeared from the altar's farther side, his smoking service revolver in his hand, a smile of satisfaction on his face. "*Tiens*, my aim is true as yours, *mon* Jules," he announced matter-of-factly. "Shall I give the woman one as well?"

"By no means, no," de Grandin answered quickly. "Give her rather the charity of covering for her all-charming nudity, my friend. Quick, spread the robe over her."

Renouard obeyed, and as he dropped the desecrated alb on the still body I saw a look of wonder come into his face. "She is unconscious," he breathed. "She faints, my Jules; will you revive her?"

"All in good time," the other answered. "First let us look at this." He stirred the prostrate Konstantin with the toe of his boot.

How it happened I could not understand, for de Grandin's bullet had surely pierced his frontal bone, inflicting an instantly-fatal wound, but the prone man stirred weakly and whimpered like a child in pain.

"Have mercy!" he implored. "I suffer. Give me a second shot to end my misery. Quick, for pity's sake; I am in agony!"

De Grandin smiled unpleasantly. "So the lieutenant of the firing-party thought," he answered. "So the corporal who administered *le coup de grâce* believed, my friend. Them you could fool; you can not make a monkey out of Jules de Grandin. No; by no means. Lie here and die, my excellent adorer of the Devil, but do not take too long in doing it, for we fire the building within the quarter-hour, and if you have not finished dying by that time, *tiens*"—he raised his shoulders in a shrug—"the fault is yours, not ours. No."

"Hi, there, Doctor de Grandin, sor; don't be after settin' fire to this bloody devils' roost wid me an Doctor Trowbridge cooped up in here!" Costello roared.

"*Morbleu*," the little Frenchman laughed as he unlocked our prison, "upon occasion I have roasted both of you, my friends, but luckily I did not do it actually tonight. Come, let us hasten. We have work to do."

Within the suite which Konstantin had occupied in the deserted house we found sufficient blankets to wrap Sonia against the outside cold, and having thus prepared her for the homeward trip, we set fire to the ancient house in a dozen different spots and hastened toward my waiting car.

Red, mounting flames illuminated our homeward way, but we made no halt to watch our handiwork, for Sonia was moaning in delirium, and her hands and face were hot and dry as though she suffered from typhoid.

"To bed with her," de Grandin ordered when we reached my house. "We shall administer hyoscine and later give her strychinia and brandy; meanwhile we must inform her husband that the missing one is found and safe. Yes; he will be pleased to hear us say so, I damn think."

8. The Tangled Skein Unraveled

Jules de Grandin, smelling most agreeably of *Giboulées de Mas* toilet water and dusting-powder, extremely dapper-looking in his dinner clothes and matching black-pearl stud and cuff-links, decanted a fluid ounce or so of Napoleon brandy from the silver-mounted pinch bottle standing handily upon the tabouret beside his easy-chair, passed the wide-mouthed goblet beneath his nose, sniffing the ruby liquor's aroma with obvious approval, then sipped a thimbleful with evident appreciation.

"Attend me," he commanded, fixing small bright eyes in turn on Donald Tanis and his wife, Detective Sergeant Costello, Renouard and me. "When dear Madame Sonia told us of her strange adventures with this Konstantin, I was amazed, no less. It is not given every woman to live through such excitement and retain her faculties, much less to sail at last into the harbor of a happy love, as she has done. Her father's fate also intrigued me. I'd heard of his strange suicide and how he did denounce the Bolshevik spy, so I was well prepared to join with Monsieur Tanis and tell her that she was mistaken when she declared the man who kidnapped her was Konstantin. I knew the details of his apprehension and his trial; also I knew he fell before the firing-squad.

"Ah, but Jules de Grandin has the open mind. To things which others call impossible he gives consideration. So when I heard the tale of Konstantin's execution at Vincennes, and heard how he had been at pains to learn if they would give him the mercy-shot, and when I further heard how he did not die at once, although eight rifle-balls had pierced his breast; I thought, and thought right deeply. Here were the facts—" he checked them off upon his outspread fingers:

"Konstantin was Russian; Konstantin had been shot by eight skilled riflemen—four rifles in the firing-squad of twelve were charged with blanks—he had not died at once, so a mercy-shot was given, and this seemed to kill him to death. So far, so ordinary. But ah, there were extraordinary factors in the case, as well. Oui-da. Of course. Before he suffered execution Konstantin had said some things which showed he might have hope of returning once again to wreak grave mischief on those he hated. Also, Madame Sonia had deposed it had been he who kidnapped her. She was unlikely to have been mistaken. Women do not make mistakes in matters of that kind. No. Assuredly not. Also, we must remember, Konstantin was Russian. That is of great importance.

"Russia is a mixture, a potpourri of mutual conflicting elements. Neither European nor Asiatic, neither wholly civilized nor savage, modern on the surface, she is unchanging as the changeless East in which her taproots lie. Always she has harbored evil things which were incalculably old when the first deep stones of Egypt's mighty pyramids were laid.

"Now, together with the werewolf and the vampire, the warlock and the witch, the Russian knows another demon-thing called callicantzaros, who is a being neither wholly man nor devil, but an odd and horrifying mixture of the two. Some call them foster-children of the Devil, stepsons of Satan; some say they are the progeny of evil, sin-soaked women and the incubi who are their paramours. They are imbued with semi-immortality, also; for though they may be killed like other men, they must be slain with a single fatal blow; a second stroke, although it would at once kill ordinary humankind, restores their lives—and their power for wickedness.

"So much for the means of killing a callicantzaros—and the means to be avoided. To continue:

"Every so often, preferably once each year about the twenty-fifth of February, the olden feast of St. Walburga, or at the celebration of St. Peter's Chains on August 1, he must perform the sacrilege known as the Black Mass or Mass to Lucifer, and hold thereby Satanic favor and renew his immortality.

"Now this Black Mass must be performed with certain rules and ceremonies, and these must be adhered to to the letter. The altar is the body of an unclothed woman, and she must lend herself with willingness to the dreadful part she plays. If she be tricked or made to play the part by force, the rite is null and void. Moreover, she must be without a taint or spot of wickedness, a virtuous woman, pure in heart—to find a one like that for such a service is no small task, you will agree.

"When we consider this we see why Konstantin desired Madame Sonia for wife. She was a Russian like himself, and Russian women are servient to their men. Also, by beatings and mistreatment he soon could break what little independence she possessed, and force her to his will. Thus he would be assured of the 'altar' for his Devil's Mass.

"But when he had procured the 'altar' the work was but begun. The one who celebrated this unclean rite must do so fully vested as a priest, and he must wear the sacred garments which have been duly consecrated. Furthermore he must use the consecrated elements at the service, and also the sacred vessels.

"If the Host can be stolen from a Latin church or the presanctified elements from an altar of the Greek communion, it is necessary only that the ritual be fulfilled, the benediction said, and then defilement of the elements be made in insult of the powers of Heaven and to the satisfaction of the Evil One. But if the Eucharist is unobtainable, then it is necessary to have a duly ordained priest, one who is qualified to cause the mystery of transubstantiation to take place, to say the office. If this form be resorted to, there is a further awful rite to be performed. A little baby, most usually a boy, who has not been baptized, but whose baby lips are too young and pure for speech and whose soft feet have never made a step, must be taken, and as the celebrant pronounces 'Hoc est enim corpus meum,' he cuts the helpless infant's throat and drains the gushing lifeblood into the chalice, thus mingling it with the transmuted wine.

"It was with knowledge of these facts that I heard Father Pophosepholos report his loss, and when he said the elements were stolen I did rejoice most greatly, for then I knew no helpless little one would have to die upon the altar of the Devil's Mass.

"And so, with Madame Sonia gone, with the elements and vestments stolen from St. Basil's Church and with my dark suspicions of this Konstantin's true character, I damn knew what was planned, but how to find this server of the Devil, this stepson of Satan, in time to stop the sacrilege? Ah, that was the question! Assuredly.

"And then came Sun Ah Poy. A bad man he had been, a very damn-bad man, as Friend Renouard can testify; but China is an old, old land and her sons are steeped in ancient lore. For generations more than we can count they've known the demon Ch'ing Shih and his ghostly brethren, who approximate the vampires of the West, and greatly do they fear him. They hate and loathe him, too, and there lay our salvation; for wicked as he was, Doctor Sun would have no dealings with this cursed Konstantin, but came to warn us and to tell us where he might be found, although his coming cost his life.

"And so we went and saw and were in time to stop the last obscenity of all—the defilement of the consecrated Eucharist in honor of the Devil. Yes. Of course."

"But, Doctor de Grandin, I was the altar at that mass," Sonia Tanis wailed, "and I *did* offer myself for the Devil's service! Is there hope for such as I? Will Heaven ever pardon me? For even though I loathed the thing I did, I *did* it, and"—she faced us with defiant, blazing eyes—"I'd do it again for—"

"*Précisément, Madame*," de Grandin interrupted. "'For—' That 'for' is your salvation; because you did the thing you did for love of him you married to save him from assassination. 'Love conquers all,' the Latin poet tells us. So in this case. Between your sin—if sin it were to act the part you did to save your husband's life—and its reward, we place the shield of your abundant love. Be assured, *chère Madame*, you have no need to fear, for kindly Heaven understands, and understanding is forgiveness."

"But," the girl persisted, her long, white fingers knit together in an agony of terror, her eyes wide-set with fear, "Donald would never have consented to my buying his safety at such a price, he—"

"*Madame*," the little Frenchman fairly thundered, "I am Jules de Grandin. I do not make mistakes. When I say something, it is so. I have assured you of your pardon; will you dispute with me?"

"Oh, Sonia," the husband soothed, "it's finished, now, there is no more—"

"*Hélas*, the man speaks truth, Friend Trowbridge," de Grandin wailed. "It is finished—there is no more! How true, my friend; how sadly true.

"The bottle, it is empty!"

The Bleeding Mummy

Outside, the midwinter wind hurled wave after wave of a sleet-barrage against the window-panes, keening a ferocious war-chant the while. Within, the glow of sawn railway ties burning on the brass fire-dogs blended pleasantly with the shaded lamplight. Jules de Grandin put aside the copy of *l'Illustration* he had been perusing since dinnertime, stretched his slender, womanishly small feet toward the fire and regarded the gleaming tips of his patent leather pumps with every evidence of satisfaction. "*Tiens*, Friend Trowbridge," he remarked lazily as he watched the leaping firelight quicken in reflection on his polished shoes, "this is most entirely pleasant. Me, not for anything would I leave the house on such a night. He is a fool who quits his cheerful fire to—"

The sharp, peremptory clatter of the front door knocker battered through his words, and before I could hoist myself from my chair the summons was repeated, louder, more insistently.

"I say, Doctor Trowbridge, will you come over to Larson's? I'm afraid something's happened to him—I hate to drag you out on such a night, but I think he really needs a doctor, and—" Young Professor Ellis half staggered into the hall as the driving wind thrust him almost bodily across the doorstep.

"I ran over to see him a few minutes ago," he added as I slammed the door against the storm, "and as I went up his front path I noticed a light burning in an upper window, though the rest of the house was dark. I knocked, but got no answer, then went into the yard to call to him, when all of a sudden I heard him give the most God-awful yell, followed by a shriek of laughter, and as I looked up at his window he seemed to be struggling with something, though there was no one else in the room. I rang his bell a dozen times and pounded on the door, but not another sound came from the house. At first I thought of notifying the police; then I remembered you lived just round the corner, so I came here, instead. If Larson's been taken ill, you can help; if we need the police, there's always time to call 'em, so—"

"*Eh bien*, my friends, why do we stand here talking while the poor Professor Larson is in need of help?" demanded Jules de Grandin from the study door. "Have you no professional pride, Friend Trowbridge? Why do we linger here?"

"Why, you've only finished saying you wouldn't budge from the house tonight," I retorted accusingly. "Do you mean—"

"But certainly I do," he interrupted. "Only two kinds of people can not change their minds, my friend, the foolish and the dead. Jules de Grandin is neither. Come, let us go."

"No use getting out the car," I murmured as we donned our overcoats. "This sleet would make driving impossible."

"Very well, then, let us walk; but let us be about it swiftly," he responded, fairly pushing me through the door and out into the raging night. Heads bent against the howling storm, we set out for Professor Larson's house.

"I didn't exactly have an engagement with Larson," Professor Ellis admitted as we trudged along the street. "Fact is, I expect he'd about as soon have seen the devil as me, but—have you heard about his latest mummy?" he broke off.

"His what?" I answered sharply.

"His mummy. He brought it in from Africa last week, and he's been talking about it ever since. This evening he was going to remove the wrappings, so I just ambled over to his house on the off chance he'd let me stick around.

"Larson's a queer chap. Good man in anthropology, and all that, of course, but a lone wolf when it comes to work. He found this mummy by accident in a cleverly hidden tomb near Naga-ed-dêr, and that country was given up as thoroughly worked out thirty years ago, you know. Funny thing about it, too. While they were excavating the sepulcher two of his workmen were bitten by tomb spiders and died in convulsions. That's unusual, for the Egyptian tomb spider's not particularly venomous, though he's an ugly-looking brute. They'd just about cleared the shaft of rubble and started working toward the funerary chamber when all Larson's *fellaheen* ran out on him, too; but he's a stubborn devil, and he and Foster stuck it out, with the help of such men as they could hire in the neighborhood.

"They had the devil of a time getting the mummy down the Nile, too. Half the crew of their *dehabeeyah* came down with some mysterious fever, and several of 'em died, and the rest deserted; and just as they were ready to sail from Alexandria, Foster, who was Larson's assistant, came down with fever and died within three days. Larson hung on like grim death, though, and brought the mummy through—smuggled it right past the Egyptian customs men disguised as a crate of Smyrna sponges."

"But see here," I interrupted, "both you and Professor Larson are members of the Harrisonville Museum staff. How does it happen he's able to treat this mummy as his personal property? Why didn't he take it to the museum instead of his house?"

Ellis gave a short laugh. "Don't know Larson very well, do you?" he asked. "Didn't I say he's a lone wolf? This expedition to Naga-ed-dêr was a fifty-fifty affair; the Museum paid half the shot, and Larson just about beggared himself to make up the difference. He had a theory there were some valuable Fifth Dynasty relics to be found at Naga, and everybody laughed at him. When he'd justified his theory he was like a spoiled kid with a stick of candy, and wouldn't share his find with anyone; when I suggested he let me help him unwrap the thing he told me to take a running jump in the lake. I hadn't an idea, really, he'd let me in when I called on him tonight, but when I heard him yelling and laughing and saw him jumping around like a chestnut on a griddle, I thought maybe he'd gone off his rocker, and ran to get you as quickly as I could. Here we are. We'll probably be told to go to hell for our trouble, but he *might* need help."

As he finished speaking, Ellis sounded a thunderous knock on Larson's door. Only the skirling of the wind around the angle of the house and the flapping of an unsecured window-blind responded.

"*Pardieu*, either he is gravely ill or most abominably deaf, that one!" declared de Grandin, sinking his chin in the fur collar of his coat and grasping at his hat as the storm-wind all but wrenched it from his head.

Ellis turned to us in indecision. "D'ye think—" he began, but:

"Think what you please, my friends, and freeze your feet while doing," the little Frenchman interrupted testily. "Me, I go into that house right away, immediately, this minute." Trying the door and nearest window, and finding both securely fastened, he dashed his gloved hand through the pane without more ado, undid the latch and raised the sash. "Do you follow, or remain behind to perish miserably with cold?" he called as he flung a leg across the sill.

De Grandin in the lead, we felt our way across the darkened drawing-room, across the hall, and up the winding staircase. Every room inside the house, save one, was black as ancient Egypt during the plague of darkness, but a thin stream of light trickling out into the hall from beneath Professor Larson's study door led our footsteps toward his sanctum as a lighthouse guides a ship to port upon a starless night. "Larson!" Ellis called softly, rapping on the study door. "Larson, are you there?"

No answer came, and he seized the door-knob, giving it a tentative twist. The handle turned in his grasp, but the door held firm, for the lock had been shot from the inside.

"One side, if you will be so kind, *Monsieur*," requested Jules de Grandin, drawing as far back as the width of the hall permitted, then dashing himself forward like a football player battering toward the goal. The flimsy door fell before his rush, and the darkened hall was flooded with a freshet of dazzling light. For a moment we paused on the threshold, blinking owlishly; then:

"Good heavens!" I exclaimed.

"For Gawd's sake!" came Ellis' rejoinder.

"*Eh bien*, I rather think it is the devil's," Jules de Grandin murmured.

The room before us was a chaos of confusion, as though its contents had been stirred with a monster spoon in the hands of a maliciously mischievous giant. Furniture was overturned; some of the chair covers had been ripped open, as though a ruthless, hurrying searcher had cut the upholstery in search of hidden valuables; pictures hung crazily upon the walls.

In the middle of the study, beneath the glare of a cluster of electric lights, stood a heavy oaken table, and on it lay a mummy-case stripped of its cover, a slender, China-tea-colored form swathed in crisscrossed linen bandages, reclining on the table by the case.

Close to the baseboard of the wall beneath the window crouched a grotesque, unhuman thing, resembling a farmer's cast-off scarecrow or a hopelessly outmoded tailor's dummy. We had to look a second time and strain our unbelieving eyes before we recognized Professor Larson in the crumpled form.

Stepping daintily as a cat on a shower-splashed pavement, de Grandin crossed the room and sank to one knee beside the huddled form, drawing his right glove off as he knelt.

"Is—is he—" Ellis whispered hoarsely, halting at the word of which laymen seem to have a superstitious fear.

"Dead?" de Grandin supplied. "*Mais oui, Monsieur*; like a herring. But he has not been so long. No; I should hazard a guess that he was still living when we left the house to come here."

"But—isn't there something we can do? There must be something—" Ellis asked tremulously.

"But certainly; we can call the coroner," de Grandin answered. "Meanwhile, we might examine this." He nodded toward the mummy lying on the table.

Ellis' humane concern for his dead colleague dropped from him like a worn-out garment as he turned toward the ancient relic, the man eclipsed completely by the anthropologist. "Beautiful—superb!" he murmured ecstatically as he gazed at the unlovely thing. "See, there's no face-mask or funerary statue, either on the mummy or the case. Fifth Dynasty work, as sure as you're alive, and the case is—I say, do you see it?" he broke off, pointing excitedly at the open cedar coffin.

"See it? But certainly," de Grandin answered sharply. "But what is it you find extraordinary, if one may ask?"

"Why, don't you see? There's not a line of writing on that mummy-case! The Egyptians always wrote the titles and biographies of the dead upon their coffins, but this one is just bare, virgin wood. See"—he leant over and tapped the thin, hard shell of cedar—"there's never been a bit of paint or varnish on it! No wonder Larson kept it to himself. Why, there's never been a thing like this discovered since Egyptology became a science!"

De Grandin's glance had wandered from the coffin to the mummy. Now he brushed past Ellis with his quick, cat-like step and bent above the bandaged form. "The *égyptologie* I do not know so well," he admitted, "but medicine I know perfectly. What do you make of this, *hein?*" His slender forefinger rested for a moment on the linen bands encircling the desiccated figure's left pectoral region.

I started at the words. There was no doubt about it. The left breast, even beneath the mummy-bands, was considerably lower than the right, and faintly, but perceptibly, through the tightly bound linen there showed the faintest trace of brown-red stain. There was no mistaking it. Every surgeon, soldier and embalmer knows that telltale stain at sight.

Professor Ellis' eyes opened till they were nearly as wide as de Grandin's. "Blood!" he exclaimed in a muted voice. "Good Lord!" Then:

"But it can't be blood; it simply can't, you know. Mummies were eviscerated and pickled in natron before desiccation; there's no possibility of any blood being left in the body—"

"Oh, no?" the Frenchman's interruption was charged with sarcasm. "Nevertheless, *Monsieur*, de Grandin is too old a fox to be instructed in the art of sucking eggs. Friend Trowbridge"—he turned to me—"how long have you been dealing pills to those afflicted with bellyache?"

"Why," I answered wonderingly, "about forty years, but—"

"No buts, my friend. Can you, or can you not recognize a blood-stain when you see it?"

"Of course, but—"

"What, then, is this, if you will kindly tell us?"

"Why, blood, of course; anyone can tell that—"

"*Précisément*—it is blood, Monsieur Ellis. The good and most reliable Doctor Trowbridge corroborates me. Now, let us examine the coffin of this so remarkable mummy which, despite your pickling in natron and your desiccation, can still shed blood." With a wave of his hand he indicated the case of plain, unvarnished cedar-wood.

"By George, this is unusual, too!" Ellis cried, bending above the coffin. "D'ye see?"

"What?" I queried, for his eyes were shining with excitement as he gazed into the violated casket.

"Why, the way the thing's fastened. Most mummy-case lids are held in place by four little flanges—two on each side—which sink into mortises cut in the lower section and held in place by hardwood dowels. This has eight, three on each side and one at each end. H'm, they must have wanted to make sure whoever was put in there couldn't break loose. And—great Scott, will you look there!" Excitedly he pointed to the bottom of the case.

Once more I looked my wonderment. The abnormalities which struck his practised eye were quite invisible to me.

"See how they've lined the case with spices? I've opened several hundred mummy-cases, but I never saw *that* before."

As he had said, the entire bottom of the coffin was strewn with loose spices to a depth of four inches or so. The aromatics had crumbled to a fine powder, but the mingled clove and cinnamon, aloes and thyme gave off a pungent, almost suffocating aroma as we bent above the bathtub-like coffin.

De Grandin's small blue eyes were very round and bright as he glanced quickly from me to Ellis, then back again. "I damn think this explains it," he announced. "Unless I am much more mistaken than I think I am, this body never was a mummy, at least not such a mummy as the old embalmers customarily produced. Will you assist me?" He bowed invitingly to Ellis, placing his hands beneath the mummy's shoulders at the same time.

"Take the feet, if you please, *Monsieur*," he bade, "and lift it gently—gently, if you please—it must be put exactly where it was until the coroner has viewed the room."

They raised the bandaged form six inches or so above the table, then set it down again, and astonishment was written on their faces as they finished.

"What is it?" I asked, completely mystified by their glances of mutual understanding.

"It weighs—" began de Grandin, and:

"Sixty pounds, at least!" completed Ellis.

"Well?"

"Well, be everlastingly consigned to Satan's lowest subcellar!" rejoined the little Frenchman sharply. "It is not well at all, my friend; it is completely otherwise. You know your physiology; you know that sixty percent or more of us is water, simply H20, such as is found in rivers, and on the tables of Americans in lieu of decent wine. Mummification is dehydration—the watery contents of the body is removed and nothing left but bone and desiccated flesh, a scant forty per cent of the body's weight in life. This body is a small one; in life it could have weighed scarcely a hundred pounds; yet—"

"Why, then, it must have been only partly mummified," I interrupted, but he cut in with:

"Or not at all, my friend. I damn think that we shall find some interesting disclosures when these wrappings are removed. A bleeding mummy, and a mummy which weighs more than half its lifetime weight—yes, the probabilities of a surprise are great, or I am more mistaken than I think.

"Meantime," he turned toward the door, "there is the routine of the law to be complied with. The coroner must be told of Monsieur Larson's death, and there is no need for us to burn these lights while we are waiting."

Bowing politely to us to precede him, he switched off the study lights before closing the door and followed us to the lower hall where the telephone was located.

"I simply can't imagine how it happened," Professor Ellis murmured, striding nervously across his late colleague's drawing-room while we waited the advent of the coroner. "Larson seemed in the pink of condition this afternoon, and—good Lord, what's that?"

The sound of a terrific struggle, like that of two men locked in a death-grip, echoed through the quiet house.

Thump—thump—thump! Heavy, pounding footsteps banged upon the floor above our heads; then crash! came a smashing impact, as of overturning furniture, a momentary pause, a strident scream and the sudden crescendo of a wild, discordant laugh. Then silence once again.

"Good heavens!" I exclaimed, panic grasping at my throat. "Why, it's directly overhead—in the study, where we left the mummy and—"

"Impossible!" Professor Ellis contradicted. "Nobody could have gotten past us to that room, and—"

"Impossible or not, Friend Trowbridge speaks the truth, by damn!" the little Frenchman shouted, springing from his chair and racing toward the stairs. "*En avant, mes enfants*—follow me!"

Three steps at a stride he mounted headlong up the stairway, paused a moment at the closed door of the study while he whipped a pistol from his pocket, then his weapon swinging in a circle before him, advanced with a quick leap, snapped on the lights and:

"Hands up!" he shouted warningly. "A single offer of resistance and you breakfast with the devil in the morning—*grand Dieu*, my friends, behold!"

Save that one or two chairs had been overset, the room was just as we had left it. Upon the table lay the supine, bandaged mummy, its spice-filled case uncovered by its side; the thing which had been Larson crouched shoulders-to-the wall, as though stricken in an attempt to turn a somersault; the window-blind flapped cracklingly in the chilling winter wind.

"The window—it's open!" cried Professor Ellis. "It was closed when we were here, but—"

"*Dieu de Dieu de Dieu de Dieu*—does not one know it?" de Grandin interrupted angrily, striding toward the open casement. "*Parbleu*, the way in which you pounce upon the obvious is greatly trying to my nerves, Friend Ellis, and— ah? A-a-a-ah? One sees, one perceives, one understands—almost!"

Abreast of him, we gazed across the sill, and obedient to the mute command of his pointing finger, looked at the snow-encrusted roof of the first floor bay-window which joined the house-wall something like two feet below the study window. Gouged in the dead-white veneer of snow were four long, parallel streaks, exposing the slate beneath. "U'm," he murmured, lowering the sash and turning toward the door, "the mystery is in part explained, my friends.

"That window, it would be the logical place for a burglar to force entry," he added as we trooped down the stairs. "The roof of the bay-window has but very little slope, and stands directly underneath the window of Professor Larson's study. One bent on burglary could hardly fail to note its possibilities as an aid to crime, and the fact that we had light going only in the downstairs room was notice to the world that the upper story was untenanted. So—"

"Quite so, but there wasn't any burglar there," Ellis interrupted practically.

De Grandin favored him with such a stare as a teacher might bestow on a more than ordinarily dull pupil. "One quite agrees, *mon ami*," he replied. "However, if you will have the exceeding goodness to restrain your curiosity—and conversation—for a time, it may be we shall find that which we seek."

The dark, hunched-up object showed with startling vividness against the background of the snow-powdered lawn as we descended from the porch. De Grandin knelt beside it and struck a match to aid in his inspection. It was a ragged, unkempt figure, unwashed, unshaven; a typical low-class sneak-thief who had varied his customary sorry trade with an excursion into the higher profession of housebreaking with disastrous results to himself. He crouched as he had fallen from the bay-window's sloping roof, one arm twisted underneath him, his head bent oddly to one side, his battered, age-discolored hat mashed in at the crown and driven comically down upon his head till his ears were bent beneath it. Little lodes of sleety snow had lodged within the wrinkles of his ragged coat, and tiny threads of icicles had formed on his mustache.

The man was dead, no doubt of it. No one, not even the most accomplished contortionist, could twist his neck at that sharp angle. And the manner of his death was obvious. Frightened at sight of the mummy, the poor fellow had endeavored to effect a hasty exit by the open window, had slipped upon the sleet-glazed roof of the bay-window and fallen to the ground, striking head-first and skidding forward with his full weight on his twisted neck.

I voiced my conclusions hastily, but de Grandin shook a puzzled head. "One understands the manner of his death," he answered thoughtfully. "But the reason, that is something else again. We can well think that such a creature would have a paralyzing fear when he beheld the mummy stretched upon the table, but that does not explain the antics he went through before he fell or jumped back through the window he had forced. We heard him thrash about; we heard him kick the furniture; we heard him scream with mirthless laughter. For why? Frightened men may scream, they sometimes even laugh hysterically, but what was there for him to wrestle with?"

"That's just what Larson did!" Professor Ellis put in hastily. "Don't you remember—"

"*Exactement*," the Frenchman answered with a puzzled frown. "Professor Larson cries aloud and fights with nothing; this luckless burglar breaks into the very room where Monsieur Larson died so strange a death, and he, too, wrestles with the empty air and falls to death while laughing hideously. There is something very devilish here, my friends."

When we had gone back in the house young Ellis looked at us with something very near to panic in his eyes. "You say that we must leave that mummy as it is until the coroner has seen it?" he demanded.

"Your understanding is correct, my friend," de Grandin answered.

"All right, we'll leave the dam' thing there, but just as soon as Mr. Martin has finished with it, I think we'd better take it out and burn it."

"Eh, what is it that you say? Burn it, *Monsieur?*" de Grandin asked.

"Just that. It's what the Egyptologists call an 'unlucky' mummy, and the sooner we get rid of it the healthier it'll be for all of us, I'm thinking. See here"— he glanced quickly upward, as though fearing a renewed outbreak in the room above, then turned again to us—"do you recall the series of fatalities following Tutankhamen's exhumation?"

De Grandin made no answer, but the fixed, unwinking stare he leveled on the speaker, and the nervous way his trimly waxed mustache quivered at the corners of his mouth betrayed his interest.

Ellis hurried on: "Call it nonsense if you will—and you probably will—but the fact is there seems something in this talk of the ancient gods of Egypt having power to curse those disturbing the mummies of people dying in apostasy. You know, I assume, that there are certain mummies known as 'unlucky'—unlucky for those who find them, or have anything to do with them? Tutankhamen is probably the latest, as well as the most outstanding example of this class. He was a heretic in his day, and had offended the 'old ones' or their priests, which amounted to the same thing. So, when he died, they buried him with elaborate ceremonies, but set no image of Amen-Ra at the bow of the boat which carried him across the lake of the dead, and the plaques of Tem, Seb, Nephthys, Osiris and Isis were not prepared to go with him into the tomb. Tutankhamen, notwithstanding his belated efforts at reconciliation with the priesthood, was little better than an atheist according to contemporary Egyptian belief, and the wrath of the gods went into the tomb with him. It was not their wish that his name be preserved to posterity or that any of his relics be brought to light again.

"Now, think what happened: When Lord Carnarvon located the tomb, he had four associates. Carnarvon and three of his helpers are dead today. Colonel Herbert and Doctor Evelyn-White were among the first to go into Tut's tomb. Both died within a year. Sir Archibald Douglas was engaged to make an X-ray— he died almost before the plates could be developed. Six out of seven French journalists who went into the tomb shortly after it was opened died in less than a year, and almost every workman engaged in the excavations died before he had a chance to spend his pay. Some of these men died one way, some another, but the point is: they all died.

"Not only that; even minor articles taken from the tomb seem to exercise a malign influence. There is absolute proof that attendants in the Cairo Museum whose duties keep them near the Tutankhamen relics sicken and die for no apparent reason. D'ye wonder they call him an 'unlucky' mummy?"

"Very good, *Monsieur*; what then?" de Grandin prompted as the other lapsed into a moody silence.

"Just this: That mummy-case upstairs is bare of painting as the palm of your hand, and the orthodox Egyptians of the Fifth Dynasty would no more have thought of putting a body away without suitable biographical and religious writings on the coffin than the average American family today would think of holding a funeral without religious services of some sort. Further than that, the evidence points to that body's never having been embalmed at all—apparently it was merely wrapped and put into a coffin with a layer of spices around it. Embalming had religious significance in ancient Egypt. If the flesh corrupted, the spirit could not return at the end of the prescribed cycle and reanimate it, and to be buried unembalmed was tantamount to a denial of immortality. This body had only the poorest makeshift attempt at preservation. It looks as though this person, whoever he was, died outside the religious pale, doesn't it?"

"You make out a strong case, *Monsieur*," de Grandin nodded, "but—"

"All right, then look at the thing's history so far: Larson's workmen died while working in the tomb. How? By tomb-spider bite!

"Bosh! A tomb-spider is hardly more poisonous than our own garden spiders. I know; I've been bitten by the things, and suffered less inconvenience than when a scorpion stung me in Yucatan.

"Then, on the passage down the Nile most of the boat crew sickened, and some of 'em died, with a strange fever; yet they were hardy devils, used to the climate and in all probability immune to anything in the way of illness the country could produce. Then Foster, Larson's assistant, pegged out just as they were setting sail from Egypt. Looks as though some evil influence were working, doesn't it?

"Now, tonight: Larson was all ready to unwrap the mummy, but never got past taking it from the box. He's dead—'dead like a herring,' as you put it—and only God knows how he died. Right while we're waiting for the coroner to come, this poor devil of a burglar breaks into the house, *fights with some unseen thing*, just as Larson did, and dies. Say what you will"—his voice rose almost to a scream—"there's an aura of terrible misfortune round that mummy, and death is waiting for whoever ventures near it!"

De Grandin patted the waxed ends of his diminutive mustache affectionately. "What you say may all be true, *Monsieur*," he conceded, "but the fact remains that both Doctor Trowbridge and I have been near the mummy; yet we were never better in our lives—though I could do nicely with a gulp or so of brandy at this time. Not only that, Professor Larson spent nearly his entire fortune and a considerable portion of the Museum's funds in finding this so remarkable cadaver. It would be larceny, no less, for us to burn it as you suggest."

"All right," Ellis answered with a note of finality in his voice. "Have it your own way. As soon as the coroner's through with me I'm going home. I wouldn't go near that cursed mummy again for a fortune."

"Hullo, Doctor de Grandin," Coroner Martin greeted, stamping his feet and shaking the snow from his coat. "Bad business, this, isn't it? Any idea as to the cause of death?"

"The one outside unquestionably died from a broken neck," the Frenchman answered. "As for Professor Larson's—"

"Eh, the one outside?" Mr. Martin interrupted. "Are there *two* of 'em?"

"Humph, we're lucky there aren't five," Ellis cut in bitterly. "They have been dying so fast we can't keep track of 'em since Larson started to unwrap that—"

"One moment, if you please, *Monsieur*," de Grandin interrupted as he raised a deprecating hand. "Monsieur the Coroner is a busy man and has his duties to perform. When they have been completed I make no doubt he will be glad to listen to your interesting theories. At present"—he bowed politely to the coroner—"will you come with us, *Monsieur?*" he asked.

"Count me out," said Ellis. "I'll wait down here, and I want to warn you that—"

We never heard the warning he had for us; for, de Grandin in the lead, we mounted the stairs to the study where Professor Larson and the mummy lay.

"H'm," Mr. Martin, who in addition to being coroner was also the city's leading funeral director, surveyed the room with a quick, practised glance, "this looks almost as if—" he strode across the room toward Larson's hunched-up body and extended one hand, but:

"*Grand Dieu des cochons*—stand back, *Monsieur!*" de Grandin's shouted admonition halted Mr. Martin in mid-stride. "Back, *Monsieur*; back, Friend Trowbridge—for your lives!" Snatching me by the elbow and Mr. Martin by the skirt of his coat, he fairly dragged us from the room.

"What on earth—" I began as we reached the hall, but he pushed us toward the stairway.

"Do not stand and parley!" he commanded shortly. "Out—out into the friendly cold, while there is still time, my friends! *Pardieu*, I see it now—Monsieur Ellis has right; that mummy—"

"Oh—*oh—o-o-o-oh!*" The sudden cry came to us from the floor below, followed by the sound of scuffling, as though Ellis and another were struggling madly. Then came an awful, marrow-freezing laugh, shrill, mirthless, sardonic.

"*Sang du diable*—it has him!" de Grandin shouted, as he rushed madly toward the stair, leaped to the balustrade and shot downward like a meteor.

Coroner Martin and I followed sedately, and found the Frenchman standing mute and breathless at the entrance of the drawing-room, his thin, red lips pursed as though emitting a soundless whistle. Professor Larson's parlor was furnished in the formal, stilted style so popular in the late years of the last century, light chairs and couches of gilded wood upholstered in apple-green satin, a glass-doored cabinet for bric-à-brac, a pair of delicate spindle-legged tables adorned with bits of Dresden china. The furniture had been tossed about the room, the light-gray velvet rug turned up, the china-cabinet smashed and flung upon its side. In the midst of the confusion Ellis lay, his hands clenched at his sides, his knees drawn up, his lips retracted in a grim, sardonic grin.

"Good God!" Coroner Martin viewed the poor, tensed body with staring eyes. "This is dreadful—"

"*Cordieu*, it will he more so if we linger here!" de Grandin cried. "Outside, my friends. Do not wait to take your coats or hats—come out at once! I tell you death is lurking in each shadow of this cursed place!"

He herded us before him from the house, and bade us stand a moment, hatless and coatless, in the chilling wind. "I say," I protested through chattering teeth, "this is carrying a joke too far, de Grandin. There's no need to—"

"Joke?" he echoed sharply. "Do you consider it a joke that Professor Larson died the way he did tonight; that the misguided burglar perished in the same way; that even now the poor young Ellis lies all stiff and dead inside that cursed hellhole of a house? Your sense of humor is peculiar, my friend."

"What was it?" Coroner Martin asked practically. "Was there some infection in the house that made Professor Ellis scream like that before he died, or was it—"

"Tell me, *Monsieur*," de Grandin interrupted, "have you facilities for fumigation at your mortuary?"

"Of course," the coroner returned wonderingly. "We've apparatus for making both formaldehyde and cyanogen gas, depending on the class of fumigation required, but—"

"Very good. Be so good as to hasten to your place of business and return as quickly as may be with *materiel* for cyanogen fumigation. I shall await you here. Make haste, *Monsieur*, this matter is of utmost urgency, I assure you."

While Mr. Martin was obtaining the apparatus for fumigation, de Grandin and I hastened to my house, procured fresh outdoor clothing and retraced our steps. Though I made several attempts to discover what he had found at Larson's, his only answers were impatient shrugs and half-articulate exclamations, and I finally gave over the attempt, knowing he would explain in detail when he thought it proper. Hands deep in pockets, heads drawn well down into our collars, we waited for the coroner's return.

With the deftness of long practise Mr. Martin's assistants set the tanks of mercuric cyanide in place at the front and back doors of the Larson house, ran rubber hose from them to the keyholes and lighted spirit lamps beneath them. When Mr. Martin suggested that the bodies be removed before fumigation began, de Grandin shook his head decidedly. "It would be death—or most unnecessary risk of death, at best—to permit your men to enter till the gas has had at least a day to work within the house," he answered.

"But those bodies should be cared for," the coroner contended, speaking from the professional knowledge of one who had practised mortuary science for more than twenty years.

"They will undergo no putrefactive changes worthy of account," the Frenchman answered. "The gas will act to some extent as a preservative, and the risk to be avoided is worth the trouble."

As Coroner Martin was about to counter, he continued: "Demonstration outweighs explanation ten to one, my friend. Permit that I should have my way, and by this time tomorrow night you will be convinced of the good foundation for my seeming stubbornness."

Shortly after eight o'clock the following evening we met once more at Larson's house, and as calmly as though such crazy actions were an everyday affair with him, de Grandin smashed window after window with his walking-stick, and bade us wait outside for upward of a quarter-hour. At last:

"I think that it is safe to enter now," he said. "The gas should be dispelled. Come, let us go in."

We tiptoed down the hall to the drawing-room where Professor Ellis lay, and de Grandin turned on every available light before entering the room. Beside the young man's rigid body he went to his knees, and seemed to be examining the floor with minutest care. "Whatever are you doing—" I began, when:

"*Triomphe*, I have found him!" he announced. "Come and see."

We crossed the room and stared in wonder at the tiny object which he held between the thumb and finger of his gloved right hand. It was a tiny, ball-like thing, scarcely larger than a dried bean, a little, hairy spider with a black body striped about the abdomen with lines of vivid vermilion. "You observe him?" he asked simply. "Was I not wise to order our retreat last night?"

"What is the thing?" I demanded. "It's harmless-looking enough, but—"

"*Eh bien*, there is a very great but there, my friend," he retorted with a mirthless smile. "You saw what had been Monsieur Larson; you looked upon the poor, new-dead young Ellis? This—this little, seemingly so harmless thing it was which killed them. It is a *katipo*, or *latrodectus Nasselti*, the deadliest spider in the world.

Even the cobra's bite is but a sweetheart's kiss beside the sting of this so small, deadly thing. Those bit by him are seized immediately with convulsions—they beat the air, they stumble and they whirl, at length they give vent to a dreadful scream which simulates a laugh. And then they fall and die.

"Does not that make it clear? The wholly irrational antics performed by Professor Larson ere he died could be explained in no sane manner. They puzzled me. I was not willing to accept Professor Ellis' theory that the mummy was 'unlucky,' although, as the good God knows, it proved so for him. However, that Professor Larson was entirely dead could not be doubted, nor could one readily assign a reason for his death. *Tiens*, in such a case the coroner must be called, and so we telephoned for Monsieur Martin.

"Meantime, as we sat waiting in this room, a poor, half-starving devil of a man decided he would break into the house and steal whatever he could find. He mounted the bay-window's roof, and, guided by his evil star, set foot inside the chamber where the mummy and Professor Larson lay. We heard him trample on the floor; we heard him give that dreadful, laughing scream; we searched for him, and found him dead upon the lawn.

"Very good. In due time Monsieur Martin comes; we lead him to the place where Monsieur Larson is, and as we go into the room I chance to look into the spices strewn about the bottom of that mummy-case. *Ha*—what is it that I see? *Parbleu*, I see a movement! Spices do not move, my friend, except they be blown on by the wind, and there is no wind in that room. Moreover, spices are not jettyblack with bands of red about their bellies. *Non, pardieu*, but certain spiders are. I see him and I know him. In the Eastern Islands, in Java, in Australia, I have seen him, and I have also seen his deadly work. He is the *latrodectus Nasselti*, called *katipo* by the natives, and his bite is almost instant and most painful death. More, those bitten by him dance about insanely in a sort of frantic seizure; they laugh—but not with happiness!—they scream with mirthless laughter; then they die. I did not wish to dance and laugh and die, my friends; I did not wish that you should do so, either. There was no time for talk or explanation; our only safety lay in flight, for they are tropic things, those spiders, and once we were outside the cold would kill them. I was about to call a warning to Monsieur Ellis, too; but I was, *hélas*, too late.

"Beyond a doubt one of the spiders had fastened on his clothing while he bent over to inspect that mummy-case. The insect clung to him when he left the room, and while he waited downstairs for us it crawled until it came in contact with his naked skin; then, angered, it may be, by some movement which he made, it bit him and he died.

"When I saw him lying here upon the floor I took incontinently to flight. Jules de Grandin is no coward, but who could say how many of those cursed spiders had crawled from the mummy-case and found hiding-places in the shadows—even in our clothing, as in the case of Monsieur Ellis? To stay here was to court a quick and highly disagreeable death; accordingly I rushed you out into the storm and asked Monsieur Martin to provide fumigation for the house forthwith. Now, since the cyanogen gas has killed every living thing inside this house, it is safe for us to enter.

"The bodies may safely be taken away by your assistants at any time, Monsieur," he finished with a bow to Mr. Martin.

"Eh bien, were he but here, we could set poor Monsieur Ellis' mind at rest concerning many things," de Grandin murmured as we drove toward my house. "He could not understand how Professor Larson's servants died by spider-bite, since the Egyptian tomb-spider is known to be innocuous, or nearly so. The answer now is obvious. In some way which we do not understand, a number of those poisonous black spiders found their way into that mummy-case. They are terrestrial in their habits, living in the earth and going forth by night. Light irritates them, and when the workmen brought their torches into the tomb they showed their annoyance by biting them. Death, accompanied by convulsions, followed, and because the small black spiders were invisible in the shadows, the harmless tomb-spiders received the blame. Some few of the black spiders came overseas with Professor Larson; when he pried the lid from that mummy-case—perhaps when he thrust his hand into the scattered spices to lift the mummy out—they fastened on him, bit him; killed him. You apprehend?"

"H'm, it sounds logical enough," I answered thoughtfully, "but have you any idea how those spices came in that coffin? Poor Ellis seemed to think we'd hit on something extraordinary when he saw them; but he's gone now and—great Scott, de Grandin, d'ye suppose those old Egyptian priests could have planted spider eggs among the spices, hoping they would hatch eventually, so that whoever molested the body in years to come would stand a chance of being bitten and killed?"

For a moment he drummed soundlessly with gloved fingers on the silver head of his stick. At length: "My friend, you interest me," he declared solemnly. "I do not know that what you say is probable, but the manner of that mummy's preparation is unusual. I think we owe it as a debt to poor, dead Ellis to look into the matter thoroughly."

"Look into it? How—"

"Tomorrow we shall unwrap the body," he responded as casually as though unshrouding centuries-old dead Egyptians were an everyday activity with us. "If we can find some explanation hidden in the mummy-clothes, well and good. If we do not—eh bien, the dead have spoken before; why not again?"

"The—dead—have—spoken?" I echoed slowly, incredulously. "What in the world—"

"Not in this world, precisely," he interrupted with the shadow of a smile, "but there are those who look behind the veil which separates us from the ones we call the dead, my friend. We shall try other methods first. Those failing—" he recommenced his drumming on the handle of his cane, humming softly:

Sacré de nom,
Ron, ron et ron;
La vie est brêve,
La nuit est longue—

Next evening we unwrapped the mummy.

It was an oddly assorted group which gathered in the basement of Harrisonville Museum to denude the ancient dead of its cerements. Hodgson, the assistant curator of the department of archeology, a slender little man in gold-bowed, rimless spectacles, bald to the ears and much addicted to the habit of buttoning and unbuttoning his primly untidy double-breasted jacket, stood by in a state of twittering nervousness as de Grandin set to work.

"Who sups with the devil needs a long spoon," the little Frenchman quoted with a smile as he drew a pair of heavy rubber gloves on his hands before taking up his scissors and snipping one of the criss-crossed linen bands with which the body was tightly wrapped. "I do not greatly fear that any of those small black imps of hell survived Monsieur Martin's gas," he added, laying back a fold of yellowed linen, "but it is well to be prepared. The cemeteries are full to overflowing with those who have thought otherwise."

Yard after endless yard of linen he reeled off, coming at length to a strong, seamless shroud drawn sackwise over the body and tied at the feet with a stout cord. The cloth of which the sack was made seemed stronger and heavier than the bandages, and was thickly coated with wax or some ceraceous substance, the whole being, apparently, airtight and watertight.

"Why, bless my soul, I never saw anything like *this* before," stammered Doctor Hodgson, leaning forward across de Grandin's shoulder to stare curiously at the inner shroud.

"So much we gathered from Monsieur Ellis before—when he first viewed this body," de Grandin answered dryly, and Professor Hodgson retreated with an odd little squeaking exclamation, for all the world like that of an intimidated mouse.

"*Sale lâche!*" the Frenchman whispered softly, his contempt of Hodgson's cowardice written plainly on his face. Then, as he cut the binding string away and began twitching the waxed shroud upward from the mummy's shoulders:

"*Ah ha? Ah-ha-ha—que diable?*"

The body brought to view beneath the blue-white glare of the electric bulbs was not technically a mummy; though the aromatic spices and the sterile, arid atmosphere of Egypt had combined to keep it in a state of most unusual preservation. The feet, first parts to be exposed, were small and beautifully formed, with long, straight toes and narrow heels, the digits and soles, as well as the whole plantar region, stained brilliant red. There was surprizingly little desiccation, and though the terminal tendons of the *brevis digitorum* showed prominently through the skin, the effect was by no means revolting; I had seen equal prominence of flexor muscles in living feet where the patient had suffered considerable emaciation.

The ankles were sharp and shapely, the legs straight and well turned, with the leanness of youth, rather than the wasted look of death; the hips were narrow, the waist slender and the gentle swelling bosoms high and sharp. Making allowance for the early age at which women of the Orient mature, I should have said the girl died somewhere in her middle teens; certainly well under twenty.

"Ah?" de Grandin murmured as the waxed sack slid over the body's shoulders. "I think that here we have the explanation of those stains, Friend Trowbridge, *n'est-ce-pas?*"

I looked and gulped back an exclamation of horrified amazement. The slim, tapering arms had been folded on the breast, in accordance with the Egyptian custom, but the humerus of the left arm had been cruelly crushed, a compound comminutive fracture having resulted, so that a quarter-inch or more of splintered bone thrust through the skin above and below the deltoid attachment. Not only this: the same blow which had crushed the arm had smashed the bony structure of the chest, the third and fourth left ribs being snapped in two, and through the smooth skin underneath the breast a prong of jagged bone protruded. A hemorrhage of considerable extent had followed, and the long-dried blood lay upon the body from left breast to hip in a dull, brown-red veneer. Waxed though the mummy-sack had been, the welling blood had found its way through some break in the coating, had soaked the tightly knotted outer bandages, and borne mute testimony of an ancient tragedy.

The finely cut features were those of a woman in her early youth. Semitic in their cast, they had a delicacy of line and contour which bespoke patrician breeding. The nose was small, slightly aquiline, high-bridged, with narrow nostrils. The lips were thin and sensitive, and where they had retracted in the process of partial desiccation, showed small, sharp teeth of startling whiteness. The hair was black and lustrous, cut short off at the ears, like the modern Dutch bob affected by young women, parted in the middle and bound about the brows with a circlet of hammered gold set with small studs of lapis lazuli. For the rest, a triple-stranded necklace of gold and blue enamel, armlets of the same design and a narrow golden girdle fashioned like a snake composed the dead girl's costume. Originally a full, plaited skirt of sheer white linen had been appended to the girdle, but the fragile fabric had not withstood the years of waiting in the grave, and only one or two thin wisps of it remained.

"*La pauvre!*" exclaimed the Frenchman, gazing sadly at the broken little body. "I think, my friends, that we see here a demonstration of that ancient saying that the blood of innocents can not be concealed. Unless I am more wrong than I admit, this is a case of murder, and—"

"But it might as well have been an accident," I cut in. "I've seen such injuries in motor-wrecks, and this poor child might have been the victim of a chariot smashup."

"I do not think so," he returned. "This case has all the marks of ritual murder, my friend. Observe the—"

"I think we'd better wrap the body up again," Hodgson broke in hastily. "We've gone as far as we can tonight, and—well, I'm rather tired, gentlemen, and if you don't mind, we'll call the session off." He coughed apologetically, but there was the mild determination of weak men who have authority to make their wishes law in his manner as he spoke.

"You mean that you're afraid of something that might happen?" de Grandin countered bluntly. "You fear the ancient gods may take offense at our remaining here to speculate on the manner of this poor one's death?"

"Well," Hodgson took his glasses off and wiped them nervously, "of course, I don't believe those stories that they tell of these 'unlucky' mummies, but—you're bound to admit there have been some unexplained fatalities connected with this case. Besides—well, frankly, gentlemen, this body's less a mummy than a corpse, and I've a terrible aversion to being around the dead, unless they've been mummified."

De Grandin smiled sarcastically. "The old-time fears die hard," he assented. "Nevertheless, *Monsieur*, we shall respect your sensibilities. You have been most kind, and we would not try your nerves still further. Tomorrow, if you do not mind, we shall pursue our researches. It may be possible that we shall discover something hitherto unknown about the rites and ceremonies of those old ones who ruled the world when Rome had scarce been thought of."

"Yes, yes; of course," Hodgson coughed as he edged near the door. "I'm sure I shall be happy to give you a pass to the Museum tomorrow—only"—he added as an afterthought—"I must ask that you refrain from mutilating the body in any way. It belongs to the Museum, you know, and I simply can not give permission for an autopsy."

"*Morbleu*, but you are the shrewd guesser, *Monsieur*," de Grandin answered with a laugh. "I think you must have read intention in my eyes. Very well; we consent. There shall be no post-mortem of the body made. *Bon soir, Monsieur*."

"I'm sorry, Doctor de Grandin," Hodgson greeted us the next morning, "but I'm afraid you'll not be able to pursue any further investigations with the mummy—the body, I mean—we unwrapped last night."

The little Frenchman stiffened in both body and manner. "You mean that you have altered your decision, *Monsieur?*" he asked with cold politeness.

"Not at all. I mean the body's disintegrated with exposure to the air, and only a few wisps of hair, the skull and some unarticulated bones remain. While they weren't quite airtight, the bandages and the wax-coated shroud seem to have been able to keep the flesh intact, but exposure to our damp atmosphere has reduced them to a heap of bone and dust."

"U'm," the Frenchman answered. "That is unfortunate, but not irreparable. I think our chance of finding out the cause and manner of the poor young lady's death is not yet gone. Would you be good enough to lend us the ornaments, some of the mummy-cloth and several of the bones, *Monsieur?* We guarantee their safe return."

"Well," Hodgson hesitated momentarily, "it's not quite regular, but if you're sure you will return them—"

"*Monsieur,*" de Grandin's voice broke sharply through the curator's apologetic half-refusal, "I am Jules de Grandin; I am not accustomed to having my good faith assailed. No matter, the experiment which I have in mind will not take long, and you are welcome to accompany us. Thus you need never have the relics out of sight at any time. Will that assure you of their safe return?"

Hodgson undid the buttons of his jacket, then did them up again. "Oh, don't think I was doubting your *bona fides,*" he returned, "but this body cost the Museum a considerable sum, and was the indirect cause of our losing two valuable members of the staff. I'm personally responsible for it, and—"

"No matter," de Grandin interrupted, "if you will come with us I can assure you that the articles will be within your sight at all times, and you may have them back again this morning."

Accordingly, Hodgson superintending fussily, we selected the gold and lapis lazuli diadem, the broken humerus, one of the fractured ribs and several lengths of mummy-cloth which bore the dull-red blood stains, and thrust them into a traveling-bag. De Grandin paused to call a number on the 'phone, talked for a moment in a muted tone, then directed me to an address in Scotland Road.

Half an hour's drive through the brisk winter air brought us to a substantial brownstone-fronted residence in the decaying but still eminently respectable neighborhood. Lace curtains hung at the tall windows of the first floor and the windows of the basement dining-room were neatly draped with scrim. Beside the carefully polished bell-pull a brass plate with the legend, *Creighton, Clairvoyant,* was set. A neat maid in black and white uniform responded to de Grandin's ring and led us to a drawing-room rather overfurnished with heavy pieces of the style popular in the middle nineties. "Mrs. Creighton will be down immediately, sir; she's expecting you," she told him as she left the room.

My experience with those who claim ability to "look beyond the veil" was limited, but I had always imagined that they set their stages more effectively than this. The carpet, patterned with impossible roses large as cabbages, the heavy and not especially comfortable golden oak chairs upholstered in green plush, the stereotyped oil paintings of the Grand Canal, of Capri by moonlight and Vesuvius in action, were pragmatic as a plate of prunes, and might have been duplicated, item by item, in the "parlor" of half a hundred non-fashionable but respectable boarding-houses. Even the faint aroma of cooking food which wafted up to us from the downstairs kitchen had a reassuring and worldly tang which seemed entirely out of harmony with the ghostly calling of our hostess.

Madame Creighton fitted her surroundings perfectly. She was short, stout and matronly, and her high-necked white linen blouse and plain blue skirts were far more typical of the busy middle-class housewife than of the self-admitted medium. Her eyes, brown and bright, shone pleasantly behind the lenses of neat, rimless spectacles; her hair, already shot with gray, was drawn tightly back from her forehead and twisted in a commonplace knot above her occiput. Even her hands were plump, short-fingered, slightly workworn and wholly commonplace. Nowhere was there any indication of the "psychic" in her dress, face, form or manner.

"You brought the things?" she asked de Grandin when introductions were completed.

Nodding, he placed the relics on the oaken table beside which she was seated. "These were discovered—" he began, but she raised her hand in warning.

"Please don't tell me anything about them," she requested. "I'd rather my controls did all that, for one never can be sure how much information secured while one is conscious may be carried over into the subconscious while the trance is on, you know."

Opening a drawer in the table she took out a hinged double slate and a box of thin, white chalk.

"Will you hold this, Doctor Trowbridge?" she asked, handing me the slate. "Take it in both hands, please, and hold it in your lap. Please don't move it or attempt to speak to me until I tell you."

Awkwardly I took the blank-faced slate and balanced it on my knees while Mrs. Creighton drew a small crystal ball from a little green-felt bag, placed it on the table between the broken arm-bone and the fractured rib, then, with a snap of the switch, set an electric light in a gooseneck fixture standing on the table aglow. The luminance from the glowing bulb shone directly on the crystal sphere, causing it to glow as though with inward fire.

For a little time—two minutes, perhaps—she gazed intently at the glass ball; then her eyes closed and her head, resting easily against the crocheted doily on the back of her rocking-chair, moved a little sidewise as her neck muscles relaxed. For a moment she rested thus, her regular breathing only slightly audible.

Suddenly, astonishingly, I heard a movement of the chalk between the slates. I had not moved or tilted them, there was no chance the little pencil could have rolled, yet unquestionably the thing was moving. Now, I distinctly *felt* it as it traveled slowly back and forth across the tightly folded leaves of the slate, gradually increasing its speed till it seemed like a panic-stricken prisoned thing rushing wildly round its dungeon in search of escape.

I had a momentary wild, unreasoning desire to fling that haunted slate away from me and rush out of that stuffy room, but pride held me in my chair, pride made me grip those slates as a drowning man might grip a rope; pride kept my gaze resolutely on Mrs. Creighton and off of the uncanny thing which balanced on my knees.

I could hear de Grandin breathing quickly, hear Hodgson moving restlessly in his chair, clearing his throat and (I knew this without looking) buttoning and unbuttoning his coat.

Mrs. Creighton's sleep became troubled. Her head rolled slowly, fretfully from side to side, and her breathing became stertorous; once or twice she gave vent to a feeble moan; finally the groaning, choking cry of a sleeper in a nightmare. Her smooth, plump hands clenched nervously and doubled into fists, her arms and legs twitched tremblingly; at length she straightened stiffly in her chair, rigid as though shocked by a galvanic battery, and from her parted lips there came a muffled, strangling cry of horror. Little flecks of foam formed at the corners of her mouth, she arched her body upward, then sank back with a low, despairing whimper, and her firm chin sagged down toward her breast—I knew the symptoms! No medical practitioner can fail to recognize those signs.

"*Madame!*" de Grandin cried, rising from his chair and rushing to her side. "You are unwell—you suffer?"

She struggled to a sitting posture, her brown eyes bulging as though a savage hand were on her throat, her face contorted with some dreadful fear. For a moment she sat thus; then, with a shake of her head, she straightened, smoothed her hair, and asked matter-of-factly: "Did I say anything?"

"No, *Madame*, you said nothing articulate, but you seemed in pain, so I awakened you."

"Oh, that's too bad," she answered with a smile. "They tell me I often act that way when in a trance, but I never remember anything when I wake up, and I never seem any the worse because of anything I dream while I'm unconscious. If you had only waited we might have had a message on the slate."

"We have!" I interrupted. "I heard the pencil writing like mad, and nearly threw the thing away!"

"Oh, I'm so glad," responded Mrs. Creighton. "Bring it over, and we'll see what it says."

The slate was covered with fine writing, the minute characters, distinct as script etched on a copper plate, running from margin to margin, spaces between the lines so narrow as to be hardly recognizable.

For a moment we studied the calligraphy in puzzled silence; then.

"*Mort de ma vie*, we have triumphed over Death and Time, my friends!" de Grandin cried excitedly. "*Attendez, si'l vous plait*." Opening the slates before him like a book he read:

Revered and awful judges of the world, ye awful ones who sit upon the parapets of hell, I answer guilty to the charge ye bring against me. Aye, Atoua, who now stands on the brink of deathless death, whose body waits the crushing stones of doom, whose spirit, robbed for ever of the hope of fleshly tegument, must wander in Amenti till the end of time has come, confesses that the fault was hers, and hers alone.

Behold me, awesome judges of the living and the dead, am I not a woman, and a woman shaped for love? Are not my members beautiful to see, my lips like apricots and pomegranates, my eyes like milk and beryl, my breasts like ivory set with coral? Yea, mighty ones, I am a woman, and a woman formed for joy.

Was it my fault or my volition that I was pledged to serve the great All-Mother, Isis, or ever I had left the shelter of my mother's flesh? Did I abjure the blissful agony of love and seek a life of sterile chastity, or was the promise spoken for me by another's lips?

I gave all that a woman has to give, and gave it freely, knowing that the pains of death and after death the torment of the gods awaited me, nor do I deem the price too great to pay.

Ye frown? Ye shake your dreadful heads upon which rest the crowns of Amun and of Kneph, of Seb and Tem, of Suti and Osiris' mighty self? Ye say that I speak sacrilege? Then hear me yet awhile: She who stands in chains before ye, shorn of reverence as a priestess of Great Mother Isis, shorn of all honor as a woman, tells ye these things to your teeth, knowing that ye can not do her greater hurt than that she stands already judged to undergo. Your reign and that of those ye serve draws near its end. A little while ye yet may strut and preen yourselves and mouth the judgments of your gods, but in the days that wait your very names shall be forgot, save when some stranger delves into your tombs and drags your violated bodies forth for men to make a show of. Aye, and the very gods ye serve shall be forgotten—they shall sink so low that none shall call their names, not even as a curse, and in their ruined temples none shall do them reverence, and no living thing be found, save only the white-bellied lizard and the fearful jackal.

And who shall do this thing? An offspring of the Hebrews! Yea, from the people ye despise a child shall spring, and great shall be His glory. He shall put down your gods beneath his feet and spoil them of all glory and respect; they shall become but shadow-gods of a forgotten past.

My name ye've stricken from the roll of priestesses, no writing shall be graven on my tomb, and I shall be forgotten for all time by gods and men. So reads your judgment. I give ye, then, the lie. Upon a day far in the future strange men from a land across the sea shall open wide my tomb and take my body from it, nor shall my flesh taste of corruption until those strangers look upon my face and see my broken bones, and seeing, wonder how I died. *And I shall tell them.* Yea, by Osiris' self I swear that though I have been dead for centuries, I shall relate the manner of my judgment and my death, and they shall know my name and weep for me, and on your heads they shall heap curses for this thing ye do to me.

Pile now your stones of doom upon my breast, break my bones and still the fevered beating of my heart. I go to death, but not from out the memory of men as ye shall go. I have spoken.

Below the writing was a little scrawl of drawing, as crudely executed as a child's rough chalk-sketch on a wall; yet as we looked at it we seemed to see the outline of a woman held upon the ground by kneeling slaves while a man above her poised a heavy rock to crush her exposed breast and another stood in readiness to aid the executioner:

"*Cordieu!*" de Grandin exclaimed as we gazed upon the drawing. "I shall say she told the truth, my friends. She was a priestess of the goddess Isis, and as such was sworn to lifelong chastity, with awful death by torture as the penalty for violation of her vow. Undoubtlessly she loved not wisely, but too well, as women have been wont to love since time began, and upon discovery she was sentenced to the death decreed for those who did forget their obligations to the goddess. Her chest was broken in with stones, and without benefit of mummification her mutilated body was put in a casket void of any writing which might give a clue to her identity. Without a single invocation to the gods who held the fate of her poor spirit in their hands, they buried her. But did she triumph? Who says otherwise? We know her name, Atoua, we know the reason and the manner of her death. But those old priests who judged her and decreed her doom—who knows their names, yes, *parbleu*, who knows or cares a single, solitary damn where their vile mummies lie? They are assuredly gone into oblivion, while she—*tiens*, at least she is a personality to us, and we are very much alive."

"Excuse me, gentlemen, if you're quite finished with these relics, I'll take them, now," Professor Hodgson interrupted. "This little séance has been interesting, but you must admit nothing sufficiently authentic to be incorporated in our archives has been developed here. I fear we shall have to label these bones and ornaments as belonging to an unidentified body found by Doctor Larson at Naga-ed-dêr. Now, if you don't mind I shall get—"

"Get anywhere you wish, *Monsieur*, and get there quickly," de Grandin broke in furiously. "You have presided over relics of the dead so long your brain is clogged with mummy-dust. As for your heart—*mort d'un rat mort*, I do not think you have one!

"As for me," he added with a sudden smile, "I return at once to Doctor Trowbridge's. This poor young lady's tragic fate affects me deeply, and unless some urgent business interferes, I plan to drown my sorrow—*morbleu*, I shall do more. Within the hour I shall be most happily intoxicated!"

The Thing in the Fog

"*Tiens*, on such a night as this the Devil must congratulate himself!" Jules de Grandin forced his chin still deeper in the upturned collar of his trench-coat, and bent his head against the whorls of chilling mist which eddied upward from the bay in token that autumn was dead and winter come at last.

"Congratulate himself?" I asked in amusement as I felt before me for the curbstone with the ferrule of my stick. "Why?"

"Why? *Pardieu*, because he sits at ease beside the cozy fires of hell, and does not have to feel his way through this eternally-to-be-execrated fog! If we had but the sense—

"*Pardon, Monsieur*, one of us is very clumsy, and I do not think that it is I!" he broke off sharply as a big young man, evidently carrying a heavier cargo of ardent spirits than he could safely manage, lurched against him in the smothering mist, then caromed off at an unsteady angle to lose himself once more in the enshrouding fog.

"Dolt!" the little Frenchman muttered peevishly. "If he can not carry liquor he should abstain from it. Me, I have no patience with these—*grand Dieu*, what is that?"

Somewhere behind us, hidden in the curtains of the thick, gray vapor, there came a muffled exclamation, half of fright, half of anger, the sound of something fighting threshingly with something else, and a growling, snarling noise, as though a savage dog had leapt upon its prey, and, having fleshed its teeth, was worrying it; then: "Help!" The cry was muffled, strangled, but laden with a weight of helpless terror.

"Hold fast, my friend, we come!" de Grandin cried, and, guided by the sounds of struggle, breasted through the fog as if it had been water, brandishing his silver-headed sword-stick before him as a guide and a defense.

A score of quick steps brought us to the conflict. Dim and indistinct as shadows on a moonless night, two forms were struggling on the sidewalk, a large one lying underneath, while over it, snarling savagely, was a thing I took for a police dog which snapped and champed and worried at the other's throat.

"Help!" called the man again, straining futilely to hold the snarling beast away and turning on his side the better to protect his menaced face and neck.

"*Cordieu*, a war-dog!" exclaimed the Frenchman. "Stand aside, Friend Trowbridge, he is savage, this one; mad, perhaps, as well." With a quick, whipping motion he ripped the chilled-steel blade from the barrel of his stick and, point advanced, circled round the struggling man and beast, approaching with a cautious, cat-like step as he sought an opportunity to drive home the sword.

By some uncanny sense the snarling brute divined his purpose, raised its muzzle from its victim's throat and backed away a step or two, regarding de Grandin with a stare of utter hatred. For a moment I caught the smoldering glare of a pair of fire-red eyes, burning through the fogfolds as incandescent charcoal might burn through a cloth, and:

"A dog? *Non, pardieu,* it is—" began the little Frenchman, then checked himself abruptly as he lunged out swiftly with his blade, straight for the glaring, fiery eyes which glowered at him through the mist.

The great beast backed away with no apparent haste, yet quickly enough to avoid the needle-point of Jules de Grandin's blade, and for an instant I beheld a row of gleaming teeth bared savagely beneath the red eyes' glare; then, with a snarling growl which held more defiance than surrender in its throaty rumble, the brute turned lithely, dodged and made off through the fog, disappearing from sight before the clicking of its nails against the pavement had been lost to hearing.

"Look to him, Friend Trowbridge," de Grandin ordered, casting a final glance about us in the mist before he put his sword back in its sheath. "Does he survive, or is he killed to death?"

"He's alive, all right," I answered as I sank to my knees beside the supine man, "but he's been considerably chewed up. Bleeding badly. We'd best get him to the office and patch him up before—"

"Wha—what was it?" our mangled patient asked abruptly, rising on his elbow and staring wildly round him. "Did you kill it—did it get away? D'ye think it had hydrophobia?"

"Easy on, son," I soothed, locking my hands beneath his arms and helping him to rise. "It bit you several times, but you'll be all right as soon as we can stop the bleeding. Here"—I snatched a handkerchief from the breast pocket of my dinner coat and pressed it into his hand—"hold this against the wound while we're walking. No use trying to get a taxi tonight, the driver'd never find his way about. I live only a little way from here and we'll make it nicely if you'll lean on me. So! That's it!"

The young man leaned heavily upon my shoulder and almost bore me down, for he weighed a good fourteen stone, as we made our way along the vapor-shrouded street.

"I say, I'm sorry I bumped into you, sir," the youngster apologized as de Grandin took his other arm and eased me somewhat of my burden. "Fact is, I'd taken a trifle too much and was walkin' on a side hill when I passed you." He pressed the already-reddened handkerchief closer to his lacerated neck as he continued with a chuckle: "Maybe it's a good thing I did, at that, for you were within hearing when I called because you'd stopped to cuss me out."

"You may have right, my friend," de Grandin answered with a laugh. "A little drunkenness is not to be deplored, and I doubt not you had reason for your drinking—not that one needs a reason, but—"

A sudden shrill, sharp cry for help cut through his words, followed by another call which stopped half uttered on a strangled, agonizing note; then, in a moment, the muffled echo of a shot, another, and, immediately afterward, the shrilling signal of a police whistle.

"*Tête bleu*, this night is full of action as a pepper-pot is full of spice!" exclaimed de Grandin, turning toward the summons of the whistle. "Can you manage him, Friend Trowbridge? If so I—"

Pounding of heavy boots on the sidewalk straight ahead told us that the officer approached, and a moment later his form, bulking gigantically in the fog, hove into view. "Did anny o' yez see—" he started, then raised his hand in half-formal salute to the vizor of his cap as he recognized de Grandin.

"I don't suppose ye saw a dar-rg come runnin' by this way, sor?" he asked. "I wuz walkin' up th' street a moment since, gettin' ready to report at th' box, when I heard a felly callin' for help, an' what should I see next but th' biggest, ugliest baste of a dar-rg ye iver clapped yer eyes upon, a-worryin' at th' pore lad's throat. I wus close to it as I'm standin' to you, sor, pretty near, an' I shot at it twict, but I'm damned if I didn't miss both times, slick as a whistle—an' me holdin' a pistol expert's medal from th' department, too!"

"U'm?" de Grandin murmured. "And the unfortunate man beset by this great beast your bullets failed to hit, what of him?"

"Glory be to God; I plumb forgot 'im!" the policeman confessed. "Ye see, sor, I wuz that overcome wid shame, as th' felly says, whin I realized I'd missed th' baste that I run afther it, hopin' I'd find it agin an' maybe put a slug into it this time, so—"

"Quite so, one understands," de Grandin interrupted, "but let us give attention to the man; the beast can wait until we find him, and—*mon Dieu!* It is as well you did not stay to give him the first aid, my friend, your efforts would have been without avail. His case demands the coroner's attention."

He did not understate the facts. Stretched on his back, hands clenched to fists, legs slightly spread, one doubled partly under him, a man lay on the sidewalk; across the white expanse of evening shirt his opened coat displayed there spread a ruddy stickiness, while his starched white-linen collar was already sopping with the blood which oozed from his torn and mangled throat. Both external and anterior jugulars had been ripped away by the savagery which had torn the integument of the neck to shreds, and so deeply had the ragged wound gone that a portion of the hyoid bone had been exposed. A spate of blood had driveled from the mouth, staining lips and chin, and the eyes, forced out between the lids, were globular and fixed and staring, though the film of death had hardly yet had time to set upon them.

"Howly Mither!" cried the officer in horror as he looked upon the body. "Sure, it were a hound from th' Divil's own kennels done this, sor!"

"I think that you have right," de Grandin nodded grimly, "Call the department, if you will be so good. I will stand by the body." He took a kerchief from his pocket and opened it, preparatory to veiling the poor, mangled face which stared appealingly up at the fog-bound night, but:

"My God, it's Suffrige!" the young man at my side exclaimed. I left him just before I blundered into you, and—oh, what could have done it?"

"The same thing which almost did as much for you, Monsieur," the Frenchman answered in a level, toneless voice. "You had a very narrow escape from being even as your friend, I do assure you."

"You mean that dog—" he stopped, incredulous, eyes fairly starting from his face as he stared in fascination at his friend's remains.

"The dog, yes, let us call it that," de Grandin answered.

"But—but—" the other stammered, then, with an incoherent exclamation which was half sigh, half groaning hiccup, slumped heavily against my shoulder and slid unconscious to the ground.

De Grandin shrugged in irritation. "Now we have two of them to watch," he complained. "Do you recover him as quickly as you can, my friend, while I—" he turned his back to me, dropped his handkerchief upon the dead man's face and bent to make a closer examination of the wounds in the throat.

I took the handkerchief from my overcoat pocket, ran it lightly over the trunk of a leafless tree which stood beside the curb and wrung the moisture from it on the unconscious man's face and forehead. Slowly he recovered, gasped feebly, then, with my assistance, got upon his feet, keeping his back resolutely turned to the grisly thing upon the sidewalk. "Can—you—help—me—to—your—office?" he asked slowly, breathing heavily between the words.

I nodded, and we started toward my house, but twice we had to stop; for once he became sick, and I had to hold him while he retched with nausea, and once he nearly fainted again, leaning heavily against the iron balustrade before a house while he drew great gulps of chilly, fog-soaked air into his lungs.

At last we reached my office, and helping him up to the examination table I set to work. His wounds were more extensive than I had at first supposed. A deep cut, more like the raking of some heavy, blunt-pointed claw than a bite, ran down his face from the right temple almost to the angle of the jaw, and two deep parallel scores showed on his throat above the collar. A little deeper, a little more to one side, and they would have nicked the interior jugular. About his hands were several tears, as though they had suffered more from the beast's teeth than had his face and throat, and as I helped him with his jacket I saw his shirt-front had been slit and a long, raking cut scored down his chest, the animal's claws having ripped through the stiff, starched linen as easily as though it had been muslin.

The problem of treatment puzzled me. I could not cauterize the wounds with silver nitrate, and iodine would be without efficiency if the dog were rabid. Finally I compromised by dressing the chest and facial wounds with potassium permanganate solution and using an electric hot-point on the hands, applying laudanum immediately as an anodyne.

"And now, young fellow," I announced as I completed my work, "I think you could do nicely with a tot of brandy. You were drunk enough when you ran into us, heaven knows, but you're cold sober now, and your nerves have been badly jangled, so—"

"So you would be advised to bring another glass," de Grandin's hail sounded from the surgery door. "My nerves have been on edge these many minutes, and in addition I am suffering from an all-consuming thirst, my friend."

The young man gulped the liquor down in one tremendous swallow, seeing which de Grandin gave a shudder of disgust. Drinking fifty-year-old brandy was a rite with him, and to bolt it as if it had been common bootlegged stuff was grave impropriety, almost sacrilege.

"Doctor, do you think that dog had hydrophobia?" our patient asked half diffidently. "He seemed so savage—"

"Hydrophobia is the illness human beings have when bitten by a rabid dog or other animal, *Monsieur*," de Grandin broke in with a smile. "The beast has rabies, the human victim develops hydrophobia. However, if you wish, we can arrange for you to go to Mercy Hospital early in the morning to take the Pasteur treatment; it is effective and protective if you are infected, quite harmless if you are not."

"Thanks," replied the youth. "I think we'd better, for—"

"*Monsieur*," the Frenchman cut him short again, "is your name Maxwell, by any chance? Since I first saw you I have been puzzled by your face; now I remember, I saw your picture in *le Journal* this morning."

"Yes," said our visitor, "I'm John Maxwell, and, since you saw my picture in the paper, you know that I'm to marry Sarah Leigh on Saturday; so you realize

why I'm so anxious to make sure the dog didn't have hydro—rabies, I mean. I
don't think Sallie'd want a husband she had to muzzle for fear he'd bite her on the
ankle when she came to feed him."

The little Frenchman smiled acknowledgment of the other's pleasantry, but
though his lips drew back in the mechanics of a smile, his little, round, blue eyes
were fixed and studious.

"Tell me, *Monsieur*," he asked abruptly, "how came this dog to set upon you
in the fog tonight?"

Young Maxwell shivered at the recollection. "Hanged if I know," he
answered. "Y'see, the boys gave me a farewell bachelor dinner at the Carteret
this evening, and there was the usual amount of speech-making and toast-drink-
ing, and by the time we broke up I was pretty well paralyzed—able to find my
way about, but not very steadily, as you know. I said good-night to the bunch at
the hotel and started out alone, for I wanted to walk the liquor off. You see"—a
flush suffused his blond, good-looking face—"Sallie said she'd wait up for me to
telephone her—just like old married folks!—and I didn't want to talk to her
while I was still thick-tongued. Ray Suffrige, the chap who—the one you saw
later, sir—decided he'd walk home, too, and started off in the other direction,
and the rest of 'em left in taxis.

"I'd walked about four blocks, and was getting so I could navigate pretty well,
when I bumped into you, then brought up against the railing of a house. While I
was hanging onto it, trying to get steady on my legs again, all of a sudden, out of
nowhere, came that big police-dog and jumped on me. It didn't bark or give any
warning till it leaped at me; then it began growling. I flung my hands up, and it
fastened on my sleeve, but luckily the cloth was thick enough to keep its teeth
from tearing my arm.

"I never saw such a beast. I've had a tussle or two with savage dogs before,
and they always jumped away and rushed in again each time I beat 'em off, but
this thing stood on its hind legs and fought me, like a man. When it shook its
teeth loose from my coat-sleeve it clawed at my face and throat with its fore-
paws—that's where I got most of my mauling—and kept snapping at me all the
time; never backed away or even sank to all-fours once, sir.

"I was still unsteady on my legs, and the brute was heavy as a man; so it
wasn't long before it had me down. Every time it bit at me I managed to get my
arms in its way; so it did more damage to my clothes than it did to me with its
teeth, but it surely clawed me up to the Queen's taste, and I was beginning to
tire when you came running up. It would have done me as it did poor Suffrige in
a little while, I'm sure."

He paused a moment, then, with a shaking hand, poured out another drink of
brandy and tossed it off at a gulp. "I guess I *must* have been drunk," he admitted with
a shamefaced grin, "for I could have sworn the thing *talked* to me as it growled."

"Eh? The Devil!" Jules de Grandin sat forward suddenly, eyes wider and rounder than before, if possible, the needle-points of his tightly waxed wheat-blond mustache twitching like the whiskers of an irritated tomcat. "What is it that you say?"

"Hold on," the other countered, quick blood mounting to his cheeks. "I didn't say it; I said it *seemed* as if its snarls were words."

"*Précisément, exactement,* quite so," returned the Frenchman sharply. "And what was it that he *seemed* to snarl at you, *Monsieur?* Quickly, if you please."

"Well, I was drunk, I admit, but—"

"Ten thousand small blue devils! We bandy words. I have asked you a question; have the courtesy to reply, *Monsieur.*"

"Well, it sounded—sort of—as if it kept repeating Sallie's name, like this—" he gave an imitation of a throaty, growling voice: "'Sarah Leigh, Sarah Leigh—you'll never marry Sarah Leigh!'

"Ever hear anything so nutty? I reckon I must have had Sallie in my mind, subconsciously, while I was having what I thought was my death-struggle."

It was very quiet for a moment. John Maxwell looked half sullenly, half defiantly from de Grandin to me. De Grandin sat as though lost in contemplation, his small eyes wide and thoughtful, his hands twisting savagely at the waxed ends of his mustache, the tip of his patent-leather evening shoe beating a devil's tattoo on the white-tiled floor. At length, abruptly:

"Did you notice any smell, any peculiar odor, when we went to Monsieur Maxwell's rescue this evening, Friend Trowbridge?" he demanded.

"Why—" I bent my brows and wagged my head in an effort at remembrance. "Why, no, I didn't—" I stopped, while somewhere from the file-cases of my subconscious memory came a hint of recollection: Soldiers' Park—a damp and drizzling day—the open air dens of the menagerie. "Wait," I ordered, closing both eyes tightly while I bade my memory catalogue the vague, elusive scent; then: "Yes, there was an odor I've noticed at the zoo in Soldiers' Park; it was the smell of the damp fur of a fox, or wolf!"

De Grandin beat his small, white hands together softly, as though applauding at a play. "Capital, perfect!" he announced. "I smelt it too, when first we did approach, but our senses play strange tricks on us at times, and I needed the corroboration of your nose's testimony, if it could be had. Now—" he turned his fixed, unwinking stare upon me as he asked: "Have you ever seen a wolf's eyes—or a dog's—at night?"

"Yes, of course," I answered wonderingly.

"*Très bien.* And they gleamed with a reflected greenness, something like Madame Pussy's, only not so bright, *n'est-ce-pas?*"

"Yes."

"*Très bon.* Did you see the eyes of what attacked Monsieur Maxwell this evening? Did you observe them?"

"I should say I did," I answered, for never would I forget those fiery, glaring orbs. "They were red, red as fire!"

"Oh, excellent Friend Trowbridge; oh, prince of all the recollectors of the world!" de Grandin cried delightedly. "Your memory serves you perfectly, and upholds my observations to the full. Before, I guessed; I said to me, 'Jules de Grandin, you are generally right, but once in many times you may be wrong. See what Friend Trowbridge has to say.' And you, *parbleu*, you said the very thing I needed to confirm me in my diagnosis.

"*Monsieur*," he turned to Maxwell with a smile, "you need not fear that you have hydrophobia. No. You were very near to death, a most unpleasant sort of death, but not to death by hydrophobia. *Morbleu*, that would be an added refinement which we need not take into consideration."

"Whatever are you talking about?" I asked in sheer amazement. "You ask me if I noticed the smell that beast gave off, and if I saw its eyes, then tell Mr. Maxwell he needn't fear he's been inoculated. Of all the hare-brained—"

He turned his shoulder squarely on me and smiled assuringly at Maxwell. "You said that you would call your *amoureuse* tonight, *Monsieur*; have you forgotten?" he reminded, then nodded toward the phone.

The young man picked the instrument up, called a number and waited for a moment; then: "John speaking, honey," he announced as we heard a subdued click sound from the monophone. Another pause, in which the buzzing of indistinguishable words came faintly to us through the quiet room; then Maxwell turned and motioned me to take up the extension 'phone.

"—and please come right away, dear," I heard a woman's voice plead as I clapped the instrument against my ear. "No, I can't tell you over the 'phone, but I must see you right away, Johnny—I must! You're sure you're all right? Nothing happened to you?"

"Well," Maxwell temporized, "I'm in pretty good shape, everything considered. I had a little tussle with a dog, but—"

"A—*dog?*" Stark, incredulous horror sounded in the woman's fluttering voice. "What sort of dog?"

"Oh, just a dog, you know; not very big and not very little, sort o' betwixt and between, and—"

"You're sure it was a *dog?* Did it look like a—a police-dog, for instance?"

"Well, now you mention it, it *did* look something like a police-dog, or collie, or airedale, or something, but—"

"John, dear, don't try to put me off that way. This is terribly, dreadfully important. Please hurry over—no, don't come out at night—yes, come at once, but be sure not to come alone. Have you a sword, or some sort of steel or iron weapon you can carry for defense when you come?"

Young Maxwell's face betrayed bewilderment. "A sword?" he echoed. "What d'ye think I am, dear, a knight of old? No, I haven't a sword to my name, not even a jack-knife, but—I say, there's a gentleman I met tonight who has a bully little sword; may I bring him along?"

"Oh, yes, please do, dear; and if you can get some one else, bring him too. I'm terribly afraid to have you venture out tonight, dearest, but I have to see you right away!"

"All right," the young man answered. "I'll pop right over, honey."

As he replaced the instrument, he turned bewilderedly to me. "Wonder what the deuce got into Sally?' he asked. "She seemed all broken up about something, and I thought she'd faint when I mentioned my set-to with that dog. What's it mean?"

Jules de Grandin stepped through the doorway connecting surgery with consulting-room, where he had gone to listen to the conversation from the desk extension. His little eyes were serious, his small mouth grimly set. "*Monsieur*," he announced gravely, "it means that Mademoiselle Sarah knows more than any of us what this business of the Devil is about. Come, let us go to her without delay."

As we prepared to leave the house he paused and rummaged in the hall coat closet, emerging in a moment, balancing a pair of blackthorn walking-sticks in his hands.

"What—" I began, but he cut me short.

"These may prove useful," he announced, handing one to me, the other to John Maxwell. "If what I damn suspect is so, he will not greatly relish a thwack from one of these upon the head. No, the thorn-bush is especially repugnant to him."

"Humph, I should think it would be particularly repugnant to anyone," I answered, weighing the knotty bludgeon in my hand. "By the way, who is 'he'?"

"Mademoiselle Sarah will tell us that," he answered enigmatically. "Are we ready? *Bon*, let us be upon our way."

The mist which had obscured the night an hour or so before had thinned to a light haze, and a drizzle of rain was commencing as we set out. The Leigh house was less than half a mile from my place, and we made good time as we marched through the damp, cold darkness.

I had known Joel Leigh only through having shared committee appointments with him in the local Republican organization and at the archdeaconry. He had entered the consular service after being retired from active duty with the Marine Corps following a surgeon's certificate of disability, and at the time of his death two years before had been rated as one of the foremost authorities on Near East commercial conditions. Sarah, his daughter, whom I had never met, was, by all accounts, a charming young woman, equally endowed with brains, beauty and money, and keeping up the family tradition in the big house in Tuscarora Avenue, where she lived with an elderly maiden aunt as duenna.

Leigh's long residence in the East was evidenced in the furnishings of the long, old-fashioned hall, which was like a royal antechamber in miniature. In the softly diffused light from a brass-shaded Turkish lamp we caught gleaming reflections from heavily carved blackwood furniture and the highlights of a marvelously inlaid Indian screen. A carved table flanked by dragon-chairs stood against the wall, the floor was soft as new-mown turf with rugs from China, Turkey and Kurdistan.

"Mis' Sarah's in the library," announced the Negro butler who answered our summons at the door, and led us through the hall to the big, high-ceilinged room where Sarah Leigh was waiting. Books lined the chamber's walls from floor to ceiling on three sides; the fourth wall was devoted to a bulging bay-window which overlooked the garden. Before the fire of cedar logs was drawn a deeply padded divan, while flanking it were great armchairs upholstered in red leather. The light which sifted through the meshes of a brazen lamp-shade disclosed a tabouret of Indian mahogany on which a coffee service stood. Before the fire the mistress of the house stood waiting us. She was rather less than average height, but appeared taller because of her fine carriage. Her mannishly close-cropped hair was dark and inclined toward curliness, but as she moved toward us I saw it showed bronze glints in the lamplight. Her eyes were large, expressive, deep hazel, almost brown. But for the look of cynicism, almost hardness, around her mouth, she would have been something more than merely pretty.

Introductions over, Miss Leigh looked from one of us to the other with something like embarrassment in her eyes. "If—" she began, but de Grandin divined her purpose, and broke in:

"*Mademoiselle*, a short time since, we had the good fortune to rescue *Monsieur* your *fiancé* from a dog which I do not think was any dog at all. That same creature, I might add, destroyed a gentleman who had attended Monsieur Maxwell's dinner within ten minutes of the time we drove it off. Furthermore, Monsieur Maxwell is under the impression that this dog-thing talked to him while it sought to slay him. From what we overheard of your message on the telephone, we think you hold the key to this mystery. You may speak freely in our presence, for I am Jules de Grandin, physician and occultist, and my friend, Doctor Trowbridge, has most commendable discretion."

The young woman smiled, and the transformation in her taut, strained face was startling. "Thank you," she replied; "if you're an occultist you will understand, and neither doubt me nor demand explanations of things I can't explain."

She dropped cross-legged to the hearth rug, as naturally as though she were more used to sitting that way than reclining in a chair, and we caught the gleam of a great square garnet on her forefinger as she extended her hand to Maxwell.

"Hold my hand while I'm talking, John," she bade. "It may be for the last time." Then, as he made a gesture of dissent, abruptly:

"I can not marry you—or anyone," she announced.

Maxwell opened his lips to protest, but no sound came. I stared at her in wonder, trying futilely to reconcile the agitation she had shown when telephoning with her present deadly, apathetic calm.

Jules de Grandin yielded to his curiosity. "Why not, *Mademoiselle?*" he asked. "Who has forbid the banns?"

She shook her head dejectedly and turned a sad-eyed look upon him as she answered: "It's just the continuation of a story which I thought was a closed chapter in my life." For a moment she bent forward, nestling her check against young Maxwell's hand; then:

"It began when Father was attached to the consulate in Smyrna," she continued. "France and Turkey were both playing for advantage, and Father had to find out what they planned, so he had to hire secret agents. The most successful of them was a young Greek named George Athanasakos, who came from Crete. Why he should have taken such employment was more than we could understand; for he was well educated, apparently a gentleman, and always well supplied with money. He told us he took the work because of his hatred of the Turks, and as he was always successful in getting information, Father didn't ask questions.

"When his work was finished he continued to call at our house as a guest, and I—I really didn't love him, I *couldn't* have, it was just infatuation, meeting him so far from home, and the water and that wonderful Smyrna moonlight, and—"

"Perfectly, *Mademoiselle*, one fully understands," de Grandin supplied softly as she paused, breathless; "and then—"

"Maybe you never succumbed to moonlight and water and strange, romantic poetry and music," she half whispered, her eyes grown wider at the recollection, "but I was only seventeen, and he was very handsome, and—and he swept me off my feet. He had the softest, most musical voice I've ever heard, and the things he said sounded like something written by Byron at his best. One moonlit night when we'd been rowing, he begged me to say I loved him, and—and I did. He held me in his arms and kissed my eyes and lips and throat. It was like being hypnotized and conscious at the same time. Then, just before we said good-night he told me to meet him in an old garden on the outskirts of the city where we sometimes rested when we'd been out riding. The rendezvous was made for midnight, and though I thought it queer that he should want to meet me at that time in such a place—well, girls in love don't ask questions, you know. At least, I didn't.

"There was a full moon the next night, and I was fairly breathless with the beauty of it all when I kept the tryst. I thought I'd come too early, for George was nowhere to be seen when I rode up, but as I jumped down from my horse and looked around I saw something moving in the laurels. It was George, and he'd thrown a cape or cloak of some sort of fur across his shoulders. He startled me dreadfully at first; for he looked like some sort of prowling beast with the animal's head hanging half down across his face, like the beaver of an ancient helmet. It seemed to me, too, that his eyes had taken on a sort of sinister greenish tinge, but when he took me in his arms and kissed me I was reassured.

"Then he told me he was the last of a very ancient clan which had been wiped out warring with the Turks, and that it was a tradition of their blood that the woman they married take a solemn oath before the nuptials could be celebrated. Again I didn't ask questions. It all seemed so wonderfully romantic," she added with a pathetic little smile.

"He had another skin cloak in readiness and dropped it over my shoulders, pulling the head well forward above my face, like a hood. Then he built a little fire of dry twigs and threw some incense on it. I knelt above the fire and inhaled the aromatic smoke while he chanted some sort of invocation in a tongue I didn't recognize, but which sounded harsh and terrible—like the snarling of a savage dog.

"What happened next I don't remember clearly, for that incense did things to me. The old garden where I knelt seemed to fade away, and in its place appeared a wild and rocky mountain scene where I seemed walking down a winding road. Other people were walking with me, some before, some behind, some beside me, and all were clothed in cloaks of hairy skin like mine. Suddenly, as we went down the mountainside, I began to notice that my companions were dropping to all-fours, like beasts. But somehow it didn't seem strange to me; for, without realizing it, I was running on my hands and feet, too. Not crawling, you know, but actually running—like a dog. As we neared the mountain's foot we ran faster and faster; by the time we reached a little clearing in the heavy woods which fringed the rocky hill we were going like the wind, and I felt myself panting, my tongue hanging from my mouth.

"In the clearing other beasts were waiting for us. One great, hairy creature came trotting up to me, and I was terribly frightened at first, for I recognized it as a mountain wolf, but it nuzzled me with its black snout and licked me, and somehow it seemed like a caress—I liked it. Then it started off across the unplowed field, and I ran after it, caught up with it, and ran alongside. We came to a pool and the beast stopped to drink, and I bent over the water too, lapping it up with my tongue. Then I saw our images in the still pond, and almost died of fright, for the thing beside me was a mountain wolf, and I was a she-wolf!

"My astonishment quickly passed, however, and somehow I didn't seem to mind having been transformed into a beast; for something deep inside me kept urging me on, on to something—I didn't quite know what.

"When we'd drunk we trotted through a little patch of woodland and suddenly my companion sank to the ground in the underbrush and lay there, red tongue lolling from its mouth, green eyes fixed intently on the narrow, winding path beside which we were resting. I wondered what we waited for, and half rose on my haunches to look, but a low, warning growl from the thing beside me warned that something was approaching. It was a pair of farm laborers, Greek peasants I knew them to be by their dress, and they were talking in low tones and looking fearfully about, as though they feared an ambush. When they came abreast of us the beast beside me sprang—so did I.

"I'll never forget the squeaking scream the nearer man gave as I leaped upon him, or the hopeless, terrified expression in his eyes as he tried to fight me off. But I bore him down, sank my teeth into his throat and began slowly tearing at his flesh. I could feel the blood from his torn throat welling up in my mouth, and its hot saltiness was sweeter than the most delicious wine. The poor wretch's struggles became weaker and weaker, and I felt a sort of fierce elation. Then he ceased to fight, and I shook him several times, as a terrier shakes a rat, and when he didn't move or struggle, I tore at his face and throat and chest till my hairy muzzle was one great smear of blood.

"Then, all at once, it seemed as though a sort of thick, white fog were spreading through the forest, blinding me and shutting out the trees and undergrowth and my companion beasts, even the poor boy whom I had killed, and—there I was kneeling over the embers of the dying fire in the old Smyrna garden, with the clouds of incense dying down to little curly spirals.

"George was standing across the fire from me, laughing, and the first thing I noticed was that *his lips were smeared with blood.*

"Something hot and salty stung my mouth, and I put my hand up to it. When I brought it down the fingers were red with a thick, sticky liquid.

"I think I must have started to scream; for George jumped over the fire and clapped his hand upon my mouth—*ugh*, I could taste the blood more than ever, then!—and whispered, 'Now you are truly mine, Star of the Morning. Together we have ranged the woods in spirit as we shall one day in body, O true mate of a true *vrykolakas!*'

"*Vrykolakas* is a Greek word hard to translate into English. Literally it means 'the restless dead', but it also means a vampire or a werewolf, and the *vrykolakas* are the most dreaded of all the host of demons with which Greek peasant-legends swarm.

"I shook myself free from him. 'Let me go; don't touch me; I never want to see you again!' I cried.

"'Nevertheless, you shall see me again—and again and again—Star of the Sea!' he answered with a mocking laugh. 'You belong to me, now, and no one shall take you from me. When I want you I will call, and you will come to me, for'—he looked directly into my eyes, and his own seemed to merge and run together, like two pools of liquid, till they were one great disk of green fire— 'thou shalt have no other mate than me, and he who tries to come between us dies. See, I put my mark upon you!'

"He tore my riding-shirt open and pressed his lips against my side, and next instant I felt a biting sting as his teeth met in my flesh. See—"

With a frantic, wrenching gesture she snatched at the low collar of her red-silk lounging pajamas, tore the fabric asunder and exposed her ivory flesh. Three inches or so below her left axilla, in direct line with the gently swelling bulge of her firm, high breast, was a small whitened cicatrix, and from it grew a little tuft of long, grayish-brown hair, like hairs protruding from a mole, but unlike any body hairs which I had ever seen upon a human being.

"*Grand Dieu*," exclaimed de Grandin softly. "*Poil de loup!*"

"Yes," she agreed in a thin, hysterical whisper, "it's wolf's hair! I know. I cut it off and took it to a biochemist in London, and he assured me it was unquestionably the hair of a wolf. I've tried and tried to have the scar removed, but it's useless. I've tried cautery, electrolysis, even surgery, but it disappears for only a little while, then comes again."

For a moment it was still as death in the big dim-lighted room. The little French-gilt clock upon the mantelpiece ticked softly, quickly, like a heart that palpitates with terror, and the hissing of a burning resined log seemed loud and eery as night-wind whistling round a haunted tower. The girl folded the torn silk of her pajama jacket across her breast and pinned it into place; then, simply, desolately, as one who breaks the news of a dear friend's death:

"So I can not marry you, you see, John, dear," she said.

"Why?" asked the young man in a low, fierce voice. "Because that scoundrel drugged you with his devilish incense and made you think you'd turned into a wolf? Because—"

"Because I'd be your murderess if I did so," she responded quiveringly. "Don't you remember? He said he'd call me when he wanted me, and anyone who came between him and me would die. He's come for me, he's called me, John; it was he who attacked you in the fog tonight. Oh, my dear, my dear, I love you so; but I must give you up. It would be murder if I were to marry you!"

"Nonsense!" began John Maxwell bruskly. "If you think that man can—"

Outside the house, seemingly from underneath the library's bow-window, there sounded in the rain-drenched night a wail, long-drawn, pulsating, doleful as the cry of an abandoned soul: "*O-u-o—o-u-oo—o-u-o—o-u-oo!*" it rose and fell, quavered and almost died away, then resurged with increased force. "*O-u-o—o-u-o-o—o-u-o—o-u-oo!*"

The woman on the hearth rug cowered like a beaten beast, clutching frantically with fear-numbed fingers at the drugget's pile, half crawling, half writhing toward the brass bars where the cheerful fire burned brightly. "Oh," she whimpered as the mournful ululation died away, "that's he; he called me once before today; now he's come again, and—"

"*Mademoiselle*, restrain yourself," de Grandin's sharp, whip-like order cut through her mounting terror and brought her back to something like normality. "You are with friends," he added in a softer tone; "three of us are here, and we are a match for any *sacré loup-garou* that ever killed a sheep or made night hideous with his howling. *Parbleu*, but I shall say damn yes. Did I not, all single-handed, already put him to flight once tonight? But certainly. Very well, then, let us talk this matter over calmly, for—"

With the suddenness of a discharged pistol a wild, vibrating howl came through the window once again. "O-u-o—o-u-oo—o-u-o!" it rose against the stillness of the night, diminished to a moan, then suddenly crescendoed upward, from a moan to a wail, from a wail to a howl, despairing, pleading, longing as the cry of a damned spirit, fierce and wild as the rally-call of the fiends of hell.

"*Sang du diable*, must I suffer interruption when I wish to talk? *Sang des tous les saints*—it is not to be borne!" de Grandin cried furiously, and cleared the distance to the great bay-window in two agile, cat-like leaps.

"*Allez!*" he ordered sharply, as he flung the casement back and leaned far out into the rainy night. "Be off, before I come down to you. You know me, *hein?* A little while ago you dodged my steel, but—"

A snarling growl replied, and in the clump of rhododendron plants which fringed the garden we saw the baleful glimmer of a pair of fiery eyes.

"*Parbleu*, you dare defy me—*me?*" the little Frenchman cried, and vaulted nimbly from the window, landing sure-footed as a panther on the rain-soaked garden mold, then charging at the lurking horror as though it had been harmless as a kitten,

"Oh, he'll be killed; no mortal man can stand against a *vrykolakas!*" cried Sarah Leigh, wringing her slim hands together in an agony of terror. "Oh, God in heaven, spare—"

A fusillade of crackling shots cut through her prayer, and we heard a short, sharp yelp of pain, then the voice of Jules de Grandin hurling imprecations in mingled French and English. A moment later:

"Give me a hand, Friend Trowbridge," he called from underneath the window. "It was a simple matter to come down, but climbing back is something else again."

"*Merci*," he acknowledged as he regained the library and turned his quick, elfin grin on each of us in turn. Dusting his hands against each other, to clear them of the dampness from the windowsill, he felt for his cigarette case, chose a Maryland and tapped it lightly on his finger-nail.

"*Tiens*, I damn think he will know his master's voice in future, that one," he informed us. "I did not quite succeed in killing him to death, unfortunately, but

I think that it will be some time before he comes and cries beneath this lady's window again. Yes. Had the *sale poltron* but had the courage to stand against me, I should certainly have killed him; but as it was"—he spread his hands and raised his shoulders eloquently—"it is difficult to hit a running shadow, and he offered little better mark in the darkness. I think I wounded him in the left hand, but I can not surely say."

He paused a moment, then, seeming to remember, turned again to Sarah Leigh with a ceremonious bow. "*Pardon, Mademoiselle,*" he apologized, "you were saying, when we were so discourteously interrupted—" he smiled at her expectantly.

"Doctor de Grandin," wondering incredulity was in the girl's eyes and voice as she looked at him, "you shot him—wounded him?"

"Perfectly, *Mademoiselle,*" he patted the waxed ends of his mustache with affectionate concern, "my marksmanship was execrable, but at least I hit him. That was something."

"But in Greece they used to say—I've always heard that only silver bullets were effective against a *vrykolakas*; either silver bullets or a sword of finely tempered steel, so—"

"*Ah bah!*" he interrupted with a laugh. "What did they know of modern ordnance, those old-time ritualists? Silver bullets were decreed because silver is a harder metal than lead, and the olden guns they used in ancient days were not adapted to shoot balls of iron. The pistols of today shoot slugs encased in cupronickel, far harder than the best of iron, and with a striking-force undreamed of in the days when firearms were a new invention. *Tiens,* had the good Saint George possessed a modern military rifle he could have slain the dragon at his leisure while he stood a mile away. Had Saint Michel had a machine-gun, his victory over Lucifer could have been accomplished in thirty seconds by the watch."

Having delivered himself of this scandalous opinion, he reseated himself on the divan and smiled at her, for all the world like the family cat which has just breakfasted on the household canary.

"And how was it that this so valiant runner-away-from-Jules-de-Grandin announced himself to you, *Mademoiselle?*" he asked.

"I was dressing to go out this morning," she replied, "when the 'phone rang, and when I answered it no one replied to my 'hello.' Then, just as I began to think they'd given some one a wrong number, and was about to put the instrument down, there came one of those awful, wailing howls across the wire. No word at all, sir, just that long-drawn, quavering howl, like what you heard a little while ago.

"You can imagine how it frightened me. I'd almost managed to put George from my mind, telling myself that the vision of lycanthropy which I had in Smyrna was some sort of hypnotism, and that there really weren't such things as werewolves, and even if there were, this was practical America, where I needn't fear them—then came that dreadful howl, the sort of howl I'd heard—and given!—in my vision in the Smyrna garden, and I knew there *are* such things as werewolves, and that one of them possessed me, soul and body, and that I'd have to go to him if he demanded it.

"Most of all, though, I thought of John, for if the werewolf were in America he'd surely read the notice of our coming marriage, and the first thing I remembered was his threat to kill anyone who tried to come between us."

She turned to Maxwell with a pensive smile. "You know how I've been worrying you all day, dear," she asked, "how I begged you not to go out to that dinner tonight, and when you said you must how I made you promise that you'd call me as soon as you got home, but on no account to call me before you were safely back in your apartment?

"I've been in a perfect agony of apprehension all evening," she told us, "and when John called from Doctor Trowbridge's office I felt as though a great weight had been lifted from my heart."

"And did you try to trace the call?" the little Frenchman asked.

"Yes, but it had been dialed from a downtown pay station, so it was impossible to find it."

De Grandin took his chin between his thumb and forefinger and gazed thoughtfully at the tips of his patent-leather evening shoes. "U'm?" he murmured; then: "What does he look like, this so gallant persecutor of women, *Mademoiselle?* 'He is handsome,' you have said, which is of interest, certainly, but not especially instructive. Can you be more specific? Since he is a Greek, one assumes that he is dark, but—"

"No, he's not," she interrupted. "His eyes are blue and his hair is rather light, though his beard—he used to wear one, though he may be smooth-shaven now—is quite dark, almost black. Indeed, in certain lights it seems to have an almost bluish tinge."

"Ah, so? *Une barbe bleu?*" de Grandin answered sharply. "One might have thought as much. Such beards, *ma chère*, are the sign-manual of those who traffic with the Devil. Gilles de Retz, the vilest monster who ever cast insult on the human race by wearing human form, was light of hair and blue-black as to beard. It is from him we get the most unpleasant fairy-tale of Bluebeard, though the gentleman who dispatched his wives for showing too much curiosity was a lamb and sucking dove beside the one whose name he bears.

"Very well. Have you a photograph of him, by any happy chance?"

"No; I did have one, but I burned it years ago."

"A pity, *Mademoiselle*; our task would be made easier if we had his likeness as a guide. But we shall find him otherwise."

"How?" asked Maxwell and I in chorus.

"There was a time," he answered, "when the revelations of a patient to his doctor were considered privileged communications. Since prohibition came to blight your land, however, and the gangster's gun has written history in blood, the physicians are required to note the names and addresses of those who come to them with gunshot wounds, and this information is collected by the police each day. Now, we know that I have wounded this one. He will undoubtlessly seek medical assistance for his hurt. *Voilà*, I shall go down to the police head-quarters, look upon the records of those treated for injuries from bullets, and by a process of elimination we shall find him. You apprehend?"

"But suppose he doesn't go to a physician?" young Maxwell interposed.

"In that event we have to find some other way to find him," de Grandin answered with a smile, "but that is a stream which we shall cross when we have arrived upon its shore. Meantime"—he rose and bowed politely to our host-ess—"it is getting late, *Mademoiselle*, and we have trespassed on your time too long already. We shall convoy Monsieur Maxwell safely home, and see him lock his door, and if you will keep your doors and windows barred, I do not think that you have anything to fear. The gentleman who seems also to be a wolf has his wounded paw to nurse, and that will keep him busy the remainder of the night."

With a movement of his eyes he bade me leave the room, following closely on my heels and closing the door behind him. "If we must separate them the least which we can do is give them twenty little minutes for good-night," he murmured as we donned our mackintoshes.

"Twenty minutes?" I expostulated. "Why, he could say good-night to twenty girls in twenty minutes!"

"*Oui-da, certainement*; or a hundred," he agreed, "but not to the one girl, my good friend. *Ah bah*, Friend Trowbridge, did you never love; did you never worship at the small, white feet of some beloved woman? Did you never feel your breath come faster and your blood pound wildly at your temples as you took her in your arms and put your lips against her mouth? If not—*grand Dieu des porcs*—then you have never lived at all, though you be older than Methuselah!"

Running our quarry to earth proved a harder task than we had anticipated. Daylight had scarcely come when de Grandin visited the police, but for all he discovered he might have stayed at home. Only four cases of gunshot wounds had been reported during the preceding night, and two of the injured men were Negroes, a third a voluble but undoubtedly Italian laborer who had quarreled with some fellow countrymen over a card game, while the fourth was a thin-faced, tight-lipped gangster who eyed us saturninely and murmured, "Never mind who done it; I'll be seein' 'im," evidently under the misapprehension that we were emissaries of the police.

The next day and the next produced no more results. Gunshot wounds there were, but none in the hand, where de Grandin declared he had wounded the nocturnal visitant, and though he followed every lead assiduously, in every case he drew a blank.

He was almost beside himself on the fourth day of fruitless search; by evening I was on the point of prescribing triple bromides, for he paced the study restlessly, snapping his fingers, tweaking the waxed ends of his mustache till I made sure he would pull the hairs loose from his lip, and murmuring appalling blasphemies in mingled French and English.

At length, when I thought that I could stand his restless striding no longer, diversion came in the form of a telephone call. He seized the instrument peevishly, but no sooner had he barked a sharp "*Allo?*" than his whole expression changed and a quick smile ran across his face, like sunshine breaking through a cloud.

"But certainly; of course, assuredly!" he cried delightedly. Then, to me:

"Your hat and coat, Friend Trowbridge, and hurry, *pour l'amour d'un têtard*—they are marrying!"

"Marrying?" I echoed wonderingly. "Who—"

"Who but Mademoiselle Sarah and Monsieur Jean, *parbleu?*" he answered with a grin. "*Oh, la, la*, at last they show some sense, those ones. He had broken her resistance down, and she consents, werewolf or no werewolf. Now we shall surely make the long nose at that *sacré singe* who howled beneath her window when we called upon her!"

The ceremony was to be performed in the sacristy of St. Barnabas' Church, for John and Sarah, shocked and saddened by the death of young Fred Suffrige, who was to have been their best man, had recalled the invitations and decided on a private wedding with only her aunt and his mother present in addition to de Grandin and me.

"Dearly beloved, we are gathered together here in the sight of God and in the face of this company to join together this man and this woman in holy matrimony," began the rector, Doctor Higginbotham, who, despite the informality of the occasion, was attired in all the panoply of a high church priest and accompanied by two gorgeously accoutered and greatly interested choir-boys who served as acolytes. "Into this holy estate these two persons come now to be joined. If any man can show just cause why they should not lawfully be joined together let him now speak, or else hereafter forever hold his peace—"

"Jeez!" exclaimed the choir youth who stood upon the rector's left, letting fall the censer from his hands and dodging nimbly back, as from a threatened blow.

The interruption fell upon the solemn scene like a bombshell at a funeral, and one and all of us looked at the cowering youngster, whose eyes were fairly bulging from his face and whose ruddy countenance had gone a sickly, pasty gray, so that the thick-strewn freckles started out in contrast, like spots of rouge upon a corpse's pallid cheeks.

"Why, William—" Doctor Higginbotham began in a shocked voice; but:

Rat, tat-tat! sounded the sudden sharp clatter of knuckles against the window-pane, and for the first time we realized it had been toward this window the boy had looked when his sacrilegious exclamation broke in on the service.

Staring at us through the glass we saw a great, gray wolf! Yet it was not a wolf, for about the lupine jaws and jowls was something hideously reminiscent of a human face, and the greenish, phosphorescent glow of those great, glaring eyes had surely never shone in any face, animal or human. As I looked, breathless, the monster raised its head, and strangling horror gripped my throat with fiery fingers as I saw a human-seeming neck beneath it. Long and grisly-thin it was, corded and sinewed like the desiccated gula of a lich, and, like the face, covered with a coat of gray-brown fur. Then a hand, hair-covered like the throat and face, slim as a woman's—or a mummy's!—but terribly misshapen, fingers tipped with blood-red talon-nails, rose up and struck the glass again. My scalp was fairly crawling with sheer terror, and my breath came hot and sulfurous in my throat as I wondered how much longer the frail glass could stand against the impact of those bony, hair-gloved hands.

A strangled scream behind me sounded from Sarah's aunt, Miss Leigh, and I heard the muffled thud as she toppled to the floor in a dead faint, but I could no more turn my gaze from the horror at the window than the fascinated bird can tear its eyes from the serpent's numbing stare.

Another sighing exclamation and another thudding impact. John Maxwell's mother was unconscious on the floor beside Miss Leigh, but still I stood and stared in frozen terror at the thing beyond the window.

Doctor Higginbotham's teeth were chattering, and his ruddy, plethoric countenance was death-gray as he faced the staring horror, but he held fast to his faith.

"*Conjuro te, sceleratissime, abire ad tuum locum*"—he began the sonorous Latin exorcism, signing himself with his right hand and advancing his pectoral cross toward the thing at the window with his left—"I exorcise thee, most foul spirit, creature of darkness—"

The corners of the wolf-thing's devilish eyes contracted in a smile of malevolent amusement, and a rim of scarlet tongue flicked its black muzzle. Doctor Higginbotham's exorcism, bravely begun, ended on a wheezing, stifled syllable, and he stared in round-eyed fascination, his thick lips, blue with terror, opening and closing, but emitting no sound.

"*Sang d'un cochon*, not that way, Monsieur—this!" cried Jules de Grandin, and the roar of his revolver split the paralysis of quiet which had gripped the little chapel. A thin, silvery tinkle of glass sounded as the bullet tore through the window, and the grisly face abruptly disappeared, but from somewhere in the outside dark there echoed back a braying howl which seemed to hold a sort of obscene laughter in its quavering notes.

"*Sapristi!* Have I missed him?" de Grandin asked incredulously. "No matter; he is gone. On with the service, *Monsieur le Curé*. I do not think we shall be interrupted further."

"No!" Doctor Higginbotham backed away from Sarah Leigh as though her breath polluted him. "I can perform no marriage until that thing has been explained. Some one here is haunted by a devil—a malign entity from hell which will not heed the exorcism of the Church—and until I'm satisfied concerning it, and that you're all good Christians, there'll be no ceremony in this church!"

"*Eh bien, Monsieur*, who can say what constitutes a good Christian?" de Grandin smiled unpleasantly at Doctor Higginbotham. "Certainly one who lacks in charity as you do can not be competent to judge. Have it as you wish. As soon as we have recovered these fainting ladies we shall leave, and may the Devil grill me on the grates of hell if ever we come back until you have apologized."

Two hours later, as we sat in the Leigh library, Sarah dried her eyes and faced her lover with an air of final resolution: "You see, my dear, it's utterly impossible for me to marry you, or anyone," she said. "That awful thing will dog my steps, and—"

"My poor, sweet girl, I'm more determined than ever to marry you!" John broke in. "If you're to be haunted by a thing like that, you need me every minute, and—"

"*Bravo!*" applauded Jules de Grandin. "Well said, *mon vieux*, but we waste precious time. Come, let us go."

"Where?" asked John Maxwell, but the little Frenchman only smiled and shrugged his shoulders.

"To Maidstone Crossing, quickly, if you please, my friend," he whispered when he had led the lovers to my car and seen solicitously to their comfortable seating in the tonneau. "I know a certain justice of the peace there who would marry the Witch of Endor to the Emperor Nero though all the wolves which ever plagued Red Riding-Hood forbade the banns, provided only we supply him with sufficient fee."

Two hours' drive brought us to the little hamlet of Maidstone Crossing, and de Grandin's furious knocking on the door of a small cottage evoked the presence of a lank, lean man attired in a pair of corduroy trousers drawn hastily above the folds of a canton-flannel nightshirt.

A whispered colloquy between the rustic and the slim, elegant little Parisian; then: "O.K., Doc," the justice of the peace conceded. "Bring 'em in; I'll marry 'em, an'—hey, Sam'l!" he called up the stairs. "C'mon down, an' bring yer shotgun. There's a weddin' goin' to be pulled off, an' they tell me some fresh guys may try to interfere!"

"Sam'l," a lank, lean youth whose costume duplicated that of his father, descended the stairway grinning, an automatic shotgun cradled in the hollow of his arm. "D'ye expect any real rough stuff?" he asked.

"Seems like they're apt to try an' set a dawg on 'em," his father answered, and the younger man grinned cheerfully.

"Dawgs, is it?" he replied. "Dawgs is my dish. Go on, Pap, do yer stuff. Good luck, folks," he winked encouragingly at John and Sarah and stepped out on the porch, his gun in readiness.

"Do you take this here woman fer yer lawful, wedded wife?" the justice inquired of John Maxwell, and when the latter answered that he did:

"An' do you take this here now man to be yer wedded husband?" he asked Sarah.

"I do," the girl responded in a trembling whisper, and the roaring bellow of a shotgun punctuated the brief pause before the squire concluded:

"Then by virtue of th' authority vested in me by th' law an' constitootion of this state, I do declare ye man an' wife—an' whoever says that ye ain't married lawfully 's a danged liar," he added as a sort of afterthought.

"What wuz it that ye shot at, Sam'l?" asked the justice as, enriched by fifty dollars, and grinning appreciatively at the evening's profitable business, he ushered us from the house.

"Durned if I know, Pap," the other answered. "Looked kind o' funny to me. He wuz about a head taller'n me—an' I'm six foot two,—an' thin as Job's turkey-hen, to boot. His clothes looked skintight on 'im, an' he had on a cap, or sumpin with a peak that stuck out over his face. I first seen 'im comin' up th' road, kind o' lookin' this way an' that, like as if he warn't quite certain o' his way. Then, all of a suddent, he kind o' stopped an' threw his head back, like a dawg sniffin' th' air, an' started to go down on his all-fours, like he wuz goin' to sneak up on th' house. So I hauls off an' lets 'im have a tickle o' buckshot. Don't know whether I hit 'im or not, an' I'll bet he don't, neether; he sure didn't waste no time stoppin' to find out. Could he run! I'm tellin' ye, that feller must be in Harrisonville by now, if he kep' on goin' like he started!"

Two days of feverish activity ensued. Last-minute traveling arrangements had to be made, and passports for "John Maxwell and wife, Harrisonville, New Jersey, U.S.A.," obtained. De Grandin spent every waking hour with the newly married couple and even insisted on occupying a room in the Leigh house at night; but his precautions seemed unnecessary, for not so much as a whimper sounded under Sarah's window, and though the little Frenchman searched the garden every morning, there was no trace of unfamiliar footprints, either brute or human, to be found.

"Looks as if Sallie's Greek boy friend knows when he's licked and has decided to quit following her about," John Maxwell grinned as he and Sarah, radiant with happiness, stood upon the deck of the *Île de France*.

"One hopes so," de Grandin answered with a smile. "Good luck, *mes amis*, and may your *lune de miel* shine as brightly throughout all your lives as it does this night.

"*La lune*—ha?" he repeated half musingly, half with surprise, as though he just remembered some important thing which had inadvertently slipped his memory. "May I speak a private warning in your ear, Friend Jean?" He drew the bridegroom aside and whispered earnestly a moment.

"Oh, bosh!" the other laughed as they rejoined us. "That's all behind us, Doctor; you'll see; we'll never hear a sound from him. He's got *me* to deal with now, not just poor Sarah."

"Bravely spoken, little cabbage!" the Frenchman applauded. "*Bon voyage*." But there was a serious expression on his face as we went down the gangway.

"What was the private warning you gave John?" I asked as we left the French Line piers. "He didn't seem to take it very seriously."

"No," he conceded. "I wish he had. But youth is always brave and reckless in its own conceit. It was about the moon. She has a strange influence on lycanthropy. The werewolf metamorphoses more easily in the full of the moon than at any other time, and those who may have been affected with his virus, though even faintly, are most apt to feel its spell when the moon is at the full. I warned him to be particularly careful of his lady on moonlit nights, and on no account to go anywhere after dark unless he were armed.

"The werewolf is really an inferior demon," he continued as we boarded the Hoboken ferry. "Just what he is we do not know with certainty, though we know he has existed from the earliest times; for many writers of antiquity mention him. Sometimes he is said to be a magical wolf who has the power to become a man. More often he is said to be a man who can become a wolf at times, sometimes of his own volition, sometimes at stated seasons, even against his will. He has dreadful powers of destructiveness; for the man who is also a wolf is ten times more deadly than the wolf who is only a wolf. He has the wolf's great strength and savagery, but human cunning with it. At night he quests and kills his prey, which is most often his fellow man, but sometimes sheep or hares, or his ancient enemy, the dog. By day he hides his villainy—and the location of his lair—under human guise.

"However, he has this weakness: Strong and ferocious, cunning and malicious as he is, he can be killed as easily as any natural wolf. A sharp sword will slay him, a well-aimed bullet puts an end to his career; the wood of the thorn-bush and the mountain ash are so repugnant to him that he will slink away if beaten or merely threatened with a switch of either. Weapons efficacious against an ordinary physical foe are potent against him, while charms and exorcisms which would put a true demon to flight are powerless.

"You saw how he mocked at Monsieur Higginbotham in the sacristy the other night, by example. But he did not stop to bandy words with me. Oh, no. He knows that I shoot straight and quick, and he had already felt my lead on one occasion. If young Friend Jean will always go well-armed, he has no need to fear; but if he be taken off his guard—*eh bien*, we can not always be on hand to rescue him as we did the night when we first met him. No, certainly."

"But why do you fear for Sarah?" I persisted.

"I hardly know," he answered. "Perhaps it is that I have what you Americans so drolly call the hunch. Werewolves sometimes become werewolves by the aid of Satan, that they may kill their enemies while in lupine form, or satisfy their natural lust for blood and cruelty while disguised as beasts. Some are transformed as the result of a curse upon themselves or their families, a few are metamorphosed by accident. These are the most unfortunate of all. In certain parts of Europe, notably in Greece, Russia and the Balkan states, the very soil seems cursed with lycanthropic power. There are certain places where, if the unwary traveler lies down to sleep, he is apt to wake up with the curse of werewolfism on him. Certain streams and springs there are which, if drunk from, will render the drinker liable to transformation at the next full moon, and regularly thereafter. You will recall that in the dream, or vision, which Madame Sarah had while in the Smyrna garden so long ago, she beheld herself drinking from a woodland pool? I do not surely know, my friend, I have not even good grounds for suspicion, but something—something which I can not name—tells me that in some way this poor one, who is so wholly innocent, has been branded with the taint of lycanthropy. How it came about I can not say, but—"

My mind had been busily engaged with other problems, and I had listened to his disquisition on lycanthropy with something less than full attention. Now, suddenly aware of the thing which puzzled me, I interrupted:

"Can you explain the form that werewolf—if that's what it was—took on different occasions? The night we met John Maxwell he was fighting for his life with as true a wolf as any there are in the zoological gardens. O'Brien, the policeman, saw it, too, and shot at it, after it had killed Fred Suffrige. It was a sure-enough wolf when it howled under Sarah's window and you wounded it; yet when it interrupted the wedding it was an awful combination of wolf and man, or man and wolf, and the thing the justice's son drove off with his shotgun was the same, according to his description."

Surprisingly, he did not take offense at my interruption. Instead, he frowned in thoughtful silence at the dashboard lights a moment; then: "Sometimes the werewolf is completely transformed from man to beast," he answered; "sometimes he is a hideous combination of the two, but always he is a fiend incarnate. My own belief is that this one was only partly transformed when we last saw him because he had not time to wait complete metamorphosis. It is possible he could not change completely, too, because—" he broke off and pointed at the sky significantly.

"Well?" I demanded as he made no further effort to proceed.

"*Non*, it is not well," he denied, "but it may be important. Do you observe the moon tonight?"

"Why, yes."

"What quarter is it in?"

"The last; it's waning fast."

"*Précisément*. As I was saying, it may be that his powers to metamorphose himself were weakened because of the waning of the moon. Remember, if you please, his power for evil is at its height when the moon is at the full, and as it wanes, his powers become less and less. At the darkening of the moon, he is at his weakest, and then is the time for us to strike—if only we could find him. But he will lie well hidden at such times, never fear. He is clever with a devilish cunningness, that one."

"Oh, you're fantastic!" I burst out.

"You say so, having seen what you have seen?"

"Well, I'll admit we've seen some things which are mighty hard to explain," I conceded, "but—"

"But we are arrived at home; Monsieur and Madame Maxwell are safe upon the ocean, and I am vilely thirsty," he broke in. "Come, let us take a drink and go to bed, my friend."

With midwinter came John and Sarah Maxwell, back from their honeymoon in Paris and on the Riviera. A week before their advent, notices in the society columns told of their homecoming, and a week after their return an engraved invitation apprised de Grandin and me that the honor of our presence was requested at a reception in the Leigh mansion, where they had taken residence. ". . . and please come early and stay late; there are a million things I want to talk about," Sarah pencilled at the bottom of our card.

Jules de Grandin was more than usually ornate on the night of the reception. His London-tailored evening clothes were knife-sharp in their creases; about his neck hung the insignia of the *Legion d'Honneur*; a row of miniature medals, including the French and Belgian war crosses, the *Médaille Militaire* and the Italian Medal of Valor, decorated the left breast of his faultless evening coat; his little, wheat-blond mustache was waxed to needle-sharpness and his sleek blond hair was brilliantined and brushed till it fitted flat upon his shapely little head as a skull-cap of beige satin.

Lights blazed from every window of the house as we drew up beneath the porte-cochère. Inside all was laughter, staccato conversation and the odd, not unpleasant odor rising from the mingling of the hundred or more individual scents affected by the women guests. Summer was still near enough for the men to retain the tan of mountain and seashore on their faces and for a velvet vestige of veneer of painfully acquired sun-tan to show upon the women's arms and shoulders.

We tendered our congratulations to the homing newlyweds; then de Grandin plucked me by the sleeve. "Come away, my friend," he whispered in an almost tragic voice. "Come quickly, or these thirsty ones will have drunk up all the punch containing rum and champagne and left us only lemonade!"

The evening passed with pleasant swiftness, and guests began to leave. "Where's Sallie—seen her?" asked John Maxwell, interrupting a rather Rabelaisian story which de Grandin was retailing with gusto to several appreciative young men in the conservatory. "The Carter-Brooks are leaving, and—"

De Grandin brought his story to a close with the suddenness of a descending theater curtain, and a look of something like consternation shone in his small, round eyes. "She is not here?" he asked sharply. "When did you last see her?"

"Oh," John answered vaguely, "just a little while ago; we danced the 'Blue Danube' together, then she went upstairs for something, and—"

"Quick, swiftly!" de Grandin interrupted. "*Pardon, Messieurs,*" he bowed to his late audience and, beckoning me, strode toward the stairs.

"I say, what's the rush—" began John Maxwell, but:

"Every reason under heaven," the Frenchman broke in shortly. To me: "Did you observe the night outside, Friend Trowbridge?"

"Why, yes," I answered. "Its a beautiful moonlit night, almost bright as day, and—"

"And there you are, for the love of ten thousand pigs!" he cut in. "Oh, I am the stupid-headed fool, me! Why did I let her from my sight?"

We followed in wondering silence as he climbed the stairs, hurried down the hall toward Sarah's room and paused before her door. He raised his hand to rap, but the portal swung away, and a girl stood staring at us from the threshold.

"Did it pass you?" she asked, regarding us in wide-eyed wonder.

"*Pardon, Mademoiselle?*" de Grandin countered. "What is it that you ask?"

"Why, did you see that lovely collie, it—"

"*Cher Dieu,*" the words were like a groan upon the little Frenchman's lips as he looked at her in horror. Then, recovering himself: "Proceed, *Mademoiselle*, it was of a dog you spoke?"

"Yes," she returned. "I came upstairs to freshen up, and found I'd lost my compact somewhere, so I came to Sallie's room to get some powder. She'd come up a few moments before, and I was positive I'd find her here, but—" she paused in puzzlement a moment; then: "But when I came in there was no one here. Her dress was lying on the chaiselongue there, as though she'd slipped it off, and by the window, looking out with its paws up on the sill, was the loveliest silver collie.

"I didn't know you had a dog, John," she turned to Maxwell. "When did you get it? It's the loveliest creature, but it seemed to be afraid of me; for when I went to pat it, it slunk away, and before I realized it had bolted through the door, which I'd left open. It ran down the hall."

"A dog?" John Maxwell answered bewilderedly. "We haven't any dog, Nell; it must have been—"

"Never mind what it was," de Grandin interrupted as the girl went down the hall, and as she passed out of hearing he seized us by the elbows and fairly thrust us into Sarah's room, closing the door quickly behind us.

"What—" began John Maxwell, but the Frenchman motioned him to silence.

"Behold, regard each item carefully; stamp them upon your memories," he ordered, sweeping the charming chamber with his sharp, stock-taking glance.

A fire burned brightly in the open grate, parchment-shaded lamps diffused soft light. Upon the bed there lay a pair of rose-silk pajamas, with a sheer crêpe negligée beside them. A pair of satin mules were placed toes in upon the bedside rug. Across the chaise-longue was draped, as though discarded in the utmost haste, the white-satin evening gown that Sarah had worn. Upon the floor beside the lounge were crumpled wisps of ivory crêpe de Chine, her bandeau and trunks. Sarah, being wholly modern, had worn no stockings, but her white-and-silver evening sandals lay beside the lingerie, one on its sole, as though she had stepped out of it, the other on its side, gaping emptily, as though kicked from her little pink-and-white foot in panic haste. There was something ominous about that silent room; it was like a body from which the spirit had departed, still beautiful and warm, but lifeless.

"Humph," Maxwell muttered, "the Devil knows where she's gone—"

"He knows very, exceedingly well, I have no doubt," de Grandin interrupted. "But we do not. Now—ah? Ah-ah-ah?" his exclamation rose steadily, thinning to a sharpness like a razor's cutting-edge. "What have we here?"

Like a hound upon the trail, guided by scent alone, he crossed the room and halted by the dressing-table. Before the mirror stood an uncorked flask of perfume, lovely thing of polished crystal decorated with silver basketwork. From its open neck there rose a thin but penetrating scent, not wholly sweet nor wholly acrid, but a not unpleasant combination of the two, as though musk and flower-scent had each lent it something of their savors.

The little Frenchman put it to his nose, then set it down with a grimace. "Name of an Indian pig, how comes this devil's brew here?" he asked.

"Oh, that?" Maxwell answered. "Hanged if I know. Some unknown admirer of Sallie's sent it to her. It came today, all wrapped up like something from a jeweler's. Rather pleasant-smelling, isn't it?"

De Grandin looked at him as Torquemada might have looked at one accusing him of loving Martin Luther. "Did you by any chance make use of it, *Monsieur?*" he asked in an almost soundless whisper.

"I? Good Lord, do I look like the sort of he-thing who'd use perfume?" the other asked.

"*Bien*, I did but ask to know," de Grandin answered as he jammed the silver-mounted stopper in the bottle and thrust the flask into his trousers pocket.

"But where the deuce *is* Sallie?" the young husband persisted. "She's changed her clothes, that's certain; but what did she go out for, and if she didn't go out, where is she?"

"Ah, it may be that she had a sudden feeling of faintness, and decided to go out into the air," the Frenchman temporized. "Come, *Monsieur*, the guests are waiting to depart, and you must say *adieu*. Tell them that your lady is indisposed, make excuses, tell them anything, but get them out all quickly; we have work to do."

John Maxwell lied gallantly, de Grandin and I standing at his side to prevent any officious dowager from mounting the stairs and administering homemade medical assistance. At last, when all were gone, the young man turned to Jules de Grandin, and:

"Now, out with it," he ordered gruffly. "I can tell by your manner something serious has happened. What is it, man; what is it?"

De Grandin patted him upon the shoulder with a mixture of affection and commiseration in the gesture. "Be brave, *mon vieux*," he ordered softly. "It is the worst. He has her in his power; she has gone to join him, for—*pitié de Dieu!*—she has become like him."

"Wha—what?" the husband quavered. "You mean she—that Sallie, my Sallie, has become a were—" his voice balked at the final syllable, but de Grandin's nod confirmed his guess.

"*Hélas*, you have said it, my poor friend," he murmured pitifully.

"But how?—when?—I thought surely we'd driven him off—" the young man faltered, then stopped, horror choking the words back in his throat.

"Unfortunately, no," de Grandin told him. "He was driven off, certainly, but not diverted from his purpose. Attend me."

From his trousers pocket he produced the vial of perfume, uncorked it and let its scent escape into the room. "You recognize it, *hein?*" he asked.

"No, I can't say I do," Maxwell answered.

"Do you, Friend Trowbridge?"

I shook my head.

"Very well. I do, to my sorrow."

He turned once more to me. "The night Monsieur and Madame Maxwell sailed upon the *Île de France*, you may recall I was explaining how the innocent became werewolves at times?" he reminded.

"Yes, and I interrupted to ask about the different shapes that thing assumed," I nodded.

"You interrupted then," he agreed soberly, "but you will not interrupt now. Oh, no. You will listen while I talk. I had told you of the haunted dells where travelers may unknowingly become werewolves, of the streams from which the drinker may receive contagion, but you did not wait to hear of *les fleurs des loups*, did you?"

"*Fleurs des loups*—wolf-flowers?" I asked.

"*Précisément*, wolf-flowers. Upon those cursed mountains grows a kind of flower which, plucked and worn at the full of the moon, transforms the wearer into a *loup-garou*. Yes. One of these flowers, known popularly as the *fleur de sang*, or blood-flower, because of its red petals, resembles the marguerite, or daisy, in form; the other is a golden yellow, and is much like the snapdragon. But both have the same fell property, both have the same strong, sweet, fascinating scent.

"This, my friends," he passed the opened flagon underneath our noses, "is a perfume made from the sap of those accursed flowers. It is the highly concentrated venom of their devilishness. One applying it to her person, anointing lips, ears, hair and hands with it, as women wont, would as surely be translated into wolfish form as though she wore the cursed flower whence the perfume comes. Yes.

"That silver collie of which the young girl spoke, *Monsieur*"—he turned a fixed, but pitying look upon John Maxwell—"she was your wife, transformed into a wolf-thing by the power of this perfume.

"Consider: Can you not see it all? Balked, but not defeated, the vile *vryko-lakas* is left to perfect his revenge while you are on your honeymoon. He knows that you will come again to Harrisonville; he need not follow you. Accordingly, he sends to Europe for the essence of these flowers, prepares a philtre from it, and sends it to Madame Sarah today. Its scent is novel, rather pleasing; women like strange, exotic scents. She uses it. Anon, she feels a queerness. She does not realize that it is the metamorphosis which comes upon her, she only knows that she feels vaguely strange. She goes to her room. Perhaps she puts the perfume on her brow again, as women do when they feel faint; then, *pardieu*, then there comes the change all quickly, for the moon is full tonight, and the essence of the flowers very potent.

"She doffed her clothes, you think? *Mais non*, they fell from her! A woman's raiment does not fit a wolf; it falls off from her altered form, and we find it on the couch and on the floor.

"That other girl comes to the room, and finds poor Madame Sarah, transformed to a wolf, gazing sadly from the window—*la pauvre*, she knew too well who waited outside in the moonlight for her, and she must go to him! Her friend puts out a hand to pet her, but she shrinks away. She feels she is 'unclean', a thing apart, one of 'that multitudinous herd not yet made fast in hell'—*les loups-garous!* And so she flies through the open door of her room, flies where? Only *le bon Dieu*—and the Devil, who is master of all werewolves—knows!"

"But we must find her!" Maxwell wailed. "We've got to find her!"

"Where are we to look?" de Grandin spread his hands and raised his shoulders. "The city is wide, and we have no idea where this wolf-man makes his lair. The werewolf travels fast, my friend; they may be miles away by now."

"I don't care a damn what you say, I'm going out to look for her!" Maxwell declared as he rose from his seat and strode to the library table, from the drawer of which he took a heavy pistol. "You shot him once and wounded him, so I know he's vulnerable to bullets, and when I find him—"

"But certainly," the Frenchman interrupted. "We heartily agree with you, my friend. But let us first go to Doctor Trowbridge's house where we, too, may secure weapons. Then we shall be delighted to accompany you upon your hunt."

As we started for my place he whispered in my ear: "Prepare the knock-out drops as soon as we are there, Friend Trowbridge. It would be suicide for him to seek that monster now. He can not hit a barn-side with a pistol, can not even draw it quickly from his pocket. His chances are not one in a million if he meets the wolf, and if we let him go we shall be playing right into the adversary's hands."

I nodded agreement as we drove along, and when I'd parked the car, I turned to Maxwell. "Better come in and have a drink before we start," I invited. "It's cold tonight, and we may not get back soon."

"All right," agreed the unsuspecting youth. "But make it quick, I'm itching to catch sight of that damned fiend. When I meet him he won't get off as easily as he did in his brush with Doctor de Grandin."

Hastily I concocted a punch of Jamaica rum, hot water, lemon juice and sugar, adding fifteen grains of chloral hydrate to John Maxwell's, and hoping the sugar and lemon would disguise its taste while the pungent rum would hide its odor. "To our successful quest," de Grandin proposed, raising his steaming glass and looking questioningly at me for assurance that the young man's drink was drugged.

Maxwell raised his goblet, but ere he set it to his lips there came a sudden interruption. An oddly whining, whimpering noise it was, accompanied by a scratching at the door, as though a dog were outside in the night and importuning for admission.

"*Ah?*" de Grandin put his glass down on the hall table and reached beneath his left armpit where the small but deadly Belgian automatic pistol nestled in its shoulder-holster. "*Ah-ha?* We have a visitor, it seems." To me he bade:

"Open the door, wide and quickly, Friend Trowbridge; then stand away, for I shall likely shoot with haste, and it is not your estimable self that I desire to kill."

I followed his instructions, but instead of the gray horror I had expected at the door, I saw a slender canine form with hair so silver-gray that it was almost white, which bent its head and wagged its tail, and fairly fawned upon us as it slipped quickly through the opening then looked at each of us in turn with great, expressive topaz eyes.

"*Ah, mon Dieu,*" exclaimed the Frenchman, sheathing his weapon and starting forward, "it is Madame Sarah!"

"Sallie!" cried John Maxwell incredulously, and at his voice the beast leaped toward him, rubbed against his knees, then rose upon its hind feet and strove to lick his face.

"*Ohé, quel dommage!*" de Grandin looked at them with tear-filled eyes; then:

"Your pardon, Madame Sarah, but I do not think you came to us without a reason. Can you lead us to the place where he abides? If so we promise you shall be avenged within the hour."

The silver wolf dropped to all fours again, and nodded its sleek head in answer to his question; then, as he hesitated, came slowly up to him, took the cuff of his evening coat gently in its teeth and drew him toward the door.

"*Bravo, ma chère,* lead on, we follow!" he exclaimed; then, as we donned our coats, he thrust a pistol in my hand and cautioned: "Watch well, my friend, she seems all amiable, but wolves are treacherous, man-wolves a thousand times more so; it may be he has sent her to lead us to a trap. Should anything untoward transpire, shoot first and ask your foolish questions afterward. That way you shall increase your chances of dying peacefully in bed."

The white beast trotting before us, we hastened down the quiet, moonlit street. After forty minutes' rapid walk, we stopped before a small apartment house. As we paused to gaze, the little wolf once more seized Jules de Grandin's sleeve between her teeth and drew him forward.

It was a little house, only three floors high, and its front was zigzagged with iron fire escapes. No lights burned in any of the flats, and the whole place had in air of vacancy, but our lupine guide led us through the entrance way and down the ground floor hall until we paused before the door of a rear apartment.

De Grandin tried the knob cautiously, found the lock made fast, and after a moment dropped to his knees, drew out a ringful of fine steel instruments and began picking the fastening as methodically as though he were a professional burglar. The lock was "burglar-proof" but its makers had not reckoned with the skill of Jules de Grandin. Before five minutes had elapsed he rose with a pleased exclamation, turned the knob and thrust the door back.

"Hold her, Friend Jean," he bade John Maxwell, for the wolf was trembling with a nervous quiver, and straining to rush into the apartment. To me he added: "Have your gun ready, good Friend Trowbridge, and keep by me. He shall not take us unawares."

Shoulder to shoulder we entered the dark doorway of the flat, John Maxwell and the wolf behind us. For a moment we paused while de Grandin felt along the wall, then click; the snapping of a wall-switch sounded, and the dark room blazed with sudden light.

The wolf-man's human hours were passed in pleasant circumstances. Every item of the room proclaimed it the abode of one whose wealth and tastes were well matched. The walls were hung with light gray paper, the floor was covered with a Persian rug and wide, low chairs upholstered in long-napped mohair invited the visitor to rest. Beneath the arch of a marble mantelpiece a wood fire had been laid, ready for the match, while upon the shelf a tiny French-gilt clock beat off the minutes with sharp, musical clicks. Pictures in profusion lined the walls, a landscape by an apt pupil of Corot, an excellent imitation of Botticelli, and, above the mantel, a single life-sized portrait done in oils.

Every item of the portrait was portrayed with photographic fidelity, and we looked with interest at the subject, a man in early middle life, or late youth, dressed in the uniform of a captain of Greek cavalry. His cloak was thrown back from his braided shoulders, displaying several military decorations, but it was the face which captured the attention instantly, making all the added detail of no consequence. The hair was light, worn rather long, and brushed straight back from a high, wide forehead. The eyes were blue, and touched with an expression of gentle melancholy. The features were markedly Oriental in cast, but neither coarse nor sensual. In vivid contrast to the hair and eyes was the pointed beard upon the chin; for it was black as coal, yet by some quaint combination of the artist's pigments it seemed to hide blue lights within its sable depths. Looking from the blue-black beard to the sad blue eyes it seemed to me I saw a hint, the merest faint suggestion, of wolfish cruelty in the face.

"It is undoubtlessly he," de Grandin murmured as he gazed upon the portrait. "He fits poor Madame Sarah's description to a nicety. But where is he in person? We can not fight his picture; no, of course not."

Motioning us to wait, he snapped the light off and drew a pocket flashlight from his waistcoat. He tiptoed through the door, exploring the farther room by the beam of his searchlight, then rejoined us with a gesture of negation.

"He is not here," he announced softly; "but come with me, my friends, I would show you something."

He led the way to the adjoining chamber, which, in any other dwelling, would have been the bedroom. It was bare, utterly unfurnished, and as he flashed his light around the walls we saw, some three or four feet from the floor, a row of paw-prints, as though a beast had stood upon its hind legs and pressed its forefeet to the walls. And the prints were marked in reddish smears—blood.

"You see?" he asked, as though the answer to his question were apparent. "He has no bed; he needs none, for at night he is a wolf, and sleeps denned down upon the floor. Also, you observe, he has not lacked for provender—*le bon Dieu* grant it was the blood of animals that stained his claws!"

"But where is he?" asked Maxwell, fingering his pistol.

"*S-s-sh!*" warned the Frenchman. "I do not think that he is far away. The window, you observe her?"

"Well?"

"*Précisément.* She is a scant four feet from the ground, and overlooks the alley. Also, though she was once fitted with bars, they have been removed. Also, again, the sash is ready-raised. Is it not all perfect?"

"Perfect? For what?"

"For him, *parbleu!* For the werewolf's entrances and exits. He comes running down the alley, leaps agilely through the open window, and *voilà*, he is here. Or leaps out into the alleyway with a single bound, and goes upon his nightly hunts. He may return at any moment; it is well that we await him here."

The waiting minutes stretched interminably. The dark room where we crouched was lighted from time to time, then cast again into shadow, as the racing clouds obscured or unveiled the full moon's visage. At length, when I felt I could no longer stand the strain, a low, harsh growl from our four-footed companion brought us sharply to attention. In another moment we heard the soft patter-patter, scratch-scratch of a long-clawed beast running lightly on the pavement of the alleyway outside, and in a second more a dark form bulked against the window's opening and something landed upon the floor.

For a moment there was breathless silence; then: "*Bon soir, Monsieur Loup-garou*," de Grandin greeted in a pleasant voice. "You have unexpected visitors.

"Do not move," he added threateningly as a hardly audible growl sounded from the farther corner of the room and we heard the scraping of long nails upon the floor as the wolf-thing gathered for a spring; "there are three of us, and each one is armed. Your reign of terror draws to a close, *Monsieur.*"

A narrow, dazzling shaft of light shot from his pocket torch, clove through the gloom and picked the crouching wolf-thing's form out of the darkness. Fangs bared, black lips drawn back in bestial fury, the gaunt, gray thing was backed into the corner, and from its open jaws we saw a thin trickle of slabber mixed with blood. It had been feeding, so much was obvious. "But what had been its food?" I wondered with a shudder.

"It is your shot, Friend Jean," the little Frenchman spoke. "Take careful aim and do not jerk the pistol when you fire." He held his flashlight steadily upon the beast, and a second later came the roar of Maxwell's pistol.

The acrid smoke stung in our nostrils, the reverberation of the detonation almost deafened us, and—a little fleck of plaster fell down from the wall where Maxwell's bullet was harmlessly embedded.

"Ten thousand stinking camels!" Jules de Grandin cried, but got no further, for with a maddened, murderous growl the wolf-man sprang, his lithe body describing a graceful arc as it hurtled through the air, his cruel, white fangs flashing terribly as he leaped upon John Maxwell and bore him to the floor before he could fire a second shot.

"*Nom de Dieu de nom de Dieu de nom de Dieu!*" de Grandin swore, playing his flashlight upon the struggling man and brute and leaping forward, seeking for a chance to use his pistol.

But to shoot the wolf would have meant that he must shoot the man, as well; for the furry body lay upon the struggling Maxwell, and as they thrashed and wrestled on the floor it was impossible to tell, at times, in the uncertain light, which one was man and which was beast.

Then came a deep, low growl of pent-up, savage fury, almost an articulate curse, it seemed to me, and like a streak of silver-plated vengeance the little she-wolf leaped upon the gray-brown brute which growled and worried at the young man's throat.

We saw the white teeth bared, we saw them flesh themselves in the wolf-thing's shoulder, we saw her loose her hold, and leap back, avoiding the great wolf's counter-stroke, then close with it again, sinking needle-fangs in the furry ruff about its throat.

The great wolf shook her to and fro, battered her against the walls and floor as a vicious terrier mistreats a luckless rat, but she held on savagely, though we saw her left forepaw go limp and knew the bone was broken.

De Grandin watched his chance, crept closer, closer, till he almost straddled the contending beasts; then, darting forth his hand he put his pistol to the tawny-gray wolf's ear, squeezed the trigger and leaped back.

A wild, despairing wail went up, the great, gray form seemed suddenly to stiffen, to grow longer, heavier, to shed its fur and thicken in limbs and body-structure. In a moment, as we watched the horrid transformation, we beheld a human form stretched out upon the floor; the body of a handsome man with fair hair and black beard, at the throat of which a slender silver-gray she-wolf was worrying.

"It is over, finished, little brave one," de Grandin announced, reaching out a hand to stroke the little wolf's pale fur. "Right nobly have you borne yourself this night; but we have much to do before our work is finished."

The she-wolf backed away, but the hair upon her shoulders was still bristling, and her topaz eyes were jewel-bright with the light of combat. Once or twice, despite de Grandin's hand upon her neck, she gave vent to throaty growls and started toward the still form which lay upon the floor in a pool of moonlight, another pool fast gathering beneath its head where de Grandin's bullet had crashed through its skull and brain.

John Maxwell moved and moaned a tortured moan, and instantly the little wolf was by his side, licking his cheeks with her pink tongue, emitting little pleading whines, almost like the whimpers of a child in pain.

When Maxwell regained consciousness it was pathetic to see the joy the wolf showed as he sat up and feebly put a groping hand against his throat.

"Not dead, my friend, you are not nearly dead, thanks to the bravery of your noble lady," de Grandin told him with a laugh. Then, to me:

"Do you go home with them, Friend Trowbridge. I must remain to dispose of this"—he prodded the inert form with his foot—"and will be with you shortly.

"Be of good cheer, *ma pauvre*," he told the she-wolf, "you shall be soon released from the spell which binds you; I swear it; though never need you be ashamed of what you did this night, whatever form you might have had while doing it."

John Maxwell sat upon the divan, head in hands, the wolf crouched at his feet, her broken paw dangling pitifully, her topaz eyes intent upon his face. I paced restlessly before the fire. De Grandin had declared he knew how to release her from the spell—but what if he should fail? I shuddered at the thought. What booted it that we had killed the man-wolf if Sarah must be bound in wolfish form henceforth?

"*Tiens* my friends," de Grandin announced himself at the library door, "he took a lot of disposing of, that one. First I had to clean the blood from off his bedroom floor, then I must lug his filthy carcass out into the alley and dispose of it as though it had been flung there from a racing motor. Tomorrow I doubt not the papers will make much of the mysterious murder. 'A gangster put upon the spot by other gangsters,' they will say. And shall we point out their mistake? I damn think no."

He paused with a self-satisfied chuckle; then: "Friend Jean, will you be good enough to go and fetch a negligee for Madame Sarah?" he asked. "Hurry, *mon vieux*, she will have need of it anon."

As the young man left us: "Quick, my friends," he ordered. "You, Madame Sarah, lie upon the floor before the fire, thus. *Bien*.

"Friend Trowbridge, prepare bandages and splints for her poor arm. We can not set it now, but later we must do so. Certainly.

"Now, my little brave one," he addressed the wolf again, "this will hurt you sorely, but only for a moment."

Drawing a small flask from his pocket he pulled the cork and poured its contents over her.

"It's holy water," he explained as she whined and shivered as the liquid soaked into her fur. "I had to stop to steal it from a church."

A knife gleamed in the firelight, and he drove the gleaming blade into her head, drew it forth and shook it toward the fire, so that a drop of blood fell hissing in the leaping flames. Twice more he cut her with the knife, and twice more dropped her blood into the fire; then, holding the knife lightly by the handle, he struck her with the flat of the blade between the ears three times in quick succession, crying as he did so: "Sarah Maxwell, I command that you once more assume your native form in the name of the Most Holy Trinity!"

A shudder passed through the wolf's frame. From nose to tail-tip she trembled, as though she lay in her death agony; then suddenly her outlines seemed to blur. Pale fur gave way to paler flesh, her dainty lupine paws became dainty human hands and feet, her body was no more that of a wolf, but of a soft, sweet woman.

But life seemed to have gone from her. She lay flaccid on the hearth rug, her mouth a little open, eyes closed, no movement of her breast perceptible. I looked at her with growing consternation, but:

"Quickly, my friends, the splints, the bandages!" de Grandin ordered.

I set the broken arm as quickly as I could, and as I finished young John Maxwell rushed into the room.

"Sallie, beloved!" he fell beside his wife's unconscious form, tears streaming down his face.

"Is she—is she—" he began, but could not force himself to finish, as he looked imploringly at Jules de Grandin.

"Dead?" the little man supplied. "By no means; not at all, my friend. She is alive and healthy. A broken arm mends quickly, and she has youth and stamina. Put on her robe and bear her up to bed. She will do excellently when she has had some sleep.

"But first observe this, if you please," he added, pointing to her side. Where the cicatrix with its tuft of wolf-hair had marred her skin, there was now only smooth, unspotted flesh. "The curse is wholly lifted," he declared delightedly. "You need no more regard it, except as an unpleasant memory."

"John, dear," we heard the young wife murmur as her husband bore her from the room, "I've had such a terrible dream. I dreamed that I'd been turned into a wolf, and—"

"Come quickly, good Friend Trowbridge," de Grandin plucked me by the arm. "I, too, would dream."

"Dream? Of what?" I asked him.

"Perchance of youth and love and springtime, and the joys that might have been," he answered, something like a tremble in his voice. "And then, again, perchance of snakes and toads and elephants, all of most unauthentic color—such things as one may see when he has drunk himself into the blissful state of delirium tremens. I do not surely know that I can drink that much, but may the Devil bake me if I do not try!"

The Hand of Glory

1. The Shrieking Woman

"Th' tip o' th' marnin' to yez, gintlemen." Officer Collins touched the vizor of his cap as Jules de Grandin and I rounded the corner with none too steady steps. The night was cold, and our host's rum punch had a potency peculiarly its own, which accounted for our decision to walk the mile or so which stretched between us and home.

"*Holà, mon brave*," responded my companion, now as ever ready to stop and chat with any member of the gendarmerie. "It is morning, you say? *Ma foi*, I had not thought it much past ten o'clock."

Collins grinned appreciatively. "Arrah, Doctor de Grandin, sor," he answered, "wid a bit o' th' crayter th' likes o' that ye've had, 'tis meself as wouldn't be bodderin' wid th' time o' night, ayther, fer—"

His witticism died birth-strangled, for, even as he paused to guffaw at the intended thrust, there came stabbing through the pre-dawn calm a cry of such thin-edged, unspeakable anguish as I had not heard since the days when as an intern I rode an ambulance's tail and amputations often had to be performed without the aid of anesthesia.

"*Bon Dieu!*" de Grandin cried, dropping my elbow and straightening with the suddenness of a coiled spring released from its tension. "What is that, in pity's gracious name?"

His answer followed fast upon his question as a pistol's crack succeeds the powder-flash, for round the shoulder of the corner building came a girl on stumbling, fear-hobbled feet, arms spread, eyes wide, mouth opened for a scream which would not come, a perfect fantasm of terror.

"Here, here, now, phwat's up?" demanded Collins gruffly, involuntary fright lending harshness to his tones. "'Tis a foin thing ye're after doin', runnin' through th' strates in yer nighties, scarin' folks out o' their sivin senses, an'—"

The woman paid him no more heed than if he'd been a shadow, for her dilated eyes were blinded by extremity of fear, as we could see at a glance, and had de Grandin not seized her by the shoulder she would have passed us in her headlong, stumbling flight. At the touch of the Frenchman's hand she halted suddenly, swayed uncertainly a moment; then, like a marionette whose strings are cut, she buckled suddenly, fell half kneeling, I half sprawling to the sidewalk and lifted trembling hands to him beseechingly.

"It was afire!" she babbled thickly. "Afire—blazing, I tell you—and the door flew open when they held it out. They—they—*aw-wah-wah!*—" her words degenerated into unintelligible syllables as the tautened muscles of her throat contracted with a nervous spasm, leaving her speechless as an infant, her thin face a white wedge of sheer terror.

"D.T.'s, sor?" asked Collins cynically, bending for a better view of the trembling woman.

"Hysteria," denied de Grandin shortly. Then, to me:

"Assist me, Friend Trowbridge, she goes into the paroxysmal stage." As he uttered the sharp warning the woman sank face-downward to the pavement, lay motionless a moment, then trembled with convulsive shudders, the shudders becoming twitches and the twitches going into wild, abandoned gestures, horribly reminiscent of the reflex contortions of a decapitated fowl.

"Good Lord, I'll call the wagon," Collins offered; but:

"A cab, and quickly, if you please," de Grandin countermanded. "This is no time for making of arrests, my friend; this poor one's sanity may depend upon our ministrations."

Luckily, a cruising taxi hove in sight even as he spoke, and with a hasty promise to inform police headquarters of the progress of the case, we bundled our patient into the vehicle and rushed at breakneck speed toward my office.

"Morphine, quickly, if you please," de Grandin ordered as he bore the struggling woman to my surgery, thrust her violently upon the examination table and drew up the sleeve of her georgette pajama jacket, baring the white flesh for the caress of the mercy-bearing needle.

Swabbing the skin with alcohol, I pinched the woman's trembling arm, inserted the hypo point in the folded skin and thrust the plunger home, driving a full three-quarter grain dose into her system; then, with refilled syringe, stood in readiness to repeat the treatment if necessary.

But the opiate took effect immediately. Almost instantly the clownish convulsions ceased, within a minute the movements of her arms and legs had subsided to mere tremblings, and the choking, anguished moans which had proceeded from her throat died to little, childish whimpers.

"Ah, so," de Grandin viewed the patient with satisfaction. "She will be better now, I think. Meantime, let us prepare some stimulant for the time of her awakening. She has been exposed, and we must see that she does not take cold."

Working with the speed and precision of one made expert by long service in the war's field hospitals, he draped a steamer rug across the back of an easy-chair in the study, mixed a stiff dose of brandy and hot water and set it by the open fire; then, calm-eyed but curious, resumed his station beside the unconscious girl upon the table.

We had not long to wait. The opiate had done its work quickly, but almost as quickly had found its antidote in the intensely excited nervous system of the patient. Within five minutes her eyelids fluttered, and her head rolled from side to side, like that of a troubled sleeper. A little moan, half of discomfort, half involuntary protest at returning consciousness, escaped from her.

"You are in the office of Doctor Samuel Trowbridge, *Mademoiselle*," de Grandin announced in a low, calm voice, anticipating the question which nine patients out of ten propound when recovering from a swoon. "We found you in the street in a most deplorable condition and brought you here for treatment. You are better now? Good. *Permettez-moi.*"

Taking her hands in his, he raised her from the table, eased her to the floor and, his arms about her waist, guided her gently to the study, where, with the adeptness of a deck steward, he tucked the steamer rug about her feet and knees, placed a cushion at her back and before she had a chance to speak, held the glass of steaming toddy to her lips.

She drank the torrid liquid greedily, like a starving child gulping at a goblet of warm milk; then, as the potent draft raced through her, leaving a faint flush on her dead-pale cheeks, gave back the glass and viewed us with a pathetic, drowsy little smile.

"Thank you," she murmured. "I—oh, I remember now!" Abruptly her half-somnolent manner vanished and her hands clutched claw-like at the chair-arms. "It was afire!" she told us in a hushed, choking voice. "It was blazing, and—"

"*Mademoiselle!* You will drink this, if you please!" Sharply, incisively, the Frenchman's command cut through her fearful utterance as he held forward a cordial glass half full of cloudy liquid.

Startled but docile, she obeyed, and a look of swift bewilderment swept across her pale, peaked features as she finished drinking. "Why"—she exclaimed— "why—" Her voice sank lower, her lids closed softly and her head fell back against the cushion at her shoulders.

"*Voilà*, I feared that recollection might unsettle her and had it ready," he announced. "Do you go up to bed, my friend. Me, I shall watch beside her, and should I need you I shall call. I am inured to sleeplessness and shall not mind the vigil, but it is well that one of us has rest, for tomorrow—*eh bien*, this poor one's case has the smell of herring on it and I damn think that we shall have more sleepless nights than one before we see the end of it."

Murmuring, I obeyed. Delightful companion, thoughtful friend, indefatigable co-worker that he was, Jules de Grandin possessed a streak of stubbornness beside which the most refractory mule ever sired in the State of Missouri was docility personified, and I knew better than to spend the few remaining hours of darkness in fruitless argument.

2. The Hand of Glory

A gentle murmur of voices sounded from the study when I descended from my room after something like four hours' sleep. Our patient of the night before still sat swathed in rugs in the big wing chair, but something approximating normal color had returned to her lips and cheeks, and though her hands fluttered now and again in tremulous gesticulation as she talked, it required no second glance to tell me that her condition was far from bordering on nervous collapse. "Taut, but not stretched dangerously near the snapping-point," I diagnosed as I joined them. De Grandin reclined at ease across the fire from her, a pile of burned-out cigarettes in the ash-tray beside him, smoke from a freshly lighted Maryland slowly spiraling upward as he waved his hand back and forth to emphasize his words.

"What you tell is truly interesting, *Mademoiselle*," he was assuring her as I entered the study.

"'Trowbridge, *mon vieux*, this is Mademoiselle Wickwire. *Mademoiselle*, my friend and colleague, Doctor Samuel Trowbridge. Will you have the goodness to repeat your story to him? I would rather that he had it from your own lips."

The girl turned a wan smile toward me, and I was struck by her extreme slenderness. Had her bones been larger, she would have been distressfully thin; as it was the covering of her slight skeletal structure was so scanty as to make her almost as ethereal as a sprite. Her hair was fair, her eyes of an indeterminate shade somewhere between true blue and amethyst, and their odd coloration was picked up and accentuated by a chaplet of purple stones about her slender throat and the purple settings of the rings she wore upon the third finger of each hand. Limbs and extremities were fine-drawn as silver wire and elongated to an extent which was just short of grotesque, while her profile was robbed of true beauty by its excessive clarity of line. Somehow, she reminded me more of a statuette carved from crystal than of a flesh-and-blood woman, while the georgette pajamas of sea-green trimmed with amethyst and the absurd little boudoir cap which perched on one side of her fair head helped lend her an air of tailor's-dummy unreality.

I bowed acknowledgment of de Grandin's introduction and waited expectantly for her narrative, prepared to cancel ninety percent of all she told me as the vagary of an hysterical young woman.

"Doctor de Grandin tells me I was screaming that 'it was burning' when you found me in the street last night," she began without preamble. "It was."

"Eh?" I ejaculated, turning a quick glance of inquiry on de Grandin. "What?"

"The hand."

"Bless my soul! The *what?*"

"The hand," she returned with perfect aplomb. Then: "My father is Joseph Wickwire, former Horner Professor of Orientology and Ancient Religion at De Puy University. You know his book, *The Cult of the Witch in Assyria?*"

I shook my head, but the girl, as though anticipating my confession of ignorance, went on without pause:

"I don't understand much about it, for Father never troubled to discuss his studies with me, but from some things he's told me, he became convinced of the reality of ancient witchcraft—or magic—some years ago, and gave up his chair at De Puy to devote himself to private research. While I was at school he made several trips to the Near East and last year spent four months in Mesopotamia, supervising some excavations. He came home with two big cases—they looked more like casket-boxes than anything else—which he took to his study, and since then no one's been allowed in the room, not even I or Fanny, our maid. Father won't permit anything, not even so much as a grain of dust, to be taken from that room; and one of the first things he did after receiving those boxes was to have an iron-plated door made for the study and have heavy iron bars fitted to all the windows.

"Lately he's been spending practically all his time at work in the study, sometimes remaining there for two or three days at a time, refusing to answer when called to meals or to come out for rest or sleep. About a month ago something happened which upset him terribly. I think it was a letter he received, though I'm not sure, for he wouldn't tell me what it was; but he seemed distracted, muttering constantly to himself and looking over his shoulder every now and then as though he expected some one, or something, to attack him from behind. Last week he had some workmen come and reinforce all the doors with inch-wide strips of cast iron. Then he had special combination locks fitted to the outside doors and Yale locks to all the inside ones, and every night, just at dusk, he sets the combinations, and no one may enter or leave the house till morning. It's been rather like living in prison."

"More like a madhouse," I commented mentally, looking at the girl's thin face with renewed interest. "Delusions of persecution on the part of the parent might explain abnormal behavior on the part of the offspring, if—"

The girl's recital broke in on my mental diagnosis: "Last night I couldn't sleep. I'd gone to bed about eleven and slept soundly for an hour or so; then suddenly I sat up, broad awake, and nothing I could do would get me back to sleep. I tried bathing the back of my neck with cologne, turning my pillows, even taking ten grains of allonal; nothing was any good, so finally I gave up trying and went down to the library. There was a copy of Hallam's *Constitutional History of England* there, and I picked that out as being the dullest reading I could find, but I read over a hundred pages without the slightest sign of drowsiness. Then I decided to take the book upstairs. Possibly, I thought, if I tried reading it in bed I might drop off without realizing it.

"I'd gotten as far as the second floor—my room's on the third—and was almost in front of Father's study when I heard a noise at the front door. 'Any burglar who tries breaking into this house will be wasting his talents,' I remember saying to myself, when, just as though they were being turned by an invisible hand, the dials of the combination lock started to spin. I could see them in the light of the hall ceiling-lamp, which Father insists always be kept burning, and they were turned not slowly, but swiftly, as though being worked by one who knew the combination perfectly.

"At the same time the queerest feeling came over me. It was like one of those dreadful nightmares people sometimes have, when they're being attacked or pursued by some awful monster, and can't run or cry out, or even *move*. There I stood, still as a marble image, every faculty alert, but utterly unable to make a sound or move a finger—or even wink an eye.

"And as I watched in helpless stillness, the front door swung back silently and two men entered the hall. One carried a satchel or suitcase of some sort, the other"—she paused and caught her breath like a runner nearly spent, and her voice sank to a thin, harsh whisper—"the other was holding a blazing hand in front of him!"

"A *what?*" I demanded incredulously. There was no question in my mind that the delusions of the sire were ably matched by the hallucinations of the daughter.

"A blazing hand," she answered, and again I saw the shudder of a nervous chill run through her slender frame. "He held it forward, like a candle, as though to light his way; but there was no need of it for light, for the hall lamp has a hundred-watt bulb, and its luminance reached up the stairs and made everything in the upper passage plainly visible. Besides, the thing burned with more fire than light. There seemed to be some sort of wick attached to each of the fanned-out fingers, and these burned with a clear, steady blue flame, like blazing alcohol. It—"

"But my dear young lady," I expostulated, "that's impossible."

"Of course it is," she agreed with unexpected calmness. "So is this: As the man with the blazing hand mounted the stairs and paused before my father's study, I heard a distinct *click*, and the door swung open, unlocked. Through the opening I could see Father standing in the middle of the room, the light from an unshaded ceiling-lamp making everything as clear as day. On a long table was some sort of object which reminded me of one of those little marble stones they put over soldiers' graves in national cemeteries, only it was gray instead of white, and a great roll of manuscript lay beside it. Father had risen and stood facing the door with one hand resting on the table, the other reaching toward a sawed-off shotgun which lay beside the stone and manuscript. But he was paralyzed—frozen in the act of reaching for the gun as I had been in the act of walking down the hall. His eyes were wide and set with surprise—no, not quite that, they were more like the painted eyes of a window-figure in a store, utterly expressionless—and I remember wondering, in that odd way people have of thinking of inconsequential things in moments of intense excitement, whether mine looked the same.

"I saw it all. I saw them go through the study's open door, lift the stone off the table, bundle up Father's manuscript and stuff everything into the bag. Then, the man with the burning hand going last, walking backward and holding the thing before him, they left as silently as they came. The doors swung to behind them without being touched. The study door had a Yale snap-lock in addition to its combination fastenings, so it was fastened when it closed, but the bolts of the safe lock on the front door didn't fly back in place when it closed.

"I don't know how long that strange paralysis held me after the men with the hand had gone; but I remember suddenly regaining my power of motion and finding myself with one foot raised—I'd been overcome in the act of stepping and had remained helpless, balanced on one foot, the entire time. My first act, of course, was to call Father, but I could get no response, even when I beat and kicked on the door.

"Then panic seized me. I didn't quite know what I was doing, but something seemed urging me to get away from that house as though it had been haunted, and the horrifying memory of that blazing hand with those combination-locked doors flying open before it came down on me like a cloud of strangling, smothering gas. The front door was still unfastened, as I've told you, and I flung it open, fighting for a breath of fresh outdoors air, and—ran screaming into the street. You know the rest."

"You see?" asked Jules de Grandin.

I nodded understandingly. I saw only too well. A better symptomatized case of dementia praecox it had never been my evil fortune to encounter.

There was a long moment of silence, broken by de Grandin. "*Eh bien, mes amis*, we make no progress here," he announced. "Grant me fifteen small minutes for my toilette, *Mademoiselle*, and we shall repair to the house of your father. There, I make no doubt, we shall learn something of interest concerning last night's so curious events."

He was as good as his promise, and within the stipulated time had rejoined us, freshly shaved, washed and brushed, a most agreeable odor of bath salts and dusting-powder emanating from his spruce, diminutive person.

"Come, let us go," he urged, assisting our patient to her feet and wrapping the steamer rug about her after the manner of an Indian's blanket.

3. The House of the Magician

The front entrance of Professor Wickwire's house was closed, but unfastened, when we reached our destination, and I looked with interest at the formidable iron reinforcements and combination locks upon the door. Thus far the girl's absurd story was borne out by facts, I was forced to admit, as we mounted the stairs to the upper floor where Wickwire had his barricaded sanctum.

No answer coming to de Grandin's peremptory summons, Miss Wickwire tapped lightly on the iron-bound panels. "Father, it is I, Diane," she called.

Somewhere beyond the door we heard a shuffling step and a murmuring voice, then a listless fumbling at the locks which held the portal fast.

The man who stood revealed as the heavy door swung back looked like a Fundamentalist cartoonist's caricature of Charles Darwin. The pate was bald, the jaw bearded, the brows heavy and prominent, but where the great evolutionist's forehead bulged with an intellectual swell, this man's skull slanted back obliquely, and the temples were flat, rather than concave. Also, it required no second glance to tell us that the full beard covered a soft, receding chin, and the eyes beneath the shaggy brows were weak with a weakness due to more than mere poor vision. He looked to me more like the sort of person who would spend spare time reading books on development of willpower and personality than poring over ponderous tomes on Assyriology. And though he seemed possessed of full dentition, he mumbled like a toothless ancient as he stared at us, feeble eyes blinking owlishly behind the pebbles of his horn-rimmed spectacles.

"*Magna Mater* . . . *trismegistus* . . . *salve* . . ." we caught the almost unintelligible Latin of his mumbled incantation.

"Father!" Diane Wickwire exclaimed in distress. "Father, here are—"

The man's head rocked insanely from side to side, as though his neck had been a flaccid cord, and: "*Magna Mater* . . ." he began again with a whimpering persistence.

"*Monsieur!* Stop it. I command it, and I am Jules de Grandin!" Sharply the little Frenchman's command rang out; then, as the other goggled at him and began his muttered prayer anew, de Grandin raised his small gloved hand and dealt him a stinging blow across the face. "*Parbleu*, I will be obeyed, me!" he snorted wrathfully. "Save your conjurations for another time, *Monsieur*; at present we would talk with you."

Brutal as his treatment was, it was efficacious. The blow acted like a douche of cold water on a swooning person, and Wickwire seemed for the first time to realize we were present.

"These gentlemen are Doctors Trowbridge and de Grandin," his daughter introduced. "I met them when I ran for help last night, and they took me with them. Now, they are here to help you—"

Wickwire stopped her with uplifted hand. "I fear there's no help for me—or you, my child," he interrupted sadly. "They have the Sacred Meteorite, and it is only a matter of time till they find the Word of Power, then—"

"*Nom d'un coq, Monsieur*, let us have things logically and in decent order, if you please," de Grandin broke in sharply. "This sacred meteorite, this word of powerfulness, this so mysterious 'they' who have the one and are about to have the other, in Satan's name, who and what are they? Tell us from the start of the beginning. We are intrigued, we are interested; *parbleu*, we are consumed with the curiosity of a dying cat!"

Professor Wickwire smiled at him, the weary smile a tired adult might give a curious child. "I fear you wouldn't understand," he answered softly.

"By blue, you do insult my credulity, *Monsieur!*" the Frenchman rejoined hotly. "Tell us your tale, all—every little so small bit of it—and let us be the judges of what we shall believe. Me, I am an occultist of no small ability, and this so strange adventure of last night assuredly has the flavor of the superphysical. Yes, certainly."

Wickwire brightened at the other's words. "An occultist?" he echoed. "Then perhaps you can assist me. Listen carefully, if you please, and ask me anything which you may not understand:

"Ten years ago, while assembling data for my book on witchcraft in the ancient world, I became convinced of the reality of sorcery. If you know anything at all of mediæval witchcraft, you realize that Diana was the patroness of the witches, even in that comparatively late day, Burchard, Bishop of Worms, writing of sorcery, heresy and witchcraft in Germany in the year 1000 says: 'Certain wretched women, seduced by the sorcery of demons, affirm that during the night they ride with Diana, goddess of the heathens, and a host of other women, and that they traverse immense spaces.'

"Now, Diana, whom most moderns look upon as a clean-limbed goddess of chastity, was only one name for the great Female Principle among the pantheon of ancient days. Artemis, or Diana, is typified by the moon, but there is also Hecate, goddess of the black and fearful night, queen of magic, sorcery and witchcraft, deity of goblins and the underworld and guardian of crossroads; she was another attribute of the same night-goddess whom we know best today as Diana.

"But back of all the goddesses of night, whether they be styled Diana, Artemis, Hecate, Rhea, Astarte or Ishtar, is the Great Mother—*Magna Mater*. The origin of her cult is so ancient that recorded history does not even touch it, and even oral tradition tells of it only by indirection. Her worship is so old that the Anatolian meteorite brought to Rome in 204 b.c. compares to it as Christian Science or New Thought compare in age with Buddhism.

"Piece by piece I traced back the chain of evidence of her worship and finally became convinced that it was not in Anatolia at all that her mother-shrine was located, but in some obscure spot, so many centuries forgotten as to be no longer named, near the site of the ancient city of Uruck. An obscure Roman legionary mentions the temple where the goddess he refers to by the Syro-Phœnician name of Astarte was worshipped by a select coterie of adepts, both men and women, to whom she gave dominion over earth and sea and sky—power to raise tempests or to quiet them, to cause earthquakes, to cause fertility or sterility in men and beasts, or cause the illness or death of an enemy. They were also said to have the power of levitation, or flying through the air for great distances, or even to be seen in several places at the same time. This, you see, is about the sum total of all the powers claimed for witches and wizards in mediæval times. In fine, this obscure goddess of our nameless centurion is the earliest ascertainable manifestation of the female divinity who governed witchcraft in the ancient world, and whose place has been usurped by the Devil in Christian theology.

"But this was only the beginning: The Roman chronicler stated definitely that her idol was a 'stone from heaven, wrapped in an envelope of earth,' and that no man durst break the tegument of the celestial stone for fear of rousing Astarte's wrath; yet to him who had the courage to do so would be given the *Verbum Magnum*, or Word of Power—an incantation whereby all majesty, might, power and dominion of all things visible and invisible would be put into his hands, so that he who knew the word would be, literally, Emperor of the Universe.

"As I said before, I became convinced of the reality of witchcraft, both ancient and modern, and the deeper I delved into the records of the past the more convinced I was that the greatest claims made by latter-day witches were mere childish nonsense compared to the mighty powers actually possessed by the wizards of olden times. I spent my health and bankrupted myself seeking that nameless temple of Astarte—but at last *I found it*. I found the very stone of which the Roman wrote and brought it back to America—here."

Wickwire paused, breathing in labored gasps, and his pale eyes shone with the quenchless ardor of the enthusiast as he looked triumphantly from one of us to the other.

"*Bien, Monsieur*, this stone of the old one is brought here; what then?" de Grandin asked as the professor showed no sign of proceeding further with his narrative.

"Eh? Oh, yes." Once more Wickwire lapsed into semisomnolence. "Yes, I brought it back, and was preparing to unwrap it, studying my way carefully, of course, in order to avoid being blasted by the goddess' infernal powers when I broke the envelope, but—but they came last night and stole it."

"*Bon sang d'un bon poisson*, must we drag information from you bit by little bit, *Monsieur?*" blazed the exasperated Jules de Grandin. "Who was it pilfered your unmentionable stone?"

"Kraus and Steinert stole it," Wickwire answered tonelessly. "They are German *illuminati*, Hanoverians whose researches paralleled mine in almost every particular, and who discovered the approximate location of the mystic meteorite shortly after I did. Fortunately for me their data were not so complete as mine, and they lost some time trying to locate the ancient temple. I had dug up the stone and was on my way home when they finally found the place.

"Can you imagine what it would mean to any mortal man to be suddenly translated into godhood, to sway the destinies of nations—of all mankind—as a wind sways a wheatfield? If you can, you can imagine what those two adepts in black magic felt when they arrived and found the key to power gone and on its way to America in the possession of a rival. They sent astral messengers after me, first offering partnership, then, when I laughed at them, making all manner of threats. Several times they attempted my life, but my magic was stronger than theirs, and each time I beat their spirit-messengers off.

"Lately, though, their emissaries have been getting stronger. I began to realize this when I found myself weaker and weaker after each encounter. Whether they have found new sources of strength, or whether it is because two of them work against me I do not know, but I began to realize we were becoming more evenly matched and it was only a matter of time before they would master me. Yet there was much to be done before I dared remove the envelope from that stone; to attempt it unprepared would be fool-hardy. Such forces as would be unleashed by the cracking of that wrapping are beyond the scope of human imagining, and every precaution had go be taken. Any dunce can blow himself up handling gunpowder carelessly; only the skilled artillerist can harness the explosive and make it drive a projectile to a given target.

"While I was perfecting my spiritual defenses I took all physical precautions, also, barring my windows and so securing my doors that if my enemies gave up the battle of magic in disgust and fell back upon physical force, I should be more than a match for them. Then, because I thought myself secure, for a little time at least, I overlooked one of the most elementary forms of sorcery, and last night they entered my house as though there had been no barriers and took away the magic stone. With that in their possession I shall be no match for them; they will work their will on me, then overwhelm the world with the forces of their wizardry. If only—"

"Excuse me, Professor," I broke in, for, wild as his story was, I had become interested despite myself; "what was the sorcery these men resorted to in order to force entrance? Your daughter told us something of a blazing hand, but—"

"It was a hand of glory," he returned, regarding me with something of the look a teacher might bestow upon a backward schoolboy, "one of the oldest, simplest bits of magic known to adepts. A hand—preferably the sinister—is cut from the body of an executed murderer, and five locks of hair are clipped from his head. The hand is smoked over a fire of juniper wood until it becomes dry and mummified; after this the hair is twisted into wicks which are affixed to the finger tips. If the proper invocations are recited while the hand and wicks are being prepared and the words of power pronounced when the wicks are lighted, no lock can withstand the light cast by the blazing glory hand, and—"

"*Ha*, I remember him," de Grandin interrupted delightedly. "Your so droll Abbé Barham tells of him in his exquisitely humorous poem:

Now open lock to the dead man's knock,
Fly bolt and bar and band;
Nor move nor swerve joint, muscle or nerve,
At the spell of the dead man's hand.
Sleep all who sleep, wake all who wake,
But be as the dead for the dead man's sake.

Wickwire nodded grimly. "There's a lot of truth in those doggerel rimes," he answered. "We laugh at the fairy-story of Bluebeard today, but it was no joke in fifteenth century France when Bluebeard was alive and making black magic."

"*Tu parles, mon vieux*," agreed de Grandin, "and—"

"Excuse me, but you've spoken several times of removing the envelope from this stone, Professor," I broke in again. "Do you mean that literally, or—"

"Literally," Wickwire responded. "In Babylonia and Assyria, you know, all 'documents' were clay tablets on which the cuneiform characters were cut while they were still moist and soft, and which were afterward baked in a kiln. Tablets of special importance, after having been once written upon and baked, were covered with a thin coating of clay upon which an identical inscription was impressed, and the tablets were once more baked. If the outer writing were then defaced by accident or altered by design, the removal of the outer coating would at once show the true text. Such a clay coating has been wrapped about the mystic meteorite of the Great Mother-Goddess, but even in the days of the Roman historian most of the inscription had been obliterated by time. When I found it I could distinguish only one or two characters, such as the double triangle, signifying the moon, and the eight-pointed asterisks meaning the lord of lords and god of gods, or lady of ladies and goddess of goddesses. These, I may add, were not in the Assyrian cuneiforms of 700 b.c. or even the archaic characters dating back to 2500, but the early, primitive cuneiform, which was certainly not used later than 4500 b.c., probably several centuries earlier."

"And how did you propose removing the clay integument without hurt to yourself, *Monsieur?*" de Grandin asked.

Wickwire smiled, and there was something devilish, callous, in his expression as be did so. "Will you be good enough to examine my daughter's rings?" he asked.

Obedient to his nodded command, the girl stretched forth her thin, frail hands, displaying the purple settings of the circlets which adorned the third finger of each. The stones were smoothly polished, though not very bright, and each was deeply incised with this inscription:

"It's the ancient symbol of the Mother-Goddess," Wickwire explained, "and signifies 'Royal Lady of the Night, Ruler of the Lights of Heaven, Mother of Gods, Men and Demons.' Diane would have racked the envelope for me, for only the hands of a virgin adorned with rings of amethyst bearing the Mother-Goddess' signet can wield the hammer which can break that clay—and the maid must do the act without fear or hesitation; otherwise she will be powerless."

"U'm?" de Grandin twisted fiercely at his little blond mustache. "And what becomes of this ring-decorated virgin, *Monsieur?*"

Again that smile of fiendish indifference transformed Wickwire's weak face into a mask of horror. "She would die," he answered calmly. "That, of course, is certain, but"—some lingering light of parental sanity broke through the look of wild fanaticism—"unless she were utterly consumed by the tremendous forces liberated when the envelope was cracked, I should have power to restore her to life, for all power, might, dominion and majesty in the world would have been mine; death should bow before me, and life should exist only by my sanction. I—"

"You are a scoundrel and a villain and a most unpleasant species of a malodorous camel," cut in Jules de Grandin.

"*Mademoiselle*, you will kindly pack a portmanteau and come with us. We shall esteem it a privilege to protect you till danger from those *sales bêtes* who invaded your house last night is past."

Without a word, or even a glance at the man who would have sacrificed her to his ambition, Diane Wickwire left the room, and we heard the clack-clack of her bedroom mules as she ascended to her chamber to procure a change of clothing.

Professor Wickwire turned a puzzled look from de Grandin to me, then back to the Frenchman. That we could not understand and sympathize with his ambition and condone his willingness to sacrifice his daughter's life never seemed to enter his mad brain. "But me—what's to become of me?" he whimpered.

"*Eh bien*, one wonders," answered Jules de Grandin. "As far as I am concerned, *Monsieur*, you may go to the Devil, nor need you delay your departure in anywise out of consideration for my feelings."

"**M**ad," I diagnosed. "Mad as hatters, both of 'em. The man's a potential homicidal maniac; only heaven knows how long it will be before we have to put the girl under restraint."

De Grandin looked cautiously about; then, satisfied that Diane Wickwire was still in the chamber to which she had been conducted by Nora McGinnis, my efficient household factotum, he replied: "You think that story of the glory hand was madness, *hein?*"

"Of course it was," I answered. "What else could it be?"

"*Le bon Dieu* knows, not I," he countered; "but I would that you read this item in today's *Journal* before consigning her to the madhouse." Picking up a copy of the morning paper he indicated a boxed item in the center of the first page:

> Police are seeking the ghouls who broke into James Gibson's funeral parlor, 1037 Ludlow St., early last night and stole the left hand from the body of José Sanchez, which was lying in the place awaiting burial today. Sanchez had been executed Monday night at Trenton for the murder of Robert Knight, caretaker in the closed Steptens iron foundry, last summer, and relatives had commissioned Gibson to bring the body to Harrisonville for interment.
>
> Gibson was absent on a call in the suburbs last night, and as his assistant, William Lowndes, was confined to bed at home by unexpected illness, had left the funeral parlor unattended, having arranged to have any telephone calls switched to his residence in Winthrop St. On his return he found a rear door of his establishment had been jimmied and the left hand of the executed murderer severed at the wrist.
>
> Strangely enough, the burglars had also shorn a considerable amount of hair from the corpse's head. A careful search of the premises failed to disclose anything else had been taken, and a quantity of money lying in the unlocked safe was untouched.

"Well!" I exclaimed, utterly nonplussed; but:

"*Non*," he denied shortly. "It is not at all well, my friend, it is most exceedingly otherwise. It is fiendish, it is diabolical: it is devilish. There are determined miscreants against whom we have set ourselves, and I damn think that we shall lose some sleep ere all is done. Yes."

4. The Sending

However formidable Professor Wickwire's rivals might have been, they gave no evidence of ferocity that I could see. Diane settled down comfortably in our midst, fitting perfectly into the quiet routine of the household, giving no trouble and making herself so generally agreeable that I was heartily glad of her presence. There is something comforting about the pastel shades of filmy dresses and white arms and shoulders gleaming softly in the candle-light at dinner. The melody of a well-modulated feminine voice, punctuated now and again with little rippling notes of quiet laughter, is more than vaguely pleasant to the bachelor ear, and as the time of our companionship lengthened I often found myself wondering if I should have had a daughter such as this to sit at table or before the fire with me if fate had willed it otherwise and my sole romance had ended elsewhere than an ivy-covered grave with low white headstone in St. Stephen's churchyard. One night I said as much to Jules de Grandin, and the pressure of his hand on mine was good to feel.

"*Bien*, my friend," he whispered, "who are we to judge the ways of heaven? The grass grows green above the lips you used to kiss—me, I do not know if she I loved is in the world or gone away. I only know that never may I stand beside her grave and look at it, for in that cloistered cemetery no man may come, and—eh, what is that? *Un chaton?*" Outside the window of the drawing-room, scarce heard above the shrieking of the boisterous April wind, there sounded a plaintive mew, as though some feline Wanderer begged entrance and a place before our fire.

Crossing the room, I drew aside the casement curtain, staining my eyes against the murky darkness. Almost level with my own, two eyes of glowing green looked through the pane, and another pleading miaul implored my charity.

"All right, Pussy, come in," I invited, drawing back the sash to permit an entrance for the little waif, and through the opening jumped a plump, soft-haired angora cat, black as Erebus, jade-eyed, velvet-pawed. For a moment it stood at gaze, as though doubtful of the worthiness of my abode to house one of its distinction; then, with a satisfied little cat-chuckle, it crossed the room, furry tail waving jauntily, came to halt before the fire and curled up on the hearth rug, where, with paws tucked demurely in and tail curled about its body, it lay blinking contentedly at the leaping flames and purring softly. A saucer of warm milk further cemented cordial relations, and another member was added to our household personnel.

The little cat, on which we had bestowed the name of Eric Brighteyes, at once attached himself to Diane Wickwire, and could hardly be separated from her. Toward de Grandin and me it showed disdainful tolerance. For Nora McGinnis it had supreme contempt.

It was the twenty-ninth of April, a raw, wet night when the thermometer gave the lie to the calendars assertion that spring had come. Three of us, de Grandin, Diane and I sat in the drawing-room. The girl seemed vaguely nervous and distraught, toying with her coffee cup, puffing at her cigarette, grinding out its fire against the ash-tray, then lighting another almost instantly. Finally she went to the piano and began to play. For a time she improvised softly, white fingers straying at random over the white keys; then, as though led by some subconscious urge for the solace of ecclesiastical music, she began the opening bars of Gounod's *Sanctus*:

Holy, Holy, Holy,
Lord God of Hosts,
Heaven and earth are full of Thy Glory . . .

The music ended on a sharply dissonant note and a gasp of horrified surprise broke the echoing silence as the player lifted startled fingers from the keys. We turned toward the piano, and:

"*Mon Dieu!*" exclaimed de Grandin. "Hell is unchained against us!"

The cat, which had been contentedly curled up on the piano's polished top, had risen and stood with arched back, bristling tail and gaping, blood-red mouth, gazing from blazing ice-green eyes at Diane with such a look of murderous hate as made the chills of sudden blind, unreasoning fear run rippling down my spine.

"Eric—Eric Brighteyes!" Diane extended a shaking hand to soothe the menacing beast, and in a moment it was its natural, gentle self again, its back still arched, but arched in seeming playfulness, rubbing its fluffy head against her fingers and purring softly with contented friendliness. "And did the horrid music hurt its eardrums? Well, Diane won't play it any more," the girl promised, taking the jet-black ball of fur into her arms and nursing it against her shoulder. Shortly afterward she said goodnight, and, the cat still cuddled in her arms, went up to bed.

"I hardly like the idea of her taking that brute up with her," I told de Grandin. "It's always seemed so kind and gentle, but—well"—I laughed uneasily—"when I saw it snarling at her just now I was heartily glad it wasn't any bigger."

"U'm," returned the Frenchman, looking up from his silent study of the fire, "one wonders."

"Wonders what?"

"Much, by blue. Come, let us go."

"Where?"

"Upstairs, *cordieu*, and let us step softly while we are about it."

De Grandin in the lead, we tiptoed to the upper floor and paused before the entrance to Diane's chamber. From behind the white-enameled panels came the sound of something like a sob; then, in a halting, faltering voice:

"Amen. Evil from us deliver but temptation into not us lead, and us against trespass who those forgive we as . . ."

"*Grand Dieu—la prière renversée!*" de Grandin cried, snatching savagely at the knob and dashing back the door.

Diane Wickwire knelt beside her bed, purple-ringed hands clasped before her, tears streaming down her cheeks, while slowly, haltingly, like one wrestling with the vocables of an unfamiliar tongue, she painfully repeated the Lord's Prayer backward.

And on the counterpane, it's black muzzle almost forced against her face, crouched the black cat. But now its eyes were not the cool jade-green which we had known; they were red as embers of a dying fire when blown to life by some swift draft of air, and on its feline face, in hellish parody of humanity, there was a *grin*, a smile as cold and menacing, yet wicked and triumphant as any mediæval artist ever painted on the lips of Satan!

We stood immovable a moment, taking in the tableau with a quickening gaze of horror, then:

"Say it, *Mademoiselle*, say it after me—*properly!*" commanded Jules de Grandin, raising his right hand to sign the cross above the girl's bowed head and beginning slowly and distinctly: "Our Father, which art in Heaven, hallowed be Thy name . . ."

A terrifying screech, a scream of unsupportable agony, as though it had been plunged into a blazing fire, broke from the cowering cat-thing on the bed. Its reddened eyes flashed savagely, and its gaping mouth showed gleaming, knife-sharp teeth as it turned its gaze from Diane Wickwire and fixed it on de Grandin. But the Frenchman paid no heed.

". . . and lead us not into temptation, but deliver us from evil. Amen," he finished the petition.

And Diane prayed with him. Catching her cue from his slowly spoken syllables, she repeated the prayer word by painful word, and at the end collapsed, a whimpering, flaccid thing, against the bedstead.

But the cat? It was gone. As the girl and Frenchman reached "Amen" the beast snarled savagely, gave a final spiteful hiss, and whirled about and bolted through the open window, vanishing into the night from which it had come a week before, leaving but the echo of its menacing sibilation and the memory of its dreadful transformation as mementoes of its visit.

"In heaven's name, what was it?" I asked breathlessly.

"A spy," he answered. "It was a sending, my old one, an emissary from those evil ones to whom we stand opposed."

"A—a sending?"

"Perfectly. Assist me with Mademoiselle Diane and I shall elucidate."

The girl was sobbing bitterly, trembling like a wind-shaken reed, but not hysterical, and a mild sedative was sufficient to enable her to sleep. Then, as we once more took our seats before the fire, de Grandin offered:

"I did not have suspicion of the cat, my friend. He seemed a natural animal, and as I like cats, I was his friend from the first. Indeed, it was not until tonight when he showed aversion for the sacred music that I first began to realize what I should have known from the beginning. He was a sending."

"Yes, you've said that before," I reminded him, "but what the devil is a 'sending'?"

"The crystallized, physicalized desires and passions of a sorcerer or wizard," he returned. "Somewhat—as the medium builds a semi-physical, semi-spiritual body out of that impalpability which we call psychoplasm or ectoplasm, so the skilled adept in magic can evoke a physical-seeming entity out of his wicked thoughts and send it where he will, to do his bidding and work his evil purposes. These ones against whom we are pitted, these burglar-thieves who entered Monsieur Wickwire's house with their accursed glory hand and stole away his unnamable stone of power are no good, my friend. No, certainly. On the contrary, they are all bad. They are drunk with lust for the power which they think will come into their hands when they have stripped the wrapping off that unmentionable stone. They know also, I should say, that Wickwire—may he eat turnips and drink water throughout eternity!—had ordained his daughter for the sacrifice, had chosen her for the rôle of envelope-stripper-off for that stone, and they accordingly desire to avail themselves of her services. To that end they evoke that seeming-cat and send it here, and it did work their will—conveyed their evil suggestions to the young girl's mind. She, who is all innocent of any knowledge of witchery or magic-mongering, was to be perverted; and right well the work was done, for tonight when she knelt to say her prayers she could not frame to pronounce them aright, but, was obliged perforce to pray witch-fashion."

"Witch-fashion?"

"But certainly. Of course. Those who have taken the vows of witchhood and signed their names in Satan's book of blackness are unable to pray like Christians from that time forward; they must repeat the holy words in reverse. Mademoiselle Diane, she is no professed witch, but I greatly fear she is infected by the virus. Already she was unable to pray like others, though when I said the prayer aright, she was still able to repeat it after me. Now—"

"Is there any way we can find these scoundrels and free Diane?" I interrupted. Not for a moment did I grant his premises, but that the girl was suffering some delusion I was convinced; possibly it was long-distance hypnotic suggestion, but whatever its nature, I was determined to seek out the instigators and break the spell.

For a moment he was silent, pinching his little pointed chin between a thoughtful thumb and forefinger and gazing pensively into the fire. At length: "Yes," he answered. "We can find the place where they lair, my friend; she will lead us to them."

"She? How—"

"*Exactement*. Tomorrow is May Eve, Witch-Night—Walpurgis-Nacht. Of all the nights which go to make the year, they are most likely to try their deviltry then. It was not for nothing that they sent their spy into this house and established rapport with Mademoiselle Diane. Oh, no. They need her in their business, and I think that all unconsciously she will go to them some time tomorrow evening. Me, I shall make it my especial duty to keep in touch with her, and where she goes, there will I go also."

"I, too," I volunteered, and we struck hands upon it.

5. Walpurgis-Nacht

Covertly, but carefully, we noted every movement the girl made next day. Shortly after luncheon de Grandin looked in at the consulting-room and nodded significantly. "She goes; so do I," he whispered, and was off.

It was nearly time for the evening meal when Diane returned, and a moment after she had gone upstairs to change for dinner I heard de Grandin's soft step in the hall.

"Name of a name," he ejaculated, dropping into the desk-side chair and lighting a cigarette, "but it is a merry chase on which she has led me today, that one!"

I raised interrogative brows, and:

"From pharmacy to pharmacy she has gone, like a hypochondriac seeking for a cure. Consider what she bought"—he checked the items off upon his fanned-out fingers—"aconitum, belladonna, solanin, mandragora officinalis. Not in any one, or even any two places did she buy these things. No, she was shrewd, she was clever, by blue, but she was subtle! Here she bought a *flaçon* of perfume, there a box of powder, again, a cake of scented soap, but mingled with her usual purchases would be occasionally one of these strange things which no young lady can possibly be supposed to want or need. What think you of it, my friend?"

"H'm, it sounds like some prescription from the mediæval pharmacopœia," I returned.

"Well said, my old astute one!" he answered. "You have hit the thumb upon the nail, my Trowbridge. That is exactly what it is, a prescription from the *Pharmacopœia Maleficorum*—the witches' book of recipes. Every one of those ingredients is stipulated as a necessary part of the witch's ointment—"

"The what?"

"The unguent with which those about to attend a sabbat, or meeting of a coven of witches, anointed themselves. If you will stop and think a moment, you will realize that nearly every one of those ingredients is a hypnotic or sedative. One thoroughly rubbed with a concoction of them would to a great degree lose consciousness, or, at the least, a sense of true responsibility."

"Yes? And—"

"Quite yes. Today foolish people think of witches as rather amiable, sadly misunderstood and badly persecuted old females. That is quite as silly as the vapid modern belief that fairies, elves and goblins are a set of well-intentioned folk. The truth is that a witch or wizard was—and is—one who by compact with the powers of darkness attains to power not given to the ordinary man, and uses that power for malevolent purposes; for a part of the compact is that he shall love evil and hate good. Very well. *Et puis?* Just as your modern gunmen of America and the *apaches* of Paris drug themselves with cocaine in order to stifle any flickering remnant of morality and remorse before committing some crime of monstrous ruthlessness, so did—and do—the witch and wizard drug themselves with this accursed ointment that they might utterly forget the still small voice of conscience urging them to hold their hands from evil unalloyed. It was not merely magic which called for this anointing, it was practical psychology and physic which prescribed it, my friend."

"Yes, well—"

"By damn," he hurried on, heedless of my interruption, "I think that we have congratulated ourselves all too soon. Mademoiselle Diane is not free from the wicked influence of those so evil men; she is very far from free, and tonight, unconsciously and unwillingly, perhaps, but nevertheless surely, she will anoint herself with this witch prescription, and, her body shining like something long dead and decomposing, will go to them."

"But what are we to do? Is there anything—"

"But yes; of course. You will please remain here, as close as may be to her door, and if she leaves the house, you follow her. Me, I have important duties to perform, and I shall do them quickly. Anon I shall return, and if she has not gone by then, I shall join you in your watch. If—"

"Yes, that's just it. Suppose she leaves while you're away," I broke in. "How am I to get in touch with you? How will you know where to come?"

"Call this number on the 'phone," he answered, scratching a memorandum on a card. "Say but 'She is gone and I go with her,' and I shall come at once. For safety's sake I would suggest that you take a double pocketful of rice, and scatter it along your way. I shall see the small white grains and follow hard upon your trail as though you were a hare and I a hound."

O bedient to his orders, I mounted to the second floor and took my station where I could see the door of Diane's room. Half an hour or more I waited in silence, feeling decidedly foolish, yet fearing to ignore his urgent request. At length the soft creaking of hinges brought me alert as a fine pencil of light cut through the darkened hall. Walking so softly that her steps were scarcely audible, Diane Wickwire came from her room. From throat to insteps she was muffled in a purple cloak, while a veil or scarf of some dark-colored stuff was bound about her head, concealing the bright beacon of her glowing golden hair. Hoping desperately that I should not lose her in the delay, I dialed the number which de Grandin had given me and as a man's voice challenged "Hello?" repeated the formula he had stipulated:

"She goes, and I go with her."

Then, without waiting for reply, I clashed the monophone back into its hooks, snatched up my hat and topcoat, seized a heavy blackthorn cane and crept as silently as possible down the stairs behind the girl.

She was fumbling at the front door lock as I reached the stairway's turn, and I flattened myself against the wall, lest she descry me; then, as she let herself through the portal, I dashed down the stairs, stepped soft-footedly across the porch, and took up the pursuit.

She hastened onward through the thickening dusk, her muffled figure but a faint shade darker than the surrounding gloom, led me through one side street to another, gradually bending her way toward the old East End of town where ramshackle huts of squatters, abandoned factories, unofficial dumping-grounds and occasional tumbledown and long-vacated dwellings of the better sort disputed for possession of the neighborhood with weed-choked fields of yellow clay and partly inundated swamp land—the desolate backwash of the tide of urban growth which every city has as a memento of its early settlers' bad judgment of the path of progress.

Where field and swamp and desolate tin-can-and-ash-strewn dumping-ground met in dreary confluence, there stood the ruins of a long-abandoned church. Immediately after the Civil War, when rising Irish immigration had populated an extensive shantytown down on the flats, a young priest, more ambitious than practical, had planted a Catholic parish, built a brick chapel with funds advanced by sympathetic co-religionists from the richer part of town, and attempted to minister to the spiritual needs of the newcomers. But prosperity had depopulated the mean dwellings of his flock who, offered jobs on the railway or police force, or employment in the mills then being built on the other side of town, had moved their humble household gods to new locations, leaving him a shepherd without sheep. Soon he, too, had gone and the church stood vacant for two-score years or more, time and weather and ruthless vandalism taking toll of it till now it stood amid the desolation which surrounded it like a lich amid a company of sprawling skeletons, its windows broken out, its doors unhinged, its roof decayed and fallen in, naught but its crumbling walls and topless spire remaining to bear witness that it once had been a house of prayer.

The final grains of rice were trickling through my fingers as I paused before the barren ruin, wondering what my next move was to be. Diane had entered through the doorless portal at the building's front, and the darkness of the black interior had swallowed her completely. I had a box of matches in my pocket, but they, I knew, would scarcely give me light enough to find my way about the ruined building. The floors were broken in a dozen places, I was sure, and where they were not actually displaced they were certain to be so weakened with decay that to step on them would be courting swift disaster. I had no wish to break a leg and spend the night, and perhaps the next day and the next, in an abandoned ruin where the chances were that anyone responding to my cries for help would only come to knock me on the head and rob me.

But there was no way out but forward. I had promised Jules de Grandin that I'd keep Diane in sight, and so, with a sigh which was half a prayer to the God of Foolish Men, I grasped my stick more firmly and stepped across the threshold of the old, abandoned church.

Stygian darkness closed about me as waters close above the head of one who dives, and like foul, greasy water, so it seemed to me, the darkness pressed upon me, clogging eyes and nose and throat, leaving only the sense of hearing—and of apprehension—unimpaired. The wind soughed dolefully through the broken arches of the nave and whistled with a sort of mocking ululation among the rotted cross-beams of the transept. Drops of moisture accumulated on the studdings of the broken roof fell dismally from time to time. The choir and sanctuary were invisible, but I realized they must be at the farther end of the building, and set a cautious foot forward, but drew it quickly back, for only empty air responded to the pressure of my probing boot. "Where was the girl? Had she fallen through an opening in the floor, to be precipitated on the rubble in the basement?" I asked myself.

"Diane? Oh, Diane?" I called softly.

No answer.

I struck a match and held the little torch aloft, its feeble light barely staining the surrounding blackness with the faintest touch of orange, then gasped involuntarily.

Just for a second, as the match-head kindled into flame, I saw a vision. Vision, perhaps, is not the word for it; rather, it was like one of those phosphenes or subjective sensations of light which we experience when we press our fingers on our lowered eyelids, not quite perceived, vague, dancing and elusive, yet, somehow, definitely *felt*. The molding beams and uprights of the church, long denuded of their pristine coat of paint and plaster, seemed to put on new habiliments, or to have been mysteriously metamorphosed; the bare brick walls were sheathed in stone, and I was gazing down a long and narrow colonnaded corridor, agleam with glowing torches, which terminated in a broad, low flight of steps leading to a marble platform. A giant statue dominated all, a figure hewn from stone and representing a tall and bearded being with high, virgin female breasts, clothed below the waist in woman's robes, a scepter tipped with an acornlike ornament in the right hand, a new-born infant cradled in the crook of the left elbow. Music, not heard, but rather felt, filled the air until the senses swooned beneath its overpowering pressure, and a line of girls, birth-nude, save for the veilings of their long and flowing hair, entered from the right and left, formed twos and stepped with measured, mincing tread in the direction of the statue. With them walked shaven-headed priests in female garb, their weak and beardless faces smirking evilly.

Brow-down upon the tessellated pavement dropped the maiden priestesses, their hands, palms forward, clasped above their heads while they beat their foreheads softly on the floor and the eunuch priests stood by impatiently.

And now the groveling women rose and formed a circle where they stood, hands crossed above their breasts, eyes cast demurely down, and four shaven-pated priests, came marching in, a gilded litter on their shoulders. On it, garlanded in flowers, but otherwise unclothed, lay a young girl, eyes closed, hands clasped as if in prayer, slim ankles crossed. They put the litter on the floor before the statue of the monstrous hermaphroditic god-thing; the circling maidens clustered round; a priest picked up a golden knife and touched the supine girl upon the insteps. There was neither fear nor apprehension on the face of her upon the litter, but rather an expression of ecstatic longing and anticipation as she uncrossed her feet. The flaccid-faced, emasculated priest leaned over her, gloating . . .

As quickly as it came the vision vanished. A drop of gelid moisture fell from a rafter overhead, extinguishing the quivering flame of my match, and once more I stood in the abandoned church, my head whirling, my senses all but gone, as I realized that through some awful power of suggestion I had seen a tableau of the worship of the great All-Mother, the initiation of a virgin priestess to the ranks of those love-slaves who served the worshippers of the goddess of fertility, Diana, Milidath, Astarte, Cobar or by whatever name men knew her in differing times and places.

But there was naught of vision in the flickering lights which now showed in the ruined sanctuary-place. Those spots of luminance were torches in the hands of living, mortal men, men who moved soft-footedly across the broken floor and set up certain things—a tripod with a brazen bowl upon its top, a row of tiny brazen lamps which flickered weakly in the darkness, as though they had been votive lamps before a Christian altar. And by their faint illumination I saw an odd-appearing thing stretched east and west upon the spot where the tabernacle had been housed, a gray-white, leprous-looking thing which might have been a sheeted corpse or lichened tombstone, and before it the torch-bearers made low obeisance, genuflecting deeply, and the murmur of their chant rose above the whispering reproaches of the wind.

It was an obscene invocation. Although I could not understand the words, or even classify the language which was used, I felt that there was something wrong about it. It was something like a phonographic record played in reverse. Syllables which I knew instinctively should be sonorously noble were oddly turned and twisted in pronunciation . . . "*diuq sirairolg.*" With a start I found the key. It was Latin—spoke backward. They were intoning the fifty-second Psalm: "*Quid gloriaris* . . . why boastest thou thyself . . . whereas the goodness of God endureth yet daily?"

A stench, as of burning offal, stole through the building as the incense pot upon the tripod began to belch black smoke into the air.

And now another voice was chanting. A woman's rich contralto. "*Oitani-mulli sunimod . . .*" I strained my ears and bent my brows in concentration, and at last I had the key. It was the twenty-seventh Psalm recited in reverse Latin: "The Lord is my light and my salvation . . ."

From the shadows Diane Wickwire came, straight and supple as a willow wand, unclothed as for the bath, but smeared from soles to hair-line with some luminous concoction, so that her slim, nude form stood out against the blackness like a spirit out of Purgatory visiting the earth with the incandescence of the purging fires still clinging to it.

Silently, on soft-soled naked feet, she stepped across the long-deserted sanctuary and passed before the object lying there. And as her voice mingled with the chanting of the men I seemed to see a monstrous form take shape against the darkness. A towering, obscene, freakish form, bearded like a hero of the *Odyssey*, its pectoral region thick-hung with multiple mammae, its nether limbs encased in a man's chiton, a lingam-headed scepter and a child held in its hands.

I shuddered. A chill not of the storm-swept night, but colder than any physical cold, seemed creeping through the air, as the ghostly, half-defined form seemed taking solidarity from the empty atmosphere. Diane Wickwire paused a moment, then stepped forward, a silver hammer gleaming in the lambent light rays of the little brazen lamps.

But suddenly, like a draft of clear, fresh mountain breeze cutting through the thick, mephitic vapors of swamp, there came another sound. Out of the darkness it came, yet not long was it in darkness, for, his face picked out by candlelight, a priest arrayed in full canonicals stepped from the shadows, while beside him, clothed in cassock and surplice, a lighted taper in his hand, walked Jules de Grandin.

They were intoning the office of exorcism. "Remember not, Lord, our offenses nor the offenses of our forefathers, neither take Thou vengeance of our sins. . . ."

As though struck dumb by the singing of the holy chant, the evocators ceased their sacrilegious intonation and stared amazed as de Grandin and the cleric approached. Abreast of them, the priest raised the aspergillum which be bore and sprinkled holy water on the men, the woman and the object of their veneration.

The result was cataclysmic. Out went the light of every brazen lamp, vanished was the hovering horror from the air above the stone, the luminance on Diane's body faded as though wiped away, and from the sky's dark vault there came the rushing of a mighty wind.

It shook the ancient ruined church, broke joists and timbers from their places, toppled tattered edges of brick walls into the darkened body of the rotting pile. I felt the floor swaying underneath my feet, heard a woman's wild, despairing scream, and the choking, suffocated roar of something in death-agony, as though a monster strangled in its blood; then:

"Trowbridge, *mon brave*; Trowbridge, *mon cher*, do you survive? Are you still breathing?" I heard de Grandin's hail, as though from a great distance.

I sat up gingerly, his arm behind my shoulders. "Yes, I think so," I answered doubtfully. "What was it, an earthquake?"

"Something very like it," he responded with a laugh.

"It might have been coincidence—though I do not think it was—but a great wind came from nowhere and completed the destruction which time began. That ruined church will never more give sanctuary to wanderers of the night. It is only debris, now."

"Diane—" I began, and:

"She is yonder," he responded, nodding toward an indistinct figure lying on the ground a little distance off. "She is still unconscious, and I think her arm is broken, but otherwise she is quite well. Can you stand?"

With his assistance I rose and took a few tottering steps, then, my strength returning, helped him lift the swooning girl and bear her to a decrepit Ford which was parked in the muddy apology for a road beside the marshy field. "*Mon Père*," de Grandin introduced, "this is the good physician, Doctor Trowbridge, of whom I told you, he who led us to this place. Friend Trowbridge, this is Father Ribet of the French Mission, without whom we should—*eh bien*, who can say what we should have done?"

The priest, who, like most members of his calling, drove well but furiously, took us home, but declined to stay for refreshment, saying he had much to do the next day.

We put Diane to bed, her fractured arm carefully set and bandaged. De Grandin sponged her with a Turkish cloth, drying her as deftly as any trained hospital nurse could have done; then, when we'd put her night-clothes on her and tucked her in between the sheets, he bore the basin of bath-water to the sink, poured it out and followed it with a liberal libation of carbolic antiseptic. "See can you withstand that, vile essence of the old one?" he demanded as the strong scent of phenol filled the room.

"Well, I'm listening," I informed him as we lighted our cigars. "What's the explanation, if any?"

He shrugged his shoulders. "Who can say?" he answered. "You know from what I told you that Mademoiselle Diane prepared to go to them; from what you did observe yourself, you know she went.

"To meet their magic with a stronger counter-agent, I had recourse to the good Père Ribet. He is a Frenchman, therefore he was sympathetic when I laid the case before him, and readily agreed to go with me and perform an exorcism of the evil spirit which possessed our dear Diane and was ruled by those vile miscreants. It was his number which I bade you call, and fast we followed on your message, tracing you by the trail of rice you left and making ready to perform our office when all was ready. We waited till the last safe minute; then, while they were chanting their so blasphemous inverted Psalms, we broke in on them and—"

"What was that awful, monstrous thing I saw forming in the air just before you and Father Ribet came in?" I interrupted.

"*Tiens*, who can say?" he answered with another shrug. "Some have called it one thing, some another. Me, I think it was the visible embodiment of the evil thing which man worshipped in the olden days and called the Mother Principle. These things, you know, my friend, were really demons, but their strength was great, for they drew form and substance from the throngs which worshipped them. But demons they were and are, and so are subject to the rite of exorcism, and accordingly, when good Père Ribet did sprinkle—"

"D'ye mean you actually believe a few phrases of ecclesiastical Latin and a few drops of holy water could dissipate that dreadful thing?" I asked incredulously.

He puffed slowly at his cigar; then: "Have it this way, if you prefer," he answered. "The power of evil which this thing we call the *Magna Mater* for want of a better name possesses comes from her—or its—worshippers. Generation after superstitious generation of men worshipped it, pouring out daily praise and prayer to it, believing in it. Thereby they built up a very great psychological power, a very exceedingly great power, indeed; make no doubt about that.

"But the olden gods died when Christianity came. Their worshippers fell off; they were weakened for very lack of psychic nourishment. Christianity, the new virile faith, upon the other hand, grew strong apace. The office of exorcism was developed by the time-honored method of trial and error, and finally it was perfected. Certain words—certain sounds, if you prefer—pronounced in certain ways, produced certain ascertainable effects, precisely as a note played upon a violin produces a responsive note from a piano. You have the physical explanation of that? Good; this is a spiritual analogy. Besides, generations of faithful Christians have believed, firmly believed, that exorcism is effective. *Voilà*; it is, therefore, effective. A psychological force of invincible potency has been built up for it.

"And so, when Père Ribet exorcised the demon goddess in that old and ruined church tonight—*tiens*, you saw what happened."

"What became of those men?" I asked.

"One wonders," he responded. "Their bodies I can vouch for. They are broken and buried under tons of fallen masonry. Tomorrow the police emergency squad will dig them out, and speculation as to who they were, and how they met their fate, will be a nine days' wonder in the newspapers."

"And the stone?"

"Crushed, my friend. Utterly crushed and broken. Père Ribet and I beheld it, smashed into a dozen fragments. It was all clay, not clay surrounding a meteorite, as the poor, deluded Wickwire believed. Also—"

"But look here, man," I broke in. "This is all the most fantastic lot of balderdash I've ever heard. D'ye think I'm satisfied with any such explanation as this? I'm willing to concede part of it, of course, but when it comes to all that stuff about the *Magna Mater* and—"

"*Ah hah*," he cut me off, "as for those explanations, they satisfy me no more than they do you. There *is* no explanation for these happenings which will meet a scientific or even logical analysis, my friend. Let us not be too greatly concerned with whys and wherefores. The hour grows late and I grow very thirsty. Come, let us take a drink and go to bed."

The Mansion of Unholy Magic

"**C**AR, SIR? TAKE YOU anywhere you want to go."

It was a quaint-looking figure which stood before us on the railway station platform, a figure difficult to classify as to age, status, or even sex. A man's gray felt hat which had seen better days, though not recently, was perched upon a head of close-cropped, tightly, curling blond hair, surmounting a face liberally strewn with freckles. A pull-over sweater of gray cardigan sheathed boyishly broad shoulders and boyishly narrow hips and waist, while the straight, slim legs were encased in a pair of laundry-faded jodhpurs of cotton corduroy. A pair of bright pink coral ear-drops completed the ensemble.

Jules de Grandin eased the strap by which his triple-barreled Knaak combination gun swung from his left shoulder and favored the solicitor with a look denoting compound interest. "A car?" he echoed. "But no, I do not think we need one. The motor stage—"

"The bus isn't running," the other interrupted. "They had an accident this afternoon and the driver broke his arm; so I ran over to see if I could pick up any passengers. I've got my car here, and I'll be glad to take you where you want to go—if you'll hurry."

"But certainly," the Frenchman agreed with one of his quick smiles. "We go to Monsieur Sutter's hunting-lodge. You know the way?"

A vaguely troubled look clouded the clear gray eyes regarding him as he announced our destination. "Sutter's lodge?" the girl—by now I had determined that it was a girl—repeated as she cast a half-calculating, half-fearful glance at the lengthening lines of red and orange which streaked the western sky. "Oh, all right; I'll take you there, but we'll have to hurry. I don't want to—come on, please."

She led the way to a travel-stained Model T Ford touring-car, swung open the tonneau door and climbed nimbly to the driving-seat.

"All right?" she asked across her shoulder, and ere we had a chance to answer put the ancient vehicle in violent motion, charging down the unkempt country road as though she might be driving for a prize.

"*Eh bien*, my friend, this is a singularly unengaging bit of country," de Grandin commented as our rattling chariot proceeded at breakneck speed along a road which became progressively worse. "At our present pace I estimate that we have come five miles, yet not one single habitation have we passed, not a ray of light or wreath of smoke have we seen, nor—" he broke off, grasping at his cap as the almost springless car catapulted itself across a particularly vicious hummock in the road.

"Desist, *ma belle chauffeuse*," he cried. "We desire to sleep together in one piece tonight; but one more bump like that and—" he clutched at the car-side while the venerable flivver launched itself upon another aerial excursion.

"Mister," our driver turned her serious, uncompromising face upon us while she drove her foot still harder down on the accelerator, "this is no place to take your time. We'll all be lucky to sleep in bed tonight, I'm thinkin', in one piece or several, if I don't—"

"Look out, girl!" I shouted, for the car, released from her guiding hand while she answered de Grandin's complaint, had lurched across the narrow roadway and was headed for a great, black-boled pine which grew beside the trail. With a wrench she brought the vehicle once more to the center of the road, putting on an extra burst of speed as she did so.

"If we ever get out of this," I told de Grandin through chattering teeth, "I'll never trust myself to one of these modern young fools' driving, you may be—"

"If we emerge from this with nothing more than *Mademoiselle's* driving to trouble us, I think we shall be more lucky than I think," he cut in seriously.

"What d'ye mean?" I asked exasperated. "If—"

"If you will look behind us, perhaps you will be good enough to tell me what it is you see," he interrupted, as he began unfastening the buckles of his gun-case.

"Why," I answered as I glanced across the lurching car's rear cushion, "it's a man, de Grandin. A running man."

"*Eh*, you are sure?" he answered, slipping a heavy cartridge into the rifle barrel of his gun. "A man who runs like that?"

The man was certainly running with remarkable speed. Tall, almost gigantic in height, and dressed in some sort of light-colored stuff which clung to his spare figure like a suit of tights, he covered the ground with long, effortless strides reminiscent of a hound upon the trail. There was something oddly furtive in his manner, too, for he did not keep to the center of the road, but dodged in a sort of zigzag, swerving now right, now left, keeping to the shadows as much as possible and running in such manner that only for the briefest intervals was he in direct line with us without some bush or tree-trunk intervening.

De Grandin nursed the forestock of his gun in the crook of his left elbow, his narrowed eyes intent upon the runner.

"When he comes within fifty yards I shall fire," he told me softly. "Perhaps I should shoot now, but—"

"Good heavens, man; that's murder!" I expostulated. "If—"

"Be still!" he told me in a low, sharp whisper. "I know what I am doing."

The almost nighttime darkness of the dense pine woods through which we drove was thinning rapidly, and as we neared the open land the figure in our wake seemed to redouble its efforts. Now it no longer skulked along the edges of the road, but sprinted boldly down the center of the trail, arms flailing wildly, hands outstretched as though to grasp the rear of our car.

Amazingly the fellow ran. We were going at a pace exceeding forty miles an hour, but this long, thin woodsman seemed to be outdistancing us with ease. As we neared the margin of the wood and came into the dappled lights and shadows of the sunset, he put on a final burst of speed and rushed forward like a whirlwind, his feet scarce seeming to touch the ground.

Calmly, deliberately, de Grandin raised his gun and sighted down its gleaming blue-steel barrels.

"No!" I cried, striking the muzzle upward as he squeezed the trigger. "You can't do that, de Grandin; it's murder!"

My gesture was in time to spoil his aim, but not in time to stop the shot. With a roar the gun went off and I saw a tree-limb crack and hurtle downward as the heavy bullet sheared it off. And, as the shot reverberated through the autumn air, drowning the rattling of our rushing flivver, the figure in our wake dissolved. Astonishingly, inexplicably, but utterly, it vanished in the twinkling of an eye, gone completely—and as instantly—as a soap-bubble punctured with a pin.

The screeching grind of tortured brakes succeeded, and our car bumped to a stop within a dozen feet. "D-did you shoot?" our driver asked tremulously. Her fair and sunburned face had gone absolutely corpse-gray with terror, making the golden freckles stand out with greater prominence, and her lips were blue and cyanotic.

"Yes, Mademoiselle, I shot," de Grandin answered in a low and even voice. "I shot, and had it not been for my kind and empty-headed friend, I should have scored a hit." He paused; then, lower still, he added: "And now one understands why you were in a hurry, Mademoiselle."

"Th-then, you saw—you saw—" she began through trembling lips, plucked feverishly at the steering-wheel with fear-numbed fingers for a moment, then, with a little, choking, gasping moan, slumped forward in her seat, unconscious.

"Parbleu, now one can sympathize with that Monsieur Crusoe," the little Frenchman murmured as he looked upon the fainting girl. "Here we are, a dozen miles from anywhere, with most unpleasant neighbors all about, and none to show us to our destination." Matter-of-factly he fell to chafing the girl's wrists,

slapping her cheeks softly from time to time, massaging her brow with deft, practised fingers.

"Ah, so, you are better now, n'est-ce-pas?" he asked as her eyelids fluttered
upward. "You can show us where to go if my friend will drive the car?"

"Oh, I can drive all right, I think," she answered shakily, "but I'd be glad if
you would sit by me."

Less speedily, but still traveling at a rate which seemed to me considerably
in excess of that which our decrepit car could make with safety, we took up our
journey, dipping into desolate, uninhabited valleys, mounting rocky elevations,
finally skirting an extensive growth of evergreens and turning down a narrow,
tree-lined lane until we reached the Sutter lodge, a squat, substantial log house
with puncheon doors and a wide chimney of field stone. The sun had sunk below
the western hills and long, purple-gray shadows were reaching across the little
clearing round the cabin as we came to halt before the door.

"How much?" de Grandin asked as he clambered from the car and began
unloading our gear.

"Oh, two dollars," said the girl as she slid down from the driving-seat and
bent to lift a cowskin bag. "The bus would have brought you over for a dollar, but
they'd have let you down at the foot of the lane, and you'd have had to lug your
duffle up here. Besides—"

"Perfectly, Mademoiselle," he interrupted, "we are not disposed to dicker over
price. Here is five dollars, and you need not trouble to make change; neither is
it necessary that you help us with our gear; we are quite content to handle it
ourselves, and—"

"Oh, but I want to help you," she broke in, staggering toward the cabin with
the heavy bag. "Then, if there's anything I can do to make you comfortable—"
She broke off, puffing with exertion, set the bag down on the door-sill and hastened to the car for another burden.

Our traps stored safely in the cabin, we turned once more to bid our guide
adieu, but she shook her head. "It's likely to be cold tonight," she told us. "This
fall weather's right deceptive after dark. Better let me bring some wood in, and
then you'll be needing water for your coffee and washing in the morning. So—"

"No, Mademoiselle, you need not do it," Jules de Grandin protested as she
came in with an armful of cut wood. "We are able-bodied men, and if we find
ourselves in need of wood or water we can—mordieu!"

Somewhere, faint and far-off seeming, but growing in intensity till it seemed
to make our very eardrums ache, there rose the quavering, mournful howling
of a dog, such a slowly rising and diminishing lament as hounds are wont to
make at night when baying at the moon—or when bemoaning death in the
family of their master. And, like an echo of the canine yowling, almost like an
orchestrated part of some infernal symphony, there came from very near a little

squeaking, skirking noise, like the squealing of a hollow rubber toy or the gibbering of an angry monkey. Not one small voice, but half a dozen, ten, a hundred of the chattering things seemed passing through the woodland at the clearing's edge, marching in a sort of disorderly array, hurrying, tumbling, rushing toward some rendezvous, and gabbling as they went.

The firewood clattered to the cabin door, and once again the girl's tanned face went pasty-gray.

"Mister," she told de Grandin solemnly, "this is no place to leave your house o' nights, for wood or water or anything else."

The little Frenchman tweaked the needle-points of his mustache as he regarded her. Then: "One understands, *Mademoiselle*—in part, at least," he answered. "We thank you for your kindness, but it is growing late; soon it will be dark. I do not think we need detain you longer."

Slowly the girl walked toward the door, swung back the sturdy rough-hewn panels, and gazed into the night. The sun had sunk and deep-blue darkness spread across the hills and woods; here and there an early star winked down, but there was no hint of other light, for the moon was at the dark. A moment she stood thus upon the sill, then, seeming to take sudden resolution, slammed the door and turned to face us, jaw squared, but eyes suffused with hot tears of embarrassment.

"I can't," she announced; then, as de Grandin raised his brows interrogatively: "I'm afraid—scared to go out there. Will—will you let me spend the night here?"

"Here?" the Frenchman echoed.

"Yes, sir; here. I—I *daren't* go out there among those gibbering things. I can't. I can't; *I can't!*"

De Grandin laughed delightedly. "*Morbleu*, but prudery dies hard in you Americans, *Mademoiselle*," he chuckled, "despite your boasted modernism and emancipation. No matter, you have asked our hospitality, and you shall have it. You did not really think that we would let you go among those—those whatever-they-may-bes, I hope? But no. Here you shall stay till daylight makes your going safe, and when you have eaten and rested you shall tell us all you know of this strange business of the monkey. Yes, of course."

As he knelt to light the fire he threw me a delighted wink. "When that so kind Monsieur Sutter invited us to use his lodge for hunting we little suspected what game we were to hunt, *n'est-ce-pas?*" he asked.

COFFEE, FRIED BACON, PANCAKES and a tin of preserved peaches constituted dinner. De Grandin and I ate with the healthy appetite of tired men, but our guest was positively ravenous, passing her plate for replenishment again and again. At last, when we had filled the seemingly bottomless void within her and

I had set my pipe aglow while she and Jules de Grandin lighted cigarettes, the little Frenchman prompted. "And now, *Mademoiselle?*"

"I'm glad you saw something in Putnam's woods and heard those things squeaking in the dark outside tonight," she answered. "It'll make it easier for you to believe me." She paused a moment, then:

"Did you notice the white house in the trees just before we came here?" she demanded.

We shook our heads, and she went on, without pausing for reply:

"That's Colonel Putnam's place, where it all started. My dad is postmaster and general storekeeper at Bartlesville, and Putnam's mail used to be delivered through our office. I was graduated from high school last year, and went to help Dad in the store, sometimes giving him a lift with the letters, too. I remember, it was in the afternoon of the twenty-third of June a special delivery parcel came for Colonel Putnam, and Dad asked me if I'd like to drive him over to deliver it after supper. We could make the trip in an hour, and Dad and Colonel Putnam had been friends since boyhood; so he wanted to do him the favor of getting the package to him as soon as possible.

"Folks had started telling some queer tales about Colonel Putnam, even then, but Dad pooh-poohed 'em all. You see, the colonel was the richest man in the county, and lived pretty much to himself since he came back here from Germany. He'd gone to school in that country as a young man, and went back on trips every year or so until about twenty years ago, when he married a Bavarian lady and settled there. His wife, we heard, died two years after they were married, when their little girl was born; then, just before the War, the daughter was drowned in a boating accident and Colonel Putnam came back to his old ancestral home and shut himself in from everybody, an old, broken and embittered man. I'd never seen him, but Dad had been to call once, and said he seemed a little touched in the head. Anyway, I was glad of the chance to see the old fellow when Dad suggested we drive over with the parcel.

"There was something queer about the Putnam house—something I didn't like, without actually knowing what it was. You know, just as you might be repelled by the odor of tuberoses, even though you didn't realize their connection with funerals and death? The place seemed falling apart; the drive was overgrown with weeds, the lawns all gone to seed, and a general air of desolation everywhere.

"There didn't seem to be any servants, and Colonel Putnam let us in himself. He was tall and spare, almost cadaverous, with white hair and beard, and wore a long, black, double-breasted frock coat and a stiff white-linen collar tied with a black stock. At first he hardly seemed to know Dad, but when he saw the parcel we brought, his eyes lighted up with what seemed to me a kind of fury.

"'Come in, Hawkins,' he invited; 'you and your daughter are just in time to see a thing which no one living ever saw before.'

"He led us down a long and poorly lighted hall, furnished in old-fashioned walnut and haircloth, to a larger apartment overlooking his weed-grown back yard.

"'Hawkins,' he told my father, 'you're in time to witness a demonstration of the uncontrovertible truth of the Pythagorean doctrine—the doctrine of metempsychosis.'

"'Good Lord, Henry, you don't mean to say you believe such non—' Dad began, but Colonel Putnam looked at him so fiercely that I thought he'd spring on him.

"'Silence, impious fool!' he shouted. 'Be silent and witness the exemplification of the Truth!' Then he calmed down a little, though he still continued walking up and down the room twitching his eyebrows, shrugging his shoulders and snapping his fingers every now and then.

"'Just before I came back to this country,' he went on, 'I met a master of the occult, a Herr Doktor von Meyer, who is not only the seventh son of a seventh son, but a member of the forty-ninth generation in direct descent from the Master Magician, Simon of Tyre. He possesses the ability to remember incidents in his former incarnations as you and I recall last night's dreams in the morning, Hawkins. Not only that: he has the power of reading other people's pasts. I sat with him in his *atelier* in Leipzig and saw my whole existence, from the time I was an insensate amoeba crawling in the primordial slime to the minute of my birth in this life, pass before me like the episodes of a motion picture.'

"'Did he tell you anything of this life; relate any incident of your youth known only to yourself, for instance, Henry?' Father asked him.

"'Be careful, scoffer, the Powers know how to deal with unbelievers such as you!' Colonel Putnam answered, flushing with rage, then calmed down again and resumed pacing the floor.

"'Back in the days when civilization was in the first flush of its youth,' he told us, 'I was a priest of Osiris in a temple by the Nile. And she, my darling, my dearest daughter, orphaned then as later, was a priestess in the temple of the Mother Goddess, Isis, across the river from my sanctuary.

"'But even in that elder day the fate which followed us was merciless. Then as later, water was the medium which was to rob me of my darling, for one night when her service to the Divine Mother was ended and temple slaves were rowing her across the river to my house, an accident overturned her boat, and she, the apple of my doting eyes, was thrown from her couch and drowned in the waters of Nilus. Drowned, drowned in the Egyptian river even as her latest earthly body was drowned in the Rhine.'

"Colonel Putnam stopped before my father, and his eyes were fairly blazing as he shook his finger in Dad's face and whispered:

"'But von Meyer told me how to overcome my loss, Hawkins. By his supernatural powers he was able to project his memory backward through the ages to the rock-tomb where they had laid the body of my darling, the very flesh in which she walked the streets of hundred-gated Thebes when the world was young. I sought it out, together with the bodies of those who served her in that elder life, and brought them here to my desolated house. Behold—'

"With a sort of dancing step he crossed the room and swept aside a heavy curtain. There, in the angle of the wall, with vases of fresh-cut flowers before them, stood three Egyptian mummy-cases.

"'It is she!' Colonel Putnam whispered tensely. 'It is she, my own little daughter, in her very flesh, and these'—he pointed to the other two—'were her attendants in that former life.'

"'Look!' He lifted the lid from the center coffin and revealed a slender form closely wrapped in overlying layers of dust-colored linen. 'There she stands, exactly as the priestly craftsmen wrapped her for her long, long rest, three thousand years ago! Now all is prepared for the great work I purpose; only the contents of that parcel you brought were needed to call the spirits of my daughter and her servants back to their earthly tenements, here, tonight, in this very room, Hawkins!'

"'Henry Putnam,' my father cried, 'do you mean to say you intend to play with this Devil's business? You'd really try to call back the spirit of one whose life on earth is done?'

"'I would; by God, *I will!*' Colonel Putnam shouted.

"'You shan't!' Father told him. 'That kind of thing is denounced by the laws of Moses, and mighty good sense he showed when he forbade it, too!'

"'Fool!' Colonel Putnam screamed at him. 'Don't you know Moses stole all his knowledge from the priesthood of Egypt, to which I belonged? Centuries before Moses was, we knew the white arts of life and the black arts of death. Moses! How dare you quote that ignorant charlatan and thief?'

"'Well, I'll have no part in any such Devil's mummery,' Father told him, but Colonel Putnam was like a madman.

"'You shall!' he answered, drawing a revolver from his pocket. 'If either of you tries to leave this room I'll shoot him dead!'

The girl stopped speaking and covered her face with her hands. "If we'd only let him shoot us!" she said wearily "Maybe we'd have been able to stop it."

De Grandin regarded her compassionately. "Can you continue, *Mademoiselle?*" he asked gently. "Or would you, perhaps, wait till later?"

"No, I might as well get it over with," she answered with a sigh. "Colonel Putnam ripped the cover off the package Father had brought and took out seven little silver vessels, each about as large as a hen's egg, but shaped something like a pineapple—having a pointed top and a flat base. He set them in a semicircle before the three coffins and filled them from an earthenware jug which was fitted with a spout terminating in a knob fashioned like a woman's head crowned with a diadem of hawks' wings. Then he lighted a taper and blew out the oil-lamp which furnished the only illumination for the room.

"It was deathly still in the darkened room; outside we could hear the crickets cheeping, and their shrill little cries seemed to grow louder and louder, to come closer and closer to the window. Colonel Putnam's shadow, cast by the flickering taper's light, lay on the wall like one of those old-time pictures of the Evil One.

"'The hour!' he breathed. 'The hour has come!'

Quickly he leaned forward, touching first one, then another of the little silver jars with the flame of his taper.

"The room's darkness yielded to an eery, bluish glow. Wherever the fire came in contact with a vase a tiny, thin, blue flame sprang up.

"Suddenly the corner of the room where the mummy-cases stood seemed wavering and rocking, like a ship upon a troubled ocean. It was hot and sultry in the house, shut in as it was by the thick pine woods, but from somewhere a current of cold—freezing cold!—air began to blow. I could feel its chill on my ankles, then my knees, finally on my hands as I held them in my lap.

"'Daughter, little daughter—daughter in all the ages past and all the ages yet to be, I call to you. Come, your father calls!' Colonel Putnam intoned in a quavering voice. 'Come. Come, I command it! Out of the illimitable void of eternity, come to me. In the name of Osiris, Dread Lord of the Spirit World, I command it. In the name of Isis, wife and sister of the Mighty One, I command it! In the names of Horus and Anubis, I command it!'

"Something—I don't know what—seemed entering the room. The windows were tight-latched; yet we saw the dusty curtains flutter, as though in a sudden current of air, and a light, fine mist seemed to obscure the bright blue flames burning in the seven silver lamps. There was a creaking sound, as though an old and rusty-hinged door were being slowly opened, and the lids of the two mummy-cases to right and left of the central figure began to swing outward. And as they moved, the linen-bandaged thing in the center coffin seemed to writhe like a hibernating snake recovering life, and stepped out into the room!

"Colonel Putnam forgot Father and me completely. 'Daughter—Gretchen, Isabella, Francesca, Musepa, T'ashamt, by whatever name or names you have been known throughout the ages, I charge you speak!' he cried, sinking on his knees and stretching out his hands toward the moving mummy.

"There came a gentle, sighing noise, then a light, tittering laugh, musical, but hard and metallic, as a thin, high voice replied. 'My father, you who loved and nurtured me in ages gone, I come to you at your command with those who served me in the elder world; but we are weak and worn from our long rest. Give us to eat, my father.'

"'Aye, food shall ye have, and food in plenty,' Colonel Putnam answered. 'Tell me, what is it that ye crave?'

"'Naught but the life-force of those strangers at your back,' the voice replied with another light, squeaking laugh. 'They must die if we would live—' and the sheeted thing moved nearer to us in the silver lamps' blue light.

"Before the Colonel could snatch up the pistol which had fallen from his hand, Father grabbed it, seized me with his free hand and dragged me from the house. Our car was waiting at the door, its engine still going, and we jumped in and started for the highroad at top speed.

"We were nearly out of the woods surrounding Putnam's house—the same woods I drove you through this afternoon—I happened to look back. There, running like a rabbit, coming so fast that it was actually overtaking our speeding car, was a tall, thin man, almost fleshless as a skeleton, and aptly dressed in some dust-colored, close-fitting kind of tights.

"But I recognized it! It was one of those things from the mummy-cases we'd seen in Colonel Putnam's parlor!

"Dad crowded on more speed, but the dreadful running mummy kept gaining on us. It had almost overtaken us when we reached the edge of the woods and I happened to remember Father still had Colonel Putnam's pistol. I snatched the weapon from his pocket and emptied it at the thing that chased us, almost at pointblank range. I know I must have hit it several times, for I'm a pretty good shot and the distance was too short for a miss, even allowing for the way the car was lurching, but it kept right on; then, just as we ran out into the moonlight at the woodland's edge, it stopped in its tracks, waved its arms at us and—vanished."

De Grandin tweaked the sharply waxed ends of his little wheat-blond mustache. "There is more, *Mademoiselle*," he said at length. "I can see it in your eyes. What else?"

Miss Hawkins cast a startled look at him, and it seemed to me she shuddered slightly, despite the warming glow of the fire.

"Yes," she answered slowly, "there's more. Three days after that a party of young folks came up here on a camping-trip from New York. They were at the Ormond cabin down by Pine Lake, six of 'em; a young man and his wife, who acted as chaperons, and two girls and two boys. The second night after they came, one of the girls and her boy friend went canoeing on the lake just at sundown. They paddled over to this side, where the Putnam farm comes down to the water, and came ashore to rest."

There was an air of finality in the way she paused. It was as if she had announced, "Thus the tale endeth," when she told us of the young folks' beaching their canoe, and de Grandin realized it, for, instead of asking what the next occurrence was, he demanded simply:

"And when were they found, *Mademoiselle?*"

"Next day, just before noon. I wasn't with the searching-party, but they told me it was pretty dreadful. The canoe paddles were smashed to splinters, as though they'd used them as clubs to defend themselves and broken them while doing so, and their bodies were literally torn limb from limb. If it hadn't been there was no evidence of any of them being eaten, the searchers would have thought a pair of panthers had pounced on them, for their faces were clawed almost beyond recognition, practically every shred of clothing ripped off them, and their arms and legs and heads completely separated from their bodies."

"U'm? And blood was scattered all around, one imagines?" de Grandin asked.

"No! Not a single drop of blood was anywhere in sight. Job Denham, the undertaker who received the bodies from the coroner, told me their flesh was pale and dry as veal. He said he couldn't understand it, but I—"

She halted in her narrative, glancing apprehensively across her shoulder at the window; then, in a low, almost soundless whisper. "The Bible says the blood's the life, doesn't it?" she asked. "And that voice we heard in Colonel Putnam's house told him those mummies wanted the vital force from Dad and me, didn't it? Well, I think that's the answer. Whatever it was Colonel Putnam brought to life in his house three days before was what set on that boy and girl in Putnam's woods, and it—they—attacked them for their blood."

"Have similar events occurred, *Mademoiselle?*"

"Did you notice the farm land hereabouts as we drove over?" she asked irrelevantly.

"Not particularly."

"Well, it's old land; sterile. You couldn't raise so much as a mortgage on it. No one's tried to farm it since I can remember, and I'll be seventeen next January."

"U'm; and so—"

"So you'd think it kind of funny for Colonel Putnam suddenly to decide to work his land, wouldn't you?"

"Perhaps."

"And with so many men out of work hereabouts, you'd think it queer for him to advertise for farmhands in the Boston papers, wouldn't you?"

"*Précisément, Mademoiselle.*"

"And for him to pay their railway fare up here, and their bus fare over from the station, and then get dissatisfied with 'em all of a sudden, and discharge 'em in a day or two—and for 'em to leave without anybody's knowing when they went, or *where* they went; then for him to hire a brand-new crew in the same way, and discharge them in the same way in a week or less?"

"*Mademoiselle,*" de Grandin answered in a level, almost toneless voice, "we consider these events somewhat more than merely queer. We think they have the smell of fish upon them. Tomorrow we shall call upon this estimable Putnam person, and he would be well advised to have a credible explanation in readiness."

"Call on Colonel Putnam? Not I." the girl rejoined. "I wouldn't go near that house of his, even in daylight, for a million dollars!"

"Then I fear we must forego the pleasure of your charming company," he returned with a smile, "for we shall visit him, most certainly. Yes, of course.

"Meantime," he added, "we have had a trying day; is it agreeable that we retire? Doctor Trowbridge and I shall occupy the bunks in this room; you may have the inner room, *Mademoiselle*."

"Please," she pleaded, and a flush mantled her face to the brows, "please let me sleep out here with you. I'd—well, I'd be scared to death sleeping in there by myself, and I'll be just as quiet—honestly, I won't disturb you."

She was unsupplied with sleeping-wear, of course; so de Grandin, who was about her stature, cheerfully donated a pair of lavender-and-scarlet striped silk pajamas, which she donned in the adjoining room, expending so little time in process that we had scarcely had time to doff our boots, jackets and cravats ere she rejoined us, looking far more like an adolescent lad than a young woman, save for those absurd pink-coral ear-studs.

"I wonder if you'd mind my using the 'phone?" she asked as she pattered across the rough-board floor on small and amazingly white bare feet. "I don't think it's been disconnected, and I'd like to call Dad and tell him I'm all right."

"By all means, do so," bade de Grandin as he hitched the blanket higher on his shoulder. "We can understand his apprehension for your safety in the circumstances."

The girl raised the receiver from the old-fashioned wall fixture, took the magneto crank in her right hand and gave it three vigorous turns, then seven slow ones.

"Hello? Dad?" she called. "This is Audrey; I'm—*oh!*" The color drained from her cheeks as though a coat of liquid white were sprayed across her face. "Dad— Dad—what *is* it?" she cried shrilly; then slowly, like a marionette being lowered by its strings, she wavered totteringly a moment, let fall the telephone receiver and slumped in a pathetic little heap upon the cabin floor.

De Grandin and I were out of bed with a bound, the little Frenchman bending solicitously above the fainting girl, I snatching at the telephone receiver.

"Hullo, hullo?" I called through the transmitter. "Mr. Hawkins?"

"*Huh—hoh—huh-hoh-huh!*" the most fiendish, utterly diabolical chuckle I ever heard came to me across the wire. "*Huh—hoh—huh-hoh-huh!*"

Then click! the telephone connection broke, and though I repeated the three-seven ring I'd heard the girl give several times, I could obtain no answer, not even the faint buzzing which denotes an open wire.

"My father! Something dreadful has happened to him, I know!" moaned the girl as she recovered consciousness. "Did you hear it, too, Doctor Trowbridge?"

"I heard something, certainly; it sounded like a poor connection roaring in the wire," I lied. Then, as hopeful disbelief lightened in her eyes: "Yes, I'm sure that's what it was, for the instrument's quite dead, now."

Reluctantly reassured, Audrey Hawkins clambered into bed, and though she moaned once or twice with a little, whimpering sound, her buoyant youth and healthily tired young muscles stood her in good stead, and she was sleeping peacefully within an hour.

Several times, as de Grandin and I lay in silence, waiting for her to drop off, I fancied I heard the oddly terrifying squeaking sounds we'd noticed earlier in the evening, but I resolutely put all thought of what their probable origin might be from my mind, convinced myself they were the cries of nocturnal insects, and—lay broad awake, listening for their recurrence.

"What was it that you heard in the telephone, Friend Trowbridge?" the little Frenchman asked me in a whisper when her continued steady, even breathing had assured us that our youthful guest was sound asleep.

"A laugh," I answered, "the most hideous, hellish chuckle I've ever listened to. You don't suppose her father could have laughed like that, just to frighten—"

"I do not think *Monsieur* her father has either cause for laughter or ability to laugh," he interrupted. "What it is that haunts these woods I do not surely know, my friend, though I suspect that the crack-brained Colonel Putnam let loose a horde of evil elementals when he went through that mummery at his house last summer. However that may be, there is no doubt that these things, whatever be their nature, are of a most unpleasant disposition, intent on killing any one they meet, either from pure lust for killing or in order to secure the vital forces of their victims and thus increase their strength in a material form. It is my fear that they may have a special grudge against Monsieur Hawkins and his daughter, for they were the first people whose lives they sought, and they escaped, however narrowly. Therefore, having failed in their second attempt to do the daughter mischief this afternoon, they may have wreaked vengeance on the father. Yes, it is entirely possible."

"But it's unlikely," I protested. "He's over in Bartlesville, ten miles away, while she's right here; yet—"

"Yes, you were saying—" he prompted as a sudden unpleasant thought forced itself into my mind and stopped my speech.

"Why, if they're determined to do mischief to either Hawkins or his daughter, haven't they attempted to enter this house, which is so much nearer than her home?"

"*Eh bien*, I thought you might be thinking that," he answered dryly. "And are you sure that they have made no attempt to enter here? Look at the door, if you will be so good, and tell me what it is you see."

I glanced across the cabin toward the stout plank door and caught the ruddy reflection of the firelight on a small, bright object lying on the sill. "It looks like your hunting-knife," I told him.

"*Précisément*, you have right; it *is* my hunting-knife," he answered. "My hunting-knife, unsheathed, with its sharp point directed toward the door-sill. Yours is at the other entrance, while I have taken the precaution to place a pair of heavy shears on the window-ledge. I do not think I wasted preparations, either, as you will probably agree if you will cast your eyes toward the window."

Obediently, I glanced at the single window of the room, then stifled an involuntary cry of horror; for there, outlined against the flickering illumination of the dying fire, stood an evil-looking, desiccated thing, skeleton-thin, dark, leather-colored skin stretched tightly as drum parchment on its skull, broken teeth protruding through retracted lips, tiny sparks of greenish light glowing malevolently in its cavernous, hollow eye-sockets. I recognized it at a glance; it was a mummy, an Egyptian mummy, such as I had seen scores of times while walking through the museums. And yet it was no mummy, either, for while it had the look of death and unnaturally delayed decay about it, it was also endued with some kind of dreadful life-in-death; for its little, glittering eyes were plainly capable of seeing, while its withered, leathery lips were drawn back in a grin of snarling fury, and even as I looked, they moved back from the stained and broken teeth in the framing of some phrase of hatred.

"Do not be afraid," de Grandin bade. "He can look and glare and make his monkey-faces all he wishes, but he can not enter here. The shears and knives prevent him."

"Y-you're sure?" I asked, terror gripping at my throat.

"Sure? To be sure I'm sure, He and his unpleasant playfellows would have been inside the cabin, and at our throats, long since, could they have found a way to enter. The sharpened steel, my friend, is very painful to him. Iron and steel are the most earthly of all metals, and exercise a most uncomfortable influence on elementals. They can not handle it, they can not even approach it closely, and when it is sharpened to a point it seems to be still more efficient, for its pointed end appears to focus and concentrate radiations of psychic force from the human body, forces which are highly destructive to them. Knowing this, and suspecting what it is that we have to do with from the story Mademoiselle Hawkins told us, I took precautions to place these discouragers at doors and window before we went to bed. *Tiens*, I have lain here something like an hour, hearing them squeak and gibber as they prowled around the house; only a moment since I noticed that thin gentleman peering in the window, and thought you might he interested."

Rising, he crossed the cabin on tiptoe, so as not to wake the sleeping girl, and drew the burlap curtain across the window. "Look at that until your ugly eyes are tired, *Monsieur le Cadavre*," he bade. "My good Friend Trowbridge does not care to have you watch him while he sleeps."

"Sleep!" I echoed. "D'ye think I could sleep knowing *that's* outside?"

"*Parbleu*, he is much better outside than in, I think," returned the Frenchman with a grin. "However. if you care to lie awake and think of him, I have no objections. But me, I am tired. I shall sleep; nor shall I sleep the worse for knowing that he is securely barred outside the house. No."

R EASSURED, I FINALLY FELL asleep, but my rest was broken by unpleasant dreams. Sometime toward morning I awoke, not from any consciousness of impending trouble nor from any outward stimulus; yet, once my eyes were open, I was as fully master of my faculties as though I had not slept at all. The predawn chill was in the air, almost bitter in its penetrating quality; the fire which had blazed merrily when we said good-night now lay a heap of whitened ashes and feebly smoldering embers. Outside the cabin rose a furious chorus of light, swishing, squeaking noises, as though a number of those whistling rubber toys with which small children are amused were being rapidly squeezed together. At first I thought it was the twittering of birds, then realized that the little feathered friends had long since flown to southern quarters; besides, there was an eery unfamiliarity in this sound, totally unlike anything I had ever heard until the previous evening, and it rose and gathered in shrill tone and volume as I listened. Vaguely, for no conscious reason, I likened it to the clamoring of caged brutes when feeding-time approaches in the zoo.

Then, as I half rose in my bunk, I saw an indistinct form move across the cabin. Slowly, very slowly, and so softly that the rough, uneven floor forbore to creak beneath her lightly pressing feet, Audrey Hawkins tiptoed toward the cabin door, creeping with a kind of feline grace. Half stupefied, I saw her pause before the portal, sink stealthily to one knee, reach out a cautious hand—

"*Non, non; dix mille fois non*—you shall not do it!" de Grandin cried, emerging from his bunk and vaulting across the cabin, seemingly with a single movement, then grasping the girl by the shoulders with such force that he hurled her half across the room. "What business of the fool do you make here, *Mademoiselle?*" he asked her angrily. "Do not you know that once the barriers of steel have been removed we should be—*mon Dieu*, one understands!"

Audrey Hawkins' hands were at her temples as she looked at him with innocent amazement while he raged at her. Clearly, she had wakened from a sound and dreamless sleep when she felt his hands upon her shoulders. Now she gazed at him in wonder mixed with consternation.

"Wh-what is it? What was I doing?" she asked.

"Ah, *parbleu*, you did nothing of your own volition, *Mademoiselle*," he answered, "but those other ones, those very evil ones outside the house, in some way they reached you in your sleep and made you pliable to their desires. *Ha*, but they forgot de Grandin; he sleeps, yes, but he sleeps the sleep of the cat. They do not catch him napping. But no."

We piled fresh wood upon the fire and, wrapped in blankets, sat before the blaze, smoking, drinking strong black coffee, talking with forced cheerfulness till the daylight came again, and when de Grandin put the curtain back and looked out in the clearing round the cabin, there was no sign of any visitants, nor were there any squeaking voices in the woods.

B REAKFAST FINISHED, WE CLIMBED into the ancient Ford and set out for Bartlesville, traveling at a speed I had not thought the ancient vehicle could make.

Hawkins' general store was a facsimile of hundreds of like institutions to be found in typical American villages from Vermont to Vancouver. Square as a box, it faced the village main street. Shop windows, displaying a miscellany of tinned groceries, household appliances and light agricultural equipment, occupied its front elevation. Shuttered windows piercing the second-story walls denoted where the family living-quarters occupied the space above the business premises.

Audrey tried the red-painted door of the shop, found it locked securely, and led the way through a neat yard surrounded by a fence of white pickets, took a key from her trousers pockets and let us through the private family entrance.

Doctors and undertakers have a specialized sixth sense. No sooner had we crossed the threshold than I smelled death inside that house. De Grandin sensed it, too, and I saw his smooth brow pucker in a warning frown as he glanced at me across the girl's shoulder.

"Perhaps it would be better if we went first, *Mademoiselle*," he offered. "*Monsieur* your father may have had an accident, and—"

"Dad—oh, Dad, are you awake?" the girl's call interrupted. "It's I. I was caught in Putnam's woods last evening and spent the night at Sutter's camp, but I'm—*Dad!* Why don't you answer me?"

For a moment she stood silent in an attitude of listening; then like a flash she darted down the little hall and up the winding stairs which led to the apartment overhead.

We followed her as best we could, cannoning into unseen furniture, barking our shins on the narrow stairs, but keeping close behind her as she raced down the upper passageway into the large bedroom which overlooked the village street.

The room was chaos. Chairs were overturned, the clothing had been wrenched from the big, old-fashioned bed and flung in a heap in the center of the floor, and from underneath the jumbled pile of comforter and sheets and blankets a man's bare foot protruded.

I hesitated at the doorway, but the girl rushed forward, dropped to her knees and swept aside the veiling bedclothes. It was a man past early middle life, but looking older, she revealed. Thin, he was, with that starved-turkey kind of lean-ness characteristic of so many native New Englanders. His gray head was thrown back and his lean, hard-shaven chin thrust upward truculently. In pinched nos-tril, sunken eye and gaping open mouth his countenance bore the unmistakable seal of death. He lay on his back with arms and legs sprawled out at grotesque angles from the inadequate folds of his old-fashioned Canton flannel nightshirt, and at first glance I recognized the unnaturalness of his posture, for human anat-omy does not alter much with death, and this man's attitude would have been impossible for any but a practised contortionist.

Even as I bent my brows in wonder, de Grandin knelt beside the body. The cause of death was obvious, for in the throat, extending almost down to the left clavicle, there gaped a jagged wound, not made by any sharp, incising weapon, but rather, apparently, the result of some savage lancination, for the whole integ-ument was ripped away, exposing the trachea to view—yet not a clot of blood lay round the ragged edges of the laceration, nor was there any sign of staining on the nightrobe. Indeed, to the ordinary pallor of the dead there seemed to be a different sort of pallor added, a queer, unnatural pallor which rendered the man's weather-stained countenance not only absolutely colorless, but curiously transparent, as well.

"Good heavens—" I began, but:

"Friend Trowbridge, if you please, observe," de Grandin ordered, lifting one of the dead man's hands and rotating it back and forth. I grasped his meaning instantly. Even allowing for the passage of *rigor mortis* and ensuing *post mortem* flaccidity, it would have been impossible to move that hand in such a manner if the radius and ulna were intact. The man's arm-bones had been fractured, probably in several places, and this, I realized, accounted for the posture of his hands and feet.

"Dad—oh, Daddy, Daddy!" cried the distracted girl as she took the dead man's head in her arms and nursed it on her shoulder. "Oh, Daddy dear, I knew that something terrible had happened when—"

Her outburst ended in a storm of weeping as she rocked her body to and fro, moaning with the helpless, inarticulate piteousness of a dumb thing wounded unto death. Then, abruptly:

"You heard that laugh last night!" she challenged me. "You know you did, Doctor Trowbridge—and there's where we heard it from," she pointed with a shaking finger at the wall-telephone across the room.

As I followed the line of her gesture I saw that the instrument had been ripped clear from its retaining bolts, its wires, its mouthpiece and receiver broken as though by repeated hammer-blows.

"They—those dreadful things that tried to get at us last night came over here when they found they couldn't reach me and murdered my poor father!"

she continued in a low, sob-choked voice. "I know! The night Colonel Putnam raised those awful mummies from the dead the she-thing said they wanted our lives, and one of the others chased us through the woods. They've been hungering for us ever since, and last night they got Daddy. I—"

She paused, her slender bosom heaving, and we could see the tear drops dry away as fiery anger flared up in her eyes.

"Last night I said I wouldn't go near Putnam's house again for a million dollars," she told de Grandin. "Now I say I wouldn't stay away from there for all the money in the world. I'm going over now—this minute—and pay old Putnam off. I'll face that villain with his guilt and make him pay for Daddy's life if it's the last thing I do!"

"It probably would be, *Mademoiselle*," de Grandin answered dryly. "Consider, if you please: This so odious Monsieur Putnam is undoubtlessly responsible for loosing those evil things upon the countryside, but while his life is forfeit for his crimes of necromancy, merely to kill him would profit us—and the community—not at all. These most unpleasant pets of his have gotten out of hand. I make no doubt that he himself is in constant, deadly fear of them, and that they, who came as servants of his will, are now his undisputed masters. Were we to kill him, we should still have those evil ones to reckon with, and till they have been utterly destroyed the country will be haunted by them; and others—countless others, perhaps—will share the fate of your poor father and that unfortunate young man and woman who perished on their boating-trip, not to mention those misguided workingmen who answered Monsieur Putnam's advertisements. You comprehend? This is a war of extermination on which we are embarked; we must destroy or be destroyed. Losing our lives in a gallant gesture would be a worthless undertaking. Victory, not speedy vengeance, must be our first and great consideration."

"Well, then, what are we to do, sit here idly while they range the woods and kill more people?"

"By no means, *Mademoiselle*. First of all, we must see that your father has the proper care; next, we must plan the work which lies before us. That done, it is for us to work the plans which we have made."

"All right, then, let's call the coroner," she agreed. "Judge Lindsay knows me, and he knew Dad all his life. When I tell him how old Putnam raised those mummies from the dead, and—"

"*Mademoiselle!*" the Frenchman expostulated. "You will tell him nothing about anything which Monsieur Putnam has done. It has been two hundred years, unfortunately, since your kin and neighbors ceased paying such creatures as this Putnam for their sins with rope and flame. To tell your truthful story to the coroner would be but signing your commitment to the madhouse. Then, doubly protected by your incarceration and public disbelief in their existence,

Monsieur Putnam's mummy-things could range the countryside at will. Indeed, it is altogether likely that the first place they would visit would be the madhouse where you were confined, and there, defenseless, you would be wholly at their mercy. Your screams for help would be regarded as the ravings of a lunatic, and the work of extirpation of your family which they began last night would be concluded. Your life, which they have sought since first they came, would be snuffed out, and, with none to fight against them, the countryside would fall an easy prey to their vile depredations. *Eh bien,* who can say how far the slaughter would go before the pig-ignorant authorities, at last convinced that you had told the sober truth when they thought you raving, would finally arouse themselves and take befitting action? You see why we must guard our tongues, *Mademoiselle?"*

N EWS OF THE MURDER spread like wildfire through the village. Zebulon Lindsay, justice of the peace, who also acted as coroner, empaneled a jury before noon; by three o'clock the inquisition had been held and a verdict of death by violence at the hands of some person or persons unknown was rendered.

Among the agricultural implements in Hawkins' stock de Grandin noted a number of billhooks, pike-like instruments with long, curved blades resembling those of scythes fixed on the ends of their strong helves.

"These we can use tonight, my friends," he told us as he laid three carefully aside.

"What for?" demanded Audrey.

"For those long, cadaverous things which run through Monsieur Putnam's woods, by blue!" he answered with a rather sour smile. "You will recall that on the first occasion when you saw them you shot one of their number several times?"

"Yes."

"And that notwithstanding you scored several hits, it continued its pursuit?"

"Yes, sir."

"Very well. You know the reason? Your bullets tore clear through its desiccated flesh, but had not force to stop it. *Tiens,* could you have knocked its legs off at the knees, however, do you think that it could still have run?"

"Oh, you mean—"

"Precisely, exactly; quite so, *ma chère,* I purpose dividing them, anatomizing them, striking them limb from limb. What lead and powder would be powerless to do, these instruments of iron will accomplish very nicely. We shall go to their domain at nightfall; that way we shall be sure of meeting them. Were we to go by daylight, it is possible they would be hidden in some secret place, for like all their kind they wait the coming of darkness because their doings are evil.

"Should you see one of them, remember what he did to your poor father, *Mademoiselle,* and strike out with your iron. Strike and do not spare your blows.

It is not as foeman unto foe we go tonight, but as executioners to criminals. You understand?"

W E SET OUT JUST at sundown, Audrey Hawkins driving, de Grandin and I, each armed with a stout billhook, in the rear seat.

"It were better that you stopped here, *Mademoiselle*," de Grandin whispered as the big white pillars of the mansion's antique portico came in view between the trees. "There is no need to advertise our advent; surprise is worth a thousand men in battle."

We dismounted from the creaking vehicle and, our weapons on our shoulders, began a stealthy advance.

"*S-s-st!*" Audrey warned as we paused a moment by a little opening in the trees, our eyes intent upon the house. "Hear it?"

Very softly, like the murmur of a sleepy little bird, there came a subdued squeaking noise from a hemlock thicket twenty feet or so away. I felt the short hair on my neck begin to rise against my collar and a little chill of mingled hate and apprehension run rippling through my scalp and cheeks. It was like the sensation felt when one comes unexpectedly upon a serpent in the path.

"Softly, friends," Jules de Grandin ordered, grasping the handle of his billhook like a quarterstaff and leaning toward the sound; "do you stand by me, good Friend Trowbridge, and have your flashlight ready. Play its beam on him the minute he emerges, and keep him visible for me to work on."

Cautiously, quietly as a cat stalking a mouse, he stepped across the clearing, neared the clump of bushes whence the squeaking came, then leant forward, eyes narrowed, weapon ready.

It burst upon us like a charging beast, one moment hidden from our view by the screening boughs of evergreen, next instant leaping through the air, long arms flailing, skeleton-hands grasping for de Grandin's throat, its withered, leather-like face a mask of hatred and ferocity.

I shot the flashlight's beam full on it, but its terrifying aspect caused my hand to tremble so that I could scarcely hold the shaft of light in line with the leaping horror's movements.

"*Ça-ha, Monsieur le Cadavre*, we meet again, it seems!" de Grandin greeted in a whisper, dodging nimbly to the left as the mummy-monster reached out scrawny hands to grapple with him. He held the billhook handle in the center, left hand upward, right hand down, and as the withered leather talons missed their grasp he whirled the iron-headed instrument overhand from left to right, turning it as he did so, so that the carefully whetted edge of the heavy blade crashed with devastating force upon the mummy's withered biceps. The limb dropped helpless from the desiccated trunk, but, insensible to pain, the creature whirled and grasped out with its right hand.

Once more the billhook circled whistling through the air, this time reversed, striking downward from right to left. The keen-edged blade sheared through the lich's other arm, cleaving it from the body at the shoulder.

And now the withered horror showed a trace of fear. Sustained by supernatural strength and swiftness, apparently devoid of any sense of pain, it had not entered what intelligence the thing possessed that a man could stand against it. Now it paused, irresolutely a moment, teetering on its spindle legs and broad, splay feet, and while it hesitated thus the little Frenchman swung his implement again, this time like an ax, striking through dry, brown flesh and aged, brittle bone, lopping off the mummy's legs an inch or so above the knees.

Had it not been so horrible I could have laughed aloud to see the withered torso hurtle to the ground and lie there, flopping grotesquely on stumps of arms and legs, seeking to regain the shelter of the hemlock copse as it turned its fleshless head and gazed across its bony shoulder at de Grandin.

"Hit it on the head! Crush its skull!" I advised, but:

"*Non*, this is better," he replied as he drew a box of matches from his pocket and lighted one.

Now utter terror seized the limbless lich. With horrid little squeaking cries it redoubled its efforts to escape, but the Frenchman was inexorable. Bending forward, he applied the flaming match to the tinder-dry body, and held it close against the withered skin. The fire caught instantly. As though it were compounded of a mass of oil-soaked rags, the mummy's body sent out little tongues of fire, surmounted by dense clouds of aromatic smoke, and in an instant was a blaze of glowing flame. De Grandin seized the severed arms and legs and piled them on the burning torso so that they, too, blazed and snapped and crackled like dry wood thrown on a roaring fire.

"And that, I damn think, denotes the end of that," he told me as he watched the body sink from flames to embers, then to white and scarcely glowing ashes. "Fire is the universal solvent, the one true cleanser, my friend. It was not for nothing that the olden ones condemned their witches to be burned. This elemental force, this evil personality which inhabited that so unsavory mummy's desiccated flesh, not only can it find no other place to rest now that we have destroyed its tenement, but the good, clean, clarifying flames have dissipated it entirely. Never again can it materialize, never more enter human form through the magic of such necromancers as that *sacré* Putnam person. It is gone, disposed of—*pouf!* it is no longer anything at all.

"What think you of my scheme, *Mademoiselle?*" he asked. "Was I not the clever one to match iron and fire against them? Was it not laughable to see— *grand Dieu*, Friend Trowbridge—*where is she?*"

He leant upon his billhook, looking questingly about the edges of the clearing while I played my searchlight's beam among the trees. At length:

"One sees it perfectly," he told me. "While we battled with that one, another of them set on her and we could not hear her cries because of our engagement. Now—"

"Do—do you suppose it killed her as it did her father?" I asked, sick with apprehension.

"We can not say; we can but look," he answered. "Come."

Together we searched the woodland in an ever-widening circle, but no trace of Audrey Hawkins could we find.

"Here's her billhook," I announced as we neared the house.

Sticking in the hole of a tree, almost buried in the wood, was the head of the girl's weapon, some three inches of broken shaft adhering to it. On the ground twenty feet or more away lay the main portion of the helve, broken across as a match-stem might he broken by a man.

The earth was moist beneath the trees, and at that spot uncovered by fallen leaves or pine needles. As I bent to pick up Audrey's broken billhook, I noticed tracks in the loam—big, barefoot tracks, heavy at the toe, as though their maker strained forward as he walked, and beside them a pair of wavy parallel lines—the toe-prints of Audrey's boots as she was dragged through the woods and toward the Putnam house.

"What now?" I asked. "They've taken her there, dead or alive, and—"

He interrupted savagely: "What can we do but follow? Me, I shall go into that *sacré* house, and take it down, plank by single plank, until I find her; also I shall find those others, and when I do—"

No LIGHTS SHOWED IN the Putnam mansion as we hurried across the weed-grown, ragged lawn, tiptoed up the veranda steps and softly tried the handle of the big front door. It gave beneath our pressure, and in a moment we were standing in a lightless hall, our weapons held in readiness as we strove to pierce the gloom with straining eyes and held our breaths as we listened for some sound betokening an enemy's approach.

"Can you hear it, Trowbridge, *mon ami?*" he asked me in a whisper. "Is it not their so abominable squealing?"

I listened breathlessly, and from the passageway's farther end it seemed there came a series of shrill skirking squeaks, as though an angry rat were prisoned there.

Treading carefully, we advanced along the corridor, pausing at length as a vague, greenish-blue glow appeared to filter out into the darkness, not exactly lightening into the darkness, making the gloom a little less abysmal.

We gazed incredulously at the scene presented in the room beyond. The windows were all closed and tightly shuttered, and in a semicircle on the floor there burned a set of seven little silver lamps which gave off a blue-green, phosphorescent glow, hardly sufficient to enable us to mark the actions of a group of figures gathered there. One was a man, old and white-haired, disgustingly unkempt, his deep-set dark eyes burning with a fanatical glow of adoration as he kept them fixed upon a figure seated in a high, carved chair which occupied a sort of dais beyond the row of glowing silver lamps. Beside the farther wall there stood a giant form, a great brown skinned man with bulging muscles like a wrestler's and the knotted torso of a gladiator. One of his mighty hands was twined in Audrey Hawkins' short, blond hair; with the other he was stripping off her clothes as a monkey skins a fruit. We heard the cloth rip as it parted underneath his wrenching fingers, saw the girl's slim body show white and lissome as a new-peeled hazel wand, then saw her thrown birth-naked on the floor before the figure seated on the dais.

Bizarre and terrifying as the mummy-creatures we had seen had been, the seated figure was no less remarkable. No mummy, this, but a soft and sweetly rounded woman-shape, almost divine in bearing and adornment. Out of olden Egypt she had come, and with her she had brought the majesty that once had ruled the world. Upon her head the crown of Isis sat, the vulture cap with wings of beaten gold and blue enamel, and the vulture's head with gem-set eyes, above it rearing upright horns of Hathor between which shone the polished-silver disk of the full moon, beneath them the uraeus, emblem of Osiris.

About her neck was hung a collar of beaten gold close-studded with emeralds and blue lapis lazuli, and round her wrists were wide, bright bands of gold which shone with figures worked in red and blue enamel. Her breasts were bare, but high beneath the pointed bosoms was clasped a belt of blue and gold from which there draped a robe of thin, transparent linen gathered in scores of tiny, narrow pleats and fringed about the hem with little balls of gleaming gold which hung an inch or so above the arching insteps of her long and narrow feet, on every toe of which there gleamed a jewel-set ring. In her left hand she held a golden instrument fashioned like a T-cross with a long loop at its top, while in her right she bore a three-lashed golden scourge, the emblem of Egyptian sovereignty.

All this I noted in a sort of wondering daze, but it was her glaring, implacable eyes which held me rooted to the spot. Like the eyes of a tigress or a leopardess they were, and glowing with a horrid, inward light as though illumined from behind by the phosphorescence of an all consuming, heatless flame.

Even as we halted spellbound at the turning of the corridor we saw her raise her golden scourge and point it like an aiming weapon at Audrey Hawkins. The girl lay huddled in a small white heap where the ruthless giant had thrown her, but as the golden scourge was leveled at her she half rose to a crouching posture and crept forward on her knees and elbows, whimpering softly, half in pleading, half in fear, it seemed.

The fixed, set stare of hatred never left the seated woman's eyes as Audrey crawled across the bare plank floor, groveled for an instant at the dais' lowest step, then raised her head and began to lick the other's white, jeweled feet as though she were a beaten dog which sued for pardon from its mistress.

I saw de Grandin's small white teeth flash in the lamps' weird light as he bared them in a quick grimace. "I damn think we have had enough of this, by blue!" he whispered as he stepped out of the shadows.

While I had watched the tableau of Audrey's degradation with a kind of sickened horror, the little Frenchman had been busy. From the pockets of his jacket and his breeches he extracted handkerchiefs and knotted them into a wad, then, drawing out a tin of lighter-fluid, he doused the knotted linen with the liquid. The scent of benzine mixed with ether spread through the quiet air as, his drenched handkerchiefs on his billhook's iron head, he left the shadows, paused an instant on the door-sill, then struck a match and set the cloth ablaze.

"*Messieurs, Madame*, I think this little comedy is ended," he announced as he waved the fire-tipped weapon back and forth, causing the flames to leap and quicken with a ruddy, orange glow.

Mingled terror and surprise showed on the naked giant's face as de Grandin crossed the threshold. He fell away a pace, then, with his back against the wall, crouched for a spring.

"You first, *Monsieur*," the Frenchman told him almost affably, and with an agile leap cleared the few feet separating them and thrust the blazing torch against the other's bare, brown breast.

I gasped with unbelief as I saw the virile, sun-tanned flesh take fire as though it had been tinder, blaze fiercely and crumble into ashes as the flames spread hungrily, eating up his chest and belly, neck and head, finally destroying writhing arms and legs.

The seated figure on the dais was cowering back in fright. Gone was her look of cold, contemptuous hatred; in its place a mask of wild, insensate fear had overspread her clear-cut, haughty features. Her red lips opened, showing needle-sharp white teeth, and I thought she would have screamed aloud in her terror, but all that issued from her gaping mouth was a little, squeaking sound, like the squealing of a mouse caught in a trap.

"And now, *Madame*, permit that I may serve you, also!" De Grandin turned his back upon the blazing man and faced the cringing woman on the throne.

She held up trembling hands to ward him off, and her frightened, squeaking cries redoubled, but inexorably as a mediæval executioner advancing to ignite the faggots round a condemned witch, the little Frenchman crossed the room, held out his blazing torch and forced the fire against her bosom.

The horrifying process of incineration was repeated. From rounded breast to soft, white throat, from omphalos to thighs, from chest to arms and from thighs to feet the all-devouring fire spread quickly, and the woman's white and gleaming flesh blazed fiercely, as if it had been oil-soaked wood. Bones showed a moment as the flesh was burned away, then took the fire, blazed quickly for an instant, glowed to incandescence, and crumbled to white ash before our gaze. Last of all, it seemed, the fixed and staring eyes, still gleaming with a greenish inward light, were taken by the fire, blazed for a second with a mixture of despair and hatred, then dissolved to nothingness.

"*Mademoiselle*," de Grandin laid his hand upon the girl's bare shoulder, "they have gone."

Audrey Hawkins raised her head and gazed at him, the puzzled, non-comprehending look of one who wakens quickly from sound sleep upon her face. There was a question in her eyes, but her lips were mute.

"*Mademoiselle*," he repeated, "they have gone; I drove them out with fire. But *he* remains, my little one." With a quick nod of his head he indicated Colonel Putnam, who crouched in a corner of the room, fluttering fingers at his bearded lips, his wild eyes roving restlessly about, as though he could not understand the quick destruction of the beings he had brought to life.

"He?" the girl responded dully.

"*Précisément, Mademoiselle*—he. The accursed one; the one who raised those mummies from the dead; who made this pleasant countryside a hell of death and horror; who made it possible for them to slay your father while he slept."

One of those unpleasant smiles which seemed to change the entire character of his comely little face spread across his features as he leant above the naked girl and held his billhook toward her.

"The task is yours by right of bereavement, *ma pauvre*," he told her, "but if you would that I do it for you—"

"No—no; let me!" she cried and leapt to her feet, snatching the heavy iron weapon from his hand. Not only was she stripped of clothing; she was stripped of all restraint, as well. Not Audrey Hawkins, civilized descendant of a line of prudishly respectable New England rustics, stood before us in the silver lamps' blue light, but a primordial cave-woman, a creature of the dawn of time, wild with the lust for blood-vengeance; armed, furious, naked and unashamed.

"Come, Friend Trowbridge, we can safely leave the rest to her," de Grandin told me as he took my elbow and forced me from the room.

"But, man, that's murder!" I expostulated as he dragged me down the unlit hall. "That girl's a maniac, and armed, and that poor, crazy old man—"

"Will soon be safe in hell, unless I miss my guess," he broke in with a laugh. "Hark, is it not magnificent, my friend?"

A wild, high scream came to us from the room beyond, then a woman's cachinnating laugh, hysterical, thin-edged, but gloating; and the thudding beat of murderous blows. Then a weak, thin moaning, more blows; finally a little, groaning gasp and the sound of quick breath drawn through fevered lips to laboring lungs.

"And now, my friend, I think we may go back," said Jules de Grandin.

"ONE MOMENT, IF YOU please, I have a task to do," he called as we paused on the portico. "Do you proceed with Mademoiselle Audrey. I shall join you in a minute."

He disappeared inside the old, dark house, and I heard his boot-heels clicking on the bare boards of the hall as he sought the room where all that remained of Henry Putnam and the things he brought back from the dead were lying. The girl leaned weakly against a tall porch pillar, covering her face with trembling hands. She was a grotesque little figure, de Grandin's jacket buttoned round her torso, mine tied kilt-fashion round her waist.

"Oh," she whispered with a conscience-stricken moan, "I'm a murderess. I killed him—beat him to death. I've committed murder!"

I could think of nothing comforting to say, so merely patted her upon the shoulder, but de Grandin, hastening from the house, was just in time to hear her tearful self-arraignment.

"Pardonnez-moi, Mademoiselle," he contradicted, "you are nothing of the kind. Me, once in war I had to head the firing-party which put a criminal to death. Was I then his murderer? But no. My conscience makes no accusation. So it is with you. This Putnam one, this rogue, this miscreant, this so vile necromancer who filled these pleasant woods with squeaking, gibbering horrors, was his life not forfeit? Did not he connive at the death of that poor boy and girl who perished in the midst of their vacation? But yes. Did not he advertise for laborers, that they might furnish sustenance for those evil things he summoned from the tomb? Certainly. Did not he loose his squeaking, laughing thing upon your father, to kill him in his sleep? Of course.

"Yet for these many crimes the law was powerless to punish him. We should have sent ourselves to lifelong confinement in a madhouse had we attempted to invoke the law's processes. Alors, it was for one of us to give him his deserts, and you, my little one, as the one most greatly wronged, took precedence.

"Eh bien," he added with a tug at his small, tightly waxed mustache, "you did make extremely satisfactory work of it."

Since Audrey was in no condition to drive, I took the ancient flivver's steering-wheel.

"Look well upon that bad old house, my friends," de Grandin bade as we started on our homeward road. "Its time is done."

"What d'ye mean?" I asked.

"Precisely what I say. When I went back I made a dozen little fires in different places. They should be spreading nicely by this time."

"I CAN UNDERSTAND WHY THAT mummy we met in the woods caught fire so readily," I told him as we drove through the woods, "but how was it that the man and woman in the house were so inflammable?"

"They, too, were mummies," he replied.

"Mummies? Nonsense! The man was a magnificent physical specimen, and the woman—well, I'll admit she was evil-looking, but she had one of the most beautiful bodies I've ever seen. If she were a mummy, I—"

"Do not say it, my friend," he broke in with a laugh; "eaten words are bitter on the tongue. They were mummies—I say so. In the woods, in Monsieur Hawkins' home, when they made unpleasant faces at us through the window of our cabin, they were mummies, you agree? *Ha*, but when they stood in the blue light of those seven silver lamps, the lights which first shone on them when they came to plague the world, they were to outward seeming the same as when they lived and moved beneath the sun of olden Egypt. I have heard such things.

"That necromancer, von Meyer, of whom Monsieur Putnam spoke, I know of him by reputation. I have been told by fellow occultists whose word I can not doubt that he has perfected a light which when shone on a corpse will give it every look of life, roll back the ravages of years and make it seem in youth and health once more. A very brilliant man is that von Meyer, but a very wicked one, as well. Some day when I have nothing else to do I shall seek him out and kill him to death for the safety of society.

"Can you drive a little faster?" he inquired as we left the woods behind.

"Cold without your jacket?" I asked.

"Cold? *Mais non*. But I would reach the village soon, my friend. *Monsieur le juge* who also acts as coroner has a keg of most delicious cider in his cellar, and this afternoon he bade me call on him whenever I felt thirsty. *Morbleu*, I feel most vilely thirsty now!

"Hurry, if you please, my friend."

Red Gauntlets of Czerni

1. Revenant

OUR VISITOR LEANT FORWARD in his chair and fixed his oddly light colored eyes on Jules de Grandin with an almost pleading expression. "It is about my daughter that I come," he said in a flat, accentless voice, only his sharp-cut, perfect enunciation disclosing that English had not been his mother tongue. "She is gravely ill, *Monsieur*."

"But I do not practise medicine," the little Frenchman answered. "There are thousands of good American practitioners to whom you could apply, Monsieur—"

"Szekler," supplied the other with an inclination of his head. "Andor Szekler, sir."

"Very well, Monsieur Szekler; as I say, I am not a practitioner of medicine, and—"

"But no, it is not a medical practitioner whom I seek," the other interrupted eagerly. "My daughter, her illness is more of the spirit than the body, and I have heard of your abilities to fight back those who dwell upon the threshold of the door between our world and theirs, to conquer such ills as now afflict my child. Say that you will take the case, I beg, *Monsieur*."

"*Eh bien*, you put a different aspect upon things," de Grandin answered. "What are the symptoms of *Mademoiselle* your daughter, it you please?"

Our visitor sucked the breath between his large and firm white teeth with a sort of hissing sigh, and a look of relief, something almost like a gleam of secret triumph, flashed in his narrow eyes. He was a man in late middle life, not fat, but heavily built, blond, regular of features save that his cheek-bones were set so high that they seemed to crowd his light, indefinitely colored eyes, making them seem narrow, and pushing them into a slight slant. Dry-skinned, clean-shaven save for a heavy cavalry mustache waxed into twin uprearing horns, he had that peculiarly well-groomed aspect that denotes the professional soldier, even out of uniform, and though his forehead was broad and benevolent, his queerly narrowed slanting eyes modified its kindliness, and the large, firm mouth, with its almost wolfishly white teeth, lent his face a slightly sinister expression. Now, however, it was the father, not the soldier trained in Old World traditions of blood and iron, who spoke.

"We are Hungarian," he began, then paused a moment, as though at a loss how to proceed.

"One surmised as much," de Grandin murmured politely. "One also assumed you are a soldier, *Monsieur*. Now, as to *Mademoiselle* your daughter, you were about to say—?" He raised his brows and bent a questioning look upon the visitor.

"You are correct, *Monsieur*," responded Szekler. "I am—I was—a soldier; a colonel of hussars in the army of the old monarchy. You know what happened when the war was done, how Margyarország and Austria separated when the poltroon Charles gave up his birthright, and how our poor land, bereft of Transylvania, Croatia and Slavonia was racked by civil war and revolution. Things went badly for our caste. Reduced to virtual beggary, we were harried through the streets like beasts, for to have worn the Emperor's uniform was sufficient cause to send a man before the execution squad. With what little of our fortune that remained I took my wife and little daughter and fled for sanctuary to America.

"The new land has been good to us; in the years which I have spent here I have recouped the fortune which I lost, and added to it. We were very happy here until—"

He paused and once more drew in his breath with that peculiar, eager sound, then passed his tongue-tip across his lower lip. The sight affected me unpleasantly. His tongue was red and pointed like an animal's, and in his oddly oblique eyes there shone a look of scarcely veiled desire.

De Grandin watched him narrowly, his little, round blue eyes intent upon the stranger's face, recording every movement, every feature with photographic fidelity. His air of unsuspecting innocence, it seemed to me, was a piece of superb acting as he prompted gently: "Yes, *Monsieur*, and what occurred to spoil the happiness you found here?"

"Zita, my daughter, was always delicate," Colonel Szekler answered. "For a long time we feared she might be marked by that disease the Turks call *gusel vereni*, which is akin to the consumption of the Western world, except that the patient loses nothing of her looks and often seems to grow more beautiful as the end approaches. It is painless, progressive and incurable, so—"

"One understands, *Monsieur*," de Grandin nodded; "I have seen it in the Turkish hospitals. *Et puis?*"

"Our Magyar girls attain the bloom of womanhood early," answered Colonel Szekler. "When Zita was fourteen she was mature as any American girl four years her senior, and for a time her delicacy seemed to pass away. We sent her off to school, and each season she came home more strengthened, more robust, more like the Zita we would have her be. A month ago, however, her old malady returned. She shows profound lassitude, often complaining of being too tired to rise. Doctors we have had, five, eight of them; all said there is no trace of physical illness, yet there she is, growing weaker day by day. Two days ago I think I found the cause!"

Again that whistling, eager sigh as he drew in his breath before proceeding: "Zita was lying on the chaise-longue in her room, and I went upstairs to ask if she felt well enough to come to luncheon. She was asleep. She was wearing purple-silk pajamas, and a shawl of purple silk was draped across her knees, which enabled me to see it more distinctly.

"As I opened the door to her chamber I saw a patch of white, cloud-like substance, becoming denser and bigger as I watched, issuing from her left side just below the breast. I say it was like cloud, but that is not quite accurate; it had more substance than a cloud, it was more like some ponderable gas, or a great bubble of some gelatinous substance being gradually inflated, and as it grew, it seemed to thicken and become more opaque, or opalescent. Then, taking form as though modeled out of wax by the clever hands of an unseen sculptor, a face took shape and looked at me out of the bubble. It was a living face, Monsieur de Grandin, normal in size, with skin as white as the scraped bone of a fleshless skull, and thick, red lips and rolling, glaring eyes that made my blood run cold.

"I stood there horror-frozen for a moment, repeating to myself: 'Jesus, Mary and Joseph have pity on us!' and then, just as it had come, that cursed, milky cloud began to disappear. Slowly at first, but with ever-increasing speed, as though it were being sucked back into Zita's body, the great, cloudy bubble shrank, the dreadful, leering face flattened out and elongated, melting imperceptibly into its frame of hazy, gleaming cloudiness; finally the whole mass vanished through the fabric of the purple garment which my daughter wore.

"She still continued sleeping peacefully, apparently, and I shook her gently by the shoulder. She wakened and smiled at me and told me she had had a lovely dream. She—"

"Tell me, *Monsieur*," de Grandin interrupted, "you say you saw a face inside this so strange bubble emanating from Mademoiselle Zita's side. Did you by any chance recognize it? Was it just a face, or was it, possibly, the countenance of someone whom you know?"

Colonel Szekler started violently, and a look of frightened surprise swept across his face. "Why should I have recognized it?" he demanded in a dry, harsh voice.

"*Tiens*, why should crockery show cracks, or knives dismember chickens, or table legs be built without knees?" de Grandin countered irritably. "I asked you if you recognized the face, not why."

Szekler seemed to age visibly, to put on ten more years, as he bent his head as though in tortured thought. "Yes, I recognized him," he answered slowly. "It was the face of Red-gauntlet Czerni."

"Ah, and one infers that your relations with this Monsieur Czerni were not always of the pleasantest?"

"I killed him."

De Grandin pursed his lips and raised inquiring brows. "Doubtless he was immeasurably improved by killing," he returned, "but why, specifically, did you bestow the happy dispatch on him, *Monsieur?*"

Colonel Szekler flicked his tongue across his nether lip again, and again I caught myself comparing him to something lupine.

"The vermin!" he gritted. "While I and my son—eternal rest grant him, O Lord!—were fighting at the front for Emperor and country, that toad-creature was skulking in the backwaters of Pest, evading military service. At last they caught him; shipped him off with other conscripts to the Eastern front. Two days later he deserted and went over to the Russians. An avowed Communist, he and Bela Kun and other traitors were hired by the Russians to foment Bolshevist cells among Hungarian prisoners of war.

The colonel's breath was coming fast, and his odd, light eyes were glazed as though a film had dropped over them, as he fairly hurled a question at us:

"Do you know—have you heard how two hundred loyal Hungarian officer-prisoners—prisoners of war, mind you, entitled to protection and respect by the law of nations—were butchered by the Russians and their traitorous Hungarian accomplices, because they could not be corrupted?"

De Grandin nodded shortly. "I was with the French Intelligence, *Monsieur*," he answered.

"My son Stephan was one of those whom Tibor Czerni helped to massacre—the swine boasted of it later!

"Back he came when war was done, led home to Hungary by the instinct that leads the vulture to the helpless, dying beast; and when the puppet-republic fell and bolshevism rose up in its place this vermin, this slacker and deserter, this traitor and murderer, was given the post of Commissar of the Tribunal of Summary Jurisdiction in Buda-Pest. You know what that meant, *hein?* That anyone whom he accused was doomed, that he was lord of life and death, a court from whose decisions there was no appeal throughout the city.

"You heard me call him 'Red-gauntlet'. You know why? Because, when it did not suit his whim to order unfortunate members of the bourgeoisie or gentry to be shot or hanged, he 'put the red gauntlets on them'—had his company of butchers take them out and beat their hands to bloody pulp with mauls upon a chopping-block. Then, crippled hopelessly, suffering torment almost unendurable, they were given liberty to serve as warning to others of their kind whose only crime was that they loved their country and were loyal to their king.

"One day the wretch conceived another scheme. He had been pampered, fawned upon and flattered since his rise to power till he thought himself omnipotent. Even women of our class—more shame to them!—had not withheld their favors to purchase safety for their men or the right to retain what little property they had. My wife—the Countess Szekler she was then—was noted for her beauty, and this slug, this toad, this monstrous parody of humankind determined to have *her*. This Galician cur presumed to raise his eyes to Irina Szekler—*kreuzsakrament*, he who was not fit to lap the water which had laved her feet!

"Out to our villa in the hills beyond Buda he went, forced himself into our house and made his vile proposals, telling my wife that he had captured me and only her complaisance could buy me immunity from the Red Gauntlets. But Szeklers do not buy immunity at such a price, and well she knew it. She ordered the vile creature from her presence as though she still were Countess Szekler and he but Tibor Czerni, son of a Galician money-lender and police court journalist of Pest.

"He left her, vowing dreadful vengeance. Only the fact that he had not brought his bullies with him saved her from immediate arrest, for an hour later a squadron of 'Lenin Boys' drove up to the house, looted it of everything which they could carry, then burned it to the ground.

"But we escaped. I came home almost as the scoundrel left, and we fled to friends in Buda who concealed us till I had time to grow a beard and so alter my appearance that I dared to venture on the street without certainty of summary arrest.

"Then I began my hunt. Systematically, day by day, I dogged the villain's steps, seeking for the chance to wash away the insult he had offered in his blood. Finally we met face to face in a side street just off Franz Joseph Square. He was armed, as always, but without his bodyguard of cutthroats. Despite my beard and shabby clothes he recognized me instantly and bawled out frantically for help, dragging at his pistol as he did so.

"But to draw the rapier from my sword-stick and run him through the throat was but an instant's work. He strangled in his blood before he could repeat his hail for help; so I dispatched the monster and escaped, for no one witnessed our encounter. Next day I fled with my wife and little daughter, and through a miracle we were able to cross the border to freedom."

"And had you ever seen this revenant—this materialization—before the painful incident in *Mademoiselle's* boudoir?" de Grandin asked.

Colonel Szekler flushed. "Yes," he answered. "Once. Though Stephan died a hero, and our loss was years ago, the wound has never healed in his mother's heart. Indeed, her sorrow seems increasing as the years go by. She has been leaning more and more toward spiritism of late years, and though we knew the Church forbids such things, my daughter and I could not bring ourselves to dissuade her, since she seemed to get some solace from the mediums' mummery. A month ago, when the first symptoms of Zita's returning illness were beginning to make their appearance, she prevailed on us to attend a séance with her.

"The sitting was held at the house of a medium who calls herself Madame Claire. The psychic sat at the end of a long table on which a gramophone's tin trumpet had been placed, and her wrists were fastened to the back of her chair with tape which was sewed, not tied. Her ankles were similarly secured to the front legs of the chair, and a blindfold was tied about her eyes. Then the lights were turned off and we sat with our hands upon the table, staring out into the darkness.

"We had waited some time without any manifestation, and I felt myself growing sleepy with the monotony of it, when a sharp rap sounded suddenly from the tin cone lying on the table. *Rat-tat-tat*, it came with a quick, clicking beat, then ended with a heavier blow, which caused a distinct metallic clang. No sooner had this ceased than the table began to move, as though pushed by the medium's feet; yet we had seen her ankles lashed securely to her chair and the knots sewed with thick linen thread.

"Next instant we heard the tin horn scraping slowly across the table-top, as though being lifted with an effort, only to fall back again. This kept up several minutes; then a voice came to us, rather weakly, but still strong enough to be understood:

A, B, C, D, E, F, G,
All good people hark to me,
Where you sit there, one two, three—

"The senseless doggerel was spouted at us through the trumpet which had risen and floated through the air to the far corner of the room. I was about to rise in anger at the childishness of it all when something happened which arrested my attention. The room in which we sat was closed up tightly. We had seen the medium shut and lock the door, and all the windows were latched and heavy curtains hung before them. The place was intolerably hot, and the air had begun to grow stale and flat; but as I made a move to rise, there was a sudden chilling of the atmosphere, as though a draft of winter wind had blown into the room. No, that is not quite accurate. There was no wind nor any stirring of the air; rather, it was as though we had all been put into some vast refrigerator where the temperature was absolute zero. What gave me the impression of an air-current was an odd, whistling sound which accompanied the sudden change of temperature—something like the whirring which one hears when wind blows through telegraph wires in wintertime.

"And as the chilling cold replaced the sultry heat, the piping, mincing voice reciting its inane drivel through the trumpet was replaced by another, a stronger voice, which laughed a cackling, spiteful laugh, then choked and retched and strangled, as though the throat from which it came were suddenly filled up with blood. The words it spoke were almost unintelligible, but not quite. I'd heard them fifteen years before, but they came back to me clearly, as though it had been yesterday:

"'Pig-dog, I'll have her yet. Next time, I'll come in such a way that you can not prevail against me!'

"They broke off with in awful, gurgling rattle, and I recognized them. It was the threat that Tibor Czerni spewed at me that day in Buda-Pest when I ran my rapier through his throat and he lay choking in his blood upon the sidewalk of Maria Valeria Street!

"Just then the trumpet fell crashing to the floor, and where it had been floating in the air there showed a spot of something luminous, like a monster bubble rising from some foul, miasmic swamp, and inside it, outlined by a sort of phosphorescence, showed the grinning, malignant face of Tibor Czerni.

"The medium woke up shrieking from her trance. 'Lights! For God's sake, turn on the lights!' she screamed. Then, as the lamps were lighted: 'I'm a trumpet psychic; my controls never materialize, yet—' she struggled with the bonds that held her to the chair in a perfect ecstasy of terror, crying, groaning, begging to be released, and it was not till we had cut the tapes that she could talk coherently. Then she ordered: 'Get out; get out, all of you—someone here is followed by an evil spirit; one of you must have done it a great wrong when it was in the flesh—one of you is a murderer! Out of my house, the lot of you, and take your Nemesis with you!'"

De Grandin tweaked the needle-points of his tightly waxed, diminutive mustache. "And the luminous globe, the one with Monsieur the Dead Man's face in it, did it disappear when the lights went up?" he asked.

"Yes," responded Colonel Szekler, "but—"

"But what, if you please, Monsieur?"

"There was a distinct odor in the room, an odor which had not been present before Czerni's cursed face appeared—it was the faint but unmistakable odor of decomposing flesh. Trust a soldier who has seen a hundred battlefield cemeteries plowed up by shell-fire weeks after the dead have been buried to recognize that smell!"

For a long moment there was silence. Colonel Szekler looked at Jules de Grandin expectantly. Jules de Grandin turned a speculative eye on Colonel Szekler. At length: "Very well, Monsieur," he agreed with a nod. "The case intrigues me. Let us go and see Mademoiselle your daughter."

2. Zita

COLONEL SZEKLER'S HOUSE FACED the Albemarle Road, a mile or so outside of town. It was a big house, bowered in Norway spruce and English holly and flowering rhododendron, well back from the highway, with a stretch of smoothly mown lawn before and a well-tended rose garden on each side. There was no hallway, and we stepped directly into a big room which seemed to combine the functions of library, music room and living-room. And as a mirror gives back the image of the face which looks in it, so this single room reflected the character of the family we had come to serve. Books, piano, easy-chairs and sofas loomed in the dim light filtering through the close-drawn silken curtains. An easel with a partly finished water color on it stood by a north window; beside it was a table of age-mellowed cherry laden with porcelain dishes, tubes of color and scattered badger-hair brushes.

Beside the concert-grand piano was a music-stand on which a violin rested, and the polished barrel of a cello showed beyond the music-bench. A bunch of snowballs nodded from a crystal vase upon a table, a spray of mimosa let its saffron grains fall in a graceful shower across a violet lampshade. Satsuma ash-trays stood on little tables beside long cigarette boxes of cedar cased in silver. Everywhere were books; books in French, German, Italian and English, some few in Danish, Swedish and Norwegian.

De Grandin took the room in with a quick, appraising glance. "*Pardieu*, they live with happy richness, these ones," he advised me in a whisper. "If *Mademoiselle* makes good one-tenth the promise of this room, *cordieu*, it will have been a privilege to have served her!"

"*Mademoiselle*" did. When she came in answer to her father's call she proved to be a slender, straight young thing of middle height, blond like her sire, betraying her Tartar ancestry, as he did, in her high cheek-bones and slightly slanting eyes. Her face, despite the hallmark of non-Aryan stock, was sweet and delicate as the blossom of an almond tree— "but a wilting blossom," I told myself as I noted white, transparent skin through which showed veins in fine blue lines. There was no flush upon her cheek, no light of fever in her eyes, but had she been my patient I should have ordered her to bed at once, and then to Saranac or Colorado.

"Mother's gone downtown," she told her father in a soft and gentle voice. "I know that she'll be sorry when she hears these gentlemen have called while she was out."

"Perhaps it's just as well she's out," the colonel answered. "Doctor de Grandin is a very famous occultist, as well as a physician, and I've called him into consultation because I am convinced that something more than bodily fatigue is responsible for your condition, dear. Will you be kind enough to tell him everything he wants to know?"

"Of course," she answered with a faint and rather wistful smile. "What is it that you'd like to hear about, Doctor? My illness? I'm not really ill, you know, just terribly, terribly tired. Rest and sleep don't seem to do me any good, for I rise as exhausted as when I go to bed, and the tonics they have given me"—she pulled a little face, half comic, half pathetic—"all they do is make my stomach ache."

"*Ah bah*, those tonics, those noisome medicines!" the little Frenchman nodded in agreement. "I know them. They pucker up the mouth, they make the tongue feel rough and sore—*mon Dieu*, what must they do to the poor stomach!"

Abruptly he sobered, and: "Let us have the physical examination first," he ordered.

At the end of half an hour I was more than puzzled, I was utterly bewildered. Her temperature and pulse were normal, her skin was neither dry nor moist, but exactly as a healthy person's skin should be; fremitus was in nowise more than usual; upon percussion there was no indication of impaired resonance, and the stethoscope could find no trace of mucous rales. Whatever else the young girl suffered from, I was prepared to stake my reputation it was not tuberculosis.

"Now, *Mademoiselle*," de Grandin asked as he completed jotting down our findings in his notebook, "do you recall the night that you and your parents attended Madame Claire's séance?"

"Of course; perfectly."

"Tell us, if you please, when first you saw the face within the globe of light. How did it look to you? Describe it, if you will."

"I didn't see it, sir."

"*Morbleu*, you did not see it? How was that?"

A faint flush crept across the girl's pale cheeks, then she laughed a soft, low, gurgling laugh, half embarrassment, half amusement. "I was asleep," she confessed. "Somehow, I'd been very tired that day—not as tired as I am now, but far more tired than my usual wont, and the air in Madame Claire's drawing-room seemed close and stuffy. Almost as soon as the lights were shut off I began to feel drowsy, and I closed my eyes—just for a minute, as I thought. The next thing I knew the lights were up and Madame Claire was trying to shriek and talk and cry, all at the same time. I couldn't make out what it was about, and it was several days before I heard about the face; the only way I know about it now is from piecing scraps of conversation together, for I didn't like to ask. It would have hurt poor Mother dreadfully if she knew I'd gone to sleep at one of her precious sittings with the spirits."

"Ah? So she has attended these séances often?"

"Gracious, yes! She pretended to Father that the one we went to was her first, but she'd been going to Madame Claire for over a year before she plucked up courage to ask Dad to go with her."

"And had you ever gone with her before?"

"No, sir."

"U'm. Now tell me: have you been subject to unusual dreams since that night at Madame Claire's?"

The blush which mantled her pale face and throat and mounted to her brow was startling in its vividness. Her long, pansy-blue eyes were suddenly suffused with tears, and she cast her glance demurely down until it rested on the silver cross-straps of her boudoir sandals. "Y-yes," she answered hesitantly. "I—I've had dreams."

"And they are—?" he paused with lifted brows, and I could see the sudden flicker in his little, round blue eyes which presaged keen excitement or sudden, murderous rage.

"I'd rather not describe them, sir," her answer was a muted whisper, but the deep flush stained her face and throat and brow again.

"No matter, *Mademoiselle*, you need not do so," he told her with a quick and reassuring smile. "Some things are better left unsaid, even in the medical consulting-room or the confessional."

"INVITE US OUT TO dinner, if you please," he told the colonel as we parted on the porch. "Already I have formed a theory of the case, and if I am not right, *parbleu*, I am much more mistaken than I think."

"DON'T YOU THINK YOU should have pushed the examination further?" I demanded as we drove back to town. "If Zita Szekler's trouble is psychic, or spiritual, if you prefer, an analysis of her dreams should prove helpful. You know Freud says—"

"*Ah bah*," he interrupted with a laugh, "who in Satan's naughty name cares what that old one says? Was it necessary that she should tell her secret dreams to me? *Cordieu*, I should say otherwise! That melting eye, that lowered glance, that quick, face-burning blush, do they mean nothing in your life, my friend, or is it that you grow so old and chilly-blooded that the sweet and subtle memories—"

"Confound you, be quiet!" I cut in. "If externals are any indication, I'd say the girl's in love; madly, infatuatedly in love, and—by George"—I broke off with a sudden inspiration—"that may be it! 'Love sickness' isn't just a jesting term; I've seen adolescents actually made ill by the thwarting of suppressed desire, and Zita Szekler's an Hungarian. They're different from the colder-blooded Nordics; like the Turks and Greeks and even the Italians and Spaniards, they actually suffer from an excess of pent-up emotion and—"

"*Oh là, là*—hear him spout!" the little Frenchman cut in with a chuckle. "You are positively droll, my olden one. And yet," he sobered suddenly, "you have arrived at half—no, a quarter—of the truth in your so awkward, blundering fashion. She *is* in love; sick—drunk—exhausted with it, *mon ami*; but not the kind of love you think of.

"Consider all the facts, if you will be so kind: What do we discover? This very devil of a fellow, Tibor Czerni, has made overtures to Madame Szekler while her husband is away. For that the colonel kills him, very properly. But what does Czerni say while he is dying on the sidewalk? He promises to come back, to have the object of his black and evil heart's desire, and to come in such a way that all resistance to his coming shall be unavailing. *N'est-ce-pas?*

"Very well, then. What next? The years have come and gone. Madame Szekler has grown older. Doubtless she is charming still, but Time has little pity on a woman. She has grown older. Ah, but her little, infant daughter, *she* has ripened with the passing of the seasons. She has grown to sweet and blooming womanhood. Have we not seen her? But certainly. And"—he put his gathered fingers to his lips and wafted an ecstatic kiss up toward the evening sky—"she is the very blossom of the peach, the flower of the jasmine; she is the morning dew upon the rose—*mordieu*, she is not trying on the eyes!

"Now, what turned Madame Szekler's thoughts to spiritism? One does not surely know, but one may guess. Was it only the preying thought of her loneliness at the loss of her first child, or was it not, perhaps, the evil influence of that wicked one who was constantly hovering over the house of Szekler like the shadow of a pestilence; ever dwelling on the threshold of their lives with intent to do them evil?"

"You mean to intimate—" I started, but:

"Be quiet," he commanded sharply. "I am thinking.

"At any rate his opportunity arrived at last. Poor Madame Szekler sought out the medium and let her guard be lowered. There was the opening through which this evil, discarnate entity could inject himself, the doorway, all unguarded, through which he might proceed to spoil the very treasure-house of Szekler. Yes.

"You realize, my friend, that a spiritualistic séance is as unsafe to the spirit as a smallpox case is to the body?"

"How's that?"

"Because there are low-grade discarnate entities, just as there are low-grade mortals, spirits which have never inhabited human form—but which would like to—and the lowest and most vicious spirits whose human lives have been but cycles of wickedness and debauchery. These invariably infest the sittings of the spiritists, ever seeking for an opening through which they may once more regain the world and work their wicked wills. You know the mediums work through 'controls'? *Ha*, I tell you the line of demarcation between innocent 'control' by some benevolently-minded spirit and possession by an evil entity is a very, very narrow one. Sometimes there is no line at all.

"Now, how can an evil spirit enter in a human body—gain possession of it? Chiefly by dominating that body's human will. It is this will-dominance, which is akin to hypnotism, that is the starting, the danger-point from which all evil things work forward. You have been to séances; you know their technique. The dual state of mental concentration and muscular relaxation which is necessary on the part of everyone for the evocation of the medium's control is closely analogous to that state of passive consent which the hypnotist demands of his subject. If a person attending a séance chances to be in delicate health, so much the worse for him—or her. The evil spirit, striving for control of mortal flesh, can force his way into that body more easily than if it were a vigorous one, precisely as the germ of a physical disease can find a favorable place to incubate where the phagocytic army of defense is weak.

"Now, consider Mademoiselle Zita's condition on the evening of that so abominable séance. She was 'tired', she said, so tired that when she 'closed her eyes just for a moment' she fell into instant slumber. Was her sleep a natural one, or was it but a state of trance induced by the wicked spirit of the wicked Czerni? Who can say?

"At any rate, we know that Czerni's spirit materialized, though Madame Claire declared no spirits ever did so in her séances before. Moreover, while the innocuous control of Madame Claire was making a fool of itself by reciting that so silly verse, it was roughly shouldered from the way, and Czerni's dying threat was bellowed through the trumpet, after which the trumpet tumbled to the floor and Czerni showed his wicked face.

"He has come back, even as he promised, my friend. The materialization which the colonel witnessed in his home the other day establishes the fact. And he has come back to fulfill his threat; only, instead of possessing the mother, as he swore to do when he was dying, he has transferred his vile attentions to the young and lovely daughter. Yes, of course.

"Oh, you're fantastic!" I derided.

"Possibly," he nodded gloomily. "But I am also right, my friend. I would that I were not."

3. The Phantom Lover

MADAME SZEKLER, WHO PRESIDED at dinner, proved as representative of the old, vanished order of Hungarian society as her husband. Well beyond the borderline of middle age, she still retained appealing charm and beauty, with a slender, exquisitely formed figure which lent distinction to her Viennese dinner gown, a face devoid of lines or wrinkles as a girl's, high-browed but heavy-lidded eyes of pansy blue and a pale but flawless skin. Her hair, close-cropped as a man's and brushed straight back with a flat marcelle, was gleaming-white as a cloud adrift upon a summer sky, and gave added charm, rather than any impression of age, to her cameo-clear features.

"Zita was too tired to come to dinner; I left her sleeping soundly shortly after you had gone," Colonel Szekler apologized, and de Grandin bowed assent.

"It is well for her to get as much rest as she can," he answered; then, in an aside to me:

"It is better so, Friend Trowbridge; I would observe *Madame* at dinner, and I can do so better in her daughter's absence. Do you regard her, too, if you will be so kind. Ladies of her age are apt to become neurotic. I should value your opinion."

Dinner was quite gay, for de Grandin's spirits rose perceptibly when the main course proved to be boned squab, basted in wine, stuffed with Carolina wild rice and served with orange ice. When the glasses were filled with vintage Tokay he seemed to have forgotten the existence of such a thing as trouble, and his witty sallies brought repeated chuckles from the colonel and even coaxed a smile to Madame Szekler's sad, aristocratic lips.

The meal concluded, we adjourned to the big living-room, where coffee and liqueurs were served while de Grandin and I smoked cigars and our host and hostess puffed at long, slim cigarettes which were one-third paper mouthpiece.

"But it grows late," the little Frenchman told us as he concluded one of his inimitable anecdotes; "let us go upstairs and see how Mademoiselle Zita does."

The girl was sleeping peacefully when we looked into her room, and I was about to go downstairs again when de Grandin plucked me by the sleeve.

"Wait here, my friend," he bade. "It yet wants a half-hour until midnight, and it is then that he is most likely to appear."

'You think she's apt to have another—visitation?" Madame Szekler asked. "Oh, if I thought that wretched séance were the cause of this, I'd kill myself. I only wanted to be near my boy, but—"

"Do not distress yourself, *Madame*," de Grandin interrupted. "He was bound to find a way to enter in, that one. The séance did at most but hasten his advent—and that of Jules de Grandin. Leave us with her, if you please. If nothing happens, all is well; if she is visited, we shall be here to take such steps as may be necessary."

For hours our vigil by the sleeping girl was uneventful. Her breath came soft and regular: she did not even change position as she slept; and I stood by the window, smothering back a yawn and wishing that I had not drunk so much Tokay at dinner. Abruptly:

"Trowbridge, my friend, observe!" de Grandin's low, sharp whisper summoned my attention.

Turning, I saw that the girl had cast aside the covers and lay upon her bed, her slender, supple body showing pale as carven alabaster through the meshes of her black-lace sleeping-suit. As I looked I saw her head move restlessly from side to side, and heard a little moan escape her. I was reminded of a sleepy, ailing child registering protest at being waked to take unpleasant-tasting medicine.

But not for long was this reluctance shown. Slowly, almost tentatively, like one who feels her cautious way through darkness, she put forth one exquisitely small foot and then the other, hesitated for a breath, then rose up from her couch, a smile of blissful joy upon her face. And though her eyes were closed, she seemed to see her path as she walked half-way across the room, then halted suddenly, stretched out her arms, then clasped them tightly, as though she never would let go of what she held. Head back, lips parted, she raised herself and stood on tiptoe, scarcely seeming to touch the floor. It was as if, by some sort of levitation, she were lifted up and really floated in the air, anchored to earth only by the pink-tipped toes of her small feet. Or was it not—my heart stood still as the thought crashed through my mind—was it not as though she yielded herself to the embrace of someone taller than herself, someone who clasped her in his arms, all but lifting her from her feet while he rained kisses on her yearning mouth?

A little, moaning gasp escaped her, and she staggered backward dizzily, still hugging something which we could not see against her breast, her every movement more like that of one who leaned upon another for support than one who walked unaided. She fell across the bed. Her eyes were still fast-shut, but she thrust her head a little forward, as though she seemed to see ecstatic visions through the lowered lids. Her pale cheeks flushed, her lips fell back in the sweet curve of an eager, avid smile. She raised her hands, making little downward passes before her face, as though she stroked the cheeks of one who leant above her, and a gentle tremor shook her slender form as her slim bosom seemed to swell and her lips opened and closed slowly, blissfully, in a pantomime of kissing. A deep sigh issued from between her milk-white teeth; then her breath came short and jerkily in quick exhausted gasps.

"*Grand Dieu—l'incube!*" de Grandin whispered. "See, my friend?"

"*L'incube*—incubus—nightmare? I should say so!" I exclaimed. "Quick, waken her, de Grandin; this sort of thing may lead to erotomania!"

"Be still!" he whispered sharply. "I did not say *an* incubus, but *the* incubus. This is no nightmare, my friend, it is a foul being from the world beyond who woos a mortal woman—observe, behold, *regardez-vous!*"

From Zita's side, three inches or so below the gentle prominence of her left breast, there came a tiny puff of smoke, as from a cigarette. But it was renewed, sustained, growing from a puff to a stream, from a stream to a column, finally mushrooming at the top to form a nebulous, white pompon which whirled and gyrated and seemed to spin upon its axis, growing larger and more solid-seeming with each revolution. Then the grayish-whiteness of the vapor faded, took on translucence, gradually became transparent, and like a soap-bubble of gigantic size floated upward till it rested in the air a foot or so above the girl's ecstatic countenance.

And from the bubble looked a face—a man's face, evil as Mefisto's own, instinct with cruelty and lechery and wild, vindictive triumph. The features were coarse, gross, heavy; bulbous lips, not red, but rather purple as though gorged with blood; a great hooked nose, not aquiline, but rather reminiscent of a vulture; dank, matted hair which clung in greasy strands to a low forehead; deepset, lack-luster eyes which burned like corpse-lights showing through the hollow sockets of a skull.

I started back involuntarily, but de Grandin thrust his hand into the pocket of his dinner coat and advanced upon the vision. "Gutter-spawn of hell," he warned, "be off. *Conjuro te; abire ad locum tuum!*" With a wrenching motion he drew forth a *flaçon*, undid its stopper and hurled its contents straight against the gleaming bubble which encased the leering face.

The pearly drops of water struck the opalescent sphere as though it had been glass, some of them splashing on the sleeping, girl, some adhering to the globe's smooth sides, but for all the effect they produced they might as well not have been thrown.

"Now, by the horns on Satan's head—" the Frenchman began furiously, but stopped abruptly as the globe began to whirl again. As though it had derived its roundness from winding up the end of the smoke-column issuing from Zita's side, so now it seemed that it reversed itself, becoming first oval as it turned, then elliptical, then long and sausage-shaped, finally merging with the trailing wisp of vapor which floated from the girl's slim trunk, and which, even as we watched, was steadily withdrawn until it lost itself in her white flesh.

Zita was lying on her back, her arms stretched out as though she had been crucified, her breath coming in hot, fevered gasps, tears welling from beneath the lashes of her lowered lids.

"Now, look at this, my friend," de Grandin ordered. "It was from here the vapor issued, was it not?"

He placed a finger over the girl's side, and as I nodded he drew a needle from his lapel and thrust it to the eye in her soft flesh. I cried aloud at his barbarity, but he silenced me with a quick gesture, parted the wide meshes of her lace pajamas and held the bedside lamp above the acupuncture. The steel was almost wholly fleshed in her side; yet not only did she not cry out, but there was no sign of blood about the point of incision. It might as well have been dead tissue into which he thrust the needle.

"Whatever are you doing?" I demanded furiously.

"Merely testing," he replied; then, contritely: "*Non*, I would not play with you, my friend. I did desire to assure myself of a local anesthesia at the point from which the ectoplasm issued. You know the olden story that witches and all those who sold themselves to Satan bore somewhere on their bodies an area insensible to pain. This was said to be because the Devil had possessed them. I shall not say it was not so; but what if the possession be involuntary, if the evil spirit of possession comes against the will of the possessed? Will there still be such local insensitive areas? I thought there would be. *Pardieu*, now I know. I have proved it!

"Now the task remains to us to devise some method of attack against this so vile miscreant. He has become as much physical as spiritual; consequently spiritual weapons are of little avail against him. Will the purely physical prevail, one wonders?"

"How d'ye mean?"

"Why, you saw what happened when I dashed the holy water on him—it did not seem to inconvenience him at all."

"But, good heavens, man," I argued, "how can that—whatever it was we saw—be both spiritual and physical? Doesn't it have to be one or the other?"

"Not necessarily," he answered. "You and I and all the rest of us are dually constructed: part physical body, part animating spirit. This unpleasant Czerni person was once the same, till Colonel Szekler killed him. Then he became wholly spirit, but evil spirit. And because he was a spirit he was powerless to work overt harm. He lacked a body for his evil work. Then finally came opportunity. At that cursed séance of Madame Claire's, Mademoiselle Zita was an ideal tool to work his wickedness. It is a well-recognized fact among Spiritualists that the adolescent girl is regarded as the ideal medium, where it is desired that the spirits materialize. For why? Because such girls' nerves are highly strung and their physical resistance weak. It is from such as these that imponderable, but nevertheless physical substance called ectoplasm is most easily ravished by the spirit desiring to materialize, to build himself a semi-solid body. Accordingly, Mademoiselle Zita was ideal for the vile Czerni's purpose. From her he drew the ectoplasm to materialize at Madame Claire's. When the ectoplasm flowed back to her, *he went with it*. This moment, Friend Trowbridge, he dwells within her, dominating her completely while she is asleep and the conscious mind is off its guard, drawing ectoplasm from her when he would make himself apparent. He can not do so often, she is not strong enough to furnish him the power for frequent materializations; but there he is, ever present, always seeking opportunity to injure her. We must cast him out, my friend, before he takes complete possession of her, and she becomes what the ancients called 'possessed of a devil'; what we call insane.

"Come, let us go. I do not think that he will trouble her again tonight, and I have much studying to do before we come to final grips, I and this so vile revenant of the Red Gauntlets."

4. Red Gauntlets of Czerni

"TROWBRIDGE, MY FRIEND, AWAKE, arouse yourself; get up!" de Grandin's hail broke through my early-morning sleep. "Rise, dress, make haste, friend; we are greatly needed!"

"Eh?" I sat up drowsily and shook the sleep from my eyes. "What's wrong?"

"Everything, by blue!" he answered. "It is Mademoiselle Zita. She is hurt, maimed, injured. They have taken her to Mercy Hospital. We must hurry.

"No, I can not tell you the nature of her injuries," he answered as we drove through the gray light of early dawn toward the hospital. "I only know that she is badly hurt. Colonel Szekler telephoned a few minutes ago and seemed in great distress. He said it was her hands—"

"Her hands?" I echoed. "How—"

"*Cordieu*, I said I do not know," he flashed back. "But I damn suspect, and if my suspicions are well founded we must hasten and arrive before it is too late."

"Too late for what?"

"Oh, *pour l'amour des porcs*, talk less, drive faster, if you please, great stupid one!" he shouted.

COLONEL SZEKLER, GRAY-FACED AS a corpse, awaited us in the hospital's reception room. "*Himmelkreuzsakrament*," he swore through chattering teeth, "this is dreadful, unthinkable! My girl, my little Zita—" a storm of retching sobs choked further utterance, and he bowed his forehead on his arms and wept as though his heart were bursting.

"Courage, *Monsieur*," de Grandin soothed. "All is not lost; tell us how it happened; what is it that befell *Mademoiselle*—"

"All isn't lost, you say?" Colonel Szekler raised his tear-scarred face, and the wolfish gleam in his eyes was so dreadful that involuntarily I raised my arm protectively. "All isn't lost, when my little girl is hopelessly deformed?—when *she wears the red gauntlets of Czerni?*"

"*Dieu de Dieu de Dieu de Dieu*, do you say it?" the Frenchman cried. "Attention, *Monsieur*; lay by your grief and tell me all—everything—immediately. There is not a moment to be wasted. I had the presentiment that this might be what happened, and I have made plans, but first I must know all. Speak, *Monsieur!* There will be time enough to grieve if our efforts prove futile. Now is the time for action."

Laying small, white hands upon the colonel's shoulders, he shook him almost as a dog might shake a rat, and the show of unexpected strength in one so small, no less than the physical violence, brought the colonel from his maze of grief.

"It was about three-quarters of an hour ago," he began. "I'd gone to Zita's room and found her resting peacefully; so, reassured, I lay down and fell asleep.

Immediately, I began to dream. I was back in Buda-Pest again during the terror. Czerni was sitting in judgment on helpless victims of the Bolsheviki's vengeance. One after another they were brought before him, soldiers of the king, nobles, members of the *bourgeoisie*—children, old men, women, anyone and everyone who had fallen into the clutches of his rowdies of the Red Guard. Always the judgment was the same—death. As well might a lamb have looked for mercy from the wolf-pack as a member of our class seek clemency from that mockery of a court where Tibor Czerni sat in judgment.

"Then they brought Zita in. She stood before him, proud and silent, as became her ancient blood, not deigning to offer any defense to the accusation of counter-revolutionary activities which they brought against her. I saw Czerni's eyes light with lust as he looked at her, taking her in from head to foot with a lecherous glance that seemed to strip the garments from her body as he puckered up his gross, thick lips and smiled.

"'The charges are not proved to my satisfaction,' he declared when all the accusations had been made. 'At least they are not sufficiently substantiated to merit the death sentence on this young lady. It would be a pity, too, to mar that pretty body with bullets or stretch that lovely throat out of proportion with the hangman's rope. Besides, I know her parents, her charming mother and her proud, distinguished father. I owe them something, and I must pay my debt. Therefore, for their sakes, if not for her own charming self, I order this young lady to be set at liberty.'

"I saw a look of incredulous relief sweep over Zita's face as he gave the order, but it was replaced by one of horror as he finished:

"'Yes, comrades, set her free—but not until you've put red gauntlets on her!'

"And as I lay there gasping at the horror of my dream, I heard a laugh, high, cachinnating, triumphant, and awoke with the echo of it in my ears. Then, as I was about to fall asleep again, thanking heaven that I only dreamt, I heard Zita's scream. Peal after peal of frenzied shrieks came from her room as she cried for mercy, called to me and her mother for help, then, becoming inarticulate, merely wailed in agony. As I ran headlong down the hall her screaming died away, and she was only moaning weakly when I reached her room.

"She lay across her bed, groaning in exhausted agony, like a helpless beast caught in the hunter's trap, and her hands were stretched straight out before her.

"Her hands—*Gott in Himmel*, no! Her stumps! Her hands were crushed to bloody pulp and hung upon her wrists like mops of shredded cloth, sopping with red stickiness. Blood was over everything, the bed, the rug, the pillows and her sleeping-suit, and as I looked at her I could see it spurting from the mangled flesh of her poor, battered hands with every palpitation of her pounding heart.

"'This, too, is a dream,' I told myself, but when I crossed the room and touched her, I knew it was no dream. How it happened I don't know, but somehow, through some damned black magic, Tibor Czerni has been able to come back from that hell where his monstrous spirit waits throughout eternity and work this mischief to my child; to disfigure her beyond redemption and make a helpless cripple of her.

"There was little I could do. I got some dressings from the bathroom and bound her hands, trying my best to staunch the flow of blood, 'phoned to Mercy Hospital for an ambulance; finally called you. We are lost. Czerni has triumphed."

"WILL YOU SIGN THIS, sir?" the young intern, sick with revulsion at the ghastly phases of his trade, stepped almost diffidently into the reception room and presented a filled-in form to Colonel Szekler. "It's your authority as next of kin for the operation."

"Is it absolutely necessary—must they operate?" Colonel Szekler asked with a sharp intake of his breath.

"Good Lord, yes!" the young man answered. "It's dreadful, sir; I never saw anything like it. Doctor Teach will have to take both hands off above the carpus, he says—"

"*Pardonnez-moi, Monsieur,* but who will take what off above the which?" de Grandin interrupted. His voice was soft but there was murderous fury flashing in his small blue eyes.

"Doctor Teach, sir; the chief surgeon. He's in the operating-room now, and as soon as Colonel Szekler signs this authorization—"

"*Par la barbe d'un poisson,* your youngest grandchild will have grown a long white beard before that happens!" the Frenchman cried. "Give me that cursed damned, abominable, execrable paper, if you please!" He snatched the form from the young doctor's hand and tore it into shreds. "Go tell Doctor Teach that I shall do likewise to him if he so much as lays a finger on her," he added.

"But you don't understand, this is an emergency case," the intern swallowed his anger, for Jules de Grandin's reputation as a surgeon, had become a byword in the city's clinics, and my thirty years and more of practise had lent respectability, if nothing more, to my professional standing. "Just look at her card!"

From his pocket he produced a duplicate of the reception record, and I read across de Grandin's shoulder:

Right hand—Multiple fractures of carpus and metacarpus; compound comminutive fractures of first, second and third phalanges; rupture of flexor and reflexor muscles; short abductor muscle severed; multiple contusions of thenar eminence; multiple ecchymoses . . .

"Good heavens!" I exclaimed as the detailed catalogue of injuries burned itself into my brain; "he's right, de Grandin: her hands are practically destroyed."

"*Parbleu*, so will that *sacré* Doctor Teach be if he presumes to lay a hand on her!" he shot back fiercely; then, to Colonel Szekler:

"Retract your order of employment, *Monsieur*, I implore you. Tell them that they may not operate, at least until Doctor Trowbridge and I have had an opportunity to treat her. Do you realize what it means if that *sale* butcher is allowed to take her hands away?"

Colonel Szekler eyed him coldly. "I came to you in the hope of freeing her from the incubus that rested on her," he replied. "They told me you were skilled in such things, and had helped others. You failed me. Czerni's ghost took no more notice of your boasted powers than he did of the efforts of those medical fakers I'd called in. Now she is deformed, crippled past all hope of healing, and you ask another chance. You'd cure her? You haven't even seen her poor, crushed hands. What assurance have I that—"

"*Monsieur*," the little Frenchman broke in challengingly, "you are a soldier, are you not?"

"Eh? Yes, of course, but—"

"And you put the miscreant Czerni to death, *n'est-ce-pas?*"

"I did, but—"

"And you would not shrink from taking life again?"

"What—"

"Very good. I put my life in pawn for my success, *Monsieur!*" Reaching underneath his jacket he drew out the vicious little Ortgies automatic pistol cradled in its holster below his armpit and handed it to Colonel Szekler. "There are nine shots in it, Monsieur," he said. "One will be enough to finish Jules de Grandin if he fails."

"BUT THERE ISN'T A chance; not a ghost of a chance, Trowbridge!" stormed Doctor Teach when we told him that the colonel had withheld permission for the operation. "I've seen de Grandin do some clever tricks in surgery—he's a good workman, I'll give him that—but anyone who holds out hope of saving that girl's hands is a liar or a fool or both. I tell you, it's hopeless; utterly hopeless."

"Do you drink, *Monsieur?*" de Grandin interjected mildly, apropos of nothing.

Doctor Teach favored him with a stare beside which that bestowed by Cotton Mather on a Salem witch would have been a lover's ardent glance. "I don't quite see it's any of your business," he answered coldly, "but as a matter of fact I do sometimes indulge."

"Ah, *bon, meilleur; mieux.* Let us wager. When all is done, let us drink glass for glass till one of us can drink no more, and if I save her hands you pay the score; if not, I shall. You agree?"

"You've an odd sense of humor, sir, jesting at a time like this."

"Ah, *mon Dieu*, hear him!" de Grandin cried as he rolled his eyes toward heaven. "As if good brandy could ever be a cause for jest!"

"WELL, YOU'VE GOT YOURSELF into a nice fix, I must say!" I chided as we sat beside the cot where Zita Szekler lay, still drugged with morphine. "You've no more chance of saving this poor child's hands than I have of flying to the moon, and if I know anything of human nature, Colonel Szekler will take you at your word when he finds you can't make good your promise, and shoot you like a dog. Besides, you've made me look ridiculous by seeming to back you in your insane—"

"S-s-st!" his sharp hiss shut me off. "Be quiet, if you please. I would think, and can not do so for your ceaseless jabbering."

He rose, went to the wall telephone and called the office. "Is all in readiness, exactly as I ordered?" he demanded. A pause; then: "*Bon, très bon, Mademoiselle*; have them bring the sweeper to this floor immediately, and have the saline solution all in readiness in the operating-room.

"What the deuce—" I began, but he waved me silent.

"I arranged for my *matériel de siège* while they were transporting her," he answered with a smile. "Now, if *Monsieur le Revenant* will only put in his appearance—ah, *parbleu*, what have we here? By damn, I think he does!"

The drugged girl on the bed began to stir and moan as though she suffered an unpleasant dream, and I became aware of a faint, unpleasant smell which cut through the mingled aroma of disinfectant and anesthetic permeating the hospital atmosphere. For a moment I was at a loss to place it; then, suddenly, I knew. Across the span of years my memory flew to the days of my internship, when I had to make my periodic visits to the city mortuary. That odor of decaying human flesh once smelled can never be forgotten, nor can all the deodorants under heaven quite drive it from the air.

And now the girl's soft breast was heaving tremulously, and her features were distorted by a faint grimace of suffering. Her brows drew downward, and along her cheeks deep lines were cut, as though she were about to weep.

"She's coming out of anesthesia," I warned; "shall I ring for a—"

"S-s-sst! Be quiet!" de Grandin commanded, leaning toward the writhing girl, his little eyes agleam, lips drawn back from his small, white teeth in a smile which was more than half a snarl.

Slowly, almost tentatively, a little puff of gray-white, smoke-like substance issued from the moaning girl's left side, grew larger and denser, whirled spirally above her, seemed to blossom into something globular—a big and iridescent bubble-thing in which the pale malignant features of the incubus took form.

"Now for the test, by blue!" de Grandin murmured fiercely.

With a leap he crossed the room, swung back the door and jumped across the threshold to the corridor, reappearing in the twinkling of an eye with—of all things!—*a vacuum sweeper* in his hand. He set the mechanism going with a quick flick of the trigger, and as the sharp, irritable whine of the motor sounded, sprang across the room, paused a moment by the bed and thrusting his hand beneath his jacket drew forth his heavy Kukri knife and passed it with a slashing motion above the girl's stiff, quivering form. The steel sheared through the ligament of tenuous, smoke-like matter connecting the gleaming bubble-globe to Zita's side, and as the sphere raised itself, like a toy balloon released from its tether, he brought the nozzle of the vacuum cleaner up, caught the trailing, gray-white wisp of gelatinous substance which swung pendent in the air and—sucked it in.

The droning motor halted in its vicious hornet-whine, as though the burden he had placed on it were more than it could cope with; then, sharply, spitefully, began to whir again, and, bit by struggling bit, the trail of pale, pellucid stuff was sucked into the bellows of the vacuum pump.

A look of ghastly fright and horror shone upon the face within the bubble. The wide mouth opened gaspingly, the heavy-lidded eyes popped staringly, as though a throttling hand had been laid on the creature's unseen throat, and we heard a little whimpering sound, so faint that it was scarcely audible, but loud enough to be identified. It was like the shrieking of someone in mortal torment heard across a stretch of miles.

"Ha—so? And you would laugh at Jules de Grandin's face, *Monsieur?*" the little Frenchman cried exultantly. "You would make of him one louse-infested monkey? Yes? *Parbleu*, I damn think we shall see who makes a monkey out of whom before our little game is played out to a finish. But certainly!"

"Ring the bell, Friend Trowbridge," he commanded me. "Bid them take her to the operating room and infuse a quart of artificial serum by hypodermoclysis. Doctor Brundage is in readiness; he knows what to do.

"Now, come with me, if you would see what you shall see," he ordered as I made the call. "Leave *Mademoiselle* with them; they have their orders."

Twisting the connecting hose of the vacuum cleaner into a sharp V, he shut the current off; then, always the urbane Parisian, he motioned me to precede him through the door.

Down to the basement we hastened, and paused by the great furnace which kept the building well supplied with boiling water. He thrust the cleaner's plug into an electric wall fixture and: "Will you be kind enough to open up that door?" he asked, nodding toward the furnace and switching on the power in his motor.

As the machine once more began to hum he pressed the trigger sharply downward, reversing the motor and forcing air from the cleaner's bellows. There was a short, sharp, sputtering cough, as though the mechanism halted in its task, then a labored, angry groaning of the motor as it pumped and pumped against some stubborn obstacle. Abruptly, the motor started racing, and like a puff of smoke discharging from a gun, a great gray ring shot from the cleaner's nozzle into the superheated air of the furnace firebox. For an instant it hovered just above the gleaming, incandescent coals; then with an oddly splashing sound it dropped upon the fire-bed, and a sharp hissing followed while a cloud of heavy steam arose and spiraled toward the flue. I sickened as I smelled the acrid odor of incinerating flesh.

"*Très bien.* That, it appears, is that," announced de Grandin as he shut the motor off and closed the furnace door with a well-directed kick. "Come, let us go and see how Mademoiselle Zita does. They should be through with the infusion by this time."

5. Release

ZITA SZEKLER LAY UPON her bed, her bandaged hands upon her bosom. Whether she was still under anesthesia or not I could not tell, but she seemed to be resting easily. Also, strangely, there was not the dreadful pallor that had marked her when we left; instead, her cheeks were faintly, though by no means feverishly, flushed and her lips were healthy pink.

"Why, this is incredible," I told him. "She's been through an experience fit to make a nervous wreck of her, the pain she suffered must have been exquisite, she's had extensive hemorrhages; yet—"

"Yet you forget that Doctor Brundage pumped a thousand cubic centimeters of synthetic serum into her, and that such heroic measures are almost sovereign in case of shock, collapse, hemorrhage or coma. No, my friend, she lost but little blood, and what she lost was more than compensated by the saline infusion. It was against the loss of life-force I desired to insure her, and it seems the treatment was effective."

"Life-force? How do you mean?"

He grinned his quick, infectious elfin grin and, regardless of institutional prohibitions, produced a rank-smelling Maryland and set it glowing. "Ectoplasm," he replied laconically.

"Ec—what in the world—"

"*Précisément, exactement,* quite so," he answered with another grin. "Regard me, if you please: This Czerni person's soul was earthbound, as we know. It hung about the Szekler house, ever seeking opportunity for mischief, but it could accomplish little; for immaterial spirits, lacking physical co-operation of some sort, can not accomplish physical results. At last there came the chance when Madame Szekler induced her husband and child to attend that séance. Mademoiselle Zita was ill, nervous, run down, not able to withstand her assaults. Not only was he able to force himself into her mind to make her do his bidding, but he was able to withdraw from her the ectoplasmic force which supplied him with a body of a kind.

"This ectoplasm, what is it? We do not surely know, any more than we know what electricity is. But in a vague way we know that it is a solidification of the body's emanations. How? Puff out your breath. You can not see it, but you know that something vital has gone out of you. Ah, but if the temperature were low enough, you could not only feel your breath, you could see it, as well. So, when conditions are favorable, the ectoplasm, at other times unseen, becomes visible. Not only that, by a blending of the spiritual entity with its physical properties, it can become an almost-physical body. A materialization, we should call it, a 'manifestation' the Spiritists denominate it.

"Why did he do this? For two reasons. First, he craved a body of some sort again; by materializing, he could make himself seen by Colonel Szekler, whom he desired to plague. He had become a sort of semi-human once again, so far physical that physical means had to be taken to combat him.

"Last night, when I flung the holy water on him, and nothing happened, I said, 'Mon Dieu, I am lost!' Then I counseled me, 'Jules de Grandin, do not be dismayed. If holy things are unavailing, it is because he has become physical, though not corporeal, and you must use physical weapons to combat him.'

"'Very good, Jules de Grandin, it shall be that way,' I say to me.

"Thereupon I planned my scheme of warfare. He was too vague, too subtle, too incorporeal to be killed to death with a sword or pistol. The weapons would cut through him but do him little harm. 'Ah, but there is always one thing that will deal with such as he,' I remind me. 'Fire, the cleansing fire, regarded by the ancients as an element, known by the moderns as the universal solvent.'

"But how to get him to the fire? I could not bring the fire to him, for fear of hurting Mademoiselle Zita. I could not take him to the fire, for he would take refuge in her body if I attempted to seize him. Then I remembered: When he materialized in her room the bubble which enclosed his evil face wavered in the air.

"'Ah-ha, my evil one,' I say, 'I have you at the disadvantage. If you can be blown by the wind you can be sucked by in air-current. It is the vacuum sweeper which shall be your hearse to take you to the crematory. Oh, yes.'

"So then I know that we must lie in wait for him with our vacuum sweeper all in readiness. It may take months to catch him, but catch him we shall, eventually. But there is another risk. We must sever his materialized form from Mademoiselle Zita's body, and we can not put the ectoplasm back. And so I decide that we must have some saline solution ready to revive her from the shock of losing all that life-force. This seemed a condition which could not be overcome, but this wicked Czerni, by his very wickedness, provided us with the solution of our problem. By injuring Mademoiselle Zita, he made them bring her to this hospital, the one place where we should have everything ready to our hand—the sweeper, the fire which should consume him utterly, the saline solution and facilities for its quick administration. *Eh bien*, my friend, but he did us the favor, that one.

"But her hands, man, her hands," I broke in. "How—"

"It is a stigma," he replied.

"A stigma—how—what—"

"Perfectly. You understand the phenomenon of stigmata? It is akin to hypnotism. In the psychological laboratory you have seen it, but by a different name. The hypnotist can bid his subject's blood run from his hand, and the hand becomes pale and anemic; you have seen the blood transferred from one arm to another; you have seen what appears to be a wound take form upon the skin without external violence, merely the command of the hypnotist.

"Now, this Czerni had complete possession of Mademoiselle Zita's mind while she slept. He could make her do all manner of things, think of all manner of things, feel all manner of things. He had only to give her the command: 'Your hands have been beaten to a pulp, smashed by merciless mauls upon a chopping-block—you are wearing the red gauntlets!' and, to all intents, what he said became a fact. Just as the scientific hypnotist makes his subject's blood reverse itself against the course of nature, just as he makes what appears to be a bleeding cut appear upon uninjured skin—then heals it with a word—so could Czerni make Mademoiselle Zita's hands take on the appearance of wearing the red gauntlets without the use of outside force. Only a strong will, animated by a frightful hate, and operating on another will whose resistance had completely broken down could do these things; but do them he did. Yes.

"When Colonel Szekler told me how his daughter became red-gauntleted while lying in her bed, where she could not possibly have been injured by external force, I knew that this was what had happened, and so sure was I of my diagnosis that I staked my life upon it. Now—"

"You're crazy!" I broke in.

"We shall see," he answered with a smile, crossed to the bed and placed a second pillow under Zita's head, so that she was almost in a sitting posture.

"*Mademoiselle*," he called softly while he stroked her forehead gently, "Mademoiselle Zita, can you hear me?" He pressed his thumbs transversely on her brow, drawing them slowly outward with a stroking motion, then, with fingers on her temples, bore his thumbs against her throat below the ears. "*Mademoiselle*," he ordered in a low, insistent voice, "it is I, Jules de Grandin. I am the master of your thought, you can not think or act or move without my permission. Do you hear?"

"I hear," she answered in a sleepy voice.

"And you obey?"

"And I obey."

"*Très bon*. I bid you to forget all which the evil Czerni told you; to unlock your mind from the prison of his dominance—to restore your hands to their accustomed shape. Your hands are normal, unharmed in any way; they have never been scarred or hurt, not even scratched.

"*Mademoiselle, in what condition are your hands?*"

"They are normal and uninjured," she replied.

"*Bien! Triomphe!* Now, let us see."

With a pair of surgical shears he cut away the bandages. I held my breath as he drew away the gauze, but I wondered as the lower layers were drawn apart and showed no stain of blood.

The final layer was off. Zita Szekler's hands lay on the counterpane, smooth, white, pink-tipped, without a mark, or scar, or blemish.

"Merciful heavens!" I exclaimed. "This is a miracle, no less.

"Here, I say, de Grandin, where are you going, to call Colonel Szekler?"

"Not I," he answered with a chuckle. "Do you call him, good Friend Trowbridge. Me, I go to find that cocksure-of-his-diagnosis Doctor Teach and make him pay his wager.

"*Morbleu*, how I shall enjoy drinking him beneath the table!"

The Jest of Warburg Tantavul

WARBURG TANTAVUL WAS DYING. Little more than skin and bones, he lay propped up with pillows in the big sleigh bed and smiled as though he found the thought of dissolution faintly amusing.

Even in comparatively good health the man was never prepossessing. Now, wasted with disease, that smile of self-sufficient satisfaction on his wrinkled face, he was nothing less than hideous. The eyes, which nature had given him, were small, deep-set and ruthless. The mouth, which his own thoughts had fashioned through the years, was wide and thin-lipped, almost colorless, and even in repose was tightly drawn against his small and curiously perfect teeth. Now, as he smiled, a flickering light, lambent as the quick reflection of an unseen flame, flared in his yellowish eyes, and a hard white line of teeth showed on his lower lip, as if he bit it to hold back a chuckle.

"You're still determined that you'll marry Arabella?" he asked his son, fixing his sardonic, mocking smile on the young man.

"Yes, Father, but—"

"No buts, my boy"—this time the chuckle came, low and muted, but at the same time glassy-hard—"no buts. I've told you I'm against it, and you'll rue it to your dying day if you should marry her; but"—he paused, and breath rasped in his wizened throat—"but go ahead and marry her, if your heart's set on it. I've said my say and warned you—heh, boy, never say your poor old father didn't warn you!"

He lay back on his piled-up pillows for a moment, swallowing convulsively, as if to force the fleeting life-breath back, then, abruptly: "Get out," he ordered. "Get out and stay out, you poor fool; but remember what I've said."

"Father," young Tantavul began, stepping toward the bed, but the look of sudden concentrated fury in the old man's tawny eyes halted him in midstride.

"Get—out—I—said," his father snarled, then, as the door closed softly on his son:

"Nurse—hand—me—that—picture." His breath was coming slowly, now, in shallow labored gasps, but his withered fingers writhed in a gesture of command, pointing to the silver-framed photograph of a woman which stood upon a little table in the bedroom window-bay.

He clutched the portrait as if it were some precious relic, and for a minute let his eyes rove over it. "Lucy," he whispered hoarsely, and now his words were thick and indistinct, "Lucy, they'll be married, spite of all that I have said. They'll be married, Lucy, d'ye hear?" Thin and high-pitched as a child's, his voice rose to a piping treble as he grasped the picture's silver frame and held it level with his face. "They'll be married, Lucy dear, and they'll have—"

Abruptly as a penny whistle's note is stilled when no more air is blown in it, old Tantavul's cry was hushed. The picture, still grasped in his hands, fell to the tufted coverlet, the man's lean jaw relaxed and he slumped back on his pillows with a shadow of the mocking smile still in his glazing eyes.

Etiquette requires that the nurse await the doctor's confirmation at such times, so, obedient to professional dictates, Miss Williamson stood by the bed until I felt the dead man's pulse and nodded; then with the skill of years of practice she began her offices, bandaging the wrists and jaws and ankles that the body might be ready when the representative of Martin's Funeral Home came for it.

M Y FRIEND DE GRANDIN was annoyed. Arms akimbo, knuckles on his hips, his black-silk kimono draped round him like a mourning garment, he voiced his complaint in no uncertain terms. In fifteen little so small minutes he must leave for the theatre, and that son and grandson of a filthy swine who was the florist had not delivered his gardenia. And was it not a fact that he could not go forth without a fresh gardenia for his lapel? But certainly. Why did that *sale chameau* procrastinate? Why did he delay delivering that unmentionable flower till this unspeakable time of night? He was Jules de Grandin, he, and not to be oppressed by any species of a goat who called himself a florist. But no. It must not be. It should not be, by blue! He would—

"Axin' yer pardon, sir," Nora McGinnis broke in from the study door, "there's a Miss an' Mr. Tantavul to see ye, an'—"

"Bid them be gone, *ma charmeuse*. Request that they jump in the bay— Grand Dieu"—he cut his oratory short—"*les enfants dans le bois!*"

Truly, there was something reminiscent of the Babes in the Wood in the couple who had followed Nora to the study door. Dennis Tantavul looked even younger and more boyish than I remembered him, and the girl beside him was so childish in appearance that I felt a quick, instinctive pity for her. Plainly they were frightened, too, for they clung hand to hand like frightened children going past a graveyard, and in their eyes was that look of sick terror I had seen so often when the X-ray and blood test confirmed preliminary diagnosis of carcinoma.

"*Monsieur, Mademoiselle!*" The little Frenchman gathered his kimono and his dignity about him in a single sweeping gesture as he struck his heels together and bowed stiffly from the hips. "I apologize for my unseemly words. Were it not that I have been subjected to a terrible, calamitous misfortune, I should not so far have forgotten myself—"

The girl's quick smile cut through his apology. "We understand," she reassured. "We've been through trouble, too, and have come to Dr. Trowbridge—"

"Ah, then I have permission to withdraw?" he bowed again and turned upon his heel, but I called him back.

"Perhaps you can assist us," I remarked as I introduced the callers.

"The honor is entirely mine, *Mademoiselle*," he told her as he raised her fingers to his lips. "You and *Monsieur* your brother—"

"He's not my brother," she corrected. "We're cousins. That's why we've called on Dr. Trowbridge."

De Grandin tweaked the already needle-sharp points of his small blond mustache. "*Pardonnez-moi?*" he begged. "I have resided in your country but a little time; perhaps I do not understand the language fluently. It is because you and *Monsieur* are cousins that you come to see the doctor? Me, I am dull and stupid like a pig; I fear I do not comprehend."

Dennis Tantavul replied: "It's not because of the relationship, Doctor—not entirely, at any rate, but—"

He turned to me: "You were at my father's bedside when he died; you remember what he said about marrying Arabella?"

I nodded.

"There was something—some ghastly, hidden threat concealed in his warning, Doctor. It seemed as if he jeered at me—dared me to marry her, yet—"

"Was there some provision in his will?" I asked.

"Yes, sir," the young man answered. "Here it is." From his pocket he produced a folded parchment, opened it and indicated a paragraph:

To my son Dennis Tantavul I give, devise and bequeath all my property of every kind and sort, real, personal and mixed, of which I may die seized and possessed, or to which I may be entitled, in the event of his marrying Arabella Tantavul, but should he not marry the said Arabella Tantavul, then it is my will that he receive only one half of my estate, and that the residue thereof go to the said Arabella Tantavul, who has made her home with me since childhood and occupied the relationship of daughter to me."

"H'm," I returned the document, "this looks as if he really wanted you to marry your cousin, even though—"

"And see here, sir," Dennis interrupted, "here's an envelope we found in Father's papers."

Sealed with red wax, the packet of heavy, opaque parchment was addressed:

"To my children, Dennis and Arabella Tantavul, to be opened by them upon the occasion of the birth of their first child."

De Grandin's small blue eyes were snapping with the flickering light they showed when he was interested. "Monsieur Dennis," he took the thick envelope from the caller, "Dr. Trowbridge has told me something of your father's death-bed scene. There is a mystery about this business. My suggestion is you read the message now—"

"No, sir. I won't do that. My father didn't love me—sometimes I think he hated me—but I never disobeyed a wish that he expressed, and I don't feel at liberty to do so now. It would be like breaking faith with the dead. But"—he smiled a trifle shame-facedly—"Father's lawyer Mr. Bainbridge is out of town on business, and it will be his duty to probate the will. In the meantime I'd feel better if the will and this envelope were in other hands than mine. So we came to Dr. Trowbridge to ask him to take charge of them till Mr. Bainbridge gets back, meanwhile—"

"Yes, Monsieur, meanwhile?" de Grandin prompted as the young man paused.

"You know human nature, Doctor," Dennis turned to me; "no one can see farther into hidden meanings than the man who sees humanity with its mask off, the way a doctor does. D'ye think Father might have been delirious when he warned me not to marry Arabella, or—" His voice trailed off, but his troubled eyes were eloquent.

"H'm," I shifted uncomfortably in my chair, "I can't see any reason for hesitating, Dennis. That bequest of all your father's property in the event you marry Arabella seems to indicate his true feelings." I tried to make my words convincing, but the memory of old Tantavul's dying words dinned in my ears. There had been something gloating in his voice as he told the picture that his son and niece would marry.

De Grandin caught the hint of hesitation in my tone. "*Monsieur*," he asked Dennis, "will not you tell us of the antecedents of your father's warning? Dr. Trowbridge is perhaps too near to see the situation clearly. Me, I have no knowledge of your father or your family. You and *Mademoiselle* are strangely like. The will describes her as having lived with you since childhood. Will you kindly tell us how it came about?"

The Tantavuls were, as he said, strangely similar. Anyone might easily have taken them for twins. Like as two plaster portraits from the same mold were their small straight noses, sensitive mouths, curling pale-gold hair.

Now, once more hand in hand, they sat before us on the sofa, and as Dennis spoke I saw the frightened, haunted look creep back into their eyes.

"Do you remember us as children, Doctor?" he asked me.

"Yes, it must have been some twenty years ago they called me out to see you youngsters. You'd just moved into the old Stephens house, and there was a deal of gossip about the strange gentleman from the West with his two small children and Chinese cook, who greeted all the neighbors' overtures with churlish rebuffs and never spoke to anyone."

"What did you think of us, sir?"

"H'm; I thought you and your sister—as I thought her then—had as fine a case of measles as I'd ever seen."

"How old were we then, do you remember?"

"Oh, you were something like three; the little girl was half your age, I'd guess."

"Do you recall the next time you saw us?"

"Yes, you were somewhat older then; eight or ten, I'd say. That time it was the mumps. You were queer, quiet little shavers. I remember asking if you thought you'd like a pickle, and you said, 'No, thank you, sir, it hurts.'"

"It did, too, sir. Every day Father made us eat one; stood over us with a whip till we'd chewed the last morsel."

"*What?*"

The young folks nodded solemnly as Dennis answered, "Yes, sir; every day. He said he wanted to check up on the progress we were making."

For a moment he was silent, then: "Dr. Trowbridge, if anyone treated you with studied cruelty all your life—if you'd never had a kind word or gracious act from that person in all your memory, then suddenly that person offered you a favour—made it possible for you to gratify your dearest wish, and threatened to penalize you if you failed to do so, wouldn't you be suspicious? Wouldn't you suspect some sort of dreadful practical joke?"

"I don't think I quite understand."

"Then listen: In all my life I can't remember ever having seen my father smile, not really smile with friendliness, humour or affection, I mean. My life— and Arabella's, too—was one long persecution at his hands. I was two years or so old when we came to Harrisonville, I believe, but I still have vague recollections of our Western home, of a house set high on a hill overlooking the ocean, and a wall with climbing vines and purple flowers on it, and a pretty lady who would take me in her arms and cuddle me against her breast and feed me ice cream from a spoon, sometimes. I have a sort of recollection of a little baby sister in that house, too, but these things are so far back in babyhood that possibly they were no more than childish fancies which I built up for myself and which I loved so dearly and so secretly they finally came to have a kind of reality for me.

"My real memories, the things I can recall with certainty, begin with a hurried train trip through hot, dry, uncomfortable country with my father and a strangely silent Chinese servant and a little girl they told me was my cousin Arabella.

"Father treated me and Arabella with impartial harshness. We were beaten for the slightest fault, and we had faults a-plenty. If we sat quietly we were accused of sulking and asked why we didn't go and play. If we played and shouted we were whipped for being noisy little brats.

"As we weren't allowed to associate with any of the neighbors' children we made up our own games. I'd be Geraint and Arabella would be Enid of the dove-white feet, or perhaps I'd be King Arthur in the Castle Perilous, and she'd be the kind Lady of the Lake who gave him back his magic sword. And though we never mentioned it, both of us knew that whatever the adventure was, the false knight or giant I contended with was really my father. But when actual trouble came I wasn't an heroic figure.

"I must have been twelve or thirteen when I had my last thrashing. A little brook ran through the lower part of our land, and the former owners had widened it into a lily-pond. The flowers had died out years before, but the outlines of the pool remained, and it was our favourite summer play place. We taught ourselves to swim—not very well, of course, but well enough—and as we had no bathing suits we used to go in in our underwear. When we'd finished swimming we'd lie in the sun until our underthings were dry, then slip into our outer clothing. One afternoon as we were splashing in the water, happy as a pair of baby otters, and nearer to shouting with laughter then we'd ever been before, I think, my father suddenly appeared on the bank.

"'Come out o' there!' he shouted to me, and there was a kind of sharp, dry hardness in his voice I'd never heard before. 'So this is how you spend your time?' he asked as I climbed up the bank. 'In spite of all I've done to keep you decent, you do a thing like this!'

"'Why, Father, we were only swimming—' I began, but he struck me on the mouth.

"'Shut up, you little rake!' he roared. 'I'll teach you!' He cut a willow switch and thrust my head between his knees; then while he held me tight as in a vice he flogged me with the willow till the blood came through my skin and stained my soaking cotton shorts. Then he kicked me back into the pool as a heartless master might a beaten dog.

"As I said, I wasn't an heroic figure. It was Arabella who came to my rescue. She helped me up the slippery bank and took me in her arms. 'Poor Dennie,' she said. 'Poor, poor Dennie. It was my fault, Dennie, dear, for letting you take me into the water!' Then she kissed me—the first time anyone had kissed me since the pretty lady of my half-remembered dreams. 'We'll be married on the very day that Uncle Warburg dies,' she promised, 'and I'll be so sweet and good to you, and you'll love me so dearly that we'll both forget these dreadful days.'

"We thought my father'd gone, but he must have stayed to see what we would say, for as Arabella finished he stepped from behind a rhododendron bush, and for the first time I heard him laugh. 'You'll be married, will you?' he asked. 'That would be a good joke—the best one of all. All right, go ahead—see what it gets you.'

"That was the last time he ever actually struck me, but from that time on he seemed to go out of his way to invent mental tortures for us. We weren't allowed to go to school, but he had a tutor, a little rat-faced man named Ericson, come in to give us lessons, and in the evening he'd take the book and make us stand before him and recite. If either of us failed a problem in arithmetic or couldn't conjugate a French or Latin verb he'd wither us with sarcasm, and always as a finish to his diatribe he'd jeer at us about our wish to be married, and threaten us with something dreadful if we ever did it.

"So, Dr. Trowbridge, you see why I'm suspicious. It seems almost as if this provision in the will is part of some horrible practical joke my father prepared deliberately—as if he's waiting to laugh at us from the grave."

"I can understand your feelings, boy," I answered, "but—"

"'But' be damned and roasted on the hottest griddle in hell's kitchen!" Jules de Grandin interrupted. "The wicked dead one's funeral is at two tomorrow afternoon, n'est-ce-pas?

"Très bien. At eight tomorrow evening—or earlier, if it will be convenient— you shall be married. I shall esteem it a favour if you permit that I be best man; Dr. Trowbridge will give the bride away, and we shall have a merry time, by blue! You shall go upon a gorgeous honeymoon and learn how sweet the joys of love can be—sweeter for having been so long denied! And in the meantime we shall keep the papers safely till your lawyer returns.

"You fear the so unpleasant jest? Mais non, I think the jest is on the other foot, my friends, and the laugh on the other face!"

WARBURG TANTAVUL WAS NEITHER widely known nor popular, but the solitude in which he had lived had invested him with mystery; now the bars of reticence were down and the walls of isolation broken, upward of a hundred neighbors, mostly women, gathered in the Martin funeral chapel as the services began. The afternoon sun beat softly through the stained-glass windows and glinted on the polished mahogany of the casket. Here and there it touched upon bright spots of color that marked a woman's hat or a man's tie. The solemn hush was broken by occasional whispers: "What'd he die of? Did he leave much? Were the two young folks his only heirs?"

Then the burial office: "Lord, Thou hast been our refuge from one generation to another . . . for a thousand years in Thy sight are but as yesterday . . . Oh teach us to number our days that we may apply our hearts unto wisdom . . ."

As the final Amen sounded one of Mr. Martin's frock-coated young men glided forward, paused beside the casket, and made the stereotyped announcement: "Those who wish to say good-bye to Mr. Tantavul may do so at this time."

The grisly rite of passing by the bier dragged on. I would have left the place; I had no wish to look upon the man's dead face and folded hands; but de Grandin took me firmly by the elbow, held me till the final curiosity-impelled female had filed past the body, then steered me quickly toward the casket.

He paused a moment at the bier, and it seemed to me there was a hint of irony in the smile that touched the corners of his mouth as he leant forward. "*Eh bien*, my old one; we know a secret, thou and I, *n'est-ce-pas?*" he asked the silent form before us.

I swallowed back an exclamation of dismay. Perhaps it was a trick of the uncertain light, perhaps one of those ghastly, inexplicable things which every doctor and embalmer meets with sometimes in his practice—the effect of desiccation from formaldehyde, the pressure of some tissue gas within the body, or something of the sort—at any rate, as Jules de Grandin spoke the corpse's upper lids drew back the fraction of an inch, revealing slits of yellow eye which seemed to glare at us with mingled hate and fury.

"Good heavens; come away!" I begged. "It seemed as if he looked at us, de Grandin!"

"*Et puis*—and if he did? I damn think I can trade him look for look, my friend. He was clever, that one, I admit it; but do not be mistaken, Jules de Grandin is nobody's imbecile."

T HE WEDDING TOOK PLACE in the rectory of St. Chrysostom's. Robed in stole and surplice, Dr. Bentley glanced benignly from Dennis to Arabella, then to de Grandin and me as he began: "Dearly beloved, we are gathered together here in the sight of God and in the face of this company to join together this man and this woman in holy matrimony. . . ." His round and ruddy face grew slightly stern as he admonished, "If any man can show just cause why they should not lawfully be joined together, let him now speak or else hereafter for ever hold his peace."

He paused the customary short, dramatic moment, and I thought I saw a hard, grim look spread on de Grandin's face. Very faint and far off seeming, so faint that we could scarcely hear it, but gaining steadily in strength, there came a high, thin, screaming sound. Curiously, it seemed to me to resemble the long-drawn, wailing shriek of a freight train's whistle heard miles away upon a still and sultry summer night, weird, wavering and ghastly. Now it seemed to grow in shrillness, though its volume was no greater.

I saw a look of haunted fright leap into Arabella's eyes, saw Dennis' pale face go paler as the strident whistle sounded shriller and more shrill; then, as it seemed I could endure the stabbing of that needle-sound no longer, it ceased abruptly, giving way to blessed, comforting silence. But through the silence came a burst of chuckling laughter, half breathless, half hysterical, wholly devilish:

Huh—hu-u-uh—hu-u-u-uh! the final syllable drawn out until it seemed almost a groan.

"The wind, *Monsieur le Curé*; it was nothing but the wind," de Grandin told the clergyman sharply. "Proceed to marry them, if you will be so kind."

"Wind?" Dr. Bentley echoed. "I could have sworn I heard somebody laugh, but—"

"It is the wind, *Monsieur*; it plays strange tricks at times," the little Frenchman insisted, his small blue eyes as hard as frozen iron. "Proceed, if you will be so kind. We wait on you."

"Forasmuch as Dennis and Arabella have consented to be joined together in holy wedlock . . . I pronounce them man and wife," concluded Dr. Bentley, and de Grandin, ever gallant, kissed the bride upon the lips, and before we could restrain him, planted kisses on both Dennis' cheeks.

"*Cordieu*, I thought that we might have the trouble, for a time," he told me as we left the rectory.

"What *was* that awful shrieking noise we heard?" I asked.

"It was the wind, my friend," he answered in a hard, flat, toneless voice. "The ten times damned, but wholly ineffectual wind."

"So, THEN, LITTLE SINNER, weep and wail for the burden of mortality you have assumed. Weep, wail, cry and breathe, my small and wrinkled one! Ha, you will not? *Pardieu*, I say you shall!"

Gently, but smartly, he spanked the small red infant's small red posterior with the end of a towel wrung out in hot water, and as the smacking impact sounded the tiny toothless mouth opened and a thin, high, piping squall of protest sounded. "Ah, that is better, *mon petit ami*," he chuckled. "One cannot learn too soon that one must do as one is told, not as one wishes, in this world which you have just entered. Look to him, *Mademoiselle*," he passed the wriggling, bawling morsel of humanity to the nurse and turned to me as I bent over the table where Arabella lay. "How does the little mother, Friend Trowbridge?" he asked.

"U'm'mp," I answered noncommittally. "Bear a hand, here, will you? The perineum's pretty badly torn—have to do a quick repair job . . ."

"But in the morning she will have forgotten all the pain," laughed de Grandin as Arabella, swathed in blankets, was trundled from the delivery room. "She will gaze upon the little monkey-thing which I just caused to breathe the breath of life and vow it is the loveliest of all God's lovely creatures. She will hold it at her tender breast and smile on it, she will—*Sacré nom d'un rat vert*, what is that?"

From the nursery where, ensconced in wire trays, a score of newborn fragments of humanity slept or squalled, there came a sudden frightened scream—a woman's cry of terror.

We raced along the corridor, reached the glass-walled room and thrust the door back, taking care to open it no wider than was necessary, lest a draft disturb the carefully conditioned air of the place.

Backed against the farther wall, her face gone grey with fright, the nurse in charge was staring at the skylight with terror-widened eyes, and even as we entered she opened her lips to emit another scream.

"Desist, *ma bonne*, you are disturbing your small charges!" de Grandin seized the horrified girl's shoulder and administered a shake. Then: "What is it, *Mademoiselle?*" he whispered. "Do not be afraid to speak; we shall respect your confidence—but speak softly."

"It—it was up there!" she pointed with a shaking finger toward the black square of the skylight. "They'd just brought Baby Tantavul in, and I had laid him in his crib when I thought I heard somebody laughing. Oh"—she shuddered at the recollection—"it was awful! Not really a laugh, but something more like a long-drawn-out hysterical groan. Did you ever hear a child tickled to exhaustion—you know how he moans and gasps for breath, and laughs, all at once? I think the fiends in hell must laugh like that!"

"Yes, yes, we understand," de Grandin nodded, "but tell us what occurred next."

"I looked around the nursery, but I was all alone here with the babies. Then it came again, louder, this time, and seemingly right above me. I looked up at the skylight, and—there it was!

"It was a face, sir—just a face, with no body to it, and it seemed to float above the glass, then dip down to it, like a child's balloon drifting in the wind, and it looked right past me, down at Baby Tantavul, and laughed again."

"A face, you say, *Mademoiselle*—"

"Yes, sir, yes! The most awful face I've ever seen. It was thin and wrinkled—all shrivelled like a monkey—and as it looked at Baby Tantavul its eyes stretched open till their whites glared all around the irises, and the mouth opened, not widely, but as if it were chewing something it relished—and it gave that dreadful, cackling, jubilating laugh again. That's it! I couldn't think before, but it seemed as if that bodiless head were laughing with a sort of evil triumph, Dr. de Grandin!"

"H'm," he tweaked his tightly waxed mustache, "I should not wonder if it did, Mademoiselle," To me he whispered, "Stay with her, if you will, my friend, I'll see the supervisor and have her send another nurse to keep her company. I shall request a special watch for the small Tantavul. At present I do not think the danger is great, but—mice do not play where cats are wakeful."

"ISN'T HE JUST LOVELY?" Arabella looked up from the small bald head that rested on her breast, and ecstasy was in her eyes. "I don't believe I ever saw so beautiful a baby!"

"*Tiens*, Madame, his voice is excellent, at any rate," de Grandin answered with a grin, "and from what one may observe his appetite is excellent, at well."

Arabella smiled and patted the small creature's back. "You know, I never had a doll in my life," she confided. "Now I've got this dear little mite, and I'm going to be so happy with him. Oh, I wish Uncle Warburg were alive. I know this darling baby would soften even his hard heart.

"But I mustn't say such things about him, must I? He really wanted me to marry Dennis, didn't he? His will proved that. You think he wanted us to marry, Doctor?"

"I am persuaded that he did, Madame. Your marriage was his dearest wish, his fondest hope," the Frenchman answered solemnly.

"I felt that way, too. He was harsh and cruel to us when we were growing up, and kept his stony-hearted attitude to the end, but underneath it all there must have been some hidden stratum of kindness, some lingering affection for Dennis and me, or he'd never have put that clause in his will—"

"Nor have left this memorandum for you," de Grandin interrupted, drawing from an inner pocket the parchment envelope Dennis had entrusted to him the day before his father's funeral.

She started back as if he menaced her with a live scorpion, and instinctively her arms closed protectively around the baby at her bosom. "The—that—letter?" she faltered, her breath coming in short, smothered gasps. "I'd forgotten all about it. Oh, Dr. de Grandin, burn it. Don't let me see what's in it. I'm afraid!"

It was a bright May morning, without sufficient breeze to stir the leaflets on the maple trees outside the window, but as de Grandin held the letter out I thought I heard a sudden sweep of wind around the angle of the hospital, not loud, but shrewd and keen, like wind among the graveyard evergreens in autumn, and, curiously, there seemed a note of soft malicious laughter mingled with it.

The little Frenchman heard it, too, and for an instant he looked toward the window, and I thought I saw the flicker of an ugly sneer take form beneath the waxed ends of his mustache.

"Open it, *Madame*," he bade. "It is for you and Monsieur Dennis, and the little *Monsieur Bébé* here."

"I—I daren't—"

"*Tenez*, then Jules de Grandin does!" with his penknife he slit the heavy envelope, pressed suddenly against its ends so that its sides bulged, and dumped its contents on the counterpane. Ten fifty-dollar bills dropped on the coverlet. And nothing else.

"Five hundred dollars!" Arabella gasped. "Why—"

"A birthday gift for *petit Monsieur Bébé*, one surmises," laughed de Grandin. "*Eh bien*, the old one had a sense of humour underneath his ugly outward shell, it seems. He kept you on the tenterhooks lest the message in this envelope contained dire things, while all the time it was a present of congratulation."

"But such a gift from Uncle Warburg—I can't understand it!"

"Perhaps that is as well, too, *Madame*. Be happy in the gift and give your ancient uncle credit for at least one act of kindness. *Au 'voir*."

"Hanged if I can understand it, either," I confessed as we left the hospital. "If that old curmudgeon had left a message berating them for fools for having offspring, or even a new will that disinherited them both, it would have been in character, but such a gift—well, I'm surprised."

Amazingly, he halted in midstep and laughed until the tears rolled down his face. "*You* are surprised!" he told me when he managed to regain his breath, "*Cordieu*, my friend, I do not drink that you are half as much surprised as Monsieur Warburg Tantavul!"

Dennis Tantavul regarded me with misery-haunted eyes. "I just can't understand it," he admitted. "It's all so sudden, so utterly—"

"*Pardonnez-moi*," de Grandin interrupted from the door of the consulting room, "I could not help but hear your voice, and if it is not an intrusion—"

"Not at all, sir," the young man answered. "I'd like the benefit of your advice. It's Arabella, and I'm terribly afraid she's—"

"*Non*, do not try it, *mon ami*," de Grandin warned. "Do you give us the symptoms, let us make the diagnosis. He who acts as his own doctor has a fool for a patient, you know."

"Well, then, here are the facts: This morning Arabella woke me up, crying as if her heart would break. I asked her what the trouble was, and she looked at me as if I were a stranger—no, not exactly that, rather as if I were some dreadful thing she'd suddenly found at her side. Her eyes were positively round with horror, and when I tried to take her in my arms to comfort her she shrank away as if I were infected with the plague.

"'Oh, Dennie, don't!' she begged and positively cringed away from me. Then she sprang out of bed and drew her kimono around her as if she were ashamed to have me see her in her pyjamas, and ran out of the room.

"Presently I heard her crying in the nursery, and when I followed her in there—" He paused and tears came to his eyes. "She was standing by the crib where little Dennis lay, and in her hand she held a long sharp steel letter-opener. 'Poor little mite, poor little flower of unpardonable sin,' she said. 'We've got to go, Baby darling; you to limbo, I to hell—oh, God wouldn't, *couldn't* be so cruel as to damn you for our sin!—but we'll all three suffer torment endlessly, because we didn't know!'

"She raised the knife to plunge it in the little fellow's heart, and he stretched out his hands and laughed and cooed as the sunlight shone on the steel. I was on her in an instant, wrenching the knife from her with one hand and holding her against me with the other, but she fought me off.

"'Don't touch me, Dennie, please, *please* don't,' she begged. I know it's mortal sin, but I love you so, my dear, that I just can't resist you if I let you put your arms about me.'

"I tried to kiss her, but she hid her face against my shoulder and moaned as if in pain when she felt my lips against her neck. Then she went limp in my arms, and I carried her, unconscious but still moaning piteously, into her sitting room and laid her on the couch. I left Sarah the nurse-maid with her, with strict orders not to let her leave the room. Can't you come over right away?"

De Grandin's cigarette had burned down till it threatened his mustache, and in his little round blue eyes there was a look of murderous rage. "*Bête!*" he murmured savagely. "*Sale chameau*, species of a stinking goat! This is his doing, undoubtedly. Come, my friends, let us rush, hasten, fly. I would talk with Madame Arabella."

"Naw, suh, she's done gone," the portly colored nursemaid told us when we asked for Arabella. "Th' baby started squealin' sumpin awful right after Mistu Dennis lef', an' Ah knowed it wuz time fo' his breakfas', so Mis' Arabella wuz layin' nice an' still on the' sofa, an' Ah says ter her, Ah says, 'Yuh lay still dere, honey, whilst Ah goes an' sees after yo' baby;' so Ah goes ter th' nursery, an' fixes him all up, an' carries him back ter th' settin'-room where Mis' Arabella wuz, an' she ain't there no more. Naw, suh."

"I thought I told you—" Dennis began furiously, but de Grandin laid a hand upon his arm.

"Do not upbraid her, *mon ami*, she did wisely, though she knew it not; she was with the small one all the while, so no harm came to him. Was it not better so, after what you witnessed in the morning?"

"Ye-es," the other grudgingly admitted, "I suppose so. But Arabella—"

"Let us see if we can find a trace of her," the Frenchman interrupted. "Look carefully, do you miss any of her clothing?"

Dennis looked about the pretty chintz-hung room. "Yes," he decided as he finished his inspection, "her dress was on that lounge and her shoes and stockings on the floor beneath it. They're all gone."

"So," de Grandin nodded. "Distracted as she seemed, it is unlikely she would have stopped to dress had she not planned on going out. Friend Trowbridge, will you kindly call police headquarters and inform them of the situation? Ask to have all exits to the city watched."

As I picked up the telephone he and Dennis started on a room-by-room inspection of the house.

"Find anything?" I asked as I hung up the 'phone after talking with the missing persons bureau.

"*Corbleu*, but I should damn say yes!" de Grandin answered as I joined them in the upstairs living room. "Look yonder, if you please, my friend."

The room was obviously the intimate apartment of the house. Electric lamps under painted shades were placed beside deep leather-covered easy chairs, ivory-enamelled bookshelves lined the walls to a height of four feet or so, upon their tops was a litter of gay, unconsidered trifles—cinnabar cigarette boxes, bits of hammered brass. Old china, blue and red and purple, glowed mellowly from open spaces on the shelves, its colors catching up and accenting the muted blues and reds of antique Hamadan carpet. A Paisley shawl was draped scarfwise across the baby grand piano in one corner.

Directly opposite the door a carven crucifix was standing on the bookcase top. It was an exquisite bit of Italian work, the cross of ebony, the corpus of old ivory, and so perfectly executed that though it was a scant six inches high, one could note the tense, tortured muscles of the pendent body, the straining throat which overfilled with groans of agony, the brow all knotted and bedewed with the cold sweat of torment. Upon the statue's thorn-crowned head, where it made a bright iridescent halo, was a band of gem-encrusted platinum, a woman's diamond-studded wedding ring.

"*Hélas*, it is love's crucifixion!" whispered Jules de Grandin.

THREE MONTHS WENT BY, and though the search kept up unremittingly, no trace of Arabella could be found. Dennis Tantavul installed a fulltime highly trained and recommended nurse in his desolate house, and spent his time haunting police stations and newspaper offices. He aged a decade in the ninety days since Arabella left; his shoulders stooped, his footsteps lagged, and a look of constant misery lay in his eyes. He was a prematurely old and broken man.

"It's the most uncanny thing I ever saw," I told de Grandin as we walked through West Forty-Second Street toward the West Shore Ferry. We had gone over to New York for some surgical supplies, and I do not drive my car in the metropolis. Truck drivers there are far too careless and repair bills for wrecked mudguards far too high. "How a full-grown woman would evaporate this way is something I can't understand. Of course, she may have done away with herself, dropped off a ferry, or—"

"*S-s-st*," his sibilated admonition cut me short. "That woman there, my friend, observe her, if you please." He nodded toward a female figure twenty feet or so ahead of us.

I looked, and wondered at his sudden interest at the draggled hussy. She was dressed in tawdry finery much the worse for wear. The sleazy silken skirt was much too tight, the cheap fur jaquette far too short and snug, and the high heels of her satin shoes were shockingly run over. Makeup was fairly plastered on her cheeks and lips and eyes, and short black hair bristled untidily beneath the brim of her abbreviated hat. Written unmistakably upon her was the nature of her calling, the oldest and least honorable profession known to womanhood.

"Well," I answered tartly, "what possible interest can you have in a—"

"Do not walk so fast," he whispered as his fingers closed upon my arm, "and do not raise your voice. I would that we should follow her, but I do not wish that she should know."

The neighborhood was far from savory, and I felt uncomfortably conspicuous as we turned from Forty-Second Street into Eleventh Avenue in the wake of the young strumpet, followed her provocatively swaying hips down two malodorous blocks, finally pausing as she slipped furtively into the doorway of a filthy, unkempt "rooming house."

We trailed her through a dimly lighted barren hall and up a flight of shadowy stairs, then up two further flights until we reached a sort of oblong foyer bounded on one end by the stair-well, on the farther extremity by a barred and very dirty window, and on each side by sagging, paint-blistered doors. On each of these was pinned a card, handwritten with the many flourishes dear to the chirography of the professional card-writer who still does business in the poorer quarters of our great cities. The air was heavy with the odor of cheap whisky, bacon rind and fried onions.

We made a hasty circuit of the hill, studying the cardboard labels. On the farthest door the notice read *Miss Sieglinde.*

"*Mon Dieu*," he exclaimed as he read it, "*c'est le mot propre!*"

"Eh?" I returned.

"Sieglinde, do not you recall her?"

"No-o, can't say I do. The only Sieglinde I remember is the character in Wagner's *Die Walkure* who unwittingly became her brother's paramour and bore him a son—"

"*Précisément.* Let us enter, if you please." Without pausing to knock he turned the handle of the door and stepped into the squalid room.

The woman sat upon the unkempt bed, her hat pushed back from her brow. In one hand she held a cracked teacup, with the other she poised a whisky bottle over it. She had kicked her scuffed and broken shoes off; we saw that she was stockingless, and her bare feet were dark with long-accumulated dirt and black-nailed as a miner's hands. "Get out!" she ordered thickly. "Get out o' here, I ain't receivin'—" a gasp broke her utterance, and she turned her head away quickly. Then: "Get out o' here, you lousy bums!" she screamed. "Who d'ye think you are, breakin' into a lady's room like this? Get out, or—"

De Grandin eyed her steadily, and as her strident command wavered: "Madame Arabella, we have come to take you home," he announced softly.

"Good God, man, you're crazy" I exclaimed. "Arabella? This—"

"Precisely, my old one; this is Madame Arabella Tantavul whom we have sought these many months in vain." Crossing the room in two quick strides he seized the cringing woman by the shoulders and turned her face up to the light. I looked, and felt a sudden swift attack of nausea.

He was right. Thin to emaciation, her face already lined with the deep-bitten scars of evil living, the woman on the bed was Arabella Tantavul, though the shocking change wrought in her features and the black dye in her hair had disguised her so effectively that I should not have known her.

"We have come to take you home, *ma pauvre*," he repeated. "Your husband—"

"My husband!" her reply was half a scream. "Dear God, as if I had a husband—"

"And the little one who needs you," he continued. "You cannot leave them thus, Madame."

"I can't? Ah, that's where you're wrong, Doctor. I can never see my baby again, in this world or the next. Please go away and forget you've see me, or I shall have to drown myself—I've tried it twice already, but the first time I was rescued, and the second time my courage failed. But if you try to take me back, or if you tell Dennis you saw me—"

"Tell me, Madame," he broke in, "was not your flight caused by a visitation from the dead?"

Her faded brown eyes—eyes that had been such a startling contrast to her pale-gold hair—widened. "How did you know?" she whispered.

"*Tiens*, one may make surmises. Will not you tell us just what happened? I think there is a way out of your difficulties."

"No, no, there isn't; there can't be!" Her head drooped listlessly. "He planned his work too well; all that's left for me is death—and damnation afterward."

"But if there were a way—if I could show it to you?"

"Can you repeal the laws of God?"

"I am a very clever person, *Madame*. Perhaps I can accomplish an evasion, if not an absolute repeal. Now tell us, how and when did *Monsieur* your late but not at all lamented uncle come to you?"

"The night before—before I went away. I woke about midnight, thinking I heard a cry from Dennie's nursery. When I reached the room where he was sleeping I saw my uncle's face glaring at me through the window. It seemed to be illuminated by a sort of inward hellish light, for it stood out against the darkness like a jack-o'-lantern, and it smiled an awful smile at me. 'Arabella,' it said, and I could see its dun dead lips writhe back as if the teeth were burning-hot, 'I've come to tell you that your marriage is a mockery and a lie. The man you married is your brother, and the child you bore is doubly illegitimate. You can't continue living with them, Arabella. That would be an even greater sin. You must leave them right away, or'—Once more his lips crept back until his teeth were bare—'or I shall come to visit you each night, and when the baby has grown old enough to understand I'll tell him who his parents really are. Take your choice, my daughter. Leave them and let me go back to the grave, or stay and see me every night and know that I will tell your son when he is old enough to understand. If I do it he will loathe and hate you; curse the day you bore him.'

"'And you'll promise never to come near Dennis or the baby if I go?' I asked.

"He promised, and I staggered back to bed, where I fell fainting.

"Next morning when I wakened I was sure it had been a bad dream, but when I looked at Dennis and my own reflection in the glass I knew it was no dream, but a dreadful visitation from the dead.

"Then I went mad. I tried to kill my baby, and when Dennis stopped me I watched my chance to run away, came over to New York and took to this." She looked significantly around the miserable room. "I knew they'd never look for Arabella Tantavul among the city's whores; I was safer from pursuit right here than if I'd been in Europe or China."

"But, *Madame*," de Grandin's voice was jubilant with shocked reproof, "that which you saw was nothing but a dream; a most unpleasant dream, I grant, but still a dream. Look in my eyes, if you please!"

She raised her eyes to his, and I saw his pupils widen as a cat's do in the dark, saw a line of white outline the cornea, and, responsive to his piercing gaze, beheld her brown eyes set in a fixed stare, first as if in fright, then with a glaze almost like that of death.

"Attend me, Madame Arabella," he commanded softly. "You are tired—*grand Dieu*, how tired you are! You have suffered greatly, but you are about to rest. Your memory of that night is gone; so is all memory of the things which have transpired since. You will move and eat and sleep as you are bidden, but of what takes place around you till I bid you wake you will retain no recollection. Do you hear me, Madame Arabella?"

"I hear," she answered softly in a small tired voice.

"*Très bon*. Lie down, my little poor one. Lie down to rest and dreams of love. Sleep, rest, dream and forget.

"Will you be good enough to 'phone to Dr. Wyckoff?" he asked me. "We shall place her in his sanitarium, wash this *sacré* dye from her hair and nurse her back to health; then when all is ready we can bear her home and have her take up life and love where she left off. No one shall be the wiser. This chapter of her life is closed and sealed for ever.

"Each day I'll call upon her and renew hypnotic treatments that she may simulate the mild but curable mental case which we shall tell the good Wyckoff she is. When finally I release her from hypnosis her mind will be entirely cleared of that bad dream that nearly wrecked her happiness."

A RABELLA TANTAVUL LAY ON the sofa in her charming boudoir, an orchid negligee about her slender shoulders, an eiderdown rug tucked round her feet and knees. Her wedding ring was once more on her finger. Pale with a pallor not to be disguised by the most skillfully applied cosmetics, and with deep violet crescents underneath her amber eyes, she lay back listlessly, drinking in the cheerful warmth that emanated from the fire of apple-logs that snapped and crackled on the hearth. Two months of rest at Dr. Wyckoff's sanitarium had cleansed the marks of dissipation from her face, and the ministrations of beauticians had restored the pale-gold luster to her hair, but the listlessness that followed her complete breakdown was still upon her like the weakness from a fever.

"I can't remember anything about my illness, Dr. Trowbridge," she told me with a weary little smile, "but vaguely I connect it with some dreadful dream I had. And"—she wrinkled her smooth forehead in an effort at remembering—"I think I had a rather dreadful dream last night, but—"

"Ah-*ha?*" de Grandin leant abruptly forward in his chair. "What was it that you dreamed, Madame?"

"I—don't—know," she answered slowly. "Odd, isn't it, how you can remember that a dream was so unpleasant, yet not recall its details? Somehow, I connect it with Uncle Warburg; but—"

"*Parbleu*, do you say so? Has he returned? *Ah hah*, he makes me to be so mad, that one!"

" I T IS TIME WE went, my friend," de Grandin told me as the tall clock in the hall beat out its tenth deliberate stroke; "we have important duties to perform."

"For goodness' sake," I protested, "at this hour o' night?"

"Precisely. At Monsieur Tantavul's I shall expect a visitor tonight, and—we must be ready for him.

"Is Madame Arabella sleeping?" he asked Dennis as he answered our ring at the door.

"Like a baby," answered the young husband. "I've been sitting by her all evening, and I don't believe she even turned in bed."

"And you did keep the window closed, as I requested?"

"Yes, sir; closed and latched."

"*Bien.* Await us here, *mon brave*; we shall rejoin you presently."

He led the way to Arabella's bedroom, removed the wrappings from a bulky parcel he had lugged from our house, and displayed the object thus disclosed with an air of inordinate pride. "Behold him," he commanded gleefully. "Is he not magnificent?"

"Why—what the devil?—it's nothing but an ordinary window screen," I answered.

"A window screen, I grant, my friend; but not an ordinary one. Can not you see it is of copper?"

"Well—"

"*Parbleu*, but I should say it is well," he grinned. "Observe him, how he works."

From his kit bag he produced a roll of insulated wire, an electrical transformer, and some tools. Working quickly he passe-partouted the screen's wooden frame with electrician's tape, then plugged a wire in a nearby lamp socket, connected it with the transformer, and from the latter led a double strand of cotton-wrapped wire to the screen. This he clipped firmly to the copper meshes and led a third strand to the metal grille of the heat register. Last of all he filled a bulb-syringe with water and sprayed the screen, repeating the performance till it sparkled like a cobweb in the morning sun. "And now, *Monsieur le Revenant*," he chuckled as he finished, "I damn think all is ready for your warm reception!"

For something like an hour we waited, then he tiptoed to the bed and bent above Arabella.

"Madame!"

The girl stirred slightly, murmuring some half-audible response, and:

"In half an hour you will rise," he told her. "You will put your robe on and stand by the window, but on no account will you go near it or lay hands on it. Should anyone address you from outside you will reply, but you will not remember what you say or what is said to you."

He motioned me to follow, and we left the room, taking station in the hallway just outside.

H OW LONG WE WAITED I have no accurate idea. Perhaps it was an hour, perhaps less; at any rate the silent vigil seemed unending, and I raised my hand to stifle back a yawn when:

"Yes, Uncle Warburg, I can hear you," we heard Arabella saying softly in the room beyond the door.

We tiptoed to the entry: Arabella stood before the window, and from beyond it glared the face of Warburg Tantavul.

It was dead, there was no doubt about that. In sunken cheek and pinched-in nose and yellowish-grey skin there showed the evidence of death and early putrefaction, but dead through it was, it was also animated with a dreadful sort of life. The eyes were glaring horribly, the lips were red as though they had been painted with fresh blood.

"You hear me, do you?" it demanded. "Then listen, girl; you broke your bargain with me, now I'm come to keep my threat: every time you kiss your husband"—a shriek of bitter laughter cut his words, and his staring eyes half closed with hellish merriment—"or the child you love so well, my shadow will be on you. You've kept me out thus far, but some night I'll get in, and—"

The lean dead jaw dropped, then snapped up as if lifted by sheer will-power, and the whole expression of the corpse-face changed. Surprise, incredulous delight, anticipation as before a feast were pictured on it. "Why"—its cachinnating laughter sent a chill up my spine—"why your window's open! You've changed the screen and I can enter!"

Slowly, like a child's balloon stirred by a vagrant wind, the awful thing moved closer to the window. Closer to the screen it came, and Arabella gave ground before it and put up her hands to shield her eyes from the sight of its hellish grin of triumph.

"*Sapristi*," swore de Grandin softly. "Come on, my old and evil one, come but a little nearer—"

The dead thing floated nearer. Now its mocking mouth and shriveled, pointed nose were almost pressed against the copper meshes of the screen; now they began to filter through the meshes like a wisp of fog—

There was a blinding flash of blue-white flame, the sputtering gush of fusing metal, a wild, despairing shriek that ended ere it fairly started in a sob of mortal torment, and the sharp and acrid odor of burned flesh!

"Arabella—darling—is she all right?" Dennis Tantavul came charging up the stairs. "I thought I heard a scream—"

"You did, my friend," de Grandin answered, "but I do not think that you will hear its repetition unless you are unfortunate enough to go to hell when you have died."

"What was it?"

"*Eh bien*, one who thought himself a clever jester pressed his jest too far. Meantime, look to *Madame* your wife. See how peacefully she lies upon her bed. Her time for evil dreams is past. Be kind to her, *mon jeune*. Do not forget, a woman loves to have a lover, even though he is her husband." He bent and kissed the sleeping girl upon the brow. "*Au 'voir*, my little lovely one," he murmured. Then, to me:

"Come, Trowbridge, my good friend. Our work is finished here. Let us leave them to their happiness."

A N HOUR LATER IN the study he faced me across the fire. "Perhaps you'll deign to tell me what it's all about now?" I asked sarcastically.

"Perhaps I shall," he answered with a grin. "You will recall that this annoying Monsieur Who Was Dead Yet Not Dead, appeared and grinned most horrifyingly through windows several times? Always from the outside, please remember. At the hospital, where he nearly caused the *garde-malade* to have a fit, he laughed and mouthed at her through the glass skylight. When he first appeared and threatened Madame Arabella he spoke to her through the window—"

"But her window was open," I protested.

"Yes, but screened," he answered with a smile. "Screened with iron wire, if you please."

"What difference did that make? Tonight I saw him almost force his features through—"

"A copper screen," he supplied. "Tonight the screen was copper; me, I saw to that."

Then, seeing my bewilderment: "Iron is the most earthy of all metals," he explained. "It and its derivative, steel, are so instinct with the earth's essence that creatures of the spirit cannot stand its nearness. The legends tell us that when Solomon's Temple was constructed no tool of iron was employed, because even the friendly *jinn* whose help he had enlisted could not perform their tasks in close proximity to iron. The witch can be detected by the pricking of an iron pin—never by a pin of brass.

"Very well. When first I thought about the evil dead one's reappearances I noted that each time he stared outside the window. Glass, apparently, he could not pass—and glass contains a modicum of iron. Iron window-wire stopped him. 'He are not a true ghost, then,' I inform me. 'They are things of spirit only, they are thoughts made manifest. This one is a thing of hate, but also of some physical material as well; he is composed in part of emanations from the body which lies putrefying in the grave. *Voilà*, if he have physical properties he can be destroyed by physical means.'

"And so I set my trap. I procured a screen of copper through which he could effect an entrance, but I charged it with electricity. I increased the potential of the current with a step-up transformer to make assurance doubly sure, and then I waited for him like the spider for the fly, waited for him to come through that charged screen and electrocute himself. Yes, certainly."

"But is he really destroyed?" I asked dubiously.

"As the candle-flame when one has blown it out. He was—how do you say it?—short-circuited. No malefactor in the chair of execution ever died more thoroughly than that one, I assure you."

"It seems queer, though, that he should come back from the grave to haunt those poor kids and break up their marriage when he really wanted it," I murmured wonderingly.

"Wanted it? Yes, as the trapper wants the bird to step within his snare."

"But he gave them such a handsome present when little Dennis was born—"

"*La, la*, my good, kind, trusting friend, you are *naïf*. The money I gave Madame Arabella was my own. I put it in that envelope."

"Then what was the real message?"

"It was a dreadful thing, my friend; a dreadful, wicked thing. The night that Monsieur Dennis left that package with me I determined that the old one meant to do him in, so I steamed the cover open and read what lay within. It made plain the things which Dennis thought that he remembered.

"Long, long ago Monsieur Tantavul lived in San Francisco. His wife was twenty years his junior, and a pretty, joyous thing she was. She bore him two fine children, a boy and girl, and on them she bestowed the love which he could not appreciate. His surliness, his evil temper, his constant fault-finding drove her to distraction, and finally she sued for divorce.

"But he forestalled her. He spirited the children away, then told his wife the plan of his revenge. He would take them to some far off place and bring them up believing they were cousins. Then when they had attained full growth he would induce them to marry and keep the secret of their relationship until they had a child, then break the dreadful truth to them. Thereafter they would live on, bound together by their fear of censure, or perhaps of criminal prosecution, but their consciences would cause them endless torment, and the very love they had for each other would be like fetters forged of white-hot steel, holding them in odious bondage from which there was no escape. The sight of their children would be a reproach to them, the mere thought of love's sweet communion would cause revulsion to the point of nausea.

"When he had told her this his wife went mad. He thrust her into an asylum and left her there to die while he came with his babies to New Jersey, where he reared them together, and by guile and craftiness nurtured their love, knowing that when finally they married he would have his so vile revenge."

"But, great heavens, man, they're brother and sister!" I exclaimed in horror.

"Perfectly," he answered coolly. "They are also man and woman, husband and wife, and father and mother."

"But—but—" I stammered, utterly at loss for words.

"But me no buts, good friend. I know what you would say. Their child? *Ah bah*, did not the kings of ancient times repeatedly take their own sisters to wife, and were not their offspring sound and healthy? But certainly. Did not both Darwin and Wallace fail to find foundation for the doctrine that cross-breeding between healthy people with clean blood is productive of inferior progeny? Look at little Monsieur Dennis. Were you not blinded by your silly, unrealistic training and tradition—did you not know his parents' near relationship—you would not hesitate to pronounce him an unusually fine, healthy child.

"Besides," he added earnestly, "they love each other, not as brother and sister, but as man and woman. He is her happiness, she is his, and little Monsieur Dennis is the happiness of both. Why destroy this joy—*le bon Dieu* knows they earned it by a joyless childhood—when I can preserve it for them by simply keeping silent?"

Hands of the Dead

"I F THERE WERE SUCH a thing as a platinum blond tom-cat, I'm sure it would look like Doctor de Grandin." My dinner partner, a long-eyed, sleek-haired brunette in a black-crêpe gown cut to the base of her throat in front and slashed in a V below the waist behind, gestured with her oddly oblique eyes across the table toward Jules de Grandin. "He's a funny little fellow—rather a darling, though," Miss Travers added. "Just see how he looks at Virginia Bush-rod; wouldn't you think she was a particularly luscious specimen of sparrow, and he—"

"Why should he watch Miss Bushrod, particularly?" I countered. "She's very lovely, but—"

"Oh, I don't think he's interested in her face, pretty as it is," Miss Travers laughed. "He's watching her hands. Everybody does."

I looked along the candle-lighted table with its ornate Georgian silver and lace-and-linen cloth until my eye came to rest upon Virginia Bushrod. Latest of the arrivals at the Merridews' house party, she was also probably the most interesting. You could not judge her casually. A pale, white skin, lightly tanned on beach and tennis court, amber eyes, shading to brown, hair waved and parted in dull-gold ringlets, curled closely on the back curve of her small and shapely head. The dead-white gown she wore set off her bright, blond beauty, and a pair of heavy gold bracelets, tight-clasped about her wrists, drew notice to her long and slender hands.

They were extraordinary hands. Not large, not small, their shapeliness was statuesque, their form as perfect as a sculptor's dream, with straight and supple fingers and a marvelous grace of movement expressive as a spoken word. Almost, it seemed to me as she raised the spun-glass Venetian goblet of Madeira, her hands possessed an independent being of their own; a consciousness of volition which made them not a mere part of her body, but something allied with, though not subservient to it.

"Her hands are rarely beautiful," I commented. "What is she, an actress? A dancer, perhaps—"

"No," said Miss Travers, and her voice sank to a confidential whisper, "but a year ago we thought she'd be a hopeless cripple all her life. Both hands were mangled in a motor accident."

"But that's impossible," I scoffed, watching Miss Bushrod's graceful gestures with renewed interest. "I've been in medicine almost forty years; no hands which suffered even minor injuries could be as flexible as hers."

"They did, just the same," Miss Travers answered stubbornly. "The doctors gave up hope, and said they'd have to amputate them at the wrist; her father told me so. Virginia gave Phil Connor back his ring and was ready to resign herself to a life of helplessness when—"

"Yes?" I smiled as she came to a halt. Lay versions of medical miracles are always interesting to the doctor, and I was anxious to learn how the "hopeless cripple" had been restored to perfect manual health.

"Doctor Augensburg came over here, and they went to him as a last resort—"

"I should think they would," I interjected. Augensburg, half charlatan, a quarter quack, perhaps a quarter genius, was a fair example of the army of medical marvels which periodically invades America. He was clever as a workman, we all admitted that, and in some operations of glandular transplanting had achieved remarkable results, but when he came out with the statement that he had discovered how to make synthetic flesh for surgical repair work the medical societies demanded that he prove his claims or stop the grand triumphal tour that he was making of his clinics. He failed to satisfy his critics and returned to Austria several thousand dollars richer, but completely discredited in medical circles.

"Well, they went to him," Miss Travers answered shortly, "and you see what he accomplished. He—"

Her argument was stilled as Jane Merridew, who acted as her brother's hostess, gave the signal for the ladies to retire.

CHINESE LANTERNS, ORANGE, RED, pale jade, blossomed in the darkness of the garden. Farther off the vine-draped wall cast its shadow over close-clipped grass and winding flagstone paths; there were rustic benches underneath the ginkgo trees; a drinking-fountain fashioned like a lion's head with water flushing in an arc between its gaping jaws sent a musically mellow tinkle through the still night air. I sighed regretfully as I followed the men into the billiard room. The mid-Victorian custom of enforced separation of men and women for a period after dinner had always seemed to me a relic of the past we might well stuff and donate to a museum.

"Anybody want to play?" Ralph Chapman took a cue down from the rack and rubbed its felt-tipped end with chalk. "Spot you a dollar a shot, Phil; are you on?"

"Not I," the youth addressed responded with a grin. "You took me into camp last time. Go get another victim."

Young Chapman set the balls out on the table, surveyed them critically a moment, then, taking careful aim, made a three-cushion shot, and followed it with another which bunched the gleaming spheres together in one corner.

De Grandin raised a slender, well-manicured hand and patted back a yawn. "*Mon Dieu*," he moaned to me, "it is sad! Outside there is the beauty of the night and of the ladies, and we, *pardieu*, we sit and swelter here like a pack of *sacré* fools while he knocks about the relics of departed elephants. Me, I have enough. I go to join the ladies, if—"

"May I try, Ralph?" Glowing in defiant gayety, lips wine-moist, eyes bright and wandering, Virginia Bushrod poised upon the threshold of the wide French window which let out on the terrace. "I've never played," she added, "but tonight I feel an urge for billiards; I've got a yen to knock the little balls around, if you know what I mean."

"Never too late to learn," young Chapman grinned at her. "I'm game; I'll pay you five for every kiss you make."

"Kiss?" she echoed, puzzled.

"Kiss is right, infant. A purely technical term. See, here's a kiss." Deftly he brought the balls together in light contact, paused a moment, then with a quick flick of his cue repeated the maneuver twice, thrice, four times.

"O-oh, I see." Her eyes were bright with something more than mere anticipation. It seemed to me they shone like those of a drunkard long deprived of drink when liquor is at last accessible.

"See here, you take the stick like this," began young Chapman, but the girl brushed past him, took a cue down from the rack and deftly rubbed the cube of chalk against its tip.

She leant across the table, her smooth brow furrowed in a frown of concentration, thrust the cue back and forth across her fingers tentatively; then swiftly as a striking snake the smooth wood darted forward. Around the table went the cue ball, taking the cushions at a perfect angle. *Click-click*, the ivory spheres kissed each other softly, then settled down a little way apart, their polished surfaces reflecting the bright lamplight.

"Bravo, Virginia!" cried Ralph Chapman. "I couldn't have made a better shot myself. Talk about beginner's luck!"

The girl, apparently, was deaf. Eyes shining, lips compressed, she leant across the table, darted forth her cue and made an expert draw shot, gathering the balls together as though they had been magnetized. Then followed a quick volley shot, the cue ball circled round the table, spun sharply in reverse English and kissed the other balls with so light an impact that the click was hardly audible.

Again and again she shot, driving her cue ball relentlessly home against the others, never missing, making the most difficult shots with the sure precision betokening long mastery of the game. Fever-eyed, white-faced, oblivious to all about her, she made shot follow shot until a hundred marks had been run off, and it seemed to me that she was sating some fierce craving as she bent above the table, cue in hand.

Phil Connor, her young fiancé, was as puzzled as the rest, watching her inimitable skill first with wonder, then with something like stark fear. At last: "Virginia!" he cried, seizing her by the elbow and fairly dragging her away. "Virginia honey, you've played enough."

"Oh?" An oddly puzzled look gathered between her slim brows, and she shook her head from side to side, like a waking sleeper who would clear his brain of dreams. "Did I do well?"

"Very well. Very well, indeed, for one who never played the game before," Ralph Chapman told her coldly.

"But, Ralph, I never did," she answered. "Honestly, I never had a billiard cue in my hands before tonight!"

"No?" his tone was icy. "If this is your idea of being sporting—"

"See here, Chapman," young Connor's Irish blood was quick to take the implication up. "Ginnie's telling you the truth. There isn't a billiard table in her father's house or mine, there wasn't any in her sorority house; she's never had a chance to play. Don't you think I'd know it if she liked the game? I tell you it was luck; sheer luck—"

"At five dollars per lucky point?"

"Word of honor, Ralph," Miss Bushrod told him, "I—"

"You'll find my honor good as yours," he broke in frigidly. "I'll hand you my check for five hundred dollars in the morning, Miss—"

"Why, you dam' rotten swine, I'll break your neck!" Phil Connor leaped across the room, eyes flashing, face aflame; but:

"Gentlemen, this has gone quite far enough," Colonel Merridew's cold voice cut through the quarrel. "Chapman, apologize to Virginia. Connor, put your hands down!" Then, as the apology was grudgingly given:

"Shall we join the ladies, gentlemen?" asked Colonel Merridew.

"IT WAS A RATHER shoddy trick that Bushrod girl played on young Chapman, wasn't it?" I asked de Grandin as we prepared for bed. "He's a conceited pup, I grant, vain of his skill at billiards, and all that; but for her to play the wide-eyed innocent and let him offer her five dollars a point, when she's really in the championship class—well, it didn't seem quite sporting."

The little Frenchman eyed the glowing tip of his cigar in thoughtful silence for a moment; then: "I am not quite persuaded," he replied. "Mademoiselle Bushrod—*mon Dieu*, what a name!—appeared as much surprised as any—"

"But, man, did you notice her dexterity?" I cut in petulantly. "That manual skill—"

"*Précisément*," he nodded, "that manual skill, my friend. Did it not seem to you her hands betrayed a—how do you say him?—a knowledge which she herself did not possess?"

I shook my head in sheer exasperation. "You're raving," I assured him. "How the deuce—"

"*Tiens*, the devil knows, perhaps, not I," he broke in with a shrug. "Come, let us take a drink and go to bed."

He raised the chromium carafe from the bedside table, and: "Name of a devil!" he exclaimed in disappointment. "The thing holds water!"

"Of course it does, idiot," I assured him with a laugh. "You wanted a drink, didn't you?"

"A drink, but not a bath, *cordieu*. Come, species of an elephant, arise and follow me."

"Where?" I demanded.

"To find a drink; where else?" he answered with a grin. "There is a tray with glasses on the sideboard of the dining-room."

The big old house was silent as a tomb as we crept down the stairs, slipped silently along the central hall and headed for the dining-room. De Grandin paused abruptly, hand upraised, and, obedient to his signal, I, too, halted.

In the music room which opened from the hallway on the right, someone was playing the piano, very softly, with a beautiful harpsichord touch. The lovely, haunting sadness of the *Londonderry Air* came to us as we listened, the gently struck notes falling, one upon another, like water dripping from a lichened rock into a quiet woodland pool.

"Exquisite!" I began, but the Frenchman's hand raised to his lips cut short my commendation as he motioned me to follow.

Virginia Bushrod sat before the instrument, her long, slim fingers flitting fitfully across the ivory keys, the wide gold bracelets on her wrists agleam. Black-lace pajamas, less concealing than a whorl of smoke, revealed the gracious curves of her young body, with a subtle glow, as wisps of banking storm-clouds dim, but do not hide, the moon.

As we paused beside the door the sweet melody she played gave way to something else, a lecherous, macabre theme in C sharp minor, seductive and compelling, but revolting as a painted corpse already touched with putrefaction. Swaying gently to the rhythm of the music, she turned her face toward us, and in the wavering candlelight I saw her eyes were closed, long lashes sweeping against pale-gold cheeks, smooth, fine-veined eyelids gently lowered.

I turned to Jules de Grandin with a soundless question, and he nodded affirmation. "But yes, she sleeps, my friend," he whispered. "Do not waken her."

The music slowly sank to a thin echo, and Miss Bushrod rose with lowered lids and gently parted lips, swayed uncertainly a moment, then passed us with a slow and gliding step, her slim, bare feet soundless as a draft of air upon the rug-strewn door. Slowly she climbed the stairs, one shapely hand upon the carven balustrade, the dim night-light which burned up in the gallery picking little points of brightness from her golden wristlets.

"Probably neurotic," I murmured as I watched her turn left and disappear around the pillar at the stairhead. "They say she underwent an operation on her hands last year, and—"

De Grandin motioned me to silence as he teased the needle-points of his mustache between his thumb and finger. "Quite so," he said at length. "Precisely, exactly. One wonders."

"Wonders what?" I asked.

"How long we have to wait until we get that drink," he answered with a grin. "Come, let us get it quickly, or we need not go to bed at all."

BREAKFAST WAS NO FORMAL rite at Merridews'. A long buffet, ready-set with food and gay with raffia-bound Italian glassware, Mexican pottery and bowls, daisies, chicory and Queen Anne's lace, stood upon the terrace, while little tables, spread with bright-checked peasant linen, dotted the brick paving.

De Grandin piled a platter high with food, poured himself a cup of coffee and set to work upon the viands. "Tell me, good Friend Trowbridge," he commanded as he returned from the sideboard with a second generous helping of steamed sole, "what did you note, if anything, when we caught Mademoiselle Bushrod at her midnight music?"

I eyed him speculatively. When Jules de Grandin asked me questions such as that they were not based on idle curiosity.

"You're on the trail of something?" I evaded.

He spread his hands before him, imitating someone groping in the dark. "I think I am," he answered slowly, "but I can not say of what. Come, tell me what you noticed, if you please."

"Well," I bent my brows in concentration, "first of all, I'd say that she was sleep-walking; that she had no more idea what she was doing than I have what she's doing now."

He nodded acquiescence. "Precisely," he agreed. "And—"

"Then, I was struck by the fact that though she had apparently risen from bed, she had those thick, barbaric bracelets on her wrists."

"Holà, touché," he cried delightedly, "you have put the finger on it. It was unusual, was it not?"

"I'd say so," I agreed. "Then—why, bless my soul!" I paused in something like dismay as sudden recollection came to me.

He watched me narrowly, eyebrows raised.

"She turned the wrong way at the stairhead," I exclaimed. "The women's rooms are to the right of the stairs, the men's to the left. Don't you remember, Colonel Merridew said—"

"I remember perfectly," he cut in. "I also saw her turn that way, but preferred to have corroboration—"

The clatter of hoofs on the driveway cut short his remarks, and a moment later Virginia Bushrod joined us on the terrace. She looked younger and much smaller in her riding-clothes. White breeches, obviously of London cut, were topped by a white-linen peasant blouse, gay with wool embroidery, open at the throat, but with sleeves which came down to the gauntlets of her doeskin gloves. For belt she wore a brilliant knit-silk Roman scarf, and another like it knotted turbanwise around her head, its glowing reds and greens and yellows bringing out the charming colors of her vivid, laughing face. Black boots, reaching to the knee, encased her high-arched, narrow feet and slender legs.

"Hello, sleepy-heads," she greeted as she sat down at our table, "where've you been all morning? Making up for night calls and such things? I've been up for hours—and I'm famished."

"What will it be, *Mademoiselle?*" de Grandin asked as he leaped up nimbly to serve her; "a little toast, perhaps—a bowl of cereal?"

"Not for me," she denied, laughing. "I want a man's-sized breakfast. I've ridden fifteen miles this morning."

As she peeled off her white-chamois gloves I caught the glint of golden bracelets on her wrists.

"We enjoyed your playing, *Mademoiselle,*" the little Frenchman told her smilingly as, obedient to her orders, he deposited a "man's-sized" plate of food before her. "The *Londonderry Air* is beautiful, but that other composition which you played with such *verve*, such feeling, it was—"

"Is this a joke?" Miss Bushrod looked at him through narrowed eyes. "If it is, I can't quite see the humor."

"*Mais non*, it is no jest, I do assure you. Music is one of my passions, and although I play but poorly, I enjoy to hear it. Your talent—"

"Then you've mistaken me for someone else," the girl cut in, a quick flush mounting to her face. "I'm one of those unfortunates who's utterly tone-deaf; I—"

"That's right," Christine Travers, virtually naked in a sun-back tennis blouse and shorts, emerged through the French windows and dropped down beside Miss Bushrod. "Ginnie's tone-deaf as an oyster. Couldn't carry a tune in a market basket."

"But, my dear young lady," I began, when a vicious kick upon my shin cut my protest short.

"Yes?" Miss Travers smiled her slow, somewhat malicious smile. "Were you going to tell Ginnie you've a remedy for tone-deafness, Doctor? Something nice and mild, like arsenic, or corrosive sublimate? If you'll just tell her how to take it, I'll see—"

"Doctar Trowbridge, Doctar de Grannun, suh, come quick, fo' de Lawd's sake!" Noah Blackstone, Merridew's stout colored butler, burst upon the terrace, his usual serene aplomb torn to shreds by sudden terror. "Come runnin', gen'lemens, sumpin awful's happened!"

"Eh, what is it you say?" de Grandin asked. "Something awful—"

"Yas, suh; sumpin dreadful. Mistu—Mistu Chapman's done been kilt. Sumbuddy's murdered 'im. He's daid!"

"Dead? Ralph Chapman?" Horror mounted in Virginia Bushrod's amber eyes as she seemed to look past us at some scene of stark tragedy. "Ralph Chapman—dead!" Unthinkingly, mechanically as another woman might have wrung her handkerchief in similar circumstances, she took the heavy silver fork with which she had been eating and bent it in a spiral.

SPRAWLED SUPINELY ACROSS THE bed, protruding eyes staring sightlessly at the ceiling Ralph Chapman lay, mouth slightly agape, tongue thrust forward. It needed no second glance to confirm the butler's diagnosis, and it required only a second glance to confirm his suspicion of murder, for in those bulging eyes and that protruding tongue, no less than in the area of bruise upon the throat, we read the autograph of homicide.

"So!" de Grandin gazed upon the body speculatively, then crossed the room, took the dead boy's face between his hands and raised the head. It was as if the head and body joined by a cord rather than a column of bone and muscle, for there was no resistance to the little Frenchman's slender hands as the young man's chin nodded upward. "Ah—so-o-o!" de Grandin murmured. "He used unnecessary violence, this one; see, my friend"—he turned the body half-way over and pointed to a purpling bruise upon the rear of the neck—"two hands were used. In front we have the murderer's thumb and finger marks; behind is ecchymosis due to counter-pressure. And so great a force was used that not only was this poor one strangled, but his neck was broken, as well."

He passed his fingers tentatively along the outline of young Chapman's jaw; then: "How long has he been dead, my friend?" he asked.

Following his example, I felt the dead boy's jaw, then his chest and lower throat. "H'm," I glanced at my watch, "my guess is six or seven hours. There's still some stiffening of the jaw, but not much in the chest, and the forearms are definitely hard—yes, I'd say six hours at the least, eight at the most, judging by the advance of *rigor mortis*. That would place the time of death—"

"Somewhere near midnight," he supplied. Then, irrelevantly: "They were strong hands that did this thing, my friend; the muscles of our necks are tough, our vertebræ are hard; yet this one's neck is snapped as though it were a reed."

"You—you've a suspicion?" I faltered.

"I think so," he returned, sweeping the room with a quick, stock-taking glance.

"Ah, what is this?" He strode across the rug, coming to pause before the bureau. On the hanging mirror of the cabinet, outlined plainly as an heraldic device blazoned on a coat of arms, was a handprint, long slender fingers, the mounts of the palm and the delicately sweeping curve of the heel etched on the gleaming surface, as though a hand, dank with perspiration, had been pressed upon it.

"Now," his slim black brows rose in saracenic arches as he regarded me quizzically, "for why should a midnight visitant especially if bent on murder, take pains to leave an autograph upon the mirror, good Friend Trowbridge?" he demanded.

"B-but that's a woman's hand," I stammered. "Whoever broke Ralph Chapman's neck was strong as a gorilla, you just said so. A woman—"

"Tell me, my friend," he interrupted, fixing me with that level, disconcerting stare of his, "do you not wish to see that justice triumphs?"

"Why, yes, of course, but—"

"And is it your opinion—I ask you as a man of medicine—that a man's neck offers more resistance than, by example, a silver table-fork?"

I stared at him dumfounded. Ralph Chapman had publicly denounced Virginia Bushrod as a cheat; we had seen her going toward his room about the time of the murder; within five minutes we had seen her give a demonstration of manual strength scarcely to be equaled by a professional athlete. The evidence was damning, but—

"You're going to turn her over to the police?" I asked.

For answer he drew the green-silk handkerchief peeping from the pocket of his brown sports coat, wadded it into a mop and erased the handprint from the mirror. "Come, my friend," he ordered, "we must write out our report before the coroner arrives."

THE MORTICIAN TO WHOM Coroner Lordon had entrusted Chapman's body obligingly lent his funeral chapel for the inquest. The jury, picked at random from the villagers, occupied the space customarily assigned to the remains. The coroner himself sat in the clergyman's enclosure. Witnesses were made comfortable in the family room, being called out one by one to testify. Through the curtained doorway leading to the chapel—ingeniously arranged to permit the mourning family to see and hear the funeral ceremonies without being seen by those assembled in the auditorium—we saw the butler testify to finding the body and heard him say he summoned de Grandin and me immediately.

"You give it as your medical opinion that death had taken place some six or seven hours earlier?" the coroner asked me.

"Yes, sir," I replied.

"And what, in your opinion, was the cause of death?"

"Without the confirmation of an autopsy I can only hazard an opinion," I returned, "but from superficial examination I should say it was due to respiratory failure caused by a dislocation of the spinal column and rupture of the cord. The dislocation, as nearly as I could judge from feeling of the neck, took place between the second and third cervical vertebræ."

"And how was the spinal fracture caused?"

"By manual pressure, sir—pressure with the hands. The bruises on the dead man's neck show the murderer grasped him by the throat at first, probably to stifle any outcry, then placed one hand behind his head and with the other forced the chin violently upward, thereby simulating the quick pressure given the neck in cases of judicial hanging."

"It would have required a man of more than usual strength to commit this murder in the manner you have described it?"

I drew a deep breath of relief. "Yes, sir, it would have had to be such a man," I answered, emphasizing the final word, unconsciously, perhaps.

"Thank you, Doctor," said the coroner, and called de Grandin to corroborate my testimony.

As the inquisition lengthened it became apparent Coroner Lordon had a theory of his own, which he was ingeniously weaving into evidence. Rather subtly he brought out the fact that the household had retired by eleven-thirty, and not till then did he call for testimony of the quarrel which had flared up in the billiard room. The painful scene was reenacted in minute detail; six men were forced to swear they heard young Connor threaten to break Chapman's neck.

"Mr. Connor," asked the coroner, "you rowed stroke oar at Norwood, I believe?"

Phil Connor nodded, and in his eyes was growing terror.

"Day before yesterday you won a twenty-dollar bet with Colonel Merridew by tearing a telephone directory in quarters, did you not?"

A murmur ran along the jury as the question stabbed young Connor like a rapier-thrust.

I saw Virginia Bushrod blanch beneath her tan, saw her long, slim hand go out to clutch her lover's, but my interest in the by-play ceased as the final question hurtled like a crossbow bolt:

"Mr. Connor, where were you between the hours of twelve and two last night?"

The tortured youth's face flushed, then went white as tallow as the frightened blood drained back. The trap had sprung. He rose, grasping at the chair in front of him till lines of white showed on his hands as the flexor muscles stood out pallidly against his sun-tanned skin.

"I—I must refuse to answer—" he began, and I could see his throat working convulsively as he fought for breath. "What I was doing then is no affair—"

"*Pardonnez-moi, Monsieur le Coroner*," de Grandin rose and bowed respectfully, "I do not wonder that the young man is embarrassed. He was with me, and—believe me, I am grieved to mention it, and would not, if it were not necessary—he was drunk!"

"Drunk?" a slow flush stained the coroner's face as he saw his cherished case evaporating.

"Drunk?" the little Frenchman echoed, casting a grin toward the responsive jury. "But yes, *Monsieur*. Drunk like a pig; so drunk he could not mount the stairs unaided."

Before he could be interrupted he proceeded:

"Me, I am fond of liquor. I like it in the morning, I delight in it at noon; at night I utterly adore it. Last night, when I had gone to bed, I felt the need of stimulant. I rose and went downstairs, and as I reached the bottom flight I turned and saw Messieurs Connor and Chapman on the balcony above. They were in argument, and seemed quite angry. '*Holà, mes enfants*,' I called to them, 'cease your dispute and join me in a drink. It will dissolve your troubles as a cup of coffee melts a lump of sugar.'

"Monsieur Chapman would have none of it. Perhaps he was one of those unfortunates who have no love for brandy; it might have been he did not choose to drink with Monsieur Connor. At any rate, he went into his room and closed the door, while Monsieur Connor joined me in the dining-room.

"*Messieurs*," he bent another quick smile at the jurymen, "have you ever seen a man unused to liquor making the attempt to seem to like it? It is laughable is it not? So it was last night. This one"—he laid a patronizing hand upon young Connor's shoulder—"he tipped his glass and poured the brandy down, then made a face as though it had been castor oil. Ah, but he had the gameness, as you say so quaintly over here. When I essayed a second drink he held his glass for more, and when I took a third, he still desired to keep me company; but then he scarce knew what he did. Three glasses of good cognac"—he fairly smacked his lips upon the word—"are not for one who does not give his serious thought to drinking. No, certainly.

"Before you could pronounce the name of that *Monsieur Jacques Robinson* our young friend here was drunk. *Mordieu*, it was superb! Not in more than twenty years have I been able to achieve such drunkenness, *Messieurs*. He staggered, his head hung low between his shoulders, and rolled from side to side; he smiled like a pussy-cat who has lately dined on cream; he toppled from his chair and lay upon the floor!

"I raised him up. 'Come, *Monsieur*,' I told him, 'this is no way to do. You are like a little, naughty boy who creeps into his father's cellar and gets drunk on stolen wine. Be a man, *Monsieur*. Come to bed!'

"Ah, but he could not. He could not walk, he could not talk, except to beg me that I would not tell his fiancée about his indiscretion. And so I dragged him up the stairs. Yes, I, who am not half his size, must carry him upstairs, strip off his clothes, and leave him snoring in a drunken stupor. He—"

"Then you think he couldn't 'a' broke th' other feller's neck?" a juryman demanded with a grin.

De Grandin left his place, walked across the chapel till he faced his questioner and leant above him, speaking in a confidential whisper which he nevertheless managed to make audible throughout the room. "My friend," he answered solemnly, "he could not break the bow of his cravat. I saw him try it several times; at last I had to do it for him."

The verdict of the jury was that Ralph Chapman came to his death at the hands of some person or persons to them unknown.

D E GRANDIN POURED A thimbleful of old Courvoiser into his brandy sniffer, rotated the glass a moment, then held it to his nose, sighing ecstatically. "You know, my friend," he told me as he sipped the cognac slowly, "I often wonder what became of them. It was a case with possibilities, that one. I can not rid my mind of the suspicion—"

"Whatever are you vaporing about?" I cut in testily. "What case, and what suspicion—"

"Why, that of Mademoiselle Bushrod and her fiancé, the young Monsieur Connor. I—"

"You certainly lied Phil Connor out of the electric chair," I told him with a smile. "If ever I saw a death-trap closing in on anyone, it was the snare the coroner had laid for him. Whatever made you do it, man? Didn't *you* want to see justice triumph?"

"I did," he answered calmly, "but justice and law are not always cousins German, my friend. Justly, neither of those young folks was responsible for—"

"Beg pardon, sor, there's a lady an' gentleman askin' fer Doctor de Grandin," interrupted Nora McGinnis from the doorway. "A Misther Connor an' Miss Bushrod. Will I be showin' 'em in, I dunno?"

"By all means!" cried de Grandin, swallowing his brandy at a gulp. "Come, Friend Trowbridge, the angels whom we spoke of have appeared!"

P HIL CONNOR LOOKED EMBARRASSED; a darkling, haunted fear was in Virginia Bushrod's eyes as we joined them in the drawing-room.

The young man drew a deep, long breath, like a swimmer about to dive into icy water, then blurted: "You saved my life, sir, when they had me on the spot last month. Now we've come to you again for help. Something's been troubling us ever since Ralph Chapman died, and we believe that you're the only one to clear it up."

"But I am honored!" said de Grandin with a bow. "What is the nature of your worriment, my friends? Whatever I can do you may be sure I'll do if you will take me in your confidence.

Young Connor rose, a faint flush on his face, and shifted from one foot to the other, like a schoolboy ill at ease before his teacher. "It's more a matter of your taking us into your confidence, sir," he said at length. "What really happened on the night Ralph Chapman's neck was broken? Of course, that story which you told was pure invention—even though it saved me from a trial for murder—but both Virginia and I have been haunted by the fear that something which we do not know about happened, and—"

"How do you say, you fear that something which you do not know about," he began, but Virginia Bushrod cut in with a question:

"Is there anything to the Freudian theory that dreams are really wish-fulfilments, Doctor? I've tried to tell myself there is, for that way lies escape, but—"

"Yes, *Mademoiselle?*" de Grandin prompted as she paused.

"Well, in a misty, hazy sort of way I recollect I dreamt that Ralph was dead that night and that—oh, I might as well tell everything! I dreamt I killed him!

"It seemed to me I got up out of bed and walked a long, long way along a dark and winding road. I came to a high mountain, but oddly, I was on its summit, without having climbed it. I descended to the valley, and everything was dark; then I sat down to rest, and far away I heard a strain of music It was soft, and sweet and restful, and I thought, 'How good it is to be here listening—'

"*Pardon, Mademoiselle*, can you recall the tune you heard?" de Grandin asked, his small mustache aquiver like the whiskers of an alert tom-cat, his little, round blue eyes intent on her in an unwinking stare.

"Why, yes, I think I can. I'm totally tone-deaf, you know, utterly unable to reproduce a single note of music accurately, but there are certain tunes I recognize. This was one of them, the *Londonderry Air.*"

"Ah?" the little Frenchman flashed a warning look at me; then: "And what else did you dream?" he asked.

"The tune I listened to so gladly seemed to change. I couldn't tell you what the new air was, but it was something dreadful—terrible. It was like the shrieking and laughing of a thousand fiends together—and they were laughing at me! They seemed to point derisive fingers at me, making fun of me because I'd been insulted by Ralph Chapman and didn't dare resent it.

"I don't suppose you've ever heard of the Canadian poet Service, Doctor, but somewhere in one of his poems he tells of the effect of music on a crowd of miners gathered in a saloon:

"The thought came back of an ancient wrong,
And it stung like a frozen lash,
And the lust arose to kill—to kill . . .

"That's how that dream-tune seemed to me. The darkness round me seemed to change to dusky red, as though I looked out through a film of blood, and a single thought possessed me: 'Kill Ralph Chapman; kill Ralph Chapman! He called you a low cheat before your friends tonight; kill him for it-wring his neck!'

"Then I was climbing up the mountainside again, clambering over rocks and boulders, and always round me was that angry, bloody glow, like the red reflection of a fire at night against the sky. At last I reached the summit, weak and out of breath, and there before me, sleeping on the rocks, was Ralph Chapman. I looked at him, and as I looked the hot resentment which I felt came flooding up until it nearly strangled me. I bent over him, took his throat between my hands and squeezed, pressed till his face grew bluish-gray and his eyes and tongue were starting forward. Oh, he knew who it was, all right! Before I gave his neck the final vicious twist and felt it break beneath my fingers like a brittle stick that's bent too far, I saw the recognition in his eyes and the deadly fear in them.

"I wasn't sorry for the thing I'd done. I was deliriously happy. I'd killed my enemy, avenged the slight he'd put on me, and was nearly wild with fierce, exultant joy. I wanted to call everybody and show them what I'd done; how those who called Virginia Bushrod thief and cheat were dealt with."

Her breath was coming fast, and in her eyes there shone a bright and gleaming light, as though the mere recital of the dream brought her savage exaltation. "The woman's mad," I told myself, "a homicidal maniac, if ever I saw one."

"And then, *Mademoiselle?*" I heard de Grandin ask soothingly.

"Then I awoke. My hands and brow and cheeks were bathed in perspiration, and I trembled with a sort of chilled revulsion. 'Girl, you've certainly been on a wish-fulfillment spree in Shut-eye Town,' I told myself as I got out of bed.

'It was early, not quite five o'clock, but I knew there was no chance of further sleep, so I took a cold shower, got into my riding-clothes, and went for a long gallop. I argued with myself while riding, and had almost convinced myself that it was all a ghastly dream when I met you and Doctor Trowbridge having breakfast.

"When you mentioned hearing the *Londonderry Air* the night before, I went almost sick. The thought crashed through my brain: 'Music at midnight—music at midnight—music luring me to murder!'

"Then, when the butler ran out on the terrace and told you Ralph was dead—"

"Precisely, *Mademoiselle*, one understands," de Grandin supplied softly.

"I don't believe you do," she contradicted with a wan and rather frightened smile. "For a long time—almost ever since my accident—I've had an odd, oppressive feeling every now and then that I was not myself."

"*Eh*, that you were someone else?" he asked her sharply.

"Yes, that's it, that I was someone different from myself—"

"Who, by example, *Mademoiselle?*"

"Oh, I don't know. Someone low and vile and dreadful, someone with the basest instincts, who—who's *trying to push me out of myself.*"

De Grandin tweaked the needle-points of his mustache, leant forward in his chair and faced her with a level, almost hypnotic stare. "Explain yourself—in the smallest detail—if you will be so good," he ordered.

"I'm afraid I can't explain, sir, it's almost impossible; but—well, take the episode in the billiard room at Colonel Merridew's the night that Ralph was killed. I gave him my word then, and I give you my solemn pledge now that never before in all my life had I held a billiard cue in my hand. I don't know what made me do it, but I happened to be standing on the terrace near the windows of the billiard room, and when I heard the balls click I felt a sudden overmastering urge, like the craving of a drug fiend for his dope, to go inside and play. It was silly, I knew I couldn't even hit a ball, much less make one ball hit another, but something deep inside me seemed to force me on—no, that's not it, it was as though my hands were urging me." She wrinkled her brow in an effort to secure a precisely descriptive phrase; then:

"It seemed as though my hands, entirely independent of me, were leading—no, *pulling* me toward that billiard table. Then, when I had picked up the cue I had a sudden feeling, amounting almost to positive conviction: 'You've done this before; you know this game, no one knows it better.' But I was in a sort of daze as I shot the balls around; I didn't realize how long I'd been playing, or even whether I'd done well or not, till Ralph accused me of pretending ignorance of the game in order to win five hundred dollars from him.

"That isn't all: I'd hardly been out of the hospital a month when one day I found myself in Rodenberg's department store in the act of shoving a piece of Chantilly lace under the jumper of my dress. I can't explain it. I didn't realize I was doing it—truly I didn't—till all of a sudden I seemed to wake up and catch myself in the act of shoplifting. 'Virginia Bushrod, what *are* you doing?' I asked myself, then held the lace out to the sales girl and told her I would take it. I didn't really want it, had no earthly use for it; but I knew instinctively that if I didn't buy it I would steal it."

Abruptly she demanded: "Do you approve of brightly colored nails?"

"*Tenez, Mademoiselle*, that depends upon the time and place and personality of the wearer," he responded with a smile.

"That's it, the personality," she answered. "Bright carmine nails may be all right for some; they're not becoming to my type. Yet I've had an urge, almost in irresistible desire, from time to time to have my nails dyed scarlet. Last week I stopped in Madame Toussaint's for a manicure and pedicure. When I got home

I found the nails of both my hands and feet were varnished brilliant red. I never use a deeper shade than rose, and was horrified to find my nails all daubed that way; yet, somehow, there was a feeling of secret elation, too. I called the salon and asked for Héloise, who'd done my nails, and she said, 'I thought it strange when you insisted on that vivid shade of red, Miss Bushrod. I didn't like to put it on, but you declared you wanted it.'

"Perhaps I did; but I don't remember anything about it."

De Grandin eyed her thoughtfully a moment; then:

"You have spoken of an accident you had, *Mademoiselle*. Tell me of it, if you please."

"It was a little more than a year ago," she answered. "I'd been over to the country club by Morristown, and was hurrying back to keep a date with Phil when my car blew out a tire. At least, I think that's what happened. I remember a sharp, crackling *pop*, like the discharge of a small rifle, and next instant the road-ster fairly somersaulted from the road. I saw the earth rush up at me; then"—she spread her shapely hands in a gesture of finality—"there I was, pinned beneath the wreckage, with both hands crushed to jelly."

"Yet you recovered wholly, thanks to Doctor Augensburg, I understand?"

"Yes, it wasn't till every surgeon we had seen had said he'd have to amputate that Father called in Doctor Augensburg, and he proved they all were wrong. I was in the hospital two months, most of the time completely or partly uncon-scious from drugs, but"—her delicate, long-fingered hands spread once again with graceful eloquence—"here I am, and I'm not the helpless cripple they all said I'd be."

"Not physically, at any rate," de Grandin murmured softly; then, aloud:

"*Mademoiselle*, take off your bracelets!" he commanded sharply.

Had he hurled an insult in her face, the girl could not have looked more shocked. Surprise, anger, sudden fear showed in her countenance as she repeated: "Take—off—"

"*Précisément*," the little Frenchman answered almost harshly. "Take them off, *tout promptement*. I have the intuition; what you call the hunch."

Slowly, reluctantly, as though she were disrobing in the presence of a stranger, Miss Bushrod snapped the clasps of the wide bands of gold which spanned her slender wrists. A line of untanned skin, standing out in contrast to her sun-kissed arms, encircled each slim wrist, testifying that the bracelets had been worn on beach and tennis court, as well as in her leisure moments, but whiter still, livid, eldritch as the mocking grin of broken teeth within the gaping mouth-hole of a skull, there ran around each wrist a ring of cicatrice an inch or so above the styloid process' protuberance. Running up and down a half an inch or so from the encir-cling band of white were vertical scar-lines, interweaving, overlapping, as though the flesh had once been cut apart, then sewn together in a dove-tailed jointure.

Involuntarily I shrank from looking on the girl's deformity, but de Grandin scrutinized it closely. At length:

"*Mademoiselle*, please believe I do not act from idle curiosity," he begged, "but I must use the fluoroscope in my examination. Will you come with me?"

He led her to the surgery, and a moment later we could hear the crackling of the Crookes' tube as he turned the X-ray on.

M ISS BUSHROD'S BRACELETS WERE replaced when they returned some fifteen minutes later, and de Grandin wore a strangely puzzled look. His lips were pursed, as though he were about to whistle, and his eyes were blazing with the hard, cold light they showed when he was on a man-hunt.

"Now, my friends," he told the lovers as he glanced at them in turn, "I have seen enough to make me think that what this lady says is no mere idle vagary. These strange influences she feels, these surprising lapses from normal, they do not mean she suffers from a dual personality, at least as the term is generally used. But unless I am more mistaken than I think, we are confronted by a situation so bizarre that just to outline it would cast a doubt upon our sanity. *Alors*, we must build our case up from the ground.

"Tell me," he shot the question at young Connor, "was there anything unusual—anything at all, no matter how trivial, which occurred to Mademoiselle Bushrod a month—two months—before the accident which crushed her hands?"

The young man knit his brow in concentration. "No-o," he replied at length. "I can't remember anything."

"No altercation, no unpleasantness which might have led to vengeful thoughts, perhaps?" the Frenchman prompted.

"Why, now you speak of it," young Connor answered with a grin, "I did have a run-in with a chap at Coney Island."

"Ah? Describe it, if you please."

"It really wasn't anything. Ginnie and I had gone down to the Island for a spree. We think the summer's not complete without at least one day at Coney— shooting the chutes, riding the steeplechase and roller coasters, then taking in the side shows. This afternoon we'd just about completed the rounds when we noticed a new side show with a Professor Mysterioso or Mefisto, or something of the sort, listed as the chief attraction. He was a hypnotist."

"Ah?" de Grandin murmured softly, "and—"

"The professor was just beginning his act when we went in. He was extraordinarily good, too. Uncannily good, I thought. All dressed in red tights, like Mefistofeles, he was, and his partner—'subject' you call it, don't you?—was a girl dressed in a white gown with a blond wig, simulating Marguerite, you know. He did the darndest things with her—put her in a trance and made her lie stretched between two chairs, with neck on one and heels on the other, no support beneath her body, while men stood on her; told her to rise, rose up three feet in the air, as drawn by invisible wires; finally, he took half a dozen long, sharp knitting-needles and thrust them through her hands, her forearms, even through her cheeks. Then he withdrew them and invited us to search her for signs of scars. It was morbid, I suppose, but we looked, and there wasn't the faintest trace of wounds where he had pierced her with the needles, nor any sign of blood.

"Then he called for volunteers to come up and be hypnotized, and when no one answered, he came down among the audience. 'You, Madame?' he asked Ginnie, stopping in front of her and grinning in her face.

"When she refused he persisted; told her that it wouldn't hurt, and all that sort of thing; finally began glaring into her eyes and making passes before her.

"That was a little bit too much. I let him have it."

"Bravo!" de Grandin murmured softly. "And then?"

"I expected he'd come back at me, for he picked himself up and came across the floor with his shoulders hunched in a sort of boxer's crouch, but when he almost reached me he stopped short, raised his hands above his head and muttered something indistinctly. He wasn't swearing, at least not in English, but I felt that he was calling down a curse on us. I got Virginia out before we had more trouble with him."

"And that was all?" de Grandin asked.

"That was all."

"*Parbleu*, my friend, I think it is enough to be significant." Then, abruptly: "This feminine assistant. Did you notice her?"

"Not particularly. She had a pretty, common sort of face, and long, slim graceful hands with very brightly painted nails."

De Grandin pinched his pointed chin between a thoughtful thumb and finger. "Where did Doctor Augensburg repair your injured hands, *Mademoiselle?*" he asked.

"At the Ellis Sanitarium, out by Hackensack," she answered. "I was in Mercy Hospital at first, but the staff and Doctor Augensburg had some misunderstanding, so he took me out to Ellis Clinic for the operation.

The little Frenchman smiled benignly on the visitors. "I can understand your self-concern, *Mademoiselle*," he told Miss Bushrod. "This feeling of otherhood, this impression that a trespasser-in-possession is inside of you, displacing your personality, making you do things you do not wish to do, is disconcerting, but it is not cause for great alarm. You were greatly hurt, you underwent a trying operation. Those things shock the nervous system. I have seen other instances of it. In the war I saw men make what seemed complete recovery, only to give way to strange irregularities months afterward. Eventually they regained normality;

so should you, within, let us say"—he paused as though to make a mental calculation—"within a month or so."

"You really think so, Doctor?" she asked, pathos looking from her amber eyes.

"But yes, I am all confident of it."

"Name of a most unpleasant small blue devil!" he swore as our visitors' footsteps faded on the cement walk outside. "I must make good my promise to her, but how—death of a dyspeptic hippopotamus!—how?"

"What?" I demanded.

"You know how dreams reflect the outside world in symbolic images. By example, you have kicked the covers off the bed, you are cold. But you are, still asleep. How does the dream convert the true facts into images? By making you to think that you are in the Arctic and a polar storm is raging, or, perhaps, that you have fallen in the river, and are chilled by the cold water. So it was with Mademoiselle Bushrod. She dreams she stands upon a mountain top, that is when she leaves her chamber. She dreams that she descends the mountain; that is when she walks downstairs. She hears a tune, of course she does, her hands, those hands which can not play a single note when she is waking, produce it. She dreams she re-ascends the mountain—climbs the stairs. *Ha*, then she sees before her traducer, sleeping, helpless. She reaches forth her hands, and—

"What then, my friend? Are we to trust the symbolism of the dream still farther?"

"But," I began, and—

"*But* be damned and stewed in hell eternally!" he cut in. "*Attendez-moi:* Those hands, those lovely, graceful hands of hers, are not her own!"

"Eh?" I shot back. "Not—good Lord, man, you're raving! What d'ye mean?"

"Precisely what I say," he answered in a level, toneless voice. "Those hands were grafted on her wrists, as the rose is grafted on the dogwood tree. Her radii and ulnæ have been sawn across transversely; then other bones, processing with the wrist-joints of a pair of hands, were firmly fastened on by silver plates and rivets, the flexor muscles spliced with silver wire, the arteries and veins and nerves attached with an uncanny skill. It is bizarre, incredible, impossible; but it is so. I saw it with my own two eyes when I examined her beneath the fluoroscope."

He left the house directly after breakfast the next morning, and did not reappear till dinner had been waiting half an hour.

"*Sacré nom*," he greeted me across his cocktail glass, "what a day I had, my friend! I have been busy as a flea upon a dog, but what I have accomplished! *Parbleu*, he is a clever fellow, this de Grandin!

"I took down copious mental notes while Mademoiselle Bushrod talked last night, and so this morning I set out for Coney Island. *Grand Dieu des rats*, what a place!

"From one small show-place to another I progressed, and in between times I engaged in conversation with the hangers-on. At last I found a prize, a jewel, a paragon. He rejoices in the name of Snead—Bill Snead, to give him his full title—and when he is not occupied with drinking he proclaims the virtues of a small display of freaks. *Eh bien*, by the expenditure of a small amount of money for food, and something more for drink, I learned from him enough to put me on the trail I sought.

"Professor Mysterioso de Diablo was a hypnotist of no mean parts, I learned. He had 'played big time' for years, but by a most unfortunate combination of events he was sent to prison in the State of Michigan, The lady's husband secured a divorce, *Monsieur le Professeur* a rigidly enforced vacation from the stage.

"After that his popularity declined until finally he was forced to show his art at Coney Island side shows. He was a most unpleasant person, I was told, principally noted for the way he let his fancies for the fair sex wander. This caused his partner much annoyance, and she often reproached him bitterly and publicly.

"Now, attend me carefully. It is of this partner I would speak particularly. Her name was Agnes Fagan. She was born to the theatrical profession, for her father, Michael Fagan, had been a thrower-out of undesired patrons in a burlesque theater when he was not appearing as a strong man on the stage or lying deplorably drunk in bed. The daughter was 'educated something elegant,' my informant told me. She was especially adept at the piano, and for a time entertained ambitions to perform in concert work. However, she inherited one talent, if no other, from her estimable parent: she was astonishingly strong. Monsieur Snead had often seen her amuse her intimates by bending tableware in knots, to the great annoyance of the restaurant proprietor where she happened to perform. She could, he told me solemnly, take a heavy table fork and twist it in a corkscrew.

"*Eh bien*, the lure of the footlights was stronger than her love of music, it appears, for we next behold her as the strong woman in an acrobatic troupe. Perhaps it was another heritage from her many-sided sire, perhaps it was her own idea; at any rate, one day while playing in the city of Detroit, she appropriated certain merchandise without the formality of paying for it. Two police officers were seriously injured in the subsequent proceedings, but eventually she went to prison, was released at the same time that the professor received liberty, and became his partner, the subject of his hypnotism during his performances, and, according to the evil-minded Monsieur Snead, his mistress, as well.

"She possessed four major vanities: her musical ability, her skill at billiards, her strong, white, even teeth and the really unusual beauty of her hands. She was wont to show her strength on all occasions. Her dental vanity led her to suffer the discomfort of having a sound tooth drilled, gold-filled and set with a small diamond. She spent hours in the care of her extremities, and often bought a manicure when it was a choice of pampering her vanity or going without food.

"Now listen carefully, my friend: About a year ago she had a quarrel with her partner, the professor. I recite the facts as Monsieur Snead related them to me. It seems that the professor let his errant fancies wander, and was wont to invite ladies from the audience to join him in his acts. Usually he succeeded, for he had a way with women, Monsieur Snead assured me. But eventually he met rebuff. He also met the fist of the young lady's escort. He was, to use your quaint American expression, 'knocked for a row of ash-cans' by the gentleman.

"*La Fagan* chided him in no uncertain terms. They had a fearful fight in which she would have been the victor, had he not resorted to hypnotism for defense. 'She wuz about to tear him into little bits, when he put 'is hand up and said, "Rigid",' Monsieur Snead related. 'An' there she was, stiff as a frozen statoo, wid 'er hand up in th' air, an' her fist all doubled up, not able to so much as bat a eye. She stood that way about a hour, I expect; then suddenly she fell down flat, and slept like nobody's business. I reckon th' professor gave her th' sleepin' order from wherever he had beat it to. He had got so used to orderin' her about that he could control her at a distance 'most as well as when he looked into her eyes.'

"Thereafter he was often absent from the show where he performed. Eventually he quit it altogether, and within a month his strong and pretty-handed partner vanished. Like *pouf!* she was suddenly nowhere at all.

"By the time the estimable Monsieur Snead had finished telling me these things he could impart no further information. He was, as I have heard it described, 'stewed like a dish of prunes,' for all the while he talked I kept his tongue well oiled with whisky. Accordingly I bid him farewell and pushed my research elsewhere. I searched the files of the journals diligently, endeavoring to find some clue to the vanishment of Mademoiselle Fagan. *Cordieu*, I think I found it! Read this, if you will be so good."

Adjusting my pince-nez I scanned the clipping which he handed me:

GIRL FALLS UNCONSCIOUS WITH
STRANGE MALADY
Collapses on Roadway Near Hackensack—
Absence of Disease Symptoms
Puzzles Doctors

Hackensack, N.J., Sept. 17—Police and doctors today are endeavoring to solve the mystery of the identity and illness of an attractive young woman who collapsed on the roadway near here shortly after noon today, and has lain unconscious in the Ellis Clinic ever since.

She is described as about 30 years old, five feet two inches tall, and with fair complexion and red hair. Her hands and feet showed evidences of unusual care, and both finger- and toe-nails were dyed a brilliant scarlet. In her upper left eye-tooth was a small diamond set in a gold inlay.

She wore a ring with an oval setting of green stone, gold earrings in her pierced ears, and an imitation pearl necklace. Her costume consisted of a blue and white polka-dot dress, white fabric gloves, a black sailor hat with a small feather, and black patent leather pumps. She wore no stockings.

Alec Carter and James Heilmann, proprietors of an antique shop facing on the road, saw the young woman walking slowly toward Hackensack, staggering slightly from side to side. She fell in the roadway across from their store, and when they reached her she was unconscious. Failing to revive her by ordinary first aid methods, they placed her in an automobile and took her to the Ellis Clinic, which was the nearest point where medical aid could be secured.

Physicians at the clinic declared they could find no cause for her prolonged unconsciousness, as she was evidently neither intoxicated nor under the influence of drugs, and exhibited no symptoms of any known disease.

Nothing found upon her offered any clue to her identity.

"Well?" I demanded as I put the clipping down.

"I do not think it was," he answered. "By no means; not at all. Consider, if you please:

"Mademoiselle Bushrod's accident had occurred two weeks before, she had been given up by local surgeons; Augensburg, who was at the Ellis Clinic at the time, had just accepted her case.

"This strange young woman with the pretty hands drops down upon the roadway almost coincidentally with Mademoiselle Virginia's advent at the clinic. Do you not begin to sniff the odor of the rodent?"

"I don't think so," I replied.

"Very well, then, listen: The mysterious young woman was undoubtlessly the Fagan girl, whose disappearance occurred about this time. What was the so mysterious malady which struck her down, which had no symptoms, other than unconsciousness? It was merely that she had been once again put under the hypnotic influence, my friend. You will recall that the professor could control her almost as well when at a distance as when he stared into her eyes? Certainly. Assuredly. She had become so used to his hypnosis that his slightest word or wish was law to her; she was his slave, his thing, his chattel, to do with as he pleased. Unquestionably he commanded her to walk along that road that day, to fall unconscious near the Ellis Clinic; to lie unconscious afterward, eventually to die. Impossible? *Mais non.* If one can tell the human heart to beat more slowly, and make it do so, under power of hypnosis, why may one not command it to cease beating altogether, still under hypnotic influence? So far as the young Fagan person was concerned, she had no thought, no will, no power, either mentally or physically, which the professor could not take from her by a single word of command. No, certainly.

"We were told Mademoiselle Bushrod's accident came from a tire blow-out, *n'est-ce-pas?* I do not think it did. I inquired—most discreetly, I assure you—at and near the Ellis Clinic, and discovered that *Monsieur* the hypnotist visited that institution the very day that she was hurt, had a long conference with Doctor Augensburg in strictest privacy and—when he came he bore a small, high-powered rifle. He said he had been snake-hunting. Me, I think the serpent which he shot was the tire of Mademoiselle Bushrod's car. That was the blow-out which caused her car to leave the road and crush her hands, my friend!

"Now, again: This Professor of the Devil, as he called himself appropriately, visited Doctor Augensburg at several times. He was in the room where the unknown woman lay on more than one occasion. He was at the clinic on the day when Augensburg operated on Mademoiselle Bushrod's hands—and on that day, not fifteen minutes before the operation was performed, the unknown woman died. She had been sinking slowly for some days; her death occurred while orderlies were wheeling our poor Mademoiselle Virginia to the operating-room.

"You will recall she was unknown; that she was given shelter in an institution which maintains no beds for charity or emergency patients? But did you know that Augensburg paid her bill, and demanded in return that he be given her unclaimed body for anatomical research, that he might seek the cause of her 'strange' death? No, you did not know it, nor did I; but now I do, and I damn think that in that information lies the answer to our puzzle.

"I do not have to tell you that the period between somatic death—the mere ceasing to live—and molecular, or true death, when the tissue-cells begin to die, is often as long as three or four hours. During this period the individual body-cells remain alive, the muscles react to electrical stimuli, even the pupils of the eye can be expanded with atropine. She had suffered no disease-infection, this unknown one, her body was healthy, but run down, like an unwound clock. Moreover, fifteen minutes after her death, her hands were, histologically speaking, still alive. What easier than to make the transplantation of her sound, live hands to Mademoiselle Bushrod's wrists, then chop and maim her body in the autopsy room in such a way that none would be the wiser?

"And what of these transplanted hands? They were part and parcel of a hypnotic subject, were they not, accustomed to obey commands of the hypnotist immediately, even to have steel knitting-needles run through them, yet feel no pain? Yes, certainly.

"Very well. Are it not entirely possible that these hands which the professor have commanded so many times when they were attached to one body, will continue to obey his whim when they are rooted to another? I think so.

"In his fine story, your magnificent Monsieur Poe tells of a man who really died, yet was kept alive through hypnosis. These hands of Mademoiselle Fagan never really died, they were still technically alive when they were taken off—who knows what orders this professor gave his dupe before he ordered her to die? Those hands had been a major vanity of hers, they were skilled hands, strong hands, beautiful hands—*hélas*, dishonest hands, as well—but they formed a large part of their owner's personality. Might he not have ordered that they carry on that personality after transplantation to the end that they might eventually lead the poor Mademoiselle Bushrod to entire ruin? I think so. Yes.

"Consider the evidence: Mademoiselle Bushrod is tone-deaf, yet we heard her play exquisitely. She had no skill and no experience in billiards, yet we saw her shoot a brilliant game. For why should she, whose very nature is so foreign to the act, steal merchandise from a shopkeeper?

"Yet she tells us that she caught herself in such a crime. Whence comes this odd desire on her part to have her nails so brightly painted, a thing which she abhors? Last of all, how comes it that she, who is in nowise noted for her strength, can twist a silver table fork into a corkscrew?

"You see," he finished, "the case is perfect. I know it can not possibly be so; yet so it is. We can not face down facts, my friend."

"It's preposterous," I replied, but my denial lacked conviction.

He read capitulation in my tone, and smiled with satisfaction.

"But can't we break this spell?" I asked. "Surely, we can make this Professor What's-his-Name—"

"Not by any legal process," he cut in. "No court on earth would listen to our story, no jury give it even momentary credence. Yet"—he smiled a trifle grimly—"there is a way, my friend."

"What?" I asked.

"Have you by any chance a trocar in your instruments?" he asked irrelevantly.

"A trocar? You mean one of those long, sharp-pointed hollow needles used in paracentesis operations?"

"*Précisément. Tu parles, mon vieux.*"

"Why, yes, I think there's one somewhere."

"And may one borrow it tonight?"

"Of course, but—where are you going at this hour?"

"To Staten Island," he replied as he placed the long, deadly, stiletto-like needle in his instrument case. "Do not wait up for me, my friend, I may be very late."

HORRIFIED SUSPICION, GROWING RAPIDLY to dreadful certainty, mounted in my mind as I scanned the evening paper while de Grandin and I sipped our coffee and liqueurs in the study three nights later. "Read this," I ordered, pointing to an obscure item on the second page:

St. George, S.I, September 30—The body of George Lothrop, known professionally on the stage as Prof. Mysterioso, hypnotist, missing from his rooming-house at Bull's Head, S.I., since Tuesday night, was found floating in New York bay near the St. George ferry slip by harbor police this afternoon.

Representatives of the Medical Examiners' office said he was not drowned, as a stab wound, probably from a stiletto, had pierced his left breast and reached his heart.

Employees at the side show at Coney Island, where Lothrop formerly gave exhibitions as a hypnotist, said he was of a sullen and quarrelsome disposition and given to annoying women. From the nature of the wound which caused his death police believe the husband or admirer of some woman he accosted resented his attentions and stabbed him, afterward throwing his body into the bay.

De Grandin read the item through with elevated brows. "A fortunate occurrence, is it not?" he asked. "Mademoiselle Bushrod is now freed from any spell he might have cast on her—or on her hands. Hypnotic suggestion can not last, once the hypnotist is dead."

"But—but you—that trocar—" I began.

"I returned it to your instrument case last Tuesday night," he answered. "Will you be good enough to pour me out a little brandy? Ah, thank you, my friend."

Witch-House

STREET LIGHTS WERE COMING on and the afterglow was paling in the west beneath the first faint stars as we completed our late dinner and moved to the veranda for coffee and liqueurs. Sinking lazily into a wicker deck chair, Jules de Grandin stretched his womanishly small feet out straight before him and regarded the gleaming tips of his brightly polished calfskin pumps with every evidence of satisfaction.

"*Morbleu*," he murmured dreamily as he drained his demitasse and set his cigar glowing before he raised his tiny glass of *kaiserschmarnn*, "say what you will, Friend Trowbridge, I insist there is no process half so pleasant as the combination of digestion and slow poisoning by nicotine and alcohol. It is well worth going hungry to enjoy—ah, *pour l'amour d'une souris verte*, be quiet, great-mouthed one!" he broke off as the irritable stutter of the 'phone bell cut in on his philosophizing. "*Parbleu*, the miscreant who invented you was one of humankind's worst enemies!"

"Hullo, Trowbridge," hailed a voice across the wire, "this is Friebergh. Sorry to trouble you, but Greta's in bad shape. Can you come out right away?"

"Yes, I suppose so," I replied, not especially pleased at having my postprandial breathing-spell impinged on by a country call. "What seems to be the matter?"

"I wish I knew," he answered. "She just came home from Wellesley last week, and the new house seemed to set her nerves on edge. A little while ago her mother thought she heard a noise up in her bedroom, and when she went in, there was Greta lying on the floor in some sort of fainting-fit. We don't seem able to rouse her, and—"

"All right," I interrupted, thinking regretfully of my less than half-smoked cigar, "I'll be right out. Keep her head low and loosen any tight clothing. If you can make her swallow, give her fifteen drops of aromatic ammonia in a wine-glassful of water. Don't attempt to force any liquids down her throat, though; she might strangle."

"And this Monsieur Friebergh was unable to give you any history of the causal condition of his daughter's swoon?" de Grandin asked as we drove along the Albemarle Road toward the Friebergh place at Scandia.

"No," I responded. "He said that she's just home from college and has been nervous ever since her arrival. Splendid case history, isn't it?"

"*Eh bien*, it is far from being an exhaustive one, I grant," he answered, "but if every layman understood the art of diagnosis we doctors might be forced to go to work, *n'est-ce-pas?*"

THOUGH GRETA FRIEBERGH HAD recovered partial consciousness when we arrived, she looked like a patient just emerging from a lingering fever. Attempts to get a statement from her met with small response, for she answered slowly, almost incoherently, and seemed to have no idea concerning the cause of her illness. Once she murmured drowsily, "Did you find the kitten? Is it all right?"

"What?" I demanded. "A kitten—"

"She's delirious, poor child," whispered Mrs. Friebergh. "Ever since I found her she's been talking of a kitten she found in the bathroom.

"I thought I heard Greta cry," she added, "and ran up here to see if she were all right. Her bedroom was deserted, but the bathroom door was open and I could hear the shower running. When I called her and received no answer I went in and found her lying on the floor. She was totally unconscious, and remained so till just a few minutes ago."

"U'm?" murmured Jules de Grandin as he made a quick inspection of the patient, then rose and stalked into the bathroom which adjoined the chamber. "Tell me, Madame," he called across his shoulder, "is it customary that you leave the windows of your bathroom screenless?"

"Why, no, of course not," Mrs. Friebergh answered. "There's an opaque screen in—good gracious, it's fallen out!"

The little Frenchman turned to her with upraised brows. "Fallen, *Madame?* It was not fastened to the window-casing, then?"

"Yes, it was," she answered positively. "I saw to that myself. The carpenters attached it to the casing with two bolts, so that we could take it out and clean it, but so firmly that it could not be blown in. I can't understand—"

"No matter," he broke in. "Forgive my idle curiosity, if you please. I'm sure that Doctor Trowbridge has completed his examination, now, so we can discuss your daughter's ailment with assurance."

To me he whispered quickly as the mother left the room: "What do you make of the objective symptoms, *mon ami?* Her pulse is soft and frequent, she has a fluttering heart, her eyes are all suffused, her skin is hot and dry, her face is flushed and hectic. No ordinary fainting-fit, you'll say? No case of heat-prostration?"

"No-o," I replied as I shook my head in wonder, "there's certainly no evidence of heat-prostration. I'd be inclined to say she'd suffered an arterial hemorrhage, but there's no blood about, so—"

"Let us make a more minute examination," he ordered, and rapidly inspected Greta's face and scalp, throat, wrists and calves, but without finding so much as a pin-prick, much less a wound sufficient to cause syncope.

"*Mon Dieu*, but this is strange!" he muttered. "It has the queerness of the devil, this! Perhaps she bled internally, but—*ah-ha, regardez-vous, mon vieux!*"

Searching further for some sign of wound, he had unfastened her pajama jacket, and the livid spot he pointed to seemed the key which might unlock the mystery that baffled us. Against the smooth white flesh beneath the gentle swell of her left breast there showed a red and angry patch, such as might have shone had a vacuum cup been pressed some time against the skin, and in the center of the ecchymosis were four tiny punctures spaced so evenly apart that they seemed to make an almost perfect square three-quarters of an inch or so in size.

The discolored spot with its core of tiny wounds seemed insignificant to me, but the little Frenchman looked at it as though he had discovered a small, deadly reptile coiled against the girl's pale skin.

"*Dieu de Dieu de Dieu de Dieu!*" he murmured softly to himself. "Can such things be here, in New Jersey, in the twentieth centennial of our time?"

"What are you maundering about?" I asked him irritably, "She couldn't possibly have lost much blood through these. Why, she seems almost drained dry, yet there's not a spot of blood upon those punctures. They look to me like insect bites of some kind; even if they were wide open they're not large enough to leak a cubic centimeter of blood in half an hour."

"Blood is not entirely colloidal," he responded slowly. "It will penetrate the tissues to some slight extent, especially if sufficient suction be employed."

"But it would have required a powerful suction—"

"*Précisément*, and I make no doubt that such was used, my friend. Me, I do not like the look of this at all. No, certainly." Abruptly he raised his shoulders in a shrug. "We are here as physicians," he remarked. "I think a quarter-grain of morphine is indicated. After that, bed-rest and much rich food. Then, one hopes, she will achieve a good recovery."

"How is she, Trowbridge?" Olaf Friebergh asked as we joined him in the pleasant living-room. He was a compact, lean man in his late fifties, but appeared younger, and the illusion of youth was helped by the short mustache, still quite dark, the firm-cheeked, sunburned face and hazel eyes which, under clear-cut brows, had that brightness which betokens both good health and an interest in life.

"Why, there's nothing really serious the matter," I answered. "She seems quite weak, and there's something rather queer—"

"There's something queer about the whole dam' case," he cut in almost bruskly. "Greta's been on edge since the moment that she came here; nervous as a cat and jumpy and irritable as the very devil. D'ye suppose hysteria could have caused this fainting-fit?"

De Grandin eyed him speculatively a moment; then: "In just what way has Mademoiselle Greta's nervousness been noticeable, *Monsieur?*" he asked. "Your theory of hysteria has much to recommend it, but an outline of the case might help us greatly toward a diagnosis.

Friebergh stirred his highball thoughtfully a moment; then, "D'ye know about this house?" he asked irrelevantly.

"But no, *Monsieur*; what has it to do with *Mademoiselle* your daughter?"

"Just what I'm wondering," Friebergh answered. "Women are weird brutes, Doctor, all of 'em. You never know what fool tricks nerves will play on 'em. This place belonged to one of my remotest ancestors. You're probably aware that this section was originally settled by the Swedes under William Usselinx, and though the Dutch captured it in 1655 many of the Swedish settlers stayed on not caring much who governed them as long as they were permitted to pursue their business in peace. Oscar Friebergh my great-great-grandfather's half-brother, built this house and had his piers and warehouses down on Raritan Bay. It was from here he sent his ships to Europe and even to the Orient, and to this house he brought the girl he married late in life.

"Theirs was quite a romance. Loaded with silks and wine, the *Good Intent*, my uncle's fastest ship, put in at Portugal for a final replenishment of victuals and water before setting sail for America on the last Sunday in June, 1672. The townsfolk were making holiday, for a company of witches and wizards, duly convicted by ecclesiastical courts, had been turned over to the secular arm for execution, and a great fire had been kindled on the Monte Sao Jorge. My uncle and the master of the ship, together with several of the seamen, were curious to see what was going on, so they ascended the hill where, surrounded by a cordon of soldiers, a perfect forest of stakes had been set up, and to each of these were tied two or three poor wretches who writhed and shrieked as the faggots round their feet took fire. The tortured outcasts' screams and the stench of burning flesh fairly sickened the Swedish sailors, and they were turning away from the accursed place to seek the clear air of the harbor when my uncle's attention was attracted to a little girl who fought desperately with the soldiers to break through to the flaming stakes. She was the daughter of a witch and a warlock who were even then roasting at the same stake, chained back to back as they were said to dance at meetings of the witches' coven. The soldiers cuffed her back good-naturedly, but a Dominican friar who stood by bade them let her through to burn, since, being of the witch-folk, her body would undoubtedly burn soon or later, just as her soul was doomed to burn eternally. The sailormen protested vigorously at this, and my uncle caught the wild girl by the wrists and drew her back to safety.

"She was a thin little thing, dressed in filthy rags, half starved, and unspeakably dirty. In her arms she clutched a draggled-looking white kitten which arched its back and fluffed its tail and spat venomously at the soldiers and the priest. But when my uncle pulled the girl to him both child and kitten ceased to struggle, as if they realized that they had found a friend. The Spanish priest ordered them away with their pitiful prize, saying she was born of the witchpeople and would surely grow to witchcraft and work harm to all with whom she came in contact, but adding it was better that she work her wicked spells on Englishmen and heretics than on true children of the Church.

"My, uncle lifted the child in his arms and bore her to the *Good Intent*, and the moment that he set her down upon the deck she fell upon her knees and took his hands and kissed them and thanked him for his charity in a flood of mingled Portuguese and English.

"For many days she lay like death, only occasionally jumping from her bunk and screaming, '*Padre, Madre—el fuego! el fuego!*' then falling back, hiding her face in her hands and laughing horribly. My uncle coaxed and comforted her, feeding her with his own hands and waiting on her like a nurse; so by degrees she quieted, and long before they raised the coast of Jersey off their bow she was restored to complete health and, though she still seemed sad and troubled, her temper was so sweet and her desire to please everybody so apparent that every man aboard the ship, from cabin boy to captain, was more than half in love with her.

"No one ever knew her real age. She was very small and so thin from undernourishment that she seemed more like a child than a young woman when they brought her on the *Good Intent*. None of the seamen spoke Portuguese, and her English was so slight that they could not ask her about her parents or her birthplace while she lay ill, and when she had recovered normal health it seemed her memory was gone; for though she took to English with surprising aptitude, she seemed unable to remember anything about her former life, and for kindness' sake none would mention the *auto da fé* in which her parents perished. She didn't even know her name, apparently, so my uncle formally christened her Kristina; using the Lutheran baptismal ceremony, and for surname chose to call her Beacon as a sort of poetical commemoration of the fire from which he saved her when her parents had been burnt, It seems she—"

"My dear chap," I broke in, "this is an interesting story, I'll admit, but what possible connection can it have with—"

"Be silent, if you please, my friend," de Grandin ordered sharply. "The connection which you seek is forming like the image as the sculptor chips away the stone, or I am a far greater fool than I have reason to suspect. Say on, *Monsieur*," he ordered Friebergh, "this story is of greater import than you realize, I think. You were informing us of the strange girl your uncle-several-times-removed had rescued from the Hounds of God in Portugal?"

Friebergh smiled appreciation of the little Frenchman's interest. "The sea air and good food, and the genuine affection with which everyone on shipboard regarded her had made a great change in the half-starved, half-mad little foundling by the time the *Good Intent* came back to Jersey," he replied. "From a scrawny little ragamuffin she had grown into a lovely, blooming girl, and there's not much doubt the townsfolk held a carnival of gossip when the *Good Intent* discharged the beautiful young woman along with her cargo of Spanish wines and French silks at the quay.

"Half the young bloods of the town were out to court her; for in addition to her beauty she was Oscar Friebergh's ward, and Oscar Friebergh was the richest man for miles around, a bachelor and well past fifty. Anyone who got Kristina for his wife would certainly have done himself a handsome favor.

"Apparently the girl had everything to recommend her, too. She was as good and modest as she was lovely, her devoutness at church service was so great it won the minister's unstinted praise, her ability as a housekeeper soon proved itself, and my uncle's house, which had been left to the casual superintendence of a cook and staff of Negro slaves, soon became one of the best kept and most orderly households in New Jersey. No one could get the better of Kristina in bargain. When cheating tradesmen sought to take advantage of her obvious youth and probable inexperience, she would fix her great, unfathomable eyes on them, and they would flush and stammer like schoolboys caught in mischief and own their fault at once. Besides her church and household duties she seemed to have no interest but my uncle, and the young men who came wooing met with cool reception. Less than a year from the day she disembarked, the banns for her wedding to my uncle were posted on the church door, and before the gossip which her advent caused had time to cool, she was Mistress Friebergh, and assumed a leading place in the community.

"For nineteen years they lived quietly in this house, and while my uncle aged and weakened she grew into charming, mature womanhood, treating the old man with a combination of wifely and daughterly devotion, and taking over active management of his affairs when failing sight and memory rendered him incompetent."

Friebergh paused and drew reflectively at his cigar. "I don't suppose you'd know what happened in New England in 1692?" he asked de Grandin.

The Frenchman answered with a vigorous double nod. "*Parbleu*, I do, indeed, Monsieur. That year, in Salem, Massachusetts, there were many witchcraft trials, and—"

"Quite so," our host broke in. "Parish and the Mathers set the northern colonies afire with their witchcraft persecutions. Fortunately, not much of the contagion spread outside New England, but:

"Old Oscar Friebergh had been failing steadily, and though they cupped and leeched him and fed him mixtures of burnt toads, bezoar stone, cloves, and even moss scraped from the skull of a pirate who had been hanged in chains, he died in a coma following a violent seizure of delirium in which he cursed the day that he had taken the witch's brat to his bosom.

"Oscar had sworn his crew to secrecy concerning Kristina's origin, and it seems that they respected the vow while he lived; but some few of them, grown old and garrulous, found their memories suddenly quickened over their glasses of grog after the sexton had set the sods above old Oscar's grave, and evinced a desire to serve gossip and scandal rather than the memory of a master no longer able to reproach them for oath-breaking. There were those who recollected perfectly how the girl Kristina had passed unharmed through the flames and bid her burning parents fond farewell, then came again straight through the flames to put her hand in Oscar Friebergh's and bid him carry her beyond the seas. Others recalled how she had calmed a storm by standing at the ship's rail and reciting incantations in a language not of human origin, and still others told with bated breath how the water of baptism had scalded her as though it had been boiling when Oscar Friebergh poured it on her brow.

"The whole township knew her singing, too. When she was about her household tasks or sewing by the window, or merely sitting idly, she would sing, not loudly, but in a sort of crooning voice; yet people passing in the road before the house would pause to listen, and even children stopped their noisy play to hear her as she sang those fascinating songs in a strange tongue which the far-voyaged sailor folk had never heard and which were set to tunes the like of which were never played on flute or violin or spinet, yet for all their softness seemed to fill the air with melody as the woods are filled with bird-songs in late April. People shook their heads at recollection of those songs, remembering how witches spoke a jargon of their own, known only to each other and their master, Satan, and recalling further that the music used in praise of God was somber as befitted solemn thoughts of death and judgment and the agonies of hell.

"Her kitten caused much comment, too. The townsfolk recollected how she bore a tiny white cat beneath her arm when first she tripped ashore, and though a score of years had passed, the kitten had not grown into a cat, but still as small as when it first touched land, frisked and frolicked in the Friebergh house, and played and purred and still persisted in perpetual, supernatural youth.

"Among the villagers was a young man named Karl Pettersen, who had wooed Kristina when she first came, and took the disappointment of refusal of his marriage offer bitterly. He had married in the intervening years, but a smallpox epidemic had robbed his wife of such good looks as she originally had, and continued business failures had conspired to rob him of his patrimony and his wife's dowry as well; so when Oscar Friebergh died he held Karl's notes of hand for upward of five hundred pounds, secured by mortgages upon his goods and chattels and some farming-land which had come to him at marriage.

"When the executors of Oscar's will made inventory they found these documents which virtually made the widow mistress of the Pettersen estate, and notified the debtor that he must arrange for payment. Karl went to see Kristina late one evening, and what took place at the interview we do not know, though her servants later testified that he shrieked and shouted and cried out as though in torment, and that she replied by laughing at his agony. However that might be, the records show that he was stricken with a fit as he disrobed for bed that night, that he frothed and foamed at the mouth like a mad dog, and made queer, growling noises in his throat. It is recorded further that he lay in semi-consciousness for several days, recovering only long enough to eat his meals, then lapsing back again into delirium. Finally, weak but fully conscious, he sat up in bed, sent for the sheriff, the minister and the magistrate, and formally denounced Kristina as a witch.

"I've said that we escaped the general horror of witch persecution which visited New England, but if old records are to be believed we made up in ferocity what we lacked in quantity. Kristina's old and influential friends were dead, the Swedish Lutheran church had been taken over by the Episcopacy and the incumbent was an Englishman whose youth had been indelibly impressed by Matthew Hopkins' witch-findings. Practically every important man in the community was a former disappointed suitor, and while they might have forgotten this, their wives did not. Moreover, while care and illness and multiple maternity had left their traces on these women, Kristina was more charmingly seductive in the ripeness of maturity than she had been in youth, What chance had she?

"She met their accusations haughtily, and refused to answer vague and rambling statements made against her. It seemed the case against her would break down for want of evidence until Karl Pettersen's wife remembered her familiar. Uncontradicted testimony showed this same small animal, still a kitten, romped and played about the house, though twenty years had passed since it first came ashore. No natural cat could live so long; nothing but a devil's imp disguised in feline shape could have retained its youth so marvelously. This, the village wise ones held, was proof sufficient that Kristina was a witch and harbored a familiar spirit. The clergyman preached a sermon on the circumstance, taking for his text the twenty-seventh verse of the twentieth chapter of Leviticus: 'A man also or woman that hath a familiar spirit, or that is a wizard, shall surely be put to death.'

"They held her trial on the village green. The records say she wore a shift of scarlet silk, which is all her persecutors would allow her from her wardrobe. Preliminary search had failed to find the devil's mark or witch-teat through which her familiar was supposed to nourish itself by sucking her blood; so at her own request Mistress Pettersen was appointed to the task of hunting for it *coram judice*.

"She had supplied herself with pricking-pins, and at a signal from the magistrate ripped the scarlet mantle from Kristina, leaving her stark naked in the center of a ring of cruel and lustful eyes. A wave of smothering shame swept over her, and she would have raised her hands to shield her bosom from the lecherous stares of loafers congregated on the green, but her wrists were firmly bound behind her. As she bent her head in a paroxysm of mortification, the four-inch bodkin in the Pettersen woman's hand fleshed itself first in her thigh, then her side, her shoulder, her neck and her breast, and she writhed in agonizing postures as her tender flesh was stabbed now here, now there, while the rabble roared and shouted in delight.

"The theory, you know, was that at initiation into witch-hood the devil marked his new disciple with a bite, and from this spot the imp by which the witch worked her black magic drew its sustenance by sucking her blood. This devil's mark, or witch-teat was said to be insensible to pain, but as it often failed to differ in appearance from the rest of the body's surface, it was necessary for the searcher to spear and stab the witch repeatedly until a spot insensible to pain was found. The nervous system can endure a limited amount of shock, after which it takes refuge in defensive anesthesia. This seems to have been the case with poor Kristina; for after several minutes of torment she ceased to writhe and scream, and her torturer announced the mark found. It was a little area of flesh beneath the swell of her left breast, roughly square in shape and marked off by four small scars which looked like needle-wounds set about three-quarters of an inch apart.

"But the finding of the mark was inconclusive. While a witch would surely have it, an innocent person might possess something simulating it; so there remained the test of swimming. Water was supposed to reject a witch's body; so if she were tied and thrown into a pond or stream, proof of guilt was deemed established if she floated.

They cross-tied her, making her sit tailor-fashion and binding the thumb of her right hand so tightly to the great toe of her left foot that the digits soon turned blue for lack of circulation, then doing the same with her left thumb and right great toe, after which she was bundled in a bed-sheet which was tied at the corners above her head, and the parcel was attached to a three-fathom length of rope and towed behind a rowboat for a distance of three-quarters of a mile in Raritan Bay.

"At first the air within the sheet buoyed up the bundle and its contents, and the crowd gave vent to yells of execration. 'She floats, she floats, the water will have none of her; bring the filthy witch ashore and burn her!' they shouted, but in a little while the air escaped from the wet sheet, and though Kristina sank as far down in the water as the length of rope permitted, there was no effort made to draw her up until the boat had beached. She was dead when finally they dragged her out upon the shingle.

"Karl Pettersen confessed his error and declared the devil had misled him into making a false accusation, and, her innocence proved by her drowning, Kristina was accorded Christian burial in consecrated ground, and her husband's property, in which she had a life estate, reverted to my ancestor. One of the first things he did was to sell this house, and it went through a succession of ownerships till I bought it at auction last autumn and had it reconditioned as a summer home. We found the old barn filled with household goods, and had them reconditioned, too. This furniture was once Kristina Friebergh's."

I looked around the big, low-ceilinged room with interest. Old-fashioned chintz, patterned with quaint bouquets of roses, hung at the long windows. Deep chairs and sofas were covered with a warm rose-red that went well with the gray woodwork and pale green walls. A low coffee table of pear wood, waxed to a satin finish, stood before a couch; an ancient mirror framed in gilt hung against one wall, while against another stood a tall buhl cabinet and a chest of drawers of ancient Chinese nanmu wood, brown as withered oak leaves and still exhaling a subtly faint perfume. Above the open fireplace hung an ancient painting framed in a narrow strip of gold.

"That's Kristina," volunteered our host as he nodded toward the portrait.

The picture was of a woman not young, not at all old; slender, mysterious, black hair shining smoothly back, deep blue eyes holding a far-off vision, as though they sensed the sufferings of the hidden places of the world and brooded on them; a keen, intelligent face of a clear pallor with small, straight nose, short upper lip and a mouth which would have been quite lovely had it not been so serious. She held a tiny kitten, a mere ball of white fluffiness, at her breast, and the hand supporting the small animal was the hand of one in whom the blood of ancient races ran, with long and slimly pointed fingers tipped with rosy nails. There was something to arrest attention in that face. The woman had the cold knowledge of death, ominous and ever present, on her.

"*La pauvre!*" de Grandin murmured as he gazed with interest at the portrait. "And what became of Monsieur Pettersen and his so highly unattractive wife?"

Friebergh laughed, almost delightedly. "History seems to parallel itself in this case," he answered. "Perhaps you've heard how the feud resulting from the Salem persecutions was resolved when descendants of accusers and accused were married? Well . . . it seems that after Kristina drowned, executors of Oscar Friebergh's will could not find clue or trace of the notes and mortgages which Pettersen had signed. Everybody had suspicions how they came to disappear, for Mistress Pettersen was among the most earnest searchers of Kristina's private papers when they sought a copy of the compact she had signed with Satan, but—in any event, Karl Pettersen began to prosper from the moment that Kristina died. Every venture which he undertook met with success. His descendants prospered, too. Two years ago the last male member of his line met Greta at a Christmas dance, and"—he broke off with a chuckle—"and they've been that way about each other from the first. I'm thinking they'll be standing side by side beneath a floral bell and saying 'I do' before the ink on their diplomas has had much chance to dry."

"All of which brings us back three centuries, and down to date—and Greta," I responded somewhat sharply. "If I remember, you'd begun to tell us something about her hysterical condition and the effect this house had on her, when you detoured to that ancient family romance."

"Précisément, Monsieur, the house," de Grandin prompted. "I think that I anticipate you, but I should like to hear your statement—" He paused with interrogatively raised brows.

"Just so," our host returned. "Greta has never heard the story of Kristina, and Karl Pettersen, I'm sure, for I didn't know it very well myself till I bought this house and started digging up the ancient records. She'd certainly never been in the house, nor even seen the plans, since the work of restoration was done while she was off to school; yet the moment she arrived she went directly to her room, as if she knew the way by heart. Incidentally, her room is the same one—"

"Occupied by Madame Kristina in the olden days!" supplied de Grandin.

"Good Lord! How'd you guess?"

"I did not guess, Monsieur," the little Frenchman answered levelly; "I knew."

"Humph. Well, the child has seemed to hate the place from the moment she first entered it. She's been moody and distrait, complaining of a constant feeling of malaise and troubled sleep, and most of the time she's been so irritable that there's scarcely any living with her. D'ye suppose there's something psychic in the place—something that the rest of us don't feel, that's worked upon her nerves until she had this fainting-fit tonight?"

"Not at all," I answered positively. "The child's been working hard at school, and—"

"Very likely," Jules de Grandin interrupted, "Women are more finely attuned to such influences than men, and it is entirely possible that the tragedy these walls have witnessed has been felt subconsciously by your daughter, Monsieur Friebergh."

"DOCTOR TROWBRIDGE, I DON'T like this place," Greta Friebergh told me when we called on her next day. "It—there's something about it that terrifies me; makes me feel as though I were somebody else."

She raised her eyes to mine, half frightened, half wondering, and for a moment I had the eery sensation of being confronted with the suffering ghost of a girl in the flesh.

"Like someone else?" I echoed. "How d'ye mean, my dear?"

"I'm afraid I can't quite say, sir. Something queer, a kind of feeling of vague uneasiness coupled with a sort of 'I've been here before' sensation came to me the moment I stepped across the threshold. Everything, the house, the furniture, the very atmosphere, seemed to combine to oppress me. It was as if something old and infinitely evil—like the wiped-over memory of some terrifying childhood nightmare—were trying to break through to my consciousness. I kept reaching for it mentally, as one reaches for a half-remembered tune or a forgotten name; yet I seemed to realize that if I ever drew aside the veil of memory my sanity would crack. Do you understand me, Doctor?"

"I'm afraid I don't, quite, child," I answered. "You've had a trying time at school, and with your social program speeded up—"

Something like a grimace, the parody of a smile, froze upon de Grandin's face as he leant toward the girl. "Tell us, *Mademoiselle*," he begged, "was there something more, some tangibility, which matched this feeling of malaise?"

"Yes, there was!" responded Greta.

"And that—"

"Last night I came in rather late, all tired and out of sorts. Karl Pettersen and I had been playing tennis in the afternoon, and drove over to Keyport for dinner afterward. Karl's a sweet lad, and the moonlight was simply divine on the homeward drive, but—" The quick blood stained her face and throat as she broke off her narrative.

"Yes, *Mademoiselle*, but?" de Grandin prompted.

She smiled, half bashfully, at him, and she was quite lovely when she smiled. It brightened the faintly sad expression of her mouth and raised her eyes, ever so little, at the corners. "It can't have been so long since you were young, Doctor," she returned. "What did you do on moonlight summer nights when you were alone with someone you loved terribly?"

"*Morbleu*," the little Frenchman chuckled, "the same as you, *petite*, no more, I think, and certainly no less!"

She smiled again, a trifle sadly, this time. "That's just the trouble," she lamented. "I couldn't."

"*Hein*, how is it you say, *Mademoiselle*?"

"I wanted to, Lord knows my lips were hungry and my arms were aching for him, but something seemed to come between us. It was as if I'd had a dish of food before me and hadn't eaten for a long, long time, then, just before I tasted it, a whisper came, 'It's poisoned!'

"Karl was hurt and puzzled, naturally, and I tried my best to overcome my feeling of aversion, but for a moment when his lips were pressed to mine I had a positive sensation of revulsion. I felt I couldn't bear his touch, his kisses seemed to stifle me; if he hadn't let me go I think that I'd have fainted.

"I ran right in the house when we got home, just flinging a good-night to Karl across my shoulder, and rushed up to my room. 'Perhaps a shower will pull me out of it,' I thought, and so I started to disrobe, when—" Once more she paused, and now there was no doubt of it: the girl was terrified.

"Yes, *Mademoiselle*, and then?" the Frenchman prompted softly.

"I'd slipped my jumper and culottes off, and let down my hair, preparatory to knotting it up to fit inside my shower cap, when I chanced to look into the mirror. I hadn't turned the light on, but the moonlight slanted through the window and struck right on the glass; so I could see myself as a sort of silhouette, only"—again she paused, and her narrow nostrils dilated—"only it wasn't I!"

"*Sacré nom d'un fromage vert*, what is it that you tell us, *Mademoiselle?*" asked Jules de Grandin.

"It wasn't I reflected in that mirror. As I looked, the moonlight seemed to break and separate into a million little points of light, so that it was more like a mist powdered with diamond dust than a solid shaft of light; it seemed to be at once opaque yet startlingly translucent, with a sheen like that of flowing water, yet absorbing all reflections. Then suddenly, where I should have seen myself reflected in the mirror, I saw another form take shape, half veiled in the sparkling mist that seemed to fill the room, yet startlingly distinct. It was a woman, a girl, perhaps, a little older than I, but not much. She was tall and exquisitely slender, with full-blown, high-set breasts and skin as pale as ivory. Her hair was black and silken-fine and rippled down across her shoulders till it almost reached her knees, and her deep-blue eyes and lovely features held a look of such intense distress that I thought involuntarily of those horribly realistic mediæval pictures of the Crucifixion. Her shoulders were braced back, for she held her hands behind her as though they had been tied, and on her breast and throat and sides were numerous little wounds as though she had been stabbed repeatedly with something sharp and slender, and from every wound the fresh blood welled and trickled out upon the pale, smooth skin."

"She was—" began de Grandin, but the girl anticipated him.

"Yes," she told him, "she was nude. Nothing clothed her but her glorious hair and the bright blood streaming from her wounds.

"For a minute, maybe for an hour, we looked into each other's eyes, this lovely, naked girl and I, and it seemed to me that she tried desperately to tell me something, but though I saw the veins and muscles stand out on her throat with the effort that she made, no sound came from her tortured lips. Somehow, as we stood there, I felt a queer, uncanny feeling creeping over me. I seemed in some way to be identified with this other girl, and with that feeling of a loss of personality, a bitter, blinding rage seemed surging up in me. Gradually, it seemed to take some sort of form, to bend itself against a certain object, and with a start I realized that I was consumed with hatred; dreadful, crushing, killing hatred toward someone named Karl Pettersen. Not my Karl, especially, but toward everybody in the world who chanced to bear that name. It was a sort of all-inclusive hatred, something like the hatred of the Germans which your generation had in the World War. 'I can't—I won't hate Karl!' I heard myself exclaiming, and turned to face the other girl. But she was not there.

"There I stood alone in the darkened, empty room with nothing but the moonlight—ordinary moonlight, now-slanting down across the floor.

"I turned the lights on right away and took a dose of aromatic spirits of ammonia, for my nerves were pretty badly shot. Finally I got calmed down and went into the bathroom for my shower.

"I was just about to step into the spray, when I heard a little plaintive *mew* outside the window. When I crossed the room, there was the sweetest little fluffy white kitten perched on the sill outside the screen, its green eyes blinking in the light which streamed down from the ceiling-lamp and the tip of its pink tongue sticking out like the little end of thin-sliced ham you sometimes see peeping from behind the rolls in railway station sandwiches. I unhooked the screen and let the little creature in, and it snuggled up against my breast and puffed and blinked its knowing eyes at me, and then put up a tiny, pink-toed paw and began to wash its face.

"'Would you like to take a shower with me, pussy?' I asked it, and it stopped its washing and looked up at me as if to ask, 'What did you say?' then stuck its little nose against my side and began to lick me. You can't imagine how its little rough tongue tickled."

"And then, *Mademoiselle?*" de Grandin asked as Greta broke off smilingly and lay back on her pillows.

"Then? Oh, there wasn't any then, sir. Next thing I knew I was in bed, with you and Doctor Trowbridge bending over me and looking as solemn and learned as a pair of owls. But the funny part of it all was that I wasn't ill at all; just too tired to answer when you spoke to me."

"And what became of this small kitten, *Mademoiselle?*" de Grandin asked.

"Mother didn't see it. I'm afraid the little thing was frightened when I fell, and jumped out of the bathroom window."

"U'm?" Jules de Grandin teased the needle-points of his mustache between a thoughtful thumb and forefinger; then: "And this so mysterious lady without clothing whom you saw reflected in your mirror, *Mademoiselle?* Could you, by any chance, identify her?"

"Of course," responded Greta, matter-of-factly as though he'd asked her if she had studied algebra at school, "she was the girl whose portrait's in the living-room downstairs, Kristina Friebergh."

"WILL YOU LEAVE ME in the village?" asked de Grandin as we left the Friebergh house. "I would supplement the so strange story which we heard last night by searching through the records at the church and court-house, too."

Dinner was long overdue when he returned that evening, and, intent upon his dressing, he waved my questioning aside while he shaved and took a hasty shower. Finally, when he had done justice to the salad and meringue glacé, he leant his elbows on the table, lit a cigarette and faced me with a level, serious glance.

"I have found out many things today, my friend," he told me solemnly. "Some supplement the story which Monsieur Friebergh related; some cast new light upon it; others are, I fear, disquieting.

"By example: There is a story of the little kitten of which Monsieur Friebergh told us, the kitten which refused to grow into a cat. When poor Madame Kristina was first haled before the magistrates for trial, a most careful search was made for it, but nowhere could the searchers find it; yet during the al fresco trial several persons saw it now here, now there, keeping just outside the range of stone-throw, but at all times present. Further, when the ban of witchcraft had apparently been lifted by Madame Kristina's inability to float and her burial within the churchyard close had been permitted, this so little kitten was seen nightly at her grave, curled up like a patch of snow against the greenery of the growing grass. Small boys shied stones at it, and more than once the village men went to the graveyard and took shots at it, but stone and bullet both were ineffective; the small animal would raise its head and look at those who sought to harm it with a sadly thoughtful glance, then go back to its napping on the grave. Only when approached too closely would it rouse itself, and when the hunter had almost succeeded in tiptoeing close enough to strike it with a club or sword it would completely vanish, only to reappear upon the grave when, tired out with waiting, its assailant had withdrawn to a safe distance.

"Eventually the townsfolk became used to it, but no horse would pass the cemetery while it lay upon its mistress' grave without shying violently, and the most courageous of the village dogs shunned the graveyard as a place accursed. Once, indeed, a citizen took out a pair of savage mastiffs, determined to exterminate the little haunting beast, but the giant dogs, which would attack a maddened bull without a moment's hesitation, quailed and cowered from the tiny bit of fluffy fur, nor could their master's kicks and blows and insults force them past the graveyard gateway."

"Well, what's disquieting in that?" I asked. "It seems to me that if there were any sort of supernatural intervention in the case, it was more divine than diabolical. Apparently the townsfolk tried to persecute the little harmless cat to death exactly as they had its mistress. The poor thing died eventually, I suppose?"

"One wonders," he returned as he pursed his lips and blew a geometrically perfect smoke-ring.

"Wonders what?"

"Many things, *parbleu*. Especially concerning its death and its harmlessness. Attend me, if you please: For several years the small cat persisted in its nightly vigils at the grave. Then it disappeared, and people thought no more about it. One evening Sarah Spotswood, a young farmer's daughter, was passing by the graveyard, when she was accosted by a small white cat. The little creature came out in the road near where it winds within a stone's-throw of the grave of Kristina Friebergh. It was most friendly, and when she stooped to fondle it, it leaped into her arms."

He paused and blew another smoke-ring.

"Yes?" I prompted as he watched the cloudy circle sail a lazy course across the table-candles.

"Quite yes," he answered imperturbably. "Sarah Spotswood went insane within a fortnight. She died without regaining reason. Generally she was a harmless, docile imbecile, but occasionally she broke out raving in delirium. At such times she would shriek and writhe as though in torment, and bleeding wounds appeared upon her sides and breast and throat. The madhouse-keepers thought she had inflicted injury upon herself, and placed her in a straitjacket when they saw the signs of the seizure coming on. It made no difference: the wounds accompanied each spell of madness, as though they were stigmata. Also, I think it worth while mentioning, a small white kitten, unknown to anybody in the madhouse, was always observed somewhere about the place when Sarah's periods of mania came.

"Her end came tragically, too. She escaped surveillance on a summer afternoon, fled to a little near-by stream and cast herself into it. Though the water was a scant six inches deep, she lay upon her face until she died by drowning.

"Two other similar cases are recorded. Since Sarah Spotswood died in 1750 there have been three young women similarly seized, the history of each case revealing that the maniac had taken a stray white kitten for pet shortly before the onset of incurable madness, and that in every instance the re-appearance of this kitten, or an animal just like it, had coincided with return of manic seizures. Like their predecessor, each of these unfortunate young women succeeded in drowning herself. In view of these things would you call this kitten either dead or harmless?"

"You have a theory?" I countered.

"Yes—and no," he answered enigmatically. "From such information as we have I am inclined to think the verdict rendered in Madame Kristina's witch trial was a false one. While not an ill-intentioned one—unknowingly, indeed, perhaps—I think the lady was what we might call a witch; one who had power, whether she chose to exercise it or not, of working good or bad to fellow humans by means of supernatural agencies. It seems this little kitten which never grew to cathood, which lay in mourning on her grave and which afflicted four unfortunate young women with insanity, was her familiar—a beast-formed demon through whose aid she might accomplish magic."

"But that's too utterly absurd!" I scoffed. "Kristina Friebergh died three centuries ago, while this kitten—"

"Did not necessarily die with her," he interjected. "Indeed, my friend, there are many instances in witch-lore where the familiar has outlived its witch."

"But why should it seek out other girls—"

"*Précisément*," he answered soberly. "That, I damn think, is most significant. Witches' imps, though they may be ambassadors from hell, are clothed in pseudo-natural bodies. Thus they have need of sustenance. This the witch supplies with her blood. It is at the insensitive spot known as the witch-mark or witch's teat that the familiar is suckled. When Monsieur Friebergh told us of Madame Kristina's trial, you will recall that he described the spot in which she felt no pain as an area roughly square in shape marked off by four small scars which looked like needle-wounds set about three-quarters of an inch apart? Consider, my friend—think carefully—where have you seen a cicatrix like that within the last few days?" His eyes, round and unwinking as those of a thoughtfully inclined tom-cat, never left mine as he asked the question.

"Why"—I temporized—"oh, it's too absurd, de Grandin!"

"You do not answer, but I see you recognize the similarity," he returned. "Those little 'needle-wounds,' *mon vieux*, were made by little kitten-teeth which pierced the white and tender skin of Mademoiselle Greta just before she swooned. She exhibited the signs of hemorrhage, that you will agree; yet we found no blood. *Pourquoi?* Because the little fluffy kitten which she took into her arms, the little beast which licked her with its tongue a moment before she lost consciousness, *sucked it from her body*. This cat-thing seems immortal, but it is not truly so. Once in so many years it must have sustenance, the only kind of sustenance which will enable it to mock at time, the blood of a young woman. Sarah Spotswood gave it nourishment, and lost her reason in the process, becoming, apparently, identified with the unfortunate Madame Kristina, even to showing the stigmata of the needle-wounds which that poor creature suffered at her trial. The manner of her death—by drowning—paralleled Kristina's, also, as did those of the other three who followed her in madness—*after having been accosted by a small white kitten*."

"Then what d'ye suggest?" I asked him somewhat irritably, but the cachinnation of the telephone cut in upon the question.

"Good Lord!" I told him as I hung up the receiver. "Now it's young Karl Pettersen! His mother 'phoned to tell me he's been hurt, and—"

"Right away, at once; immediately," he broke in. "Let us hasten to him with all speed. Unless I make a sad mistake, his is no ordinary hurt, but one which casts a challenge in our faces. Yes, assuredly!"

I DO NOT THINK I ever saw a man more utterly unstrung than young Karl Pettersen. His injury was trivial, amounting to scarcely more than a briar-scratch across his throat, but the agony of grief and horror showing in his face was truly pitiful, and when we asked him how the accident occurred his only answer was a wild-eyed stare and a sob-torn sentence he reiterated endlessly: "Greta, oh, Greta, how could you?"

"I think that there is something devilish here, Friend Trowbridge," whispered Jules de Grandin.

"So do I," I answered grimly. "From that wound I'd say the little fool has tried to kill himself after a puppy-lovers' quarrel. See how the cut starts underneath the condyle of the jaw, and tapers off and loses depth as it nears the median line? I've seen such cuts a hundred times, and—"

"But no," he interrupted sharply. "Unless the young *Monsieur* is left-handed he would have made the cut across the left side of his throat; this wound describes a slant across the right side. It was made by someone else—someone seated on his right, as, by example, in a motorcar.

"*Monsieur!*" he seized the boy by both his shoulders and shook him roughly. "Stop this childish weeping. Your wound is but a skin-scratch. It will heal almost with one night's sleep, but its cause is of importance. How did you get it, if you please?"

"Oh, Greta—" Karl began again, but the smacking impact of de Grandin's hand against his cheek cut short his wail.

"*Nom d'un coq*, you make me to lose patience with you!" cried the Frenchman. "Here, take a dose of this!" From his jacket pocket he produced a flask of cognac, poured a liberal portion out into a cup and thrust it into Karl's unsteady hand. "Ah, so; that is better," he pronounced as the lad gulped down the liquor. "Now, take more, *mon vieux*; we need the truth, and quickly, and never have I seen a better application of the proverb that in alcohol dwells truth."

Within five minutes he had forced the better portion of a pint of brandy down the young man's throat, and as the potent draft began to work, his incoherent babbling gave way to a melancholy but considered gravity which in other circumstances would have appeared comic.

"Now, man to man, *compagnon de débauche*, inform us what took place," the Frenchman ordered solemnly.

"Greta and I were out driving after dinner," answered Karl. "We've been nuts about each other ever since we met, and today I asked her if she'd marry me. She'd been actin' sort o' queer and distant lately, so I thought that maybe she'd been fallin' for another bird, and I'd better hurry up and get my brand on her. Catch on?"

De Grandin nodded somewhat doubtfully. "I think I apprehend your meaning," he replied, "though the language which you use is slightly strange to me. And when you had completed your proposal—"

"She didn't say a word, but just pointed to the sky, as though she'd seen some object up there that astonished her."

"Quite so. One understands; and then?"

"Naturally, I looked up, and before I realized what was happening she slashed a penknife across my throat and jumped out of the car screaming with laughter. I wasn't very badly hurt, but—" He paused, and we could fairly see his alcoholic aplomb melt and a look of infantile distress spread on his features. "O-o-o!" he wailed disconsolately. "Greta, my dear, why did you—"

"The needle, if you please, Friend Trowbridge," Jules de Grandin whispered. "There is nothing further to be learned, and the opiate will give him merciful oblivion. Half a grain of morphine should be more than ample."

"THIS IS POSITIVELY THE craziest piece of business I ever heard of!" I exclaimed as we left the house. "Only the other night she told us that she loved the lad so much that her heart ached with it; this afternoon she interrupts his declaration by slashing at his throat. I never heard of anything so utterly fantastic—"

"Except, perhaps, the case of Sarah Spotswood and the other three unfortunates who followed her to madness and the grave?" he interrupted in a level voice. "I grant the little *demoiselle* has acted in a most demented manner. *Ha*, but is she crazier than—"

"Oh, for the love of mercy, stop it!" I commanded querulously. "Those cases were most likely mere coincidences. There's not a grain of proof—"

"If a thing exists we must believe it, whether it is susceptible of proof or not," he told me seriously. "As for coincidence—had only one girl graduated into death from madness after encountering a kitten such as that which figures in each of these occurrences, we might apply the term; but when three young women are so similarly stricken, *parbleu*, to fall back on coincidence is but to shut your eyes against the facts, *mon vieux*. One case, yes; two cases, perhaps; three cases—*non*, it is to pull the long arm of coincidence completely out of joint, by blue!"

"Oh, well," I answered wearily, "if you—good Lord!"

Driven at road-burning speed a small, light car with no lamps burning came careening crazily around the elbow of the highway, missed our left fender by a hair and whizzed past us like a bullet from a rifle.

"Is it any wonder our insurance rates are high with idiots like that out upon the public roads?" I stuttered, inarticulate with fury, but the whining signal of a motorcycle's siren cut my protest short as a state policeman catapulted around the bend in hot pursuit of the wild driver.

"D'ye see 'um?" he inquired as he stopped beside us with a scream of brakes. "Which way did 'e go?"

"Took the turn to the right," I answered. "Running like a streak with no lights going, and—"

"My friend mistakes," de Grandin interrupted as he smiled at the policeman; "the wild one turned abruptly to the left, and should be nearly to the village by this time."

"Why, I'm positive he took the right-hand turn—" I began, when a vicious kick upon my shin served notice that de Grandin wished deliberately to send the trooper on a wild-goose chase. Accordingly: "Perhaps I was mistaken," I amended lamely; then, as the officer set out:

"What was your idea in that?" I asked.

"The speeder whom the gendarme followed was Mademoiselle Greta," he replied. "I recognized her in our headlights' flash as she went by, and I suggest we follow her."

"Perhaps we'd better," I conceded; "driving as she was, she's likely to end up in a ditch before she reaches home."

"WHY, GREFA'S NOT BEEN out to-night," said Mrs. Friebergh when we reached the house. "She went out walking in the afternoon and came home shortly after dinner and went directly to her room. I'm sure she's sleeping."

"But may we see her anyway, *Madame?*" de Grandin asked. "If she sleeps we shall not waken her."

"Of course," the mother answered as she led the way upstairs.

It was dark and quiet as a tomb in Greta's bedroom, and when we switched on the night-light we saw her sleeping peacefully, her head turned from us, the bedclothes drawn up close about her chin.

"You see, the poor, dear child's exhausted," Mrs. Friebergh said as she paused upon the threshold.

De Grandin nodded acquiescence as he tiptoed to the bed and bent an ear above the sleeping girl. For a moment he leant forward; then, "I regret that we should so intrude, *Madame,*" he apologized, "but in cases such as this—" An eloquently non-committal shrug completed the unfinished sentence.

Outside, he ordered in a sharp-edged whisper: "This way, my friend, here, beneath this arbor!" In the vine-draped pergola which spanned the driveway running past the house, he pointed to a little single-seated roadster. "You recognize him?" he demanded.

"Well, it *looks* like the car that passed us on the road—"

"Feel him!" he commanded, taking my hand in his and pressing it against the radiator top.

I drew away with a suppressed ejaculation. The metal was hot as a teakettle full of boiling water.

"Not only that, *mon vieux*," he added as we turned away; "when I pretended to be counting Mademoiselle Greta's respiration I took occasion to turn back the covers of her bed. She was asleep, but most curiously, she was also fully dressed, even to her shoes. Her window was wide open, and a far less active one than she could climb from it to earth and back again."

"Then you think—"

"*Non, non*, I do not think; I wish I did; I merely speculate, my friend. Her mother told us that she went out walking in the afternoon. That is what she thought. Plainly, that is what she was meant to think. Mademoiselle Greta walked out, met the young Monsieur Pettersen and drove with him, cut him with her ninety-six times cursed knife, then leaped from his car and walked back home. Anon, when all the house was quiet, she clambered from her window, drove away upon some secret errand, then returned in haste, re-entered her room as she had left it, and"—he pursed his lips and raised his shoulders in a shrug—"there we are, my friend, but just where is it that we are, I ask to know."

"On our way to home and bed," I answered with a laugh. "After all this mystery and nonsense, I'm about ready for a drink and several hours' sleep."

"An excellent idea," he nodded, "but I should like to stop a moment at the cemetery, if you will be so kind. I desire to see if what I damn suspect is true."

Fifteen minutes' drive sufficed to bring us to the lich-gate of the ancient burying-ground where generations of the county's founders slept. Unerringly he led the way between the sentinel tombstones till, a little distance from the ivy-mantled wall which bordered on the highway, he pointed to a moss-grown marker.

"There is Madame Kristina's tomb," he told me in a whisper. "It was there— by blue! Behold, my friend!"

Following his indicating finger's line I saw a little spot of white against the mossy grass about the tombstone's base, and even as I looked, the little patch of lightness moved, took shape, and showed itself a small, white, fluffy kitten. The tiny animal uncoiled itself, raised to a sitting posture, and regarded us with round and shining eyes.

"Why, the poor little thing!" I began, advancing toward it with extended hand. "It's lost, de Grandin—"

"*Pardieu*, I think that it is quite at home," he interrupted as he stooped and snatched a piece of gravel from the grave beneath his feet. "*Regardez, s'il vous plait!*"

In all the years I'd known him I had never seen him do an unkind thing to woman, child or animal; so it was with something like a gasp of consternation that I saw him hurl the stone straight at the little, inoffensive kitten. But great as my surprise had been at his unwonted cruelty, it was swallowed up in sheer astonishment as I saw the stone strike through the little body, drive against the granite tombstone at its back, then bounce against the grave-turf with a muffled thud. And all the while the little cat regarded him with a fixed and slightly amused stare, making no movement to evade his missile, showing not the slightest fear at his approach.

"You see?" he asked me simply.

"I—I thought—I could have sworn—" I stammered, and the laugh with which he greeted my discomfiture was far from mirthful.

"You saw, my friend, nor is there any reason for you to forswear the testimony of your sight," he assured me. "A hundred others have done just as I did. If all the missiles which have been directed at that small white cat-thing were gathered in a pile, I think that they would reach a tall man's height; yet never one of them has caused it to forsake its vigil on this grave. It has visited this spot at will for the past two hundred years and more, and always it has meant disaster to some girl in the vicinity. Come, let us leave it to its brooding; we have plans to make and things to do. Of course."

"GRAND DIEU DES CHATS, c'est l'explication terrible!" de Grandin's exclamation called me from perusal of the morning's mail as we completed breakfast the next day.

"What is it?" I demanded.

"Parbleu, what is it not?" he answered as he passed a folded copy of the Journal to me, indicating the brief item with a well-groomed forefinger.

TREASURE HUNTERS VIOLATE THE DEAD

the headline read, followed by the short account:

Shortly after eleven o'clock last night vandals entered the home of the late Timothy McCaffrey, Argyle Road near Scandia, and stole two of the candles which were burning by his casket while he lay awaiting burial. The body was reposing in the front room of the house, and several members of the family were in the room adjoining.

Miss Monica McCaffrey, 17, daughter of the deceased, was sitting near the doorway leading to the front room where the body lay, and heard somebody softly opening the front door of the house. Thinking it was a neighbor come to pay respects to the dead, she did not rise immediately, not wishing to disturb the visitor at his devotions, but when she noticed an abrupt diminution of the light in the room in which her father's body lay, as though several of the candles had been extinguished, she rose to investigate.

As she stepped through the communicating doorway she saw what she took to be a young man in a light tan sports coat running out the front door of the house. She followed the intruder to the porch and was in time to see him jump into a small sports roadster standing by the front gate with its engine running, and drive away at breakneck speed.

Later, questioned by state troopers, she was undetermined whether the trespasser was a man or woman, as the overcoat worn by the intruder reached from neck to knees, and she could not definitely say whether the figure wore a skirt or knickerbockers underneath the coat.

When Miss McCaffrey returned to the house she found that all the vigil lights standing by the coffin had been extinguished and two of the candles had been taken.

Police believe the act of wanton vandalism was committed by some member of the fashionable summer colony at Scandia who were engaged in a "treasure hunt," since nothing but two candles had been taken by the intruder.

"For goodness' sake!" I looked at de Grandin in blank amazement.

His eyes, wide, round and challenging, were fixed on mine unwinkingly. "*Non*," he answered shortly, "not for goodness' sake, my friend; far from it, I assure you. The thief who stole these candles from the dead passed us on her homeward way last night."

"Her homeward way? You mean—"

"But certainly. Mademoiselle Greta wore such a coat as that *le journal* mentions. Indubitably it was she returning from her gruesome foray."

"But what could she be wanting corpse-lights for?"

"Those candles had been exorcised and blessed, my friend; they were, as one might say, spiritually antiseptic, and it was a law of the old witch covens that things stolen from the church be used to celebrate their unclean rites. All evidence points to a single horrid issue, and tonight we put it to the test."

"Tonight?"

"*Précisément.* This is the twenty-third of June, Midsummer's Eve. Tonight in half the world the bonfires spring in sudden flame on mountain and in valley, by rushing river and by quiet lake. In France and Norway, Hungary and Spain, Rumania and Sweden, you could see the flares stand out against the blackness of the night while people dance about them and chant charms against the powers of Evil. On Midsummer's Eve the witches and the wizards wake to power; tonight, if ever, that which menaces our little friend will manifest itself. Let us be on hand to thwart it—if we can."

"GRETA'S DANCING AT THE Country Club," said Mrs. Friebergh when we called to see our patient late that evening. "I didn't want her to go, she's seemed so feverish and nervous all day long, but she insisted she was well enough, so—"

"Precisely, *Madame*," Jules de Grandin nodded. "It is entirely probable that she will feel no ill effects, but for precaution's sake we will look in at the dance and see how she sustains the strain of exercise."

"But I thought you said that we were going to the club," I remonstrated as he touched my arm to signal a left turn. "But we are headed toward the cemetery—"

"But naturally, my friend; there is the grave of Madame Kristina; there the small white cat-thing keeps its watch; there we must go to see the final act played to its final curtain."

He shifted the small bundle on his knees and began unfastening the knots which bound it.

"What's that?" I asked.

For answer he tore off the paper and displayed a twelve-gage shotgun, its double barrels sawed off short against the wood.

"Good Lord!" I murmured; "whatever have you brought that for?"

He smiled a trifle grimly as he answered, "To test the soundness of the advice which I bestowed upon myself this morning."

"Advice you gave yourself—good heavens, man, you're raving!"

"Perhapsly so," he grinned. "There are those who would assure you that de Grandin's cleverness is really madness, while others will maintain his madness is but cleverness disguised. We shall know more before we grow much older, I damn think."

THE AIR SEEMED THICK and heavy with a brooding menace as we made our way across the mounded graves. Silence, choking as the dust of ages in a mummy-tomb, seemed to bear down on us, and the chirping of a cricket in the grass seemed as loud and sharp as the scraping of metal against metal as we picked our path between the tombstones. The stars, caught in a web of overhanging cloud, were paling in the luminance which spread from the late-rising moon, and despite myself I felt the ripple of a chill run up my back and neck. The dead had lain here quietly two hundred years and more, they were harmless, powerless, but—reason plays no part when instinct holds the reins, and my heart beat faster and my breathing quickened as we halted by the tombstone which marked Kristina Friebergh's grave.

I cannot compute the time we waited. Perhaps it was an hour, perhaps several, but I felt as though we had crouched centuries among the moon-stained shrubbery and the halftones of the purple shadows when de Grandin's fingers on my elbow brought me from my semi-dream to a sort of terrified alertness. Down by the ancient lich-gate through which ten generations of the village dead had come to their last resting-place, a shadow moved among the shadows. Now it lost itself a moment; now it stood in silhouette against the shifting highlights on the corpse-road where the laurel bushes swayed in the light breeze. Terror touched me like a blast of icy wind. I was like a little, frightened boy who finds himself deserted in the darkness.

Now a tiny spot of lightness showed against the blackened background of the night; a second spot of orange light shone out, and I descried the form of Greta Friebergh coming slowly toward us. She was dressed in red, a bright-red evening dress of pleated net with surplice sleeves and fluted hem, fitted tightly, at the waistline, molding her slender, shapely hips, swirling about her toeless silver sandals. In each hand she bore a candle which licked hungrily against the shadows with its little, flickering tongue of orange flame. Just before her, at the outer fringe of candlelight, walked a little chalk-white kitten, stepping soundlessly on dainty paws, leading her unhurriedly toward the grave where Kristina Friebergh lay as a blind man's poodle might escort its master.

I would have spoken, but de Grandin's warning pressure on my arm prevented utterance as he pointed silently across the graveyard to the entrance through which Greta had just come.

Following cautiously, dodging back of tombstones, taking cover behind bushes, but keeping at an even distance from the slowly pacing girl, was another figure. At a second glance I recognized him. It was young Karl Pettersen.

Straight across the churchyard Greta marched behind her strange conductor, halted by the tombstone at the head of Kristina's grave, and set her feebly flaring candles in the earth as though upon an altar.

For a moment she stood statue-still, profiled against the moon, and I saw her fingers interlace and writhe together as if she prayed for mercy from inexorable fate; then she raised her hands, undid snap-fasteners beneath her arms and shook her body with a sort of lazy undulation, like a figure in a slowed-down motion picture, freeing herself from the scarlet evening gown and letting it fall from her.

Straight, white and slim she posed her ivory nakedness in silhouette against the moon, so still that she seemed the image of a woman rather than a thing of flesh and blood, and we saw her clasp her hands behind her, straining wrists and elbows pressed together as though they had been bound with knotted thongs, and on her features came a look of such excruciating pain that I was forcibly reminded of the pictures of the martyrs which the mediæval artists painted with such dreadful realism.

She turned and writhed as though in deadly torment, her head swayed toward one shoulder, then the other; her eyes were staring, almost starting from their sockets; her lips showed ruddy froth where she gnashed them with her teeth; and on her sides and slim, white flanks, upon her satin-gleaming shoulders, her torture-corded neck and sweetly rounded breasts, there flowered sudden spots of red, cruel, blood-marked wounds which spouted little streams of ruby fluid as though a merciless, sharp skewer probed and stabbed and pierced the tender, wincing flesh.

A wave of movement at the grave's foot drew our glance away from the tormented girl. Karl Pettersen stood there at the outer zone of candlelight, his face agleam with perspiration, eyes bright and dilated as though they had been filled with belladonna. His mouth began to twist convulsively and his hands shook in a nervous frenzy.

"Look—look," he slobbered thickly, "she's turning to the witch! She's not my Greta, but the wicked witch they killed so long ago. They're testing her to find the witch-mark; soon they'll drown her in the bay—I know the story; every fifty years the witch-cat claims another victim to go through the needle-torture, then—"

"You have right, *mon vieux*, but I damn think it has found its last one," interrupted Jules de Grandin as he rested his shotgun in the crook of his left elbow and pulled both triggers with a jerk of his right hand.

Through a smoky pompon flashed twin flares of flame, and the shotgun's bellow was drowned out by a strangling scream of agony. Yet it was not so much a cry of pain as of wild anger, maniacal, frenzied with thwarted rage. It spouted up, a marrow-freezing geyser of terrifying sound, and the kitten which had crouched at Greta's feet seemed literally to fly to pieces. Though the double charge of shotgun slugs had hit it squarely, it did not seem to me that it was ripped to shreds, but rather as though its tiny body had been filled with some form of high explosive, or a gas held at tremendous pressure, and that the penetrating slugs had liberated this and caused a detonation which annihilated every vestige of the small, white, furry form.

As the kitten vanished, Greta dropped down to the ground unconscious, and, astoundingly, as though they had been wiped away by magic, every sign of pulsing, bleeding wounds was gone, leaving her pale skin unscarred and without blemish in the faintly gleaming candlelight.

"And now, *Monsieur, s'il vous plait!*" With an agile leap de Grandin crossed the grave, drew back his sawed-off shotgun and brought its butt-plate down upon Karl's head.

"Good heavens, man, have you gone crazy?" I demanded as the youngster slumped down like a pole-axed ox.

"Not at all, by no means; otherwise, entirely, I assure you," he answered as he gazed down at his victim speculatively. "Look to *Mademoiselle*, if you will be so kind; then help me carry this one to the motorcar."

Clumsily, I drew the scarlet ballgown over Greta's shoulders, then grasped her underneath the arms, stood her on unconscious feet a moment and let the garment fall about her. She was scarcely heavier than a child, and I bore her to the car with little effort, then returned to help de Grandin with Karl Pettersen.

"What ever made you do it?" I demanded as we set out for my office.

Pleased immensely with himself, he hummed a snatch of tune before he answered: "It was expedient that he should be unconscious at this time, my friend. Undoubtlessly he followed Mademoiselle Greta from the dance, saw her light the candles and disrobe herself, then show the bleeding stigma of the witch. You heard what he cried out?"

"Yes."

"*Très bon.* They love each other, these two, but the memory of the things which he has seen tonight would come between them and their happiness like a loathsome specter. We must eliminate every vestige of that memory, and of the wound she dealt him, too. But certainly. When they recover consciousness I shall be ready for them. I shall wipe their memories clean of those unpleasant things. Assuredly; of course."

"How can you do that?"

"By hypnotism. You know I am an adept at it, and these two, exhausted, all weakened with the slowly leaving burden of unconsciousness, will offer little opposition to my will. To implant suggestions which shall ripen and bear fruit within their minds will be but child's play for me."

We drove along in silence a few minutes; then, chuckling, he announced: "*Tiens*, she is the lucky girl that Jules de Grandin is so clever. Those other ones were not so fortunate. There was no Jules de Grandin to rescue Sarah Spotswood from her fate, nor the others, either. No. The same process was beginning in this case. First came a feeling of aversion for her lover, a reluctance to embrace him. That was the will of wickedness displacing her volition. Then, all unconsciously, she struck him with a knife, but the subjugation of her will was not complete. The will of evilness forced her hand to strike the blow, but her love for him withheld it, so that he suffered but a little so small scratch."

"Do you mean to tell me Kristina Friebergh was responsible for all these goings-on?" I asked.

"No-o, I would not say it," he responded thoughtfully. "I think she was a most unfortunate young woman, more sinned against than sinning. That *sacré petit chat*—that wicked little cat-thing—was her evil genius, and that of Sarah Spotswood and the other girls, as well as Mademoiselle Greta. You remember Monsieur Friebergh's story, how his several times great-uncle found the little Kristina trying to force her way into the flames which burnt her parents, with a little kitten clutched tight in her arms? That is the explanation. Her parents were undoubtlessly convicted justly for the crime of witchcraft, and the little cat-thing was the imp by which they worked their evil spells. When they were burnt, the cat-familiar lingered on and attached itself to their poor daughter. It had no evil work to do, for there is no record that Kristina indulged in witchery. But it was a devil's imp, instinct with wickedness, and her very piety and goodness angered it; accordingly it brought her to a tragic death. Then it must find fresh source of nourishment, since witches' imps, like vampires, perpetuate themselves by sucking human blood. Accordingly it seized on Sarah Spotswood as a victim, and took her blood and sanity, finally her life. For half a century it lived on the vitality it took from that unfortunate young woman, then—*pouf!*—another victim suffers, goes insane and dies. Each fifty years the process is repeated till at last it comes to Mademoiselle Greta—and to me. Now all is finished."

"But I saw you toss a stone at it last night without effect," I argued, "yet tonight—"

"*Précisément.* That gave me to think. 'It can make a joke of ordinary missiles,' I inform me when I saw it let the stone I threw pass through its body. 'This being so, what are we to do with it, Jules de Grandin?'

"'Phantoms and werewolves which are proof against the ordinary bullet can be killed by shots of silver,' I reply.

"'Very well, then, Jules de Grandin,' I say to me; 'let us use a silver bullet.'

"'*Ha*, but this small cat-thing are an artful dodger, you might miss it,' I remind me; so I make sure there shall be no missing. From the silversmith I get some silver filings, and with these I stuff some shotgun shells. 'Now, *Monsieur le Chat*,' I say, 'if you succeed in dodging these, you will astonish me.'

"*Eh bien*, it was not I who was astonished, I damn think."

W E TOOK THE CHILDREN to my surgery, and while I went to seek some wine and biscuit at de Grandin's urgent request, he placed them side by side upon the couch and took his stance before them.

When I tiptoed back some fifteen minutes later, Greta lay sleeping peacefully upon the sofa, while Karl was gazing fascinated into Jules de Grandin's eyes.

". . . and you will remember nothing but that you love her and she loves you, *Monsieur*," I heard de Grandin say, and heard the boy sigh sleepily in acquiescence.

"Why, we're in Doctor Trowbridge's surgery!" exclaimed Greta as she opened her eyes.

"But yes, of course," de Grandin answered. "You and Monsieur Karl had a little, trifling accident upon the road, and we brought you here."

"Karl dear"—for the first time she seemed to notice the scratch upon his neck—"you've been hurt!"

"*Ah bah*, it is of no importance, *Mademoiselle*," de Grandin told her with a laugh. "Those injuries are of the past, and tonight the past is dead. See, we are ready to convey you home, but first"—he filled the glasses with champagne and handed them each one—"first we shall drink to your happiness and forgetfulness of all the things which happened in the bad old days."

Suicide Chapel

LTHOUGH THE CALENDAR DECLARED it was late May the elements and
the thermometer denied it. All day the rain had streamed torrentially and
the wind keened like a moaning banshee through the newly budded leaves
that furred the maple boughs. Now the raving tempest laid a lacquer-like veneer
of driven water on the window-pane and howled a bawdy chanson down the
chimney where a four-log fire was blazing on the hearth. Fresh from a steaming
shower and smelling most agreeably of Roman Hyacinth, Jules de Grandin sat
before the fire and gazed with unconcealed approval at the toe tip of his purple
leather slipper. A mauve silk scarf was knotted Ascot fashion round his throat,
his hands were drawn up in the sleeves of his deep violet brocade dressing-gown,
and on his face was that look of somnolent content which well-fed tomcats wear
when they are thoroughly at peace with themselves and the world. "Not for a
thousand gold Napoléons would I set foot outside this house again tonight," he
told me as he dipped into the pocket of his robe, fished out a pack of "Marylands"
and set one of the evil-smelling things alight. "Three times, three separate, distinct times, have I been soaked to saturation in this *sacré* rain today. Now, if the
Empress Josèphine came to me in the flesh and begged that I should go with her,
I would refuse the assignation. Regretfully, *mais certainement*, but definitely. Me,
I would not stir outside the door for—"

"Sergeant Costello, if ye plaze, sor," came the rich Irish brogue of Nora McGinnis, my household factotum, who appeared outside the study entrance like a figure
materialized in a vaudeville illusion. "He says it's most important, sor."

"*Tiens*, bid him enter, *ma petite*, and bring a bottle of the Irish whisky from
the cellar," de Grandin answered with a smile; then:

"*C'est véritablement toi, ami?*" he asked as the big Irishman came in and held
cold-reddened fingers to the fire. "What evil wind has blown you out on such a
fetid night?"

"Evil is th' word, sor," Costello answered as he drained the glass de Grandin proffered. "Have ye been radin' in th' papers of th' Cogswell gur-rl's disappearin', I dunno?"

"But yes, of course. Was she not the young woman who evaporated from her dormitory at the Shelton School three months ago? You have found her, *mon vieux*? You are to be congratulated. In my experience—"

"Would yer experience tell ye what to do when a second gur-rl pops outa sight in pracizely th' same manner, lavin' nayther hide nor hair o' clue?"

De Grandin's small blue eyes closed quickly, then opened wide, for all the world like an astonished cat's. "But surely, there is some little trace of evidence, some hint of hidden romance, some—"

"Some nothin' at all, sor. Three months ago today th' Cogswell gur-rl went to 'er room immejiately afther class. Th' elevator boy who took her up seen her walk down th' hall, two classmates said hello to her. Then she shut her door, an' shut herself outa th' wor-rld entirely, so it seems. Nobody's seen or heard o' her since then. This afthernoon, just afther four o'clock, th' Lefètre gur-rl comes from th' lab'ratory, goes straight to 'er room an'"—he paused and raised his massive shoulders in a ponderous shrug—"there's another missin'-persons case fer me to wrastle wid. I've come to ask yer help, sor."

De Grandin pursed his lips and arched his narrow brows. "I am not interested in criminal investigation, *mon sergent*."

"Not even to save an old pal in a hot spot, sor?"

"*Hein?* How is it you say?"

"'Tis this way, sor. When th' Cogswell gur-rl evaporated, as ye say, they gave th' case to me, though be rights it b'longed to th' Missin' Persons Bureau. Well, sor, when a gur-rl fades out that way there may be anny number o' good reasons fer it, but mostly it's because she wants to. An' th' more ye asks th' family questions th' less ye learn. 'Had she anny, love affairs?' sez you, an' 'No!' sez they, as if ye'd been set on insultin' her. 'Wuz she happy in her home?' ye asks, an' 'Certainly, she wuz!' they tells ye, an' they imply ye've hinted that they bate her up each night at eight o'clock an' matinees at two-fifteen. So it goes. Each time ye try to git some reason for her disappearin' act they gits huffier an' huffier till finally they sez they're bein' persecuted, an' ye git th' wor-rks, both from th' chief an' newspapers."

"Perfectly," de Grandin nodded. "As Monsieur Gilbert says, a policeman's life is not a happy one."

"Ye're tellin' me! But this time it's still worse, sor. When I couldn't break th' Cogswell case they hinted I wuz slowin' down, an' had maybe seen me best days. Now they goes an' dumps this here new case in me lap an' tells me if I fail to break it I'll be back in harness wid a nightsthick in me hand before I've checked another birthday off. So, sor, if ye could—"

"*Pas possible!* They dare say this to you, the peerless officer, the pride of the *gendarmerie*—"

"They sure did, sor. An' lots more—"

"Aside, Friend Trowbridge; aside, *mon sergent*—make passageway for me. Await while I put on my outside clothing. I shall show them, me. We shall see if they can do such things to my tried friend—*les crétins!*"

So INCREDIBLY SHORT WAS the interval elapsing before he rejoined us with his hat pulled down above his eyes, trench coat buttoned tight beneath his chin, that I could not understand until I caught a flash of violet silk pajama leg bloused out above the top of his laced boots.

"Lead on, my *sergent*," he commanded. "Take us to the place which this so foolish girl selected for her disappearance. We shall find her or otherwise!"

"Would ye be manin' 'or else,' sor, I dunno?"

"*Ah bah*, who cares? Let us be about our task!"

"Sure, we got a full description o' th' clothes she wore when she skedaddled," Costello told us as we drove out toward the fashionable suburb where the Shelton School was located. "She wuz wearin' orange-colored lounging pajamas an' pegged orange-colored slippers."

"Pegged?" de Grandin echoed. "Was she then poor—"

"Divil a bit o' it, sor. Her folks is rich as creases, but she wuz overdrawn on her allowance, and had to cut th' corners til her next check came."

"One comprehends. And then—"

"There ain't no then, sor. We've inventoried all her wardrobe, an' everything is present but th' duds she wore when she came in from class. Not even a hat's missin'. O' course, that don't mean nothin' much. If she'd set her heart or lammin', she coulda had another outfit waitin' for her somewheres else, but—"

"Quite but, my friend," de Grandin nodded. "Until the contrary appears, we must assume she went away *sans trousseau*."

With characteristic fickleness the shrewish storm had blown itself away while we drove from the city, and a pale half-waning moon tossed like a bit of lucent jetsam in a purling surf of broken clouds as we drew up beneath the porte-cochère of the big red brick dormitory whence Emerline Lefètre had set forth for her unknown goal six hours earlier.

"Yas, suh," replied the colored elevator operator, visibly enjoying the distinction of being questioned by the police. "Ah remembers puffickly erbout hit all. Miss Lefètre come in from lab. She seemed lak she was in a powerful hurry, an' didn't say a thing, 'ceptin' to thank me for de letters."

"The letters? Do you by any happy circumstance remember whence they came?"

"Naw, suh. Ah don' look at de young ladies' mail, 'ceptin' to see who hit's for. I recolleck dese letters mos' partickler, though, 'cause one of 'em wuz smelled up so grand."

"Perfumed?"

"An' how, suh. Jus' lak de scents de conjur doctors sell, on'y more pretty-smellin'. Dat one wuz in a big vanilla envelope. All sealed up, it wuz, but de odor come right through de paper lak hit wuz nothin' a-tall."

"*Merci bien*. Now, if you will kindly take us up—"

THE LITTLE ROOM WHERE Emerline Lefètre dwelt was neat and colorless as only hospital, barrack or dormitory rooms can be. No trace of dust marred imitation mahogany furniture. Indifferent reproductions of several of the less rowdy Directoire prints were ranged with mathematical precision on the walls. The counterpane was squared with blocks of blue and white so virginally chaste as to seem positively spinsterish. "*Mon Dieu*, it is a dungeon, nothing less," de Grandin murmured as he scanned the place. "Can anybody blame a girl for seeking sanctuary from such terrible surround—*quel parfum horrible!*" His narrow nostrils quivered as he sniffed the air. "She had atrocious taste in scent, this so mysteriously absent one."

"Perhaps it's the elegant perfume the elevator operator mentioned," I ventured. "He'd have admired something redolent of musk—"

"*Dis donc!* You put your finger on the pulse, my friend! It is the musk. But yes. I did not recognize him instantly, but now I do. The letter she received was steeped in musk. Why, in Satan's name? one wonders."

Thoughtfully, he walked slowly to the window, opened it and thrust his head out, looking down upon the cement walk some fifty feet below. Neither ivy, waterspout nor protuberance of the building offered foothold for a mouse upon the flat straight wall.

"I do not think she went that way," he murmured as he turned to look up at the overhanging roof.

"Nor that way, either, sor," Costello rejoined, pointing to the overhanging of mansard roof some seven feet above the window-top.

"U'm? One wonders." Reaching out, de Grandin tapped an iron cleat set in the wall midway of the window's height. From the spike's tip branched a flange of a turnbuckle, evidently intended to secure a shutter at some former time. "A very active person might ascend or—*parbleu!*"

Breaking off his words half uttered, he took a jeweler's loop out of his raincoat pocket, fixed it in his eye, then played the beam of his electric torch upon the window-sill, subjecting it to a methodical inspection.

"What do you make of this, my friends?" he asked as he passed the glass to us in turn, directing his light ray along the gray stone sill and indicating several tiny scratches on the slate. "They may be recent, they may have been here since the building was erected," he admitted as we handed back the glass, "but in cases such as this there are no such things as trifles."

Once more he leant across the window-sill, then mounted it and bent out till his eyes were level with the rusty iron cleat set in the wall.

"*Morbleu*, it is a repetition!" he exclaimed as he rejoined us. "Up, my *sergent*, up, Friend Trowbridge, and see what you can see upon that iron."

Gingerly, I clambered to the sill and viewed the rusty cleat through the enlarging-glass while Costello played the flashlight's beam upon it. On the iron's reddish surface, invisible, or nearly so, to naked eyes, but clearly visible through the loop's lens, there showed a row of sharp, light scratches, exactly duplicating those upon the window-sill.

"Bedad, I don't know what it's all about, sor," Costello rumbled as he concluded his inspection, "but if it's a wild-goose chase we're on I'm thinkin' that we've found a feather in th' wind to guide us."

"*Exactement*. One is permitted to indulge that hope. Now let us mount the roof.

"Have the care," he cautioned as Costello took his ankles in a firm grip and slid him gently down the slanting, still-wet slates. "I have led a somewhat sinful life, and have no wish to be projected into the beyond without sufficient time to make my peace with heaven."

"No fear, sor," grinned Costello. "Ye're a little pip squeak, savin' yer presence, an' I can swing ye be th' heels till mornin' if this rotten brickwor-rk don't give way wid me."

Wriggling eel-like on his stomach, de Grandin searched the roof slates inch by careful inch from the leaded gutter running round the roof bank's lower edge to the lower brick ridge that marked the incline's top. His small blue eyes were shining brightly as he rejoined us.

"*Mes amis*, there is the mystery here," he announced solemnly. "Across the gutter to the slates, and up the slates until the roof's flat top is reached, there is a trail of well defined, light scratches. Moreover, they are different."

"Different, sor? How d'ye mean—"

"Like this: Upon the window-sill they are perceptibly more wide and deep at their beginning than their end—like exclamation marks viewed from above. In the gutter and upon the roof they are reversed, with deeper gashes at the lower ends and lighter scratches at their upper terminals."

"O.K., sor. Spill it. I'm not much good at riddles."

A momentary frown inscribed twin upright wrinkles between de Grandin's brows. "One cannot say with surety, but one may guess," he answered slowly, speaking more to himself than to us. "If the marks were uniform one might infer someone had crawled out of the window mounted to the gutter by the ringbolt set into the wall, then climbed upon the roof. An active person might accomplish it. But the situation is quite otherwise. The scratches on the slates reverse the scorings on the window-sill."

"You've waded out beyond me depth now, sor," Costello answered.

"*Tiens*, mine also," the Frenchman grinned. "But let us hazard a conjecture: Suppose one wearing hobnailed boots—or shoes which had been pegged, as Miss Lefètre's were—had crawled out from this window: how would he use his feet?"

"To stand on, I praysume, sor."

"*Ah bah*. You vex me, you annoy me, you get upon my goat! Standing on the sill and reaching up and out to grasp that iron cleat, he would have used his feet to brace himself and pivot on. His tendency would be to turn upon his toes, thereby tracing arcs or semicircles in the stone with the nails set in his shoes. But that is not the case here. The scorings marked into the stone are deeper at beginning, showing that the hobnailed shoes were scratching in resistance, clawing, if you please, against some force which bore the wearer of those shoes across the windowsill. Digging deeply at beginning, the nail marks taper off, as the shoes slipped from the stone and their wearer's weight was lifted from the sill.

"When we view the iron cleat we are upon less certain ground. One cannot say just how a person stepping to the iron would move his feet in climbing to the roof; but when we come to read the slates we find another chapter in this so puzzling story. Those marks were left by someone who fought not to mount the roof; but who was struggling backward with the strength of desperation, yet who was steadily forced upward. Consider, if you please: The fact that such resistance, if successful, would have resulted in this person's being catapulted to the cement path and almost surely killed, shows us conclusively the maker of those marks regarded death as preferable to going up that roof. Why? one asks."

"PARDON ME, SIR, ARE you from headquarters?" Slightly nasal but not at all unmusical, the challenge drawled at us across the corridor. From the doorway of the room set opposite to Emerline's a girl regarded us with one of the most indolent, provocative "come-hither" looks I'd ever seen a woman wear. She was of medium height, not slender and not stout, but lushly built, with bright hair, blond as a well-beaten egg, worn in a page-boy bob and curled up slightly at the ends. From round throat to high white insteps she was draped in black velvet pajamas which had obviously not been purchased ready-made, but sculptured to her perfect measure, for her high, firm, ample breasts pushed up so strongly underneath the velvet that the dip of the fabric to her flat stomach was entirely without wrinkles. Her trousers were so loose about the legs they simulated a wide skirt, but at the hips they fitted with a skin-tight snugness as revealing as a rubber bathing-suit. From high-arched, carefully penciled brows to blood-red toenails she was the perfect figure of the siren, and I heard Costello gasp with almost awe-struck admiration as his eyes swept over her.

"We are, indeed, *ma belle*," de Grandin answered. "You wish to speak with us?"

Her blue eyes widened suddenly, then dropped a veil of carefully mascaraed lashes which like an odalisque's thin gossamer revealed more than it hid. They were strange eyes to see in such a young face, meaningful and knowing, a little weary, more than a little mocking. "Yes," she drawled lazily. "You're on the case of Emerline Lefètre, aren't you?"

"Yes, *Mademoiselle*."

"Well, I'm sure she disappeared at five o'clock."

"Indeed? How is it that you place the time?"

A shrug which was a slow contortion raised her black-draped shoulders and pressed the pointed breasts more tightly still against her tucked-in jacket. "I was in bed all afternoon with a neuralgic headache. The last lab period today was out at half past four, and I heard the girls come down the hall from class. There's not much time till dinner when we come in late from lab, and a warning bell rings in the dorm at three minutes before five. When it went off this afternoon it almost split my head apart. The rain had stopped; at least I didn't hear it beating on my window, but the storm had made it dark as midnight, and at first I thought it was a dream. Then I heard some of the girls go hurrying by, and knew that it was five o'clock, or not more than a minute past. I was lying there, trying to find energy to totter to the bureau for some mentholated cologne, when I heard a funny noise across the hall. I'm sure it came from Emerline's room."

"A funny noise, *Mademoiselle*? How do you mean?"

A little wrinkle furrowed down the smooth white skin between the penciled brows. "As nearly as I can describe it, it was like the opening quaver of a screech owl's cry, but it was shut off almost as it started. Then I heard a sound of stamping, as though there were a scuffle going on in there. I s'pose I should have risen and investigated, but I was too sick and miserable to do more than lie there wondering about it. Presently I fell asleep and forgot about it till I heard you in her room just now." She paused and patted back a yawn. "Mind if I go in and have a look around?" she asked, walking toward us with a swinging, aphrodisiacally undulating gait. The aura of a heavy, penetrating perfume—musk-based patchouli essence, I determined at a hasty breath—seemed hovering round her like a cumulus of tangible vapor.

As far as Jules de Grandin was concerned her blandishments might have been directed at a granite statue. "It is utterly forbidden, *Mademoiselle*. We are most grateful for your help, but until we have the opportunity to sweep the place for clues we request that no one enter it."

"WHAT D'YE MEAN, SWEEP th' place for clues, sor?" asked Costello as we drove toward home.

"Precisely what I said, *mon vieux*. There may be clues among the very dust to make this so mysterious puzzle clear."

Arrived at the house, he rummaged in the broom cupboard, finally emerging with my newest vacuum sweeper underneath his arm. It was a cleaner I had let myself be argued into buying because, as the young salesman pointed out, instead of a cloth bag it had a sack of oiled paper which when filled could be detached and thrown away. To my mind this had much merit, but Nora McGinnis begged to disagree, and so the old cloth-bellows sweeper was in daily use while the newer, sanitary engine rested in the closet.

"Behold, my friend," he grinned, "there is a virtue to be found in everything. Madame Nora has refused to use the sweeper, thereby making it impossible for you to get return on your investment, but her stubbornness assists me greatly, for here I have a pack of clean fresh paper bags in which to gather up our evidence. You comprehend?"

"Ye mean ye're goin' to vacuum-sweep that room out to th' Shelton School?" Costello asked incredulously.

"Perfectly, my friend. The floor, the walls, perhaps the ceiling. When Jules de Grandin seeks for clues he does not play. Oh, no."

The door of Emerline Lefètre's room was open on a crack as we marched down the corridor equipped with vacuum sweeper and paper refills, and as de Grandin thrust it open with his foot we caught the heavy, almost overpowering odor of patchouli mixed with musk.

"*Dame!*" de Grandin swore. "She has been here, *cette érotofurieuse*, against my express orders. And she has raised the window, too. How can we say what valuable bit of evidence has been blown out—*morbleu!*"

Positively venomous with rage, he had stamped across the room to slam the window down, but before he lowered it he had leant across the sill. Now he rested hands upon the slate and gazed down at the cement pavement fifty feet below, a look of mingled pain and wonder on his face.

"Trowbridge Costello, *mes amis*, come quickly!" he commanded, beckoning us imperiously. "Look down and tell me what it is you see."

Spotlighted by a patch of moonlight on the dull-gray cement walk a huddled body lay, inert, grotesque, unnatural-looking as a marionette whose wires have been cut. The flash of yellow hair and pale white skin against the somber elegance of sable velvet gave it positive identification.

"How th' divil did she come to take that tumble?" Costello asked as we dashed down the stairs, disdaining to wait on the slowly moving elevator.

"*Le bon Dieu* and the devil only know," de Grandin answered as he knelt beside the crumpled remnant of the girl's bright personality and laid a hand beneath her generously swelling breast.

The impact of her fall must have been devastating. Beneath her crown of gold-blond hair her skull vault had been mashed as though it were an eggshell; through the skin above her left eye showed a staring splinter of white bone where the shattered temporal had pierced the skin; just above the round neck of her velvet jacket thrust a jagged chisel-edge of white, remnant of a broken cervical vertebra. Already purple bruises of extravasated blood were forming on her face; her left leg thrust out awkwardly, almost perpendicularly to her body's axis, and where the loose-legged trouser had turned back we saw the Z-twist of a compound comminutive fracture.

"Is she—" began Costello, and de Grandin nodded as he rose.

"Indubitably," he returned. "Dead like a herring."

"But why should she have jumped?" I wondered. "Some evil influence—a wild desire to emulate—"

He made a gesture of negation. "How far is it from here to the house wall?" he asked.

"Why, some eighteen feet, I judge."

"*Précisément*. That much, at least. Is it in your mind her fall's trajectory would have been so wide an arc?"

"What's that?"

"Simply this, by blue! Had she leaped or fallen from the window she should have struck the earth much nearer to the building's base. The distance separating ground and window is too small to account for her striking thus far out; besides it is unlikely that she would have dived head first. Men sometimes make such suicidal leaps, women scarcely ever. Yet all the evidence discloses that she struck upon her head; at least she fell face forward. Why?"

"You imply that she was—"

"I am not sure, but from the facts as we observe them I believe that she was thrown, and thrown by one who had uncommon strength. She was a heavy girl; no ordinary person could have lifted her and thrown her through a window, yet someone must have done just that; there is no evidence of struggle in the room."

"Shall I take charge, sor?" asked Costello.

De Grandin nodded. "It will expedite our work if you will be so kind. When she is taken to the morgue I wish you would prevent the autopsy until I have a chance to make a more minute inspection of the body. Meantime I have important duties elsewhere."

METHODICALLY, AS THOUGH HE'D been a janitor—but with far more care for detail—he moved the vacuum sweeper back and forth across the floor of the small tragic room, drew out the paper bag and sealed and labeled it. Then with a fresh bag in the bellows he swept the bed, the couch, the draperies. Satisfied that every latent trace of dust had been removed, he shut the current off, and, his precious bags beneath his arm, led the march toward my waiting car.

A sheet of clean white paper spread across the surgery table made background for the miscellany of fine refuse which he emptied from the sweeper's bags. Microscope to eye, he passed a glass rod vigorously rubbed with silk back and forth across the dust heap. Attracted by the static charge fine bits of rubbish adhered to the rod and were subjected to his scrutiny. As he completed his examination I viewed the salvage through a second microscope, but found it utterly uninteresting. It was the usual hodgepodge to be culled by vacuuming a broom-cleaned room. Tiny bits of paper, too fine to yield to straw brooms' pressure, little flecks of nondescript black dust, a wisp or two of wool fiber from the cheap rug, the trash was valueless from any viewpoint, as far as I could see.

"*Que diable?*" With eyes intently narrowed he was looking at some object clinging to his glass rod.

"What is it?" I demanded, leaning closer.

"See if you can classify it," he returned, moving aside to let me look down through the viewhole of the microscope.

It was a strand of hair three-quarters of an inch or so in length, curled slightly like a human body hair, but thicker, coarser in its texture. Reddish rusty brown at tip, it shaded to a dull gray at the center and bleached to white transparency about the base. I saw it was smooth-scaled upon its outer surface and terminated in a point, showing it had never been cut or, if clipped, had sufficient time to grow to its full length again.

"Let us proceed," I heard him whisper as he moved his polished rod again across the heap of sweepings. "Perhaps we shall discover something else."

Slowly he moved the rod across the furrowed edges of the dust heap, pausing now and then to view a fresh find. A splinter of straw, a tiny tag of paper, fine powdered dust, these comprised his salvage, till: "Ah?" he murmured, "ah-ha?" Adhering to the rod there was another wisp of hair, almost the counterpart of his first find, except it was more nearly uniform in color, dull lack-luster rust all over, like an aged tomcat's fur, or the hair of some misguided woman who has sought a simulation of her vanished youth by having her gray tresses dyed with henna.

"What—" I began, but he waved me silent with a nervous gesture as he continued fishing with his rod. At last he laid the rod aside and began to winnow the dust piles through a fine wire screen. Half an hour's patient work resulted in the salvaging of two or three small chocolate-colored flakes which looked for all the world like grains of bran and when field close to our noses on a sheet of folded paper gave off a sweetly penetrating odor.

"You recognize them?" he asked.

"Not by sight. By their smell I'd say they contained musk."

"Quite yes," he nodded. "They are musk. Crude musk, such as the makers of perfumery use."

"But what should that be doing in a young girl's room—"

"One wonders with the wonder of amazement. One also wonders what those hairs did there. I should say the musk flakes were contained in the brown envelope the elevator boy delivered to Mademoiselle Lefètre. As for the hairs—"

The tinkle of the telephone broke off his explanation. "Yes, my *sergent*, it is I," I heard him answer. "He is? Restrain him—forcefully, if necessary. I shall make the haste to join you.

"Come, let us hurry," he commanded as he set the 'phone down.

"Where, at this hour o' night, for pity's sake?"

"Why, to the morgue, of course. Parnell, the coroner's physician, insists on making an autopsy on the body of Miss Henrietta Sidlo within the hour. We must look at her first."

"Who the devil was Miss Henrietta Sidlo?" I asked as we commenced our hurried journey to the city morgue.

"The so attractive blond young woman who was killed because she could not mind her business and keep from the room we had forbidden her to enter."

"What makes you so sure she was killed? She might have fallen from the window, or—"

"Or?" he echoed.

"Oh, nothing. I just had a thought."

"I rejoice to hear it. What was it, if you please?"

"Perhaps she thought as you did, that Miss Lefètre had climbed to the roof, and tried to emulate the feat experimentally."

I had expected him to scout my theory, but he nodded thoughtfully. "It may be so," he answered. "It seems incredible that one should be so foolish, but the Sidlo girl was nothing if not unbelievable, *n'est-ce-pas?*"

BENEATH THE SEARING GLARE that flooded from the clustered arclights set above the concave operating-table in the morgue's autopsy room her body showed almost as pale as the white tiles that floored and walled the place. She had bled freely from the nose and ears when skull and brain were smashed at once, and the dried blood stained her chin and cheeks and throat. De Grandin took spray-nosed hose and played its thread-like stream across her face and neck sponging off the dried blood with a wad of cotton. At length: "What is it that you see?" he asked.

Where the blood and grime had washed away were five light livid patches, one some three inches in size and roughly square, and extending from it four parallel lines almost completely circling the neck. At the end of each was a deeply pitted scar, as if the talons of some predatory beast had sunk into the flesh.

"Good heavens," I exclaimed; "it's terrible!"

"But naturally. One does not look for beauty in the morgue. I asked you what you saw, not for your *impression esthetique*."

I hesitated for a breath and felt his small blue eyes upon me in a fixed, unwinking stare, quizzical, sardonic; almost, it seemed, a little pleading. Long years ago, when we had known each other but a day, he and I had stood beside another corpse in this same morgue, the corpse of a young girl who had been choked and mauled to death by a gorilla. "Sarah Humphreys—" I began; and:

"*Bravo, bravissimo!*" he whispered, "You have right, my friend. See, here is the bruise left by the heel of his hand; these encircling marks, they are his fingers; these jagged, deep-set marks the wounds left by his broken nails. Yes, it is so. There is no thumb print, for he does not grasp like men, he does not use his thumb for fulcrum."

"Then those hairs you found when you swept up the room—"

"*Précisément.* I recognized them instantly, but could not imagine how they came there. If—one moment, if you please!"

Bending quickly he took the dead girl's pale plump hands in his and with his penknife tip skimmed underneath the rims of her elaborately lacquered nails, dropping the salvage into a fresh envelope. "I think that we shall find corroboration in a microscopic test of these," he stated, but the bustling entrance of the coroner's physician cut him short.

"What's going on here?" Doctor Parnell asked. "No one should touch this body till I've finished my examination—"

"We do but make it ready for you, *cher collègue*," de Grandin answered with fictitious mildness as he turned away. Outside he muttered as we climbed into my car: "There are fools, colossal fools, damned fools, and then there is Parnell. He is superlative among all fools, friend Trowbridge."

Three-quarters of an hour later we put the scrapings from the dead girl's nails beneath a microscope. Most of the matter was sheer waste, but broken and wedged firmly in a tiny drop of nail stain we came upon the thing we sought, a tiny fragment of gorilla hair.

"*Tiens*, she fought for life with nature's weapons, *cette pauvre*," he murmured as he rose from the examination. "It is a pity she should die so young and beautiful. We must take vengeance for her death, my friend."

AMBER BROCADE CURTAINS HAD been drawn against the unseasonably chilly weather and a bright fire crackled on the hearth of the high-manteled fireplace of the lounging-room of the Lefètre home in Nyack. Harold Lefètre greeted us restrainedly. Since dinnertime the day before he had been interviewed by a succession of policemen and reporters, and his nerves and patience were stretched almost to the snapping-point.

"There isn't anything that I can add to what you've been already told," he said like one who speaks a well-learned piece. "Emerline was just past seventeen, she had no love affairs, wasn't especially interested in boys. Her scholastic standing was quite good, though she seldom got past B grades. She was not particularly studious, so it couldn't have been a nervous breakdown forced by overstudy. She stood well enough in marks not to have been worried over passing her examinations; she was happy in her home. There is no reason, no earthly reason I can think of, for her to disappear. I've told you everything I know. Suppose you try looking for her instead of quizzing me."

Costello's face flushed brick-red. He had been against the interview, expecting a rebuke would be forthcoming.

De Grandin seemed oblivious to Lefètre's censure. His eyes were traveling round the charming room in a quick, stock-taking gaze. He noted with approval the expensive furniture, the bizarre small tables with their litter of inconsequential trifles, cinnabar and silver cigarette-containers, fashionable magazines, bridge markers, the deep bookshelves right and left of the big fireplace, the blurred blues and mulberries of the antique china in the unglassed cabinets. In a far, unlighted corner of the room his questing glance seemed resting, as though he had attained the object of his search. In apposition to the modern, western, super-civilized sophistication of the other bric-à-brac the group of curios seemed utterly incongruous; a hippopotamus leg with hoof intact, brass-lined to form a cane stand and holding in its tube a sheaf of African assagais. Above the group of relics hung a little drum no bigger than a sectioned coconut, with a slackly tensioned head of dull gray parchment. "*Monsieur*," the Frenchman suddenly demanded, "you were in Africa with Willis Cogswell in 1922?"

Lefètre eyed him sharply. "What has that to do—"

"It was Monsieur Cogswell's daughter who vanished without trace three months ago, *n'est-ce-pas?*"

"I still don't see—"

"There were three members of your African adventure, were there not: yourself, and Messieurs Cogswell and Everton?"

Anger flamed in our host's face as he turned on Costello. "What has all this got to do with Emerline's case?" he almost roared. "First you come badgering me with senseless questions about her, now you bring this 'expert' here to pry into my private life—"

"You did not part with Monsieur Everton in friendship?" de Grandin broke in imperturbably. Then, as if his question were rhetorical: "But no. Quite otherwise. You and he and Monsieur Cogswell quarreled. He left you vowing vengeance—"

"See here, I've had enough of this unwarranted—"

"And ninety days ago he struck at Willis Cogswell through the dearest thing that he possessed. Attend me very carefully, *Monsieur*. You have heard that shock caused Monsieur Cogswell to collapse, that he died of a heart seizure two days following his daughter's disappearance—"

"Of course, he did. Why shouldn't he? He'd been suffering from angina for a year, had to give up business and spend half his time in bed. His doctor'd warned him anything exciting might prove fatal—"

"*Précisément*. He fell dead in his library. His butler found him dead upon the floor—"

"That's true, but what—"

De Grandin drew a slip of folded paper from his pocket. "This was in your friend's hand when the butler found him," he answered as he held the missive toward our host. It was a piece of coarse brown paper, torn, apparently from a grocery bag, and penciled on it in black chalk was one word: *Bokoli*.

The anger faded from Lefètre's face; fear drained his color, left him gray.

"You recognize the writing?" asked de Grandin.

"No, no, it can't be," Lefètre faltered. "Everton is dead—we—I saw him—"

"And these, *Monsieur*, we found among the sweepings from your daughter's room," de Grandin interrupted. "You recognize them, *hein?*" Fixed with adhesive gum to a card of plain white paper, he extended the gorilla hairs we'd found the night before.

Utter panic replaced fear in our host's face. His eyes were glassy, bright and dilated as if drugged with belladonna. They shifted here and there, as though he sought some channel of escape. His lips began to twist convulsively.

"This—this is a trick!" he mumbled, and we saw the spittle drooling from the corners of his mouth. "This couldn't be—"

His hands shook in a nervous frenzy, clawing at his collar. Then suddenly his knees seemed softening under him, and every bit of stiffness left his body so that be fell down in a heap before the hearth, the impact of his fall rattling the brass tools by the fireplace.

Involuntarily I shivered. Something evil and soft-footed seemed to shuffle in that quiet room, but there was no seeing it, no hearing it, no way of knowing what it was; only the uncanny, hideous feel of it—clammy, cold, obscenely leering.

"Now—so!" de Grandin soothed as he lowered his flask from the reviving man's lips. "That is better, *n'est-ce-pas?*"

He helped Lefètre to a chair, and, "Would it not be well to tell us all about it?" he suggested. "You have had a seething pot inside you many years, *Monsieur*; it has boiled, then simmered down, then boiled again, and it has brought much scum up in the process. Let us skim it off, *comme ça*"—he made a gesture as if with a spoon—"and throw it out. Only so shall we arrive at mental peace."

Lefètre set his face like one who contemplates a dive in icy water. "There were four of us on safari through Bokoliland," he answered; "Cogswell, his wife Lysbeth, a Boer settler's daughter, Everton and I. We'd found the going pretty rough; no ivory, no trading fit to mention, no gold, and our supplies were running low. When we reached Shamboko's village the men were all out hunting, but the women and old men were kind to us and fed and lodged us. In normal circumstances we'd have waited there until the chief came back and tried to do some trading, but on the second evening Everton came hurrying to our hut half drunken with excitement.

"'I've just been to the Ju-Ju house,' he told us. 'D'ye know what they've got there? Gold! Great heaps and stacks o' yellow dust, enough to fill our hats and pockets, and a stack o' yellow diamonds bigger than your head. Let's go!'

"Now, the Bokoli are a fairly peaceful folk, and they'd take a lot from white men, but if you monkey with their women or their Ju-Ju you'd better have your life insurance premiums all paid. I'd seen the body of a man they'd 'chopped' for sacrilege one time, and it had put the fear o' God in me. They'd flayed the skin off him, not enough to kill him, but the torment must have been almost past standing. Then they'd smeared honey on the raw nerve ends and staked him down spread-eagled in a clearing in the jungle. The ants had found him there— millions of the little red ones—and they'd cleaned the flesh off of his bones as if they had been boiled.

"I wasn't having any of that, so I turned the proposition down, but the others were all for it. Finally I yielded and we sneaked down to the Ju-Ju house. It was just as Everton had said. The gold was piled in little pyramidal heaps before the idol in a semicircle, with the diamonds stacked up in the center. The offerings must have been accumulating over several centuries, for there's little gold in the Bokoli country, and no diamonds nearer than five hundred miles. But there the stuff was, ready for our taking.

"We stuffed our haversacks and pockets and set out for the coast within an hour, anxious to put as many miles as possible between us and the village before the medicine man paid his morning visit to the Ju-Ju and found out what we'd done.

"Everton began to act queer from the start. He'd sneak away from camp at night and be gone hours at a time without an explanation. One night I followed him. He made straight for a clearing by the river and sat down on the grass as if waiting someone. Presently I saw a shadow slipping from the bush and next moment a full-grown gorilla shambled out into the moonlight. Instead of rushing Everton the monster stopped a little distance off and looked at him, and Everton looked back, then—think I'm a liar if you wish—they *talked* to one another. Don't ask me how they did it; I don't know. I only know that Everton addressed a series of deep grunts to the great beast and it answered him in kind. Then they parted and I trailed him back to camp.

"Three days later the Bokoli caught us. We'd just completed dinner and were sitting down to smoke when all at once the jungle seemed alive with 'em, great strapping blacks with four-foot throwing spears and bullhide shields and vulture feathers in their hair. They weren't noisy about it. That was the worst of it. They appeared like shadows out of nowhere and stood there in a ring, just looking at us. Old Chief Shamboko did the honors, and he was as polite about it as the villain in a play. No reproaches for the diamonds and the gold dust we'd made off with, though they must have represented his tribe's savings for a century or more. Oh, no, he put it squarely to us on the ground of sacrilege. The Ju-Ju was insulted. He'd lost face. Only blood could wash away the memory of the insult, but he'd be satisfied with one of us. Just one. We were to make the choice. Then he walked back to the ring of warriors and stood waiting for us to announce which one of us would go back to be flayed alive and eaten up by ants. Pretty fix to be in, eh?"

"You made no offer to return the loot?" de Grandin asked.

"I'll say we did. Told him he might have our whole trade stock to boot, but he wasn't interested. The treasure we had taken from the temple had been tainted by our touch, so couldn't be put back, and only things dug from the earth were suitable as offerings to the Ju-Ju, so our trade stuff had no value. Besides, they wanted blood, and blood was what they meant to have."

"One sees. Accordingly—?"

"We tossed for it. Lysbeth, Cogswell's wife, drew out a coin and whispered something to her husband. Then he and Everton and I stood by as she flipped it. Cogswell beat us to the call and shouted 'Heads!' And heads it came. That left Everton and me to try.

"He shouted 'Tails!' almost before the silver left her hand. It came up heads again, and I was safe."

"And so—"

"Just so. The Bokoli couldn't understand our words, of course, but they knew that Everton had lost by his demeanor, and they were on him in a second, pinioning his arms against his sides with grass rope before he had a chance to draw his gun and shoot himself.

"Considering what he was headed for, you could hardly blame him, but it seemed degrading, the way he begged for life. We'd seen him in a dozen desperate fixes when his chance of coming through alive seemed absolutely nil, but he seemed like another person, now, pleading with us to shoot him, or die fighting for him, making us the most outlandish offers, promising to be our slave and work for ever without wages if we'd only save him from the savages. Even old Shamboko seemed to feel embarrassed at the sight of such abysmal cowardice in a white man, and he'd ordered his young men to drag their victim off when Everton chanced to kick the silver coin which sent him to his fate. The florin shone and twinkled in the moonlight when he turned it over. Then he and I and all of us realized. It was a trick piece Lysbeth used, an old Dutch florin with two heads. There hadn't been a chance her man could lose the toss, for she'd told him to call heads, and she'd flipped the coin herself, so none of us could see it was a cheat.

"Everton turned sober in a second. Rage calmed him where his self-respect was powerless to overcome his fear of torture, and he rose with dignity to march away between the Bokoli warriors. But just before he disappeared with them into the bush he turned on us. 'You'll never know a moment's safety, any of you,' he bellowed. 'The shadow of the jungle will be on you always, and it'll take the dearest things you have. Remember, you'll each lose the thing you love most dearly.'

"That was all. The Bokoli marched him off, and we never saw him again."

"But, *Monsieur*—"

"But two weeks later, when we were almost at the outskirts of the Boer country, I woke up in the night with the sound of screaming in my ears. Cogswell lay face downward by the campfire, and just disappearing in the bush was a great silver-backed gorilla with Lysbeth struggling in his arms."

"You pursued—"

"Not right away. I was too flabbergasted to do more than gape at what I saw for several seconds, and the big ape and the woman were gone almost before you could say 'knife.' Then there was Cogswell to look after. He'd had a dreadful beating, though I don't suppose the beast had more than merely flung him from his way. They're incredibly powerful, those great apes. Cogswell had a dislocated shoulder and two broken ribs, and for a while I thought he'd not pull through. I pulled his shoulder back in place and bandaged him as best I could, but it was several weeks before he regained strength to travel, and even then we had to take it slowly.

"I kept us alive by hunting, and one day while I was gunning I found Lysbeth. It was a week since she'd been stolen, but apparently she'd never been more than a mile or so away, for her body hung up in a tree-fork less than an hour's walk from camp, and was still warm when I found it.

"The ape had ripped her clothing off as he might have peeled a fruit, and apparently he'd been none too gentle in the process, for she was overlaid with scratches like a net. Those were just play marks, though. It wasn't till he tired of her—or till she tried to run away—he really used his strength on her. Down her arms and up her thighs were terrible, great gashes, deep enough to show the bone where skin and flesh had been shorn through in places. Her face was beaten absolutely flat, nose, lips and chin all smashed down to a bloody level. Her neck was broken. Her head hung down as if suspended by a string, and on her throat were bruise marks and the nailprints of the great beast's hands where he had squeezed her neck until her spinal column snapped. I"—Lefètre faltered and we saw the shadow of abysmal horror flit across his face—"I don't like to think what had happened to the poor girl in the week between her kidnapping and killing."

Costello looked from our host to de Grandin. "'Tis a highly interestin' tale, sor," he assured the Frenchman, "but I can't say as I sees where it fits in. This here now Everton is dead—ain't he?" he turned to Lefètre.

"I've always thought—I like to think he is."

"Ye saw 'im march off wid th' savages, didn't ye? They're willin' workers wid th' knife, if what ye say is true."

De Grandin almost closed his eyes and murmured softly, like one who speaks a poem learned in childhood and more than half forgotten: "It was December 2, 1923, that Lieutenant José Garcia of the Royal Spanish Army went with a file of native troops to inspect the little outpost of Akaar, which lies close by Boko-liland. He found the place in mourning, crazed with sorrow, fear and consterna-tion. Some days before a flock of fierce gorillas had swept down upon the village, murdered several of the men and made away with numerous young women. From what the natives told him, Lieutenant Garcia learned such things had happened almost for a year in the Bokoli country, and that the village of the chief Sham-boko had been utterly destroyed by a herd of giant apes—"

"That's it!" Lefètre shrieked. "We've never known. We heard about the ape raids and that Shamboko's village had been wrecked by them, but whether they destroyed it before Everton was put to death or whether they came down on it in vengeance—Cogswell and I both thought he had been killed, but we couldn't know. When his daughter disappeared I didn't connect it with Africa, but that paper Cogswell clutched when he dropped dead, those hairs you found in Emer-line's room—"

"*Exactement*," de Grandin nodded as Lefètre's voice trailed off. "Perfectly, exactly, quite so, *Monsieur*. It is a very large, impressive 'but.' We do not know, we cannot surely say, but we can damn suspect."

"But for th' love o' mud, sor, how'd, this here felly git so chummy wid th' apes?" Costello asked. "I've seen some monkeys in th' zoo that seemed to have more sense than many a human, but—"

"You don't ask much about companions' former lives in Africa," Lefètre in-terrupted, "but from scraps of information he let drop I gathered Everton had been an animal trainer in his younger days and that he'd also been on expedi-tions to West Africa and Borneo to collect apes for zoos and circuses. It may be he had some affinity for them. I know he seemed to speak to and to understand that great ape in the jungle—d'ye suppose—"

"I do, indeed, *Monsieur*," de Grandin interrupted earnestly. "I am convinced of it."

"SURE, IT'S TH' NUTTIEST business I iver heard of, sor," Costello declared as we drove home. "'Tis wild enough when he stharts tellin' us about a man that talks to a gorilly, but when it's intaymated that a ape clomb up th' buildin' an' sthold th' gur-rl—"

"Such things have happened, *mon ami*," de Grandin answered. "The records of the Spanish army, as well as reports of explorers, vouch for such kidnappings—"

"O.K., sor; O.K. But why should th' gorillies choose th' very gur-rls this felly Everton desired to have sthold? Th' apes ye tell about just snatch a woman—any woman—that chances in their way, but these here now gorillies took th' very—"

"*Restez tranquil,*" de Grandin ordered. "I would think, I desire to cogitate. *Nom d'un porc vert,* I would meditate, consider, speculate, if you will let me have a little silence!"

"Sure, sor, I'll be afther givin' ye all ye want. I wuz only—"

"Nature strikes her balance with nicety," de Grandin murmured as though musing aloud. "Every living creature pays for what he has. Man lacks great strength, but reinforces frailty with reason; the bloodhound cannot see great distances, but his sense of smell is very keen; nocturnal creatures like the bat and owl have eyes attuned to semi-darkness. What is the gorilla's balance? He has great strength, a marvelous agility, keen sight, but—*parbleu*, he lacks the sense of smell the lesser creatures have! You comprehend?"

"No, sor, I do not."

"But it is simple. His nose is little keener than his human cousins', but even his flat snout can recognize the pungent scent of crude musk at considerable distance. We do not know, we cannot surely say the Cogswell girl received an envelope containing musk upon the night she disappeared. We know that Mademoiselle Lefètre did." Abruptly:

"What sort of day was it Miss Cogswell disappeared?" he asked Costello.

The Irishman considered for a moment; then: "It wuz a wet, warm day in March, much like yesterday," he answered.

"It must have been," de Grandin nodded. "The great apes are susceptible to colds; to risk one in our northern winter out of doors would be to sign his death warrant, and this one was required for a second job of work."

Costello looked at him incredulously. "I s'pose ye know how old th' snatchin' monkey wuz?" he asked ironically.

"Approximately, yes. Like man, gorillas gray with age, but unlike us, their gray hairs show upon their backs and shoulders. A 'silverback' gorilla may be very aged, or he may still be in the vigor of his strength. They mature fully at the age of fourteen; at twenty they are very old. I think the ape we seek is something like fifteen years old; young enough to be in his full prime, old enough to have been caught in early youth and trained consistently to recognize the scent of musk and carry off the woman who exuded it."

"TH' TELLYPHONE'S BEEN RINGIN' for a hour," Nora McGinnis told us as we drew up at my door. "'Tis a Misther Lefètre, an' he wants ye to call back—"

"*Merci bien,*" de Grandin called as he raced down the hall and seized the instrument. In a moment he was back. "Quick, at once, right away, my friends," he cried. "We must go back to Nyack."

"But, glory be, we've just come down from there," Costello started to object, but the look of fierce excitement in the Frenchman's face cut his protest short.

"Monsieur Lefètre has received a note like that which killed his friend Cogswell," de Grandin announced. "It was thrust beneath his door five minutes after we had gone."

"And this," de Grandin tapped the scrap of ragged paper, "this shall be the means of trapping him who persecutes young girls."

"Arrah, sor, how ye're goin' to find 'im through that thing is more than I can see," Costello wondered. "Even if it has his fingerprints upon it, where do we go first?"

"To the office of the sheriff."

"Excuse me, sor, did ye say th' sheriff?"

"Your hearing is impeccable, my friend. Does not *Monsieur le Shérif* keep those sad-faced, thoughtful-looking dogs, the bloodhounds?"

"Be gob, sor, sure he does, but how'll ye know which way to lead 'em to take up th' scent?"

De Grandin flashed his quick, infectious grin at him. "Let us consider local geography. Our assumption is the miscreant we seek maintains an ape to do his bidding. Twice in three months a young girl has been kidnapped from the Shelton School—by this gorilla, we assume. America is a wondrous land. Things which would be marvels otherwise pass unnoticed here, but a gorilla in the country is still sufficiently a novelty to excite comment. Therefore, the one we seek desires privacy. He lives obscurely, shielded from his neighbors' prying gaze. Gorillas are equipped to walk, but not for long. The aerial pathways of the trees are nature's high roads for them. *Alors*, this one lives in wooded country. Furthermore, he must live fairly near the Shelton School, since his ape must be able to go there without exciting comment, and bring his quarry to his lair unseen. You see? It is quite simple. Somewhere within a mile or so of Shelton is a patch of densely wooded land. When we have found that place we set our hounds upon the track of him whose scent is on this *sacré* piece of paper, and—*voilà!*"

"Be gorry, sor, ye'll have no trohble findin' land to fit yer bill," Costello assured him. "Th' pine woods grow right to th' Shelton campus on three sides, an' th' bay is on th' other."

T HE GENTLE BLOODHOUNDS WAGGED their tails and rubbed their velvet muzzles on de Grandin's faultlessly creased trousers. "Down, noble ones," he bade, dropping a morsel of raw liver to them. "Down, canine noblemen, peerless scenters-out of evil doers. We have a task to do tonight, thou and I."

He held the crudely lettered scrap of paper out to them and bade them sniff it, then began to lead them in an ever-widening circle through the thick-grown pine trees. Now and then they whimpered hopefully, their sadly thoughtful eyes upon him, then put their noses to the ground again. Suddenly one of them threw back his head and gave utterance to a short, sharp, joyous bark, followed by a deep-toned, belling bay.

"*Tallis au!*" de Grandin cried. "The chase is on, my friends. See to your weapons. That we seek is fiercer than a lion or a bear, and more stealthy than a panther."

Through bramble-bristling thicket, creeping under low-swung boughs and climbing over fallen trees, we trailed the dogs, deeper, deeper, ever deeper into the pine forest growing in its virgin vigor on the curving bay shore. It seemed to me we were an hour on the way, but probably we had not followed our four-footed guides for more than twenty minutes when the leprous white of weather-blasted clapboards loomed before us through the wind-bent boughs. "Good Lord," I murmured as I recognized the place. "It's Suicide Chapel!"

"Eh? How is it you say?" de Grandin shot back.

"That's what the youngsters used to call it. Years ago it was the meeting-place of an obscure cult, a sort of combination of the Holy Rollers and the Whitests. They believed the dead are in a conscious state, and to prove their tenets their pastors and several members of the flock committed suicide *en masse*, offering themselves as voluntary sacrifices. The police dispersed the congregation, and as far as I know the place has not been tenanted for forty years. It has an evil reputation, haunted, and all that, you know."

"*Tenez*, I damn think it is haunted now by something worse than any of the old ones' spooks," he whispered.

The ruined church was grim in aspect as a Doré etching. In the uncertain light of an ascending moon its clapboard sides, almost nude of paint, seemed glowing with unearthly phosphorescence. Patches of blue shadow lay like spilled ink on the weed-grown clearing round the edifice; the night wind keened a mournful threnody in the pine boughs. As we scrambled from the thicket of scrub evergreen and paused a moment in reconnaissance the ghostly hoot of an owl echoed weirdly, through the gloom.

De Grandin cradled his short-barreled rifle in the crook of his left arm and pointed to the tottering, broken-sided steeple. "He is there if he is here," he announced.

"I don't think that I follow ye," Costello whispered back. "D'ye mane he's here or there?"

"Both. The wounded snake or rodent seeks the nearest burrow. The cat things seek the shelter of the thickets. The monkey folk take to the heights when they are hunted. If he has heard the hounds bay he has undoubtlessly— *mordieu!*"

Something heavy, monstrous, smotheringly bulky, dropped on me with devastating force. Hot, noisome breath was in my face and on my neck, great, steelstrong hands were clutching at my legs, thick, club-like fingers closed around my arms, gripping them until I thought my biceps would be torn loose from my bones. My useless gun fell clattering from my hands, the monster's bristling hair thrust in my eyes, my nose, my mouth, choking and sickening me as I fought futilely against his overpowering strength. Half fainting with revulsion I struggled in the great ape's grasp and fell sprawling to the ground, trying ineffectually to brace myself against the certainty of being torn to pieces. I felt my head seized in a giant paw, raised till I thought my neck would snap, then bumped against the ground with thunderous force. A lurid burst of light blazed in my eyes, followed by a deafening roar. Twice more the thunderous detonations sounded, and as the third report reverberated I felt the heavy weight on top of me go static. Though the hairy chest still bore me down, there was no movement in the great encircling arms, and the vise-like hands and feet had ceased their torturing pressure on my arms and legs. A sudden sticky warmness flooded over me, wetting through my jacket and trickling down my face.

"Trowbridge, *mon vieux, mon brave, mon véritable ami*, are you alive, do you survive?" de Grandin called as he and Costello hauled the massive simian corpse off me. "I should have shot him still more quickly, but my trigger finger would not mind my brain's command."

"I'm quite alive," I answered as I got unsteadily upon my feet and stretched my arms and legs tentatively. "Pretty well mauled and shaken, but—"

"S-s-sh," warned de Grandin. "There is another we must deal with. *Holà l'haut!*" he called. "Will you come forth, *Monsieur*, or do we deal with you as we dealt with your pet?"

STARK DESOLATION REIGNED WITHIN the ruined church. Floors sagged uncertainly and groaned protestingly beneath our feet; the cheap pine pews were cracked and broken, fallen in upon themselves; throughout the place the musty, faintly acrid smell of rotting wood hung dank and heavy, like miasmic vapors of a marsh in autumn. Another smell was noticeable, too; the ammonia-laden scent of pent-up animals, such as hovers in the air of prisons, lazarets and primate houses at the zoo.

Guided by the odor and the searching beam shot by de Grandin's flashlight, we crossed the sagging floor with cautious steps until we reached the little eminence where in the former days the pulpit stood. There, like the obscene parody of a tabernacle, stood a great chest, some eight feet square, constructed of stout rough-sawn planks and barred across the front with iron uprights. A small dishpan half filled with water and the litter of melon rinds told us this had been the prison of the dead gorilla.

De Grandin stooped and looked inside the cage. "*Le pauvre sauvage*," he murmured. "It was in this pen he dwelt. It was inhuman—*pardieu!*" Bending quickly he retrieved a shred of orange satin. He raised it to his nose, then passed it to us. It was redolent of musk.

"So, then, Jules de Grandin is the fool, the *imbécile*, the simpleton, the ninny, the chaser-after-shadows, *hein?*" he demanded. "Come, let us follow through our quest."

Th' place seems empty, sor," Costello said as, following the wall, we worked our way toward the building's front. "If there wuz anny body here—Howly Mither!"

Across our path, like a doll cast aside by a peevish child there lay a grotesque object. The breath stopped in my throat, for the thing was gruesomely suggestive of a human body, but as de Grandin played his flashlight on it we saw it was a life-sized dummy of a woman. It was some five feet tall, the head was decorated by a blond bobbed wig, and it was clothed in well-made sports clothes—knit pull-over, a kilted skirt of rough tweed, Shetland socks, tan heelless shoes—the sort of costume worn by eight in ten high school and college girls. As we bent to look at it the cloyingly sweet scent of musk assailed our nostrils.

"Is not all plain?—does it not leap to meet the eye?" de Grandin asked. "This was the implement of training. That hairy one out yonder had been trained for years to seek and bring back this musk-scented dummy. When he was letter-perfect in discovering and bringing back this lifeless simulacrum, his master sent him to the harder task of seeking out and stealing living girls who had the scent of musk upon them. *Ha*, one can see it plainly—the great ape leaping through the shadowed trees, scaling the school roof as easily as you or I could walk the streets, sniffing, searching, playing at this game of hide-and-seek he had been taught. Then from the open window comes the perfume which shall tell him that his quest is finished; there in the lighted room he sees the animated version of the dummy he has learned to seize and carry to this *sacré* place. He enters. There is a scream of terror from his victim. His great hand closes on her throat and her cry dies out before it is half uttered; then through the treetops he comes to the chapel of the suicides, and underneath his arm there is—*morbleu*, and what in Satan's name is that?"

As he lectured us he swung his flashlight in an arc, and as it pointed toward the ladder-hole that led up to the ruined belfry its darting ray picked up another form which lay half bathed in shadows, like a drowned body at the water's edge.

It was—or had been—a man, but it lay across our path as awkwardly as the first dummy. Its arms and legs protruded at unnatural angles from its trunk, and though it lay breast down the head was turned, completely round so that the face looked up, and I went sick with disgust as I looked on what had once been human features, but were now so battered, flattened and blood-smeared that only staring, bulging eyes and broken teeth protruding through smashed lips told life had once pulsed underneath the hideous, shattered mask. Close beside one of the open, flaccid hands a heavy whip-stock lay, the sort of whip that animal trainers use to cow their savage pupils. A foot or so of plaited rawhide lash frayed from the weighted stock, for the long, cruel whip of braided leather had been ripped and pulled apart as though it had been made of thread.

"God rest 'is sinful soul!" Costello groaned. "Th' gorilly musta turned on 'im an' smashed 'im to a pulp. Looks like he'd tried to make a getaway, an' got pulled down from them stheps, sor, don't it?"

"By blue, it does; it most indubitably does," de Grandin agreed. "He was a cruel one, this, but the whip he used to beat his ape into submission was powerless at the last. One can find it in his heart to understand the monster's anger and desire for revenge. But pity for this one? Non! He was deserving of his fate, I damn think."

"All th' same, sor—Howly Saint Patrick, what's that?" Almost overhead, so faint and weak as to be scarcely audible, there sounded a weak, whimpering moan.

"Up, up, my friends, it may be that we are in time to save her!" the little Frenchman cried, leaping up the palsied ladder like a seaman swarming up the ratlines.

We followed him as best we could and halted at the nest of crossbeams marking the old belfry. For a moment we stood silent, then simultaneously flashed our torches. The little spears of light stabbed through the shrouding darkness for a moment, and picked up a splash of brilliant orange in the opening where the bell had hung. Lashed to the bell-wheel was a girl's slim form, arms and feet drawn back and tied with cruel knots to the spokes, her body bowed back in an arc against the wheel's periphery. Her weight had drawn the wooden cycle down so that she hung dead-center at its bottom, but the fresh, strong rope spliced to the wheel-crank bore testimony to the torment she had been subjected to, the whirling-swinging torture of the mediæval bullwheel.

"Oh, please—please kill me!" she besought as the converging light beams played upon her pain-racked face. "Don't swing me any more—I can't—stand—" her plea trailed off in a thin whimpering mewl and her head fell forward.

"Courage, Mademoiselle," the small Frenchman comforted. "We are come to take you home."

"BUT NO, MON SERGENT," Jules de Grandin shook his head in deprecation as he watched the ice cube slowly melting in his highball glass, "I have a great appreciation of myself, and am not at all averse to advertising, but in this case I must be anonymous. You it was who did it all, who figured out the African connection, and who found the hideaway to which the so unfortunate Miss Lefètre was conveyed. Friend Trowbridge and I did but go along to give you help; the credit must be yours. We shall show those fools down at headquarters if you are past your prime. We shall show them if you are unfit for crime detection. This case will make your reputation firm, and that you also found what happened to the Cogswell girl will add materially to your fame. Is it not so?"

"I only wish to God I did know what happened to poor Margaret Cogswell," the big detective answered.

De Grandin's smiling face went serious. "I have the fear that her fate was the same as that of Monsieur Cogswell's first wife. You recall how she was mauled to death by a gorilla? I should not be surprized if that ten-times-cursed Everton gave the poor girl to his great ape for sport when he had tired of torturing her. Tomorrow you would be advised to take a squad of diggers to that chapel of the suicides and have them search for her remains. I doubt not you will find them."

"An' would ye tell me one thing more, sor?"

"A hundred, if you wish."

"Why did th' gorilly kill th' Sidlo gur-rl instead o' carryin' her away?"

"The human mind is difficult enough to plumb; I fear I cannot look into an ape's mentality and see the thoughts he thinks, *mon vieux*. When he had stolen Mademoiselle Lefètre and borne her to the ruined chapel of the suicides the ape turned rebel. He did not go back to his cage as he was wont to do, but set out on another expedition. His small mind worked in circles. Twice he had taken women from the Shelton School, he seems to have enjoyed the pastime, so went back for more. He paused upon the roof-ledge, wondering where he should seek next for victims, and to him through the damp night air the pungent scent the Sidlo girl affected came. *Voilà*, down into the room he dropped, intent on seizing her. She was well built and strongly muscled. Also she was very frightened. She did not swoon, nor struggle in his grasp, but fought him valiantly. Perhaps she hurt him with her pointed fingernails. *En tout cas*, she angered him, and so he broke her neck in peevish anger, as a child might break its doll, and, again child-like, he flung the broken toy away.

"It was a pity, too. She was so young, so beautiful, so vital. That she should die before she knew the joys of love—*morbleu*, it saddens me. Trowbridge, my friend, can you sit there thus and see me suffer so? Refill my glass, I beg you!"

The House Where Time Stood Still

T HE FEBRUARY WIND WAS holding carnival outside, wrenching at the window fastenings, whooping round the corners of the house, roaring bawdy chansons down the chimney flues. But we were comfortable enough, with the study curtains drawn, the lamps aglow and two fresh oak logs upon the andirons taking up the blazing torch their dying predecessors flung them. Pleased with himself until his smugness irritated me, Jules de Grandin smiled down at the toe of his slim patent-leather pump, took a fresh sip of whisky-soda, and returned to the argument.

"But no, my friend," he told me, "medicine the art is necessarily at odds with medicine the science. As followers of Æsculapius and practitioners of the healing art we are concerned with individual cases, in alleviating suffering in the patient we attend. We regard him as a person, a complete and all-important entity. Our chief concern for the time being is to bring about his full recovery, or if that is not possible, to spare him pain as far as in our power lies, *n'est-ce-pas?*"

"Of course," I rejoined. "That's the function of the doctor—"

"*Mais non.* Your term is poorly chosen. That is the function of the physician, the healer, the practitioner of medicine as an art. The doctor, the learned savant, the experimenting scientist, has a larger field. He is unconcerned with man the individual, the *subspecies aeternitatis.* Him he cannot see for bones and cells and tissues where micro-organisms breed and multiply to be a menace to the species as a whole. He deals with large, great bodies like—"

"Sir Haddingway Ingraham an' Sergeant Costello, if ye plaze, sors," interrupted Nora McGinnis from the study entrance.

"Yes, *parbleu*, exactly like them!" de Grandin burst out laughing as the two six-footers hesitated at the doorway, unable to come through together, undecided which should take precedence.

"Regard, observe them, if you please, Friend Trowbridge!" he ordered as he looked at the big visitors. "*Quel type, mais quel type; morbleu, c'est incroyable!*"

To say that the big Briton and the even bigger Celt were of a common type seemed little less than fantastic. Ingraham—Sir Haddingway Ingraham Jamison Ingraham, known to all his friends familiarly as Hiji, was as typically an Englishman of the Empire Builder sort as could be found in literature or on the stage. So big that he was almost gigantic, his face was long and narrow, high-cheeked, almost saddle-leather tanned, with little splayed-out lines of sun-wrinkles about the outer corners of his eyes. His hair was iron-gray, center-parted, smooth as only brilliantine and careful brushing could make it, and by contrast his small military mustache was as black as the straight brows that framed his deep-set penetrating hazel eyes. His dinner clothes were cut and draped with such perfection that they might as well have borne the label Saville Row in letters half a foot in height; and in his martial bearing, his age and his complexion, you could read the record of his service to his king and country as if campaign ribbons had adorned his jacket: the Aisne, Neuve Chapelle, the second Marne, and after that the jungle or the veldt of British Africa, or maybe India. He was English as roast beef or Yorkshire pudding, but not the kind of Briton who could be at home in London or the Isles, or anywhere within a thousand miles of Nelson's monument, save for fleeting visits.

Costello was a perfect contrast. Fair as the other was dark, he still retained his ruddy countenance and smooth, fresh Irish skin, although his once-red hair was almost white. If Hiji was six feet in height the sergeant topped him by a full two inches; if the Englishman weighed fourteen stone the Celt outweighed him by a good ten pounds; if Ingraham's lean, brown, well-manicured hand could strike a blow to floor an ox, Costello's big, smooth-knuckled fist could stun a charging buffalo. His clothes were good material, but lacked elegance of cut and were plainly worn more for protective than for decorative purposes. Smooth-shaved, round-cheeked, he might have been an actor or a politician or, if his collar were reversed, a very worldly, very knowing, very Godly bishop, or a parish priest with long experience of the fallibility of human nature and the infinite compassion of the Lord.

Thus their dissidence. Amazingly, there was a subtle similarity. Each moved with positively tigerish grace that spoke of controlled power and almost limitless reserves of strength, and in the eyes of each there was that quality of seeing and appraising and recording everything they looked at, and of looking at everything within their range of vision without appearing to take note of anything. As usual, de Grandin was correct.

Each bore resemblance to the other, each was the perfect type of the born man-hunter, brave, shrewd, resourceful and implacable.

"But it is good to see you, *mes amis!*" de Grandin told them as he gave a hand to each and waved them to a seat beside the fire. "On such a night your company is like a breath of spring too long delayed. Me, I am delighted!"

"Revoltin' little hypocrite, ain't he?" Hiji turned to Costello, who nodded gloomy acquiescence.

"*Comment?* A hypocrite—I?" Amazement and quick-gathering wrath puckered the small Frenchman's face as if he tasted something unendurably sour. "How do you say—"

"Quite," Hiji cut in heavily. "Hypocrite's the word, and nothin' less. Pretendin' to be glad to see us, and not offerin' us a drink! On such a night, too. Disgustin' is the word for it."

"*Mea culpa, mea maxima culpa!*" wailed de Grandin. "Oh, I am humiliated, I am desolated, I am—"

"Never mind expressions of embarrassment, you little devil. Pour that whisky; don't be sparin' o' your elbow!"

In a moment Scotch and soda bubbled in the glasses. Ice tinkled in Costello's. "None in mine, you blighted little thimblerigger; d'ye want to take up space reserved for whisky?" Hiji forbade when de Grandin would have dropped an ice-cube in his glass.

Refreshed, we faced each other in that silence of comradery which only men who have shared common perils know.

"And now, what brings you out on such a night?" de Grandin asked. "Smile and grin and play the innocent as you will, I am not to be imposed upon. I know you for the sybarites you are. Neither of you would thrust his great nose out of doors tonight unless compulsion forced him. Speak, thou great ungainly ones, thou hulking oafs, thou species of a pair of elephants. I wait your babbling confidences, but I do not wait with patience. Not I. My patience is as small as my thirst is great—and may I never see tomorrow's sunrise if I see it sober!"

Hiji drained his glass and held it out to be refilled. "It's about young Southerby," he answered gloomily. "The poisonous little scorpion's managed to get himself lost. He's disappeared; vanished."

"Ah? One is desolated at the news." De Grandin leant back in his chair and grinned at Ingraham and Costello. "I am completely ravaged at intelligence of this one's disappearance, for since I have abandoned criminal investigation in all its phases, I can look upon the case objectively, and see how seriously it affects you. May I prescribe an anodyne?" he motioned toward the syphon and decanter.

"Drop it, you little imp o' Satan!" Ingraham replied gruffly. "This is serious business. Yesterday we had a matter of the greatest importance—and secrecy— to be transmitted to the embassy in Washington. There wasn't a king's messenger available, and we did not dare trust the papers to the post; so when young Southerby—dratted little idiot!—stepped in and told the Chief he'd do his Boy Scout's good deed by runnin' the dispatches down to Washington, they took him on. He's been knocking round the consulate a year and more, gettin' into everybody's hair, and the Chief thought it would be a holiday for the staff to get him out from under foot awhile. The little blighter does know how to drive a car, I'll say that for him; and he's made the trip to Washington so often that he knows the road as well as he knows Broadway. Twelve hours ought to do the trip and leave him time for meals to spare, but the little hellion seems to have rolled right off the earth. There ain't a trace o' hide or hair of him—"

"But surely, you need not concern yourself with it," de Grandin interrupted. "This is a matter for the police; the good Costello or the state constabulary, or the Federal agents."

"And the newspapers and the wireless, not to mention the cinema," broke in Hiji with a frown. "Costello's not here officially. As my friend he's volunteered to help me out. As a policeman he knows nothin' of the case. You'll appreciate my position when I tell you that these papers were so confidential that they're not supposed to exist at all, and we simply can't report Southerby's disappearance to the police, nor let it leak out that he's missin' or was carryin' anything to Wash-ington. All the same, we've got to find those precious papers. The Chief made a bad blunder entrustin' 'em to such a scatterbrain, and if we don't get 'em back his head is goin' to fall. Maybe his won't be the only one—"

"You are involved, my friend?" De Grandin's small eyes widened with con-cern.

"In a way, yes. I should have knocked the little blighter silly the minute that he volunteered, or at least have told the Chief he wasn't to be trusted. As it was, I rather urged him to accept the offer."

"Then what do we wait for? Let us don our outdoor clothes and go to seek this missing young man. You he may elude, but I am Jules de Grandin; though he hide in the lowest workings of a mine, or scale the sky in a balloon—"

"Easy on, son," Hiji thrust a hand out to the little Frenchman. "There's nothin' much that we can do tonight."

"I've already done some gum-shoe wor-rk, sor," Costello volunteered. "We've traced 'im through th' Holland Tunnels an' through Newark an' th' Amboys and New Brunswick. Th' trail runs out just th' other side o' Cranberry. It wuz four o'clock when he left New York, an' a storm blew up about five, so he musta slowed down, for it wuz close to eight when he passed Cranberry, headed for Phillydelphia, an'"—he spread his hands—"there th' trail ends, sor, like as if he's vanished into thin air, as th' felly says."

De Grandin lit a cigarette and leant back in his chair, drumming soundlessly on the table where his glass stood, narrowing his eyes against the smoke as he stared fixedly at the farther wall.

"There was mingled rain and snow—sleet—on all the roads last night," he murmured. "The traffic is not heavy in the early evening, for pleasure cars have reached their destinations and the nightly motorcade of freight trucks does not start till sometime near eleven. He would have had a lonely, slippery, dangerous road to travel, this one. Has inquiry been made for wrecks?"

"That it has, sor. He couldn't 'a' had a blowout widout our knowin' of it. His car wuz a Renault sports model, about as inconspicuous as a ellyphunt on a Jersey road, an' that should make it a cinch to locate 'im. That's what's drivin' me nuts, too. If a young felly in a big red car can evaporate—howly Mither, I wonder now, could that have any bearin'—" He broke off suddenly, his blue eyes opened wide, a look almost of shocked amazement on his face.

"A very pleasant pastime that, my friend," de Grandin put in acidly as the big detective remained silent. "Will you not confide your cause for wonder to us? We might wish to wonder, also."

"Eh? O' course, sor." Costello shook his shoulders with a motion reminiscent of a dog emerging from the water. "I wuz just wonderin'—"

"We gathered as much—"

"If sumpin' else that's happened, recently, could have a bearin' on this case. Th' Missin' Persons Bureau has had lookouts posted several times widin th' past three months fer persons last seen just th' other side o' Cranberry—on th' Phillydelphia side, that is. O' course, you know how so many o' these disappearances is. Mostly they disappear because they wants to. But these wuz not th' sort o' cases ye'd think that of. A truck driver wuz th' first, a fine young felly wid a wife an' two kids: then a coupla college boys, an' a young gur-rl from New York named Perinchief. Th' divil a one of 'em had a reason for vamoosin', but they all did. Just got in their cars an' drove along th' road till they almost reached Cranberry, then—bingo! no one ever heard o' one of 'em again. It don't seem natural-like. Th' state police an' th' Middlesex authorities has searched for 'em, but th' devil a trace has been turned up. Nayther they nor their cars have been seen or heard from. D'ye think that mebbe there is sumpin' more than coincidence here?"

"It may not be probable, but it is highly possible," de Grandin nodded. "As you say, when people disappear, it is often by their own volition, and that several persons should be missed in a short period may quite easily be coincidental. But when several people disappear in a particular locality, that is something else again.

"Is there not something we can do tonight?" he turned to Ingraham.

"No," the Englishman replied, "I don't believe there is. It's blacker than the inside of a cow out there, and we can't afford to attract attention lookin' for the little blighter with flashlights. Suppose we do a move tomorrow before dawn and see what we can pick up in the neighborhood where Southerby was last reported."

DAWN, A RAW, COLD February dawn well nigh as colorless and uninviting as a spoiled oyster, was seeping through the lowering storm clouds as we drove across the bridge at Perth Amboy and headed south toward Cranberry. Hiji and

Costello occupied the rear seat; de Grandin rode beside me, chin buried in his greatcoat collar, hands thrust deep in his pockets.

"See here," I asked him as an idea struck me, "d'ye suppose this lad has skipped? You heard Hiji say how valuable the papers he was carrying are, and apparently he begged to be allowed to carry them. These youngsters in the consular and diplomatic service usually live beyond their means, and sometimes they do queer things if they're tempted by a large amount of cash."

"I wish I could believe that," he returned, cowering lower in his seat. "It would have saved me the discomfort of emerging from a warm bed into a chill morning. But I know *les anglais*, my friend. They are often stupid, generally dull; socially they are insufferable in many cases, but when it comes to loyalty Gibraltar is less firm. Your English gentleman would as soon consider eating breakfast without marmalade as selling out his honor or running from an enemy or doing anything original. Yes."

A little light, but no sunshine, had strengthened in the sky when we drew up beside the roadway a half-mile beyond Cranberry. "All right," Hiji called as he dismounted; "we might as well start here and comb the terrain. We have a fairly good line on our bird up to this point, and—hullo, there's a prospect!"

He nodded toward a corduroyed Italian, obviously a laborer, who was trudging slowly up the road walking to the left and facing traffic, as pedestrians who hope to survive have to do on country highways.

"*Com' esta?*" de Grandin called. "You live near here?"

The young man drew his chin up from his tightly buttoned reefer and flashed a smile at him. "*Si, signor*," he returned courteously, and raised a finger to his cap. "I live just there, me."

With a mittened hand he waved vaguely toward a patch of bottom land whence rose a cumulus of early-morning smoke.

"And you work long hours, one surmises?"

Again the young man smiled. "*Si*, all day I worka; mornin', night, all time—"

"So you walk home in darkness?"

A smile and nod confirmed his surmise.

"Sometimes the motors cause you trouble, make you jump back from the road, *hein?*"

"Not moch," the young Italian grinned. "In mornin' when I come to work they not yet come. At night when I come back they all 'ave gone away. But sometimes I 'ave to jomp queek. Las' night I 'ave to jomp away from a beega rad car—"

"I think we are upon the scent, my friends!" de Grandin whispered. Aloud: "How was that? Could he not see you?"

The young man shrugged his shoulders. "I theenk 'e craz'," he answered. "Always I walka dees side a road, so I can see car come, but dees a one 'e come from other side, an' almost bang me down. Come ver' fast, too, not look where he go. Down there"—again he waved a vague hand down the road—"'e run into da woods. I theenk 'e get hurt, maybe, bot I not go see. I ver' tired, me, and want for to get 'ome."

De Grandin pursed his lips and rummaged in his pocket for a coin. "You say the young man left the road and ran into the woods? Did you see his car?"

"*Si, signor.* Heef I don' see heem I not be 'ere now. Eet was a beega rad car, lika dose we see in old contry, not small like dose we see 'ere."

"And where did this one leave the road?"

"You see dose talla tree down by de 'ill op dere?"

"Perfectly."

"'E go off road about a honnerd meters farther on."

"Thank you, my peerless one," the Frenchman smiled, as he handed the young man a half-dollar. "You have been most helpful." To us: "I think that we are on the trail at last."

"But I can't think that Southerby would have stopped to take a drink, much less get drunk," objected Ingraham, as we hastened toward the point the young Italian indicated. "He knew how devilishly important those things were—"

"Perhaps he was not drunk," the Frenchman cut in cryptically as we walked toward the little copse of evergreens which lay back from the road.

An earth cart-track, deeply rutted with the winter rains, ran through the unkempt field which fringed the road and wound into the heart of the small wood lot, stopping at the edge of a creek which ran clattering between abrupt banks of yellow clay.

"Be gob," Costello looked down at the swirling ochre water, "if yer little friend ran inter this, he shure got one good duckin', Hiji."

"*Eh bien*, someone has run into it, and not so long ago," de Grandin answered, pointing to a double row of tire tracks. "Observe them, if you will. They run right down the bank, and there is nothing showing that the car was stopped or that its occupant alighted."

"By Jove, you're right, Frenchy," Ingraham admitted. "See here"—he indicated a pair of notches in the bank—"here's where he went down. Last night's storm has almost washed 'em away, but there the tracks are. The blighted little fool! Wonder how deep, it is?"

"That is easily determined," de Grandin drew his knife and began hacking down a sapling growing at the water's edge. "Now"—he probed experimentally—"one may surmise that—*morbleu!*"

"What is it?" we exclaimed in chorus.

"The depth, my friends. See, I have thrust this stick six feet beneath the surface, but I have not yet felt bottom. Let us see how it is here." He poked his staff into the stream some ten feet beyond his original soundings and began to switch it tentatively back and forth. "Ah, here the bottom is, I think—*non*, it is a log or—*mon Dieu*, attend me, *mes amis!*"

We clustered around him as he probed the turbulent yellow water. Slowly he angled with his pole, swishing it back and forth, now with, now against the rushing current, then twirled it between his hands as if to entangle something in the protruding stubs of the roughly hacked-off boughs.

"*Ha!*" he heaved quickly upward, and as the stick came clear we saw some dark, sodden object clinging to its tip, rising sluggishly to the surface for a moment, then breaking free and sinking slowly back again.

"You saw it?" he demanded.

"Yes," I answered, and despite myself I felt my breath come quicker. "It looked like a coat or something."

"Indubitably it was something," he agreed. "But what?"

"An old overcoat?" I hazarded, leaning over his shoulder to watch.

"Or undercoat," he replied, panting with exertion as he fished and fished again for the elusive object. "Me, I think it was an—ah, here it is!" With a quick tug he brought up a large oblong length of checkered cloth and dragged it out upon the bank.

"Look at him, my Hiji," he commanded. "Do you recognize him?"

"I think I do," the Englishman responded gravely. "It's the tartan of the clan MacFergis. Southerby had some Scottish blood and claimed alliance with the clan. He used that tartan for a motor rug—"

"*Exactement.* Nor is that all, my friend. The minute I began exploring with this stick I knew it was not bottom that I touched. I could feel the outlines of some object, and feel something roll and give beneath my pressure every now and then. I am certain that a motor car lies hidden in this stream. What else is there we cannot surely say, but—"

"Why not make sure, sor?" Costello broke in. "We've found th' car, an' if young Misther Southerby is drownded there's nothin' to be hid. Why not git a tow-line an' drag whativer's in there out?"

"Your advice is excellent," de Grandin nodded. "Do you stay here and watch the spot, my sergeant. Hiji and I will go out to the road and see if we can hail a passing truck to drag whatever lies beneath that water out. Trowbridge, my friend, will you be kind enough to go to yonder house"—he pointed to a big building set among a knot of pines that crowned a hill which swept up from the road—"and ask them if they have a car and tow-line we may borrow?"

THE STORM WHICH HAD been threatening for hours burst with berserk fury as I plodded up the unkempt, winding road that scaled the hill on which the old house stood enshrouded in a knot of black-boughed pine trees writhing in the wind. The nearer I drew to the place the less inviting it appeared. At the turning of the driveway from which almost all the gravel had been washed long since, a giant evergreen bent wrestling with the gale, its great arms creaking, groaning, shaken but invincible against the storm. Rain lashed against the walls of weathered brick; heavy shutters swung and banged and crashed, wrenched loose from their turn-buckles by the fury of the wind; the blast tore at the vines that masked the house-front till they writhed and shuddered as in torment; even the shadowy glimmer of dim light glowing through the transom set above the door seemed less an invitation than a portent, as if warning me that something dark and stealthy moved behind the panels. I pulled my hat down farther on my brow and pushed the collar of my greatcoat higher up around my ears.

"Someone's up and stirring," I told myself aloud as I glanced up at the feeble glow above the door. "They can't very well refuse to help us." Thus for the bolstering of my morale. Actually, I was almost shaking with a sort of evil prescience, and wanted more than anything to turn and run until I reached the roadway where my friends were waiting.

"Come, man, don't be a blithering fool!" I bade myself, and seized the rusty iron knocker stapled to the weather-blasted door.

There was something reassuring in the shock of iron upon iron. Here was reality; just a commonplace old farmhouse, run down and ruinous, but natural and earthy. I struck the knocker twice more, making it sound sharply through the moaning wind and hissing rain, waited for a moment, then struck again.

What sort of response I'd expected I had no accurate idea. From the ruinous appearance of the place I had surmised it had been used as a multiple dwelling, housing several families of day-laborers, perhaps a little colony of squatters washed up by the rising tide of unemployment which engulfed our centers of industry. Perhaps a family of discouraged farmer folk used a portion of it and closed off the rest. Had a Negro or Italian answered my impatient knock I should not have been startled, but when the door swung open and a tall man in semi-military uniform looked at me with polite inquiry I was fairly breathless with surprise. A liveried chauffeur opening the door of the old ruin seemed somehow as utterly incongruous as a Zulu chieftain donning dinner-clothes for tribal ceremonies.

His expression of inquiry deepened as I told my errand. It was not until I had exhausted five minutes in futile repetitions that I realized he understood no word I spoke.

"See here," I finally exclaimed, "if you don't understand English, is there anybody here who does? I'm in a hurry, and—"

"In-gliss?" he repeated, shaking his head doubtfully. "No In-gliss 'ere."

"No," I responded tartly, "and I don't suppose you've any Eskimos or Sioux here, either. I don't want an Englishman. I have one already, and a Frenchman and an Irishman, to boot. What I want is someone who can help me haul a motor car out of the brook. Understand? Motor car—sunk—brook—pull out!" I went through an elaborate pantomime of raising a submerged vehicle from the muddy little stream.

His sallow, rat-like countenance lit up with a sudden gleam as I completed my dumb-show, and he motioned me to enter.

The door had seemed so old and weather-weakened that I'd feared my knocking might shake loose a panel, but it swung behind me with a solid bang, and the clicking of the lock that sounded as the portal closed struck a highly modern and efficient note.

Barely over the threshold, I came to a full stop. Something faintly irritating, like a swarm of small black ants, seemed crawling up my neck and on my scalp. Instinct, untrammeled and unverbalized, was giving warning: "Here is peril!" But reason scoffed at instinct: "What peril can there be in an old farmhouse burdened with decrepitude, almost on the verge of falling in upon itself?"

But as I stared about me I realized the look of desolation and decay was but a shell of camouflage about a wholly different condition. New the place might not have been, but its interior repair was perfect. The air was heavy, scented like the atmosphere that permeates cathedrals after celebration of the Mass—the sharp and sweet, yet heavy, scent of incense borne from censers swung by priests.

The floor was brightly waxed and polished, the walls encrusted with a terra-cotta colored lacquer and, as church walls are embossed with stations of the Cross, were pitted with two rows of little niches framed in polished black wood. Before each framed recess there burned a little lamp, something like a sanctus light, which shed a wavering fulgent spot upon the image nested in the cavity. Each statuette was wrought in gleaming white stone, and though each differed from the others, all had one thing in common: they were uncompleted. Scarcely human, yet not exactly bestial, were the beings portrayed. Here a creature which seemed part ape, part man, was struggling with strained muscles to emerge from the rough ashlar from which the sculptor had but partly hewn it; there a female figure, perfect as to head and throat, seemed melting at the shoulders into a vague amorphousness as misshapen and unsymmetrical as the bloated body of an octopus shorn of tentacles, and hid her grief and horror-stricken face behind an arm clipped off at the elbow. Here was a head as bald of crown as any shaven-pated mediæval monk, but with a face obscured by long and matted hair, waving wildly as a harpy's tresses whipped by tempest-winds. Beyond it was a niche in which a scarcely-started group of statuary rested. Vague and almost formless as a wisp of shifting cloud, it still showed outlines of a pair of figures, obviously masculine and feminine, as far as faces were concerned, but with bodies bulbous as the barrel of a squid, staring at each other with a look of surprised consternation, of terror mixed with loathing, as if each saw in the other a mirroring of his deformity, and abhorred his vis-à-vis as a reminder of his hideousness.

"Nightmare sculpture, hewn from dreams of madness . . ." the quotation flashed across my mind as I followed the tall man in livery down the hallway.

My guide rapped at a door set at the rear of the corridor, waited for a moment, then stood aside to let me enter. Facing me across a flat-topped desk sat a small, stoop-shouldered man, reading from a large book through a pair of Crookes'-lens spectacles.

"Doctor," my conductor introduced in perfect English, "this gentleman came knocking at our door a few moments ago, going through some most extraordinary antics and mumbling something about a motor car sunk in our brook."

I looked from one of them to the other in utter, stupefied amazement, but my astonishment increased tenfold at the seated man's reply. "Stravinsky," he said sternly, looking at me through the purplish-black of his thick glasses, "how dare you leave your quarters without permission? Go upstairs with Mishkin at once."

"I beg your pardon," I stammered, "my name's not Stravinsky. I'm Doctor Samuel Trowbridge of Harrisonville, and some friends of mine and I need help in raising a sunken motor car from the brook that runs between the highway and your place. If you'll be kind enough to tell your chauffeur to—"

"That will do," he broke in sharply. "We've heard all that before. Go to your room at once, or I shall have to order you into a strait-waistcoat again."

"See here," I began in a rage, "I don't know what this nonsense means, but if you think for one moment—"

My protest died half uttered. A pair of sinewy hands seized me by the elbows, drawing my arms sharply to my sides, a wide strap of woven webbing was thrown about my body, like a lasso, pinioning both elbows, drawn tightly through a buckle and snapped into position. I was securely bound and helpless as ever captive was.

"Confound you!" I cried. "Take this devilish harness off me! What d'ye mean—"

Something smooth and soft and smothering, like a piece of wadded silk, was thrust against my face, shutting out the light, covering mouth and nose; a sickly-sweet, pungent odor assailed my nostrils, the floor seemed suddenly to heave and billow like a sea lashed by the wind, and I felt my knees give way beneath me slowly.

"FEELING BETTER, NOW, STRAVINSKY?" the suave, low voice of the round-shouldered man woke me from a troubled sleep.

I sat up, staring round me stupidly. I lay upon a narrow iron cot of the sort used in the free wards of hospitals, uncovered except for a thin cotton blanket. The bed stood in a little cubbyhole not more than six feet square, and was the only article of furniture in the apartment. A small window, heavily barred, let in a little light and a great quantity of cold air together with occasional spatterings of rain. Directly facing me was a stout wooden door made without panels but fitted with a barred wicket through which my captor looked at me with a rather gentle, pitying smile. Close behind him, grinning with what seemed to be sadistic malice, was the liveried man who'd let me in.

"You'll be sorry for this!" I threatened, leaping from the cot. "I don't know who you are, but you'll know who *I* am before you're done with me—"

"Oh, yes, I know perfectly who you are," he corrected in a gentle, soothing voice. "You are Abraham Stravinsky, sixty-five years old, once in business as a cotton converter but adjudged a lunatic by the orphans' court three weeks ago and placed in my care by your relatives. Poor fellow"—he turned sorrowfully to his companion—"he still thinks he's a physician, Mishkin. Sad case, isn't it?"

He regarded me again, and I thought I saw a glimmer of amusement in his solicitous expression as he asked: "Wouldn't you like some breakfast? You've been sleeping here since we had to use harsh measures day before yesterday. You must be hungry, now. A little toast, some eggs, a cup of coffee—"

"I'm not hungry," I cut in, "and you know I'm not Stravinsky. Let me out of here at once, or—"

"Now, isn't that too bad?" he asked, again addressing his companion. "He doesn't want his breakfast. Never mind, he will, in time." To me:

"The treatment we pursue in cases such as yours is an unique one, Stravinsky. It inhibits the administration of food, or even water, for considerable periods of time. Indeed, I often find it necessary to withhold nourishment indefinitely. Sometimes the patient succumbs under treatment, to be sure; but then his insanity is cured, and we can't have everything, can we? After all, Stravinsky, the mission of the sanitarium is to cure the disease from which the patient suffers, isn't it, Stravinsky?

"Make yourself comfortable, Stravinsky. Your trouble will be over in a little while. If it were only food you are required to forgo your period of waiting might be longer, but prohibition of water shortens it materially—Stravinsky."

The constant repetition of the name he'd forced upon me was like caustic rubbed in a raw wound. "Damn you," I screamed, as I dashed myself against the door, "my name's not Stravinsky, and you know it! You know it—you *know it!*"

"Dear, dear, Stravinsky," he reproved, smiling gently at my futile rage. "You mustn't overtax yourself. You can't last long if you permit yourself to fly into such frenzies. Of course, your name's Stravinsky. Isn't it, Mishkin?" He turned for confirmation to the other.

"Of course," his partner echoed. "Shall we look in on the others?"

They turned away, chuckling delightedly, and I heard their footsteps clatter down the bare floor toward the other end of the corridor on which my room faced.

In a few minutes I heard voices raised in heated argument, seemingly from a room almost directly underneath my cell. Then a door slammed and there came the sound of dully, rhythmically repeated blows, as if a strap were being struck across a bed's footboard. Finally, a wail, hopeless and agonized as if wrung from tortured flesh against the protest of an undefeated spirit: "Yes, yes, anything— *anything!*"

The commotion ceased abruptly, and in a little while I heard the clack of boot heels as they went upon their rounds.

THE HOURS PASSED LIKE eons clipped from Hell's eternity. There was absolutely no way to amuse myself, for the room—cell would be a better term for it—contained no furniture except the bed. The window, unglazed, small and high-set, faced an L of the house; so there was neither sky nor scenery to be looked at, and the February wind drove gusts of gelid rain into the place until I cowered in the corner to escape its chilling wetness as though it were a live, malignant thing. I had been stripped to shirt and trousers, even shoes and stockings taken from me, and in a little while my teeth were chattering with cold. The anesthetic they had used to render me unconscious still stung the mucous membranes of my mouth and nose, and my tongue was roughened by a searing thirst. I wrenched a metal button from my trousers, thrust it in my mouth and sucked at it, gaining some slight measure of relief, and so, huddled in the sleazy blanket, shivering with cold and almost mad with thirst, I huddled on the bed for hour after endless hour till I finally fell into a doze.

How long I crouched there trembling I have no idea, nor could I guess how long I'd slept when a hand fell on my shoulder and a light flashed blindingly into my face.

"Get up!" I recognized the voice as coming from the man called Mishkin, and as I struggled to a sitting posture, still blinking from the powerful flashlight's glare, I felt a broad web strap, similar to the one with which I had at first been pinioned, dropped deftly on my arms and drawn taut with a jerk.

"Come," my jailer seized the loose end of my bond and half dragged, half led me from my cell, down the stairs and through a lower hall until we paused before a door which had been lacquered brilliant red. He thrust the panels back with one hand, seized me by the shoulder with the other, and shoved me through the opening so violently that, bound as I was, I almost sprawled upon my face.

The apartment into which I stumbled was in strong contrast to the cell in which I'd lain. It was a large room, dimly lighted and luxurious. The walls were gumwood, unvarnished but rubbed down with oil until their surface gleamed like satin. The floor of polished yellow pine was scattered with bright Cossack rugs, barbarian with primary colors. A sofa and deep easy-chairs were done in brick-red crushed leather. A log fire blazed and hissed beneath the gumwood over-mantel and the blood-orange of its light washed out across the varnished floor and ebbed and flowed like rising and receding wavelets on the dark-red walls. A parchment-shaded lamp was on the table at the center of the room, making it a sort of island in the shadows, and by its light I looked into the face of the presiding genius of this house of mystery.

He had taken off his dark-lensed glasses, and I saw his eyes full on me. As I met their level, changeless stare I felt as if the last attachments of my viscera had broken. Everything inside me had come loose, and I was weak to sickness with swift-flooding, nameless terror.

In a lifetime's practice as physician one sees many kinds of eyes, eyes of health and eyes diseased, the heaven-lighted eyes of the young mother with her first-born at her breast, the vacant eye of fever, the stricken eye of one with sure foreknowledge of impending death upon him, the criminal's eye, the idiot's lack-luster eye, the blazing eye of madness. But never had I seen a pair of eyes like these in a human face. Beast's eyes they were, unwinking, topaz, gleaming, the kind of eye you see in a house cat's round, smug face, or staring at you speculatively through the bars that barricade the carnivores' dens at the zoo. As I looked, fascinated, in these bestial eyes set so incongruously in a human countenance, I felt—I knew—that there was nothing this man would not do if he were minded to it. There was nothing in those yellow, ebony-pupiled eyes to which one could appeal; no plea addressed to pity, decency or morals would affect the owner of these eyes; he was as callous to such things as is the cat that plays so cunningly and gently with a ball one moment, and pounces on a hapless bird or mouse so savagely the next. Feline ferocity, and feline fickleness, looked at me from those round, bright, yellow eyes.

"Forgive the lack of light, please, Doctor Trowbridge," he begged in his soft, almost purring voice. "The fact is I am sensitive to it, highly photophobic. That has its compensations, though," he added with a smile. "I am also noctiloptic and have a supernormal acuity of vision in darkness, like a cat—or a tiger."

As he spoke he snapped the switch of the desk lamp, plunging the apartment into shadow relieved only by the variable fire-glow. Abruptly as a pair of miniature motor lights switched on, the twin disks of his eyes glowed at me through the dimness with a shining phosphorescent gleam of green.

"That is why I wear the Crookes'-lensed glasses in the daytime," he added with an almost soundless laugh. "You won't mind if we continue in the darkness for a little while." The vivid glow of his eyes seemed to brighten as he spoke, and I felt fresh chills of horror ripple up my spine.

Silence fell, and lengthened. Somewhere in the darkness at my back a clock ticked slowly, measuring off the seconds, minutes. . . . I caught myself remembering a passage from Marlowe's *Doctor Faustus*:

O lente, lente currite, noctis equi!
The stars move still, time runs, the clock will strike,
. . . and Faustus must be damn'd!

The shadowed room seemed full to overflowing with manifested, personalized evil as the magician's cell had been that night so long ago in Wurtemberg when Mephistopheles appeared to drag his screaming soul to everlasting torment. Had the floor opened at my feet and the red reflection of the infernal pit shone on us, I do not think I should have been surprised.

I almost screamed when he spoke. "Do you remember—have you heard of—Friedrich Friedrichsohn, Doctor Trowbridge?"

The name evoked no memories. "No," I answered.

"You lie. Everyone—even you half-trained American physicians—knows of the great Friedrichsohn!"

His taunt stung a mnemonic chord. Dimly, but with increasing clarity, recollection came. Friedrich Friedrichsohn, brilliant anatomist, authority on organic evolution . . . colonel-surgeon in the army which Franz Josef sent to meet its doom on the Piave . . . shellshocked . . . invalided home to take charge of a hospital at Innsbruck—now memory came in a swift gush. The doctors in Vienna didn't talk about it, only whispered rumors went the rounds of schools and clinics, but the fragmentary stories told about the work they'd found him at, matching bits of shattered bodies, grafting amputated limbs from some to others' blood-fresh amputation-wounds, making monsters hideous as Hindoo idols or the dreadful thing that Frankenstein concocted out of sweepings from dissecting-rooms. . . . "He died in an insane asylum at Korneusburg," I replied.

"Wrong! Wrong as your diagnoses are in most instances, *mein lieber Doktor*. I am Friedrich Friedrichsohn, and I am very far from dead. They had many things to think of when the empire fell to pieces, and they forgot me. I did not find it difficult to leave the prison where they'd penned me like a beast, nor have I found it difficult to impose on your credulous authorities. I am duly licensed by your state board as a doctor. A few forged documents were all I needed to secure my permit. I am also the proprietor of a duly licensed sanitarium for the treatment of the insane. I have even taken a few patients. Abraham Stravinsky, suffering from dementia præcox is—was—one of them. He died shortly after you arrived, but his family have not yet been notified. They will be in due course, and you—but let us save that for a later time.

"The work in which I was engaged when I was interrupted was most fascinating, Doctor. Until you try it you cannot imagine how many utterly delightful and surprising combinations can be made from the comparatively few parts offered by the human body. I have continued my researches here, and while some of my experiments have unfortunately failed, I have succeeded almost past my expectations in some others. I should like to show you them before—I'm sure you'll find them interesting, Doctor."

"You're mad!" I gasped, struggling at the strap that bound my arms.

I could feel him smiling at me through the dark. "So I have been told. I'm not mad, really, but the general belief in my insanity has its compensations. For example, if through some deplorable occurrence now unforeseen I should be interrupted at my work here, your ignorant police might not feel I was justified in all I've done. The fact that certain subjects have unfortunately expired in the process of being remodeled by me might be considered grounds for prosecuting me for murder. That is where the entirely erroneous belief that I am mad would have advantages. Restrained I might be, but in a hospital, not a tomb. I have never found it difficult to escape from hospitals. After a few months' rest I should escape again if I were ever apprehended. Is not that an advantage? How many so-called sane men have *carte blanche* to do exactly as they please, to kill as many people as they choose, and in such manner as seems most amusing, knowing all the while they are immune to the electric chair or the gallows? I am literally above the law, *mein lieber Kollege.*

"Mishkin," he ordered the attendant who stood at my elbow, "go tell Pedro we should like some music while we make our tour of inspection.

"Mishkin was confined with me at Korneusburg," he explained, as the clatter of the other's boot heels died away beyond the door. "When I left there I brought him with me. They said he was a homicidal maniac, but I have cured his mania—as much as I desired. He is a faithful servant and quite an efficient helper, Doctor Trowbridge. In other circumstances I might find it difficult to handle him, but his work with me provides sufficient outlets for his—shall we call it eccentricity? Between experiments he is as tractable as a well-trained beast. Of course, he has to be reminded that the whip is always handy—but that is the technique of good beast-training, *nicht wahr?*

"Ah, our accompaniment has commenced. Shall we go?"

Seizing the end of my tether, he assisted me to rise, held the door for me, and led me out into the hall.

Somewhere upstairs a violin was playing softly, *Di Provenza il Mar,* from *Traviata.* Its plaintive notes were fairly liquid with nostalgic longing:

From land and wave of dear Provence
What hath caused thy heart to roam?
From the love that met thee there,
From thy father and thy home? ...

"He plays well, *nicht wahr?*" Friedrichsohn's soft voice whispered. "Music must have been instinctive with him, otherwise he would not remember—but I forget, you do not know about him, do you?" In the darkness of the corridor his glowing eyes burned into mine.

"Do you remember Viki Boehm, *Herr Doktor?*"

"The Viennese coloratura? Yes. She and her husband Pedro Attavanta were lost when the *Oro Castle* burned—"

His almost silent laughter stopped me. "Lost, *lieber Kollege,* but not as you suppose. They are both here beneath this roof, guests of their loving *Landsmann.*

Oh, they are both well, I assure you; you need have no fears on that score. All my skill and science are completely at their service, night and day. I would not have one of them die for anything!"

We had halted at a narrow lacquered door with a small design like a coronet stenciled on it. In the dim light of a small lamp set high against the wall I saw his face, studious, arrogant, unsmiling. Then a frigid grimace, the mere parody of a smile, congealed upon his lips.

"When I was at the university before the war"—his voice had the hard brittleness of an icicle—"I did Viki Boehm the honor to fall in love with her. I, the foremost scientist of my time, greater in my day than Darwin and Galileo in theirs, offered her my hand and name; she might have shared some measure of my fame. But she refused. Can you imagine it? She rebuffed my condescension. When I told her of the things I had accomplished, using animals for subjects, and, of what I knew I could do later when the war put human subjects in my hands, she shrank from me in horror. She had no scientific vision. She was so naïve she thought the only office of the doctor was to treat the sick and heal the injured. She could not vision the long vistas of pure science, learning and experimenting for their own sakes. For all her winsomeness and beauty she was nothing but a woman. *Pfui!*" He spat the exclamation of contempt at me. Then:

"Ah, but she was beautiful! As lovely as the sunrise after rain, sweet as springtime in the Tyrol, fragile as a—"

"I have seen her," I cut in. "I heard her sing."

"So? You shall see her once again, *Herr Doktor*. You shall look at her and hear her voice. You recall her fragile loveliness, the contours of her arms, her slender waist, her perfect bosom—see!"

He snatched the handle of the door and wrenched it open. Behind the first door was a second, formed of upright bars like those of a jail cell, and behind that was a little cubicle not more than six feet square. A light flashed on as he shoved back the door, and by its glow I saw the place was lined with mirrors, looking-glasses on the walls and ceiling, bright-lacquered composition on the floor; so that from every angle shone reflections, multiplied in endless vistas, of the monstrous thing that squatted in the center of the cell.

In general outline it was like one of those child's toys called a humpty-dumpty, a weighted pear-shaped figure which no matter how it may be laid springs upright automatically. It was some three feet high and more than that in girth, wrinkled, edematous, knobbed and bloated like a toad, with a hide like that of a rhinoceros. If it had feet or legs they were invisible; near its upper end two arm-like stubs extended, but they bore no resemblance to human pectoral limbs. Of human contours it had no trace; rather, it was like a toad enlarged five hundred times, denuded of its rear limbs and—fitted with a human face!

Above the pachydermous mass of shapelessness there poised a visage, a human countenance, a woman's features, finely chiseled, delicate, exquisite in every line and contour with a loveliness so ethereal and unearthly that she seemed more like a fairy being than a woman made of flesh and blood and bone. The cheeks were delicately petal-like, the lips were full and sensitive, the eyes deep blue, the long, fair hair which swept down in a cloven tide of brightness rippled with a charming natural wave. Matched by a body of ethereal charm the face would have been lovely as a poet's dream; attached to that huge tumorous mass of bloated horror it was a thousand times more shocking than if it too had been deformed past resemblance to humanity.

The creature seemed incapable of voluntary locomotion, but it was faced toward us, and as we looked at it, it threw its lovely head back with a sort of slow contortion such as might be made by a half-frozen snake. There was neither horror nor hatred, not even reproach, in the deep-blue eyes that looked at Friedrichsohn. There was instead, it seemed to me, a look of awful resignation, of sorrow which had burned itself to ashes and now could burn no more, of patience which endures past all endurance and now waits calmly for whatever is to be, knowing that the worst is past and nothing which can come can match that which is already accomplished.

"Her case was relatively simple," I heard Friedrichsohn whisper. "Mishkin and I were cruising in a motorboat off shore when the *Oro Castle* burned. We picked her and her husband up, gave them a little drink which rendered them unconscious and brought them here. She gave us very little trouble. First we immobilized her by amputating both legs at the hip; then, in order to make sure that she would not destroy herself or mar her beauty, I took off both arms midway between shoulder and elbow. That left a lovely torso and an even lovelier face to work with.

"You're wondering about her beautifully swollen trunk? Nothing could be simpler, *herr Kollege*. Artificially induced elephantiasis resulted in enormous hypertrophy of the derma and subcutaneous tissue, and we infected and reinfected her until we had succeeded in producing the highly interesting result you observe. It was a little difficult to prevent the hypertrophy spreading to her neck and face, but I am not the greatest doctor in the world for nothing. She suffers nothing now, for the progress of her condition has brought a permanent insensitiveness, but there were several times during the progress of our work when we had to keep her drugged. Elephantiasis begins as an erysipelatous inflammation, you know, and the accompanying lymphangitis and fever are uncomfortable.

"Internally she's quite healthy, and Mishkin makes her face up every day with loving care—too loving, sometimes. I caught him kissing her one day and beat him for an hour with the knout.

"That put a chill upon her ardor. I do not let him feed her. That is my own delightful duty. She bit me once—the lovely little vixen!—but that was long ago. Now she's as tame and gentle as a kitten.

"Ingenious, having her room lined with mirrors, isn't it? No matter which way she may look—up, down or sidewise—she cannot fail to contemplate herself, and compare her present state of loveliness with what she once possessed.

"Viki!" he rattled the bars of her cage. "Sing for our guest, Viki!"

She regarded him a moment with incurious, thoughtful eyes, but there was no recognition in her glance, no sign that she had heard his command.

"Viki!" Again he spoke sharply. "Will you sing, or must we get the branding-iron out?"

I saw a spasm of quick pain and apprehension flash across her face, and: "That is always effective," he told me, with another soft laugh. "You see, we altered Pedro Attavanti, too. Not very much. We only blinded him and moved his scalp down to his face—a very simple little grafting operation—but he went mad while we were working on him. Unfortunately, we were short of anesthetics, and non-Aryans lack the fortitude of the superior races. Once a day we let him have his violin, and he seems quite happy while he plays. When Viki is intractable we have an excellent use for him. She can't bear to see him suffer; so when we bring him to her door and let her watch us burn him with hot irons she does whatever we ask her.

"Shall we get the irons, Viki," he turned to the monstrous woman-headed thing in the cell, "or will you sing?"

The hideous creature threw its lovely head back, breathing deeply. I could see the wattled skin beneath the throat swell like a puffing toad as it filled its lungs with breath; then, clear and sweet and true as ever Viki Boehm had sung upon the concert stage, I heard her voice raised in the final aria of *Faust*:

Holy angels, in heaven blest,
My spirit longs with thee to rest . . .

Surely, the ecstatic melody of that prison scene was never more appropriately sung than by that toad-thing with a lovely woman's head.

The song still mounted poignantly with an almost piercing clarity as Friedrichsohn slammed the door and with a jerk that almost pulled me off my feet dragged me down the hall.

"You'll be interested in my heart experiment, *Herr Doktor*," he assured me. "This is a more ambitious scheme, a far more complicated—"

I jerked against the harness that confined me. "Stop it!" I demanded. "I don't want to see your fiend's work, you sadistic devil. Why don't you kill me and have done with—"

"Kill you?" The mild, surprised reproach in his voice was almost pathetic.

"Why, Doctor Trowbridge, I would not kill anyone, intentionally. Sometimes my patients die, unfortunately, but, believe me, I feel worse about it than they do. It's terribly annoying, really, to carry an experiment almost to completion, then have your work entirely nullified by the patient's inconsiderate death. I assure you it upsets me dreadfully. A little while ago I had almost finished grafting arms and legs and half the pelt from a gorilla to an almost perfect human specimen, a truck driver whose capture caused me no end of trouble, and would you believe it, the inconsiderate fellow died and robbed me of a major triumph. That sort of thing is very disconcerting. Shall we proceed?"

"No, damn you!" I blazed back. "I'll see myself in Hell before—"

"Surely, you're not serious, Doctor?" He dropped his hand upon my shoulder, feeling with quick-kneading fingers for the middle cervical ganglion. "You really mean you will not come with me?" With a finger hard and pitiless as a steel bolt he thrust downward on my spine, and everything went red before me in a sudden blaze of torment. It was as if my head and neck and throat were an enormous exposed nerve on which he bore with fiendish pressure. I felt myself reel drunkenly, heard myself groan piteously.

"You will come with me now, won't you, *lieber Kollege?*" he asked as he released the pressure momentarily, then bore down on my spine again until it seemed to me my heart had quite stopped beating, then started up again with a cold, nauseating lurch. I could see his eyes blaze at me through the dark, feel his fingers fumbling at my skull-base.

"Don't—don't!" I panted, sick with pain. "I'll—"

"*Ist gut*. Of course you will. I knew that you would not be stubborn. As I was saying, this next experiment I propose making is more ambitious than any I have tried before. It involves the psyche quite as much as the body. Tell me, Doctor, is it your opinion that the physical attraction we call love springs more from contemplation of the loved one's face or figure?"

He tapped me on the shoulder with a rigid forefinger, and I shrank from the contact as from a heated iron. Sick revulsion flooded through me. What atrocity was hatching in the diseased mind of this completely irresponsible mad genius?

"Why—I—what do you mean?" I stammered stupidly. My head and neck still pained me so that I could hardly think.

"Precisely what I say, *mein lieber Kollege*," he snapped back acidly. "Every day we see cases which make us wonder. Men love and marry women with faces which might put Medusa to shame, but with bodies which might make a Venus jealous. Or, by contrast, they fall in love with pretty faces set on bodies which lack every element of beauty, or which may even be deformed. Women marry men with similar attributes. Can you explain these vagaries?"

"Of course not," I returned. "Human beings aren't mere animals. Physical attraction plays its part, naturally, but intellectual affinity, the soul—"

"The psyche, if you please, *mein Kollege*. Let us not be mediæval in our terminology."

"All right, the psyche, then. We see beneath the surface, find spiritual qualities that attract us, and base our love on them. A love with nothing but the outward-seeming of the body for foundation is unworthy of the name. It couldn't last—"

"Fool!" he half laughed and half snarled. "You believe in idealistic love—in the love that casteth out fear and endureth all things?"

"Absolutely."

"So do those two down there—"

He had halted at a turning of the hallway; as he spoke he pressed a lever, sliding back a silent panel in the floor. Immediately beneath us was a small room, comfortably furnished and well lighted. On a couch before the open fire a boy and girl were seated, hand in hand, fear written on their faces.

He was a lad of twenty-two or so, slightly made, with sleek, fair hair and a ruddy, fresh complexion. I did not need to hear him speak to know that he was English, or that I had the answer to the disappearance of the British consul's messenger.

The girl was younger by a year or so, and dark as her companion was blond.

Their costumes and positions were reminiscent of domestic bliss as portrayed in the more elaborate motion pictures; he wore a suit of violet pajamas beneath a lounging-robe of purple silk brocade, and a pair of purple kid house-boots. She was clothed in an elaborate hostess coat of Persian pattern, all-enveloping from throat to insteps, but so tight from neck to hips that it hid her lissome form no more than the apple's skin conceals the fruit's contours. From hips to hem it flared out like a ballerina's skirt. Laced to her feet with narrow strips of braided scarlet leather were brightly gilded sandals with cork soles at least four inches thick, and the nails of her exquisitely formed hands and feet were lacquered brilliant red to match the sandal straps.

"No," she was saying as Friedrichsohn slid back the panel, "it isn't hopeless, dear. They're sure to find us sometime—why, you were a king's messenger; the consulate will turn the country inside out—"

His bitter laugh broke in. "No chance! I've stultified myself, blasted my name past all redemption. They'll let me rot, and never turn a hand—"

"Neville! What do you mean?"

He put his elbows on his knees and hid his face in his cupped hands. "I should have let 'em kill me first," he sobbed, "but—oh, my dear, you can't imagine how they hurt me! First they beat me with a strap, and when that didn't break my spirit the little man with the black glasses did something to my neck—I don't know what—that made me feel as if I had a dentist's drill in every tooth at once. I couldn't stand the dreadful pain, and—and so I signed it, Lord, forgive me!"

"Signed what, dearest?"

"A letter to the consul tellin' him I'd sold the papers that he'd trusted with me to the Germans, and that I'd hooked it with the money. I shouldn't have found it hard to die, dear, but the pain—the awful pain—"

"Of course, my dear, my poor, sweet dear"—she took his head against her bosom and rocked it back and forth as if he were a fretful child and she his mother—"I understand. Rita understands, dear, and so will they when we get out of here. No one's responsible for things he's done when he's been tortured. Think of the people who denied their faith when they were on the rack—"

"And of the ones who had the stuff to stick it!" he sobbed miserably.

"Honey, listen. I don't love you 'cause you're strong and masterful and heroic; I love you 'cause you're you." She stopped his wild self-accusation with a kiss. Then back again to her first theme:

"They're sure to find us, dear. This is Twentieth Century America. Two people can't just disappear and stay that way. The police, the G-men—"

"How long have we been here?" he interrupted.

"I—I don't quite know. Not being able to look out and see the sun, I can't form estimates of time. We don't know even when it's night and when it's day, do we? All I remember is that I was late in leaving Philadelphia and I was hurrying to avoid the evening traffic from New York when, just outside of Cranberry, something flew against my face and stung me. I thought at first that it was a mosquito, but that was silly. Even Jersey skeeters don't come around in February. The next thing I knew I was awfully dizzy and the car was rocking crazily from one side of the road to the other; then—here I was. I found myself in a soft bed, and my clothes were gone, but these sandals and this house-coat were laid out for me. There was a bathroom letting off my chamber, and when I'd finished showering I found breakfast—or maybe it was luncheon or dinner—waiting for me on a tray beside the bed. They don't intend to starve us, sugar, that's a sure thing. Haven't you been well fed, too?"

"Yes, I have. My experience was about the same as yours, except that I've seen them, the tall, thin man who looks like a walkin' corpse, and the little pipsqueak with black glasses. But I didn't see 'em till today—or was it yesterday? I can't seem to remember."

The girl knit her smooth brows. "Neither can I. I've tried to keep count of the meals they've served, allowing three meals to a day, so I could form some estimate of the time I've been here, and I've tried so hard to lie in wait and catch the one who serves 'em; but somehow I always seem to fall asleep, no matter how I strive to keep awake, and—it's funny about sleeping, isn't it? When you wake up you can't say if you've just dozed for five minutes or slept around the clock—"

The boy sat forward suddenly, gripping both her hands in his. "That's it! I'm sure of it! No wonder time seems to stand still in this place! They drug us—dope us some way, so that we go to sleep whenever they desire it. We don't know how long these drugged sleeps last. We may have been here weeks, months—"

"No, dear," she shook her head. "It isn't summer, yet. We haven't been here months."

"We may have been." Wild panic had him in its grip, his voice was rising, growing thin, hysterical. "How can you tell?"

"Silly!" She bent and kissed him. "Call it woman's intuition if you like, but I am sure we haven't been cooped up here for a month."

They sat in silence a few minutes, hand interlaced in hand; then:

"Rita?"

"Yes, dear?"

"When we get out—if we get out, and if I square myself with the Chief—will you marry me?"

"Try to keep me from it, Mister Southerby, and you'll find yourself right in the middle of the tidiest breach-of-promise suit you ever saw! D'ye think that you can compromise me like this, sit here with me, dressed as we are, and without a chaperon, then ride off gayly? You'll make an honest woman of me, young feller me lad, or—" Her mask of badinage fell away, leaving her young face as ravaged as a garden after a hail storm. "Oh, Neville, you do think they'll find us, don't you?"

It was his turn to comfort her. "Of course, of course, my darling!" he whispered. "They'll find us. They can't help but find us. Then—"

"Yes, honey, then"—She snuggled sleepily into his arms—"then we'll always be together, dear, close—so close that your dear face will be the first thing that I see when I awake, the last I see before I go to sleep. Oh, it will be heaven . . . heaven."

"I shall be interested to find out if it will. Time will tell, and I think time will side with me." Friedrichsohn pressed the spring that slipped the silent panel back in place, and rose, helping me up from my knees. "It will be an interesting experiment to observe, *nicht wahr, mein Kollege?*"

"Wha—what d'ye mean?" I stammered, my voice almost beyond control. What dreadful plan had taken form behind that high, white brow? Would he subject this boy and girl to dreadful transformation? I had seen the remnant of the lovely Viki Boehm. Did he dare . . .

His soft, suave voice broke through my terrified imaginings. "Why, simply this, *mein lieber Kollege*: They are ideal subjects for my test; better, even, than I had dared hope. I caught the girl by the simple device of waiting by the roadside with an airgun loaded with impregnated darts. The slightest puncture of the epidermis with one of my medicated missiles paralyzes the sensory-motor nerves instantly, and as she told the young man, when she woke up she was in bed in one of my guest rooms.

"But my experiment requires Jill to have a Jack, Joan a Darby, Gretel a

Hänsel, and so I set about to find a mate for her. Eventually this young man came along, and was similarly caught. I had arranged for everything. Their sleeping-quarters open on a common sitting-room, his to one side, hers upon the other. Each morning—or each night, they can't tell the difference—I permit them to awaken, open the automatic doors to their rooms, and let them visit with each other. When I think that they have made love long enough I—ah— turn the current off and put them back to sleep."

"How do you mean—"

"Have not you noticed a peculiar odor here?"

"Yes, I smelled the incense when I first came in—"

"*Jawohl*. That is it. I have perfected an anesthetic gas which, according to the strength of its concentration, can put one in a state of perfect anesthesia in a minute, a second, or immediately. It is almost odorless, and such slight odor as it has is completely masked by the incense. Periodically I put them to sleep, then let them re-awaken. That is why they cannot guess the intervals of time between their meetings, and—what is more important—when they begin to reason out too much, I see that they become unconscious quickly. I turned the anesthetic on when he began to guess too accurately concerning my technique a moment ago. By this time both of them are sleeping soundly, and Mishkin has taken them to bed. When I see fit, I shall allow them to awake and eat and take their conversation up where they left off, but I do not think they will. They are too preoccupied with each other to give much thought to me—just now, at least."

"How long have they been here?" I asked. "I heard her say that she came first—"

"What is time?" he laughed. "She does not know how long she's been my guest; neither does he, nor you, *Herr Doktor*. It may have been a night I let you sleep, in Stravinsky's cell, or it may have been a week, or two—"

"That's nonsense," I cut in. "I should have been half starved if that were so. As it is, I'm not even feeling hungry—"

"How do you know we did not feed you with a nasal tube while you were sleeping?"

I had not thought of that. It upset my calculations utterly. Certainly in normal circumstances I should have been ravenous if I'd been there but four and twenty hours. A longer period without nourishment and I should have felt weak, yet I felt no hunger. . . .

"To return to our young lovers," Friedrichsohn reminded me. "They are better suited to my purpose; better, even, than I'd thought. When I captured him I could not know that they had known each other for some time, and were more than merely mildly interested in each other. Since they have been my guests, propinquity has made that interest blossom into full-blown love. Tomorrow, or the next day—or the next day after that—I think I shall begin to work on them."

"To—work—on—them?"

"*Jawohl, mein lieber Kollege.* You saw the fascinating beauty treatment I gave Viki Boehm? *Ist gut.* I shall put them quietly to sleep and subject them to precisely similar ministrations. When they awake they'll find themselves in the dove-cote I have prepared for them. It is a charming, cozy little place where they can contemplate each other as the little lady said, where the face of each shall be the first thing that the other sees when he awakes, the last thing he beholds before he goes to sleep. It is larger than the chamber I assigned to Viki—more than twice as large—and one of them shall rest at one end of it while the other occupies the other, facing him. It has been lined with mirrors, too, so that they can see themselves and each other from both front and back. That is necessary, *Herr Doktor*, since they will not be able to turn around. Lacking legs, a person finds himself severely handicapped in moving, *lieber Freund.*"

"But why should you do this to them?" I faltered, knowing even as I asked the question that reason had no part in his wild plans.

"Can you ask that after our discussion of the merits of the face and form as stimulants of love? I am surprised and disappointed in you, *mein Kollege*. It is to see if love—the love they pledge so tenderly to each other—can stand the sight of hideous deformity in the loved one. Their faces will be as they are now, only their forms will be altered. If they continue to express affection for each other I shall know the face is that which energizes love, but if—as I am sure they will—they turn from each other in loathing and abhorrence, I shall have proven that the form is more important. It will be a most diverting comedy to watch, *nicht wahr, Herr Doktor?*"

Horror drove my pulses to a hurrying rhythm. Something sharp, something penetrating as a cold and whetted knife-blade, seemed probing at my insides. I wanted to cry out against this outrage, to pray; but I could not. Heaven seemed unreal and infinitely far away with this phosphorescent-eyed monstrosity at my elbow, his pitiless, purring voice outlining plans which outdid Hell in hellish ingenuity.

"You can't—you can't do this!" I gasped. "You wouldn't dare! You'll be found out!"

"That's what Viki Boehm said when I told her of the future I had planned for her," he broke in with a susurrating laugh. "But they didn't find me out. They never will, *Herr Doktor*. This is a madhouse—pardon me, a sanitarium—duly licensed by the state and impervious to private inquiry. People expect to hear cries and shrieks and insane laughter from such places. Passersby and neighbors are not even curious. My grounds are posted against trespassers; your law insures my privacy, and no one, not even the police, may enter here without a warrant. I have a crematory fully equipped and ready to be used instantly. If attempts are made to search the house I can destroy incriminating evidence—inanimate and animate—in a moment and without trouble. I shall prosecute my work unin-terrupted, *lieber Kollege*—and that reminds me, I have a proposal to make you."

He had reached the red-walled room again, and he pushed me suddenly, forcing me into a chair.

"There are times when I feel Mishkin is inadequate," he said, taking out a cigarette and setting it alight. "I have taught him much, but his lack of early training often makes him bungle things. I need a skilled assistant, one with sur-gical experience, capable of helping me in operations. I think you are admirably fitted for this work. Will you enlist with me—"

"*I?*" I gasped. "I'll see you damned first."

"Or will you fill Stravinsky's coffin?"

"Stravinsky's—coffin?"

"Exactly. You remember that I told you Abraham Stravinsky was a patient here and that he died the day you came? *Jawohl.* His family have not yet been notified of his death. His body is preserved and waiting shipment. Should you accept my offer I shall notify his relatives and send his corpse to them without delay. If you decline"—the green eyes seemed to brighten in the gloom as they peered at me—"I shall put him in the crematory, and you shall take his place in the coffin. He was a Hebrew of the orthodox persuasion, and as such will have a plain pine coffin, rather than a casket. I have several boxes like that ready, one of them for you, unless you choose to join me. You are also doubtless aware that the rules of his religion require burial of the dead within twenty-four hours of death. For that reason there is small fear that the coffin will be opened. But if it should be, his family will not know that it is you and not their kinsman whom they see. I shall say he died in an insane seizure, as a consequence of which he was quite battered in the face.

"You need not fear, *mein lieber Kollege*: the body will be admirably battered—past all recognition. Mishkin will attend to all the details. He has a very dexter-ous talent with the ax, but—"

"But he will not exercise it, I damn think!" From behind me Jules de Gran-din spoke in ordinary conversational tone, but I recognized the flatness of his voice. Cyclopean fury boiled in him, I knew. Friedrichsohn might be insane, fierce and savage as a tiger; de Grandin was his match in fierceness, and his clear French brain was burdened with no trace of madness.

"*Kreuzsakrament!*" As de Grandin stepped before me Friedrichsohn launched himself across the table, leaping like a maddened leopard. "You—"

"It is I, indeed, thou very naughty fellow," de Grandin answered, and as the other clawed at him rose suddenly into the air, as if he were a bouncing ball, brought both feet up at once, and kicked his adversary underneath the chin, hurling him unconscious to the floor. "*Tiens*, a knowledge of *la savate* is very use-ful now and then," he murmured, as he turned and loosed the strap that bound my arms and transferred it to his fallen foeman. "So, my most unpleasant friend, you will do quite nicely thus," he said, then turned to me.

"*Embrasse moi!*" he commanded. "Oh, Trowbridge, *cher ami, brave camarade,* I had feared this stinking villain had done you an injury. *Alors*, I find you safe and sound, but"—he grinned as he inspected me—"you would look more better if you had more clothing on!"

"There's a chest behind you," I suggested. "Perhaps—"

He was already rummaging in the wardrobe, flinging out a miscellany of garments. "These would be those of Monsieur Southerby"—he tossed a well-cut tweed suit on the floor—"and these a little lady's"—a woolen traveling-suit with furred collar came to join the man's clothes. "And this—ah, here they are!" My own clothes came down from the hooks and he thrust them at me.

"Attire yourself, my friend," he ordered. "I have work elsewhere. If he shows signs of consciousness, knock him on the silly head. I shall return for him anon."

Hurrying footsteps clattered on the floor outside as I dragged on my clothes. A shout, the echo of a shot. . . .

I flung the door back just in time to see de Grandin lower his pistol as Mishkin staggered toward the front door, raised both arms above his head and crashed sprawling to the floor.

"My excellent de Grandin!" Jules de Grandin told himself. "You never miss, you are incomparable. *Parbleu*, but I admire you—"

"Look, look!" I shouted. "The lamp—"

Clawing blindly in the agony of death, Mishkin's hand had knocked one of the red-globed oil lamps from its place before a statuary niche. The lacquer-coated, oil-soaked walls were tinder to the flame, and already fire was running up them like a curtain.

"In there," I cried. "Southerby and a young girl are locked up there somewhere, and—"

"Hi, Frenchy, where the devil are you?" Hiji's hail came from the transverse corridor. "Find Trowbridge yet? We've got Southerby and a—" He staggered out into the central hall with the still unconscious Southerby held in his arms as if he were a sleeping babe. Behind him came Costello with the girl, who was also sunk deep in anesthesia.

"Whew, it's gettin' hotter than Dutch love in here!" the Englishman exclaimed. "We'd best be hookin' it, eh, what?"

"Indubitably what, my friend," de Grandin answered. "One moment, if you please." He dashed into the red room, reappearing in a moment with arms filled with clothes. "These are their proper raiment," he called, draping the garments over Hiji's shoulder. "Take them to the garage and bid them dress themselves becomingly for public appearance. Me, I have another task to do. Assist me, if you will, Friend Trowbridge."

Back in the red-walled room he raised the fallen madman, signing me to help him. "The place will be a furnace in a moment," he panted, "and me, I am not even one of the so estimable young Hebrews who made mock of Nebuchadnezzar's fiery wrath. We must hasten if we do not wish to cook!"

He had not exaggerated. The oil-soaked walls and floors were all ablaze; lashing, crackling flames swept up the stairway as if it were a chimney flue.

"Good heavens!" I cried, suddenly remembering. "Up there—he's got two others locked in cells—"

Down from the upper story, clear and sweet and growing stronger, came a voice, the voice of Viki Boehm:

So stürben wir, um ungetrennt,
Ewig einig ohne end . . .

So should we die, no more to part,
Ever in one endless joy . . .

The mounting notes of a violin accompanied the words of Tristan and Isolde's plea for death which should unite them in the mystic world beyond life.

"*Mon Dieu! Concede misericors, Deus . . .*" De Grandin looked up at the fire-choked stairway. "There is no chance of reaching them—"

The crash of breaking timbers drowned his words, and a gust of flame and sparks burst from the stairwell as the draft was forced down by the falling floors. The song had died; only the roar of blazing, oil-soaked wood sounded as we bent our heads against the smoke and staggered toward the door. "It is their funeral pyre—*fidelium animae per misericordiam Dei, requiescat in pace!*" de Grandin panted. "*A-a-ah!*"

"What's the matter?" I asked. "Are you—"

"Bid Hiji or Costello come at once!" he groaned. "I—am—unable—"

"You're hurt?" I cried solicitously.

"*Vite, vite*—get one of them!" he choked.

I rushed through the front door and circled around the house toward the garage. "Hiji—Costello!" I shouted. "Come quickly, de Grandin's hurt—"

"*Pardonnez-moi, mon ami*, on the contrary I am in the best of health, and as pleased as I can be in all the circumstances." At my very heels de Grandin stood and grinned at me.

"You got clear? Good!" I exclaimed. Then: "Where's Friedrichsohn?"

There was no more expression in his small blue eyes than if they had been china eyes in a doll's face. "He was detained," he answered in a level voice. "He could not come."

Suddenly I felt an overmastering weakness. It seemed to me I had not eaten for a year; the cold bit at my bones as if it were a rabid wolf. "What day is it?" I asked.

"You are unpatriotic, my friend. It is the anniversary of the Great Emancipator's birth. Did not you know?"

"February twelfth? Why, that's today!"

"*Mon Dieu*, what did you think it was, tomorrow or yesterday?"

"But—I mean—we left Harrisonville on the morning of the twelfth, and I've been in that place at least—"

He glanced down at his wrist watch. "A little over two hours. If we hasten we shall be in time to lunch at Keyport. They have delicious lobster there."

"But—but—"

"Doctor Trowbridge, Doctor de Grandin, these are Miss Perinchief and Mr. Southerby," Hiji broke in as he and Costello came from the garage shepherding a most ecstatic-looking pair of youngsters.

"I've seen—" I began; then: "I'm very glad to meet you both." I acknowledged the introduction.

He made me tell him my adventures from the moment I had left him by the brook where Southerby's car was foundered, listening with tear-filled eyes as I described the loathsome things Friedrichsohn had made of Viki Boehm and her husband, weeping unashamedly when I recounted what I'd overheard while I looked through the trap-door into the room in which young Southerby and Rita Perinchief confessed their love. "And now, in heaven's name, what were you doing all that time?" I asked.

"When you failed to return we were puzzled. Costello wished to go to the farmhouse and inquire for you, but I would not permit it. One took at that place and I knew it had the smell of fish upon it. So I posted them out by the great tree at the turning of the driveway, where they could be in plain sight while I crept around the house and sought an opening. At the last I had to cut the lock away from the back door, and that took time. I do not doubt the Mishkin rascal watched them from some point of vantage. *Bien.* While he was thus engaged Jules de Grandin was at work at the back door.

"At last I forced an entrance, tiptoed to the front door and unfastened it, signaling to them that all was well. I was waiting for them when I saw that *sale chameau* Friedrichsohn come down the stairs with you.

"'Can this be endured?' I ask me. 'Can anyone be permitted to lead my good Friend Trowbridge as if he were a dog upon a leash? *Mais non*, Jules de Grandin, you must see to this.' So I crept up to the room where he had taken you and listened at the keyhole. *Voilà tout.* The rest you know."

"No, I don't," I denied. "How did Hiji and Costello know where to look for Southerby and Rita?"

"*Tiens*, they did not know at all, my friend. They came in and looked about, and they espied the Mishkin rogue on guard before their prison door. He ran, and they broke down the door and brought the prisoners out. They should have shot him first. They have no judgment in such matters. *Eh bien*, I was there. It is perhaps as well. I have had no target practice for a long, long time—"

"Did they find the papers Southerby was carrying?"

"But yes. Friedrichsohn set no value on them. They were in the desk of the room where you first saw him. Hiji has them safely in his pocket."

"It seems incredible I was in there such a little while," I mused. "I could have sworn that I was there at least a week—"

"Ah, my friend, time passes slowly in a prison. What you thought was hours' space as you lay shivering in that cell was really only half an hour or so. Time does not pass at all, it stands entirely still while you are sleeping. They rendered you unconscious with their gas, and woke you in perhaps five minutes. Suggestion did the rest. You thought that you had slept around the clock-dial, and since you could not see the sun, you had no clue to what the hour really was. Sleep and our own imaginings play strange tricks upon us, *n'est-ce-pas?*"

THE BROILED LIVE LOBSTER was, as he had promised, delicious. Luncheon done, de Grandin, Hiji and Costello marched toward the bar, with me bringing up the rear. Neville Southerby and Rita Perinchief cuddled close together on a settle set before the fireplace in the lounge. As I passed the inglenook in which they snuggled side by side, I heard her: "Honey lamb, I think I know how Robinson Crusoe felt about his island when they'd rescued him. He kept remembering it all his life, and even though he'd undergone a lot of hardships there, he loved it. Somehow, I'll always feel that way about the place that madman shut us up in. Just suppose they'd never found us . . . suppose we'd stayed there always, just the two of us, being with each other always, looking at each other . . . we might have been changed some by being cooped up, but—"

"*Morbleu*, my friend, you look as if you'd seen a most unpleasant ghost!" de Grandin told me as I joined them at the bar and reached unsteadily for a drink.

"I have," I answered with a shudder. "A most unpleasant one."

The Green God's Ring

S T. DUNSTAN'S WAS PACKED to overflowing. Expectantly smiling ladies in cool crêpe and frilly chiffon crowded against perspiring gentlemen in formal afternoon dress while they craned necks and strained ears. Aisles, chancel, sanctuary, were embowered in July roses and long trailing garlands of southern smilax, the air was heavy with the humid warmth of summer noon, the scent of flowers and the perfume from the women's hair and clothes.

The dean of the Cathedral Chapter, the red of his Cambridge hood in pleasing contrast to the spotless white of linen surplice and sleek black cassock, pronounced the fateful words, his calm clear voice a steady mentor for the bridegroom's faltering echo:

"I, Wade, take thee Melanie to be my wedded wife, to have and to hold from this day forward—"

"From this day forward," Dean Quincy repeated, smiling with gentle tolerance. In forty years of priesthood he had seen more than one bridegroom go suddenly dumb. "From this day forward, for better, for worse—"

His smile lost something of its amusement, his florid, smooth-shaven face assumed an expression of mingled surprise and consternation which in other circumstances would have seemed comic. Swaying back and forth from toes to heels, from heels to toes, the bridegroom balanced uncertainly a moment, then with a single short, hard, retching cough fell forward like an overturned image, the gilded hilt of his dress sword jangling harshly on the pavement of the chancel.

For what seemed half a minute the bride looked down at the fallen groom with wide, horrified eyes, then, flowing lace veil billowing about her like wind-driven foam, she dropped to her knees, thrust a lace-sheathed arm beneath his neck and raised his head to pillow it against the satin and seed pearls of her bodice. "Wade," she whispered in a passionless, cold little voice that carried to the farthest corner of the death-still church. "Oh, Wade, my belovèd!"

Quickly, with the quiet efficiency bred of their training, the young Naval officers attending the fallen bridegroom wheeled in their places and strode down the aisle to shepherd panic-stricken guests from their pews.

"Nothin' serious; nothin' at all," a lad who would not see his twenty-fifth birthday for another two years whispered soothingly through trembling lips as he motioned Jules de Grandin and me from our places. "Lieutenant Hardison is subject to these spells. Quite all right, I assure you. Ceremony will be finished in private—in the vestry room when he's come out of it. See you at the reception in a little while. Everything's all right. Quite—"

The pupils of de Grandin's little round blue eyes seemed to have expanded like those of an alert tomcat, and his delicate, slim nostrils twitched as though they sought to capture an elusive scent. "*Mais oui, mon brave*," he nodded approval of the young one-striper's tact. "We understand. *Certainement*. But me, I am a physician, and this is my good friend, Dr. Trowbridge—"

"Oh, are you, sir?" the lad broke in almost beseechingly. "Then for God's sake go take a look at him; we can't imagine—"

"But of course not, *mon enfant*. Diagnosis is not your trade," the small Frenchman whispered. "Do you prevail upon the congregation to depart while we—*attendez-moi*, Friend Trowbridge," he ordered in a low voice as he tiptoed toward the chancel where the stricken bride still knelt and nursed the stricken bridegroom's head against her bosom.

"*Sacré nom!*" he almost barked the exclamation as he came to a halt by the tragic tableau formed by the kneeling bride and supine man. "*C'est cela même.*"

There was no doubting his terse comment. In the glassy-eyed, hang-jawed expression of the bridegroom's face we read the trade mark of the King of Terrors. Doctors, soldiers and morticians recognize death at a glance.

"Come, Melanie," Mrs. Thurmond put a trembling hand upon her daughter's shoulder. "We must get Wade to a doctor, and—"

"A doctor?" the girl's voice was small and still as a night breeze among the branches. "What can a doctor do for my poor murdered darling? Oh, Wade, my dear, my dear," she bent until her lips were at his ear, "I loved you so, and I'm your murderess."

"*Non, Mademoiselle*," de Grandin denied softly. "You must not say so. It may be we can help you—"

"Help? *Ha!*" she almost spit the exclamation at him. "What help can there be for him—or me? Go away—get out—all of you!" she swept the ring of pitying faces with hard bright eyes almost void of all expression. "Get out, I tell you, and leave me with my dead!"

De Grandin drew the slim black brows that were in such sharp contrast to his wheat blond hair down in a sudden frown. "*Mademoiselle*," his voice was cold as icy spray against her face, "You ask if any one can help you, and I reply they can. I, Jules de Grandin can help you, despite the evil plans of pisacha, bhirta and preta, shahini and rakshasha, I can help—"

The girl cringed from his words as from a whip. "Pisacha, bhirta and preta," she repeated in a trembling, terrified whisper. "You know—"

"Not altogether, *Mademoiselle*," he answered, "but I shall find out, you may be assured."

"What is it you would have me do?"

"Go hence and leave us to do that which must needs be done. Anon I shall call on you, and if what I have the intuition to suspect is true, *tenez*, who knows?"

She drew a kneeling cushion from the step before the altar rail and eased the dead boy's head down to it. "Be kind, be gentle with him, won't you?" she begged. "Good-by, my darling, for a little while," she laid a light kiss on the pale face pillowed on the crimson cushion. "Good-by—" Tears came at last to her relief and, weeping piteously, she stumbled to her mother's waiting arms and tottered to the vestry room.

"Heart?" I hazarded as the bridal party left us alone with the dead man. "I should think not," he denied with a shake of his head. "He was on the Navy's active list, that one, and those with cardiac affections do not rate that."

"Perhaps it was the heat—"

"Not if Jules de Grandin knows his heat prostration symptoms, and he has spent much time near the Equator. The fires of hell would have been cold beside the temperature in here when all those curious ones were assembled to see this poor one and his belovèd plight their troth, but did he not seem well enough when he came forth to meet her at the chancel steps? Men who will fall prone on their faces in heat collapse show symptoms of distress beforehand. Yes, of course. Did you see his color? Excellent, was it not? But certainly. Bronzed from the sea and sun, *au teint vermeil de bon santé*. We were not thirty feet away, and could see perfectly. He had none of that pallor that betokens heat stroke. No."

"Well, then"—I was a little nettled at the cavalier way he dismissed my diagnoses—"what d'ye think it was?"

He lifted narrow shoulders in a shrug that was a masterpiece of disavowal of responsibility. "*Le bon Dieu* knows, and He keeps His own counsel. Perhaps we shall be wiser when the autopsy is done."

We left the relatively cool shadow of the church and stepped out to the sun-baked noonday street. "If you will be so kind, I think that I should like to call on the good Sergeant Costello," he told me as we reached my parked car.

"Why Costello?" I asked. "It's a case of sudden unexplained death, and as such one for the coroner, but as for any criminal element—"

"Perhaps," he agreed, seeming only half aware of what we talked of. "Perhaps not. At any rate, I think there are some things about this case in which the Sergeant will be interested."

We drove a few blocks in silence, then: "What was that gibberish you talked to Melanie?" I asked, my curiosity bettering my pique. "That stuff about your being able to help her despite the evil plans of the thingabobs and whatchamay-callems? It sounded like pure double talk to me, but she seemed to understand it."

He chuckled softly. "The pisacha, bhirta and preta? The shahini and rak-shasha?"

"That sounds like it."

"That, my friend, was what you call the random shot, the drawing of the bow at venture. I had what you would call the hunch."

"How d'ye mean?"

"Did you observe the ring upon the index finger of her right hand?"

"You mean the big red gold band set with a green cartouche?"

"*Précisément.*"

"Not particularly. It struck me as an odd sort of ornament to wear to her wedding, more like a piece of costume jewelry than an appropriate bridal deco-ration, still these modern youngsters—"

"That modern youngster, my friend, did not wear that ring because she wanted to."

"No? Why, then?"

"Because she had to."

"Oh, come, now. You can't mean—"

"I can and do, my friend. Did not you notice the device cut into its setting?"

"Why, no. What was it?"

"It represented a four-faced, eight-armed monstrosity holding a straining woman in unbreakable embrace. The great God Siva—"

"Siva? You mean the Hindu deity?"

"Perfectly. He is a veritable chameleon, that one, and can change his form and color at a whim. Sometimes he is as mild and gentle as a lamb, but mostly he is fierce and passionate as a tiger. Indeed, his lamb-like attributes are generally a disguise, for underneath the softness is the cruelty of his base nature. *Tiens*, I think that he is best described as Bhirta, the Terrible."

"And those others with outlandish names?"

"The pisacha and preta are a race of most unlovely demons, and like them are the rakshasha and shahini. They attend Siva in his attribute of Bhirta the Terrible as imps attend on Satan, doing his foul bidding and, if such a thing be possible, bettering his instructions."

"Well?"

"By no means, my friend, not at all. It is not well, but very bad indeed. A

Christian maiden has no business wearing such a talisman, and when I saw it on her finger I assumed that she might know something of its significance. Accordingly I spoke to her of the Four-Faced One, Bhirta and his attendant implings, the shahini, raksash and pischa. *Parbleu*, she understood me well enough. Altogether too well, I damn think."

"She seemed to, but—"

"There are no buts, my friend. She understood me. Anon I shall understand her. Now let us interview the good Costello."

D ETECTIVE-SERGEANT JEREMIAH COSTELLO WAS in the act of putting down the telephone as we walked into his office. "Good afternoon, sors," he greeted as he fastened a wilted collar and began knotting a moist necktie. "'Tis glad I'd be to welcome ye at any other time, but jist now I'm in a terin' hurry. Some swell has bumped himself off at a fashionable wedding, or if he didn't exactly do it, he died in most suspicious circumstances, an'—"

"It would not be Lieutenant Wade Hardison you have reference to?"

"Bedad, sor, it ain't Mickey Mouse!"

"Perhaps, then, we can be of some assistance. We were present when it happened."

"Were ye, indeed, sor? What kilt 'im?"

"I should like to know that very much indeed, my friend. That is why I am here. It does not make the sense. One moment he is hale and hearty, the next he falls down dead before our eyes. I have seen men shot through the brain fall in the same way. Death must have been instantaneous—"

"An' ye've no hunch wot caused it?"

"I have, indeed, *mon vieux*, but it is no more than the *avis indirect*—what you would call the hunch."

"Okay, sor, let's git goin'. Where to first?"

"Will you accompany me to the bride's house? I should like to interview her, but without official sanction it might be difficult."

"Howly Mackerel! Ye're not tellin' me she done it—"

"We have not yet arrived at the telling point, *mon ami*. Just now we ask the questions and collect the answers; later we shall assemble them like the pieces of a jigsaw puzzle. Perhaps when we have completed the mosaic we shall know some things that we do not suspect now."

"I getcha," Costello nodded. "Let's be on our way, sors."

T HE THURMOND PLACE IN Chattahoochee Avenue seemed cloaked in brooding grief as we drove up the wide driveway to the low, pillared front porch. A cemetery quiet filled the air, the hushed, tiptoe silence of the sickroom or the funeral chapel. The festive decorations of the house and grounds were as incongruous in that atmosphere of tragedy as rouge and paint upon the cheeks and lips of a corpse.

"Miss Melanie is too ill to be seen," the butler informed us in answer to Costello's inquiry. "The doctor has just left, and—"

"Present our compliments to her, if you please," de Grandin interrupted suavely. "She will see us, I make no doubt. Tell her it is the gentleman with whom she talked at the church—the one who promised her protection from Bhirta. Do you understand?"

"Bhirta?" the servant repeated wonderingly.

"Your accent leaves something to be desired, but it will serve. Do not delay, if you please, for I am not a patient person. By no means."

Draped in a sheer convent-made nightrobe that had been part of her trousseau, Melanie Thurmond lay rigid as death upon the big colonial sleigh bed of her chamber, a madeira sheet covering her to the bosom, her long auburn hair spread about her corpse-pale face like a rose gold nimbus framing an ivory ikon. Straight before her, with set, unseeing eyes she gazed, only the faint dilation of her delicate nostrils and the rhythmic rise and fall of her bosom testifying she had not already joined her stricken lover in the place he had gone a short hour before.

The little Frenchman approached the bed silently, bent and took her flaccid hand in his and raised it to his lips. "*Ma pauvre*," he murmured. "It is truly I. I have come to help you, as I promised."

The ghost of a tired little smile touched her pale lips as she turned her head slowly on the pillow and looked at him with wide-set, tearless sepia eyes. "I knew that it would come," she told him in a hopeless little voice. Her words were slow and mechanical, her voice almost expressionless, as though she were rehearsing a half-learned lesson: "It had to be. I should have known it. I'm really Wade's murderess."

"Howly Mither!" Costello ejaculated softly, and de Grandin turned a sudden fierce frown on him.

"*Comment?*" he asked softly. "How do you mean that, *ma petite roitelette?*"

She shook her head wearily from side to side and a small frown gathered between her brows. "Somehow, I can't seem to think clearly. My brain seems seething—boiling like a cauldron—"

"*Précisément, exactement, au juste,*" de Grandin agreed with a vigorous nod. "You have right, my little poor one. The brain, she is astew with all this trouble, and when she stews the recrement comes to the surface. Come, let us skim it off together, thou and I"—he made a gesture as if spooning something up and tossing it away. "Thus we shall rid our minds of dross and come at last to the sweet, unadulterated truth. How did it all start, if you please? What made you know it had to happen, and why do you accuse yourself all falsely of the murder of your *amoureux?*"

A little shudder shook the girl's slim frame, but a hint of color in her pallid cheeks told of a returning interest in life. "It all began with The Light of Asia."

"*Quoi?*" de Grandin's slim brows rose in Saracenic arches. "You have reference to the poem by Sir Edward Arnold?"

"Oh, no. This Light of Asia was an Oriental bazaar in East Fifty-Sixth Street. The girls from Briarly were in the habit of dropping in there for little curios— quaint little gifts for people who already seemed to have everything, you know.

"It was a lovely place. No daylight ever penetrated there. Two great vases stood on ebony stands in the shop windows, and behind them heavy curtains of brocaded cloth of gold shut off the light from outside as effectively as solid doors. The shop—if you could call it that—was illuminated by lamps that burned scented oil and were encased in frames of carved and pierced teakwood. These, and two great green candles as tall as a man, gave all the light there was. The floors were covered with thick, shining Indian rugs, and lustrous embroideries hung against the walls. The stock was not on shelves, but displayed in cabinets of buhl and teak and Indian cedar—all sorts of lovely things: carved ivories and moulded silver, hand-worked gold and tortoise-shell, amethyst and topaz, jade and brass and lovely blue and green enamel, and over everything there hung the scent of incense, curiously and pungently sweet; it lacked the usual cloying, heavy fragrance of the ordinary incense, yet it was wonderfully penetrating, almost hypnotic."

De Grandin nodded. "An interesting place, one gathers. And then—"

"I'd been to The Light of Asia half a dozen times before I saw The Green One."

"The Green One? *Qui diable?*"

"At the back of the shop there was a pair of double doors of bright vermilion lacquer framed by exquisitely embroidered panels. I'd often wondered what lay behind them. Then one day I found out! It was a rainy afternoon and I'd dropped into The Light as much to escape getting wet as to shop. There was no other customer in the place, and no one seemed in attendance, so I just wandered about, admiring the little bits of *virtu* in the cabinets and noting new additions to the stock, and suddenly I found myself at the rear of the shop, before the doors that had intrigued me so. There was no one around, as I told you, and after a hasty glance to make sure I was not observed, I put my hand out to the nearer door. It opened to my touch, as if it needed only a slight pressure to release its catch, and there in a gilded niche sat the ugliest idol I had ever seen.

"It seemed to be carved of some green stone, not like anything I'd ever seen before—almost waxen in its texture—and it had four faces and eight arms."

"*Qu'est-ce-donc?*"

"I said four faces. One looking each way from its head. Two of the faces seemed as calm as death masks, but the one behind the head had a dreadful sneering laugh, and that which faced the front had the most horrible expression—not angry, not menacing, exactly, but—would you understand me if I said it looked inexorable?"

"I should and do, *ma chère*. And the eight arms?"

"Every hand held something different. Swords, and sprays of leafy branches, and daggers—all but two. They were empty and outstretched, not so much seeming to beg as to demand an offering.

"There was something terrible—and terrifying—about that image. It seemed to be demanding something, and suddenly I realized what it was. It wanted me! I seemed to feel a sort of secret, dark thrill emanating from it, like the electric tingle in the air before a thunderstorm. There was some power in this thing, immense and terrifying power that gave the impression of dammed-up forces waiting for release. Not physical power I could understand and combat—or run from, but something far more subtle; something uncanny and indescribable, and it was all the more frightening because I was aware of it, but could not explain nor understand it.

"It seemed as if I were hypnotized. I could feel the room begin to whirl about me slowly, like a carousel when it's just starting, and my legs began to tremble and weaken. In another instant I should have been on my knees before the green idol when the spell was broken by a pleasant voice: 'You are admiring our latest acquisition?'

"It was a very handsome young man who stood beside me, not more than twenty-two or -three. I judged, with a pale olive complexion, long brown eyes under slightly drooping lids with haughty brows, and hair so sleek and black and glossy it seemed to fit his head like a skullcap of patent leather. He wore a well-cut morning coat and striped trousers, and there was a good pearl in his black poplin ascot tie.

"He must have seen the relief in my face, for he laughed before he spoke again, a friendly, soft laugh that reassured me. 'I am Kabanta Sikra Roy,' he told me. 'My dad owns this place and I help him out occasionally. When I'm not working here I study medicine at N.Y.U.'

"'Is this image—or idol, or whatever you call it—for sale?' I asked him, more to steady my nerves by conversation than anything else.

"The look he gave me was an odd one. I couldn't make out if he were angry or amused, but in a moment he laughed again, And when he smiled his whole face lighted up. 'Of course, everything in the shop's for sale, including the proprietors—at a price,' he answered, 'but I don't think you'd be interested in buying it.'

"'I should say not. But I just wondered. Isn't it some sort of god, or something?'

"'Quite so. It is the Great Mahadeva, third, but by far the most important member of the Hindu Triad, sometimes known as Siva the Destroyer.'

"I looked at the thing again and it seemed even more repulsive than before. 'I shouldn't think you'd find a quick sale for it,' I suggested.

"'We don't expect to. Perhaps we'll not sell it at all. In case we never find a buyer for it, we can put in our spare time worshiping at its shrine.'

"The utter cynicism of his reply grated on me, then I remembered having heard that many high caste Hindus have no more real faith in their gods than the educated Greeks and Romans had in theirs. But before I could be rude enough to ask if he really believed such nonsense, he had gently shepherded me away from the niche and was showing me some exquisitely carved amethysts. Before I left we found we had a dozen friends in common and he'd extended and I'd accepted an invitation to see *Life With Father* and go dancing at the Cotillion Room afterward.

"That began the acquaintance that ripened almost overnight into intimacy. Kabanta was a delightful playfellow. His father must have been enormously rich, for everything that had come to him by inheritance had been given every chance to develop. The final result was this tall, slender olive complexioned man with the sleek hair, handsome features and confident though slightly deferential manner. Before we knew it we were desperately in love.

"No"—her listless manner gathered animation with the recital—"it wasn't what you could call love; it was more like bewitchment. When we met I felt the thrill of it; it seemed almost to lift the hair on my head and make me dizzy, and when we were together it seemed as if we were the only two people in the world, as if we were cut off from everyone and everything. He had the softest, most musical voice I had ever heard, and the things he said were like poetry by Laurence Hope. Besides that, every normal woman has a masochistic streak buried somewhere deep in her nature, and the thought of the mysterious, glamorous East and the guarded, prisoned life of the zenana has an almost irresistible appeal to us when we're in certain moods. So, one night when we were driving home from New York in his sports roadster and he asked me if I cared for him I told him that I loved him with my heart and soul and spirit. I did, too—then. There was a full moon that night, and I was fairly breathless with the sweet delirium of love when he took me in his arms and kissed me. It was like being hypnotized and conscious at the same time. Then, just before we said good night, he asked me to come to The Light of Asia next evening after closing time and plight our troth in Eastern fashion.

"I had no idea what was coming, but I was fairly palpitant with anticipation when I knocked softly on the door of the closed shop shortly after sunset the next evening.

"Kabanta himself let me in, and I almost swooned at sight of him. Every shred of his Americanism seemed to have fallen away, for he was in full Oriental dress, a long, tight-waisted frock coat of purple satin with a high neck and long, tight sleeves, tight trousers of white satin and bright red leather shoes turned up at the toes and heavily embroidered with gold, and on his head was the most gorgeous piece of silk brocade I'd ever seen wrapped into a turban and decorated with a diamond aigret. About his neck were looped not one nor two but three long strands of pearls—pink-white, green-white and pure-white—and I gasped with amazement at sight of them. There couldn't have been one in the three strands that was worth less than a hundred dollars, and each of the three strands had at least a hundred gems in it. The man wore twenty or thirty thousand dollars worth of pearls as nonchalantly as a shop girl might have worn a string of dime store beads.

"'Come in, White Moghra Blossom,' he told me. 'All is Prepared.'

"The shop was in total darkness except for the glow of two silver lamps that burned perfumed oil before the niche in which the Green God crouched. 'You'll find the garments of betrothal in there,' Kabanta whispered as he led me to a door at the rear, 'and there's a picture of a Hindu woman wearing clothes like those laid out for you to serve as a model. Do not be long, O Star of My Delight, O Sweetly Scented Bower of Jasmine. I swoon for the sight of you arrayed to vow love undying.'

"In the little anteroom was a long, three-paneled mirror in which I could see myself from all sides, a dressing-table set with toilet articles and cosmetics, and my costume draped across a chair. On the dressing-table was an exquisite small picture of a Hindu girl in full regalia, and I slipped my Western clothes off and dressed myself in the Eastern garments, copying the pictured bride as closely as I could. There were only three garments—a little sleeveless bodice like a zouave jacket of green silk dotted with bright yellow discs and fastened at the front with a gold clasp, a pair of long, tight plum-colored silk trousers embroidered with pink rosebuds, and a shawl of thin almost transparent purple silk tissue fringed with gold tassels and worked with intricate designs of lotus buds and flowers in pink and green sequins. When I'd slipped the bodice and trousers on I draped the veil around me, letting it hang down behind like an apron and tying it in front in a bow knot with the ends tucked inside the tight waistband of the trousers. It was astonishing how modest such a scanty costume could be. There was less of me exposed than if I'd been wearing a halter and shorts, and not much more than if I'd worn one of the bare-midriff evening dresses just then becoming fashionable. For my feet there was a pair of bell toe rings, little clusters of silver bells set close together like grapes in a bunch that tinkled with a whirring chime almost like a whistle each time I took a step after I'd slipped them on my little toes, and a pair of heavy silver anklets with a fringe of silver tassels that flowed down from the ankle to the floor and almost hid my feet and jingled every time I moved. On my right wrist I hung a gold slave bracelet with silver chains, each ending in a ball of somber-gleaming garnet, and over my left hand I slipped a heavy sand-moulded bracelet of silver that must have weighed a full half pound. I combed my hair straight back from my forehead, drawing it so tightly that there was not a trace of wave left in it, and then I braided it into a queue, lacing strands of imitation emeralds and garlands of white jasmine in the plait. When this was done I darkened my eyebrows with a cosmetic pencil, raising them and accenting their arch to the 'flying gull' curve so much admired in the East, and rubbed green eye-shadow upon my lids. Over my head I draped a long blue veil sewn thickly with silver sequins and crowned it with a chaplet of yellow rosebuds. Last of all there was a heavy gold circlet like a clip-earring to go into my left nostril, and a single opal screw-earring to fasten in the right, giving the impression that my nose had been pierced for the jewels, and a tiny, star-shaped patch of red court plaster to fix between my brows like a caste mark.

"There is a saying clothes don't make the man, but it's just the opposite with a woman. When I'd put those Oriental garments on I *felt* myself an Eastern woman who had never known and never wished for any other life except that behind the purdah, and all I wished to do was cast myself prostrate before Kabanta, tell him he was my lord, my master and my god, and press my lips against the gold-embroidered tips of his red slippers till he gave me leave to rise. I was shaking as if with chill when I stepped from the little anteroom accompanied by the silvery chiming of my anklets and toe rings.

"Kabanta had set a fire glowing in a silver bowl before the Green God, and when I joined him he put seven sticks of sandalwood into my hands, telling me to walk around the brazier seven times, dropping a stick of the scented wood on the fire each time I made a circuit and repeating Hindu invocations after him. When this was done he poured a little scented water from a silver pitcher into my cupped hands, and this I sprinkled on the flames, then knelt across the fire from him with outstretched hands palm-upward over the blaze while I swore to love him, and him only, throughout this life and the seven cycles to come. I remember part of the oath I took: 'To be one in body and soul with him as gold and the bracelet or water and the wave are one.'

"When I had sworn this oath he slipped a heavy gold ring—this!—on my finger, and told me I was pledged to him for all time and eternity, that Siva the Destroyer was witness to my pledge and would avenge my falseness if I broke my vow. It was then for the first time I heard of the pisacha, bhirta and preta, shahini and rakshasha. It all seemed horrible and fantastic as he told it, but I believed it implicitly—then." A little rueful smile touched her pale lips. "I'm afraid that I believe it now, too, sir; but for a little while I didn't, and so—so my poor lover is dead."

"*Pauvre enfant,*" de Grandin murmured. "*Ma pauvre belle créature.* And then?"

"Then came the war. You know how little pretense of neutrality there was. Americans were crossing into Canada by droves to join up, and everywhere the question was not 'Will we get into it?' but 'When?' I could fairly see my lover in the gorgeous uniform of a risaldar lieutenant or captain in the Indian Army, leading his troop of wild Patans into battle, but Kabanta made no move. When our own boys were drafted he was deferred as a medical student. At last I couldn't stand it any longer. One evening at the shore I found courage to speak. 'Master and Lord,' I asked him—we used such language to each other in private—'is it not time that you were belting on your sword to fight for freedom?'

"'Freedom, White Blossom of the Moghra Tree?' he answered with a laugh. 'Who is free? Art thou?'

"'Thou art my lord and I thy slave,' I answered as he had taught me.

"'And are the people of my father's country free? You know that they are not. For generations they have groaned beneath the Western tyrant's lash. Now these European dogs are at each other's throats. Should I take sides in their curs' fight? What difference does it make to me which of them destroys the others?'

"'But you're American,' I protested. 'The Japanese have attacked us. The Germans and Italians have declared war on us—'

"'Be silent!' he commanded, and his voice was no longer the soft voice that I loved. 'Women were made to serve, not to advise their masters of their duty.'

"'But, Kabanta—'

"'I told you to be still!' he nearly shouted. 'Does the slave dare disobey her master's command? Down, creature, down upon your knees and beg my pardon for your insolence—'

"'You can't be serious!' I gasped as he grasped me by the hair and began forcing my head down. We'd been playing at this game of slave and master—dancing girl and maharajah—and I'd found it amusing, even thrilling after a fashion. But it had only been pretense—like a 'dress-up party' or the ritual of a sorority where you addressed someone you'd known since childhood as Queen or Empress, or by some other high-sounding title, knowing all the while that she was just your next door neighbor or a girl with whom you'd gone to grammar school. Now, suddenly, it dawned on me that it had not been play with him. As thoroughly Americanized as he appeared, he was still an Oriental underneath, with all the Oriental's cynicism about women and all an Eastern man's exalted opinion of his own importance. Besides, he was hurting me terribly as he wound his fingers in my hair. 'Let me go!' I demanded angrily. 'How dare you?'

"'How dare I? Gracious Mahadeva, hear the brazen Western hussy speak!' he almost choked. He drew my face close to his and asked in a fierce whisper, 'Do you know what you vowed that night at The Light of Asia?'

"'I vowed I'd always love you, but—'

"'You'd always love me!' he mocked. 'You vowed far more than that, my Scented Bower of Delight. You vowed that from that minute you would be my thing and chattel—vowed yourself to Siva as a voluntary offering, and accepted me—as the God's representative. As Gods are to humanity, so am I to you, O creature lower than the dust. You're mine to do with as I please, and right now it pleases me to chastise you for your insolence.' Deliberately, while he held my head back with one band in my hair, he drew one of his moccasins off and struck me across the mouth with its heel. I could feel a thin trickle of blood between my lips and the scream I was about to utter died in my throat.

"'Down!' he commanded. 'Down on your face and beg for mercy. If you are truly penitent perhaps I shall forgive your insolence.'

"I might have yielded finally, for flesh and blood can stand only so much, and suddenly I was terribly afraid of him, but when I was almost beyond resistance we heard voices in the distance, and saw a light coming toward us on the beach. 'Don't think that I've forgiven you,' he told me as he pushed me from him. 'Before I take you back you'll have to walk barefoot across hot coals and abase yourself lower than the dust—'

"Despite the pain of my bruised lips I laughed. 'If you think I'll ever see you again, or let you come within speaking distance—' I began, but his laugh was louder than mine.

"'If you think you can get away, or ever be free from your servitude to me, you'll find that you're mistaken,' he jeered. 'You are Siva's, and mine, for all eternity. My shadow is upon you and my ring is on your finger. Try to escape the one or take the other off.'

"I wrenched at the ring he'd put on my hand. It wouldn't budge. Again and again I tried to get it off. No use. It seemed to have grown fast to the flesh; the more I tried to force it off the tighter it seemed to cling, and all the time Kabanta stood there smiling at me with a look of devilish, goading derision on his dark handsome features. At last I gave up trying and almost fainting with humiliation and the pain from my bruised mouth I turned and ran away. I found my car in the parking lot and drove home at breakneck speed. I suppose Kabanta managed to get a taxi. I don't know. I never saw him again."

"*Très bon*," de Grandin nodded approval as she completed her story. "That is good. That is very good, indeed, *ma oisillone*."

"Is it?" the irony of her reply was razor-thin.

"Is it not?"

"It is not."

"*Pourquoi? Nom d'un chameau enfumé!* For why?"

"Because he kept his word, sir. His shadow *is* upon me and his ring immovably upon my finger. Last year I met Wade Hardison, and it was love at first sight. Not fascination nor physical attraction, but love, real love; the good, clean, wholesome love a man and woman ought to have for each other if they expect to spend their lives together. Our engagement was announced at Christmas, and—"

"*Et puis?*" he prompted as her voice broke on a soundless sob.

"Then I heard from Kabanta. It was a post card—just a common penny post card, unsigned and undated, and it carried just eleven words of message: 'When you remove the ring you are absolved from your oath.' He hadn't signed it, as I said, but I knew instantly it was from him.

"I tried desperately to get the ring off, wound my fingers with silk, used soap and olive oil, held my hand in ice cold water—no use. It wouldn't budge. I couldn't even turn it on my finger. It is as if the metal had grown to my flesh and become part of me. I didn't dare tell anyone about it, they wouldn't have believed me, and somehow I didn't have the courage to go to a jeweler's and have it filed off, so ..."

The silence that ensued lasted so long one might have thought the girl had fainted, but the short, irregular, spasmodic swelling of her throat told us she was fighting hard to master her emotion. At last:

"Two days ago," she whispered so low we had to bend to catch her words, "I had another note. 'He shall never call you his,' was all it said. There was no signature, but I knew only too well who the sender was.

"Then I told Wade about it, but he just laughed. Oh, if only I had had the courage to postpone our wedding Wade might be alive now. There's no use fighting against Fate," her voice rose to a thin thread of hysteria. "I might as well confess myself defeated, go back to Kabanta and take whatever punishment he cares to inflict. I'm hopelessly enmeshed, entrapped—ensnared! I am Siva's toy and plaything, and Kabanta is the Green God's representative!" She roused to a sitting posture, then fell back, burying her face in the pillow and shaking with heart-breaking sobs.

"Kabanta is a species of a cockroach, and Siva but an ape-faced piece of green stone," de Grandin answered in a hard, sharp voice. "I, Jules de Grandin tell you so, *Mademoiselle*; anon I shall say the same thing to them, but much more forcefully. Yes, certainly, of course."

"T HAT DAME'S AS NUTTY as a fruit cake," Costello confided as we left the Thurmond house. "She goes an' gits herself involved with one o' these here fancy Hindu fellies, an' he goes an' tells her a pack o' nonsense, an' she falls fer it like a ton o' brick. As if they wuz anny such things as Shivas an' shahinnies an' raytors an' th' rest o' it! Begob, I'd sooner belave in—"

"You and I do not believe, my friend," de Grandin interrupted seriously, "but there are millions who do, and the power of their believing makes a great force—"

"Oh, come!" I scoffed. "You never mean to tell us that mere cumulative power of belief can create hobgoblins and bugaboos?"

"*Vraiment*," he nodded soberly. "It is indeed unfortunately so, my friend. Thoughta are things, and sometimes most unpleasant things. Yes, certainly."

"Nonsense!" I rejoined sharply. "I'm willing to agree that Melanie could have been imposed on. The world is full of otherwise quite sane people who are willing to believe the moon is made of green cheese if they're told so impressively enough. I'll even go so far as to concede she thinks she can't get the ring off. We've all seen the cases of strange inhibitions, people who were convinced they couldn't go past a certain spot—can't go off the block in which they live, for instance. She's probably unconsciously crooked her finger when she tried to pull it off. The very fact she found excuses to put off going to a jeweler's to have it filed off shows she's laboring under a delusion. Besides, we all know those Hindu are adepts at hypnotism—"

"*Ah, bah!*" he broke in. "You are even more mistaken than usual, Friend Trowbridge. "Have you by any chance read *Darkness Out of the East* by our good friend John Thunstone?"

"No," I confessed, "but—"

"But be damned and stewed in boiling oil for Satan's supper. In his book Friend Thunstone points out that the rite of walking barefoot seven times around a living fire and throwing fuel and water on it while sacred *mantras* are recited is the most solemn manner of pronouncing an irrevocable oath. It is thus the neophyte is oath-bound to the service of the temple where she is to wait upon the gods, it is so when the wife binds herself forever to the service and subjection of her lord and husband. When that poor one performed that ceremony she undertook an oath-bound obligation which every Hindu firmly believes the gods themselves cannot break. She is pledged by fire and water for all time and eternity to the man who put the ring of Siva on her finger. While I talked to her I observed the amulet. It bears the device of a woman held in unbreakable embrace by Four-Faced Siva, and under it is written in Hindustani, 'As the gods are to mankind so is the one to whom I vow myself to me. I have said it.'

"As for her having the ring filed off—she was wiser than she knew when she refrained from that."

"How d'ye mean?" Costello and I chorused.

"I saw an instance of it once in Goa, Portuguese India. A wealthy Portuguese planter's *femme de la main gauche* had an *affaire* with a Hindu while her protector was away on business. She was inveigled into taking such a vow as Mademoiselle Thurmond took, and into having such a ring slipped on her finger. When she would have broken with her Hindu lover and returned to her *purveyor* she too found the ring immovable, and hastened to a jeweler's to have it filed off. *Tiens*, the life went out of her as the gold band was sawn asunder."

"You mean she dropped dead of a stroke?" I asked.

"I mean she died, my friend. I was present at the autopsy, and every symptom pointed to snake bite—except the stubborn fact that there had been no snake. We had the testimony of the jeweler and his two assistants; we had the testimony of a woman friend who went with her to the shop. All were agreed there had been no snake near her. She was not bitten; she merely fell down dead as the gold band came off."

"O.K., sor; if ye say it, I'll belave it, even if I know 't'aint so," Costello agreed. "What's next?"

"I think we should go to the morgue. The autopsy should be complete by this time, and I am interested in the outcome."

D R. JASON PARNELL, THE coroner's physician, fanned himself with a sheaf of death certificates, and mopped his streaming brow with a silk handkerchief. "I'm damned if I can make it out," he confessed irritably. "I've checked and rechecked everything, and the answer's the same each time. Only it doesn't make sense."

"*Qu'est-ce donc?*" de Grandin demanded. "How do you say?"

"That youngster has no more business being dead than you or I. There wasn't a God's earthly thing the matter with him from a pathological standpoint. He was perfect. Healthiest specimen I ever worked on. If he'd been shot, stabbed or run down by a motor car I could have understood it; but here he is, as physiologically perfect as an athlete, with positively no signs of trauma of any sort—except that he's as dead as a herring."

"You mean you couldn't find a symptom—" I began, and he caught me up before I had a chance to finish.

"Just that, Trowbridge. You said it. Not a single, solitary one. There is no sign of syncope, asphyxia or coma, no trace of any functional or organic weakness. Dammit man, the fellow didn't die, he just stopped living—and for no apparent reason. What'n hell am I goin' to tell the jury at the inquest?"

"*Tiens, mon ami*, that is your problem, I damn think," de Grandin answered. "We have one of our own to struggle with. There is that to do which needs immediate doing, and how we are to do it only *le bon Dieu* knows. Name of a little blue man, but it is the enigma, I tell you."

Sergeant Costello looked unhappily from Parnell to de Grandin. "Sure, sors, 'tis th' screwiest business I've ever seen entirely," he declared. "First th' pore young felley topples over dead as mutton, then his pore forsaken bride tells us a story as would make th' hair creep on yer neck, an' now you tell us that th' pore lad died o' nothin' a-tall. Mother o' Moses, 'tis Jerry Costello as don't know if he's comin' or goin' or where from an' where to. Can I use yer 'phone, Doc?" he asked Parnell. "Belike th' bhoys at Headquarters would like to know what I'm about."

We waited while he dialed Headquarters, heard him bark a question, and saw a look of utter unbelief spread on his broad perspiring face as some one at the other end answered. "'T'ain't so!" he denied. "It couldn't be.

"We wuz just up to see her, an' she's as limp as a wet wash—"

"What is it, *mon sergent?*" de Grandin asked. "Is it that—"

"Ye can bet yer bottom dollar it is, sor," the Sergeant cut in almost savagely. "It sure is, or I'm a monkey's uncle. Miss Thurmond, her we just seen layin' in th' bed so weak she couldn't hold up her head, has taken it on th' lam."

"*Diable!*" de Grandin shot back. "It cannot be."

"That's what I told 'em at Headquarters, sor, but they insist they know what they're a-talkin' about; an' so does her old man. 'Twas him as put the call in to be on th' lookout fer her. It seems she lay in a half stupor when we left her, an' they'd left her alone, thinkin' she might git a bit o' rest, when zingo! up she bounces, runs to th' garage where her car wuz parked, an' rushes down th' street like th' divil wuz on her trail."

"*Ha!*" de Grandin's hard, dry, barking laugh had nothing whatever to do with amusement. "*Ah-ha-ha!* I am the greatest stupid-head outside of a *maison de fous, mes amis.* I might have damn anticipated it! You say she ran as if the devil were behind her? *Mais non,* it is not so. He was before her. He called her and she answered his summons!"

"Whatever—" I began, but Costello caught the little Frenchman's meaning.

"Then what th' divil are we waitin' fer, sor?" he demanded. "We know where he hangs out. Let's go an' peel th' livin' hide off 'im—"

"*Ma moi, cher sergent,* you take the words out of my mouth," the small Frenchman shot back. "Come, Friend Trowbridge, let us be upon our way."

"Where to?" I asked.

"Where to? Where in the foul name of Satan but to that so vile shop called The Light of Asia, where unless I am more greatly mistaken than I think the dove goes to a rendezvous with the serpent. Quickly. Let us hasten, let us rush; let us fly, *mes amis!*"

The rain that had been threatening since early afternoon came down in bucketsful as we crept slowly through East Fifty-Sixth Street. It poured in miniature Niagaras from cornices and rolled-up awnings, the gutters were awash, the sidewalks almost ankle-deep with water.

"*Halte la!*" ordered de Grandin, and I edged the car close to the curb. "My friends, we are arrived. Be quiet, if you please, make no move unless I request it, and—" he broke off with a muttered "*nom d'un coq!*" as a wind-whipped awning sluiced a sudden flood of icy water over him, shook himself like a spaniel emerging from a pond, and laid his hand upon the brass knob of the highly varnished door.

Amazingly the door swung open at his touch and we stepped into the dim interior of The Light of Asia.

The place was like a church whose worshipers had gone. The air was redolent of incense, the darkness was relieved by only a dim, ruddy light, and all was silent—no, not quite! At the far end of the long room a voice was singing softly, a woman's voice raised in a trembling, tear-heavy contralto:

Since I, O Lord, am nothing unto thee,
See here thy sword, I make it keen and bright . . .

"*Alons, mes enfants,* follow!" whispered Jules de Grandin as he tiptoed toward the rear of the shop.

Now the tableau came in view, clear-cut as a scene upon a stage. In an elevated niche like an altar place crouched a green stone image slightly larger than man's-size, the sightless eyes of its four faces staring out in cold, malevolent obliviousness. Below it, cross-legged on a scarlet cushion, his hands folded palm-upward in his lap, was a remarkably handsome young man dressed in an ornate Oriental costume, but these we passed by at a glance, for in the foreground, kneeling with her forehead pressed against the floor, was Melanie Thurmond dressed as she had been when she took her fateful vow and had the ring of Siva put upon her hand. Her hands were raised above her bowed head, and in them rested a long, curved scimitar, the ruddy lamplight gleaming on its jeweled hilt and bright blade with ominous redness.

"Forgive, forgive!" we heard her sob, and saw her beat her forehead on the floor in utter self-abasement. "Have pity on the worm that creeps upon the dust before thy feet—"

"Forgiveness shall be thine," the man responded slowly, "when dead kine crop the grass, when the naked rend their clothes and when a shining radiance becomes a void of blackness."

"Have mercy on the insect crawling at thy feet," the prostrate woman sobbed. "Have pity on the lowly thing—"

"Have done!" he ordered sharply. "Give me the sword."

She roused until she crouched upon her knees before him, raised the scimitar and pressed its blade against her lips and brow in turn, then, head bent low, held it out to him. He took it, balancing it between his hands for a moment, then drew a silk handkerchief from his sleeve and slowly began polishing the blade with it. The woman bent forward again to lay her brow against the floor between her outstretched hands, then straightened till she sat upon her crossed feet and bent her head back till her slender flower-like throat was exposed. "I wait the stroke of mercy, Master and Lord," she whispered as she closed her eyes. "'Twere better far to die at thy hands than to live cut off from the sunshine of thy favor. . . ."

There was something wrong with the Green God. I could not tell quite what it was; it might have been a trick of light and shadow, or the whorls of incense spiraling around it, but I could have sworn its arms were moving and its fixed, immobile features changing expression.

There was something wrong with me, too. A feeling of complete inadequacy seemed to spread through me. My self-esteem seemed oozing out of every pore, my legs felt weak, I had an almost irresistible desire to drop upon my knees before the great green idol.

"*Oom, mani padme hong!*" de Grandin cried, his voice a little high and thin with excitement. "*Oom, mani padme hong!*"

Why I did it I had no idea, but suddenly I echoed his invocation, at the top of my voice, "*Oom, mani padme hong!*"

Costello's rumbling bass took up the chant, and crying the unfamiliar syllables in chorus we advanced toward the seated man and kneeling woman and the great, green gloating idol. "*Oom, mani padme hong!*"

The man half turned and raised his hands in supplication to the image, but even as he did so something seemed to happen in the niche. The great green statue trembled on its base, swayed backward, forward—rocked as if it had been shaken by a sudden blast of wind, then without warning toppled from its embrasure, crushing the man seated at its feet as a dropped tile might crush a beetle.

For a long moment we stood staring at the havoc, the fallen idol lying athwart the crushed, broken body of the man, the blood that spread in a wide, ever-broadening pool about them, and the girl who wept through lowered lids and beat her little fists against her breast, unmindful of the tragedy.

"Quickly, my friends," bade de Grandin. "Go to the dressing room and find her clothes, then join me here.

"*Oom, mani padme hong!* The gods are dead, there is no power or potency in them, my little flower," he told the girl. "*Oom, mani padme hong!*" he bent and took her right hand in his, seizing the great ring that glowed upon her forefinger and drawing it away. "*Oom, mani padme hong!* The olden gods are powerless— they have gone back to that far hell from whence they hailed—" The ring came off as if it had been several sizes too large and he lifted her in his arms gently.

"Make haste, my friends," he urged. "None saw us enter; none shall see us leave. Tomorrow's papers will record a mystery, but there will be no mention of this poor one's name in it. Oh, be quick, I do beseech you!"

"Now," I DEMANDED AS I refilled the glasses, "are you going to explain, or must the Sergeant and I choke it out of you?"

The little laughter wrinkles at the outer corners of his eyes deepened momentarily. "*Non, mes amis,*" he replied, "violence will not be required, I assure you. First of all, I assume you would be interested to know how it was we overcame that green monstrosity and his attendant by your chant?"

"Nothin' less, sor," Costello answered. "Bedad, I hadn't anny idea what it meant, or why we sang it, but I'm here to say it sounded good to me—I got a kick out o' repeating it wid ye, but why it wuz, I dunno."

"You know the history of Gautama Buddha, one assumes?"

"I niver heard o' him before, sor."

"*Quel dommage!* However"—he paused to take a long sip from his glass, then—"here are the facts: Siddhartha Gautama Buddha was born in India some five hundred years before the opening of our era. He grew up in a land priest-ridden and god-ridden. There was no hope—no pride of ancestry nor anticipation of immortality—for the great mass of the people, who were forever fixed in miserable existence by the rule of caste and the divine commands of gods whom we

should call devils. Buddha saw the wickedness of this, and after years of medita-
tion preached a new and hopeful gospel. He first denied the power of the gods
by whose authority the priests held sway, and later denied their very existence.
His followers increased by thousands and by tens of thousands; they washed the
cursed caste marks from their foreheads, proclaimed themselves emancipated,
denied the priests' authority and the existence of the gods by whom they had
been terrorized and downtrodden for generations. Guatama Buddha, their leader,
they hailed and honored with this chant: 'Oom, *mani padme hong!*—Hail, thou
Gem of the Lotus!' From the Gulf of Bengal to the Himalayas the thunder of
their greeting to their master rolled like a mighty river of emancipation, and the
power of it emptied the rock temples of the olden deities, left the priests without
offerings on which to fatten. Sometimes it even overthrew the very evil gods
themselves. I mean that literally. There are recorded instances where bands of
Buddhists entering into heathen temples have by the very repetition of 'Oom,
Mani padme hong!' caused rock-hewn effigies of those evil forces men called
Vishnu and Siva to topple from their altars. Yes, it is so.

"*En conséquence* tonight when I saw the poor misguided *mademoiselle* about
to make a sacrifice of herself to that four-faced caricature of Satan I called to
mind the greeting to the Lord Gautama which in olden days had rocked him and
his kind from their high thrones, and raised the ancient battle cry of freedom
once more. *Tiens*, he knew his master, that one. The Lord Gautama Buddha had
driven him back to whatever hell-pool he and his kind came from in the olden
days; his strength and power to drive him back was still potent. Did not you see
it with your own four eyes, my friends?"

"U'm," I admitted somewhat grudgingly. "You think it was the power of the
Green God that called Melanie back to The Light of Asia tonight?"

"Partly, beyond question. She wore his ring, and material things have great
power on things spiritual, just as spiritual things have much influence on the
material. Also it might well have been a case of utter frustration. She might
have said in effect, 'What is the use?' Her lover had been killed, her hopes of
happiness blasted, her whole world knocked to pieces. She might well have rea-
soned: 'I am powerless to fight against my fate. The strength of the Green God is
too great. I am doomed; why not admit it; why struggle hopelessly and helplessly?
Why not go to Kabanta and admit my utter defeat, the extinction of my personality, and take whatever punishment awaits me, even though it be death?' Sooner
or later I must yield. Why not sooner than later? To struggle futilely is only to
prolong the agony and make his final triumph all the greater.' These things she
may have said to herself. Indeed, did she not intimate as much to us when we
interviewed her?

"Yes," he nodded like a china mandarin on a mantelpiece, "it is unquestionably so, my friends, and but for Jules de Grandin—and the Lord Gautama

Buddha assisted by my good friends Trowbridge and Costello—it might have been that way. *Eh bien*, I and the Buddha, with your kind assistance, put an end to their fine schemes, did we not?"

"You seriously think it was the force of the Green God that killed Wade Hardison?" I asked.

"I seriously do, my friend. That and naught else. The Green One was a burning glass that focused rays of hatred as a lens does sunlight, and through his power the never-to-be-sufficiently-anathematized Kabanta was enabled to destroy the poor young Hardison completely."

He stabbed a small, impressive forefinger at me. "Consider, if you please: What was the situation tonight? Siva had triumphed. He had received a blood-sacrifice in the person of the poor young Hardison; he was about to have another in the so unfortunate Mademoiselle Melanie, then *pouf* comes Jules de Grandin and Friend Trowbridge and Friend Costello to repeat the chant which in the olden days had driven him from power. Before the potency of our chant to the Buddha the Green One felt his power ebbing slowly from him as he retreated to that far place where he had been driven aforetime by the Lord Gautama. And what did he do as he fell back? *Tenez*, he took revenge for his defeat on Kabanta. He cast the statue of himself—a very flattering likeness, no doubt—down from its altar place and utterly crushed the man who had almost but not quite enabled him to triumph. He was like a naughty child that kicks or bites the person who has promised it a sweet, then failed to make good the promise—"

"But that idol was a senseless piece of carved stone," I protested. "How could it—"

"*Ah bah*, you irritate me, my friend. Of course the idol was a senseless piece of stone, but *that for which it stood was neither stone nor senseless*. The idol was but the representation of the evil power lurking in the outer darkness as the tiger lurks in ambush. Let us put it this way: The idol is the material and visible door through which the spiritual and invisible force of evil we call Siva is enabled to penetrate into our human world.

"Through that doorway he came into the world, through it he was forced to retreat before the power of our denial of his potency. So to speak, he slammed the door as he retreated—and caught Kabanta between door and jamb. *En tout cas*, he is dead, that miserable Kabanta. We are well rid of him, and the door is fast closed on the evil entity which he and the unwitting and unfortunate Mademoiselle Melanie let back into the world for a short time.

"Yes," be nodded solemnly again. "It is so. I say it. I also say that I should like my glass refilled, if you will be so gracious, Friend Trowbridge."

MORE JULES DE GRANDIN STORIES

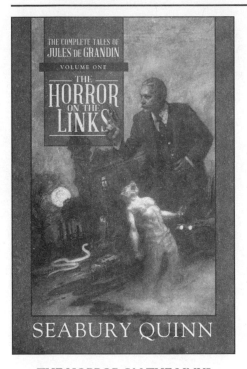

THE HORROR ON THE LINKS
978-1-59780-893-4
Hardcover / $34.99 (available now)

The first of five volumes collecting the stories of Jules de Grandin, the supernatural detective made famous in the classic pulp magazine *Weird Tales.*

Collected for the first time in trade editions, The Complete Tales of Jules de Grandin, edited by George Vanderburgh, presents all ninety-three published works featuring the supernatural detective. Presented in chronological order over five volumes, this is the definitive collection of an iconic pulp hero.

The first volume, The Horror on the Links, includes all of the Jules de Grandin stories from "The Horror on the Links" (1925) to "The Chapel of Mystic Horror" (1928), as well as an introduction by George Vanderburgh and Robert Weinberg.

MORE JULES DE GRANDIN STORIES

THE DEVIL'S ROSARY
978-1-59780-927-6
Hardcover / $34.99 (available now)

The second of five volumes collecting the stories of Jules de Grandin, the supernatural detective made famous in the classic pulp magazine *Weird Tales*.

Collected for the first time in trade editions, The Complete Tales of Jules de Grandin, edited by George Vanderburgh, presents all ninety-three published works featuring the supernatural detective. Presented in chronological order over five volumes, this is the definitive collection of an iconic pulp hero.

The second volume, The Devil's Rosary, includes all of the Jules de Grandin stories from "The Black Master" (1929) to "The Wolf of St. Bonnot" (1930), as well as a foreword by Stefan Dziemianowicz.

MORE JULES DE GRANDIN STORIES

THE DARK ANGEL
978-1-59780-944-3
Hardcover / $34.99 (available now)

The third of five volumes collecting the stories of Jules de Grandin, the supernatural detective made famous in the classic pulp magazine *Weird Tales*.

Collected for the first time in trade editions, The Complete Tales of Jules de Grandin, edited by George Vanderburgh, presents all ninety-three published works featuring the supernatural detective. Presented in chronological order over five volumes, this is the definitive collection of an iconic pulp hero.

The third volume, *The Dark Angel*, includes all of the Jules de Grandin stories from "The Lost Lady" (1931) to "The Hand of Glory" (1933), as well as "The Devil's Bride", the only novel featuring de Grandin, which was originally serialized over six issues of *Weird Tales*. It also includes a foreword by Darrell Schweitzer and an introduction by George Vanderburgh and Robert Weinberg.

MORE JULES DE GRANDIN STORIES

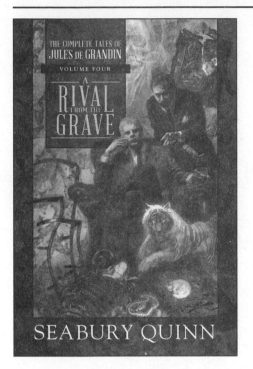

A RIVAL FROM THE GRAVE
978-1-59780-968-9
Hardcover / $34.99 (available now)

The fourth of five volumes collecting the stories of Jules de Grandin, the supernatural detective made famous in the classic pulp magazine *Weird Tales*.

Collected for the first time in trade editions, The Complete Tales of Jules de Grandin, edited by George Vanderburgh, presents all ninety-three published works featuring the supernatural detective. Presented in chronological order over five volumes, this is the definitive collection of an iconic pulp hero.

The fourth volume, A *Rival from the Grave*, includes all the stories from "The Chosen of Vishnu" (1933) to "Incense of Abomination" (1938), as well as an introduction by George Vanderburgh and Robert Weinberg and a foreword by Mike Ashley.